COLLECTED TALES, POEMS, AND OTHER WRITINGS OF EDGAR ALLAN POE

COLLECTED TALES, POEMS, AND OTHER WRITINGS OF EDGAR ALLAN POE

Edited by Carl Ostrowski

BLOOMSBURY ACADEMIC
LONDON • NEW YORK • OXFORD • NEW DELHI • SYDNEY

BLOOMSBURY ACADEMIC
Bloomsbury Publishing Plc
50 Bedford Square, London, WC1B 3DP, UK
1385 Broadway, New York, NY 10018, USA
29 Earlsfort Terrace, Dublin 2, Ireland

BLOOMSBURY, BLOOMSBURY ACADEMIC and the Diana logo are trademarks of
Bloomsbury Publishing Plc

First published in Great Britain 2021
This paperback edition published 2023

Cover design by Eleanor Rose
Photo by Dina Rudick/The Boston Globe via Getty Images

Bloomsbury Publishing Plc does not have any control over, or responsibility for, any
third-party websites referred to or in this book. All internet addresses given in this
book were correct at the time of going to press. The author and publisher
regret any inconvenience caused if addresses have changed or sites have
ceased to exist, but can accept no responsibility for any such changes.

A catalogue record for this book is available from the British Library.

A catalog record for this book is available from the Library of Congress.

ISBN: HB: 978-1-3501-8125-0
       PB: 978-1-3502-2645-6
       ePDF: 978-1-3501-8128-1
       eBook: 978-1-3501-8126-7

Typeset by RefineCatch Limited, Bungay, Suffolk

To find out more about our authors and books visit www.bloomsbury.com
and sign up for our newsletters.

CONTENTS

Acknowledgments   viii

Part I Introduction   1

Part II Tales   25
    Ms. Found in a Bottle   36
    Berenice   43
    Morella   48
    Ligeia   51
    How to Write a Blackwood Article   61
    A Predicament   68
    The Man That Was Used Up   74
    The Fall of the House of Usher   80
    William Wilson   93
    The Man of the Crowd   106
    The Murders in the Rue Morgue   111
    A Descent into the Maelström   133
    Never Bet the Devil Your Head   144
    The Masque of the Red Death   150
    The Pit and the Pendulum   154
    The Tell-Tale Heart   163
    The Gold-Bug   167
    The Black Cat   190
    The Premature Burial   196
    The Purloined Letter   205
    The System of Dr. Tarr and Prof. Fether   217
    The Balloon-Hoax   229
    The Literary Life of Thingum Bob, Esq.   237
    Some Words with a Mummy   250
    The Imp of the Perverse   261

The Facts in the Case of M. Valdemar   264

The Cask of Amontillado   271

Hop-Frog   275

Part III Poems   299

Sonnet—To Science   304

Alone   304

To Helen   304

Israfel   305

The Sleeper   306

The City in the Sea   308

The Haunted Palace   309

The Conqueror Worm   310

Dream-Land   311

The Raven   312

To —— —— —— Ulalume: A Ballad   315

The Bells   318

Annabel Lee   320

Part IV *Eureka: A Prose Poem*   327

From *Eureka: A Prose Poem*   329

Part V Letters, Prefaces, and Critical Writings   353

From "Letter to B——"   357

From *Night and Morning* (Review of Bulwer)   358

Guy Fawkes (Review of Ainsworth)   364

From *Ballads and Other Poems* (Review of Longfellow)   367

Twice-Told Tales (Review of Hawthorne)   372

Twice-Told Tales (Review of Hawthorne continued)   373

Some Secrets of the Magazine Prison-House   378

From "Anastatic Printing"   380

Preface to *The Raven and Other Poems*   382

The Philosophy of Composition   383

From "The Poetic Principle"   391

From Poe to John Allan, December 22, 1828   392

From Poe to Thomas W. White, April 30, 1835   393

From Poe to Mrs. Maria Clemm, August 29, 1835   394

From Poe to John P. Kennedy, February 11, 1836   395

From Poe to Philip P. Cooke, September 21, 1839   396

From Poe to Frederick W. Thomas, May 4, 1845   396

From Poe to Philip P. Cooke, August 9, 1846   397

From Poe to George W. Eveleth, December 15, 1846   397

From Poe to George W. Eveleth, January 4, 1848   398

ACKNOWLEDGMENTS

I would like to thank Middle Tennessee State University (MTSU) for awarding me a non-instructional assignment (NIA), allowing me to finish this project on time. My gratitude is also due to former English Department Chair Maria Bachman for supporting my NIA application and for fostering scholarly achievement within the department. At the outset of this project, I consulted with MTSU's award-winning editor of Percy Bysshe Shelley, Michael Neth, on the subject of textual editing, and I thank him for his generous assistance. My students in several iterations of an MTSU Honors College course entitled "Edgar Allan Poe's America" frequently stimulated my thinking on matters related to Poe and his contemporaries, for which I thank them here.

Among the many Poe scholars to whom I am indebted, I wish particularly to acknowledge Jeffrey A. Savoye of the Edgar Allan Poe Society of Baltimore. All Poe scholars and fans owe Jeffrey our gratitude for the Society's remarkable website, eapoe.org, to which I referred frequently while compiling this volume, as well as for his outstanding 2008 Gordian Press edition of Poe's letters.

PART I

Introduction

CHRONOLOGY OF EDGAR ALLAN POE'S LIFE AND TIMES

1809   Edgar Poe is born in Boston to actors David and Elizabeth Poe on January 19. He is the couple's second son (after William Henry). Elizabeth Poe gives birth to a daughter, Rosalie, in 1810.

1811   Upon Elizabeth Poe's death, the young Edgar Poe is taken in (but not formally adopted) by Richmond, Virginia tobacco merchant John Allan and his wife Frances.

1815   Allan moves the family to Great Britain in pursuit of improved business prospects.

1818   Poe is educated at a school run by the Reverend John Bransby at Stoke Newington, near London. Poe would later use his memories of this school in writing "William Wilson."

1820   The Allans return to Richmond.

        In an agreement known as the Missouri Compromise, Missouri is added to the union as a slave state and Maine as a free state, preserving the balance of power between free and slave states in the United States Senate. A geographical boundary line is established between free and slave states.

        Washington Irving's *The Sketchbook of Geoffrey Crayon, Gent.* completes serial publication in New York.

1823   President James Monroe announces United States opposition to further European colonialist interference in the New World, a position later codified as the Monroe Doctrine.

1826   Poe enrolls at the University of Virginia. He excels at French and Latin, but leaves the university after less than a year. Allan refuses to honor gambling debts Poe had accumulated and generally balks at financing Poe's education at the levels expected for a member of the Southern gentry.

        James Fenimore Cooper publishes *The Last of the Mohicans.*

1827   After a break with foster father John Allan, Poe moves to Boston, where he publishes his first book, *Tamerlane and Other Poems.* He joins the U.S. Army under the name Edgar A. Perry. In November, his company moves to Fort Moultrie, on Sullivan's Island, South Carolina. Sullivan's Island is later employed as the setting for his story "The Gold-Bug." The first U.S. railroad is chartered.

1828   Andrew Jackson, renowned as an Indian fighter and the hero of the Battle of New Orleans (during the War of 1812), is elected to the first of two presidential terms.

1829   Poe's foster mother Frances (Fanny) Allan dies in Richmond. Poe is discharged from the U.S. Army. He publishes a second book of poetry, *Al Aaraaf, Tamerlane, and Minor Poems*, in Baltimore.

1830   Poe is admitted to the U.S. Military Academy at West Point, New York, where he excels in French and mathematics. John Allan remarries.

The Indian Removal Act is passed with President Jackson's support, beginning the process of the forced removal of Native Americans from their homelands in the Southeast.

1831   Supported in part by a subscription list made up of fellow cadets, Poe publishes *Poems: Second Edition* in New York. Poe is discharged from the U.S. Military Academy and moves to Baltimore, where he lives with paternal aunt Maria Clemm and her daughter Virginia, among others. John Allan's second wife gives birth, effectively putting to rest Poe's hopes of receiving a significant inheritance.

Nat Turner leads a violent rebellion of slaves in Southampton County, Virginia, causing nationwide panic and outrage. *The Confessions of Nat Turner*, a pamphlet published in Baltimore, sells tens of thousands of copies.

William Lloyd Garrison founds his antislavery newspaper *The Liberator* in Boston, leading to new visibility for the abolitionist movement.

1832   The Philadelphia *Saturday Courier* publishes a story Poe had submitted to a prize contest, "Metzengerstein."

German physician Johann Spurzheim arrives in the United States for a lecture tour and popularizes the pseudo-science known as phrenology.

1833   Poe wins a prize contest sponsored by the Baltimore *Saturday Visiter* on the strength of several tales he submits, including "Ms. Found in a Bottle," which the newspaper publishes.

Slavery is abolished in the British Empire.

1834   Poe befriends novelist John Pendleton Kennedy. John Allan dies in Richmond and leaves nothing to Poe.

1835   Recommended by Kennedy to publisher Thomas W. White, Poe submits tales to White's magazine, the *Southern Literary Messenger*, published in Richmond. White publishes early Poe tales and eventually hires him as editor.

1836   Poe marries Virginia Clemm; she is thirteen and he is twenty-seven.

Ralph Waldo Emerson publishes the essay "Nature," founding the American Transcendentalist movement.

Frenchman Charles Boyen begins lecturing and publishing in New England on the subject of mesmerism, inspiring growing public interest over the next several years.

1837   Poe publishes early installments of his novel *The Narrative of Arthur Gordon Pym* in the *Southern Literary Messenger*. Poe and the *Messenger* part ways. He moves with Maria Clemm (nicknamed Muddy) and Virginia to New York City, which is soon plunged with the rest of the country into an economic depression known as the Panic of 1837. Nathaniel Hawthorne publishes the first edition of *Twice-Told Tales*.

1838   Poe publishes *The Narrative of Arthur Gordon Pym* with Harper & Brothers. He moves with Virginia and Muddy to Philadelphia.

1839   A science textbook, *The Conchologist's First Book*, is published under Poe's name in Philadelphia. Poe assumes editorial duties with William E. Burton's *Gentleman's Magazine*, contributing reviews, poems, and tales. Publishers Lea and Blanchard of Philadelphia bring out the two-volume collection *Tales of the Grotesque and Arabesque*. Henry Wadsworth Longfellow publishes *Voices of the Night*.

1840   Burton and Poe have a falling out, and Poe leaves the *Gentleman's Magazine*. The Washingtonian Temperance Society is founded in Baltimore, part of a growing national movement devoted to abstention from alcohol.

1841   Poe joins the staff of *Graham's Lady's and Gentleman's Magazine*. (George R. Graham had purchased the subscription list of the defunct *Gentleman's Magazine* from Burton.)

1842   Virginia experiences the first serious symptoms of the tuberculosis that will eventually claim her. Poe leaves the staff of *Graham's*.

1843   Poe submits "The Gold-Bug" to a prize contest sponsored by Philadelphia's *Dollar Newspaper* and wins the $100 prize. The story is widely reprinted.

1844   Poe and his family leave Philadelphia for New York. Poe joins the staff of the *New York Mirror*.
        Samuel Morse sends the message "What Hath God Wrought" on a telegraph line between Washington, D.C. and Baltimore.

1845   "The Raven" appears in January and becomes an immediate international sensation. James Russell Lowell's biographical-critical article is published in the "Our Contributors" series in *Graham's*, further raising Poe's literary profile. Poe joins the staff of the *Broadway Journal* and commences a series of attacks on beloved poet Henry Wadsworth Longfellow, accusing the poet of plagiarism. Wiley and Putnam publish two volumes by Poe in their prestigious Library of American Books series, *Tales* and *The Raven and Other Poems*. Poe accepts an invitation to deliver an original poem before the Boston Lyceum; the reading and its aftermath compromise Poe's standing in the literary world. Poe takes over proprietorship of the *Broadway Journal*.

1846   The *Broadway Journal* ceases publication. Poe is involved in an embarrassing personal scandal that leads to a fistfight with writer Thomas Dunn English. English questions Poe's sanity and morality in the *New York Mirror*. Late in the year, notices appear in newspapers soliciting help on Poe's behalf; the family is in poor financial straits and Virginia's health is in decline.

1847   Virginia dies on January 30, plunging Poe into depression. Poe wins a libel suit against English and the *Mirror*.

1848   Poe publishes his cosmological treatise *Eureka*. Sarah Helen Whitman, a widow from Providence, Rhode Island, consents to Poe's marriage proposal, provided he give up drinking. In the face of resistance from Whitman's mother and friends, however, and amid rumors of Poe's continued intemperance, the relationship ends.
        A pioneering women's rights convention is held in Seneca Falls, New York.

The Treaty of Guadalupe Hidalgo ends the U.S.–Mexican War, giving the United States vast new swaths of territory in the West.

Gold is discovered in Coloma, California, leading to the Gold Rush.

1849   Poe continues to publish poems and stories; he also lectures on poetry. He renews acquaintance with a romantic interest from his teenage years in Richmond, the now-widowed Elmira Royster Shelton. He joins the Sons of Temperance in Richmond, pledging to give up drinking. On October 3, he is discovered semi-conscious in the streets of Baltimore and taken to a hospital. He dies on October 7, forty years old. The precise cause of his death remains unknown. On October 9, Rufus Griswold publishes a mean-spirited obituary in the *New-York Daily Tribune* that paints Poe as brilliant but also arrogant, resentful, mentally unstable, and friendless. Griswold talks Maria Clemm into appointing him Poe's literary executor.

1850   Griswold publishes an edition of Poe's works; he alters the text of certain letters by Poe to discredit Poe's character. The forgeries are not discovered until almost a century later by biographer Arthur Hobson Quinn.

ROMANTICISM AND THE GOTHIC

As the timeline above indicates, Edgar Allan Poe was born in 1809, began his professional writing career in the 1830s, and died in 1849. Traditional literary-historical periodization therefore places him firmly within the Romantic era of American literature, which dates from the 1820s through the onset of the Civil War, in 1861. As practiced by an international cohort of Western writers from the late eighteenth through the mid-nineteenth centuries, Romantic literature characteristically values the mental faculties of imagination and emotion over reason, while embracing a subjective, spontaneous, organic (rather than rule-bound or classicist) approach to art. Romantic writers spiritualize the human relationship with nature, and Romantic literature typically valorizes the claims of the individual in opposition to those of a society seen as corrupt or repressive. A certain strain of British Romanticism also licensed the emergence of radical political energies, and various American Romantic-era writers, such as Margaret Fuller, Lydia Maria Child, and Henry David Thoreau, built political activism into their vision of the writer's vocation.

In light of these literary and political values, Poe seems to fit uneasily within the Romantic tradition. Poe took a keen interest in science and technology, which were conventionally regarded as antithetical to the realm of imagination. Far from being a source of spiritual redemption, the natural world in Poe's fiction usually offers humanity sites of peril and gloom. Poe engaged deeply with the ideas of certain rationalist, Enlightenment-era precursors against whose writings many Romantics tended to take an oppositional stance, including seventeenth-century philosopher John Locke and eighteenth-century Scottish common sense philosophers/rhetoricians.[1] Far from endorsing individual political liberation, Poe possessed a generally conservative temperament and distrusted average people as a potential mob easily misled by designing demagogues. Poe regarded the notion of human progress as illusory, a position that endorsed political quietism, including on the crucial subject of slavery. Finally, Poe's emphasis on literary craftsmanship as a painstaking process aimed at matching technique to effect was at odds with Romantic notions of creative spontaneity.

Poe's fit within Romanticism becomes more apparent, however, when considering his debts to British authors Lord Byron and Samuel Taylor Coleridge, two of his most important intellectual touchstones. From such popular works as *Manfred* (1817) and *Childe Harold's Pilgrimage* (1812–18), Poe borrowed Byron's characteristic poetic posture of the tortured, defiant outsider alienated from a misunderstanding world—a mood applicable to a number of Poe's poetic personas and fictional narrators. Like other young men of his generation, moreover, Poe identified with Byron's outsize personality and adventurous spirit; given the opportunity, he misrepresented or fabricated elements of his biography in imitation of famous Byronic exploits, such as swimming the Hellespont or joining the fight for Greek independence. Numerous critics have identified Coleridge (and, by extension, the German Romanticists from whom Coleridge drew his ideas, including brothers Friedrich and August Wilhelm Schlegel) as an important source for Poe's theories about the aims and methods of imaginative writing. Poe did not identify with—and, in fact, nurtured critical hostility toward—the Transcendentalist wing of Romanticism in American letters, whose most influential voice, Ralph Waldo Emerson, celebrated democratic individualism and looked to nature for spiritual and moral lessons. Poe's sensibilities instead align him with the more pessimistic practitioners of American Romantic fiction, including Herman Melville and, especially, Nathaniel Hawthorne, whose short stories Poe praised in reviews.

Poe's Romanticism partakes heavily of the Gothic tradition. Gothic literature's origins date to 1764, with the publication of Horace Walpole's novel *The Castle of Otranto*, but the mode flourished well into the Romantic period (and beyond). Gothic literature's exploration of the dark side of human psychology appealed to Poe's temperament and skill set. Poe excelled at writing stories that spoke to readers' fears and superstitions, through elements such as (apparently) supernatural occurrences, criminal violence, altered psychological states, premature burial, and imperiled women. But regarding Poe as a writer who merely peddles cheap Gothic thrills does him a disservice. For one thing, Poe's Gothic stories almost invariably involve some form of experimentation. Poe placed a high value on originality in prose fiction and strived to achieve it through constant reworking of conventions. Moreover, as G. R. Thompson has noted, Gothic-style works account for only about half of Poe's total output of stories, among which are many other forms, including hoaxes, fantastic adventures, absurdist comedic flights, and satires of the publishing industry.[2] Poe prided himself on the variety of his talents, telling a correspondent that one of his "chief aims" throughout his writing career had been achieving "the widest diversity of subject, thought, & especially *tone* & manner of handling."[3]

One of Poe's noteworthy gifts was inventing a style at the sentence level calibrated to achieving the effects he prized. Admiring critics often single out the opening sentence of "The Fall of the House of Usher" for its evocative summoning of the somber, oppressive mood that suffuses the entire story. And yet Mark Twain, representing late nineteenth-century realism's rejection of the previous era's ornate style, wrote, "To me his prose is unreadable" (an assertion Twain immediately qualified—he would condescend to read Poe "on salary").[4] According to Harry Levin, the stylistic hallmarks of Poe's prose include supposedly excessive use of "capitals, italics, dashes, and exclamation points" as well as "sham erudition, scientific pretensions, quotations from occult authorities, and misquotations from foreign languages."[5] While such elements are undoubtedly present in Poe's work, detractors such as Twain and Levin may overlook how Poe's style—which in fact embraces a number of separate styles, each appropriate to genre and content—cannot be appreciated independently of his innovative approach to first-person narration.[6] The personalities of Poe's eccentric, often violent, first-person narrators are put on display through their florid, halting, or inappropriately verbose styles of expression. Stories such as "The Black Cat" and "The Tell-Tale Heart" acquire much of their appeal from, as Peter Coviello succinctly expresses it, "the thrilling nonagreement between the lunacy of [Poe's] narrators . . . and the exquisite clarity of their narrative perceptions."[7] Poe's critical investment in the notion of carefully crafting a story to manipulate a reader's response helps to explain this obsessive attention to sentence-level expression. It also motivated Poe's preference for short stories over novels. According to Poe's way of thinking, the intensity of effect achievable within the compass of a short story, when the writer has the reader's undivided attention, was not available to the novelist, since an entire novel could not be consumed without the affairs of the world intruding.

Poe's poetry fully partakes of his Gothic sensibility. He is justly accused of a narrow range of poetic subject matter and themes, orbiting around the ideas of dreams, loss, melancholy, desolation, and, of course, the "death of a beautiful woman," identified in his critical essay "The Philosophy of Composition" (see Part V) as the "most poetical" of subjects. Poe has the slimmest output of any comparably ranked nineteenth-century poet. To some readers, moreover, Poe's attentiveness to the sonic effects of poetry seems unsubtle and artistically questionable. But popular readers have always loved Poe's poetry for exactly those features that have proven off-putting to some academic critics: its entrancing rhythms and sorrowful tone.

THE ANTEBELLUM PUBLISHING SCENE

Readers who admire Poe's stories and poems wonder how an author whose talents now seem so self-evident could have struggled with poverty for so much of his career. One explanation would cast Poe in the role of the accursed artist, or *poète maudit*, whose eccentric, self-destructive personality (including, for example, his struggles with alcohol) made him unsuited for success in the workaday world. A related line of thought suggests that his works were too visionary to appeal to the undiscriminating tastes of contemporary readers and could only be appreciated in hindsight. Nor are these explanations without some merit: Poe did behave eccentrically, to the detriment of his career (some ill-timed drunken episodes hurt his professional prospects); moreover, his literary reputation improved markedly in the decades that followed his death. Scholars have arrived at a consensus, however, that to understand Poe's lifelong financial hardship, one must look first to the material conditions of the unpredictable publishing industry in which his career unfolded.

One frequently cited estimate has the value of books manufactured and sold in the United States rising 500 percent in the years between 1820 and 1850, from $2.5 to $12.5 million.[8] Meanwhile, the premier historian of American magazines finds in the same era "a flowering of periodical publications which seemed stupendous at the time and is still notable."[9] These sound like conditions into which an aspiring author might venture with reasonable hope of success, but the obstacles facing any individual writer were nonetheless daunting. As businessmen, American literary publishers understandably preferred safe bets on known quantities to taking a chance on new authors. Given the state of copyright law at the time, the surest bets were British bestsellers, such as books by Walter Scott, Edward Bulwer, and Charles Dickens. American publishers minimized both risk and costs by reprinting these already proven works, since, in the absence of an international copyright agreement, no payments were due to authors. These conditions made it difficult for emerging American authors to establish themselves. And although, for various reasons (advances in printing and papermaking technology, the development of new distribution networks, an expanding middle-class audience), book publishing as an industry was on the rise, the broader American economy remained fearfully volatile, as evidenced by the Panic of 1837—a depression which temporarily disrupted the entire publishing industry, delaying the expected release of Poe's only novel, *The Narrative of Arthur Gordon Pym*, for about a year. In the 1840s, certain enterprising publishers took advantage of a loophole in postal regulations to flood the market with reprints of British and French novels on mammoth, single sheets of paper or in paper covers at unprecedentedly cheap prices, further depressing the prospects of American authorship.

Periodical publishing was no more stable. Magazines started up and failed frequently. As an example, Boston poet James Russell Lowell launched a magazine entitled *The Pioneer* in 1843, securing Poe as a contributor for what promised to be an ambitious literary endeavor. Although Lowell recruited well-known authors and insisted upon high-quality production standards to attract discriminating readers, the venture failed after just three months. Proprietors of new periodicals had trouble carving out a distinctive niche in a crowded marketplace; moreover, collecting payments from distant subscribers was notoriously difficult. To fill out their magazines, editors either reprinted previously published material (again, without cost) or relied on contributions from genteel amateurs. Such authors were either independently wealthy or else derived their income from other professional sources; their willingness to write for little or no compensation drove wages down for authors dependent on authorship for a livelihood. During Poe's lifetime, a growing number of publications, including magazines and gift annuals, paid contributors by the article or page, and he collected such piecemeal income whenever he could. In fact, Poe contributed articles at one time or another to most of the period's leading magazines, including *Godey's Lady's Book* (the first nationally distributed magazine to publish him); the *United States Magazine, and Democratic Review* (also a frequent publisher of Nathaniel Hawthorne); and the New York *Evening Mirror* (whose dandyish editor, Nathaniel Parker Willis, like Poe, forged a career in periodicals). These periodicals are in addition to the major magazines Poe helped to edit, where his stories and poems were also published, as discussed below.

For a short time, Poe edited and assumed sole proprietorship of a New York periodical called the *Broadway Journal*, but that venture, already struggling when Poe took over, soon failed. Believing nonetheless that cultural trends favored the magazine format ("The whole tendency of the age is Magazine-ward," he declared in *Graham's Magazine* in 1846),[10] Poe's long-held ambition, never realized, was to own and edit a high-end literary magazine featuring the contributions of the country's most accomplished writers. From this position, Poe envisioned himself becoming an influential kingmaker presiding over American literature. Though he revisited this project (alternately titled the *Penn Magazine* and *The Stylus*) numerous times in his career, preparing prospectuses, lining up contributors, and even collecting subscription pledges, he never accrued the financial capital that would make such a magazine possible.

The unforgiving conditions of the nineteenth-century publishing market can perhaps be put into perspective by considering the number of writers who supported themselves through extra-literary means. Washington Irving's *The Sketch Book* (1819–20) made him internationally famous, but he nonetheless accepted diplomatic patronage positions as attaché to the U.S. legation in Madrid and secretary to the U.S. legation in London to facilitate researching and writing subsequent works. At separate moments in his career, Nathaniel Hawthorne took advantage of political patronage to secure jobs as a customs officer, first in Boston and later in Salem, Massachusetts. Even though he famously complained in the opening sketch of *The Scarlet Letter* (1850) of the impossibility of writing productively while in the employ of the government, that did not stop him from taking a position as United States consul in Liverpool, Great Britain when opportunity offered, suspending his writing career for seven years. To earn sufficient income to pursue writing as a vocation, Thoreau helped to modernize his family's pencil-making business and worked as a surveyor in Concord, Massachusetts. His first book (*A Week on the Concord and Merrimack Rivers*, 1849) saw print only when he agreed to indemnify the publisher against losses; he was later forced to cart home hundreds of unsold copies that the publisher refused to warehouse. Emerson had a small inheritance from his first wife that provided a steady income; Longfellow collected a salary from university professorships in the early decades of his literary career, even as he was one of the most celebrated writers in the country. Poe himself sought employment in the Philadelphia Custom House through politically connected friends, traveling to Washington, DC in 1843 to speak to the son of President John Tyler about a position, but nothing came of his petitions—in part because of Poe's ill-timed drunken sprees while there. For a writer who mostly disavowed political activity and would later describe literature to a friend as the "most noble of professions" and "about the only one fit for a man,"[11] Poe's unsuccessful pursuit of government employment testifies to his painful awareness of the uncertainty of authorship as a career.

CONTEMPORARY REPUTATION

Poe's first publications were three books of poetry that brought him little public recognition—*Tamerlane and Other Poems* (1827), *Al Aaraaf, Tamerlane, and Minor Poems* (1829), and *Poems: Second Edition* (1831). He initially made his professional name as a critic in the 1830s, establishing a reputation at the *Messenger* for uncompromising critical standards (in the offhandedly racist parlance of the day, he was called the "tomahawk man" for his habit of "scalping" fellow authors). Poe modeled his acerbic style of reviewing on certain British magazines he admired, banking on the public's taste for literary conflict.[12] Notwithstanding the reservations of his employer, publisher Thomas W. White, and the genteel tone that generally prevailed in American criticism, Poe proved correct. His entertainingly caustic reviews raised the *Messenger*'s national profile. Poe realized that book reviews in the United States suffered from a pervading mediocrity; in response, he hoped to elevate the standard of criticism from mere appreciation to something more analytical. In Poe's day, magazines favorably reviewed works issued by the publishing firms with which they were affiliated, disguising advertisements (called "puffs") as criticism. Meanwhile, regional coteries (such as a powerful one in New York led by Lewis Gaylord Clark, editor of the influential magazine *The Knickerbocker*) promoted the work of favorite sons.[13] Observing this unsavory landscape, Poe undertook a career-long crusade to arbitrate literary reputations, especially to deflate those that were, in his view, unmerited (among the many contradictions in Poe's character is the fact that he was not above puffing the works of inferior authors, either out of friendship or when he thought he stood to gain from doing so).

After leaving the *Messenger* (and probably suffering through a period of abject poverty during a lost year in New York, where the trail of biographical documentation runs cold), Poe moved to Philadelphia, where he eventually secured work as an assistant editor for William Burton's *Gentleman's Magazine*. From the middle of 1839 to June 1840, at a salary of $10 per week, Poe did whatever was necessary to help Burton get out the publication, such as writing filler, soliciting contributions, proofreading, and reviewing new books. For additional pay, he also contributed original stories. After Burton sold the magazine to George Graham, Poe assumed a role as editor of the new *Graham's Lady's and Gentleman's Magazine*. Poe left this prestigious and fairly remunerative position (where he earned an annual salary of $800) because he could no longer endure what he called the "namby-pamby" character of the magazine, which prominently featured fashion plates and formulaic, sentimental fiction, which did not live up to Poe's high aesthetic standards.[14]

It had long been claimed that circulations of the *Messenger* and *Graham's* skyrocketed during Poe's periods of editorship, as if he had an unfailing instinct for identifying the demands of the literary marketplace. Such claims, it turns out, originated with Poe himself, and are now largely discredited.[15] But subscriptions are not the sole measure of a magazine's cultural impact, and Poe was widely recognized for his editorial abilities. He experimented ingeniously with the possibilities of the magazine format. For instance, Poe engaged readers of *Alexander's Weekly Messenger* interactively, challenging them to submit coded messages to test his powers of decipherment; he would then publish his solutions. (A couple of these ciphers went unsolved until the twentieth century, when literary critics published the solutions.) In the "Autography" series, Poe capitalized on a fad of collecting authors' signatures by submitting engraved signatures to a form of handwriting analysis that doubled as sly literary critique; in the "Marginalia" series, he published random thoughts supposedly scrawled at odd moments into the margins of books in his private library—a convenient fiction, since Poe could not in fact afford an extensive private library.[16]

While he continued to write poetry and work as an editor/critic (his many professional roles overlapped throughout his career), Poe next gained significant renown for his fiction. He wrote *The Narrative of Arthur Gordon Pym* (1838) in part to capitalize on public interest in South Seas exploration. The somewhat favorable reviews of this uneven (if intriguing) performance did not necessarily redound to Poe's benefit, however, since his obfuscation of authorship in the volume's confusing preface made it unclear whether Poe or the fictional Pym was the book's true author. In 1839, Poe published his first collection of stories, *Tales of the Grotesque and Arabesque*, with the respectable Philadelphia firm of Lea and Blanchard. This volume included (among others) "Morella," "William Wilson," "Ligeia," and "Berenice," all of which had been previously published in magazines. Poe forfeited the right to royalties in order to see the volume published, and sales were, as the publishers had foreseen, disappointing.

A breakthrough in Poe's national reputation occurred in 1843, with wide reprinting of his popular success "The Gold-Bug," which coupled the already popular motif of buried treasure with the "ratiocinative" skills of the story's ingenious code-breaking protagonist, William Legrand. On the strength of this performance, Poe claimed a $100 literary prize from the Philadelphia *Dollar Newspaper*. This success notwithstanding, conventions prevailing within the publishing industry made it especially difficult for a magazine writer to establish a national reputation (what we might today call a brand). Poe's works had been published across a span of years in various periodicals and geographical locations (Baltimore, Richmond, Philadelphia, New York), sometimes circulating without his name attached. Though known among his peers in the industry, and appreciated by some readers, he had nowhere near the name recognition as the country's most famous writers, figures such as Irving and James Fenimore Cooper.

Under these conditions, one grasps the importance of the profile that Lowell published in *Graham's* in February 1845, as part of a series on "Our Contributors." Accompanied by an engraving, allowing readers for the first time to pair Poe's distinctive (and now universally familiar) physiognomy with his name, Lowell's flattering biographical sketch/critical essay (re)introduced Poe to the American public, consolidating in one place an account of Poe's many activities as critic, poet, and fiction writer. Acknowledging the fugitive quality of Poe's contributions to various magazines, Lowell noted that Poe had "squared out blocks enough to build an enduring pyramid, but has left them lying carelessly and unclaimed in many different quarries." Lowell's article offered a nearly comprehensive account of Poe's publications, from *The Narrative of Arthur Gordon Pym*, to *Tales of the Grotesque and Arabesque*, to poems such as "To Helen and "The Haunted Palace." Lowell announced that "Mr. Poe has that indescribable something which men have agreed to call *genius*."[17]

The serendipitous timing of Poe's "The Raven" appeared to confirm Lowell's judgment. First appearing in January 1845, the poem achieved unprecedented popularity. One biographer compares the poem's sudden ubiquity to the cultural saturation of an "uproariously successful" hit song today.[18] The comparison seems apt, insofar as the hypnotic rhythm of the poem surely accounted for much of its appeal. With respect to "The Raven," the era's permissive copyright laws worked both for and against Poe. On the one hand, he saw no additional remuneration from the many reprintings of the poem in newspapers and magazines across the country. An author could publish one of the most popular poems of the century and harvest a payday (reportedly $15) that equaled a day laborer's compensation for a few weeks' work. On the other hand, Poe achieved international fame practically overnight (the poem was also a sensation in Great Britain). Poe shrewdly capitalized on the poem's success, first by delivering a series of lectures on poetry, and then by publishing an essay, "The Philosophy of Composition," that purported to describe the calculated, analytical process by which the poem had been composed. Meanwhile, Poe had moved to New York and been drafted into a literary and political movement known as Young America, whose members focused on the importance of an international copyright agreement as a spur to American letters. In the promotion of this nationalistic cause, the prestigious firm of Wiley and Putnam issued two volumes by Poe in its "Library of American Books" publishing series: *Tales* in July and *The Raven and Other Poems* in November.

With Poe apparently poised for ever-greater success, he suffered a series of more or less self-inflicted setbacks. On flimsy grounds, he repeatedly attacked Longfellow as a plagiarist in the *Broadway Journal*. Next came a disastrous appearance before the Boston Lyceum, where Poe had been invited to present an original poem. Apparently beset by writer's block, he instead read from *Al Aaraaf*, later claiming disingenuously (in the wake of critical newspaper coverage) that his intention all along had been to hoax the credulous Boston literary establishment. Finally, in an embarrassing scene before his wife at home, Poe was asked by acquaintances to surrender supposedly incriminating love letters in his possession from poet Frances Osgood. He lashed out verbally at another poet, Elizabeth Ellet, whom he believed responsible for the delegation, suggesting he had compromising letters from Ellet as well. The bizarre scandal led to a fistfight with writer Thomas Dunn English; English's public attack on Poe in the *New York Mirror*; and a libel suit, largely alienating Poe from New York literary society. By 1846, little more than a year after the phenomenal success of "The Raven," newspapers ran personal ads authored by members of Poe's small circle of friends, advertising his and his wife Virginia's need for charity.

In 1847, Virginia died of tuberculosis. Her death plunged Poe into a deep personal crisis; his literary output of 1847 fell precipitously. Poe's professional life rebounded to some extent with the publication of his remarkable prose-poem *Eureka*, a cosmological treatise theorizing about the origins and end of the universe, in 1848 (see Part IV); thereafter, until his death in 1849, he continued to place his poetry and fiction in various periodicals, though not publications of the same national stature as those which had once regularly bought his work. Poe never fully recovered, personally or professionally, from the events of 1845–7, and his posthumous reputation as an unstable wretch was sealed for a time by the machinations of his literary executor, Rufus W. Griswold.

RECEPTION HISTORY

Upon learning of Poe's death, Griswold composed an obituary that set the terms of Poe's critical reception for decades. Writing under the name "Ludwig," he opened the review with the startlingly cruel proclamation that "few will be grieved" by the news of Poe's death. Griswold identified resentment and an inflated ego as keys to Poe's personality (so far so good, perhaps); but he went much further, depicting Poe as a lunatic who stalked into the street during thunderstorms, muttering curses under his breath and waving his arms impotently against the fury of the elements. Griswold hereby initiated the tradition of conflating Poe with his narrators, tracing a causal relationship between his supposedly unhinged personality and his Gothic-themed literature. While various friends and employers of Poe (including Graham, Willis, and Philadelphia novelist George Lippard) rushed into print to defend his character, their efforts were only partially successful, and the question of Poe's literary achievement was tied up for decades with the issue of his supposed character failings. Scott Peeples makes the counterintuitive but highly persuasive argument that Griswold's attack ultimately benefitted Poe's literary reputation: the controversy over Poe's character kept his name in front of readers, contributing to interest in the work.[19] And indeed, since Griswold's posthumous edition, Poe's works have never been out of print.

In the late nineteenth century, Poe found a wide readership in Europe, thanks to the devoted efforts of French poet Charles Baudelaire. The author of *Les Fleurs du mal* (1857) claimed, extraordinarily, that upon reading some of Poe's works, he encountered, to his amazement, "not simply certain subjects which I had dreamed of, but *sentences* which I had thought out, written by him twenty years before."[20] Embroidering the myth of Poe as a *poète maudit* whose insistence on art for art's sake tragically clashed with the middle-class, utilitarian American attitudes of the mid-nineteenth century, Baudelaire published five volumes of Poe translations from 1856 to 1865. Among the next generation of French poets, Stéphane Mallarmé regarded Poe as a major influence, claiming to have learned English the better to read Poe (the effort yielded the dubious side benefit of a career as an English teacher), and translating Poe's poetry in the 1870s. Garnering the admiration of Paul Valéry in the subsequent generation of French Symbolist poets, Poe achieved the status of a "world figure," even as his reputation in the United States lagged.[21] It was in part through these international channels that Poe came to influence such American modernists as T. S. Eliot and William Carlos Williams. In an essay that includes some notoriously cutting remarks about Poe's body of work ("slipshod writing, puerile thinking unsupported by wide reading or profound scholarship, haphazard experiments in various types of writing, chiefly under pressure of financial need, without perfection in any detail"), Eliot mulled over Poe's legacy, acknowledging almost despite himself the possibility of Poe's influence over his work.[22] Much less ambivalently, Williams proclaimed of Poe, "in him American literature is anchored, in him alone, on solid ground."[23]

American literary critics began to take Poe seriously in the twentieth century. In a landmark work of scholarship, sympathetic biographer Arthur Hobson Quinn exposed Griswold's forgeries and judiciously evaluated Poe's achievement in 1941.[24]

By the mid-twentieth century, Poe's placement within the canon was secure, even as onetime rivals, such as Longfellow, saw their reputations plummet. The advent of the literary critical movement known as the New Criticism proved equivocal with respect to Poe's reputation. Poe's attention to craft was compatible with the New Critical methodology of close reading. The movement's bracketing off of biographical questions in the evaluation of art, moreover, would also seem suited to work in Poe's favor, disentangling the Poe legend from assessment of the work. But some New Critics distrusted the mass culture forms in which Poe worked, and such influential critics as Yvor Winters, Cleanth Brooks, and Robert Penn Warren went out of their way to denigrate Poe.[25] Despite their distrust, dissertations, articles, and books about Poe were written at a steady pace, as critics simultaneously discovered formerly unacknowledged complexity in the writings and placed them within the intellectual and philosophical currents of the nineteenth century.[26]

Poe's work gained newfound cachet with the rise of French poststructuralist theory. Baudelaire and the Symbolists were only the first of a long line of French intellectuals to show a special affinity for Poe, not the least of whom was the formidable Marie Bonaparte—French princess, sexologist, and Sigmund Freud analysand—whose full-length biographical and critical study of Poe zeroed in on supposedly sexual symbolism and located the source of Poe's creative genius in repressed grief over the loss of his mother in his early years.[27] This tradition of French appreciation continued in the work of Jacques Lacan, who found in Poe's short story "The Purloined Letter" an occasion for elaborating his theories about the linguistic origins of human psychology. Deconstructionist Jacques Derrida raised the stakes with his response to Lacan in his own seminar on the story, finding in it an exemplification of his own theories of the indeterminacy of language. Publication of both of their essays, along with further contributions to the debate by American critics, in *The Purloined Poe* (1987), was a high-water mark for the influence of poststructuralist theory on American literary criticism.[28] Perhaps the most sophisticated application to date of psychoanalytic and deconstructive theories to Poe is Jonathan Elmer's 1995 *Reading at the Social Limit*, which subtly employed these critical perspectives in the project of understanding the sociological and ideological implications of a writer whose work exemplifies the "mass culture" that first assumed shape in America during Poe's lifetime.[29]

For most of the twentieth century, critics asserted that Poe's work stood at an oblique angle with respect to that of his contemporaries. Vernon L. Parrington famously opined in 1927 that "the problem of Poe . . . lies quite outside the main current of American thought," and F. O. Matthiessen left Poe out of his field-defining survey of mid-nineteenth-century American literature, *American Renaissance*.[30] In the 1980s and 1990s, however, as historically minded commentary supplanted New Critical, deconstructionist, and psychoanalytic models, Poe criticism experienced an American/historicist turn. Scholars investigated how Poe's work exemplified or responded to nineteenth-century American ideologies of race and gender. Novelist Toni Morrison was an influential early voice in this trend. Contending that the presence of African-descended people in the New World lent a continuous but unacknowledged sub-theme to American literature, she wrote that "No early American writer is more important to the concept of American Africanism than

Poe."[31] Terence Whalen coined the memorable term "average racism" to describe Poe's writing: Poe did not commit himself to a position on matters of race and slavery in print because it was against the interests of a commercial writer to alienate potential readers on either side of the volatile debate. If an initial move of some criticism engaging racial issues was to accuse Poe of formerly unexamined implication within the period's racist ideology, subtler readings have emerged as critics realize that many Poe works engage issues of race in surprisingly complex and ambiguous ways.[32] An important anthology consolidating this line of inquiry was *Romancing the Shadow: Poe and Race*, edited by J. Gerald Kennedy and Liliane Weissberg, published in 2001.[33]

The limited roles assigned to women in his poetry and fiction (love objects whose deaths occasion dramatic stagings of male grief; passive victims of male violence; monstrous *femme fatales* with the power to return from the dead) have inspired feminist investigations into Poe and gender, with scholars arriving at a consensus view that here too, as with race, the writings offer a ripe field for undermining supposedly stable hierarchies. It has been pointed out that Poe included women writers in the magazines he edited and, in his reviews, paid them the compliment of taking their work seriously.[34] Even as he satirized "bluestockings" in his fiction, for example, he praised feminist Margaret Fuller for her intellect and writing style.

In the past couple of decades, some of the most compelling work on Poe has situated him with respect to the antebellum publishing industry. This approach harkens back to groundbreaking mid-twentieth-century studies by Sidney Moss, Perry Miller, Michael Allen, and Robert Jacobs, but received new energy in 1999 with the publication of Whalen's *Edgar Allan Poe and the Masses*.[35] Whalen finds Poe ambivalent with respect to a mass market he both courted and distrusted, and paints him as, at times, the victim of an industry that was inherently exploitative. Meredith McGill complicates this picture by giving us a Poe who was a canny exploiter of the conditions of "reprint culture." The lack of distinctively American settings in his tales (which led an earlier generation of critics to question his relevance to American culture) actually made them optimally available for reprinting in different regional and market contexts; the tales are "set" within the easily recognizable and transportable conventions of Gothicism for professional reasons, McGill argues.[36] Elements of Poe's career once thought indicative of a uniquely belligerent personality have been thoughtfully reinterpreted as responses to market conditions: Sandra Tomc contends, for example, that Poe learned from observing the careers of other magazinists that a reputation for outrageousness heightened a writer's visibility and could be leveraged into a certain amount of professional success, though not without the risk of a corresponding backlash.[37] Leon Jackson notes Poe's occasional participation in prize competitions (two wins in three tries), one of several "embedded economies" that made up an antebellum publishing scene whose economic structures were far more complicated than has been realized.[38] The essays in J. Gerald Kennedy and Jerome McGann's anthology *Poe and the Remapping of Antebellum Print Culture* explore additional insights generated from positioning Poe within a decentralized antebellum print culture.[39]

Studies focused on the economics of publishing continue to illuminate Poe's work and career up to the present moment. Carlos Martinez maintains that by defining literary success in terms of achieving an effect on the reader, Poe built marketing considerations into his paradigm of authorship, thereby "undermining the binary logic of the critical versus the popular."[40] In her most recent contribution to this line of inquiry, Tomc applies the insights of Marxist theorist James W. Moore. Moore has described how periods of capitalist expansion occur because large domains of labor or energy are rendered invisible or figured as natural resources. In Poe's day, publishers involved in debates about an international copyright law characterized the texts they published in terms of natural resources like rain or grass, effacing the labor that went into their production. Tomc contends that the picture of amateur writers flooding the market with an oversupply of manuscripts was not necessarily a true picture of affairs (editors sometimes worried about a scarcity of quality manuscripts), but was actually an "ideological construct" self-interestedly endorsed by publishers, one that excluded authors "from the realms of visibly productive workers."[41] As an author who also served for a time as the proprietor of a periodical, Poe was simultaneously a victim of and participant in such rhetoric, as Tomc finds in her analysis of "Secrets of the Magazine Prison-House," an essay by Poe included in Part V of the present volume.

EMERGING TRENDS IN POE SCHOLARSHIP

Poe's canonical status, his varied output, and the resistance of much of his fiction and poetry to interpretive closure ensure that his work will attract attention from critics working in emerging methodologies. Four approaches that have made notable inroads into Poe studies in recent years include digital humanities, queer theory, eco-criticism, and affect studies. As a technophile, Poe would undoubtedly find intriguing the work of digital humanities scholars, who apply sophisticated computer software to the analysis of literary corpora. Stefan Schöberlein applies such techniques to one of the most vexed questions of Poe scholarship over the past few decades, his supposed authorship of the notorious Paulding-Drayton review, an unsigned review that appeared during Poe's editorship of the *Southern Literary Messenger* in 1836. Much rides on the question of attribution, since the review includes a robust defense of slavery, which, if authored by Poe, would supply an interpretive context tending to resolve ambiguities on the subject of race in his work toward a presumption of bigotry. Schöberlein's study supports the re-emerging critical consensus that the review's author was Nathaniel Beverly Tucker, a sometime contributor to the *Messenger*, as many Poe scholars had long believed.[42] With a different set of digital tools, Caitlin Duffy graphs the frequency and location of words connoting emotional states in Poe's fiction, helping to map how linguistic choices create an effect of terror in selected stories.[43] Ryan Cordell uses a corrupted digital text of "The Raven," located through a searchable database, as the occasion for a sophisticated theorization of how to account bibliographically for the production of the digitized materials on which scholars increasingly (and perhaps sometimes uncritically) rely.[44]

While feminist critics have long wrestled with Poe's legacy, queer theory brings a new set of questions to representations of gender and sexuality in the work. In 2000, Gustavus T. Stadler noted that Poe was largely "absent from the map of gay and/or queer analyses of antebellum American culture,"[45] a state of affairs that scholars have since begun to rectify. Leland S. Person set an early tone when he observed a pattern of homosexual panic attending depictions of same-sex desire in Poe's fiction, a trend that helps readers "understand the inception of a powerful homophobia in the middle of the nineteenth century."[46] More recently, Suzanne Ashworth similarly finds the fiction tracking with heteronormative rejection of queer sexuality in "The Facts in the Case of M. Valdemar," where non-normative desire is associated with disgust and death.[47] David Greven arguably finds Poe's fiction somewhat more sympathetic to same-sex desire, noting, for example, how the thwarting of such desire in *The Narrative of Arthur Gordon Pym* results in the protagonist's pervasive melancholy.[48]

Taking his cue from queer theorist Lee Edelman, however, Paul Christian Jones offers a provocative reassessment of queer desire in Poe's "family fictions" ("Morella," "Ligeia," and "The Fall of the House of Usher"). Jones notes that critics have tended to vilify the narrators of "Morella" and "Ligeia," when it is the titular female characters of these stories, not the narrators, who dispossess other women of their bodies. Jones proposes that critical disapprobation of the narrators may be traceable on some level to heteronormative attitudes, whereby a character standing outside the norms of heterosexual reproduction looks suspect or even monstrous. Of the three stories in question, it is in "The Fall of the House of Usher," Jones contends, where Poe creates a narrator who most successfully manages to step outside the culture's insistence on reproductive futurism, represented in the story by Madeline and Roderick. In a noteworthy departure from much previous commentary, Jones maintains that "Poe's stories actually seem to avoid such negative characterizations of the queer; indeed, he seems largely sympathetic to these men and ultimately quite interested in the lives that await them as they negate conventional futures and attempt to invent more fulfilling ones."[49]

Because the settings of Poe's works contribute so much to the effects he aimed to cultivate, much critical attention has been profitably devoted to their analysis.[50] Ecocritical approaches offer new ways to look at settings and geography in Poe, as exemplified in Erin E. Forbes's recent analysis of "Dream-Land." Long considered one of the most purely aesthetic of Poe's works, and therefore not of interest to historically or ideologically minded critics, the poem may actually merge aesthetic and historical concerns in ways previously unrecognized. On the basis of various pieces of evidence (not least of which is the close juxtaposition of the words "dismal" and "swamp" within the poem), Forbes reads the setting for the poem as, on one level, the Great Dismal Swamp of Virginia, known in Poe's day for, among other things, harboring maroon communities in flight from slavery. Through its melding of "place and person, human and nonhuman, land and water," Forbes contends, the swamp "is broadly constitutive of Poe's aesthetic theory and practice across his fiction, poetry, and criticism"; she goes so far as to label Poe's a "swamp aesthetic."[51] Referencing *The Conchologist's First Book* (a textbook to which Poe lent his efforts early in his career), James D. Lilley takes a similar tack, crediting Poe not with a swamp aesthetic but instead with a malacological aesthetic (malacology is the study of mollusks). In *The Narrative of Arthur Gordon Pym*, among other works, Poe's aesthetic vision involves challenging the idea of stable individual personhood in favor of "an intimately interrelated living world," in which humans are consistently viewed in relation to the larger ecosystem—not unlike mollusks in relation to their shells.[52] Ellen M. Bayer turns attention to Poe's little-noticed landscape pieces, "The Domain of Arnheim" and "Landor's Cottage," making a strong case that Poe was influenced by Andrew Jackson Downing's popular landscaping manual, *A Treatise on the Theory and Practice of Landscape Gardening* (1841). Like authors combining materials in novel ways to achieve a desired effect, as Poe endorsed in his criticism, Downing encourages would-be landscapers to avail themselves of non-native plant species in order to impress viewers with the artifice of the scene. It turns out that Poe's landscape pieces refer to a number of the non-native species specifically recommended in Downing's manual. What nineteenth-century naturalists such as Downing (or their admirers, such as Poe) failed to consider were the long-term implications of importing non-native plant species, some of which have become invasive, with dire ecological consequences.[53]

The emphasis in Poe's poetics on crafting a work to inspire a particular emotion in the reader has attracted the attention of scholars working in affect studies. Critics affiliated with this loosely defined approach investigate the mechanics of how art and literature shape our emotional responses, using methods that come from fields as varied as psychology, critical theory, and neuroscience. Adam Frank notes that Poe's tales "are centrally concerned with affective communication between text and reader," and therefore reads a number of them as allegories of the writer–reader relationship, relying in part on the insights of mid-twentieth-century psychologist Silvan Tomkins.[54] In perhaps the most philosophically complex application of affect studies to Poe, Paul Hurh explores the relationship between terror and philosophical inquiry in his work. Contesting the idea that terror and philosophical thought are opposed cognitive experiences, Hurh suggests that for Poe, terror can be described as the unique, disorienting affect that accompanies deep philosophical thought.[55] Poe's story "Berenice" has become a particular site of debate for affect studies critics. Sean McAlister analyzes the story by way of the aesthetic theories of Immanuel Kant, who endorsed the disinterested contemplation of aesthetic objects. Poe rejects this idea in "Berenice," McAlister suggests, positing instead (through the figure of Egaeus and his deeply interested contemplation of Berenice's teeth) an artistic theory that depends upon interest as being more conducive to the commercial pressures of the antebellum publishing world. Chad Luck notes how European literary criticism shifted during the Romantic period from evaluating matters of taste, judgment, and beauty (an emotional response) to investigating questions of interpretation (a cognitive response). Following these trends, "Berenice" analyzes the process whereby readers react to interesting art, as Egaeus toggles between emotional and cognitive responses in his contemplation of Berenice.[56]

Inspired by the work of influential trauma theorist Cathy Caruth, critics over the past decade have investigated trauma as another key emotional state in Poe's works. Christina Zwarg examines Poe's appreciation of Margaret Fuller's travel book, *Summer on the Lakes*, as expressed in an 1846 review. In narrating her physical approach toward Niagara Falls, Fuller allowed traumatic scenes of young women pleading for their lives before scalping Indians to intrude on her present experience, unexpectedly inspiring dread in response to the sublime spectacle. Zwarg suggests that Poe appreciated Fuller's canny use of temporal dislocation, a key concept in trauma studies, to shape a reader's emotional response to incidents in the text.[57]

Marita Nadal applies trauma theory to two of Poe's most canonical stories, "Ligeia" and "The Fall of the House of Usher." In "Ligeia," the narrator's puzzling (and often-discussed) inability to remember key details of his relationship with the title character may register his trauma over her premature death, while in "Usher," Nadal contends, the family has experienced an "unspecified transgenerational family trauma," which Madeline, through her uncanny return from death, comes to embody.[58] Jeffrey Andrew Weinstock discusses trauma theory with respect to Poe's angelic dialogues, in which the speakers narrate such traumatic experiences as their individual deaths and the end of the world. Weinstock focuses on "Pre-Traumatic Stress Syndrome," a term coined by E. Ann Kaplan for the anticipatory anxiety generated in audiences by post-apocalyptic narratives in fiction and film. Poe's dialogue "The Conversation of Eiros and Charmion" conveys this emotional response through the particular manner of Eiros's narration of Earth's destruction by a comet, with implications for present-day readers mindful of the consequences of climate change: "Feeding into twenty-first-century Pre-Traumatic Stress Syndrome, Eiros's apocalyptic experience reads as prophecy of our apocalypse to come—their trauma about the world destroyed becomes our anticipatory anxiety about a precarious future."[59]

ADDITIONAL READING

Readers interested in separating fact from fiction with respect to Poe's much-mythologized life story should know about the two biographies to which Poe scholars assign special value. Despite dating from the 1940s, Arthur Hobson Quinn's *Edgar Allan Poe: A Critical Biography* is still frequently cited. Acclaimed literary biographer Kenneth Silverman updated Quinn's work with his *Edgar A. Poe: Mournful and Never-ending Remembrance* in the 1990s. In 1987, Dwight Thomas and David K. Jackson published their 900-page *The Poe Log: A Documentary Life of Edgar Allan Poe 1809–1849*, which offers, without commentary, chronological excerpts from the verifiable documentary record of Poe's life.[60] Readers not up for the challenge of hundreds of pages of biography are directed to J. Gerald Kennedy's concise biographical sketch in his edited volume *A Historical Guide to Edgar Allan Poe*, which situates Poe's life within the tumultuous political and social upheavals of the era.[61] A handsome, updated edition (in two volumes) of Poe's letters was published by the Gordian Press in 2008.[62]

An essential internet-based resource for Poe is the website of the Edgar Allan Poe Society of Baltimore (eapoe.org), which collects, along with texts of Poe's works and a certain amount of secondary literature (including the texts of Quinn's biography and *The Poe Log* in full), a reliable and illuminating series of essays on general topics about Poe, including such perennially intriguing topics as his alcoholism (and supposed drug use) and the unresolved mystery surrounding his death. For an overview of the contemporary state of Poe scholarship as of 2002, I recommend Kevin J. Hayes' entry in the prestigious Cambridge Companion series, *The Cambridge Companion to Edgar Allan Poe*. In 2012, Hayes edited an omnibus collection of thirty-seven short essays contextualizing Poe's work alongside numerous biographical, social, and cultural developments: *Edgar Allan Poe in Context*.[63]

The latest attempt to consolidate scholarship on Poe is the magisterial *Oxford Handbook of Edgar Allan Poe*, edited by J. Gerald Kennedy and Scott Peeples in 2019.[64] This landmark volume includes forty-five essays on distinct elements of Poe's life and writing, written by leading scholars of Poe and of nineteenth-century American literature more generally. The essays simultaneously bring readers up to date on the present state of knowledge and offer fresh perspectives on the field; the volume will be indispensable reading for the coming generation of Poe scholars. That Poe claims two academic journals devoted to his work—*Poe Studies: History, Theory, Interpretation* and the *Edgar Allan Poe Review*—testifies to his commanding presence on the literary-critical landscape and ensures that exegetes will continue to enrich our understanding of his works for the foreseeable future.

SCOPE OF THE PRESENT VOLUME

The remaining four sections of this book offer an overview of Poe's contributions to American and world literature in the areas of fiction, non-fiction prose, and poetry. The guiding selection principles for the literary pieces have been to include (1) works that have proven popular and influential among generations of non-academic readers, and (2) works that occupy a significant presence in the extensive secondary literature on Poe, particularly those that have enjoyed renewed (or continuing) scholarly attention in recent years. Part II covers Poe's short stories; Part III is devoted to poetry; Part IV offers excerpts from Poe's book-length cosmological treatise *Eureka*; and Part V includes critical writings and letters. The aim is to present in one volume a comprehensive gathering of the indispensable Poe canon as currently conceived, with sufficient commentary to allow readers entrée into ongoing scholarly conversations.

The short fiction included in Part II ranges across Poe's career, from the early prize-winning "Ms. Found in a Bottle" to the last tale published in his lifetime, "Hop-Frog." Stories are arranged chronologically by date of initial publication. This section includes representative selections from all of the major sub-genres in which Poe distinguished himself: Gothic thrillers, tales of sensation, satires, detective stories, and hoaxes. The length of Poe's only completed novel, *The Narrative of Arthur Gordon Pym*, made inclusion in a single-volume collection impractical; interested readers will turn to a stand-alone edition. Also not included are various pieces that have garnered minimal attention from critics in recent years. These include, among other minor works, the early satirical tales intended for insertion in the aborted *Tales of the Folio Club* project; Poe's so-called angelic dialogues, in which disembodied spirits discourse to each other from the afterlife; and "plate articles" written to accompany engravings in magazines.

The poems in Part III are arranged chronologically by date of initial publication (excepting the posthumously published "Alone," inserted by estimated date of composition). The major poems on which Poe's poetic reputation rests, such as "To Helen," "The Raven," and "Annabel Lee," are of course included, along with ten others frequently referenced in the secondary literature. I have chosen not to include Poe's early narrative poem "Al Aaraaf" (his longest poem), his verse drama "Politian," or various minor performances, including once popular but now infrequently anthologized poems such as "Lenore" and "Eldorado." The prospect of a sudden rise in critical fortunes for these works seems remote.

Excerpts from *Eureka* in Part IV capture the book's main scientific argument as well as its most interesting digressions. *Eureka* has often been regarded as an anomaly in Poe's oeuvre, but it seems poised for recuperation, judging by the recent publication of two full-length critical studies.[65] *Eureka*'s vision of a universe cataclysmically contracting in upon itself evidently speaks to an age preoccupied with the effects of climate change, when Poe's vision of humanity's ultimate annihilation (or transcendence) suddenly seems more than purely speculative.

Part V covers Poe's essays, prefaces, and selected letters. The critical works occupy one chronological grouping, the letters another. Poe's most important critical statements, his initial review of Hawthorne's *Twice-Told Tales* and his essay "The Philosophy of Composition," are included in their entirety. Excerpts from other writings convey the full range of critical principles for which Poe campaigned in his reviews. Passages from a handful of Poe's letters either reflect his uniquely histrionic personality or else include candid and illuminating opinions about his own creative work.

A particular aim of this volume has been to present works that comment in some way on Poe's embeddedness within the complicated world of antebellum publishing. This intention explains the inclusion in Part II of two rarely discussed literary satires—"Never Bet the Devil Your Head" and "The Literary Life of Thingum Bob, Esq."—and two non-fiction prose pieces in Part V: "Some Secrets of the Magazine Prison-House" and excerpts from "Anastatic Printing." Poe had an insider's knowledge of the business of writing surpassed by few if any of his peers, giving his insights into the industry's workings particular value, especially for readers interested in book history, print culture, and the history of authorship methodologies.

NOTES

1. See Robert D. Jacobs, *Poe: Journalist & Critic* (Baton Rouge: Louisiana University Press, 1969), and Joan Dayan, *Fables of Mind: An Inquiry into Poe's Fiction* (New York: Oxford University Press, 1987). Poe's affinity with eighteenth-century rhetoricians is explored in Gero Guttzeit, *Edgar Allan Poe: Authorship, Antebellum Literature, and Transatlantic Rhetoric* (Berlin and Boston: De Gruyter, 2017).

2. G. R. Thompson, Poe's Fiction: *Romantic Irony in the Gothic Tales* (Madison: University of Wisconsin Press, 1973).

3. Poe to Philip P. Cooke, New York, August 9, 1846, in *The Collected Letters of Edgar Allan Poe*, eds. John Ward Ostrom, Burton R. Pollin, and Jeffrey A. Savoye (New York: Gordian Press, 2008), 1:596.

4. Twain to William Dean Howells, Redding, CT, January 18, 1809, in *Mark Twain's Letters*, ed. Alfred Bigelow Paine (New York: Harper & Brothers Publishers, 1917), 2:830.

5. Harry Levin, *The Power of Blackness: Hawthorne, Poe, Melville* (New York: Alfred A. Knopf, 1967), 133, 135.

6. Brent Zimmerman, *Edgar Allan Poe: Rhetoric and Style* (Montreal: McGill-Queen's University Press, 2005).

7. Peter Coviello, "Poe in Love: Pedophilia, Morbidity, and the Logic of Slavery," *English Literary History* 70, no. 3 (2003): 883.

8. John Tebbel, *A History of Publishing in the United States*, vol. 1, *The Creation of an Industry, 1630–1865* (New York: R. R. Bowker, 1972), 221.

9. Frank Luther Mott, *A History of American Magazines, 1741–1930* (Cambridge, MA: Harvard University Press, 1930), 1:341.

10. Edgar A. Poe, "Marginalia," *Graham's Magazine of Literature, Art, and Fashion*, December 1846, 312.

11. Poe to Frederick W. Thomas, Fordham, February 14, 1849, *The Collected Letters*, 2:770.

12. Michael Allen, *Poe and the British Magazine Tradition* (New York: Oxford University Press, 1969).

13. Perry Miller, *The Raven and the Whale: The War of Words and Wits in the Era of Poe and Melville* (New York: Harcourt, Brace and Company, 1956).

14. Poe to Frederick W. Thomas, Philadelphia, May 25, 1842, *The Collected Letters*, 1:333.

15. Terence Whalen, *Edgar Allan Poe and the Masses: The Political Economy of Literature in Antebellum America* (Princeton, NJ: Princeton University Press, 1999).

16. Kevin J. Hayes, *Poe and the Printed Word* (Cambridge: Cambridge University Press, 2003).

17. James Russell Lowell, "Our Contributors.—No. XVII," *Graham's Magazine of Literature, Art, and Fashion*, February 1845, 50, 51.

18. Kenneth Silverman, *Edgar A. Poe: Mournful and Never-ending Remembrance* (New York: HarperPerennial, 1992), 237.

19. Scott Peeples, *The Afterlife of Edgar Allan Poe* (Rochester, NY: Camden House, 2004), 11.

20. Quoted in Patrick F. Quinn, *The French Face of Edgar Poe* (Carbondale: Southern Illinois University Press, 1957), 15.

21. Quinn, *The French Face of Edgar Poe*, 10.

22. T. S. Eliot, "From Poe to Valéry," *Hudson Review* 2, no. 3 (1949): 327.

23. William Carlos Williams, *In the American Grain* (1925; repr., New York: New Directions, 1956), 226.

24. Arthur Hobson Quinn, *Edgar Allan Poe: A Critical Biography* (1941; repr., Baltimore, MD: Johns Hopkins University Press, 1998).

25. Peeples, *The Afterlife of Edgar Allan Poe*, 64, 69.

26. Edward H. Davidson's *Poe: A Critical Study* (Cambridge, MA: Harvard University Press, 1957) is probably the most significant work of scholarship from this period, along with Levin's *The Power of Blackness*, cited above in note 5.

27. Marie Bonaparte, *The Life and Works of Edgar Allan Poe: A Psycho-Analytic Interpretation* (London: Imago Publishing Co. Ltd., 1949).

28. John P. Muller and William P. Richardson, eds., *The Purloined Poe: Lacan, Derrida, and Psychoanalytic Reading* (Baltimore, MD: Johns Hopkins University Press, 1987).

29. Jonathan Elmer, *Reading at the Social Limit: Affect, Mass Culture, and Edgar Allan Poe* (Stanford, CA: Stanford University Press, 1995).

30. Vernon Louis Parrington, *Main Currents in American Thought*, vol. 2, *The Romantic Revolution in America, 1800–1860* (1927; repr. Norman: University of Oklahoma Press, 1987), 58; F. O. Matthiessen, *American Renaissance: Art and Expression in the Age of Emerson and Whitman* (New York: Oxford University Press, 1941).

31. Toni Morrison, *Playing in the Dark: Whiteness and the Literary Imagination* (New York: Vintage Books, 1992), 32.

32. One of the most influential readings along these lines is Joan Dayan, "Amorous Bondage: Poe, Ladies, and Slaves," in *The American Face of Edgar Allan Poe*, eds. Shawn Rosenheim and Stephen Rachman (Baltimore, MD: Johns Hopkins University Press, 1995), 179–209.

33. J. Gerald Kennedy and Liliane Weissberg, eds., *Romancing the Shadow: Poe and Race* (New York: Oxford University Press, 2001).

34. Eliza Richards, *Gender and the Poetics of Reception in Poe's Circle* (Cambridge: Cambridge University Press, 2004).

35. Sidney P. Moss, *Poe's Literary Battles: The Critic in the Context of His Literary Milieu* (Durham, NC: Duke University Press, 1963); Miller, *The Raven and the Whale*; Michael Allen, *Poe and the British Magazine Tradition* (New York: Oxford University Press, 1969); Jacobs, *Poe: Journalist & Critic*.

36. Meredith McGill, *American Literature and the Culture of Reprinting, 1834–1853* (Philadelphia: University of Pennsylvania Press, 2003).

37. Sandra Tomc, *Industry and the Creative Mind: The Eccentric Writer in American Literature and Entertainment, 1790–1860* (Ann Arbor: University of Michigan Press, 2012).

38. Leon Jackson, *The Business of Letters: Authorial Economies in Antebellum America* (Stanford, CA: Stanford University Press, 2008).

39. Jerome McGann and J. Gerald Kennedy, eds., *Poe and the Remapping of Antebellum Print Culture* (Baton Rouge: Louisiana State University Press, 2012).

40. Carlos Martinez, "'The Heresy of the Didactic': Poe, the Literary Field, and the Aestheticization of the Market," *Arizona Quarterly* 74, no. 2 (2018): 104.

41. Sandra Tomc, "Cheap Poe and Other Bargains: Unpaid Work and Energy in Early Nineteenth-Century U.S. Publishing," *English Literary History* 86, no. 1 (2019): 192.

42. Stefan Schöberlein, "Poe or not Poe? A Stylometric Analysis of Edgar Allan Poe's Disputed Writings," *Digital Scholarship in the Humanities* 32, no. 3 (2017): 643–59.

43. Caitlin Duffy, "Sensory Overload and Poe's Mechanics of Terror," *Poe Studies* 52 (2019): 69–90.

44. Cordell, Ryan. "'Q i-jtb the Raven': Taking Dirty OCR Seriously," *Book History* 20 (2017): 188–225.

45. Gustavus T. Stadler, "Poe and Queer Studies," *Poe Studies/Dark Romanticism: History, Theory, Interpretation* 33, no. 1–2 (2000): 19.

46. Leland S. Person, "Queer Poe: The Tell-Tale Heart of His Fiction," *Poe Studies* 41, no. 1 (2008): 8.

47. Suzanne Ashworth, "Cadaverous Intimacies: Disgust, Desire, and the Corpse in Edgar Allan Poe's 'Valdemar,'" *Criticism* 58, no. 4 (2016): 565–92.

48. David Greven, *Gender Protest and Same-Sex Desire in Antebellum Literature: Margaret Fuller, Edgar Allan Poe, Nathaniel Hawthorne, and Herman Melville* (London: Ashgate, 2014).

49. Paul Christian Jones, "Resisting Reproduction in Edgar Allan Poe's Family Fictions," *Studies in American Fiction* 45, no. 2 (2018): 185. See also Paul Christian Jones, "'Nevermore!': Non-Normative Desire and Queer Temporality in Poe's 'The Raven,'" *Poe Studies* 49 (2016): 80–98.

50. One recent book devotes an entire volume to Poe's settings: Philip Edward Phillips, ed., *Poe and Place* (New York: Palgrave Macmillan, 2018).

51. Erin E. Forbes, "Edgar Allan Poe and the Great Dismal Swamp: Reading Race and Environment after the Aesthetic Turn," *Modern Philology* 114, no. 2 (2016): 370, 387.

52. James D. Lilley, "Poe, Movement, and Matter: The Malacological Aesthetics of *The Narrative of Arthur Gordon Pym*," *Arizona Quarterly* 73, no. 4 (2017): 2.

53. Ellen M. Bayer, "The Ecocritical Implications of Downing's Influence on Poe's Landscape Aesthetic," *Edgar Allan Poe Review* 19, no. 2 (2018): 250–73.

54. Adam Frank, *Transferential Poetics, from Poe to Warhol* (New York: Fordham University Press, 2015), 55.

55. Paul Hurh, *American Terror: The Feeling of Thinking in Edwards, Poe, and Melville* (Stanford, CA: Stanford University Press, 2015).

56. Sean McAlister, "Revolution of Thought/Revulsion of Feeling: Edgar Allan Poe and the Interest Concept," *Criticism* 55, no. 3 (2013): 471–506; Chad Luck, "Poe's 'Berenice' and the Aesthetic of the Interesting," *Poe Studies* 52 (2019): 9–27.

57. Christina Zwarg, "Temporal Effects: Trauma, Margaret Fuller, and Graphicality in Poe," in *The Oxford Handbook of Edgar Allan Poe*, eds. J. Gerald Kennedy and Scott Peeples (New York: Oxford University Press, 2019), 773–91.

58. Marita Nadal, "Trauma and the Uncanny in Edgar Allan Poe's 'Ligeia' and 'The Fall of the House of Usher,'" *Edgar Allan Poe Review* 17, no. 2 (2016): 185.

59. Jeffrey Andrew Weinstock, "Before the After: Anticipatory Anxiety and Experience Claimed in Poe's Angelic Dialogues," *Poe Studies* 52 (2019): 100.

60. Silverman and Quinn's biographies are cited above, notes 18 and 24; Dwight Thomas and David K. Jackson, *The Poe Log: A Documentary Life of Edgar Allan Poe 1809– 1849* (Boston: G. K. Hall & Co., 1987).

61. J. Gerald Kennedy, ed., *A Historical Guide to Edgar Allan Poe* (New York: Oxford University Press, 2001).

62. John Ward Ostrom, Burton R. Pollin, and Jeffrey A. Savoye, eds., *The Collected Letters of Edgar Allan Poe*, 2 vols. (New York: Gordian Press, 2008).

63. Kevin J. Hayes, ed., *The Cambridge Companion to Edgar Allan Poe* (Cambridge: Cambridge University Press, 2002); Kevin J. Hayes, ed., *Edgar Allan Poe in Context* (Cambridge: Cambridge University Press, 2013).

64. Kennedy and Peeples, *The Oxford Handbook of Edgar Allan Poe*.

65. David N. Stamos, *Edgar Allan Poe,* Eureka, *and the Scientific Imagination* (Albany, NY: SUNY Press, 2017); Robert J. Scholnick, *Poe's* Eureka, *Erasmus Darwin, and Discourses of Radical Science in Britain and America, 1770–1850* (Lewiston, NY: Edwin Mellen Press, 2018).

PART II

Tales

POE'S FICTION-WRITING CAREER

Edgar Allan Poe first came to public recognition as a fiction writer thanks to literary contests held by newspapers.[1] Poe did not win the prize contest sponsored by Philadelphia's *Saturday Courier* in the spring of 1831, but during a period of months in 1832, the newspaper published several of his submissions; that such publication was apparently uncompensated served as Poe's introduction to the harsh realities of the antebellum fiction market. In 1833, the still virtually unknown author (only one of the tales published in the *Saturday Courier* had been printed over Poe's name) won the fiction-writing portion of a prize contest sponsored by the Baltimore *Saturday Visiter* on the strength of his story "Ms. Found in a Bottle." Letters suggest that at this point in his career, Poe contemplated publishing a series of tales under the title *Tales of the Folio Club,* which would have consisted primarily of burlesques of popular writers in a number of genres, but this book project never came to fruition.

By 1834, Poe had begun to publish tales in prominent magazines with national distribution. Two of the early tales included here, "Berenice" and "Morella," appeared in the *Southern Literary Messenger* of Richmond, Virginia in March and April of 1835, respectively, during Poe's association with that magazine. The period's expanding literary marketplace afforded Poe a number of arenas in which to publish stories, even though industry conditions, as described in Part I of this volume, ensured that the income to be derived from such piecemeal work was minimal at best. Some of these venues included the Baltimore *American Museum*, where Poe published "Ligeia" and "The Psyche Zenobia" (later titled "How to Write a Blackwood Article") in the fall of 1838, and Christmas annuals, such as *The Gift* ("William Wilson" in 1840 and "The Purloined Letter" in 1844), lavish volumes intended for holiday gift-giving. On the advice of an editor at Harper and Brothers that readers preferred full-length novels to collections of stories, Poe completed his only novel, *The Narrative of Arthur Gordon Pym*, in 1837. Unfortunately for Poe, a disastrous financial panic engulfed the U.S. economy at that time, delaying publication until 1838. While the novel includes a number of thrilling and memorable incidents, its loose structure and extended descriptive passages, some virtually cribbed from encyclopedias and travel books, confirm that Poe's talents were best suited to the short story format.

In the next phase of his career, Poe held editorial posts with magazines published out of Philadelphia. These posts accorded him the financial stability that came with a salaried position, as well as the opportunity to earn additional income by providing the magazines with original fiction. "The Man That Was Used Up" and "The Fall of the House of Usher," among other pieces, appeared in William Burton's *Gentleman's*

Magazine during Poe's editorship. In 1839, Poe's first published collection of stories, *Tales of the Grotesque and Arabesque*, gathered together twenty-five tales that had previously appeared in various magazines. Poe began contributing stories to George Graham's new *Graham's Lady's and Gentleman's Magazine* after taking an editorial position there in 1840. These include "The Murders in the Rue Morgue," "A Descent into the Maelström," "Never Bet the Devil Your Head," "The Masque of the Red Death," and, some time after Poe had left his editorial position with *Graham's*, "The Imp of the Perverse."

One must admire Poe's self-assurance in withdrawing "The Gold-Bug" from its scheduled appearance in *Graham's* in 1843, for which he had already been paid, to submit it instead to a $100 prize contest sponsored by Philadelphia's *Dollar Magazine*. In pursuit of a bigger payday, Poe risked the sure thing (he had to compensate Graham in the form of additional material) for the uncertainty of competition. "The Gold-Bug" won the prize and went on to become the most popular tale Poe published in his lifetime. That year saw the publication of two more of Poe's best-known tales: "The Tell-Tale Heart" appeared in editor and poet James Russell Lowell's newly established magazine, *The Pioneer*, and "The Black Cat" was published in the *United States Saturday Post*. After moving to New York in 1844, Poe hoaxed New Yorkers with his account of a transatlantic balloon flight in the famous penny paper the *Sun* (a periodical whose credibility in such matters had somehow not been compromised when, nine years earlier, it had published a story, later acknowledged as a hoax, announcing the discovery of life on the moon). In 1845, Poe took over editorial duties and part-ownership of a New York periodical called the *Broadway Journal*. Upon becoming its sole owner for a short time (until it failed), Poe filled its pages with revised versions of previously published tales, the source of some of the texts included here.

The prominent New York firm Wiley and Putnam published a volume of Poe's *Tales* in its prestigious and canon-shaping Library of American Books series in 1845. From then on, Poe's fiction appeared in a variety of American magazines, including the *American Review: A Whig Journal* ("Some Words with a Mummy" and "The Facts in the Case of M. Valdemar") and *Godey's Lady's Book* ("The Cask of Amontillado"). In the last years of his career, Poe's fictional output declined due to the trauma of Virginia's death, in 1847, and the attention he devoted to his book-length cosmological treatise *Eureka*, published in 1848 (see Part IV for excerpts). The final short story to appear during Poe's lifetime, "Hop-Frog," was published in a Boston periodical, the *Flag of Our Union*, in March 1849. Poe died in October of that year.

GENERIC CONSIDERATIONS

Poe initially achieved national prominence (if not to say notoriety) as a reviewer, but his contemporary Nathaniel Hawthorne anticipated later judgments when he wrote to Poe in 1846: "I admire you rather as a writer of tales than as a critic upon them." (In this short note, Hawthorne slighted Poe's poetry altogether.) Hawthorne wrote that he "could never fail to recognize [Poe's] force and originality" in the latter's short fiction.[2] While Poe's criticism has undeniably been influential, and he wrote some of the most famous poems of the nineteenth century, the scholarly consensus holds his fiction to be his chief claim on modern readers. The tales selected here showcase the force and originality Poe displayed across a variety of genres. Among readers today, Poe is beloved as an author of Gothic fiction. The Gothic is easier to recognize than to define with precision, but its key elements are familiar to modern readers (and other media consumers): foreboding settings such as decaying manors and midnight graveyards; doppelgängers, ghosts, and other supernatural figures that trouble clear distinctions between the living and the dead; scenes of crime, violence, and torture; experiences that arouse feelings of anxiety and terror, such as burial alive; hallucinatory or otherwise altered states of consciousness; and invocation of traditional sources of superstition, such as witches and black cats. All of these elements can be found in the selections to follow.

Poe distinguished himself among practitioners of the Gothic by devoting superior craftsmanship to stories made up of these well-known materials. In 1835, the editor of the *Southern Literary Messenger*, Thomas W. White, wrote to Poe suggesting that the story "Berenice," which had appeared in the magazine, may have been in bad taste (the story's narrator, while in a trance, attacks the prematurely buried but still-living body of his fiancée). In his revealing response, included in Part V of this volume, Poe made the surprising claim that the tale "originated in a bet." He went on to note that such articles, whether in poor taste or not, frequently aroused a sensation among readers, cannily informing White, "to be appreciated, you must be *read*, and these things are invariably sought after with avidity." Poe's comments suggest that he turned his hand to Gothic fiction because he saw it as a route to popularity. If subsequent writings proved that Poe had a rare gift for the form, his success is best regarded as a marriage of innate ability with market-savvy opportunism. In the same letter, Poe stressed that when writing such tales, "great attention must be paid to style, and much labour spent in their composition, or they will degenerate into the turgid or the absurd." A meticulous reviser, Poe in his best tales availed himself of a number of carefully modulated stylistic techniques through which he invested every sentence with the singular force that Hawthorne appreciated.[3] Poe's curious characterization of Gothic fiction in this letter is also worth quoting here: "the ludicrous heightened into the grotesque: the fearful coloured into the horrible: the witty exaggerated into the burlesque: the singular wrought out into the strange and mystical." The use of words such as *ludicrous*, *burlesque*, and *witty* to describe Gothic fiction opens the possibility, most notably elaborated by critic G. R. Thompson, that Poe's Gothic stories retain a parodic element alongside their more serious implications.[4]

One of Poe's best-known stories, "The Fall of the House of Usher," exemplifies his handling of the form. The story assembles a surfeit of traditional Gothic trappings: a creepily stagnant landscape; a claustrophobic, decaying mansion; a neurotic aesthete and his dying sister (with a hint of incestuous desire, another Gothic trope); a ghoulish physician; an exposed family crypt; a midnight storm; and interment alive. Commentators have arrived at a number of theories explaining what all this excess finally amounts to, but the narrator's persistent attention to how the setting affects his own psychological state suggests that the story's overriding concern may be to expose, self-reflexively, the mechanics of Gothicism itself.[5] The presence within the tale of a self-consciously ridiculous passage from an invented romance, "The Mad Trist," in perilously close proximity to the story's serious denouement, also raises the possibility of the self-parodic undercurrent alluded to above.

Poe's originality resides in his conscious experimentation with traditional Gothic forms. For example, "The Premature Burial" lures the reader into expecting a tale of burial alive and then offers something very different, with the newly enlightened narrator unexpectedly disavowing Gothic thrills at the end of the story. In "The Man of the Crowd," a narrator sets out to uncover the mystery behind a presumed criminal figure who haunts London streets, yet leaves readers wondering if they have discovered anything beyond the narrator's own obsessions (and the fearful urban squalor endemic to the nineteenth-century metropolis toward which the story gestures). "The Imp of the Perverse" starts out sounding like a non-fictional, philosophical disquisition on human psychology in the author's own voice but ends, unexpectedly, with a murderer's confession of having (temporarily) pulled off the perfect crime—until he is overtaken by an irresistible impulse to confess.

Poe was self-conscious enough about Gothic fiction to mock its conventions in the diptych "How to Write a Blackwood Article/A Predicament." Here Poe takes on a particular sub-genre of the Gothic: the tale of sensation. The idea behind this popular type of story was to place the protagonist in a circumstance of extreme peril, discomfort, or strangeness, and to record his or her imagined sensations with precision. A well-known example was William Maginn's "The Man in the Bell," which had appeared in the magazine Poe references, *Blackwood's Edinburgh Magazine* (as the title suggests, the narrator found himself trapped in the belfry of a church and recorded the disorienting experience of enduring the bell's deafening peals). Poe facetiously has the magazine's famous editor instruct a neophyte author to write a sensation tale by exposing herself to a situation of extreme peril, which she promptly (and disastrously) does. Poe mocks not the sensation tale per se, but authors and readers who fail to understand the literary craftsmanship needed to write one successfully—as well as presumptuous female writers. In the present volume, "A Descent into the Maelström" and "The Pit and the Pendulum" may be classified as Poe's serious approaches to the sensation tale form.

An endearing facet of Poe's career is his mischievous impulse to hoax a credulous public. It's impossible to say if "The Balloon-Hoax" (not originally published under that title, of course) really fooled readers of the New York *Sun* as much as Poe would later claim.[6] The story nonetheless demonstrates Poe's ability to shepherd guileless readers from the plausible to the fantastic through the careful deployment of verisimilitude. Using similar techniques, Poe's "The Facts in the Case of M. Valdemar" also qualifies as a hoax, insofar as it was apparently taken seriously by readers upon republication in Great Britain.[7] After initially promoting the story in the *Broadway Journal* in such a way as to lengthen out any controversy regarding its generic status, Poe eventually wrote to an earnest correspondent clarifying the story's premise to be entirely fictional.[8]

Poe may have been unduly modest—not a character trait for which he was known—when he dismissed the inventiveness of the detective story, asking a correspondent (see the August 9, 1846 letter to Philip P. Cooke in Part V), "where is the ingenuity of unraveling a web which you yourself (the author) have woven for the express purpose of unraveling?" While scholars have identified a handful of precursors, the modern detective story as a genre emerged fully formed in Poe's three Dupin stories, of which two, "The Murders in the Rue Morgue" and "The Purloined Letter," are included here. That Poe, often living on the edge of destitution, fantasized figures such as Dupin and William Legrand of "The Gold-Bug," whose powers of ratiocination (Poe's term for the analytical intelligence at work in these stories) brought spectacular financial windfalls, lends his invention of the genre a special poignancy, especially in light of the vast commercial success that so many of his imitators would later derive from his enduring formula.

I have elsewhere interpreted "The Purloined Letter" as an allegory of alienated intellectual labor, insofar as the presumptive author of the original purloined letter stands by to see Minister D___ and Dupin serially profit from the document that he (or she) composed.[9] If the story can bear this meaning, then it gives the tale an unexpected affinity with the satires of the antebellum publishing scene through which Poe occasionally worked out his frustrations with the industry. In "The Literary Life of Thingum Bob, Esq.," Poe suggests that behind-the-scenes forces elevate certain writers to reputations incommensurate with their modest gifts, while "Never Bet the Devil Your Head" includes Poe's dissatisfaction with critics who claimed that his fiction was insufficiently moralistic. Nor was the industry in which he worked the only target of Poe's wide-ranging satire. "The Man That Was Used Up" criticizes the public's tendency to lionize military heroes beyond their merits. "Some Words with a Mummy" takes on many targets, including Americans' excessive patriotism (often commented upon by nineteenth-century travelers from abroad), their ignorance of ancient history, the Egyptomania craze of the mid-nineteenth century, and the pitfalls of democratic governance.

THEMATIC CONSIDERATIONS

Poe's modern reputation for delivering Gothic thrills, nurtured by his omnipresence in popular culture, should not distort understanding of his fiction. While Gothic fiction of the period allowed for treatment of supernatural themes, for example, such treatment could be complex. A popular approach to the Gothic among some of Poe's predecessors and contemporaries involved the "supernatural explained," in which an author toyed with invocations of the supernatural before explaining away most of the story's ambiguous events by rational means. Poe's American predecessor Charles Brockden Brown achieved success in this mode with his pioneering novel *Wieland* (1798), in which apparently supernatural voices turn out to have been produced by a character with the power of ventriloquism. Hawthorne, too, sometimes availed himself of this formula, as in the famous "was it all a dream?" ending of his short story "Young Goodman Brown." Poe's variation involved leaving readers clues enough to infer a rational explanation for events while never completely discounting a supernatural explanation. Tales collected here in which Poe teases readers with ambiguity regarding the presence of the supernatural include "Ligeia," "The Fall of the House of Usher," "William Wilson," and "The Black Cat." The number of tales in which something unambiguously supernatural transpires is smaller than readers might expect given Poe's modern reputation.

The norms structuring nineteenth-century American fiction held that evil characters had to be held to account for their actions; to write a story otherwise was thought to be socially irresponsible, threatening to corrupt immature readers.[10] While Poe in his criticism sought to discredit *overtly* moralistic fiction and poetry, this critical opinion does not presuppose an entirely amoral approach to writing, as is sometimes claimed. Instead, through his innovative use of unreliable narration, Poe explored human impulses toward violence, cruelty, and revenge while keeping readers at arm's length from a morally compromising identification with his narrators. Some of Poe's narrators display apparent remorse for their actions in the distorted guise of an uncontrollable impulse toward self-incrimination. This formula allowed Poe to lavish exquisite, suspenseful, even loving detail on the narration of horrific acts of violence, while leaving readers to infer (yet without certainty) that the narrators' confessional compulsions manifest the anguish of a guilty conscience. Poe rarely depicts characters committing vicious acts without remorse—a number of the violent characters in Poe's tales can be read as being tortured or otherwise undone by their consciences, with the notable exception of the insurrectionist Hop-Frog. The implication that violence exacts its own psychological price may derive from the period's prominent penal reform movement; the invention of the penitentiary was premised on the notion that criminals forced to meditate in solitude on their actions would be led by their consciences toward remorse and penitence.[11]

Unreliable narration is bound up with Poe's inventive treatment of what he labeled the perverse. In "The Black Cat" and "The Imp of the Perverse," Poe's narrators claim that philosophy does not account for this primitive psychological motivation, an irresistible impulse to do that which one knows to be morally wrong or destructive to one's best interests. The philosophical discussion of perversity actually goes back to St. Augustine, but Poe deserves credit for realizing its fictional potential. The spirit of the perverse in Poe's fiction acts in paradoxical ways: it may drive his narrators toward violence, or it may prompt them into gratuitous acts of self-exposure. While Poe held the perverse to be a universally experienced (if under-theorized) psychological state, he showed a complementary interest in depicting individual psychological aberrations, including cataleptic trances, drug-induced hallucinations, paralyzing anxiety, sensory hyper-acuteness, and inexplicable obsessions. That Poe rendered these troubled psychological states so convincingly by way of first-person narration helps to explain why naive readers sometimes assume that he himself suffered from these or similar conditions, imputing his fiction to the workings of a depraved or diseased mind. Such readers make the mistake Poe implicitly warns against in "How to Write a Blackwood Article": to assume that to write an extreme psychological state requires first-hand experience is to undervalue the power of a writer's imagination.

ANTEBELLUM CONTEXTS

While Poe was once thought to stand apart from the preoccupations of other accomplished American writers of his era, a generation of commentary has fully dispelled this view. Many of the most compelling recent readings of Poe's fiction have situated his work with respect to the political, cultural, and social issues pertinent to the antebellum period, of which none is more central, of course, than the institution of slavery. One event that seems likely to have made an impression on Poe occurred in 1831, when Nat Turner led a band of slaves and free Blacks across Southampton County, Virginia, killing dozens of white victims, including women and children, before Turner was captured, tried, and executed. Turner's jailhouse confession (as told to a white lawyer, Thomas Gray) became a sensational bestseller; it was published in Baltimore, where the twenty-two-year old Poe happened to be living at the time. And just as Poe forged a professional identity as an author in the mid-1830s, the abolitionist movement, led by William Lloyd Garrison, surged into American consciousness, inciting the nationwide debate over slavery that would eventually result in the Civil War. Poe left no record of his specific opinion on slavery (a review sometimes thought to capture his views cannot be definitively attributed to him),[12] but as someone who was raised for a time in Richmond, Virginia, and who tended to identify with Southern interests, Poe seems likely to have supported the peculiar institution. That he disdained abolitionists, at least, is clear from various comments in his letters and reviews, but then many Americans in the period regarded abolitionists with distrust, at least until the publication of *Uncle Tom's Cabin* turned the tide of public opinion against slavery in 1851–2, a few years after Poe's death.

In "Some Words with a Mummy," Poe's revivified Count Allamistakeo endorses a polygenism-friendly account of human creation, a view that aligned with that of spurious race scientists. The idea that humans arose in separate tribes at different locations implicitly supported the notion of superior and inferior human types. One such race scientist, George Gliddon, is actually a character in the story (though it should be noted that the story came out before Gliddon co-authored two influential quasi-scientific works on racial classification, *Types of Mankind* (1854) and *Indigenous Races of the Earth* (1857)). In certain tales, Poe employs demeaning racial codes inherited from a longer history of texts comparing the capacities of people of different races, harkening back to Thomas Jefferson's *Notes on the State of Virginia* (1787), which, besides labeling people of African descent as intellectually inferior to whites, also included the bizarre claim that orangutans mated with Black women.[13] Imagery linking people of color to orangutans on an ersatz evolutionary scale hovers in the background of "The Murders in the Rue Morgue," wherein the murderous orangutan, captured from a distant region of the globe, escapes captivity only to direct its violence toward white women. Slave or servant characters in "How to Write a Blackwood Article/A Predicament," "The Gold-Bug," and "The Man That Was Used Up" show Poe relying upon stereotypes that painted African Americans as ignorant, ugly, servile, and passive.

Yet even as Poe apparently trades in racial stereotypes, his stories also sometimes slyly indicate the ways that ridiculous figures such as Psyche Zenobia in "How to Write a Blackwood Article/A Predicament" and General John A. B. C. Smith in "The Man That Was Used Up" are in fact dependent upon the labors of their Black servants for their genteel self-presentation. Himself excluded from the ranks of Southern gentility by foster father John Allan's disinheritance, and resentful of the cliques of New England's college-educated literati, Poe often appears to harbor sympathy for those fictional characters who rebel against unjust structures of authority. On a comical level, this pattern appears in "The System of Dr. Tarr and Professor Fether," where a genial group of lunatics temporarily take over their asylum. On a more serious note, the institution of slavery is an unavoidable context against which to consider the morally complex revenge fantasy "Hop-Frog," in which a jester abducted from far-off lands, with the help of a co-conspirator, enacts a terrifying retribution upon his lazy, stupid enslavers—and then escapes scot-free. Carrying the discussion in a more abstract, figurative direction, commentators have posited that Poe's undead characters exist in an undefined region not unlike the legal limbo that slaves occupied between personhood and civil non-existence, an insight that resurfaces the slavery-related subtexts embedded but long unrecognized within Gothic tales such as "Morella" and "Ligeia." Pets, too, such as Pluto in "The Black Cat," subtly invoke antebellum legal discourse surrounding slavery, insofar as they are simultaneously living beings with a will of their own yet mere property in the eyes of the law.[14] The readings generated from such interpretive moves have tended to complicate any facile attribution of Poe's endorsement of Southern racial ideology.

Another social movement to take into account when reading Poe's fiction is the women's rights campaign. British writer Mary Wollstonecraft's *A Vindication of the Rights of Woman* (1792) was well known in the United States by Poe's time, and a growing domestic women's rights movement inspired by Wollstonecraft would famously hold a convention at Seneca Falls, New York in 1848, a year before Poe's death. The writers and activists involved with this movement called into question the antebellum era's sentimental idealization of womanhood, whose consequence was the segregation of the sexes that modern historians refer to as separate spheres ideology.[15] Given his general attitude of cultural conservatism, Poe would be expected to express hostility toward proto-feminist activism, and he clearly has fun at the expense of a would-be bluestocking in "How to Write a Blackwood Article/A Predicament." While a troubling number of women characters fall victim to horrific acts of violence in Poe's fiction, a pattern he obviously inherited from Gothic forebears, Poe also conjured women characters of enormous potency, such as Morella and Ligeia. The erudition these women possess is a source of attraction and power—though arguably some relationship exists between their intellectual superiority and their nefarious agendas. Poe singled out the writing of America's pre-eminent literary feminist of the time, Margaret Fuller, for being "nervous [this was a compliment], forcible, thoughtful, suggestive," and "brilliant," while averring she unquestionably possessed "high genius."[16] This assessment is even more notable considering widespread condemnation of Fuller's then-radical views on women's rights as well as her close association with the New England Transcendentalists, whom Poe frequently abused in print. Poe himself was not personally averse to ambitious intellectual women, as suggested by his having entered into friendships and public flirtations with several women writers and having promoted a number of them in the *Broadway Journal* during his editorship of the periodical. As with the issues of race and slavery, no simplistic idea about Poe's view of womanhood arises from a full parsing of the evidence.

The temperance campaign was one of the most significant social movements of Poe's lifetime, garnering millions of adherents at a time when consuming alcohol was even more engrained in American social customs than it is today.[17] When Poe's own lifelong struggle with the effects of his drinking habit is taken into account—he evidently lost more than one job due to his drinking and joined the Sons of Temperance movement late in life—readers must look anew at tales such as "The Black Cat" and "The Cask of Amontillado," which both turn upon the imagery of alcohol abuse. Poe's often-stated aversion to didactic literature prohibits reading these stories as simplistic cautionary tales against the dangers of alcohol. Rather, the stories show Poe capitalizing on popular literary trends (temperance literature was a significant genre that spawned popular stories and bestselling novels) and, perhaps, satirizing with dark humor what he may have considered the faulty assumptions and ludicrous excesses of such productions.

Ideas about mental illness circulating in the antebellum years influenced a number of the tales included here. Beginning in the late eighteenth century, reformers guided by Enlightenment-era principles lobbied for more humane treatment of the mentally ill, who had formerly been confined in cruel conditions alongside violent criminals. In the United States, under the influence of figures such as Dorothea Dix, individual states began to construct asylums for the treatment of mental illness during Poe's lifetime.[18] Reformers sometimes touted in exaggerated terms the benefits accruing from one or another novel system of treatment; Poe's skepticism regarding such claims is probably registered in the absurd outcome of the "soothing system" employed in "The System of Dr. Tarr and Professor Fether." The criminal justice system was called upon to reckon with newly minted psychological theories during Poe's lifetime as well, as courts first in Great Britain, and subsequently in the United States, increasingly accepted an insanity defense for violent crimes. Emergent legal standards asked whether the criminal knew the moral difference between right and wrong at the time of committing a crime, suggesting that in some cases, individuals were subject temporarily to an irresistible (and therefore exculpatory) impulse to violence. Poe's specific opinion on use of the insanity defense cannot necessarily be inferred from his fiction; however, the frightening prospect that an individual could retain intellectual faculties while possessing a disordered moral sense seems to find expression in a number of his tales, where his narrators unite a seemingly rational intelligence with a chilling disregard for the sanctity of human life.[19]

Phrenology furnishes one final context relevant to a number of Poe's tales. (Poe reviewed more than one treatise on phrenology in the course of his career.) Following in the wake of German physician Johan Spurzheim, who arrived in the U.S. to proselytize on behalf of phrenology in 1832, phrenologists promoted the notion that human character comes down to brain development, locating various character traits (such as benevolence, cautiousness, and self-esteem) in discrete, identifiable organs of the brain. Practitioners therefore claimed the ability to read individual personalities by mapping the bumps on a person's head. The claims of phrenology fed into evolving ideas about criminal justice referenced above, since supporters proposed that aberrant moral behavior sometimes resulted from physical damage to the brain. In the eyes of critics, however, such defenses risked becoming a purely deterministic, amoral theory of criminal behavior, absolving criminals of personal guilt for their actions. While Poe offered qualified praise of phrenology in reviews, he also evoked its limits in selected stories. Phrenology posited that physiological examination rendered the human personality knowable, whereas Poe proposed perversity as marking off an unpredictable domain of individual psychology.[20] Poe similarly challenges the idea that human character can be indexed through external signs, be they bumps on the head or features of the face (as claimed by proponents of physiognomy, another pseudo-science popular at the time), in "The Man of the Crowd," whose narrator finds that the eponymous old man he trails for a day and night evades final accountability.

MODERN RESONANCES

It may seem a mere critical commonplace to assert that Poe's fiction, like the work of any acclaimed artist of the past, continues to resonate in the present. Because Gothic fiction deals with human universals such as fear, violence, and madness, its appeal supposedly transcends historical circumstance. But Poe's fiction reminds us that the expression of universal fears is mediated through specific medical, legal, cultural, social, and political contexts. On the medical front, for example, yellow fever, cholera, and other communicable diseases swept across international borders and struck fear into nineteenth-century Americans. When he composed "The Masque of the Red Death," Poe knew earlier tales of plague, such as Daniel Defoe's *A Journal of the Plague Year* (1722), which recounts the experiences of Londoners during the bubonic plague outbreak of 1665–6, and Mary Shelley's *The Last Man* (1826), the story of a future world in which a global plague leaves a single man alive. He must also have had in mind an Asiatic cholera outbreak that spread to North America in 1832, killing 853 residents of Baltimore during Poe's residence there.[21] Some readers discern a moral question at the center of the story: in a situation where the afflicted are beyond hope of recovery and assisting them gives the disease opportunity to spread, does Prince Prospero deserve credit for attempting to preserve the lives of a thousand courtiers, and the values of pleasure and art, against the plague's encroachment, or is he blameworthy for turning his back on the suffering of the rest of his subjects? It may be worth remarking that the situation of populations differentially vulnerable to disease based on social class (only courtiers are to be spared in Prospero's vision) was as prevalent in Poe's age as it is in the era of Covid-19. That the prince's fortified abbey finally proves no defense against the Red Death looks forward to the dilemmas of the present, when leaders are pressed to consider the utility of closing national borders to slow the spread of a global pandemic.

Mesmerism is the nineteenth-century term for a practice akin to hypnosis, which furnished the basis for popular entertainments on the period's lecture circuits. Mesmerists claimed that the subjects they put into trances acquired, through unknown means, wondrous abilities to predict the future and diagnose disease. If the possibilities of mesmerism seemed miraculous to some observers in the 1840s, "The Facts in the Case of M. Valdemar" takes a notably more skeptical view. Under the guise of medical experimentation, the narrator proposes to forestall death in a terminal patient by placing him in a mesmeric trance. The story gains added interest today from widely publicized cases of individuals in comas who have been kept alive through extraordinary medical intervention. Sometimes desperate loved ones insist on every available means being employed to keep a patient alive; at other times, medical institutions committed to upholding faith-based principles resist withdrawing life support in spite of relatives' pleas to let the patient die. When the creepily self-possessed narrator "P" enters the public sphere to defend his actions against competing accounts, Poe anticipates the unseemly media coverage that these tragic cases spark. Activating our fears respecting the real-life quandaries attendant upon end-of-life care, Poe's story might also lead modern readers to reflect on the proposition that the concept of "brain death" as understood by the general public is in reality little more than a quasi-medical fiction, and that physicians today, though somewhat advanced beyond the nineteenth-century state of knowledge on the subject, remain uncertain about where precisely to draw a line between life and death.[22]

The antebellum journalistic scene was thrown into upheaval by the rise of the penny paper in the 1830s. Outlets such as James Gordon Bennett's scandal-mongering New York *Herald* led onlookers to worry about the cultural influence of a sensation-driven, factually unreliable media culture. Parallels to the mediascape enabled by the internet are both justified and telling. When Poe exploited the uncertainties of the age's communication environment by fabricating an account of a transatlantic balloon voyage from Europe to America in "The Balloon-Hoax," did he in some distant way (along with contemporaries such as P. T. Barnum, also known for hoaxing a complicit public) seed the rise of politically toxic disinformation tactics known today as fake news, or did he encourage healthy skepticism toward media content by exposing the mechanisms through which dubious information gains credibility?

In an era when populist, authoritarian leaders have gained strength around the world, readers might discover renewed interest in stories with political subtexts, such as "The Man That Was Used Up" and "Some Words with a Mummy." In different ways, both stories give fictional expression to growing fears about the populist trends of the 1830s and 1840s in the United States, which enfranchised vast new swaths of the white male working class, bringing a new set of leaders to power. In the latter tale, the aristocratic mummy Count Allamistakeo, acting as Poe's mouthpiece, proffers a transparent political allegory whose lesson is that democratic governance inevitably devolves over time into mob rule, implicitly predicting the eventual failure of the American experiment. And if the cyborg character at the center of "The Man That Was Used Up" foreshadows twenty-first-century attempts to supplement human biology through prosthetic technologies (as advocated, for example, by the transhumanist movement), the story also speaks in less obvious ways to recent political concerns. One of several figures who have been proposed as the inspiration for General John A. B. C. Smith is Andrew Jackson. Like the fictional Smith, Jackson came to public attention on the strength of his military prowess, first in the War of 1812, and later as a so-called Indian fighter, leading American forces against the Creeks and Seminoles in the 1810s. Once in office, the populist favorite, who supported the removal of Native Americans from their homelands in order to make room for white settlers, was regarded by political opponents as a demagogue harboring dangerous authoritarian ambitions. Jackson would be embraced as a model nearly two centuries later by newly elected U.S. President Donald Trump, who directed that a portrait of the seventh president be hung in the White House shortly after his January 2017 inauguration. If Poe intuited certain dynamics of Trump's rise a century and a half before it transpired, in the figure of the racist and bizarrely overpraised General John A. B. C. Smith—who, contrary to his bluff outward persona, turns out to be empty at the core—it suggests that no nightmare scenario, however fearful or seemingly far-fetched, lay beyond his ability to conjure.

Ms. Found in a Bottle[1]

Qui n'a plus qu'un moment à vivre
N'a plus rien à dissimuler.—*Quinault—Atys.*[2]

OF my country and of my family I have little to say. Ill usage and length of years have driven me from the one, and estranged me from the other. Hereditary wealth afforded me an education of no common order, and a contemplative turn of mind enabled me to methodize the stores which early study very diligently garnered up.— Beyond all things, the works of the German moralists gave me great delight; not from any ill-advised admiration of their eloquent madness, but from the ease with which my habits of rigid thought enabled me to detect their falsities. I have often been reproached with the aridity of my genius; a deficiency of imagination has been imputed to me as a crime; and the Pyrrhonism[3] of my opinions has at all times rendered me notorious. Indeed, a strong relish for physical philosophy has, I fear, tinctured my mind with a very common error of this age—I mean the habit of referring occurrences, even the least susceptible of such reference, to the principles of that science. Upon the whole, no person could be less liable than myself to be led away from the severe precincts of truth by the *ignes fatui*[4] of superstition. I have thought proper to premise thus much, lest the incredible tale I have to tell should be considered rather the raving of a crude imagination, than the positive experience of a mind to which the reveries of fancy have been a dead letter and a nullity.

After many years spent in foreign travel, I sailed in the year 18--, from the port of Batavia, in the rich and populous island of Java, on a voyage to the Archipelago of the Sunda islands. I went as passenger—having no other inducement than a kind of nervous restlessness which haunted me as a fiend.

Our vessel was a beautiful ship of about four hundred tons, copper-fastened, and built at Bombay of Malabar teak. She was freighted with cotton-wool and oil, from the Lachadive islands. We had also on board coir, jaggeree, ghee, cocoa-nuts, and a few cases of opium.[5] The stowage was clumsily done, and the vessel consequently crank.

We got under way with a mere breath of wind, and for many days stood along the eastern coast of Java, without any other incident to beguile the monotony of our course than the occasional meeting with some of the small grabs of the Archipelago to which we were bound.

One evening, leaning over the taffrail, I observed a very singular, isolated cloud, to the N. W. It was remarkable, as well for its color, as from its being the first we had seen since our departure from Batavia. I watched it attentively until sunset, when it spread all at once to the eastward and westward, girting in the horizon with a narrow strip of vapor, and looking like a long line of low beach. My notice was soon afterwards attracted by the dusky-red appearance of the moon, and the peculiar character of the sea. The latter was undergoing a rapid change, and the water seemed more than usually transparent. Although I could distinctly see the bottom, yet, heaving the lead, I found the ship in fifteen fathoms. The air now became intolerably hot, and was loaded with spiral exhalations similar to those arising from heated iron. As night came on, every breath of wind died away, and a more entire calm it is impossible to conceive. The flame of a candle burned upon the poop without the least perceptible motion, and a long hair, held between the finger and thumb, hung without the possibility of detecting a vibration. However, as the captain said he could perceive no indication of danger, and as we were drifting in bodily to shore, he ordered the sails to be furled, and the anchor let go. No watch was set, and the crew, consisting principally of Malays, stretched themselves deliberately upon deck. I went below—not without a full presentiment of evil. Indeed, every appearance warranted me in apprehending a Simoom.[6] I told the captain my fears; but he paid no attention to what I said, and left me without deigning to give a reply. My uneasiness, however, prevented me from sleeping, and about midnight I went upon deck.—As I placed my foot upon the upper step of the companion-ladder, I was startled by a loud, humming noise, like that occasioned by the rapid revolution of a millwheel, and before I could ascertain its meaning, I found the ship quivering to its centre. In the next instant, a wilderness of foam hurled us upon our beam-ends, and, rushing over us fore and aft, swept the entire decks from stem to stern.

The extreme fury of the blast proved, in a great measure, the salvation of the ship. Although completely water-logged, yet, as her masts had gone by the board, she rose, after a minute, heavily from the sea, and, staggering awhile beneath the immense pressure of the tempest, finally righted.

By what miracle I escaped destruction, it is impossible to say. Stunned by the shock of the water, I found myself, upon recovery, jammed in between the stern-post and rudder. With great difficulty I gained my feet, and looking dizzily around, was, at first, struck with the idea of our being among breakers; so terrific, beyond the wildest imagination, was the whirlpool of mountainous and foaming ocean within which we were engulfed. After a while, I heard the voice of an old Swede, who had shipped with us at the moment of our leaving port. I hallooed to him with all my strength, and presently he came reeling aft. We soon discovered that we were the sole survivors of the accident. All on deck, with the exception of ourselves, had been swept overboard;—the captain and mates must have perished as they slept, for the cabins were deluged with water. Without assistance, we could expect to do little for the security of the ship, and our exertions were at first paralyzed by the momentary expectation of going down. Our cable had, of course, parted like pack-thread, at the first breath of the hurricane, or we should have been instantaneously overwhelmed. We scudded with frightful velocity before the sea, and the water made clear breaches over us. The framework of our stern was shattered excessively, and, in almost every respect, we had received considerable injury; but to our extreme joy we found the pumps unchoked, and that we had made no great shifting of our ballast.—The main fury of the blast had already blown over, and we apprehended little danger from the violence of the wind; but we looked forward to its total cessation with dismay; well believing, that, in our shattered condition, we should inevitably perish in the tremendous swell which would ensue. But this very just apprehension seemed by no means likely to be soon verified. For five entire days and nights—during which our only subsistence was a small quantity of jaggeree, procured with great difficulty from the forecastle—the hulk flew at a rate defying computation, before rapidly succeeding flaws of wind, which, without equalling the first violence of the Simoom, were still more terrific than any tempest I had before encountered. Our course for the first four days was, with trifling variations, S. E. and by S.; and we must have run down the coast of New Holland.—On the fifth day the cold became extreme, although the wind had hauled round a point more to the northward.—The sun arose with a sickly yellow lustre, and clambered a very few degrees above the horizon—emitting no decisive light. There were no clouds apparent, yet the wind was upon the increase, and blew with a fitful and unsteady fury. About noon, as nearly as we could guess, our attention was again arrested by the appearance of the sun. It gave out no light, properly so called, but a dull and sullen glow without reflection, as if all its rays were polarized. Just before sinking within the turgid sea, its central fires suddenly went out, as if hurriedly extinguished by some unaccountable power. It was a dim, silver-like rim, alone, as it rushed down the unfathomable ocean.

We waited in vain for the arrival of the sixth day—that day to me has not arrived—to the Swede, never did arrive. Thenceforward we were enshrouded in pitchy darkness, so that we could not have seen an object at twenty paces from the ship. Eternal night continued to envelop us, all unrelieved by the phosphoric sea-brilliancy to which we had been accustomed in the tropics. We observed too, that, although the tempest continued to rage with unabated violence, there was no longer to be discovered the usual appearance of surf, or foam, which had hitherto attended us. All around were horror, and thick gloom, and a black sweltering desert of ebony.—Superstitious terror crept by degrees into the spirit of the old Swede, and my own soul was wrapped up in silent wonder. We neglected all care of the ship, as worse than useless, and securing ourselves, as well as possible to the stump of the mizen-mast, looked out bitterly into the world of ocean. We had no means of calculating time, nor could we form any guess of our situation. We were, however, well aware of having made farther to the southward than any previous navigators, and felt great amazement at not meeting with the usual impediments of ice. In the meantime every moment threatened to be our last—every mountainous billow hurried to overwhelm us. The swell surpassed anything I had imagined possible, and that we were not instantly buried is a miracle. My companion spoke of the lightness of our cargo, and reminded me of the excellent qualities of our ship; but I could not help feeling the utter hopelessness of hope itself, and prepared myself gloomily for that death which I thought nothing could defer beyond an hour, as, with every knot of way the ship made, the swelling of the black stupendous seas became more dismally appalling. At times we gasped for breath at an elevation beyond the albatross—at times became dizzy with the velocity of our descent into some watery hell, where the air grew stagnant, and no sound disturbed the slumbers of the kraken.

We were at the bottom of one of these abysses, when a quick scream from my companion broke fearfully upon the night. "See! see!" cried he, shrieking in my ears, "Almighty God! see! see!" As he spoke, I became aware of a dull, sullen glare of red light which streamed down the sides of the vast chasm where we lay, and threw a fitful brilliancy upon our deck. Casting my eyes upwards, I beheld a spectacle which froze the current of my blood. At a terrific height directly above us, and upon the very verge of the precipitous descent, hovered a gigantic ship of, perhaps, four thousand tons. Although upreared upon the summit of a wave more than a hundred times her own altitude, her apparent size still exceeded that of any ship of the line or East Indiaman in existence. Her huge hull was of a deep dingy black, unrelieved by any of the customary carvings of a ship. A single row of brass cannon protruded from her open ports, and dashed from their polished surfaces the fires of innumerable battle-lanterns, which swung to and fro about her rigging. But what mainly inspired us with horror and astonishment, was that she bore up under a press of sail in the very teeth of that supernatural sea, and of that ungovernable hurricane. When we first discovered her, her bows were alone to be seen, as she rose slowly from the dim and horrible gulf beyond her. For a moment of intense terror she paused upon the giddy pinnacle, as if in contemplation of her own sublimity, then trembled and tottered, and—came down.

At this instant, I know not what sudden self-possession came over my spirit. Staggering as far aft as I could, I awaited fearlessly the ruin that was to overwhelm. Our own vessel was at length ceasing from struggles, and sinking with her head to the sea. The shock of the descending mass struck her, consequently, in that portion of her frame which was already under water, and the inevitable result was to hurl me, with irresistible violence, upon the rigging of the stranger.

As I fell, the ship hove in stays, and went about; and to the confusion ensuing I attributed my escape from the notice of the crew. With little difficulty I made my way unperceived to the main hatchway, which was partially open, and soon found an opportunity of secreting myself in the hold. Why I did so I can hardly tell. An indefinite sense of awe, which at first sight of the navigators of the ship had taken hold of my mind, was perhaps the principle of my concealment. I was unwilling to trust myself with a race of people who had offered, to the cursory glance I had taken, so many points of vague novelty, doubt, and apprehension. I therefore thought proper to contrive a hiding-place in the hold. This I did by removing a small portion of the shifting-boards, in such a manner as to afford me a convenient retreat between the huge timbers of the ship.

I had scarcely completed my work, when a footstep in the hold forced me to make use of it. A man passed by my place of concealment with a feeble and unsteady gait. I could not see his face, but had an opportunity of observing his general appearance. There was about it an evidence of great age and infirmity. His knees tottered beneath a load of years, and his entire frame quivered under the burthen. He muttered to himself, in a low broken tone, some words of a language which I could not understand, and groped in a corner among a pile of singular-looking instruments, and decayed charts of navigation. His manner was a wild mixture of the peevishness of second childhood, and the solemn dignity of a God. He at length went on deck, and I saw him no more.

    *   *   *   *   *   *   *   *   *   *   *

A feeling, for which I have no name, has taken possession of my soul—a sensation which will admit of no analysis, to which the lessons of by-gone time are inadequate, and for which I fear futurity itself will offer me no key. To a mind constituted like my own, the latter consideration is an evil. I shall never—I know that I shall never—be satisfied with regard to the nature of my conceptions. Yet it is not wonderful that these conceptions are indefinite, since they have their origin in sources so utterly novel. A new sense—a new entity is added to my soul.

    *   *   *   *   *   *   *   *   *   *   *

It is long since I first trod the deck of this terrible ship, and the rays of my destiny are, I think, gathering to a focus. Incomprehensible men! Wrapped up in meditations of a kind which I cannot divine, they pass me by unnoticed. Concealment is utter folly on my part, for the people *will not* see. It was but just now that I passed directly before the eyes of the mate—it was no long while ago that I ventured into the captain's own private cabin, and took thence the materials with which I write, and have written. I shall from time to time continue this journal. It is true that I may not find an opportunity of transmitting it to the world, but I will not fail to make the endeavor. At the last moment I will enclose the MS. in a bottle, and cast it within the sea.

   *   *   *   *   *   *   *   *   *   *   *

An incident has occurred which has given me new room for meditation. Are such things the operation of ungoverned Chance? I had ventured upon deck and thrown myself down, without attracting any notice, among a pile of ratlin-stuff and old sails, in the bottom of the yawl. While musing upon the singularity of my fate, I unwittingly daubed with a tar-brush the edges of a neatly-folded studding-sail which lay near me on a barrel. The studding-sail is now bent upon the ship, and the thoughtless touches of the brush are spread out into the word DISCOVERY.

   *   *   *   *   *   *   *   *   *   *   *

I have made many observations lately upon the structure of the vessel. Although well armed, she is not, I think, a ship of war. Her rigging, build, and general equipment, all negative a supposition of this kind. What she *is not*, I can easily perceive—what she *is* I fear it is impossible to say. I know not how it is, but in scrutinizing her strange model and singular cast of spars, her huge size and overgrown suits of canvass, her severely simple bow and antiquated stern; there will occasionally flash across my mind a sensation of familiar things, and there is always mixed up with such indistinct shadows of recollection, an unaccountable memory of old foreign chronicles and ages long ago.

   *   *   *   *   *   *   *   *   *   *   *

I have been looking at the timbers of the ship. She is built of a material to which I am a stranger. There is a peculiar character about the wood which strikes me as rendering it unfit for the purpose to which it has been applied. I mean its extreme *porousness*, considered independently of the worm-eaten condition which is a consequence of navigation in these seas, and apart from the rottenness attendant upon age. It will appear perhaps an observation somewhat over-curious, but this wood would have every characteristic of Spanish oak, if Spanish oak were distended by any unnatural means.

In reading the above sentence a curious apothegm of an old weather-beaten Dutch navigator comes full upon my recollection. "It is as sure," he was wont to say, when any doubt was entertained of his veracity, "as sure as there is a sea where the ship itself will grow in bulk like the living body of the seaman."

   *   *   *   *   *   *   *   *   *   *   *

About an hour ago, I made bold to thrust myself among a group of the crew. They paid me no manner of attention, and, although I stood in the very midst of them all, seemed utterly unconscious of my presence. Like the one I had at first seen in the hold, they all bore about them the marks of a hoary old age. Their knees trembled with infirmity; their shoulders were bent double with decrepitude; their shrivelled skins rattled in the wind; their voices were low, tremulous and broken; their eyes glistened with the rheum of years; and their gray hairs streamed terribly in the tempest. Around them, on every part of the deck, lay scattered mathematical instruments of the most quaint and obsolete construction.

  * * * * * * * * * * *

I mentioned some time ago the bending of a studding-sail. From that period the ship, being thrown dead off the wind, has continued her terrific course due south, with every rag of canvass packed upon her, from her trucks to her lower studding-sail booms, and rolling every moment her top-gallant yard-arms into the most appalling hell of water which it can enter the mind of man to imagine. I have just left the deck, where I find it impossible to maintain a footing, although the crew seem to experience little inconvenience. It appears to me a miracle of miracles that our enormous bulk is not swallowed up once and forever. We are surely doomed to hover continually upon the brink of Eternity, without taking a final plunge into the abyss. From billows a thousand times more stupendous than any I have ever seen, we glide away with the facility of the arrowy sea-gull; and the colossal waters rear their heads above us like demons of the deep, but like demons confined to simple threats and forbidden to destroy. I am led to attribute these frequent escapes to the only natural cause which can account for such effect.—I must suppose the ship to be within the influence of some strong current, or impetuous under-tow.

  * * * * * * * * * * *

I have seen the captain face to face, and in his own cabin—but, as I expected, he paid me no attention. Although in his appearance there is, to a casual observer, nothing which might bespeak him more or less than man—still a feeling of irrepressible reverence and awe mingled with the sensation of wonder with which I regarded him. In stature he is nearly my own height; that is, about five feet eight inches. He is of a well-knit and compact frame of body, neither robust nor remarkably otherwise. But it is the singularity of the expression which reigns upon the face—it is the intense, the wonderful, the thrilling evidence of old age so utter, so extreme, which excites within my spirit a sense—a sentiment ineffable. His forehead, although little wrinkled, seems to bear upon it the stamp of a myriad of years.—His gray hairs are records of the past, and his grayer eyes are Sybils[7] of the future. The cabin floor was thickly strewn with strange, iron-clasped folios, and mouldering instruments of science, and obsolete long-forgotten charts. His head was bowed down upon his hands, and he pored, with a fiery unquiet eye, over a paper which I took to be a commission, and which, at all events, bore the signature of a monarch. He muttered to himself, as did the first seaman whom I saw in the hold, some low peevish syllables of a foreign tongue, and although the speaker was close at my elbow, his voice seemed to reach my ears from the distance of a mile.

    *   *   *   *   *   *   *   *   *   *   *

The ship and all in it are imbued with the spirit of Eld. The crew glide to and fro like the ghosts of buried centuries; their eyes have an eager and uneasy meaning; and when their figures fall athwart my path in the wild glare of the battle-lanterns, I feel as I have never felt before, although I have been all my life a dealer in antiquities, and have imbibed the shadows of fallen columns at Balbec, and Tadmor, and Persepolis, until my very soul has become a ruin.

    *   *   *   *   *   *   *   *   *   *   *

When I look around me I feel ashamed of my former apprehensions. If I trembled at the blast which has hitherto attended us, shall I not stand aghast at a warring of wind and ocean, to convey any idea of which the words tornado and simoom are trivial and ineffective! All in the immediate vicinity of the ship is the blackness of eternal night, and a chaos of formless water; but, about a league on either side of us, may be seen, indistinctly and at intervals, stupendous ramparts of ice, towering away into the desolate sky, and looking like the walls of the universe.

    *   *   *   *   *   *   *   *   *   *   *

As I imagined, the ship proves to be in a current; if that appellation can properly be given to a tide which, howling and shrieking by the white ice, thunders on to the southward with a velocity like the headlong dashing of a cataract.

    *   *   *   *   *   *   *   *   *   *   *

To conceive the horror of my sensations is, I presume, utterly impossible; yet a curiosity to penetrate the mysteries of these awful regions, predominates even over my despair, and will reconcile me to the most hideous aspect of death. It is evident that we are hurrying onwards to some exciting knowledge—some never-to-be-imparted secret, whose attainment is destruction. Perhaps this current leads us to the southern pole itself. It must be confessed that a supposition apparently so wild has every probability in its favor.

    *   *   *   *   *   *   *   *   *   *   *

The crew pace the deck with unquiet and tremulous step; but there is upon their countenances an expression more of the eagerness of hope than of the apathy of despair.

In the meantime the wind is still in our poop, and, as we carry a crowd of canvass, the ship is at times lifted bodily from out the sea———Oh, horror upon horror! the ice opens suddenly to the right, and to the left, and we are whirling dizzily, in immense concentric circles, round and round the borders of a gigantic amphitheatre, the summit of whose walls is lost in the darkness and the distance. But little time will be left me to ponder upon my destiny—the circles rapidly grow small—we are plunging madly within the grasp of the whirlpool—and amid a roaring, and bellowing, and thundering of ocean and of tempest, the ship is quivering, oh God! and—going down.

Berenice[1]

Dicebant mihi sodales, si sepulchrum amicae visitarem, curas meas aliquantulum
fore levatas.—*Ebn Zaiat.*[2]

MISERY is manifold. The wretchedness of earth is multiform. Overreaching the wide
horizon as the rainbow, its hues are as various as the hues of that arch,—as distinct
too, yet as intimately blended. Overreaching the wide horizon as the rainbow! How
is it that from beauty I have derived a type of unloveliness?—from the covenant of
peace a simile of sorrow? But as, in ethics, evil is a consequence of good, so, in fact,
out of joy is sorrow born. Either the memory of past bliss is the anguish of to-day, or
the agonies which *are* have their origin in the ecstasies which *might have been*.

My baptismal name is Egæus; that of my family I will not mention. Yet there are
no towers in the land more time-honored than my gloomy, gray, hereditary halls.
Our line has been called a race of visionaries; and in many striking particulars—in
the character of the family mansion—in the frescos of the chief saloon—in the
tapestries of the dormitories—in the chiselling of some butresses in the armory—but
more especially in the gallery of antique paintings—in the fashion of the library
chamber—and, lastly, in the very peculiar nature of the library's contents, there is
more than sufficient evidence to warrant the belief.

The recollection of my earliest years are connected with that chamber, and with its
volumes—of which latter I will say no more. Here died my mother. Herein was I born.
But it is mere idleness to say that I had not lived before—that the soul has no previous
existence. You deny it?—let us not argue the matter. Convinced myself, I seek not to
convince. There is, however, a remembrance of aerial forms—of spiritual and meaning
eyes—of sounds, musical yet sad—a remembrance which will not be excluded; a
memory like a shadow, vague, variable, indefinite, unsteady; and like a shadow, too, in
the impossibility of my getting rid of it while the sunlight of my reason shall exist.

In that chamber was I born. Thus awaking from the long night of what seemed,
but was not, nonentity, at once into the very regions of fairy-land—into a palace of
imagination—into the wild dominions of monastic thought and erudition—it is not
singular that I gazed around me with a startled and ardent eye—that I loitered away
my boyhood in books, and dissipated my youth in reverie; but it *is* singular that as
years rolled away, and the noon of manhood found me still in the mansion of my
fathers—it *is* wonderful what stagnation there fell upon the springs of my life
wonderful how total an inversion took place in the character of my commonest
thought. The realities of the world affected me as visions, and as visions only, while
the wild ideas of the land of dreams became, in turn,—not the material of my
everyday existence—but in very deed that existence utterly and solely in itself.

    *   *   *   *   *   *   *   *   *   *   *

Berenice and I were cousins, and we grew up together in my paternal halls. Yet
differently we grew—I ill of health and buried in gloom—she agile, graceful, and
overflowing with energy—hers the ramble on the hill-side—mine the studies of the
cloister—I living within my own heart, and addicted body and soul to the most
intense and painful meditation—she roaming carelessly through life with no thought

of the shadows in her path, or the silent flight of the raven-winged hours. Berenice!—I call upon her name—Berenice!—and from the gray ruins of memory a thousand tumultuous recollections are startled at the sound! Ah! vividly is her image before me now, as in the early days of her light-heartedness and joy! Oh! gorgeous yet fantastic beauty! Oh! sylph amid the shrubberies of Arnheim!—Oh! Naiad among its fountains!—and then—then all is mystery and terror, and a tale which should not be told. Disease—a fatal disease—fell like the simoom upon her frame, and, even while I gazed upon her, the spirit of change swept over her, pervading her mind, her habits, and her character, and, in a manner the most subtle and terrible, disturbing even the identity of her person! Alas! the destroyer came and went, and the victim— where was she? I knew her not—or knew her no longer as Berenice.

Among the numerous train of maladies superinduced by that fatal and primary one which effected a revolution of so horrible a kind in the moral and physical being of my cousin, may be mentioned as the most distressing and obstinate in its nature, a species of epilepsy not unfrequently terminating in *trance* itself—trance very nearly resembling positive dissolution, and from which her manner of recovery was, in most instances, startlingly abrupt. In the mean time my own disease—for I have been told that I should call it by no other appellation—my own disease, then, grew rapidly upon me, and assumed finally a monomaniac character of a novel and extraordinary form—hourly and momently gaining vigor—and at length obtaining over me the most incomprehensible ascendancy. This monomania, if I must so term it, consisted in a morbid irritability of those properties of the mind in metaphysical science termed the *attentive*. It is more than probable that I am not understood; but I fear, indeed, that it is in no manner possible to convey to the mind of the merely general reader, an adequate idea of that nervous *intensity of interest* with which, in my case, the powers of meditation (not to speak technically) busied and buried themselves, in the contemplation of even the most ordinary objects of the universe.

To muse for long unwearied hours with my attention riveted to some frivolous device on the margin, or in the typography of a book; to become absorbed for the better part of a summer's day in a quaint shadow falling aslant upon the tapestry, or upon the floor; to lose myself for an entire night in watching the steady flame of a lamp, or the embers of a fire; to dream away whole days over the perfume of a flower; to repeat monotonously some common word, until the sound, by dint of frequent repetition, ceased to convey any idea whatever to the mind; to lose all sense of motion or physical existence, by means of absolute bodily quiescence long and obstinately persevered in:—such were a few of the most common and least pernicious vagaries induced by a condition of the mental faculties, not, indeed, altogether unparalleled, but certainly bidding defiance to anything like analysis or explanation.

Yet let me not be misapprehended.—The undue, earnest, and morbid attention thus excited by objects in their own nature frivolous, must not be confounded in character with that ruminating propensity common to all mankind, and more especially indulged in by persons of ardent imagination. It was not even, as might be at first supposed, an extreme condition, or exaggeration of such propensity, but primarily and essentially distinct and different. In the one instance, the dreamer, or enthusiast, being interested by an object usually *not* frivolous, imperceptibly loses sight of this object in a wilderness of deductions and suggestions issuing therefrom, until, at the conclusion of a day dream *often replete with luxury*, he finds the *incitamentum* or first cause of his musings entirely vanished and forgotten. In my case the primary object was *invariably frivolous*, although assuming, through the medium of my distempered vision, a refracted and unreal importance. Few deductions, if any, were made; and those few pertinaciously returning in upon the original object as a centre. The meditations were *never* pleasurable; and, at the termination of the reverie, the first cause, so far from being out of sight, had attained that supernaturally exaggerated interest which was the prevailing feature of the disease. In a word, the powers of mind more particularly exercised were, with me, as I have said before, the *attentive*, and are, with the day-dreamer, the *speculative*.

My books, at this epoch, if they did not actually serve to irritate the disorder, partook, it will be perceived, largely, in their imaginative and inconsequential nature, of the characteristic qualities of the disorder itself. I well remember, among others, the treatise of the noble Italian Cœlius Secundus Curio "*de Amplitudine Beati Regni Dei;*" St. Austin's great work, the "City of God;" and Tertullian "*de Carne Christi,*" in which the paradoxical sentence "*Mortuus est Dei filius; credibile est quia ineptum est: et sepultus resurrexit; certum est quia impossible est*" occupied my undivided time, for many weeks of laborious and fruitless investigation.[3]

Thus it will appear that, shaken from its balance only by trivial things, my reason bore resemblance to that ocean-crag spoken of by Ptolemy Hephestion, which steadily resisting the attacks of human violence, and the fiercer fury of the waters and the winds, trembled only to the touch of the flower called Asphodel. And although, to a careless thinker, it might appear a matter beyond doubt, that the alteration produced by her unhappy malady, in the *moral* condition of Berenice, would afford me many objects for the exercise of that intense and abnormal meditation whose nature I have been at some trouble in explaining, yet such was not in any degree the case. In the lucid intervals of my infirmity, her calamity, indeed, gave me pain, and, taking deeply to heart that total wreck of her fair and gentle life, I did not fail to ponder frequently and bitterly upon the wonder-working means by which so strange a revolution had been so suddenly brought to pass. But these reflections partook not of the idiosyncrasy of my disease, and were such as would have occurred, under similar circumstances, to the ordinary mass of mankind. True to its own character, my disorder revelled in the less important but more startling changes wrought in the *physical* frame of Berenice—in the singular and most appalling distortion of her personal identity.

During the brightest days of her unparalleled beauty, most surely I had never loved her. In the strange anomaly of my existence, feelings with me, *had never been* of the heart, and my passions *always were* of the mind. Through the gray of the early morning—among the trellised shadows of the forest at noon-day—and in the silence of my library at night, she had flitted by my eyes, and I had seen her—not as the living and breathing Berenice, but as the Berenice of a dream—not as a being of the earth, earthy, but as the abstraction of such a being—not as a thing to admire, but to analyze—not as an object of love, but as the theme of the most abstruse although desultory speculation. And *now*—now I shuddered in her presence, and grew pale at her approach; yet bitterly lamenting her fallen and desolate condition, I called to mind that she had loved me long, and, in an evil moment, I spoke to her of marriage.

And at length the period of our nuptials was approaching, when, upon an afternoon in the winter of the year,—one of those unseasonably warm, calm, and misty days which are the nurse of the beautiful Halcyon,[4]—I sat, (and sat, as I thought, alone,) in the inner apartment of the library. But uplifting my eyes I saw that Berenice stood before me.

Was it my own excited imagination—or the misty influence of the atmosphere—or the uncertain twilight of the chamber—or the gray draperies which fell around her figure—that caused in it so vacillating and indistinct an outline? I could not tell. She spoke no word, and I—not for worlds could I have uttered a syllable. An icy chill ran through my frame; a sense of insufferable anxiety oppressed me; a consuming curiosity pervaded my soul; and sinking back upon the chair, I remained for some time breathless and motionless, with my eyes riveted upon her person. Alas! its emaciation was excessive, and not one vestige of the former being, lurked in any single line of the contour. My burning glances at length fell upon the face.

The forehead was high, and very pale, and singularly placid; and the once jetty hair fell partially over it, and overshadowed the hollow temples with innumerable ringlets now of a vivid yellow, and jarring discordantly, in their fantastic character, with the reigning melancholy of the countenance. The eyes were lifeless, and lusterless, and seemingly pupil-less, and I shrank involuntarily from their glassy stare to the contemplation of the thin and shrunken lips. They parted; and in a smile of peculiar meaning, *the teeth* of the changed Berenice disclosed themselves slowly to my view. Would to God that I had never beheld them, or that, having done so, I had died!

    *   *   *   *   *   *   *   *   *   *   *

The shutting of a door disturbed me, and looking up, I found that my cousin had departed from the chamber. But from the disordered chamber of my brain, had not, alas! departed, and would not be driven away, the white and ghastly *spectrum* of the teeth. Not a speck on their surface—not a shade on their enamel—not an indenture in their edges—but what that brief period of her smile had sufficed to brand in upon my memory. I saw them *now* even more unequivocally than I beheld them *then*. The teeth!—the teeth!—they were here, and there, and every where, and visibly and palpably before me; long, narrow, and excessively white, with the pale lips writhing about them, as in the very moment of their first terrible development. Then came the full fury of my *monomania*, and I struggled in vain against its strange and irresistible influence. In the multiplied objects of the external world I had no thoughts but for the teeth. For these I longed with a phrenzied desire. All other matters and all different interests became absorbed in their single contemplation. They—they alone were present to the mental eye, and they, in their sole individuality, became the essence of my mental life. I held them in every light. I turned them in every attitude. I surveyed their characteristics. I dwelt upon their peculiarities. I pondered upon their conformation. I mused upon the alteration in their nature. I shuddered as I assigned to them in imagination a sensitive and sentient power, and even when unassisted by the lips, a capability of moral expression. Of Mad'selle Sallé it has been well said, "*que tous ses pas etaient des sentiments,*" and of Berenice I more seriously believed *que tous ses dents etaient des idées.*[5] *Des idées!*—ah here was the idiotic thought that destroyed me! *Des idées!*—ah therefore it was that I coveted them so madly! I felt that their possession could alone ever restore me to peace, in giving me back to reason.

And the evening closed in upon me thus—and then the darkness came, and tarried, and went—and the day again dawned—and the mists of a second night were now gathering around—and still I sat motionless in that solitary room, and still I sat buried in meditation, and still the *phantasma* of the teeth maintained its terrible ascendancy as, with the most vivid and hideous distinctness, it floated about amid the changing lights and shadows of the chamber. At length there broke in upon my dreams a cry as of horror and dismay; and thereunto, after a pause, succeeded the sound of troubled voices, intermingled with many low moanings of sorrow, or of pain. I arose from my seat, and throwing open one of the doors of the library, saw standing out in the antechamber a servant maiden, all in tears, who told me that Berenice was—no more. She had been seized with epilepsy in the early morning, and now, at the closing in of the night, the grave was ready for its tenant, and all the preparations for the burial were completed.[6]

    *   *   *   *   *   *   *   *   *   *   *

I found myself sitting in the library, and again sitting there alone. It seemed that I had newly awakened from a confused and exciting dream. I knew that it was now midnight, and I was well aware that since the setting of the sun Berenice had been interred. But of that dreary period which intervened I had no positive—at least no definite comprehension. Yet its memory was replete with horror—horror more horrible from being vague, and terror more terrible from ambiguity. It was a fearful page in the record of my existence, written all over with dim, and hideous, and unintelligible recollections. I strived to decypher them, but in vain; while ever and anon, like the spirit of a departed sound, the shrill and piercing shriek of a female voice seemed to be ringing in my ears. I had done a deed—what was it? I asked myself the question aloud, and the whispering echoes of the chamber answered me, *"what was it?"*

On the table beside me burned a lamp, and near it lay a little box. It was of no remarkable character, and I had seen it frequently before, for it was the property of the family physician; but how came it *there,* upon my table, and why did I shudder in regarding it? These things were in no manner to be accounted for, and my eyes at length dropped to the open pages of a book, and to a sentence underscored therein. The words were the singular but simple ones of the poet Ebn Zaiat. *"Dicebant mihi sodales si sepulchrum amicae visitarem, curas meas aliquantulum fore levatas."* Why then, as I perused them, did the hairs of my head erect themselves on end, and the blood of my body become congealed within my veins?

There came a light tap at the library door, and pale as the tenant of a tomb, a menial entered upon tiptoe. His looks were wild with terror, and he spoke to me in a voice tremulous, husky, and very low. What said he?—some broken sentences I heard. He told of a wild cry disturbing the silence of the night—of the gathering together of the household—of a search in the direction of the sound;—and then his tones grew thrillingly distinct as he whispered me of a violated grave—of a disfigured body enshrouded, yet still breathing, still palpitating, *still alive!*

He pointed to my garments;—they were muddy and clotted with gore. I spoke not, and he took me gently by the hand;—it was indented with the impress of human nails. He directed my attention to some object against the wall;—I looked at it for some minutes;—it was a spade. With a shriek I bounded to the table, and grasped the box that lay upon it. But I could not force it open; and in my tremor it slipped from my hands, and fell heavily, and burst into pieces; and from it, with a rattling sound, there rolled out some instruments of dental surgery, intermingled with thirty-two small, white and ivory-looking substances that were scattered to and fro about the floor.

Morella[1]

Αυτο καθ᾽ αυτο μεθ᾽ αυτου, μονο ειδες αιει ον.
Itself, by itself solely, ONE everlastingly, and single.
Plato. Sympos[2]

With a feeling of deep yet most singular affection I regarded my friend Morella. Thrown by accident into her society many years ago, my soul, from our first meeting, burned with fires it had never before known; but the fires were not of Eros, and bitter and tormenting to my spirit was the gradual conviction that I could in no manner define their unusual meaning, or regulate their vague intensity. Yet we met; and fate bound us together at the altar; and I never spoke of passion, nor thought of love. She, however, shunned society, and attaching herself to me alone, rendered me happy. It is a happiness to wonder;—it is a happiness to dream.

Morella's erudition was profound. As I hope to live, her talents were of no common order—her powers of mind were gigantic. I felt this, and, in many matters, became her pupil. I soon, however, found that, perhaps on account of her Presburg education, she placed before me a number of those mystical writings which are usually considered the mere dross of the early German literature. These, for what reason I could not imagine, were her favorite and constant study—and that, in process of time they became my own, should be attributed to the simple but effectual influence of habit and example.

In all this, if I err not, my reason had little to do. My convictions, or I forget myself, were in no manner acted upon by the ideal, nor was any tincture of the mysticism which I read, to be discovered, unless I am greatly mistaken, either in my deeds or in my thoughts. Persuaded of this, I abandoned myself implicitly to the guidance of my wife, and entered with an unflinching heart into the intricacies of her studies. And then—then, when, pouring over forbidden pages, I felt a forbidden spirit enkindling within me—would Morella place her cold hand upon my own, and rake up from the ashes of a dead philosophy some low, singular words, whose strange meaning burned themselves in upon my memory. And then, hour after hour, would I linger by her side, and dwell upon the music of her voice—until, at length, its melody was tainted with terror,—and there fell a shadow upon my soul—and I grew pale, and shuddered inwardly at those too unearthly tones. And thus, joy suddenly faded into horror, and the most beautiful became the most hideous, as Hinnon became Ge-Henna.[3]

It is unnecessary to state the exact character of those disquisitions which, growing out of the volumes I have mentioned, formed, for so long a time, almost the sole conversation of Morella and myself. By the learned in what might be termed theological morality they will be readily conceived, and by the unlearned they would, at all events, be little understood. The wild Pantheism of Fichte; the modified Παλιγγενεσια of the Pythagoreans; and, above all, the doctrines of *Identity* as urged by Schelling, were generally the points of discussion presenting the most of beauty to the imaginative Morella.[4] That identity which is termed personal, Mr. Locke, I think, truly defines to consist in the sameness of a rational being. And since by person we understand an intelligent essence having reason, and since there is a consciousness which always *accompanies* thinking, it is this which makes us all to be that which we call *ourselves*—thereby distinguishing us from other beings that think, and giving us our personal identity. But the *principium individuationis*—the notion of that identity *which at death is or is not lost forever*, was to me—at all times, a consideration of intense interest; not more from the perplexing and exciting nature of its consequences, than from the marked and agitated manner in which Morella mentioned them.

But, indeed, the time had now arrived when the mystery of my wife's manner oppressed me as a spell. I could no longer bear the touch of her wan fingers, nor the low tone of her musical language, nor the lustre of her melancholy eyes. And she knew all this, but did not upbraid; she seemed conscious of my weakness or my folly, and, smiling, called it Fate. She seemed, also, conscious of a cause, to me unknown, for the gradual alienation of my regard; but she gave me no hint or token of its nature. Yet was she woman, and pined away daily. In time, the crimson spot settled steadily upon the cheek, and the blue veins upon the pale forehead became prominent; and, one instant, my nature melted into pity, but, in the next, I met the glance of her meaning eyes, and then my soul sickened and became giddy with the giddiness of one who gazes downward into some dreary and unfathomable abyss.

Shall I then say that I longed with an earnest and consuming desire for the moment of Morella's decease? I did; but the fragile spirit clung to its tenement of clay for many days— for many weeks and irksome months—until my tortured nerves obtained the mastery over my mind, and I grew furious through delay, and, with the heart of a fiend, cursed the days, and the hours, and the bitter moments, which seemed to lengthen and lengthen as her gentle life declined—like shadows in the dying of the day.

But one autumnal evening, when the winds lay still in heaven, Morella called me to her bed-side. There was a dim mist over all the earth, and a warm glow upon the waters, and, amid the rich October leaves of the forest, a rainbow from the firmament had surely fallen.

"It is a day of days," she said, as I approached; "a day of all days either to live or die. It is a fair day for the sons of earth and life—ah, more fair for the daughters of heaven and death!"

I kissed her forehead, and she continued:

"I am dying, yet shall I live."

"Morella!"

"The days have never been when thou couldst love me—but her whom in life thou didst abhor, in death thou shalt adore."

"Morella!"

"I repeat that I am dying. But within me is a pledge of that affection—ah, how little!—which thou didst feel for me, Morella. And when my spirit departs shall the child live—thy child and mine, Morella's. But thy days shall be days of sorrow—that sorrow which is the most lasting of impressions, as the cypress is the most enduring of trees. For the hours of thy happiness are over; and joy is not gathered twice in a life, as the roses of Pæstum[5] twice in a year. Thou shalt no longer, then, play the Teian with time, but, being ignorant of the myrtle and the vine, thou shalt bear about with thee thy shroud on earth, as do the Moslemin at Mecca."

"Morella!" I cried, "Morella! how knowest thou this?"—but she turned away her face upon the pillow, and, a slight tremor coming over her limbs, she thus died, and I heard her voice no more.

Yet, as she had foretold, her child—to which in dying she had given birth, and which breathed not until the mother breathed no more—her child, a daughter, lived. And she grew strangely in stature and intellect, and was the perfect resemblance of her who had departed, and I loved her with a love more fervent than I had believed it possible to feel for any denizen of earth.

But, ere long, the heaven of this pure affection became darkened, and gloom, and horror, and grief, swept over it in clouds. I said the child grew strangely in stature and intelligence.—Strange indeed was her rapid increase in bodily size—but terrible, oh! terrible were the tumultuous thoughts which crowded upon me while watching the development of her mental being. Could it be otherwise, when I daily discovered in the conceptions of the child the adult powers and faculties of the woman?—when the lessons of experience fell from the lips of infancy? and when the wisdom or the passions of maturity I found hourly gleaming from its full and speculative eye? When, I say, all this became evident to my appalled senses—when I could no longer hide it from my soul, nor throw it off from those perceptions which trembled to receive it—is it to be wondered at that suspicions, of a nature fearful and exciting, crept in upon my spirit, or that my thoughts fell back aghast upon the wild tales and thrilling theories of the entombed Morella? I snatched from the scrutiny of the world a being whom destiny compelled me to adore, and in the rigorous seclusion of my home, watched with an agonizing anxiety over all which concerned the beloved.

And, as years rolled away, and I gazed, day after day, upon her holy, and mild, and eloquent face, and poured over her maturing form, day after day did I discover new points of resemblance in the child to her mother, the melancholy and the dead. And, hourly, grew darker these shadows of similitude, and more full, and more definite, and more perplexing, and more hideously terrible in their aspect. For that her smile was like her mother's I could bear; but then I shuddered at its too perfect *identity*— that her eyes were like Morella's I could endure; but then they too often looked down into the depths of my soul with Morella's own intense and bewildering meaning. And in the contour of the high forehead, and in the ringlets of the silken hair, and in the wan fingers which buried themselves therein, and in the sad musical tones of her speech, and above all—oh, above all—in the phrases and expressions of the dead on the lips of the loved and the living, I found food for consuming thought and horror—for a worm that *would* not die.

Thus passed away two lustra[6] of her life, and, as yet, my daughter remained nameless upon the earth. "My child" and "my love" were the designations usually prompted by a father's affection, and the rigid seclusion of her days precluded all other intercourse. Morella's name died with her at her death. Of the mother I had never spoken to the daughter;—it was impossible to speak. Indeed, during the brief period of her existence the latter had received no impressions from the outward world such as might have been afforded by the narrow limits of her privacy. But at length the ceremony of baptism presented to my mind, in its unnerved and agitated condition, a present deliverance from the terrors of my destiny. And at the baptismal fount I hesitated for a name. And many titles of the wise and beautiful, of old and modern times, of my own and foreign lands, came thronging to my lips, with many, many fair titles of the gentle, and the happy, and the good. What prompted me, then, to disturb the memory of the buried dead? What demon urged me to breathe that sound, which, in its very recollection was wont to make ebb the purple blood in torrents from the temples to the heart? What fiend spoke from the recesses of my soul, when, amid those dim aisles, and in the silence of the night, I whispered within the ears of the holy man the syllables—Morella? What more than fiend convulsed the features of my child, and overspread them with hues of death, as starting at that scarcely audible sound, she turned her glassy eyes from the earth to heaven, and, falling prostrate on the black slabs of our ancestral vault, responded—"I am here!"

Distinct, coldly, calmly distinct, fell those few simple sounds within my ear, and thence, like molten lead, rolled hissingly into my brain. Years—years may pass away, but the memory of that epoch—never! Nor was I indeed ignorant of the flowers and the vine—but the hemlock and the cypress overshadowed me night and day. And I kept no reckoning of time or place, and the stars of my fate faded from heaven, and therefore the earth grew dark, and its figures passed by me, like flitting shadows, and among them all I beheld only—Morella. The winds of the firmament breathed but one sound within my ears, and the ripples upon the sea murmured evermore—Morella. But she died; and with my own hands I bore her to the tomb; and I laughed with a long and bitter laugh as I found no traces of the first, in the charnel where I laid the second—Morella.

Ligeia[1]

And the will therein lieth, which dieth not. Who knoweth the mysteries of the will, with its vigor? For God is but a great will pervading all things by nature of its intentness. Man doth not yield himself to the angels, nor unto death utterly, save only through the weakness of his feeble will.

Joseph Glanvill[2]

I cannot, for my soul, remember how, when, or even precisely where, I first became acquainted with the lady Ligeia. Long years have since elapsed, and my memory is feeble through much suffering. Or, perhaps, I cannot *now* bring these points to mind, because, in truth, the character of my beloved, her rare learning, her singular yet placid cast of beauty, and the thrilling and enthralling eloquence of her low musical language, made their way into my heart by paces so steadily and stealthily progressive that they have been unnoticed and unknown. Yet I believe that I met her first and most frequently in some large, old, decaying city near the Rhine. Of her family—I have surely heard her speak. That it is of a remotely ancient date cannot be doubted. Ligeia! Ligeia! Buried in studies of a nature more than all else adapted to deaden impressions of the outward world, it is by that sweet word alone—by Ligeia—that I bring before mine eyes in fancy the image of her who is no more. And now, while I write, a recollection flashes upon me that I have *never known* the paternal name of her who was my friend and my betrothed, and who became the partner of my studies, and finally the wife of my bosom. Was it a playful charge on the part of my Ligeia? or was it a test of my strength of affection, that I should institute no inquiries upon this point? or was it rather a caprice of my own—a wildly romantic offering on the shrine of the most passionate devotion? I but indistinctly recall the fact itself—what wonder that I have utterly forgotten the circumstances which originated or attended it? And, indeed, if ever that spirit which is entitled *Romance*—if ever she, the wan and the misty-winged *Ashtophet*[3] of idolatrous Egypt, presided, as they tell, over marriages ill-omened, then most surely she presided over mine.

There is one dear topic, however, on which my memory fails me not. It is the *person* of Ligeia. In stature she was tall, somewhat slender, and, in her latter days, even emaciated. I would in vain attempt to portray the majesty, the quiet ease, of her demeanor, or the incomprehensible lightness and elasticity of her footfall. She came and departed as a shadow. I was never made aware of her entrance into my closed study save by the dear music of her low sweet voice, as she placed her marble hand upon my shoulder. In beauty of face no maiden ever equaled her. It was the radiance of an opium dream—an airy and spirit-lifting vision more wildly divine than the phantasies which hovered about the slumbering souls of the daughters of Delos. Yet her features were not of that regular mould which we have been falsely taught to worship in the classical labors of the heathen. "There is no exquisite beauty," says Bacon, Lord Verulam, speaking truly of all the forms and *genera* of beauty, "without some *strangeness* in the proportion." Yet, although I saw that the features of Ligeia were not of a classic regularity—although I perceived that her loveliness was indeed "exquisite," and felt that there was much of "strangeness" pervading it, yet I have tried in vain to detect the irregularity and to trace home my own perception of "the strange." I examined the contour of the lofty and pale forehead—it was faultless— how cold indeed that word when applied to a majesty so divine!—the skin rivalling the purest ivory, the commanding extent and repose, the gentle prominence of the regions above the temples; and then the raven-black, the glossy, the luxuriant and naturally-curling tresses, setting forth the full force of the Homeric epithet, "hyacinthine!" I looked at the delicate outlines of the nose—and nowhere but in the graceful medallions of the Hebrews had I beheld a similar perfection. There were the same luxurious smoothness of surface, the same scarcely perceptible tendency to the aquiline, the same harmoniously curved nostrils speaking the free spirit. I regarded the sweet mouth. Here was indeed the triumph of all things heavenly—the magnificent turn of the short upper lip—the soft, voluptuous slumber of the under— the dimples which sported, and the color which spoke—the teeth glancing back, with a brilliancy almost startling, every ray of the holy light which fell upon them in her serene and placid, yet most exultingly radiant of all smiles. I scrutinized the formation of the chin—and here, too, I found the gentleness of breadth, the softness and the majesty, the fullness and the spirituality, of the Greek—the contour which the God Apollo revealed but in a dream, to Cleomenes, the son of the Athenian. And then I peered into the large eyes of Ligeia.

For eyes we have no models in the remotely antique. It might have been, too, that in these eyes of my beloved lay the secret to which Lord Verulam alludes. They were, I must believe, far larger than the ordinary eyes of our own race. They were even fuller than the fullest of the gazelle eyes of the tribe of the valley of Nourjahad.[4] Yet it was only at intervals—in moments of intense excitement—that this peculiarity became more than slightly noticeable in Ligeia. And at such moments was her beauty—in my heated fancy thus it appeared perhaps—the beauty of beings either above or apart from the earth—the beauty of the fabulous Houri of the Turk.[5] The hue of the orbs was the most brilliant of black, and, far over them, hung jetty lashes of great length. The brows, slightly irregular in outlines, had the same tint. The "strangeness," however, which I found in the eyes, was of a nature distinct from the formation, or the color, or the brilliancy of the features, and must, after all, be referred to the *expression*. Ah, word of no meaning! behind whose vast latitude of mere sound we intrench our ignorance of so much of the spiritual. The expression of the eyes of Ligeia! How for long hours have I pondered upon it! How have I, through the whole of a midsummer night, struggled to fathom it! What was it—that something more profound than the well of Democritus[6]—which lay far within the pupils of my beloved? What *was* it? I was possessed with a passion to discover. Those eyes! those large, those shining, those divine orbs! they became to me twin stars of Leda, and I to them devoutest of astrologers.

There is no point, among the many incomprehensible anomalies of the science of the mind, more thrillingly exciting than the fact—never, I believe, noticed in the schools—that, in our endeavors to recall to memory something long forgotten, we often find ourselves *upon the very verge* of remembrance, without being able, in the end, to remember. And thus how frequently, in my intense scrutiny of Ligeia's eyes, have I felt approaching the full knowledge of their expression—felt it approaching—yet not quite be mine—and so at length entirely depart! And (strange, oh strangest mystery of all!) I found, in the commonest objects of the universe, a circle of analogies to that expression. I mean to say that, subsequently to the period when Ligeia's beauty passed into my spirit, there dwelling as in a shrine, I derived, from many existences in the material world, a sentiment such as I felt always around within me by her large and luminous orbs. Yet not the more could I define that sentiment, or analyze, or even steadily view it. I recognized it, let me repeat, sometimes in the survey of a rapidly-growing vine—in the contemplation of a moth, a butterfly, a chrysalis, a stream of running water. I have felt it in the ocean; in the falling of a meteor. I have felt it in the glances of unusually aged people. And there are one or two stars in heaven—(one especially, a star of the sixth magnitude, double and changeable, to be found near the large star in Lyra) in a telescopic scrutiny of which I have been made aware of the feeling. I have been filled with it by certain sounds from stringed instruments, and not unfrequently by passages from books.

Among innumerable other instances, I well remember something in a volume of Joseph Glanvill, which (perhaps merely from its quaintness—who shall say?) never failed to inspire me with the sentiment;—"And the will therein lieth, which dieth not. Who knoweth the mysteries of the will, with its vigor? For God is but a great will pervading all things by nature of its intentness. Man doth not yield him to the angels, nor unto death utterly, save only through the weakness of his feeble will."

Length of years, and subsequent reflection, have enabled me to trace, indeed, some remote connection between this passage in the English moralist and a portion of the character of Ligeia. An *intensity* in thought, action, or speech, was possibly, in her, a result, or at least an index, of that gigantic volition which, during our long intercourse, failed to give other and more immediate evidence of its existence. Of all the women whom I have ever known, she, the outwardly calm, the ever-placid Ligeia, was the most violently a prey to the tumultuous vultures of stern passion. And of such passion I could form no estimate, save by the miraculous expansion of those eyes which at once so delighted and appalled me—by the almost magical melody, modulation, distinctness and placidity of her very low voice—and by the fierce energy (rendered doubly effective by contrast with her manner of utterance) of the wild words which she habitually uttered.

I have spoken of the learning of Ligeia: it was immense—such as I have never known in woman. In the classical tongues was she deeply proficient, and as far as my own acquaintance extended in regard to the modern dialects of Europe, I have never known her at fault. Indeed upon any theme of the most admired, because simply the most abstruse of the boasted erudition of the academy, have I *ever* found Ligeia at fault? How singularly—how thrillingly, this one point in the nature of my wife has forced itself, at this late period only, upon my attention! I said her knowledge was such as I have never known in woman—but where breathes the man who has traversed, and successfully, *all* the wide areas of moral, physical, and mathematical science? I saw not then what I now clearly perceive, that the acquisitions of Ligeia were gigantic, were astounding; yet I was sufficiently aware of her infinite supremacy to resign myself, with a child-like confidence, to her guidance through the chaotic world of metaphysical investigation at which I was most busily occupied during the earlier years of our marriage. With how vast a triumph—with how vivid a delight—with how much of all that is ethereal in hope—did I *feel*, as she bent over me in studies but little sought—but less known—that delicious vista by slow degrees expanding before me, down whose long, gorgeous, and all untrodden path, I might at length pass onward to the goal of a wisdom too divinely precious not to be forbidden!

How poignant, then, must have been the grief with which, after some years, I beheld my well-grounded expectations take wings to themselves and fly away! Without Ligeia I was but as a child groping benighted. Her presence, her readings alone, rendered vividly luminous the many mysteries of the transcendentalism in which we were immersed. Wanting the radiant lustre of her eyes, letters, lambent and golden, grew duller than Saturnian lead. And now those eyes shone less and less frequently upon the pages over which I pored. Ligeia grew ill. The wild eyes blazed with a too—too glorious effulgence; the pale fingers became of the transparent waxen hue of the grave, and the blue veins upon the lofty forehead swelled and sank impetuously with the tides of the most gentle emotion. I saw that she must die—and

I struggled desperately in spirit with the grim Azrael.[7] And the struggles of the passionate wife were, to my astonishment, even more energetic than my own. There had been much in her stern nature to impress me with the belief that, to her, death would have come without its terrors;—but not so. Words are impotent to convey any just idea of the fierceness of resistance with which she wrestled with the Shadow. I groaned in anguish at the pitiable spectacle. I would have soothed—I would have reasoned; but, in the intensity of her wild desire for life,—for life—*but* for life— solace and reason were alike the uttermost of folly. Yet not until the last instance, amid the most convulsive writhings of her fierce spirit, was shaken the external placidity of her demeanor. Her voice grew more gentle—grew more low—yet I would not wish to dwell upon the wild meaning of the quietly uttered words. My brain reeled as I hearkened entranced, to a melody more than mortal—to assumptions and aspirations which mortality had never before known.

That she loved me I should not have doubted; and I might have been easily aware that, in a bosom such as hers, love would have reigned no ordinary passion. But in death only, was I fully impressed with the strength of her affection. For long hours, detaining my hand, would she pour out before me the overflowing of a heart whose more than passionate devotion amounted to idolatry. How had I deserved to be so blessed by such confessions?—how had I deserved to be so cursed with the removal of my beloved in the hour of her making them? But upon this subject I cannot bear to dilate. Let me say only, that in Ligeia's more than womanly abandonment to a love, alas! all unmerited, all unworthily bestowed, I at length recognized the principle of her longing with so wildly earnest a desire for the life which was now fleeing so rapidly away. It is this wild longing—it is this eager vehemence of desire for life—*but* for life—that I have no power to portray—no utterance capable of expressing.

At high noon of the night in which she departed, beckoning me, peremptorily, to her side, she bade me repeat certain verses composed by herself not many days before. I obeyed her.—They were these:

Lo! 'tis a gala night
  Within the lonesome latter years!
An angel throng, bewinged, bedight
  In veils, and drowned in tears,
Sit in a theatre, to see
  A play of hopes and fears,
While the orchestra breathes fitfully
  The music of the spheres.

Mimes, in the form of God on high,
  Mutter and mumble low,
And hither and thither fly—
  Mere puppets they, who come and go
At bidding of vast formless things
  That shift the scenery to and fro,
Flapping from out their Condor wings
  Invisible Wo!

That motley drama!—oh, be sure
   It shall not be forgot!
With its Phantom chased forevermore,
   By a crowd that seize it not,
Through a circle that ever returneth in
   To the self-same spot,
And much of Madness and more of Sin,
   And Horror the soul of the plot.

But see, amid the mimic rout,
   A crawling shape intrude!
A blood-red thing that writhes from out
   The scenic solitude!
It writhes!—it writhes!—with mortal pangs
   The mimes become its food,
And the seraphs sob at vermin fangs
   In human gore imbued.

Out—out are the lights—out all!
   And over each quivering form,
The curtain, a funeral pall,
   Comes down with the rush of a storm,
And the angels, all pallid and wan,
   Uprising, unveiling, affirm
That the play is the tragedy, "Man,"
   And its hero the Conqueror Worm.

"O God!" half shrieked Ligeia, leaping to her feet and extending her arms aloft with a spasmodic movement, as I made an end of these lines—"O God! O Divine Father!—shall these things be undeviatingly so?—shall this Conqueror be not once conquered? Are we not part and parcel in Thee? Who—who knoweth the mysteries of the will with its vigor? Man doth not yield him to the angels, *nor unto death utterly*, save only through the weakness of his feeble will."

And now, as if exhausted with emotion, she suffered her white arms to fall, and returned solemnly to her bed of Death. And as she breathed her last sighs, there came mingled with them a low murmur from her lips. I bent to them my ear and distinguished, again, the concluding words of the passage in Glanvill—"*Man doth not yield him to the angels, nor unto death utterly, save only through the weakness of his feeble will.*"

She died;—and I, crushed into the very dust with sorrow, could no longer endure the lonely desolation of my dwelling in the dim and decaying city by the Rhine. I had no lack of what the world calls wealth. Ligeia had brought me far more, very far more than ordinarily falls to the lot of mortals. After a few months, therefore, of weary and aimless wandering, I purchased, and put in some repair, an abbey, which I shall not name, in one of the wildest and least frequented portions of fair England. The gloomy and dreary grandeur of the building, the almost savage aspect of the domain, the many melancholy and time-honored memories connected with both, had much in unison with the feelings of utter abandonment which had driven me into that remote and unsocial region of the country. Yet although the external abbey, with its verdant decay hanging about it, suffered but little alteration, I gave way, with a child-like perversity, and perchance with a faint hope of alleviating my sorrows, to a display of more than regal magnificence within.—For such follies, even in childhood, I had imbibed a taste and now they came back to me as if in the dotage of grief. Alas, I feel how much even of incipient madness might have been discovered in the gorgeous and fantastic draperies, in the solemn carvings of Egypt, in the wild cornices and furniture, in the Bedlam patterns of the carpets of tufted gold! I had become a bounden slave in the trammels of opium, and my labors and my orders had taken a coloring from my dreams. But these absurdities I must not pause to detail. Let me speak only of that one chamber, ever accursed, whither in a moment of mental alienation, I led from the altar as my bride—as the successor of the unforgotten Ligeia—the fair-haired and blue-eyed Lady Rowena Trevanion, of Tremaine.

There is no individual portion of the architecture and decoration of that bridal chamber which is not now visibly before me. Where were the souls of the haughty family of the bride, when, through thirst of gold, they permitted to pass the threshold of an apartment *so* bedecked, a maiden and a daughter so beloved? I have said that I minutely remember the details of the chamber—yet I am sadly forgetful on topics of deep moment—and here there was no system, no keeping, in the fantastic display, to take hold upon the memory. The room lay in a high turret of the castellated abbey, was pentagonal in shape, and of capacious size. Occupying the whole southern face of the pentagon was the sole window—an immense sheet of unbroken glass from Venice—a single pane, and tinted of a leaden hue, so that the rays of either the sun or moon, passing through it, fell with a ghastly lustre on the objects within. Over the upper portion of this huge window, extended the trellice-work of an aged vine, which clambered up the massy walls of the turret. The ceiling, of gloomy-looking oak, was excessively lofty, vaulted, and elaborately fretted with the wildest and most grotesque specimens of a semi-Gothic, semi-Druidical device. From out the most central recess of this melancholy vaulting, depended, by a single chain of gold with long links, a huge censer of the same metal, Saracenic[8] in pattern, and with many perforations so contrived that there writhed in and out of them, as if endued with a serpent vitality, a continual succession of parti-colored fires.

Some few ottomans and golden candelabra, of Eastern figure, were in various stations about—and there was the couch, too—the bridal couch—of an Indian model, and low, and sculptured of solid ebony, with a pall-like canopy above. In each of the angles of the chamber stood on end a gigantic sarcophagus of black granite, from the tombs of the kings over against Luxor, with their aged lids full of immemorial sculpture. But in the draping of the apartment lay, alas! the chief phantasy of all. The lofty walls, gigantic in height—even unproportionably so—were hung from summit to foot, in vast folds, with a heavy and massive-looking tapestry—tapestry of a material which was found alike as a carpet on the floor, as a covering for the ottomans and the ebony bed, as a canopy for the bed, and as the gorgeous volutes of the curtains which partially shaded the window. The material was the richest cloth of gold. It was spotted all over, at irregular intervals, with arabesque figures, about a foot in diameter, and wrought upon the cloth in patterns of the most jetty black. But these figures partook of the true character of the arabesque only when regarded from a single point of view. By a contrivance now common, and indeed traceable to a very remote period of antiquity, they were made changeable in aspect. To one entering the room, they bore the appearance of simple monstrosities; but upon a farther advance, this appearance gradually departed; and step by step, as the visiter moved his station in the chamber, he saw himself surrounded by an endless succession of the ghastly forms which belong to the superstition of the Norman, or arise in the guilty slumbers of the monk. The phantasmagoric effect was vastly heightened by the artificial introduction of a strong continual current of wind behind the draperies— giving a hideous and uneasy animation to the whole.

In halls such as these—in a bridal chamber such as this—I passed, with the Lady of Tremaine, the unhallowed hours of the first month of our marriage—passed them with but little disquietude. That my wife dreaded the fierce moodiness of my temper—that she shunned me and loved me but little—I could not help perceiving; but it gave me rather pleasure than otherwise. I loathed her with a hatred belonging more to demon than to man. My memory flew back, (oh, with what intensity of regret!) to Ligeia, the beloved, the august, the beautiful, the entombed. I revelled in recollections of her purity, of her wisdom, of her lofty, her ethereal nature, of her passionate, her idolatrous love. Now, then, did my spirit fully and freely burn with more than all the fires of her own. In the excitement of my opium dreams (for I was habitually fettered in the shackles of the drug) I would call aloud upon her name, during the silence of the night, or among the sheltered recesses of the glens by day, as if, through the wild eagerness, the solemn passion, the consuming ardor of my longing for the departed, I could restore her to the pathway she had abandoned— ah, *could* it be forever?—upon the earth.

About the commencement of the second month of the marriage, the Lady Rowena was attacked with sudden illness, from which her recovery was slow. The fever which consumed her rendered her nights uneasy; and in her perturbed state of half-slumber, she spoke of sounds, and of motions, in and about the chamber of the turret, which I concluded had no origin save in the distemper of her fancy, or perhaps in the phantasmagoric influences of the chamber itself. She became at length convalescent—finally well. Yet but a brief period elapsed, ere a second more violent disorder again threw her upon a bed of suffering; and from this attack her frame, at all times feeble, never altogether recovered. Her illnesses were, after this epoch, of alarming character, and of more alarming recurrence, defying alike the knowledge and the great exertions of her physicians. With the increase of the chronic disease which had thus, apparently, taken too sure hold upon her constitution to be eradicated by human means, I could not fail to observe a similar increase in the nervous irritation of her temperament, and in her excitability by trivial causes of fear. She spoke again, and now more frequently and pertinaciously, of the sounds— of the slight sounds—and of the unusual motions among the tapestries, to which she had formerly alluded.

One night, near the closing in of September, she pressed this distressing subject with more than usual emphasis upon my attention. She had just awakened from an unquiet slumber, and I had been watching, with feelings half of anxiety, half of a vague terror, the workings of her emaciated countenance. I sat by the side of her ebony bed, upon one of the ottomans of India. She partly arose, and spoke, in an earnest low whisper, of sounds which she *then* heard, but which I could not hear—of motions which she *then* saw, but which I could not perceive. The wind was rushing hurriedly behind the tapestries, and I wished to show her (what, let me confess it, I could not *all* believe) that those almost inarticulate breathings, and those very gentle variations of the figures upon the wall, were but the natural effects of that customary rushing of the wind. But a deadly pallor, over-spreading her face, had proved to me that my exertions to reassure her would be fruitless. She appeared to be fainting, and no attendants were within call. I remembered where was deposited a decanter of light wine which had been ordered by her physicians, and hastened across the chamber to procure it. But, as I stepped beneath the light of the censer, two circumstances of a startling nature attracted my attention. I had felt that some palpable although invisible object had passed lightly by my person; and I saw that there lay upon the golden carpet, in the very middle of the rich lustre thrown from the censer, a shadow—a faint, indefinite shadow of angelic aspect—such as might be fancied for the shadow of a shade. But I was wild with the excitement of an immoderate dose of opium, and heeded these things but little, nor spoke of them to Rowena. Having found the wine, I recrossed the chamber, and poured out a goblet-ful, which I held to the lips of the fainting lady. She had now partially recovered, however, and took the vessel herself, while I sank upon an ottoman near me, with my eyes fastened upon her person. It was then that I became distinctly aware of a gentle foot-fall upon the carpet, and near the couch; and in a second thereafter, as Rowena was in the act of raising the wine to her lips, I saw, or may have dreamed that I saw, fall within the goblet, as if from some invisible spring in the atmosphere of the room, three or four large drops of a brilliant and ruby colored fluid. If this I saw—not so Rowena. She swallowed the wine unhesitatingly, and I forbore to speak to her of a circumstance which must, after all, I considered, have been but the suggestion of a vivid imagination, rendered morbidly active by the terror of the lady, by the opium, and by the hour.

Yet I cannot conceal it from my own perception that, immediately subsequent to the fall of the ruby-drops, a rapid change for the worse took place in the disorder of my wife; so that, on the third subsequent night, the hands of her menials prepared her for the tomb, and on the fourth, I sat alone, with her shrouded body, in that fantastic chamber which had received her as my bride.—Wild visions, opium-engendered, flitted, shadow-like, before me. I gazed with unquiet eye upon the sarcophagi in the angles of the room, upon the varying figures of the drapery, and upon the writhing of the parti-colored fires in the censer overhead. My eyes then fell, as I called to mind the circumstances of a former night, to the spot beneath the glare of the censer where I had seen the faint traces of the shadow. It was there, however, no longer; and breathing with greater freedom, I turned my glances to the pallid and rigid figure upon the bed. Then rushed upon me a thousand memories of Ligeia—and then came back upon my heart, with the turbulent violence of a flood, the whole of that unutterable wo with which I had regarded *her* thus enshrouded. The night waned; and still, with a bosom full of bitter thoughts of the one only and supremely beloved, I remained gazing upon the body of Rowena.

It might have been midnight, or perhaps earlier, or later, for I had taken no note of time, when a sob, low, gentle, but very distinct, startled me from my revery.—I *felt* that it came from the bed of ebony—the bed of death. I listened in an agony of superstitious terror—but there was no repetition of the sound. I strained my vision to detect any motion in the corpse—but there was not the slightest perceptible. Yet I could not have been deceived. I *had* heard the noise, however faint, and my soul was awakened within me. I resolutely and perseveringly kept my attention riveted upon the body. Many minutes elapsed before any circumstance occurred tending to throw any light upon the mystery. At length it became evident that a slight, a very feeble, and barely noticeable tinge of color had flushed up within the cheeks, and along the sunken small veins of the eyelids. Through a species of unutterable horror and awe, for which the language of mortality has no sufficiently energetic expression, I felt my heart cease to beat, my limbs grow rigid where I sat. Yet a sense of duty finally operated to restore my self-possession. I could no longer doubt that we had been precipitate in our preparations—that Rowena still lived. It was necessary that some immediate exertion be made; yet the turret was altogether apart from the portion of the abbey tenanted by the servants—there were none within call—I had no means of summoning them to my aid without leaving the room for many minutes—and this I could not venture to do. I therefore struggled alone in my endeavors to call back the spirit still hovering. In a short period it was certain, however, that a relapse had taken place; the color disappeared from both eyelid and cheek, leaving a wanness even more than that of marble; the lips became doubly shrivelled and pinched up in the ghastly expression of death; a repulsive clamminess and coldness overspread rapidly the surface of the body; and all the usual rigorous stiffness immediately supervened. I fell back with a shudder upon the couch from which I had been so startlingly aroused, and again gave myself up to passionate waking visions of Ligeia.

An hour thus elapsed when (could it be possible?) I was a second time aware of some vague sound issuing from the region of the bed. I listened—in extremity of horror. The sound came again—it was a sigh. Rushing to the corpse, I saw—distinctly saw—a tremor upon the lips. In a minute afterward they relaxed, disclosing a bright line of the pearly teeth. Amazement now struggled in my bosom with the profound awe which had hitherto reigned there alone. I felt that my vision grew dim, that my reason wandered; and it was only by a violent effort that I at length succeeded in nerving myself to the task which duty thus once more had pointed out. There was now a partial glow upon the forehead and upon the cheek and throat; a perceptible warmth pervaded the whole frame; there was even a slight pulsation at the heart. The lady *lived*; and with redoubled ardor I betook myself to the task of restoration. I chafed and bathed the temples and the hands, and used every exertion which experience, and no little medical reading, could suggest. But in vain. Suddenly, the color fled, the pulsation ceased, the lips resumed the expression of the dead, and, in an instant afterward, the whole body took upon itself the icy chilliness, the livid hue, the intense rigidity, the sunken outline, and all the loathsome peculiarities of that which has been, for many days, a tenant of the tomb.

And again I sunk into visions of Ligeia—and again, (what marvel that I shudder while I write?) *again* there reached my ears a low sob from the region of the ebony bed. But why shall I minutely detail the unspeakable horrors of that night? Why shall I pause to relate how, time after time, until near the period of the gray dawn, this hideous drama of revivification was repeated; how each terrific relapse was only into a sterner and apparently more irredeemable death; how each agony wore the aspect of a struggle with some invisible foe; and how each struggle was succeeded by I know not what of wild change in the personal appearance of the corpse? Let me hurry to a conclusion.

The greater part of the fearful night had worn away, and she who had been dead, once again stirred—and now more vigorously than hitherto, although arousing from a dissolution more appalling in its utter hopelessness than any. I had long ceased to struggle or to move, and remained sitting rigidly upon the ottoman, a helpless prey to a whirl of violent emotions, of which extreme awe was perhaps the least terrible, the least consuming. The corpse, I repeat, stirred, and now more vigorously than before. The hues of life flushed up with unwonted energy into the countenance—the limbs relaxed—and, save that the eyelids were yet pressed heavily together, and that the bandages and draperies of the grave still imparted their charnel character to the figure, I might have dreamed that Rowena had indeed shaken off, utterly, the fetters of Death. But if this idea was not, even then, altogether adopted, I could at least doubt no longer, when, arising from the bed, tottering, with feeble steps, with closed eyes, and with the manner of one bewildered in a dream, the thing that was enshrouded advanced boldly and palpably into the middle of the apartment.

I trembled not—I stirred not—for a crowd of unutterable fancies connected with the air, the stature, the demeanor of the figure, rushing hurriedly through my brain, had paralyzed—had chilled me into stone. I stirred not—but gazed upon the apparition. There was a mad disorder in my thoughts—a tumult unappeasable. Could it, indeed, be the *living* Rowena who confronted me? Could it indeed be Rowena *at all*—the fair-haired, the blue-eyed Lady Rowena Trevanion of Tremaine? Why, *why* should I doubt it? The bandage lay heavily about the mouth—but then might it not be the mouth of the breathing Lady of Tremaine? And the cheeks—there were the roses as in her noon of life—yes, these might indeed be the fair cheeks of the living Lady of Tremaine. And the chin, with its dimples, as in health, might it not be hers?—but *had she then grown taller since her malady?* What inexpressible madness seized me with that thought? One bound, and I had reached her feet! Shrinking from my touch, she let fall from her head, unloosened, the ghastly cerements which had confined it, and there streamed forth, into the rushing atmosphere of the chamber, huge masses of long and disshevelled hair; *it was blacker than the raven wings of the midnight!* And now slowly opened *the eyes* of the figure which stood before me. "Here then, at least," I shrieked aloud, "can I never—can I never be mistaken—these are the full, and the black, and the wild eyes—of my lost love—of the lady—of the LADY LIGEIA!"

How to Write a Blackwood Article[1]

"In the name of the Prophet—figs!!"
     Cry of the Turkish fig-pedler

I presume every body has heard of me. My name is the Signora Psyche Zenobia. This I know to be a fact. No body but my enemies ever calls me Suky Snobbs. I have been assured that Suky is but a vulgar corruption of Psyche, which is good Greek, and means "the soul" (that's me, I'm *all* soul) and sometimes "a butterfly," which latter meaning undoubtedly alludes to my appearance in my new crimson satin dress, with the sky-blue Arabian *mantelet*, and the trimmings of green *agraffas*, and the seven flounces of orange-colored *auriculas*.[2] As for Snobbs—any person who should look at me would be instantly aware that my name wasn't Snobbs. Miss Tabitha Turnip propagated that report through sheer envy. Tabitha Turnip indeed! Oh the little wretch! But what can we expect from a turnip? Wonder if she remembers the old adage about "blood out of a turnip, &c." [Mem: put her in mind of it the first opportunity.] [Mem again—pull her nose.] Where was I? Ah! I have been assured that Snobbs is a mere corruption of Zenobia, and that Zenobia was a queen—(So am I. Dr. Moneypenny, always calls me the Queen of Hearts)—and that Zenobia, as well as Psyche, is good Greek, and that my father was "a Greek," and that consequently I have a right to our patronymic, which is Zenobia, and not by any means Snobbs. Nobody but Tabitha Turnip calls me Suky Snobbs. I am the Signora Psyche Zenobia.

As I said before, every body has heard of me. I am that very Signora Psyche Zenobia, so justly celebrated as corresponding secretary to the *"Philadelphia, Regular, Exchange, Tea, Total, Young, Belles, Lettres, Universal, Experimental, Bibliographical, Association, To, Civilize, Humanity."* Dr. Moneypenny made the title for us, and says he chose it because it sounded big like an empty rum-puncheon. (A vulgar man that sometimes—but he's deep.) We all sign the initials of the society after our names, in the fashion of the R.S.A., Royal Society of Arts—the S.D.U.K., Society for the Diffusion of Useful Knowledge, &c. &c. Dr. Moneypenny says that S stands for *stale*, and that D.U.K. spells duck (but it don't), and that S.D.U.K. stands for Stale Duck, and not for Lord Brougham's society[3]—but then Dr. Moneypenny is such a queer man that I am never sure when he is telling me the truth. At any rate we always add to our names the initials P.R.E.T.T.Y.B.L.U.E.B.A.T.C.H.—that is to say, Philadelphia, Regular, Exchange, Tea, Total, Young, Belles, Lettres, Universal, Experimental, Bibliographical, Association, To, Civilize, Humanity—one letter for each word, which is a decided improvement upon Lord Brougham. Dr. Moneypenny will have it that our initials give our true character—but for my life I can't see what he means.

Notwithstanding the good offices of the Doctor, and the strenuous exertions of the association to get itself into notice, it met with no very great success until I joined it. The truth is, members indulged in too flippant a tone of discussion. The papers read every Saturday evening were characterized less by depth than buffoonery. They were all whipped syllabub. There was no investigation of first causes, first principles. There was no investigation of anything at all. There was no attention paid to that great point the "fitness of things." In short there was no fine writing like this. It was all low—very! No profundity, no reading, no metaphysics—nothing which the learned call spirituality, and which the unlearned choose to stigmatise as cant. [Dr. M. says I ought to spell "cant" with a capital K—but I know better.]

When I joined the society it was my endeavor to introduce a better style of thinking and writing, and all the world knows how well I have succeeded. We get up as good papers now in the P.R.E.T.T.Y.B.L.U.E.B.A.T.C.H. as any to be found even in Blackwood. I say, Blackwood, because I have been assured that the finest writing, upon every subject, is to be discovered in the pages of that justly celebrated Magazine. We now take it for our model upon all themes, and are getting into rapid notice accordingly. And, after all, it's not so very difficult a matter to compose an article of the genuine Blackwood stamp, if one only goes properly about it. Of course I don't speak of the political articles. Every body knows how *they* are managed, since Dr. Moneypenny explained it. Mr. Blackwood has a pair of tailor's shears, and three apprentices who stand by him for orders. One hands him the "Times," another the "Examiner," and a third a "Gulley's New Compendium of Slang-Whang." Mr. B. merely cuts out and intersperses. It is soon done—nothing but Examiner, Slang-Whang, and Times—then Times, Slang-Whang, and Examiner—and then Times, Examiner, and Slang-Whang.

But the chief merit of the Magazine lies in its miscellaneous articles; and the best of these come under the head of what Dr. Moneypenny calls the *bizarreries* (whatever that may mean) and what every body else calls the *intensities*. This is a species of writing which I have long known how to appreciate, although it is only since my late visit to Mr. Blackwood (deputed by the society) that I have been made aware of the exact method of composition. This method is very simple, but not so much so as the politics. Upon my calling at Mr. B's, and making known to him the wishes of the society, he received me with great civility, took me into his study, and gave me a clear explanation of the whole process.

"My dear madam," said he, evidently struck with my majestic appearance, for I had on the crimson satin, with the green *agraffas*, and orange-coloured *auriculas*, "My *dear* madam," said he, "sit down. The matter stands thus. In the first place, your writer of intensities must have very black ink, and a very big pen, with a very blunt nib. And, mark me, Miss Psyche Zenobia!" he continued, after a pause, with the most impressive energy and solemnity of manner, "mark me!—*that pen—must—never be mended!* Herein, madam, lies the secret, the soul, of intensity. I assume it upon myself to say, that no individual, of however great genius, ever wrote with a good pen,—understand me,—a good article. You may take it for granted, that when manuscript can be read it is never worth reading. This is a leading principle in our faith, to which if you cannot readily assent, our conference is at an end."

He paused. But, of course, as I had no wish to put an end to the conference, I assented to a proposition so very obvious, and one, too, of whose truth I had all along been sufficiently aware. He seemed pleased, and went on with his instructions.

"It may appear invidious in me, Miss Psyche Zenobia, to refer you to any article, or set of articles, in the way of model or study; yet perhaps I may as well call your attention to a few cases. Let me see. There was '*The Dead Alive*,' a capital thing!—the record of a gentleman's sensations when entombed before the breath was out of his body—full of taste, terror, sentiment, metaphysics, and erudition. You would have sworn that the writer had been born and brought up in a coffin. Then we had the '*Confessions of an Opium-eater*'—fine, very fine!—glorious imagination—deep philosophy—acute speculation—plenty of fire and fury, and a good spicing of the decidedly unintelligible. That was a nice bit of flummery, and went down the throats of the people delightfully. They would have it that Coleridge wrote the paper—but not so. It was composed by my pet baboon, Juniper, over a rummer of Hollands and water, 'hot, without sugar.'" [This I could scarcely have believed had it been any body but Mr. Blackwood, who assured me of it.] "Then there was '*The Involuntary Experimentalist*,' all about a gentleman who got baked in an oven, and came out alive and well, although certainly done to a turn. And then there was '*The Diary of a Late Physician*,' where the merit lay in good rant, and indifferent Greek—both of them taking things, with the public. And then there was '*The Man in the Bell*,' a paper by-the-bye, Miss Zenobia, which I cannot sufficiently recommend to your attention. It is the history of a young person who goes to sleep under the clapper of a church bell, and is awakened by its tolling for a funeral. The sound drives him mad, and accordingly, pulling out his tablets, he gives a record of his sensations. Sensations are the great things after all. Should you ever be drowned or hung, be sure and make a note of your sensations—they will be worth to you ten guineas a sheet. If you wish to write forcibly, Miss Zenobia, pay minute attention to the sensations."[4]

"That I certainly will, Mr. Blackwood," said I.

"Good!" he replied. "I see you are a pupil after my own heart. But I must put you *au fait* to the details necessary in composing what may be denominated a genuine Blackwood article of the sensation stamp—the kind which you will understand me to say I consider the best for all purposes.

"The first thing requisite is to get yourself into such a scrape as no one ever got into before. The oven, for instance,—that was a good hit. But if you have no oven, or big bell, at hand, and if you cannot conveniently tumble out of a balloon, or be swallowed up in an earthquake, or get stuck fast in a chimney, you will have to be contented with simply imagining some similar misadventure. I should prefer, however, that you have the actual fact to bear you out. Nothing so well assists the fancy, as an experimental knowledge of the matter in hand. 'Truth is strange,' you know, 'stranger than fiction'—besides being more to the purpose."

Here I assured him I had an excellent pair of garters, and would go and hang myself forthwith.

"Good!" he replied, "do so;—although hanging is somewhat hacknied. Perhaps you might do better. Take a dose of Brandreth's pills,[5] and then give us your sensations. However, my instructions will apply equally well to any variety of misadventure, and in your way home you may easily get knocked in the head, or run over by an omnibus, or bitten by a mad dog, or drowned in a gutter. But, to proceed.

"Having determined upon your subject, you must next consider the tone, or manner, of your narration. There is the tone didactic, the tone enthusiastic, the tone natural—all common-place enough. But then there is the tone laconic, or curt, which has lately come much into use. It consists in short sentences. Somehow thus. Can't be too brief. Can't be too snappish. Always a full stop. And never a paragraph.

"Then there is the tone elevated, diffusive, and interjectional. Some of our best novelists patronize this tone. The words must be all in a whirl, like a humming-top, and make a noise very similar, which answers remarkably well instead of meaning. This is the best of all possible styles where the writer is in too great a hurry to think.

"The tone metaphysical is also a good one. If you know any big words this is your chance for them. Talk of the Ionic and Eleatic schools—of Archytas, Gorgias and Alcmœon. Say something about objectivity and subjectivity. Be sure and abuse a man called Locke. Turn up your nose at things in general, and when you let slip anything a little *too* absurd, you need not be at the trouble of scratching it out, but just add a foot-note, and say that you are indebted for the above profound observation to the '*Kritik der reinem Vernunft,*' or to the '*Metaphysische Anfangsgrunde der Naturwissenschaft.*'[6] This will look erudite and—and—and frank.

"There are various other tones of equal celebrity, but I shall mention only two more—the tone transcendental and the tone heterogeneous. In the former the merit consists in seeing into the nature of affairs a great deal farther than any body else. This second sight is very efficient when properly managed. A little reading of the 'Dial' will carry you a great way. Eschew, in this case, big words; get them as small as possible, and write them upside down. Look over Channing's[7] poems and quote what he says about a 'fat little man with a delusive show of Can.' Put in something about the Supernal Oneness. Don't say a syllable about the Infernal Twoness. Above all, study innuendo. Hint every thing—assert nothing. If you feel inclined to say 'bread and butter' do not by any means say it outright. You may say anything and every thing *approaching* to 'bread and butter.' You may hint at buck-wheat cake, or you may even go so far as to insinuate oat-meal porridge, but if bread and butter be your real meaning, be cautious, my *dear* Miss Psyche, not on any account to say 'bread and butter!'"

I assured him that I should never say it again as long as I lived. He kissed me and continued:

"As for the tone heterogeneous, it is merely a judicious mixture, in equal proportions, of all the other tones in the world, and is consequently made up of everything deep, great, odd, piquant, pertinent, and pretty.

"Let us suppose now you have determined upon your incidents and tone. The most important portion,—in fact the soul of the whole business, is yet to be attended to—I allude to *the filling up*. It is not to be supposed that a lady or gentleman either has been leading the life of a bookworm. And yet above all things it is necessary that your article have an air of erudition, or at least afford evidence of extensive general reading. Now I'll put you in the way of accomplishing this point. See here!" (pulling down some three or four ordinary looking volumes, and opening them at random.) "By casting your eye down almost any page of any book in the world, you will be able to perceive at once a host of little scraps of either learning or *bel-esprit-ism*, which are the very thing for the spicing of a Blackwood article. You might as well note down a few while I read them to you. I shall make two divisions: first, *Piquant Facts for the Manufacture of Similes*; and second, *Piquant Expressions to be introduced as occasion may require*. Write now!—" and I wrote as he dictated.

"PIQUANT FACTS FOR SIMILES. 'There were originally but three Muses— Melete, Mneme, and Aœde—meditation, memory, and singing.' You may make a great deal of that little fact if properly worked. You see it is not generally known, and looks *recherché*. You must be careful and give the thing with a downright improviso air.

"Again. 'The river Alpheus passed beneath the sea, and emerged without injury to the purity of its waters.' Rather stale that, to be sure, but, if properly dressed and dished up, will look quite as fresh as ever.

"Here is something better. 'The Persian Iris appears to some persons to possess a sweet and very powerful perfume, while to others it is perfectly scentless.' Fine that, and very delicate! Turn it about a little, and it will do wonders. We'll have something else in the botanical line. There's nothing goes down so well, especially with the help of a little Latin. Write!

"'*The Epidendrum Flos Aeris*, of Java, bears a very beautiful flower, and will live when pulled up by the roots. The natives suspend it by a cord from the ceiling, and enjoy its fragrance for years.' That's capital! That will do for the similes. Now for the Piquant Expressions.

PIQUANT EXPRESSIONS. '*The venerable Chinese novel Ju-Kiao-Li.*' Good! By introducing these few words with dexterity you will evince your intimate acquaintance with the language and literature of the Chinese. With the aid of this you may possibly get along without either Arabic, or Sanscrit, or Chickasaw. There is no passing muster, however, without Spanish, Italian, German, Latin, and Greek. I must look you out a little specimen of each. Any scrap will answer, because you must depend upon your own ingenuity to make it fit into your article. Now write!

"'*Aussi tendre que Zaïre*'—as tender as Zaïre—French. Alludes to the frequent repetition of the phrase, *la tendre Zaïre*, in the French tragedy of that name. Properly introduced, will show not only your knowledge of the language, but your general reading and wit. You can say, for instance, that the chicken you were eating (write an article about being choked to death by a chicken-bone) was not altogether *aussi tendre que Zaïre*. Write!

'Van muerte tan escondida,
    Que no te sienta venir,
Porque el plazer del morir
    No me torne a dar la vida.'

That's Spanish—from Miguel de Cervantes. 'Come quickly O death! but be sure and don't let me see you coming, lest the pleasure I shall feel at your appearance should unfortunately bring me back again to life.' This you may slip in quite *à propos* when you are struggling in the last agonies with the chicken-bone. Write!

'Il pover 'huomo che non se'n era accorto,
Andava combattendo, e era morto.'

That's Italian, you perceive,—from Ariosto. It means that a great hero, in the heat of combat, not perceiving that he had been fairly killed, continued to fight valiantly, dead as he was. The application of this to your own case is obvious—for I trust, Miss Psyche, that you will not neglect to kick for at least an hour and a half after you have been choked to death by that chicken-bone. Please to write!

'Und sterb'ich doch, no sterb'ich den
Durch sie—durch sie!'

That's German—from Schiller. 'And if I die, at least I die—for thee—for thee!' Here it is clear that you are apostrophising the *cause* of your disaster, the chicken. Indeed what gentleman (or lady either) of sense, *wouldn't* die, I should like to know, for a well fattened capon of the right Molucca breed, stuffed with capers and mushrooms, and served up in a salad-bowl, with orange-jellies *en mosäiques*. Write! (You can get them that way at Tortoni's,)—Write, if you please!

"Here is a nice little Latin phrase, and rare too, (one can't be too *recherché* or brief in one's Latin, it's getting so common,)—*ignoratio elenchi*. He has committed an *ignoratio elenchi*—that is to say, he has understood the words of your proposition, but not the ideas. The man was *a fool*, you see. Some poor fellow whom you addressed while choking with that chicken-bone, and who therefore didn't precisely understand what you were talking about. Throw the *ignoratio elenchi* in his teeth, and, at once, you have him annihilated. If he dare to reply, you can tell him from Lucan (here it is) that speeches are mere *anemonae verborum*, anemone words. The anemone, with great brilliancy, has no smell. Or, if he begin to bluster, you may be down upon him with *insomnia Jovis*, reveries of Jupiter—a phrase which Silius Italicus (see here!) applies to thoughts pompous and inflated. This will be sure and cut him to the heart. He can do nothing but roll over and die. Will you be kind enough to write?

"In Greek we must have something pretty—from Demosthenes, for example. Ανερ ο φεογων και παλιν μαχεσεται. [Aner o pheogon kai palin makesetai.] There is a tolerably good translation of it in Hudibras—

For he that flies may fight again,
Which he can never do that's slain.

In a Blackwood article nothing makes so fine a show as your Greek. The very letters have an air of profundity about them. Only observe, madam, the astute look of that Epsilon! That Phi ought certainly to be a bishop! Was ever there a smarter fellow than that Omicron? Just twig that Tau! In short, there is nothing like Greek for a genuine sensation-paper. In the present case your application is the most obvious thing in the world. Rap out the sentence, with a huge oath, and by way of *ultimatum*, at the good-for-nothing dunder-headed villain who couldn't understand your plain English in relation to the chicken-bone. He'll take the hint and be off, you may depend upon it."

These were all the instructions Mr. B. could afford me upon the topic in question, but I felt they would be entirely sufficient. I was, at length, able to write a genuine Blackwood article, and determined to do it forthwith. In taking leave of me, Mr. B. made a proposition for the purchase of the paper when written; but as he could offer me only fifty guineas a sheet, I thought it better to let our society have it, than sacrifice it for so paltry a sum. Notwithstanding this niggardly spirit, however, the gentleman showed his consideration for me in all other respects, and indeed treated me with the greatest civility. His parting words made a deep impression upon my heart, and I hope I shall always remember them with gratitude.

"My dear Miss Zenobia," he said, while the tears stood in his eyes, "is there *any*thing else I can do to promote the success of your laudable undertaking? Let me reflect! It is just possible that you may not be able, so soon as convenient, to—to—get yourself drowned, or—choked with a chicken-bone, or—or hung,—or—bitten by a—but stay! Now I think me of it, there are a couple of very excellent bull dogs in the yard—fine fellows, I assure you—savage, and all that—indeed just the thing for your money—they'll have you eaten up, *auriculas* and all, in less than five minutes (here's my watch!)—and then only think of the sensations! Here! I say— Tom!—Peter!—Dick, you villain!—let out those"—but as I was really in a great hurry, and had not another moment to spare, I was reluctantly forced to expedite my departure, and accordingly took leave *at once*—somewhat more abruptly, I admit, than strict courtesy would have, otherwise, allowed.

It was my primary object, upon quitting Mr. Blackwood, to get into some immediate difficulty, pursuant to his advice, and with this view I spent the greater part of the day in wandering about Edinburgh, seeking for desperate adventures— adventures adequate to the intensity of my feelings, and adapted to the vast character of the article I intended to write. In this excursion I was attended by my negro- servant Pompey, and my little lap-dog Diana, whom I had brought with me from Philadelphia. It was not, however, until late in the afternoon that I fully succeeded in my arduous undertaking. An important event then happened, of which the following Blackwood article, in the tone heterogeneous, is the substance and result.

A Predicament[1]

What chance, good lady, hath bereft you thus?—COMUS.[2]

IT was a quiet and still afternoon when I strolled forth in the goodly city of Edina. The confusion and bustle in the streets were terrible. Men were talking. Women were screaming. Children were choking. Pigs were whistling. Carts they rattled. Bulls they bellowed. Cows they lowed. Horses they neighed. Cats they caterwauled. Dogs they danced. *Danced!* Could it then be possible? *Danced!* Alas, thought I, *my* dancing days are over! Thus it is ever. What a host of gloomy recollections will ever and anon be awakened in the mind of genius and imaginative contemplation, especially of a genius doomed to the everlasting, and eternal, and continual, and, as one might say, the—*continued*—yes, the *continued and continuous*, bitter, harassing, disturbing, and, if I may be allowed the expression, the *very* disturbing influence of the serene, and godlike, and heavenly, and exalting, and elevated, and purifying effect of what may be rightly termed the most enviable, the most *truly* enviable— nay! the most benignly beautiful, the most deliciously ethereal, and, as it were, the most *pretty* (if I may use so bold an expression) *thing* (pardon me, gentle reader!) in the world—but I am led away by my feelings. In *such* a mind, I repeat, what a host of recollections are stirred up by a trifle! The dogs danced! I—I *could* not! They frisked—I wept. They capered—I sobbed aloud. Touching circumstances! which cannot fail to bring to the recollection of the classical reader that exquisite passage in relation to the fitness of things, which is to be found in the commencement of the third volume of that admirable and venerable Chinese novel, the *Jo-Go-Slow*.

In my solitary walk through the city I had two humble but faithful companions. Diana, my poodle! sweetest of creatures! She had a quantity of hair over her one eye, and a blue ribband tied fashionably around her neck. Diana was not more than five inches in height, but her head was somewhat bigger than her body, and her tail, being cut off exceedingly close, gave an air of injured innocence to the interesting animal which rendered her a favorite with all.

And Pompey, my negro!—sweet Pompey! how shall I ever forget thee? I had taken Pompey's arm. He was three feet in height (I like to be particular) and about seventy, or perhaps eighty, years of age. He had bow-legs and was corpulent. His mouth should not be called small, nor his ears short. His teeth, however, were like pearl, and his large full eyes were deliciously white. Nature had endowed him with no neck, and had placed his ankles (as usual with that race) in the middle of the upper portion of the feet. He was clad with a striking simplicity. His sole garments were a stock of nine inches in height, and a nearly-new drab overcoat which had formerly been in the service of the tall, stately, and illustrious Dr. Moneypenny. It was a good overcoat. It was well cut. It was well made. The coat was nearly new. Pompey held it up out of the dirt with both hands.

There were three persons in our party, and two of them have already been the subject of remark. There was a third—that third person was myself. I am the Signora Psyche Zenobia. I am *not* Suky Snobbs. My appearance is commanding. On the memorable occasion of which I speak I was habited in a crimson satin dress, with a sky-blue Arabian mantelet. And the dress had trimmings of green agraffas, and seven graceful flounces of the orange colored auricula. I thus formed the third of the party. There was the poodle. There was Pompey. There was myself. We were *three*. Thus it is said there were originally but three Furies—Melty, Nimmy and Hetty—Meditation, Memory, and Fiddling.

Leaning upon the arm of the gallant Pompey, and attended at a respectful distance by Diana, I proceeded down one of the populous and very pleasant streets of the now deserted Edina. On a sudden, there presented itself to view a church—a Gothic cathedral—vast, venerable, and with a tall steeple, which towered into the sky. What madness now possessed me? Why did I rush upon my fate? I was seized with an uncontrollable desire to ascend the giddy pinnacle, and thence survey the immense extent of the city. The door of the cathedral stood invitingly open. My destiny prevailed. I entered the ominous archway. Where then was my guardian angel?—if indeed such angels there be. *If!* Distressing monosyllable! what a world of mystery, and meaning, and doubt, and uncertainty is there involved in thy two letters! I entered the ominous archway! I entered; and, without injury to my orange-colored auriculas, I passed beneath the portal, and emerged within the vestibule! Thus it is said the immense river Alfred passed, unscathed, and unwetted, beneath the sea.

I thought the staircases would never have an end. *Round!* Yes, they went round and up, and round and up and round and up, until I could not help surmising, with the sagacious Pompey, upon whose supporting arm I leaned in all the confidence of early affection—I *could* not help surmising that the upper end of the continuous spiral ladder had been accidentally, or perhaps designedly, removed. I paused for breath; and, in the meantime, an incident occurred of too momentous a nature in a moral, and also in a metaphysical point of view, to be passed over without notice. It appeared to me—indeed I was quite confident of the fact—I could not be mistaken—no! I had, for some moments, carefully and anxiously observed the motions of my Diana—I say that *I could not be* mistaken—Diana *smelt a rat!* At once I called Pompey's attention to the subject, and he—he agreed with me. There was then no longer any reasonable room for doubt. The rat had been smelled—and by Diana. Heavens! shall I ever forget the intense excitement of that moment? Alas! what is the boasted intellect of man? The rat!—it was there—that is to say, it was somewhere. Diana smelled the rat. I—I *could* not! Thus it is said the Prussian Isis has, for some persons, a sweet and very powerful perfume, while to others it is perfectly scentless.

The staircase had been surmounted, and there were now only three or four more upward steps intervening between us and the summit. We still ascended, and now only one step remained. One step! One little, little step! Upon one such little step in the great staircase of human life how vast a sum of human happiness or misery often depends! I thought of myself, then of Pompey, and then of the mysterious and inexplicable destiny which surrounded us. I thought of Pompey!—alas, I thought of love! I thought of the many false *steps* which have been taken, and may be taken again. I resolved to be more cautious, more reserved. I abandoned the arm of Pompey, and, without his assistance, surmounted the one remaining step, and gained the chamber of the belfry. I was followed immediately afterwards by my poodle. Pompey alone remained behind. I stood at the head of the staircase, and encouraged him to ascend. He stretched forth to me his hand, and unfortunately in so doing was forced to abandon his firm hold upon the overcoat. Will the gods never cease their persecution? The overcoat it dropped, and with one of his feet, Pompey stepped upon the long and trailing skirt of the overcoat. He stumbled and fell—this consequence was inevitable. He fell forwards, and, with his accursed head, striking me full in the——in the breast, precipitated me headlong, together with himself, upon the hard, filthy and detestable floor of the belfry. But my revenge was sure, sudden and complete. Seizing him furiously by the wool with both hands, I tore out a vast quantity of the black, and crisp, and curling material, and tossed it from me with every manifestation of disdain. It fell among the ropes of the belfry and remained. Pompey arose, and said no word. But he regarded me piteously with his large eyes and—sighed. Ye gods—that sigh! It sunk into my heart. And the hair—the wool! Could I have reached that wool I would have bathed it with my tears, in testimony of regret. But alas! it was now far beyond my grasp. As it dangled among the cordage of the bell, I fancied it still alive. I fancied that it stood on end with indignation. Thus the *happy dandy Flos Aeris* of Java, bears, it is said, a beautiful flower, which will live when pulled up by the roots. The natives suspend it by a cord from the ceiling and enjoy its fragrance for years.

Our quarrel was now made up, and we looked about the room for an aperture through which to survey the city of Edina. Windows there were none. The sole light admitted into the gloomy chamber proceeded from a square opening, about a foot in diameter, at a height of about seven feet from the floor. Yet what will the energy of true genius not effect? I resolved to clamber up to this hole. A vast quantity of wheels, pinions, and other cabalistic-looking machinery stood opposite the hole, close to it; and through the hole there passed an iron rod from the machinery. Between the wheels and the wall where the hole lay, there was barely room for my body—yet I was desperate, and determined to persevere. I called Pompey to my side.

"You perceive that aperture, Pompey. I wish to look through it. You will stand here just beneath the hole—so. Now, hold out one of your hands, Pompey, and let me step upon it—thus. Now, the other hand, Pompey, and with its aid I will get upon your shoulders."

He did everything I wished, and I found, upon getting up, that I could easily pass my head and neck through the aperture. The prospect was sublime. Nothing could be more magnificent. I merely paused a moment to bid Diana behave herself, and assure Pompey that I would be considerate and bear as lightly as possible upon his shoulders. I told him I would be tender of his feelings—*ossi tender que beefsteak*. Having done this justice to my faithful friend, I gave myself up with great zest and enthusiasm to the enjoyment of the scene which so obligingly spread itself out before my eyes.

Upon this subject, however, I shall forbear to dilate. I will not describe the city of Edinburgh. Every one has been to Edinburgh—the classic Edina. I will confine myself to the momentous details of my own lamentable adventure. Having, in some measure, satisfied my curiosity in regard to the extent, situation, and general appearance of the city, I had leisure to survey the church in which I was, and the delicate architecture of the steeple. I observed that the aperture through which I had thrust my head was an opening in the dial-plate of a gigantic clock, and must have appeared, from the street, as a large keyhole, such as we see in the face of French watches. No doubt the true object was to admit the arm of an attendant, to adjust, when necessary, the hands of the clock from within. I observed also, with surprise, the immense size of these hands, the longest of which could not have been less than ten feet in length, and, where broadest, eight or nine inches in breadth. They were of solid steel apparently, and their edges appeared to be sharp. Having noticed these particulars, and some others, I again turned my eyes upon the glorious prospect below, and soon became absorbed in contemplation.

From this, after some minutes, I was aroused by the voice of Pompey, who declared he could stand it no longer, and requested that I would be so kind as to come down. This was unreasonable, and I told him so in a speech of some length. He replied, but with an evident misunderstanding of my ideas upon the subject. I accordingly grew angry, and told him in plain words that he was a fool, that he had committed an *ignoramus e-clench-eye*, that his notions were mere *insommary Bovis*, and his words little better than *an enemy-werryhor'em*. With this he appeared satisfied, and I resumed my contemplations.

It might have been half an hour after this altercation when, as I was deeply absorbed in the heavenly scenery beneath me, I was startled by something very cold which pressed with a gentle pressure upon the back of my neck. It is needless to say that I felt inexpressibly alarmed. I knew that Pompey was beneath my feet, and that Diana was sitting, according to my explicit directions, upon her hind legs in the farthest corner of the room. What could it be? Alas! I but too soon discovered. Turning my head gently to one side, I perceived, to my extreme horror, that the huge, glittering, scimetar-like minute-hand of the clock, had, in the course of its hourly revolution, *descended upon my neck*. There was, I knew, not a second to be lost. I pulled back at once—but it was too late. There was no chance of forcing my head through the mouth of that terrible trap in which it was so fairly caught, and which grew narrower and narrower with a rapidity too horrible to be conceived. The agony of that moment is not to be imagined. I threw up my hands and endeavoured, with all my strength, to force upwards the ponderous iron bar. I might as well have tried to lift the cathedral itself. Down, down, down it came, closer, and yet closer. I screamed to Pompey for aid: but he said that I had hurt his feelings by calling him "an ignorant old squint eye." I yelled to Diana; but she only said "bow-wow-wow," and that "I had told her on no account to stir from the corner." Thus I had no relief to expect from my associates.

Meantime the ponderous and terrific *Scythe of Time* (for I now discovered the literal import of that classical phrase) had not stopped, nor was it likely to stop, in its career. Down and still down, it came. It had already buried its sharp edge a full inch in my flesh, and my sensations grew indistinct and confused. At one time I fancied myself in Philadelphia with the stately Dr. Moneypenny, at another in the back parlor of Mr. Blackwood receiving his invaluable instructions. And then again the sweet recollection of better and earlier times came over me, and I thought of that happy period when the world was not all a desert, and Pompey not altogether cruel.

The ticking of the machinery amused me. *Amused me,* I say, for my sensations now bordered upon perfect happiness, and the most trifling circumstances afforded me pleasure. The eternal *click-clack, click-clack, click-clack,* of the clock was the most melodious of music in my ears, and occasionally even put me in mind of the grateful sermonic harangues of Dr. Ollapod. Then there were the great figures upon the dial-plate—how intelligent, how intellectual, they all looked! And presently they took to dancing the Mazurka, and I think it was the figure V who performed the most to my satisfaction. She was evidently a lady of breeding. None of your swaggerers, and nothing at all indelicate in her motions. She did the pirouette to admiration—whirling round upon her apex. I made an endeavor to hand her a chair, for I saw that she appeared fatigued with her exertions—and it was not until then that I fully perceived my lamentable situation. Lamentable indeed! The bar had buried itself two inches in my neck. I was aroused to a sense of exquisite pain. I prayed for death, and, in the agony of the moment, could not help repeating those exquisite verses of the poet Miguel De Cervantes:

Vanny Buren, tan escondida
Query no te senty venny
Pork and pleasure, delly morry
Nommy, tomy, darry, widdy!

But now a new horror presented itself, and one indeed sufficient to startle the strongest nerves. My eyes, from the cruel pressure of the machine, were absolutely starting from their sockets. While I was thinking how I should possibly manage without them, one actually tumbled out of my head, and, rolling down the steep side of the steeple, lodged in the rain gutter which ran along the eaves of the main building. The loss of the eye was not so much as the insolent air of independence and contempt with which it regarded me after it was out. There it lay in the gutter just under my nose, and the airs it gave itself would have been ridiculous had they not been disgusting. Such a winking and blinking were never before seen. This behaviour on the part of my eye in the gutter was not only irritating on account of its manifest insolence and shameful ingratitude, but was also exceedingly inconvenient on account of the sympathy which always exists between two eyes of the same head, however far apart. I was forced, in a manner, to wink and to blink, whether I would or not, in exact concert with the scoundrelly thing that lay just under my nose. I was presently relieved, however, by the dropping out of the other eye. In falling it took the same direction (possibly a concerted plot) as its fellow. Both rolled out of the gutter together, and in truth I was very glad to get rid of them.

The bar was now four inches and a half deep in my neck, and there was only a little bit of skin to cut through. My sensations were those of entire happiness, for I felt that in a few minutes, at farthest, I should be relieved from my disagreeable situation. And in this expectation I was not at all deceived. At twenty-five minutes past five in the afternoon precisely, the huge minute-hand had proceeded sufficiently far on its terrible revolution to sever the small remainder of my neck. I was not sorry to see the head which had occasioned me so much embarrassment at length make a final separation from my body. It first rolled down the side of the steeple, then lodged, for a few seconds, in the gutter, and then made its way, with a plunge, into the middle of the street.

I will candidly confess that my feelings were now of the most singular—nay of the most mysterious, the most perplexing and incomprehensible character. My senses were here and there at one and the same moment. With my head I imagined, at one time, that I the head, was the real Signora Psyche Zenobia—at another I felt convinced that myself, the body, was the proper identity. To clear my ideas upon this topic I felt in my pocket for my snuff-box, but, upon getting it, and endeavoring to apply a pinch of its grateful contents in the ordinary manner, I became immediately aware of my peculiar deficiency, and threw the box at once down to my head. It took a pinch with great satisfaction, and smiled me an acknowledgement in return. Shortly afterwards it made me a speech, which I could hear but indistinctly without ears. I gathered enough, however, to know that it was astonished at my wishing to remain alive under such circumstances. In the concluding sentences it quoted the noble words of Ariosto—

Il pover hommy che non sera corty
And have a combat tenty erry morty.

thus comparing me to the hero who, in the heat of combat, not perceiving that he was dead, continued to contest the battle with inextinguishable valor. There was nothing now to prevent my getting down from my elevation, and I did so. What it was that Pompey saw so *very* peculiar in my appearance I have never yet been able to find out. The fellow opened his mouth from ear to ear, and shut his two eyes as if he were endeavoring to crack nuts between the lids. Finally, throwing off his overcoat, he made one spring for the staircase and disappeared. I hurled after the scoundrel those vehement words of Demosthenes—

Andrew O'Phlegethon, you really make haste to fly,

and then turned to the darling of my heart, to the one-eyed! the shaggy-haired Diana. Alas! what horrible vision affronted my eyes? *Was* that a rat I saw skulking into his hole? *Are* these the picked bones of the little angel who has been cruelly devoured by the monster? Ye Gods! and what *do* I behold—*is* that the departed spirit, the shade, the ghost of my beloved puppy, which I perceive sitting with a grace so melancholy, in the corner? Harken! for she speaks, and, heavens! it is in the German of Schiller—

> "Unt stubby duk, so stubby dun
> Duk she! duk she!"

Alas!—and are not her words too true?

> And if I died at least I died
> For thee—for thee.

Sweet creature! she *too* has sacrificed herself in my behalf. Dogless, niggerless, headless, what *now* remains for the unhappy Signora Psyche Zenobia? Alas— *nothing!* I have done.

The Man That Was Used Up[1]

A Tale of the Late Bugaboo and Kickapoo Campaign

Pleurez, pleurez, mes yeux, et fondez vous en eau!
La moitié de ma vie a mis l'autre au tombeau.
                    CORNEILLE[2]

I CANNOT just now remember when or where I first made the acquaintance of that truly fine-looking fellow, Brevet Brigadier General John A. B. C. Smith. Some one *did* introduce me to the gentleman, I am sure—at some public meeting, I know very well—held about something of great importance, no doubt—at some place or other, I feel convinced,—whose name I have unaccountably forgotten. The truth is—that the introduction was attended, upon my part, with a degree of anxious embarrassment which operated to prevent any definite impressions of either time or place. I am constitutionally nervous—this, with me, is a family failing, and I can't help it. In especial, the slightest appearance of mystery—of any point I cannot exactly comprehend—puts me at once into a pitiable state of agitation.

There was something, as it were, remarkable—yes, *remarkable,* although this is but a feeble term to express my full meaning—about the entire individuality of the personage in question. He was, perhaps, six feet in height, and of a presence singularly commanding. There was an *air distingué* pervading the whole man, which spoke of high breeding, and hinted at high birth. Upon this topic—the topic of Smith's personal appearance—I have a kind of melancholy satisfaction in being minute. His head of hair would have done honor to a Brutus;—nothing could be more richly flowing, or possess a brighter gloss. It was of a jetty black;—which was also the color, or more properly the no color, of his unimaginable whiskers. You perceive I cannot speak of these latter without enthusiasm; it is not too much to say that they were the handsomest pair of whiskers under the sun. At all events, they encircled, and at times partially overshadowed, a mouth utterly unequalled. Here were the most entirely even, and the most brilliantly white of all conceivable teeth.

From between them, upon every proper occasion, issued a voice of surpassing clearness, melody, and strength. In the matter of eyes, also, my acquaintance was pre-eminently endowed. Either one of such a pair was worth a couple of the ordinary ocular organs. They were of a deep hazel, exceedingly large and lustrous; and there was perceptible about them, ever and anon, just that amount of interesting obliquity which gives pregnancy to expression.

The bust of the General was unquestionably the finest bust I ever saw. For your life you could not have found a fault with its wonderful proportion. This rare peculiarity set off to great advantage a pair of shoulders which would have called up a blush of conscious inferiority into the countenance of the marble Apollo. I have a passion for fine shoulders, and may say that I never beheld them in perfection before. The arms altogether were admirably modelled. Nor were the lower limbs less superb. These were, indeed, the *ne plus ultra* of good legs. Every connoisseur in such matters admitted the legs to be good. There was neither too much flesh, nor too little,—neither rudeness nor fragility. I could not imagine a more graceful curve than that of the *os femoris,* and there was just that due gentle prominence in the rear of the *fibula* which goes to the conformation of a properly proportioned calf. I wish to God my young and talented friend Chiponchipino, the sculptor, had but seen the legs of Brevet Brigadier General John A. B. C. Smith.

But although men so absolutely fine-looking are neither as plenty as reasons or blackberries, still I could not bring myself to believe that *the remarkable* something to which I alluded just now,—that the odd air of *je ne sais quoi* which hung about my new acquaintance,—lay altogether, or indeed at all, in the supreme excellence of his bodily endowments. Perhaps it might be traced to the *manner;*—yet here again I could not pretend to be positive. There *was* a primness, not to say stiffness, in his carriage—a degree of measured, and, if I may so express it, of rectangular precision, attending his every movement, which, observed in a more diminutive figure, would have had the least little savor in the world, of affectation, pomposity or constraint, but which, noticed in a gentleman of his undoubted dimension, was readily placed to the account of reserve, *hauteur*—of a commendable sense, in short, of what is due to the dignity of colossal proportion.

The kind friend who presented me to General Smith whispered in my ear some few words of comment upon the man. He was a *remarkable* man—a *very* remarkable man—indeed one of the *most* remarkable men of the age. He was an especial favorite, too, with the ladies—chiefly on account of his high reputation for courage.

"In *that* point he is unrivalled—indeed he is a perfect desperado—a down-right fire-eater, and no mistake," said my friend, here dropping his voice excessively low, and thrilling me with the mystery of his tone.

"A downright fire-eater, and *no* mistake. Showed *that*, I should say, to some purpose, in the late tremendous swamp-fight away down South, with the Bugaboo and Kickapoo Indians."[3] [Here my friend opened his eyes to some extent.] "Bless my soul!—blood and thunder, and all that!—*prodigies* of valor! heard of him of course?—you know he's the man"—

"Man alive, how *do* you do? why how *are* ye? *very* glad to see ye, indeed!" here interrupted the General himself, seizing my companion by the hand as he drew near, and bowing stiffly, but profoundly, as I was presented. I then thought, (and I think so still,) that I never heard a clearer nor a stronger voice, nor beheld a finer set of teeth: but I *must* say that I was sorry for the interruption just at that moment, as, owing to the whispers and insinuations aforesaid, my interest had been greatly excited in the hero of the Bugaboo and Kickapoo campaign.

However, the delightfully luminous conversation of Brevet Brigadier General John A. B. C. Smith soon completely dissipated this chagrin. My friend leaving us immediately, we had quite a long *tête-à-tête*, and I was not only pleased but *really*—instructed. I never heard a more fluent talker, or a man of greater general information. With becoming modesty, he forebore, nevertheless, to touch upon the theme I had just then most at heart—I mean the mysterious circumstances attending the Bugaboo war—and, on my own part, what I conceive to be a proper sense of delicacy forbade me to broach the subject; although, in truth, I was exceedingly tempted to do so. I perceived, too, that the gallant soldier preferred topics of philosophical interest, and that he delighted, especially, in commenting upon the rapid march of mechanical invention. Indeed, lead him where I would, this was a point to which he invariably came back.

"There is nothing at all like it," he would say; "we are a wonderful people, and live in a wonderful age. Parachutes and rail-roads—man-traps and spring guns! Our steam-boats are upon every sea, and the Nassau balloon packet is about to run regular trips (fare either way only twenty pounds sterling) between London and Timbuctoo. And who shall calculate the immense influence upon social life—upon arts—upon commerce—upon literature—which will be the immediate result of the great principles of electro-magnetics? Nor is this all, let me assure you! There is really no end to the march of invention. The most wonderful—the most ingenious—and let me add, Mr.—Mr.—Thompson, I believe, is your name—let me add, I say, the most *useful*—the most truly *useful* mechanical contrivances, are daily springing up like mushrooms, if I may so express myself, or, more figuratively, like—ah—grasshoppers—like grasshoppers, Mr. Thompson—about us and ah—ah—ah—around us!"

Thompson, to be sure, is not my name; but it is needless to say that I left General Smith with a heightened interest in the man, with an exalted opinion of his conversational powers, and a deep sense of the valuable privileges we enjoy in living in this age of mechanical invention. My curiosity, however, had not been altogether satisfied, and I resolved to prosecute immediate inquiry among my acquaintances touching the Brevet Brigadier General himself, and particularly respecting the tremendous events *quorum pars magna fuit*,[4] during the Bugaboo and Kickapoo campaign.

The first opportunity which presented itself, and which (*horresco referens*) I did not in the least scruple to seize, occurred at the Church of the Reverend Doctor Drummummupp, where I found myself established, one Sunday just at sermon time, not only in the pew, but by the side, of that worthy and communicative little friend of mine, Miss Tabitha T. Thus seated, I congratulated myself, and with much reason, upon the very flattering state of affairs. If any person knew anything about Brevet Brigadier General John A. B. C. Smith, that person, it was clear to me, was Miss Tabitha T. We telegraphed a few signals, and then commenced, *sotto voce*, a brisk *tête-à-tête*.

"Smith!" said she, in reply to my very earnest inquiry; "Smith!—why, not General John A. B. C.? Bless me, I thought you *knew* all about *him!* This is a wonderfully inventive age! Horrid affair that!—a bloody set of wretches, those Kickapoos!—fought like a hero—prodigies of valor—immortal renown. Smith!—Brevet Brigadier General John A. B. C.!—why, you know he's the man"——

"Man," here broke in Doctor Drummummupp, at the top of his voice, and with a thump that came near knocking the pulpit about our ears; "man that is born of a woman hath but a short time to live; he cometh up and is cut down like a flower!" I started to the extremity of the pew, and perceived by the animated looks of the divine, that the wrath which had nearly proved fatal to the pulpit had been excited by the whispers of the lady and myself. There was no help for it; so I submitted with a good grace, and listened, in all the martyrdom of dignified silence, to the balance of that very capital discourse.

Next evening found me a somewhat late visitor at the Rantipole theatre, where I felt sure of satisfying my curiosity at once, by merely stepping into the box of those exquisite specimens of affability and omniscience, the Misses Arabella and Miranda Cognoscenti. That fine tragedian, Climax, was doing Iago to a very crowded house, and I experienced some little difficulty in making my wishes understood; especially as our box was next the slips, and completely overlooked the stage.

"Smith?" said Miss Arabella, as she at length comprehended the purport of my query; "Smith?—why, not General John A. B. C.?"

"Smith?" inquired Miranda, musingly. "God bless me, did you ever behold a finer figure?"

"Never, madam, but *do* tell me"——

"Or so inimitable grace?"

"Never, upon my word!—but pray inform me"——

"Or so just an appreciation of stage effect?"

"Madam!"

"Or a more delicate sense of the true beauties of Shakespeare? Be so good as to look at that leg!"

"The devil!" and I turned again to her sister.

"Smith?" said she, "why, not General John A. B. C.? Horrid affair that, wasn't it?—great wretches, those Bugaboos—savage and so on—but we live in a wonderfully inventive age!—Smith!—O yes! great man!—perfect desperado—immortal renown—prodigies of valor! *Never heard!*" [This was given in a scream.] "Bless my soul!—why he's the man"——

"——mandragora
Nor all the drowsy syrups of the world
Shall ever medicine thee to that sweet sleep
Which thou owd'st yesterday!"[5]

here roared out Climax just in my ear, and shaking his fist in my face all the time, in a way that I *couldn't* stand, and I *wouldn't*. I left the Misses Cognoscenti immediately, went behind the scenes forthwith, and gave the beggarly scoundrel such a thrashing as I trust he will remember to the day of his death.

At the *soirée* of the lovely widow, Mrs. Kathleen O'Trump, I was confident that I should meet with no similar disappointment. Accordingly, I was no sooner seated at the card table, with my pretty hostess for a *vis-à-vis*, than I propounded those questions the solution of which had become a matter so essential to my peace.

"Smith?" said my partner, "why, not General John A. B. C.? Horrid affair that, wasn't it?—diamonds, did you say?—terrible wretches those Kickapoos!—we are playing *whist*, if you please, Mr. Tattle—however, this is the age of invention, most certainly—*the* age, one may say, *the* age *par excellence*—speak French?—oh, quite a hero—perfect desperado!—*no hearts*, Mr. Tattle? I don't believe it!—immortal renown and all that—prodigies of valor! *Never heard!!*—why, bless me, he's the man"——

"Mann?—*Captain* Mann?" here screamed some little feminine interloper from the farthest corner of the room. "Are you talking about Captain Mann and the duel?—oh, I *must* hear—do tell—go on, Mrs. O'Trump!—do now go on!" And go on Mrs. O'Trump did—all about a certain Captain Mann who was either shot or hung, or should have been both shot and hung. Yes! Mrs. O'Trump, she went on, and I—I went off. There was no chance of hearing anything farther that evening in regard to Brevet Brigadier General John A. B. C. Smith.

Still I consoled myself with the reflection that the tide of ill luck would not run against me forever, and so determined to make a bold push for information at the rout of that bewitching little angel, the graceful Mrs. Pirouette.

"Smith?" said Mrs. P., as we twirled about together in a *pas de zephyr*, "Smith?— why not General John A. B. C.? Dreadful business that of the Bugaboos, wasn't it?—terrible creatures those Indians!—*do* turn out your toes! I really am ashamed of you—man of great courage, poor fellow!—but this is a wonderful age for invention—O dear me, I'm out of breath—quite a desperado—prodigies of valor— *never heard!!*—can't believe it—I shall have to sit down and enlighten you—Smith! why he's the man"——

"Man-*Fred*, I tell you!" here bawled out Miss Bas-Bleu, as I led Mrs. Pirouette to a seat. "Did ever anybody hear the like? It's Man-*Fred*, I say, not at all by any means Man-*Friday*." Here Miss Bas-Bleu beckoned to me in a very peremptory manner; and I was obliged, will I nill I, to leave Mrs. P. for the purpose of deciding a dispute touching the title of a certain poetical drama of Lord Byron's. Although I pronounced, with great promptness, that the true title was Man-*Friday*, and not by any means Man-*Fred*, yet when I returned to seek Mrs. Pirouette she was not to be discovered, and I made my retreat from the house in a very bitter spirit of animosity against the whole race of the Bas-Bleus.

Matters had now assumed a really serious aspect, and I resolved to call at once upon my particular friend, Mr. Theodore Sinivate; for I knew that here at least I should get something like definite information.

"Smith?" said he, in his well known peculiar way of drawling out his syllables; "Smith?—why, not General John A—B—C? Savage affair that with the Kickapo-o-o-os, wasn't it? Say! don't you think so?—perfect despera-a-ado—great pity, 'pon my honor!—wonderfully inventive age!—pro-o-odigies of valor! By the by, did you ever hear about Captain Ma-a-a-n?"

"Captain Mann be d—d!" said I, "please to go on with your story."

"Hem!—oh well!—quite *la meme cho-o-ose*, as we say in France. Smith, eh? Brigadier General John A—B—C.? I say"—[here Mr. S. thought proper to put his finger to the side of his nose]—"I say, you don't mean to insinuate now, really, and truly, and conscientiously, that you don't know all about that affair of Smith's, as well as I do, eh? Smith? John A—B—C.? Why bless me, he's the ma-a-an"——

"*Mr.* Sinivate," said I imploringly, "*is* he the man in the mask?"

"No-o-o!" said he, looking wise, "nor the man in the mo-o-o-on."

This reply I considered a pointed and positive insult, and so left the house at once in high dudgeon, with a firm resolve to call my friend, Mr. Sinivate, to a speedy account for his ungentlemanly conduct and ill breeding.

In the meantime, however, I had no notion of being thwarted touching the information I desired. There was one resource left me yet. I would go to the fountain head. I would call forthwith upon the General himself, and demand, in explicit terms, a solution of this abominable piece of mystery. Here at least there should be no chance for equivocation. It would be plain, positive, peremptory—as short as pie-crust—as concise as Tacitus or Montesquieu.

It was early when I called, and the general was dressing; but I pleaded urgent business, and was shown at once into his bed-room by an old negro valet, who remained in attendance during my visit. As I entered the chamber, I looked about, of course, for the occupant, but did not immediately perceive him. There was a large and exceedingly odd looking bundle of something which lay close by my feet on the floor, and, as I was not in the best humor in the world, I gave it a kick out of the way.

"Hem! ahem! rather civil that, I should say!" said the bundle, in one of the smallest, and altogether the funniest little voices, between a squeak and a whistle, that I ever heard in all the days of my existence.

"Ahem! rather civil that, I should observe."

I fairly shouted with terror, and made off, at a tangent, into the farthest extremity of the room.

"God bless me! my dear fellow," here again whistled the bundle "what—what—what—why, what *is* the matter? I really believe you don't know me at all."

What *could* I say to all this—what *could* I? I staggered into an arm chair, and, with staring eyes and open mouth, awaited the solution of the wonder.

"Strange you shouldn't know me though, isn't it?" presently re-squeaked the nondescript, which I now perceived was performing, upon the floor, some inexplicable evolution, very analogous to the drawing on of a stocking. There was only a single leg, however, apparent.

"Strange you shouldn't know me, though, isn't it? Pompey, bring me that leg!" Here Pompey handed the bundle a very capital cork leg, all ready dressed, which it screwed on in a trice; and then it stood upright before my eyes.

"And a bloody action it *was*," continued the thing, as if in a soliloquy; "but then one mustn't fight with the Bugaboos and Kickapoos, and think of coming off with a mere scratch. Pompey, I'll thank you now for that arm. Thomas" [turning to me] "is decidedly the best hand at a cork leg; but if you should ever want an arm, my dear fellow, you must really let me recommend you to Bishop." Here Pompey screwed on an arm.

"We had rather hot work of it, that you may say. Now, you dog, slip on my shoulders and bosom! Pettitt makes the best shoulders, but for a bosom you will have to go to Ducrow."

"Bosom!" said I.

"Pompey, will you *never* be ready with that wig? Scalping is a rough process after all; but then you can procure such a capital scratch at De L'Orme's."

"Scratch!"

"Now, you nigger, my teeth! For a *good* set of these you had better go to Parmly's at once; high prices, but excellent work. I swallowed some very capital articles, though, when the big Bugaboo rammed me down with the butt end of his rifle."

"Butt end! ram down!! my eye!!!"

"O yes, by the by, my eye—here, Pompey, you scamp, screw it in! Those Kickapoos are not so very slow at a gouge; but he's a belied man, that Dr. Williams, after all; you can't imagine how well I see with the eyes of his make."

I now began very clearly to perceive that the object before me was nothing more nor less than my new acquaintance, Brevet Brigadier General John A. B. C. Smith. The manipulations of Pompey had made, I must confess, a very striking difference in the appearance of the personal man. The voice, however, still puzzled me no little; but even this apparent mystery was speedily cleared up.

"Pompey, you black rascal," squeaked the General, "I really do believe you would let me go out without my palate."

Hereupon the negro, grumbling out an apology, went up to his master, opened his mouth with the knowing air of a horse-jockey, and adjusted therein a somewhat singular-looking machine, in a very dexterous manner, that I could not altogether comprehend. The alteration, however, in the entire expression of the General's countenance was instantaneous and surprising. When he again spoke, his voice had resumed all that rich melody and strength which I had noticed upon our original introduction.

"D—n the vagabonds!" said he, in so clear a tone that I positively started at the change, "D—n the vagabonds! they not only knocked in the roof of my mouth, but took the trouble to cut off at least seven-eighths of my tongue. There isn't Bonfanti's equal, however, in America, for really good articles of this description. I can recommend you to him with confidence," [here the General bowed,] "and assure you that I have the greatest pleasure in so doing."

I acknowledged his kindness in my best manner, and took leave of him at once, with a perfect understanding of the true state of affairs—with a full comprehension of the mystery which had troubled me so long. It was evident. It was a clear case. Brevet Brigadier General John A. B. C. Smith was the man——was *the man that was used up.*[6]

The Fall of the House of Usher[1]

Son cœur est un luth suspendu;
Sitôt qu'on le touche il rèsonne.
        De Béranger.[2]

DURING the whole of a dull, dark, and soundless day in the autumn of the year, when the clouds hung oppressively low in the heavens, I had been passing alone, on horseback, through a singularly dreary tract of country; and at length found myself, as the shades of the evening drew on, within view of the melancholy House of Usher. I know not how it was—but, with the first glimpse of the building, a sense of insufferable gloom pervaded my spirit. I say insufferable; for the feeing was unrelieved by any of that half-pleasurable, because poetic, sentiment, with which the mind usually receives even the sternest natural images of the desolate or terrible. I looked upon the scene before me—upon the mere house, and the simple landscape features of the domain—upon the bleak walls—upon the vacant eye-like windows— upon a few rank sedges—and upon a few white trunks of decayed trees—with an utter depression of soul which I can compare to no earthly sensation more properly than to the after-dream of the reveler upon opium—the bitter lapse into everyday life—the hideous dropping off of the veil. There was an iciness, a sinking, a sickening of the heart—an unredeemed dreariness of thought which no goading of the imagination could torture into aught of the sublime. What was it—I paused to think—what was it that so unnerved me in the contemplation of the House of Usher? It was a mystery all insoluble; nor could I grapple with the shadowy fancies that crowded upon me as I pondered. I was forced to fall back upon the unsatisfactory conclusion, that while, beyond doubt, there *are* combinations of very simple natural objects which have the power of thus affecting us, still the analysis of this power lies among considerations beyond our depth. It was possible, I reflected, that a mere different arrangement of the particulars of the scene, of the details of the picture, would be sufficient to modify, or perhaps to annihilate its capacity for sorrowful impression; and, acting upon this idea, I reined my horse to the precipitous brink of a black and lurid tarn that lay in unruffled lustre by the dwelling, and gazed down— but with a shudder even more thrilling than before—upon the remodelled and inverted images of the gray sedge, and the ghastly tree-stems, and the vacant and eye-like windows.

Nevertheless, in this mansion of gloom I now proposed to myself a sojourn of some weeks. Its proprietor, Roderick Usher, had been one of my boon companions in boyhood; but many years had elapsed since our last meeting. A letter, however, had lately reached me in a distant part of the country—a letter from him—which, in its wildly importunate nature, had admitted of no other than a personal reply. The MS. gave evidence of nervous agitation. The writer spoke of acute bodily illness—of a mental disorder which oppressed him—and of an earnest desire to see me, as his best, and indeed his only personal friend, with a view of attempting, by the cheerfulness of my society, some alleviation of his malady. It was the manner in which all this, and much more was said—it was the apparent *heart* that went with his request—which allowed me no room for hesitation; and I accordingly obeyed forthwith what I still considered a very singular summons.

Although, as boys, we had been even intimate associates, yet I really knew little of my friend. His reserve had always been excessive and habitual. I was aware, however, that his very ancient family had been noted, time out of mind, for a peculiar sensibility of temperament, displaying itself, through long ages, in many works of exalted art, and manifested, of late, in repeated deeds of munificent yet unobtrusive charity, as well as in a passionate devotion to the intricacies, perhaps even more than to the orthodox and easily recognisable beauties, of musical science. I had learned, too, the very remarkable fact, that the stem of the Usher race, all time-honored as it was, had put forth, at no period, any enduring branch; in other words, that the entire family lay in the direct line of descent, and had always, with very trifling and very temporary variation, so lain. It was this deficiency, I considered, while running over in thought the perfect keeping of the character of the premises with the accredited character of the people, and while speculating upon the possible influence which the one, in the long lapse of centuries, might have exercised upon the other— it was this deficiency, perhaps, of collateral issue, and the consequent undeviating transmission, from sire to son, of the patrimony of the name, which had, at length, so identified the two as to merge the original title of the estate in the quaint and equivocal appellation of the "House of Usher"—an appellation which seemed to include, in the minds of the peasantry who used it, both the family and the family mansion.

I have said that the sole effect of my somewhat childish experiment—that of looking down within the tarn—had been to deepen the first singular impression. There can be no doubt that the consciousness of the rapid increase of my superstition—for why should I not so term it?—served mainly to accelerate the increase itself. Such, I have long known, is the paradoxical law of all sentiments having terror as a basis. And it might have been for this reason only, that, when I again uplifted my eyes to the house itself, from its image in the pool, there grew in my mind a strange fancy—a fancy so ridiculous, indeed, that I but mention it to show the vivid force of the sensations which oppressed me. I had so worked upon my imagination as really to believe that about the whole mansion and domain there hung an atmosphere peculiar to themselves and their immediate vicinity—an atmosphere which had no affinity with the air of heaven, but which had reeked up from the decayed trees, and the gray wall, and the silent tarn—a pestilent and mystic vapor, dull, sluggish, faintly discernible, and leaden-hued.

Shaking off from my spirit what *must* have been a dream, I scanned more narrowly the real aspect of the building. Its principal feature seemed to be that of an excessive antiquity. The discoloration of ages had been great. Minute fungi overspread the whole exterior, hanging in a fine tangled web-work from the eaves. Yet all this was apart from any extraordinary dilapidation. No portion of the masonry had fallen; and there appeared to be a wild inconsistency between its still perfect adaptation of parts, and the crumbling condition of the individual stones. In this there was much that reminded me of the specious totality of old wood-work which has rotted for long years in some neglected vault, with no disturbance from the breath of the external air. Beyond this indication of extensive decay, however, the fabric gave little token of instability. Perhaps the eye of a scrutinizing observer might have discovered a barely perceptible fissure, which, extending from the roof of the building in front, made its way down the wall in a zigzag direction, until it became lost in the sullen waters of the tarn.

Noticing these things, I rode over a short causeway to the house. A servant in waiting took my horse, and I entered the Gothic archway of the hall. A valet, of stealthy step, thence conducted me, in silence, through many dark and intricate passages in my progress to the *studio* of his master. Much that I encountered on the way contributed, I know not how, to heighten the vague sentiments of which I have already spoken. While the objects around me—while the carvings of the ceilings, the sombre tapestries of the walls, the ebon blackness of the floors, and the phantasmagoric armorial trophies which rattled as I strode, were but matters to which, or to such as which, I had been accustomed from my infancy—while I hesitated not to acknowledge how familiar was all this—I still wondered to find how unfamiliar were the fancies which ordinary images were stirring up. On one of the staircases, I met the physician of the family. His countenance, I thought, wore a mingled expression of low cunning and perplexity. He accosted me with trepidation and passed on. The valet now threw open a door and ushered me into the presence of his master.

The room in which I found myself was very large and lofty. The windows were long, narrow, and pointed, and at so vast a distance from the black oaken floor as to be altogether inaccessible from within. Feeble gleams of encrimsoned light made their way through the trellissed panes, and served to render sufficiently distinct the more prominent objects around; the eye, however, struggled in vain to reach the remoter angles of the chamber, or the recesses of the vaulted and fretted ceiling. Dark draperies hung upon the walls. The general furniture was profuse, comfortless, antique, and tattered. Many books and musical instruments lay scattered about, but failed to give any vitality to the scene. I felt that I breathed an atmosphere of sorrow. An air of stern, deep, and irredeemable gloom hung over and pervaded all.

Upon my entrance, Usher arose from a sofa on which he had been lying at full length, and greeted me with a vivacious warmth which had much in it, I at first thought, of an overdone cordiality—of the constrained effort of the *ennuyé* man of the world. A glance, however, at his countenance, convinced me of his perfect sincerity. We sat down; and for some moments, while he spoke not, I gazed upon him with a feeling half of pity, half of awe. Surely, man had never before so terribly altered, in so brief a period, as had Roderick Usher! It was with difficulty that I could bring myself to admit the identity of the wan being before me with the companion of my early boyhood. Yet the character of his face had been at all times remarkable. A cadaverousness of complexion; an eye large, liquid, and luminous beyond comparison; lips somewhat thin and very pallid, but of a surpassingly beautiful curve; a nose of a delicate Hebrew model, but with a breadth of nostril unusual in similar formations; a finely moulded chin, speaking in its want of prominence, of a want of moral energy; hair of a more than web-like softness and tenuity; these features, with an inordinate expansion of the regions of the temple, made up altogether a countenance not easily to be forgotten. And now in the mere exaggeration of the prevailing character of these features, and of the expression they were wont to convey, lay so much of change that I doubted to whom I spoke. The now ghastly pallor of the skin, and the now miraculous lustre of the eye, above all things startled and even awed me. The silken hair, too, had been suffered to grow all unheeded, and as, in its wild gossamer texture, it floated rather than fell about the face, I could not, even with effort, connect its Arabesque expression with any idea of simple humanity.

In the manner of my friend I was at once struck with an incoherence—an inconsistency; and I soon found this to arise from a series of feeble and futile struggles to overcome an habitual trepidancy—an excessive nervous agitation. For something of this nature I had indeed been prepared, no less by his letter, than by reminiscences of certain boyish traits, and by conclusions deduced from his peculiar physical conformation and temperament. His action was alternately vivacious and sullen. His voice varied rapidly from a tremulous indecision (when the animal spirits seemed utterly in abeyance) to that species of energetic concision—that abrupt, weighty, unhurried, and hollow-sounding enunciation—that leaden, self-balanced and perfectly modulated guttural utterance, which may be observed in the lost drunkard, or the irreclaimable eater of opium, during the periods of his most intense excitement.

It was thus that he spoke of the object of my visit, of his earnest desire to see me, and of the solace he expected me to afford him. He entered, at some length, into what he conceived to be the nature of his malady. It was, he said, a constitutional and a family evil, and one for which he despaired to find a remedy—a mere nervous affection, he immediately added, which would undoubtedly soon pass off. It displayed itself in a host of unnatural sensations. Some of these, as he detailed them, interested and bewildered me; although, perhaps, the terms, and the general manner of the narration had their weight. He suffered much from a morbid acuteness of the senses; the most insipid food was alone endurable; he could wear only garments of certain texture; the odors of all flowers were oppressive; his eyes were tortured by even a faint light; and there were but peculiar sounds, and these from stringed instruments, which did not inspire him with horror.

To an anomalous species of terror I found him a bounden slave. "I shall perish," said he, "I *must* perish in this deplorable folly. Thus, thus, and not otherwise, shall I be lost. I dread the events of the future, not in themselves, but in their results. I shudder at the thought of any, even the most trivial, incident, which may operate upon this intolerable agitation of soul. I have, indeed, no abhorrence of danger, except in its absolute effect—in terror. In this unnerved—in this pitiable condition—I feel that the period will sooner or later arrive when I must abandon life and reason together, in some struggle with the grim phantasm, FEAR."

I learned, moreover, at intervals, and through broken and equivocal hints, another singular feature of his mental condition. He was enchained by certain superstitious impressions in regard to the dwelling which he tenanted, and whence, for many years, he had never ventured forth—in regard to an influence whose suppositious force was conveyed in terms too shadowy here to be re-stated—an influence which some peculiarities in the mere form and substance of his family mansion, had, by dint of long sufferance, he said, obtained over his spirit—an effect which the *physique* of the gray walls and turrets, and of the dim tarn into which they all looked down, had, at length, brought about upon the *morale* of his existence.

He admitted, however, although with hesitation, that much of the peculiar gloom which thus afflicted him could be traced to a more natural and far more palpable origin—to the severe and long-continued illness—indeed to the evidently approaching dissolution—of a tenderly beloved sister—his sole companion for long years—his last and only relative on earth. "Her decease," he said, with a bitterness which I can never forget, "would leave him (the hopeless and the frail) the last of the ancient race of the Ushers." While he spoke, the lady Madeline (for so was she called) passed slowly through a remote portion of the apartment (and, without having noticed my presence, disappeared. I regarded her with an utter astonishment not unmingled with dread—and yet I found it impossible to account for such feelings. A sensation of stupor oppressed me, as my eyes followed her retreating steps. When a door, at length, closed upon her, my glance sought instinctively and eagerly the countenance of the brother—but he had buried his face in his hands, and I could only perceive that a far more than ordinary wanness had overspread the emaciated fingers through which trickled many passionate tears.

The disease of the lady Madeline had long baffled the skill of her physicians. A settled apathy, a gradual wasting away of the person, and frequent although transient affections of a partially cataleptical character, were the unusual diagnosis. Hitherto she had steadily borne up against the pressure of her malady, and had not betaken herself finally to bed; but, on the closing in of the evening of my arrival at the house, she succumbed (as her brother told me at night with inexpressible agitation) to the prostrating power of the destroyer; and I learned that the glimpse I had obtained of her person would thus probably be the last I should obtain—that the lady, at least while living, would be seen by me no more.

For several days ensuing, her name was unmentioned by either Usher or myself: and during this period I was busied in earnest endeavors to alleviate the melancholy of my friend. We painted and read together; or I listened, as if in a dream, to the wild improvisations of his speaking guitar. And thus, as a closer and still closer intimacy admitted me more unreservedly into the recesses of his spirit, the more bitterly did I perceive the futility of all attempt at cheering a mind from which darkness, as if an inherent positive quality, poured forth upon all objects of the moral and physical universe, in one unceasing radiation of gloom.

I shall ever bear about me a memory of the many solemn hours I thus spent alone with the master of the House of Usher. Yet I should fail in any attempt to convey an idea of the exact character of the studies, or of the occupations, in which he involved me, or led me the way. An excited and highly distempered ideality threw a sulphureous lustre over all. His long improvised dirges will ring forever in my ears. Among other things, I hold painfully in mind a certain singular perversion and amplification of the wild air of the last waltz of Von Weber. From the paintings over which his elaborate fancy brooded, and which grew, touch by touch, into vaguenesses at which I shuddered the more thrillingly, because I shuddered knowing not why;—from these paintings (vivid as their images now are before me) I would in vain endeavor to educe more than a small portion which should lie within the compass of merely written words. By the utter simplicity, by the nakedness of his designs, he arrested and overawed attention. If ever mortal painted an idea, that mortal was Roderick Usher. For me at least—in the circumstances then surrounding me—there arose out of the pure abstractions which the hypochondriac contrived to throw upon his canvass, an intensity of intolerable awe, no shadow of which felt I ever yet in the contemplation of the certainly glowing yet too concrete reveries of Fuseli.[3]

One of the phantasmagoric conceptions of my friend, partaking not so rigidly of the spirit of abstraction, may be shadowed forth, although feebly, in words. A small picture presented the interior of an immensely long and rectangular vault or tunnel, with low walls, smooth, white, and without interruption or device. Certain accessory points of the design served well to convey the idea that this excavation lay at an exceeding depth below the surface of the earth. No outlet was observed in any portion of its vast extent, and no torch, or other artificial source of light was discernible; yet a flood of intense rays rolled throughout, and bathed the whole in a ghastly and inappropriate splendor.

I have just spoken of that morbid condition of the auditory nerve which rendered all music intolerable to the sufferer, with the exception of certain effects of stringed instruments. It was, perhaps, the narrow limits to which he thus confined himself upon the guitar, which gave birth, in great measure, to the fantastic character of his performances. But the fervid *facility* of his *impromptus* could not be so accounted for. They must have been, and were, in the notes, as well as in the words of his wild fantasias (for he not unfrequently accompanied himself with rhymed verbal improvisations), the result of that intense mental collectedness and concentration to which I have previously alluded as observable only in particular moments of the highest artificial excitement. The words of one of these rhapsodies I have easily remembered. I was, perhaps, the more forcibly impressed with it, as he gave it, because, in the under or mystic current of its meaning, I fancied that I perceived, and for the first time, a full consciousness on the part of Usher, of the tottering of his lofty reason upon her throne. The verses, which were entitled "The Haunted Palace," ran very nearly, if not accurately, thus:

I.

In the greenest of our valleys,
    By good angels tenanted,
Once a fair and stately palace—
    Radiant palace—reared its head.
In the monarch Thought's dominion—
    It stood there!
Never seraph spread a pinion
    Over fabric half so fair.

II.

Banners yellow, glorious, golden,
    On its roof did float and flow;
(This—all this—was in the olden
    Time long ago)
And every gentle air that dallied,
    In that sweet day,
Along the ramparts plumed and pallid,
    A winged odor went away.

III.

Wanderers in that happy valley
    Through two luminous windows saw
Spirits moving musically
    To a lute's well-tunéd law,
Round about a throne, where sitting
    (Porphyrogene!)[4]
In state his glory well befitting,
    The ruler of the realm was seen.

IV.

And all with pearl and ruby glowing
   Was the fair palace door,
Through which came flowing, flowing, flowing,
   And sparkling evermore,
A troop of Echoes whose sweet duty
   Was but to sing,
In voices of surpassing beauty,
   The wit and wisdom of their king.

V.

But evil things, in robes of sorrow,
   Assailed the monarch's high estate;
(At, let us mourn, for never morrow
   Shall dawn upon him, desolate!)
And, round about his home, the glory
   That blushed and bloomed
Is but a dim-remembered story
   Of the old time entombed.

VI.

And travelers now within that valley,
   Through the red-litten windows, see
Vast forms that move fantastically
   To a discordant melody;
While, like a rapid ghastly river,
   Through the pale door,
A hideous throng rush out forever,
   And laugh—but smile no more.

I well remember that suggestions arising from this ballad, led us into a train of thought wherein there became manifest an opinion of Usher's which I mention not so much on account of its novelty, (for other men[5] have thought thus,) as on account of the pertinacity with which he maintained it. This opinion, in its general form, was that of the sentience of all vegetable things. But, in his disordered fancy, the idea had assumed a more daring character, and trespassed, under certain conditions, upon the kingdom of inorganization. I lack words to express the full extent, or the earnest *abandon* of his persuasion. The belief, however, was connected (as I have previously hinted) with the gray stones of the home of his forefathers. The conditions of the sentience had been here, he imagined, fulfilled in the method of collocation of these stones—in the order of their arrangement, as well as in that of the many *fungi* which overspread them, and of the decayed trees which stood around—above all, in the long undisturbed endurance of this arrangement, and in its reduplication in the still waters of the tarn. Its evidence—the evidence of the sentience—was to be seen, he said, (and I here started as he spoke,) in the gradual yet certain condensation of an atmosphere of their own about the waters and the walls. The result was discoverable, he added, in that silent, yet importunate and terrible influence which for centuries had moulded the destinies of his family, and which made *him* what I now saw him— what he was. Such opinions need no comment, and I will make none.

Our books—the books which, for years, had formed no small portion of the mental existence of the invalid—were, as might be supposed, in strict keeping with this character of phantasm. We pored together over such works as the Ververt et Chartreuse of Gresset; the Belphegor of Machiavelli; the Heaven and Hell of Swedenborg; the Subterranean Voyage of Nicholas Klimm by Holberg; the Chiromancy of Robert Flud, of Jean D'Indaginé, and of De la Chambre; the Journey into the Blue Distance of Tieck; and the City of the Sun of Campanella. Our favorite volume was a small octavo edition of the *Directorium Inquisitorium*, by the Dominican Eymeric de Gironne; and there were passages in Pomponius Mela, about the old African Satyrs and Œgipans, over which Usher would sit dreaming for hours. His chief delight, however, was found in the perusal of an exceedingly rare and curious book in quarto Gothic—the manual of a forgotten church—the *Vigiliae Mortuorum secundum Chorum Ecclesiae Maguntinae.*[6]

I could not help thinking of the wild ritual of this work, and of its probable influence upon the hypochondriac, when, one evening, having informed me abruptly that the lady Madeline was no more, he stated his intention of preserving her corpse for a fortnight, (previously to its final interment,) in one of the numerous vaults within the main walls of the building. The worldly reason, however, assigned for this singular proceeding, was one which I did not feel at liberty to dispute. The brother had been led to his resolution (so he told me) by consideration of the unusual character of the malady of the deceased, of certain obtrusive and eager inquiries on the part of her medical men, and of the remote and exposed situation of the burial-ground of the family. I will not deny that when I called to mind the sinister countenance of the person whom I met upon the staircase, on the day of my arrival at the house, I had no desire to oppose what I regarded as at best but a harmless, and by no means an unnatural, precaution.

At the request of Usher, I personally aided him in the arrangements for the temporary entombment. The body having been encoffined, we two alone bore it to its rest. The vault in which we placed it (and which had been so long unopened that our torches, half smothered in its oppressive atmosphere, gave us little opportunity for investigation) was small, damp, and entirely without means of admission for light; lying, at great depth, immediately beneath that portion of the building in which was my own sleeping apartment. It had been used, apparently, in remote feudal times, for the worst purposes of a donjon-keep, and, in later days, as a place of deposit for powder, or some other highly combustible substance, as a portion of its floor, and the whole interior of a long archway through which we reached it, were carefully sheathed with copper. The door, of massive iron, had been, also, similarly protected. Its immense weight caused an unusually sharp grating sound, as it moved upon its hinges.

Having deposited our mournful burden upon tressels within this region of horror, we partially turned aside the yet unscrewed lid of the coffin, and looked upon the face of the tenant. A striking similitude between the brother and sister now first arrested my attention; and Usher, divining, perhaps, my thoughts, murmured out some few words from which I learned that the deceased and himself had been twins, and that sympathies of a scarcely intelligible nature had always existed between them. Our glances, however, rested not long upon the dead—for we could not regard her unawed. The disease which had thus entombed the lady in the maturity of youth, had left, as usual in all maladies of strictly cataleptical character, the mockery of a faint blush upon the bosom and the face, and that suspiciously lingering smile upon the lip which is so terrible in death. We replaced and screwed down the lid, and, having secured the door of iron, made our way, with toil, into the scarcely less gloomy apartments of the upper portion of the house.

And now, some days of bitter grief having elapsed, an observable change came over the features of the mental disorder of my friend. His ordinary manner had vanished. His ordinary occupations were neglected or forgotten. He roamed from chamber to chamber with hurried, unequal, and objectless step. The pallor of his countenance had assumed, if possible, a more ghastly hue—but the luminousness of his eye had utterly gone out. The once occasional huskiness of his tone was heard no more; and a tremulous quaver, as if of extreme terror, habitually characterized his utterance. There were times, indeed, when I thought his unceasingly agitated mind was laboring with some oppressive secret, to divulge which he struggled for the necessary courage. At times, again, I was obliged to resolve all into the mere inexplicable vagaries of madness, for I beheld him gazing upon vacancy for long hours, in an attitude of the profoundest attention, as if listening to some imaginary sound. It was no wonder his condition terrified—that it infected me. I felt creeping upon me, by slow yet certain degrees, the wild influences of his own fantastic yet impressive superstitions.

It was, especially, upon retiring to bed late in the night of the seventh or eighth day after the placing of the lady Madeline within the donjon, that I experienced the full power of such feelings. Sleep came not near my couch—while the hours waned and waned away. I struggled to reason off the nervousness which had dominion over me. I endeavored to believe that much, if not all of what I felt, was due to the bewildering influence of the gloomy furniture of the room—of the dark and tattered draperies, which, tortured into motion by the breath of a rising tempest, swayed fitfully to and fro upon the walls, and rustled uneasily about the decorations of the bed. But my efforts were fruitless. An irrepressible tremor gradually pervaded my frame; and, at length, there sat upon my very heart an incubus of utterly causeless alarm. Shaking this off with a gasp and a struggle, I uplifted myself upon the pillows, and, peering earnestly within the intense darkness of the chamber, harkened—I know not why, except that an instinctive spirit prompted me—to certain low and indefinite sounds which came, through the pauses of the storm, at long intervals, I knew not whence. Overpowered by an intense sentiment of horror, unaccountable yet unendurable, I threw on my clothes with haste (for I felt that I should sleep no more during the night), and endeavored to arouse myself from the pitiable condition into which I had fallen, by pacing rapidly to and fro through the apartment.

I had taken but few turns in this manner, when a light step on an adjoining staircase arrested my attention. I presently recognised it as that of Usher. In an instant afterward he rapped, with a gentle touch, at my door, and entered, bearing a lamp. His countenance was, as usual, cadaverously wan—but, moreover, there was a species of mad hilarity in his eyes—an evidently restrained *hysteria* in his whole demeanor. His air appalled me—but anything was preferable to the solitude which I had so long endured, and I even welcomed his presence as a relief.

"And you have not seen it?" he said abruptly, after having stared about him for some moments in silence—"you have not then seen it?—but, stay! you shall." Thus speaking, and having carefully shaded his lamp, he hurried to one of the casements, and threw it freely open to the storm.

The impetuous fury of the entering gust nearly lifted us from our feet. It was, indeed, a tempestuous yet sternly beautiful night, and one wildly singular in its terror and its beauty. A whirlwind had apparently collected its force in our vicinity; for there were frequent and violent alterations in the direction of the wind; and the exceeding density of the clouds (which hung so low as to press upon the turrets of the house) did not prevent our perceiving the life-like velocity with which they flew careering from all points against each other, without passing away into the distance. I say that even their exceeding density did not prevent our perceiving this—yet we had no glimpse of the moon or stars—nor was there any flashing forth of the lightning. But the under surfaces of the huge masses of agitated vapor, as well as all terrestrial objects immediately around us, were glowing in the unnatural light of a faintly luminous and distinctly visible gaseous exhalation which hung about and enshrouded the mansion.

"You must not—you shall not behold this!" said I, shudderingly, to Usher, as I led him, with a gentle violence, from the window to a seat. "These appearances, which bewilder you, are merely electrical phenomena not uncommon—or it may be that they have their ghastly origin in the rank miasma of the tarn. Let us close this casement;—the air is chilling and dangerous to your frame. Here is one of your favorite romances. I will read, and you shall listen;—and so we will pass away this terrible night together."

The antique volume which I had taken up was the "Mad Trist" of Sir Launcelot Canning;[7] but I had called it a favorite of Usher's more in sad jest than in earnest; for, in truth, there is little in its uncouth and unimaginative prolixity which could have had interest for the lofty and spiritual ideality of my friend. It was, however, the only book immediately at hand; and I indulged a vague hope that the excitement which now agitated the hypochondriac, might find relief (for the history of mental disorder is full of similar anomalies) even in the extremeness of the folly which I should read. Could I have judged, indeed, by the wild overstrained air of vivacity with which he harkened, or apparently harkened, to the words of the tale, I might well have congratulated myself upon the success of my design.

I had arrived at that well-known portion of the story where Ethelred, the hero of the Trist, having sought in vain for peaceable admission into the dwelling of the hermit, proceeds to make good an entrance by force. Here, it will be remembered, the words of the narrative run thus:

"And Ethelred, who was by nature of a doughty heart, and who was now mighty withal, on account of the powerfulness of the wine which he had drunken, waited no longer to hold parley with the hermit, who, in sooth, was of an obstinate and maliceful turn, but, feeling the rain upon his shoulders, and fearing the rising of the tempest, uplifted his mace outright, and, with blows, made quickly room in the plankings of the door for his gauntleted hand; and now pulling therewith sturdily, he so cracked, and ripped, and tore all asunder, that the noise of the dry and hollow-sounding wood alarummed and reverberated throughout the forest."

At the termination of this sentence I started, and for a moment, paused; for it appeared to me (although I at once concluded that my excited fancy had deceived me)—it appeared to me that, from some very remote portion of the mansion, there came, indistinctly, to my ears, what might have been, in its exact similarity of character, the echo (but a stifled and dull one certainly) of the very cracking and ripping sound which Sir Launcelot had so particularly described. It was, beyond doubt, the coincidence alone which had arrested my attention; for, amid the rattling of the sashes of the casements, and the ordinary commingled noises of the still increasing storm, the sound, in itself, had nothing, surely, which should have interested or disturbed me. I continued the story:

"But the good champion Ethelred, now entering within the door, was sore enraged and amazed to perceive no signal of the maliceful hermit; but, in the stead thereof, a dragon of a scaly and prodigious demeanor, and of a fiery tongue, which sate in guard before a palace of gold, with a floor of silver; and upon the wall there hung a shield of shining brass with this legend enwritten—

Who entereth herein, a conqueror hath bin;
Who slayeth the dragon, the shield he shall win;

And Ethelred uplifted his mace, and struck upon the head of the dragon, which fell before him, and gave up his pesty breath, with a shriek so horrid and harsh, and withal so piercing, that Ethelred had fain to close his ears with his hands against the dreadful noise of it, the like whereof was never before heard."

Here again I paused abruptly, and now with a feeling of wild amazement—for there could be no doubt whatever that, in this instance, I did actually hear (although from what direction it proceeded I found it impossible to say) a low and apparently distant, but harsh, protracted, and most unusual screaming or grating sound—the exact counterpart of what my fancy had already conjured up for the dragon's unnatural shriek as described by the romancer.

Oppressed, as I certainly was, upon the occurrence of this second and most extraordinary coincidence, by a thousand conflicting sensations, in which wonder and extreme terror were predominant, I still retained sufficient presence of mind to avoid exciting, by any observation, the sensitive nervousness of my companion. I was by no means certain that he had noticed the sounds in question; although, assuredly, a strange alteration had, during the last few minutes, taken place in his demeanor. From a position fronting my own, he had gradually brought round his chair, so as to sit with his face to the door of the chamber; and thus I could but partially perceive his features, although I saw that his lips trembled as if he were murmuring inaudibly. His head had dropped upon his breast—yet I knew that he was not asleep, from the wide and rigid opening of the eye as I caught a glance of it in profile. The motion of his body, too, was at variance with this idea—for he rocked from side to side with a gentle yet constant and uniform sway. Having rapidly taken notice of all this, I resumed the narrative of Sir Launcelot, which thus proceeded:

"And now, the champion, having escaped from the terrible fury of the dragon, bethinking himself of the brazen shield, and of the breaking up of the enchantment which was upon it, removed the carcass from out of the way before him, and approached valorously over the silver pavement of the castle to where the shield was upon the wall; which in sooth tarried not for his full coming, but fell down at his feet upon the silver floor, with a mighty great and terrible ringing sound."

No sooner had these syllables passed my lips, than—as if a shield of brass had indeed, at the moment, fallen heavily upon a floor of silver—I became aware of a distinct, hollow, metallic, and clangorous, yet apparently muffled reverberation. Completely unnerved, I leaped to my feet; but the measured rocking movement of Usher was undisturbed. I rushed to the chair in which he sat. His eyes were bent fixedly before him, and throughout his whole countenance there reigned a stony rigidity. But, as I placed my hand upon his shoulder, there came a strong shudder over his whole person; a sickly smile quivered about his lips; and I saw that he spoke in a low, hurried, and gibbering murmur, as if unconscious of my presence. Bending closely over him, I at length drank in the hideous import of his words.

"Not hear it?—yes, I hear it, and *have* heard it. Long—long—long—many minutes, many hours, many days, have I heard it—yet I dared not—oh, pity me, miserable wretch that I am!—I dared not—I *dared* not speak! *We have put her living in the tomb!* Said I not that my senses were acute? I *now* tell you that I heard her first feeble movements in the hollow coffin. I heard them—many, many days ago—yet I dared not—*I dared not speak!* And now—to-night—Ethelred—ha! ha!—the breaking of the hermit's door, and the death-cry of the dragon, and the clangor of the shield!—say, rather, the rending of her coffin, and the grating of the iron hinges of her prison, and her struggles within the coppered archway of the vault! Oh whither shall I fly? Will she not be here anon? Is she not hurrying to upbraid me for my haste? Have I not heard her footstep on the stair? Do I not distinguish that heavy and horrible beating of her heart? Madman!"—here he sprang furiously to his feet, and shrieked out his syllables, as if in the effort he were giving up his soul—*"Madman! I tell you that she now stands without the door!"*

As if in the superhuman energy of his utterance there had been found the potency of a spell—the huge antique pannels to which the speaker pointed, threw slowly back, upon the instant, their ponderous and ebony jaws. It was the work of the rushing gust—but then without those doors there *did* stand the lofty and enshrouded figure of the lady Madeline of Usher. There was blood upon her white robes, and the evidence of some bitter struggle upon every portion of her emaciated frame. For a moment she remained trembling and reeling to and fro upon the threshold—then, with a low moaning cry, fell heavily inward upon the person of her brother, and in her violent and now final death-agonies, bore him to the floor a corpse, and a victim to the terrors he had anticipated.

From that chamber, and from that mansion, I fled aghast. The storm was still abroad in all its wrath as I found myself crossing the old causeway. Suddenly there shot along the path a wild light, and I turned to see whence a gleam so unusual could have issued; for the vast house and its shadows were alone behind me. The radiance was that of the full, setting, and blood-red moon, which now shone vividly through that once barely-discernible fissure, of which I have before spoken as extending from the roof of the building, in a zigzag direction, to the base. While I gazed, this fissure rapidly widened—there came a fierce breath of the whirlwind—the entire orb of the satellite burst at once upon my sight—my brain reeled as I saw the mighty walls rushing asunder—there was a long tumultuous shouting sound like the voice of a thousand waters—and the deep and dank tarn at my feet closed sullenly and silently over the fragments of the *"House of Usher."*

William Wilson[1]

What say of it? what say CONSCIENCE grim,
That spectre in my path?
CHAMBERLAIN'S PHARRONIDA[2]

LET me call myself, for the present, William Wilson. The fair page now lying before me need not be sullied with my real appellation. This has been already too much an object for the scorn—for the horror—for the detestation of my race. To the uttermost regions of the globe have not the indignant winds bruited its unparalleled infamy? Oh, outcast of all outcasts most abandoned!—to the earth art thou not forever dead? to its honors, to its flowers, to its golden aspirations?—and a cloud, dense, dismal, and limitless, does it not hang eternally between thy hopes and heaven?

I would not, if I could, here or to-day, embody a record of my later years of unspeakable misery, and unpardonable crime. This epoch—these later years—took unto themselves a sudden elevation in turpitude, whose origin alone it is my present purpose to assign. Men usually grow base by degrees. From me, in an instant, all virtue dropped bodily as a mantle. From comparatively trivial wickedness I passed, with the stride of a giant, into more than the enormities of an Elah-Gabalus.[3] What chance—what one event brought this evil thing to pass, bear with me while I relate. Death approaches; and the shadow which foreruns him has thrown a softening influence over my spirit. I long, in passing through the dim valley, for the sympathy—I had nearly said for the pity—of my fellow men. I would fain have them believe that I have been, in some measure, the slave of circumstances beyond human control. I would wish them to seek out for me, in the details I am about to give, some little oasis of *fatality* amid a wilderness of error. I would have them allow—what they cannot refrain from allowing—that, although temptation may have erewhile existed as great, man was never *thus*, at least, tempted before—certainly, never *thus* fell. And is it therefore that he has never thus suffered? Have I not indeed been living in a dream? And am I not now dying a victim to the horror and the mystery of the wildest of all sublunary visions?

I am the descendant of a race whose imaginative and easily excitable temperament has at all times rendered them remarkable; and, in my earliest infancy, I gave evidence of having fully inherited the family character. As I advanced in years it was more strongly developed; becoming, for many reasons, a cause of serious disquietude to my friends, and of positive injury to myself. I grew self-willed, addicted to the wildest caprices, and a prey to the most ungovernable passions. Weak-minded, and beset with constitutional infirmities akin to my own, my parents could do but little to check the evil propensities which distinguished me. Some feeble and ill-directed efforts resulted in complete failure on their part, and, of course, in total triumph on mine. Thenceforward my voice was a household law; and at an age when few children have abandoned their leading-strings, I was left to the guidance of my own will, and became, in all but name, the master of my own actions.

My earliest recollections of a school-life, are connected with a large, rambling, Elizabethan house, in a misty-looking village of England, where were a vast number of gigantic and gnarled trees, and where all the houses were excessively ancient. In truth, it was a dream-like and spirit-soothing place, that venerable old town. At this moment, in fancy, I feel the refreshing chilliness of its deeply-shadowed avenues, inhale the fragrance of its thousand shrubberies, and thrill anew with undefinable delight, at the deep hollow note of the church-bell, breaking, each hour, with sullen and sudden roar, upon the stillness of the dusky atmosphere in which the fretted Gothic steeple lay imbedded and asleep.

It gives me, perhaps, as much of pleasure as I can now in any manner experience, to dwell upon minute recollections of the school and its concerns. Steeped in misery as I am—misery, alas! only too real—I shall be pardoned for seeking relief, however slight and temporary, in the weakness of a few rambling details. These, moreover, utterly trivial, and even ridiculous in themselves, assume, to my fancy, adventitious importance, as connected with a period and a locality when and where I recognise the first ambiguous monitions of the destiny which afterwards so fully overshadowed me. Let me then remember.

The house, I have said, was old and irregular. The grounds were extensive, and a high and solid brick wall, topped with a bed of mortar and broken glass, encompassed the whole. This prison-like rampart formed the limit of our domain; beyond it we saw but thrice a week—once every Saturday afternoon, when, attended by two ushers, we were permitted to take brief walks in a body through some of the neighbouring fields—and twice during Sunday, when we paraded in the same formal manner to the morning and evening service in the one church of the village. Of this church the principal of our school was pastor. With how deep a spirit of wonder and perplexity was I wont to regard him from our remote pew in the gallery, as, with step solemn and slow, he ascended the pulpit! This reverend man, with countenance so demurely benign, with robes so glossy and so clerically flowing, with wig so minutely powdered, so rigid and so vast,—could this be he who, of late, with sour visage, and in snuffy habiliments, administered, ferule in hand, the Draconian laws of the academy? Oh, gigantic paradox, too utterly monstrous for solution!

At an angle of the ponderous wall frowned a more ponderous gate. It was riveted and studded with iron bolts, and surmounted with jagged iron spikes. What impressions of deep awe did it inspire! It was never opened save for the three periodical egressions and ingressions already mentioned; then, in every creak of its mighty hinges, we found a plenitude of mystery—a world of matter for solemn remark, or for more solemn meditation.

The extensive enclosure was irregular in form, having many capacious recesses. Of these, three or four of the largest constituted the play-ground. It was level, and covered with fine hard gravel. I well remember it had no trees, nor benches, nor any thing similar within it. Of course it was in the rear of the house. In front lay a small parterre, planted with box and other shrubs; but through this sacred division we passed only upon rare occasions indeed—such as a first advent to school or final departure thence, or perhaps, when a parent or friend having called for us, we joyfully took our way home for the Christmas or Midsummer holydays.

But the house!—how quaint an old building was this!—to me how veritably a palace of enchantment! There was really no end to its windings—to its incomprehensible sub-divisions. It was difficult, at any given time, to say with certainty upon which of its two stories one happened to be. From each room to every other there were sure to be found three or four steps either in ascent or descent. Then the lateral branches were innumerable—inconceivable—and so returning in upon themselves, that our most exact ideas in regard to the whole mansion were not very far different from those with which we pondered upon infinity. During the five years of my residence here, I was never able to ascertain with precision, in what remote locality lay the little sleeping apartment assigned to myself and some eighteen or twenty other scholars.

The school-room was the largest in the house—I could not help thinking, in the world. It was very long, narrow, and dismally low, with pointed Gothic windows and a ceiling of oak. In a remote and terror-inspiring angle was a square enclosure of eight or ten feet, comprising the *sanctum*, "during hours," of our principal, the Reverend Dr. Bransby.[4] It was a solid structure, with massy door, sooner than open which in the absence of the "Dominie," we would all have willingly perished by the *peine forte et dure*.[5] In other angles were two other similar boxes, far less reverenced, indeed, but still greatly matters of awe. One of these was the pulpit of the "classical" usher, one of the "English and mathematical." Interspersed about the room, crossing and re-crossing in endless irregularity, were innumerable benches and desks, black, ancient, and time-worn, piled desperately with much-bethumbed books, and so beseamed with initial letters, names at full length, grotesque figures, and other multiplied efforts of the knife, as to have entirely lost what little of original form might have been their portion in days long departed. A huge bucket with water stood at one extremity of the room, and a clock of stupendous dimensions at the other.

Encompassed by the massy walls of this venerable academy, I passed, yet not in tedium or disgust, the years of the third lustrum[6] of my life. The teeming brain of childhood requires no external world of incident to occupy or amuse it; and the apparently dismal monotony of a school was replete with more intense excitement than my riper youth has derived from luxury, or my full manhood from crime. Yet I must believe that my first mental development had in it much of the uncommon— even much of the *outré*. Upon mankind at large the events of very early existence rarely leave in mature age any definite impression. All is gray shadow—a weak and irregular remembrance—an indistinct regathering of feeble pleasures and phantasmagoric pains. With me this is not so. In childhood I must have felt with the energy of a man what I now find stamped upon memory in lines as vivid, as deep, and as durable as the *exergues*[7] of the Carthaginian medals.

Yet in fact—in the fact of the world's view—how little was there to remember! The morning's awakening, the nightly summons to bed; the connings, the recitations;

the periodical half-holidays, and perambulations; the play-ground, with its broils, its pastimes, its intrigues;—these, by a mental sorcery long forgotten, were made to involve a wilderness of sensation, a world of rich incident, an universe of varied emotion, of excitement the most passionate and spirit-stirring. *"Oh, le bon temps, que ce siecle de fer!"*[8]

In truth, the ardor, the enthusiasm, and the imperiousness of my disposition, soon rendered me a marked character among my schoolmates, and by slow, but natural gradations, gave me an ascendancy over all not greatly older than myself;—over all with a single exception. This exception was found in the person of a scholar, who, although no relation, bore the same Christian and surname as myself;—a circumstance, in fact, little remarkable; for, notwithstanding a noble descent, mine was one of those every-day appellations which seem, by prescriptive right, to have been, time out of mind, the common property of the mob. In this narrative I have therefore designated myself as William Wilson,—a fictitious title not very dissimilar to the real. My namesake alone, of those who in school phraseology constituted "our set," presumed to compete with me in the studies of the class—in the sports and broils of the play-ground—to refuse implicit belief in my assertions, and submission to my will—indeed, to interfere with my arbitrary dictation in any respect whatsoever. If there is on earth a supreme and unqualified despotism, it is the despotism of a master mind in boyhood over the less energetic spirits of its companions.

Wilson's rebellion was to me a source of the greatest embarrassment;—the more so as, in spite of the bravado with which in public I made a point of treating him and his pretensions, I secretly felt that I feared him, and could not help thinking the equality which he maintained so easily with myself, a proof of his true superiority; since not to be overcome cost me a perpetual struggle. Yet this superiority—even this equality—was in truth acknowledged by no one but myself; our associates, by some unaccountable blindness, seemed not even to suspect it. Indeed, his competition, his resistance, and especially his impertinent and dogged interference with my purposes, were not more pointed than private. He appeared to be destitute alike of the ambition which urged, and of the passionate energy of mind which enabled me to excel. In his rivalry he might have been supposed actuated solely by a whimsical desire to thwart, astonish, or mortify myself; although there were times when I could not help observing, with a feeling made up of wonder, abasement, and pique, that he mingled with his injuries, his insults, or his contradictions, a certain most inappropriate, and assuredly most unwelcome *affectionateness* of manner. I could only conceive this singular behavior to arise from a consummate self-conceit assuming the vulgar airs of patronage and protection.

Perhaps it was this latter trait in Wilson's conduct, conjoined with our identity of name, and the mere accident of our having entered the school upon the same day, which set afloat the notion that we were brothers, among the senior classes in the academy. These do not usually inquire with much strictness into the affairs of their juniors. I have before said, or should have said, that Wilson was not, in the most remote degree, connected with my family. But assuredly if we *had* been brothers we must have been twins; for, after leaving Dr. Bransby's, I casually learned that my namesake was born on the nineteenth of January, 1813—and this is a somewhat remarkable coincidence; for the day is precisely that of my own nativity.[9]

It may seem strange that in spite of the continual anxiety occasioned me by the rivalry of Wilson, and his intolerable spirit of contradiction, I could not bring myself to hate him altogether. We had, to be sure, nearly every day a quarrel in which, yielding me publicly the palm of victory, he, in some manner, contrived to make me feel that it was he who deserved it; yet a sense of pride on my part, and a veritable dignity on his own, kept us always upon what are called "speaking terms," while there were many points of strong congeniality in our tempers, operating to awake in me a sentiment which our position alone, perhaps, prevented from ripening into friendship. It is difficult, indeed, to define, or even to describe, my real feelings towards him. They formed a motley and heterogeneous admixture;—some petulant animosity, which was not yet hatred, some esteem, more respect, much fear, with a world of uneasy curiosity. To the moralist it will be unnecessary to say, in addition, that Wilson and myself were the most inseparable of companions.

It was no doubt the anomalous state of affairs existing between us, which turned all my attacks upon him, (and they were many, either open or covert) into the channel of banter or practical joke (giving pain while assuming the aspect of mere fun) rather than into a more serious and determined hostility. But my endeavours on this head were by no means uniformly successful, even when my plans were the most wittily concocted; for my namesake had much about him, in character, of that unassuming and quiet austerity which, while enjoying the poignancy of its own jokes, has no heel of Achilles in itself, and absolutely refuses to be laughed at. I could find, indeed, but one vulnerable point, and, that lying in a personal peculiarity, arising, perhaps, from constitutional disease, would have been spared by any antagonist less at his wit's end than myself;—my rival had a weakness in the faucial or guttural organs, which precluded him from raising his voice at any time *above a very low whisper*. Of this defect I did not fail to take what poor advantage lay in my power.

Wilson's retaliations in kind were many; and there was one form of his practical wit that disturbed me beyond measure. How his sagacity first discovered at all that so petty a thing would vex me, is a question I never could solve; but, having discovered, he habitually practised the annoyance. I had always felt aversion to my uncourtly patronymic, and its very common, if not plebeian prænomen. The words were venom in my ears; and when, upon the day of my arrival, a second William Wilson came also to the academy, I felt angry with him for bearing the name, and doubly disgusted with the name because a stranger bore it, who would be the cause of its twofold repetition, who would be constantly in my presence, and whose concerns, in the ordinary routine of the school business, must inevitably, on account of the detestable coincidence, be often confounded with my own.

The feeling of vexation thus engendered grew stronger with every circumstance tending to show resemblance, moral or physical, between my rival and myself. I had not then discovered the remarkable fact that we were of the same age; but I saw that we were of the same height, and I perceived that we were even singularly alike in general contour of person and outline of feature. I was galled, too, by the rumor touching a relationship, which had grown current in the upper forms. In a word, nothing could more seriously disturb me, (although I scrupulously concealed such disturbance,) than any allusion to a similarity of mind, person, or condition existing between us. But, in truth, I had no reason to believe that (with the exception of the matter of relationship, and in the case of Wilson himself,) this similarity had ever been made a subject of comment, or even observed at all by our schoolfellows. That *he* observed it in all its bearings, and as fixedly as I, was apparent; but that he could discover in such circumstances so fruitful a field of annoyance, can only be attributed, as I said before, to his more than ordinary penetration.

His cue, which was to perfect an imitation of myself, lay both in words and in actions; and most admirably did he play his part. My dress it was an easy matter to copy; my gait and general manner were, without difficulty, appropriated; in spite of his constitutional defect, even my voice did not escape him. My louder tones were, of course, unattempted, but then the key, it was identical; *and his singular whisper, it grew the very echo of my own.*

How greatly this most exquisite portraiture harassed me, (for it could not justly be termed a caricature,) I will not now venture to describe. I had but one consolation— in the fact that the imitation, apparently, was noticed by myself alone, and that I had to endure only the knowing and strangely sarcastic smiles of my namesake himself. Satisfied with having produced in my bosom the intended effect, he seemed to chuckle in secret over the sting he had inflicted, and was characteristically disregardful of the public applause which the success of his witty endeavours might have so easily elicited. That the school, indeed, did not feel his design, perceive its accomplishment, and participate in his sneer, was, for many anxious months, a riddle I could not resolve. Perhaps the *gradation* of his copy rendered it not so readily perceptible; or, more possibly, I owed my security to the masterly air of the copyist, who, disdaining the letter, (which in a painting is all the obtuse can see,) gave but the full spirit of his original for my individual contemplation and chagrin.

I have already more than once spoken of the disgusting air of patronage which he assumed toward me, and of his frequent officious interference with my will. This interference often took the ungracious character of advice; advice not openly given, but hinted or insinuated. I received it with a repugnance which gained strength as I grew in years. Yet, at this distant day, let me do him the simple justice to acknowledge that I can recall no occasion when the suggestions of my rival were on the side of those errors or follies so usual to his immature age and seeming inexperience; that his moral sense, at least, if not his general talents and worldly wisdom, was far keener than my own; and that I might, to-day, have been a better, and thus a happier man, had I less frequently rejected the counsels embodied in those meaning whispers which I then but too cordially hated and too bitterly despised.

As it was, I at length grew restive in the extreme under his distasteful supervision, and daily resented more and more openly what I considered his intolerable arrogance. I have said that, in the first years of our connexion as schoolmates, my feelings in regard to him might have been easily ripened into friendship; but, in the latter months of my residence at the academy, although the intrusion of his ordinary manner had, beyond doubt, in some measure, abated, my sentiments, in nearly similar proportion, partook very much of positive hatred. Upon one occasion he saw this, I think, and afterwards avoided, or made a show of avoiding me.

It was about the same period, if I remember aright, that, in an altercation of violence with him, in which he was more than usually thrown off his guard, and spoke and acted with an openness of demeanor rather foreign to his nature, I discovered, or fancied I discovered, in his accent, his air, and general appearance, a something which first startled, and then deeply interested me, by bringing to mind dim visions of my earliest infancy—wild, confused and thronging memories of a time when memory herself was yet unborn. I cannot better describe the sensation which oppressed me than by saying that I could with difficulty shake off the belief of my having been acquainted with the being who stood before me, at some epoch very long ago—some point of the past even infinitely remote. The delusion, however, faded rapidly as it came; and I mention it at all but to define the day of the last conversation I there held with my singular namesake.

The huge old house, with its countless subdivisions, had several large chambers communicating with each other, where slept the greater number of the students. There were, however, (as must necessarily happen in a building so awkwardly planned,) many little nooks or recesses, the odds and ends of the structure; and these the economic ingenuity of Dr. Bransby had also fitted up as dormitories; although, being the merest closets, they were capable of accommodating but a single individual. One of these small apartments was occupied by Wilson.

One night, about the close of my fifth year at the school, and immediately after the altercation just mentioned, finding every one wrapped in sleep, I arose from bed, and, lamp in hand, stole through a wilderness of narrow passages from my own bedroom to that of my rival. I had long been plotting one of those ill-natured pieces of practical wit at his expense in which I had hitherto been so uniformly unsuccessful. It was my intention, now, to put my scheme in operation, and I resolved to make him feel the whole extent of the malice with which I was imbued. Having reached his closet, I noiselessly entered, leaving the lamp, with a shade over it, on the outside. I advanced a step, and listened to the sound of his tranquil breathing. Assured of his being asleep, I returned, took the light, and with it again approached the bed. Close curtains were around it, which, in the prosecution of my plan, I slowly and quietly withdrew, when the bright rays fell vividly upon the sleeper, and my eyes, at the same moment, upon his countenance. I looked;—and a numbness, an iciness of feeling instantly pervaded my frame. My breast heaved, my knees tottered, my whole spirit became possessed with an objectless yet intolerable horror. Gasping for breath, I lowered the lamp in still nearer proximity to the face. Were these—*these* the lineaments of William Wilson? I saw, indeed, that they were his, but I shook as if with a fit of the ague in fancying they were not. What *was* there about them to confound me in this manner? I gazed; while my brain reeled with a multitude of incoherent thoughts. Not thus he appeared—assuredly not *thus*—in the vivacity of his waking hours. The same name! the same contour of person! the same day of arrival at the academy! And then his dogged and meaningless imitation of my gait, my voice, my habits, and my manner! Was it, in truth, within the bounds of human possibility, that *what I now saw* was the result, merely, of the habitual practice of this sarcastic imitation? Awe-stricken, and with a creeping shudder, I extinguished the lamp, passed silently from the chamber, and left, at once, the halls of that old academy, never to enter them again.

After a lapse of some months, spent at home in mere idleness, I found myself a student at Eton. The brief interval had been sufficient to enfeeble my remembrance of the events at Dr. Bransby's, or at least to effect a material change in the nature of the feelings with which I remembered them. The truth—the tragedy—of the drama was no more. I could now find room to doubt the evidence of my senses; and seldom called up the subject at all but with wonder at the extent of human credulity, and a smile at the vivid force of the imagination which I hereditarily possessed. Neither was this species of skepticism likely to be diminished by the character of the life I led at Eton. The vortex of thoughtless folly into which I there so immediately and so recklessly plunged, washed away all but the froth of my past hours, engulfed at once every solid or serious impression, and left to memory only the veriest levities of a former existence.

I do not wish, however, to trace the course of my miserable profligacy here—a profligacy which set at defiance the laws, while it eluded the vigilance of the institution. Three years of folly, passed without profit, had but given me rooted habits of vice, and added, in a somewhat unusual degree, to my bodily stature, when, after a week of soulless dissipation, I invited a small party of the most dissolute students to a secret carousal in my chambers. We met at a late hour of the night; for our debaucheries were to be faithfully protracted until morning. The wine flowed freely, and there were not wanting other and perhaps more dangerous seductions; so that the grey dawn had already faintly appeared in the east, while our delirious extravagance was at its height. Madly flushed with cards and intoxication, I was in the act of insisting upon a toast of more than wonted profanity, when my attention was suddenly diverted by the violent, although partial unclosing of the door of the apartment, and by the eager voice of a servant from without. He said that some person, apparently in great haste, demanded to speak with me in the hall.

Wildly excited with wine, the unexpected interruption rather delighted than surprised me. I staggered forward at once, and a few steps brought me to the vestibule of the building. In this low and small room there hung no lamp; and now no light at all was admitted, save that of the exceedingly feeble dawn which made its way through the semi-circular window. As I put my foot over the threshold, I became aware of the figure of a youth about my own height, and habited in a white kerseymere morning frock, cut in the novel fashion of the one I myself wore at the moment. This the faint light enabled me to perceive; but the features of his face I could not distinguish. Upon my entering he strode hurriedly up to me, and, seizing me by the arm with a gesture of petulant impatience, whispered the words "William Wilson!" in my ear.

I grew perfectly sober in an instant.

There was that in the manner of the stranger, and in the tremulous shake of his uplifted finger, as he held it between my eyes and the light, which filled me with unqualified amazement; but it was not this which had so violently moved me. It was the pregnancy of solemn admonition in the singular, low, hissing utterance; and, above all, it was the character, the tone, *the key*, of those few, simple, and familiar, yet *whispered* syllables, which came with a thousand thronging memories of by-gone days, and struck upon my soul with the shock of a galvanic battery. Ere I could recover the use of my senses he was gone.

Although this event failed not of a vivid effect upon my disordered imagination, yet was it evanescent as vivid. For some weeks, indeed, I busied myself in earnest inquiry, or was wrapped in a cloud of morbid speculation. I did not pretend to disguise from my perception the identity of the singular individual who thus perseveringly interfered with my affairs, and harassed me with his insinuated counsel. But who and what was this Wilson?—and whence came he?—and what were his purposes? Upon neither of these points could I be satisfied; merely ascertaining, in regard to him, that a sudden accident in his family had caused his removal from Dr. Bransby's academy on the afternoon of the day in which I myself had eloped. But in a brief period I ceased to think upon the subject; my attention being all absorbed in a contemplated departure for Oxford. Thither I soon went; the uncalculating vanity of my parents furnishing me with an outfit, and annual establishment, which would enable me to indulge at will in the luxury already so dear to my heart,—to vie in profuseness of expenditure with the haughtiest heirs of the wealthiest earldoms in Great Britain.

Excited by such appliances to vice, my constitutional temperament broke forth with redoubled ardor, and I spurned even the common restraints of decency in the mad infatuation of my revels. But it were absurd to pause in the detail of my extravagance. Let it suffice, that among spendthrifts I out-Heroded Herod,[10] and that, giving name to a multitude of novel follies, I added no brief appendix to the long catalogue of vices then usual in the most dissolute university of Europe.

It could hardly be credited, however, that I had, even here, so utterly fallen from the gentlemanly estate, as to seek acquaintance with the vilest arts of the gambler by profession, and, having become an adept in his despicable science, to practise it habitually as a means of increasing my already enormous income at the expense of the weak-minded among my fellow collegians. Such, nevertheless, was the fact. And the very enormity of this offence against all manly and honourable sentiment proved, beyond doubt, the main if not the sole reason of the impunity with which it was committed. Who, indeed, among my most abandoned associates, would not rather have disputed the clearest evidence of his sense, than have suspected of such courses, the gay, the frank, the generous William Wilson—the noblest and most liberal commoner at Oxford—him whose follies (said his parasites) were but the follies of youth and unbridled fancy—whose errors but inimitable whim—whose darkest vice but a careless and dashing extravagance?

I had been now two years successfully busied in this way, when there came to the university a young *parvenu* nobleman, Glendinning—rich, said report, as Herodes Atticus[11]—his riches, too, as easily acquired. I soon found him of weak intellect, and, of course, marked him as a fitting subject for my skill. I frequently engaged him in play, and contrived, with a gambler's usual art, to let him win considerable sums, the more effectually to entangle him in my snares. At length, my schemes being ripe, I met him (with the full intention that this meeting should be final and decisive) at the chambers of a fellow-commoner, (Mr. Preston,) equally intimate with both, but who, to do him justice, entertained not even a remote suspicion of my design. To give to this a better coloring, I had contrived to have assembled a party of some eight or ten, and was solicitously careful that the introduction of cards should appear accidental, and originate in the proposal of my contemplated dupe himself. To be brief upon a vile topic, none of the low finesse was omitted, so customary upon similar occasions that it is a just matter for wonder how any are still found so besotted as to fall its victim.

We had protracted our sitting far into the night, and I had at length effected the manœuvre of getting Glendinning as my sole antagonist. The game, too, was my favorite *écarté*. The rest of the company, interested in the extent of our play, had abandoned their own cards, and were standing around us as spectators. The *parvenu*, who had been induced by my artifices in the early part of the evening, to drink deeply, now shuffled, dealt, or played, with a wild nervousness of manner for which his intoxication, I thought, might partially, but could not altogether account. In a very short period he had become my debtor to a large amount, when, having taken a long draught of port, he did precisely what I had been coolly anticipating—he proposed to double our already extravagant stakes. With a well-feigned show of reluctance, and not until after my repeated refusal had seduced him into some angry words which gave a color of *pique* to my compliance, did I finally comply. The result, of course, did but prove how entirely the prey was in my toils; in less than an hour he had quadrupled his debt. For some time his countenance had been losing the florid tinge lent it by the wine; but now, to my astonishment, I perceived that it had grown to a pallor truly fearful. I say to my astonishment. Glendinning had been represented to my eager inquiries as immeasurably wealthy; and the sums which he had as yet lost, although in themselves vast, could not, I supposed, very seriously annoy, much less so violently affect him. That he was overcome by the wine just swallowed, was the idea which most readily presented itself; and, rather with a view to the preservation of my own character in the eyes of my associates, than from any less interested motive, I was about to insist, peremptorily, upon a discontinuance of the play, when some expressions at my elbow from among the company, and an ejaculation evincing utter despair on the part of Glendinning, gave me to understand that I had effected his total ruin under circumstances which, rendering him an object for the pity of all, should have protected him from the ill offices even of a fiend.

What now might have been my conduct it is difficult to say. The pitiable condition of my dupe had thrown an air of embarrassed gloom over all; and, for some moments, a profound silence was maintained, during which I could not help feeling my cheeks tingle with the many burning glances of scorn or reproach cast upon me by the less abandoned of the party. I will even own that an intolerable weight of anxiety was for a brief instant lifted from my bosom by the sudden and extraordinary interruption which ensued. The wide, heavy folding doors of the apartment were all at once thrown open, to their full extent, with a vigorous and rushing impetuosity that extinguished, as if by magic, every candle in the room. Their light, in dying, enabled us just to perceive that a stranger had entered, about my own height, and closely muffled in a cloak. The darkness, however, was now total; and we could only *feel* that he was standing in our midst. Before any one of us could recover from the extreme astonishment into which this rudeness had thrown all, we heard the voice of the intruder.

"Gentlemen," he said, in a low, distinct, and never-to-be-forgotten *whisper* which thrilled to the very marrow of my bones, "Gentlemen, I make no apology for this behaviour, because in thus behaving, I am but fulfilling a duty. You are, beyond doubt, uninformed of the true character of the person who has to-night won at *écarté* a large sum of money from Lord Glendinning. I will therefore put you upon an expeditious and decisive plan of obtaining this very necessary information. Please to examine, at your leisure, the inner linings of the cuff of his left sleeve, and the several little packages which may be found in the somewhat capacious pockets of his embroidered morning wrapper."

While he spoke, so profound was the stillness that one might have heard a pin drop upon the floor. In ceasing, he departed at once, and as abruptly as he had entered. Can I—shall I describe my sensations?—must I say that I felt all the horrors of the damned? Most assuredly I had little time given for reflection. Many hands roughly seized me upon the spot, and lights were immediately reprocured. A search ensued. In the lining of my sleeve were found all the court cards essential in *écarté*, and, in the pockets of my wrapper, a number of packs, fac-similes of those used at our sittings, with the single exception that mine were of the species called, technically, *arrondées*; the honors being slightly convex at the ends, the lower cards slightly convex at the sides. In this disposition, the dupe who cuts, as customary, at the length of the pack, will invariably find that he cuts his antagonist an honor; while the gambler, cutting at the breadth, will, as certainly, cut nothing for his victim which may count in the records of the game.

Any burst of indignation upon this discovery would have affected me less than the silent contempt, or the sarcastic composure, with which it was received.

"Mr. Wilson," said our host, stooping to remove from beneath his feet an exceedingly luxurious cloak of rare furs, "Mr. Wilson, this is your property." (The weather was cold; and, upon quitting my own room, I had thrown a cloak over my dressing wrapper, putting it off upon reaching the scene of play.) "I presume it is supererogatory to seek here (eyeing the folds of the garment with a bitter smile) for any farther evidence of your skill. Indeed, we have had enough. You will see the necessity, I hope, of quitting Oxford—at all events, of quitting instantly my chambers."

Abased, humbled to the dust as I then was, it is probable that I should have resented this galling language by immediate personal violence, had not my whole attention been at the moment arrested by a fact of the most startling character. The cloak which I had worn was of a rare description of fur; how rare, how extravagantly costly, I shall not venture to say. Its fashion, too, was of my own fantastic invention; for I was fastidious to an absurd degree of coxcombry, in matters of this frivolous nature. When, therefore, Mr. Preston reached me that which he had picked up upon the floor, and near the folding doors of the apartment, it was with an astonishment nearly bordering upon terror, that I perceived my own already hanging on my arm, (where I had no doubt unwittingly placed it,) and that the one presented me was but its exact counterpart in every, in even the minutest possible particular. The singular being who had so disastrously exposed me, had been muffled, I remembered, in a cloak; and none had been worn at all by any of the members of our party with the exception of myself. Retaining some presence of mind, I took the one offered me by Preston; placed it, unnoticed, over my own; left the apartment with a resolute scowl of defiance; and, next morning ere dawn of day, commenced a hurried journey from Oxford to the continent, in a perfect agony of horror and of shame.

I fled in vain. My evil destiny pursued me as if in exultation, and proved, indeed, that the exercise of its mysterious dominion had as yet only begun. Scarcely had I set foot in Paris ere I had fresh evidence of the detestable interest taken by this Wilson in my concerns. Years flew, while I experienced no relief. Villain!—at Rome, with how untimely, yet with how spectral an officiousness, stepped he in between me and my ambition! At Vienna, too—at Berlin—and at Moscow! Where, in truth, had I *not* bitter cause to curse him within my heart? From his inscrutable tyranny did I at length flee, panic-stricken, as from a pestilence; and to the very ends of the earth *I fled in vain.*

And again, and again, in secret communion with my own spirit, would I demand the questions "Who is he?—whence came he?—and what are his objects?" But no answer was there found. And now I scrutinized, with a minute scrutiny, the forms, and the methods, and the leading traits of his impertinent supervision. But even here there was very little upon which to base a conjecture. It was noticeable, indeed, that, in no one of the multiplied instances in which he had of late crossed my path, had he so crossed it except to frustrate those schemes, or to disturb those actions, which, if fully carried out, might have resulted in bitter mischief. Poor justification this, in truth, for an authority so imperiously assumed! Poor indemnity for natural rights of self-agency so pertinaciously, so insultingly denied!

I had also been forced to notice that my tormentor, for a very long period of time, (while scrupulously and with miraculous dexterity maintaining his whim of an identity of apparel with myself,) had so contrived it, in the execution of his varied interference with my will, that I saw not, at any moment, the features of his face. Be Wilson what he might, *this*, at least, was but the veriest of affectation, or of folly. Could he, for an instant, have supposed that, in my admonisher at Eton—in the destroyer of my honor at Oxford,—in him who thwarted my ambition at Rome, my revenge at Paris, my passionate love at Naples, or what he falsely termed my avarice in Egypt,—that in this, my arch-enemy and evil genius, I could fail to recognise the William Wilson of my schoolboy days,—the namesake, the companion, the rival,— the hated and dreaded rival at Dr. Bransby's? Impossible!—But let me hasten to the last eventful scene of the drama.

Thus far I had succumbed supinely to this imperious domination. The sentiment of deep awe with which I habitually regarded the elevated character, the majestic wisdom, the apparent omnipresence and omnipotence of Wilson, added to a feeling of even terror, with which certain other traits in his nature and assumptions inspired me, had operated, hitherto, to impress me with an idea of my own utter weakness and helplessness, and to suggest an implicit, although bitterly reluctant submission to his arbitrary will. But, of late days, I had given myself up entirely to wine; and its maddening influence upon my hereditary temper rendered me more and more impatient of control. I began to murmur,—to hesitate,—to resist. And was it only fancy which induced me to believe that, with the increase of my own firmness, that of my tormentor underwent a proportional diminution? Be this as it may, I now began to feel the inspiration of a burning hope, and at length nurtured in my secret thoughts a stern and desperate resolution that I would submit no longer to be enslaved.

It was at Rome, during the Carnival of 18—, that I attended a masquerade in the palazzo of the Neapolitan Duke Di Broglio. I had indulged more freely than usual in the excesses of the wine-table; and now the suffocating atmosphere of the crowded rooms irritated me beyond endurance. The difficulty, too, of forcing my way through the mazes of the company contributed not a little to the ruffling of my temper; for I was anxiously seeking, (let me not say with what unworthy motive) the young, the gay, the beautiful wife of the aged and doting Di Broglio. With a too unscrupulous confidence she had previously communicated to me the secret of the costume in which she would be habited, and now, having caught a glimpse of her person, I was hurrying to make my way into her presence.—At this moment I felt a light hand placed upon my shoulder, and that ever-remembered, low, damnable *whisper* within my ear.

In an absolute phrenzy of wrath, I turned at once upon him who had thus interrupted me, and seized him violently by the collar. He was attired, as I had expected, in a costume altogether similar to my own; wearing a Spanish cloak of blue velvet, begirt about the waist with a crimson belt sustaining a rapier. A mask of black silk entirely covered his face.

"Scoundrel!" I said, in a voice husky with rage, while every syllable I uttered seemed as new fuel to my fury, "scoundrel! impostor! accursed villain! you shall not—you *shall not* dog me unto death! Follow me, or I stab you where you stand!"—and I broke my way from the ballroom into a small ante-chamber adjoining—dragging him unresistingly with me as I went.

Upon entering, I thrust him furiously from me. He staggered against the wall, while I closed the door with an oath, and commanded him to draw. He hesitated but for an instant; then, with a slight sigh, drew in silence, and put himself upon his defence.

The contest was brief indeed. I was frantic with every species of wild excitement, and felt within my single arm the energy and power of a multitude. In a few seconds I forced him by sheer strength against the wainscoting, and thus, getting him at mercy, plunged my sword, with brute ferocity, repeatedly through and through his bosom.

At that instant some person tried the latch of the door. I hastened to prevent an intrusion, and then immediately returned to my dying antagonist. But what human language can adequately portray *that* astonishment, *that* horror which possessed me at the spectacle then presented to view? The brief moment in which I averted my eyes had been sufficient to produce, apparently, a material change in the arrangements at the upper or farther end of the room. A large mirror,—so at first it seemed to me in my confusion—now stood where none had been perceptible before; and, as I stepped up to it in extremity of terror, mine own image, but with features all pale and dabbled in blood, advanced to meet me with a feeble and tottering gait.

Thus it appeared I say, but was not. It was my antagonist—it was Wilson, who then stood before me in the agonies of his dissolution. His mask and cloak lay, where he had thrown them, upon the floor. Not a thread in all his raiment—not a line in all the marked and singular lineaments of his face which was not, even in the most absolute identity, *mine own!*

It was Wilson; but he spoke no longer in a whisper, and I could have fancied that I myself was speaking while he said:

"*You have conquered, and I yield. Yet, henceforward art thou also dead—dead to the World, to Heaven and to Hope! In me didst thou exist—and, in my death, see by this image, which is thine own, how utterly thou hast murdered thyself.*"

The Man of the Crowd[1]

Ce grand malheur, de ne pouvoir être seul.
La Bruyère[2]

IT was well said of a certain German book that *"er lasst sich nicht lesen"*—it does not permit itself to be read. There are some secrets which do not permit themselves to be told. Men die nightly in their beds, wringing the hands of ghostly confessors, and looking them piteously in the eyes—die with despair of heart and convulsion of throat, on account of the hideousness of mysteries which will not *suffer themselves* to be revealed. Now and then, alas, the conscience of man takes up a burthen so heavy in horror that it can be thrown down only into the grave. And thus the essence of all crime is undivulged.

Not long ago, about the closing in of an evening in autumn, I sat at the large bow window of the D—— Coffee-House in London. For some months I had been ill in health, but was now convalescent, and, with returning strength, found myself in one of those happy moods which are so precisely the converse of *ennui*—moods of the keenest appetency, when the film from the mental vision departs—the αχλυς νς πριν επηεν—and the intellect, electrified, surpasses as greatly its every-day condition, as does the vivid yet candid reason of Leibnitz, the mad and flimsy rhetoric of Gorgias.[3] Merely to breathe was enjoyment; and I derived positive pleasure even from many of the legitimate sources of pain. I felt a calm but inquisitive interest in every thing. With a cigar in my mouth and a newspaper in my lap, I had been amusing myself for the greater part of the afternoon, now in poring over advertisements, now in observing the promiscuous company in the room, and now in peering through the smoky panes into the street.

This latter is one of the principal thoroughfares of the city, and had been very much crowded during the whole day. But, as the darkness came on, the throng momently increased; and, by the time the lamps were well lighted, two dense and continuous tides of population were rushing past the door. At this particular period of the evening I had never before been in a similar situation, and the tumultuous sea of human heads filled me, therefore, with a delicious novelty of emotion. I gave up, at length, all care of things within the hotel, and became absorbed in contemplation of the scene without.

At first my observations took an abstract and generalizing turn. I looked at the passengers in masses, and thought of them in their aggregate relations. Soon, however, I descended to details, and regarded with minute interest the innumerable varieties of figure, dress, air, gait, visage, and expression of countenance.

By far the greater number of those who went by had a satisfied business-like demeanor, and seemed to be thinking only of making their way through the press. Their brows were knit, and their eyes rolled quickly; when pushed against by fellow-wayfarers they evinced no symptom of impatience, but adjusted their clothes and hurried on. Others, still a numerous class, were restless in their movements, had flushed faces, and talked and gesticulated to themselves, as if feeling in solitude on account of the very denseness of the company around. When impeded in their progress, these people suddenly ceased muttering, but redoubled their gesticulations, and awaited, with an absent and overdone smile upon the lips, the course of the persons impeding them. If jostled, they bowed profusely to the jostlers, and appeared overwhelmed with confusion.—There was nothing very distinctive about these two large classes beyond what I have noted. Their habiliments belonged to that order which is pointedly termed the decent. They were undoubtedly noblemen, merchants, attorneys, tradesmen, stock-jobbers—the Eupatrids[4] and the common-places of society—men of leisure and men actively engaged in affairs of their own—conducting business upon their own responsibility. They did not greatly excite my attention.

The tribe of clerks was an obvious one and here I discerned two remarkable divisions. There were the junior clerks of flash houses—young gentlemen with tight coats, bright boots, well-oiled hair, and supercilious lips. Setting aside a certain dapperness of carriage, which may be termed *deskism* for want of a better word, the manner of these persons seemed to me an exact facsimile of what had been the perfection of *bon ton*[5] about twelve or eighteen months before. They wore the cast-off graces of the gentry;—and this, I believe, involves the best definition of the class.

The division of the upper clerks of staunch firms, or of the "steady old fellows," it was not possible to mistake. These were known by their coats and pantaloons of black or brown, made to sit comfortably, with white cravats and waistcoats, broad solid-looking shoes, and thick hose or gaiters.—They had all slightly bald heads, from which the right ears, long used to pen-holding, had an odd habit of standing off on end. I observed that they always removed or settled their hats with both hands, and wore watches, with short gold chains of a substantial and ancient pattern. Theirs was the affectation of respectability;—if indeed there be an affectation so honorable.

There were many individuals of dashing appearance, whom I easily understood as belonging to the race of swell pick-pockets, with which all great cities are infested. I watched these gentry with much inquisitiveness, and found it difficult to imagine how they should ever be mistaken for gentlemen by gentlemen themselves. Their voluminousness of wristband, with an air of excessive frankness, should betray them at once.

The gamblers, of whom I descried not a few, were still more easily recognisable. They wore every variety of dress, from that of the desperate thimble-rig bully, with velvet waistcoat, fancy neckerchief, gilt chains, and filagreed buttons, to that of the scrupulously inornate clergyman, than which nothing could be less liable to suspicion. Still all were distinguished by a certain sodden swarthiness of complexion, a filmy dimness of eye, and pallor and compression of lip. There were two other traits, moreover, by which I could always detect them;—a guarded lowness of tone in conversation, and a more than ordinary extension of the thumb in a direction at right angles with the fingers.—Very often, in company with these sharpers, I observed an order of men somewhat different in habits, but still birds of a kindred feather. They may be defined as the gentlemen who live by their wits. They seem to prey upon the public in two battalions—that of the dandies and that of the military men. Of the first grade the leading features are long locks and smiles; of the second frogged coats and frowns.

Descending in the scale of what is termed gentility, I found darker and deeper themes for speculation. I saw Jew pedlars, with hawk eyes flashing from countenances whose every other feature wore only an expression of abject humility; sturdy professional street beggars scowling upon mendicants of a better stamp, whom despair alone had driven forth into the night for charity; feeble and ghastly invalids, upon whom death had placed a sure hand, and who sidled and tottered through the mob, looking every one beseechingly in the face, as if in search of some chance consolation, some lost hope; modest young girls returning from long and late labor to a cheerless home, and shrinking more tearfully than indignantly from the glances of ruffians, whose direct contact, even, could not be avoided; women of the town of all kinds and of all ages—the unequivocal beauty in the prime of her womanhood, putting one in mind of the statue in Lucian,[6] with the surface of Parian marble, and the interior filled with filth—the loathsome and utterly lost leper in rags—the wrinkled, bejewelled and paint-begrimed beldame, making a last effort at youth—the mere child of immature form, yet, from long association, an adept in the dreadful coquetries of her trade, and burning with a rabid ambition to be ranked the equal of her elders in vice; drunkards innumerable and indescribable—some in shreds and patches, reeling, inarticulate, with bruised visage and lack-lustre eyes—some in whole although filthy garments, with a slightly unsteady swagger, thick sensual lips, and hearty-looking rubicund faces—others clothed in materials which had once been good, and which even now were scrupulously well brushed—men who walked with a more than naturally firm and springy step, but whose countenances were fearfully pale, whose eyes hideously wild and red, and who clutched with quivering fingers, as they strode through the crowd, at every object which came within their reach; beside these, pie-men, porters, coal-heavers, sweeps; organ-grinders, monkey-exhibiters and ballad mongers, those who vended with those who sang; ragged artizans and exhausted laborers of every description, and all full of a noisy and inordinate vivacity which jarred discordantly upon the ear, and gave an aching sensation to the eye.

As the night deepened, so deepened to me the interest of the scene; for not only did the general character of the crowd materially alter (its gentler features retiring in the gradual withdrawal of the more orderly portion of the people, and its harsher ones coming out into bolder relief, as the late hour brought forth every species of infamy from its den,) but the rays of the gas-lamps, feeble at first in their struggle with the dying day, had now at length gained ascendancy, and threw over every thing a fitful and garish lustre. All was dark yet splendid—as that ebony to which has been likened the style of Tertullian.[7]

The wild effects of the light enchained me to an examination of individual faces; and although the rapidity with which the world of light flitted before the window, prevented me from casting more than a glance upon each visage, still it seemed that, in my then peculiar mental state, I could frequently read, even in that brief interval of a glance, the history of long years.

With my brow to the glass, I was thus occupied in scrutinizing the mob, when suddenly there came into view a countenance (that of a decrepid old man, some sixty-five or seventy years of age,)—a countenance which at once arrested and absorbed my whole attention, on account of the absolute idiosyncracy of its expression. Any thing even remotely resembling that expression I had never seen before. I well remember that my first thought, upon beholding it, was that Retzch,[8] had he viewed it, would have greatly preferred it to his own pictural incarnations of the fiend. As I endeavored, during the brief minute of my original survey, to form some analysis of the meaning conveyed, there arose confusedly and paradoxically within my mind, the ideas of vast mental power, of caution, of penuriousness, of avarice, of coolness, of malice, of blood-thirstiness, of triumph, of merriment, of excessive terror, of intense—of supreme despair. I felt singularly aroused, startled, fascinated. "How wild a history," I said to myself, "is written within that bosom!" Then came a craving desire to keep the man in view—to know more of him. Hurriedly putting on an overcoat, and seizing my hat and cane, I made my way into the street, and pushed through the crowd in the direction which I had seen him take; for he had already disappeared. With some little difficulty I at length came within sight of him, approached, and followed him closely, yet cautiously, so as not to attract his attention.

I had now a good opportunity of examining his person. He was short in stature, very thin, and apparently very feeble. His clothes, generally, were filthy and ragged; but as he came, now and then, within the strong glare of a lamp, I perceived that his linen, although dirty, was of beautiful texture; and my vision deceived me, or, through a rent in a closely-buttoned and evidently second-handed *roquelaire*[9] which enveloped him, I caught a glimpse both of a diamond and of a dagger. These observations heightened my curiosity, and I resolved to follow the stranger whithersoever he should go.

It was now fully night-fall, and a thick humid fog hung over the city, soon ending in a settled and heavy rain. This change of weather had an odd effect upon the crowd, the whole of which was at once put into new commotion, and overshadowed by a world of umbrellas. The waver, the jostle, and the hum increased in a tenfold degree. For my own part I did not much regard the rain—the lurking of an old fever in my system rendering the moisture somewhat too dangerously pleasant. Tying a handkerchief about my mouth, I kept on. For half an hour the old man held his way with difficulty along the great thoroughfare; and I here walked close at his elbow through fear of losing sight of him. Never once turning his head to look back, he did not observe me. By and bye he passed into a cross street, which, although densely filled with people, was not quite so much thronged as the main one he had quitted. Here a change in his demeanor became evident. He walked more slowly and with less object than before—more hesitatingly. He crossed and re-crossed the way repeatedly without apparent aim; and the press was still so thick that, at every such movement, I was obliged to follow him closely. The street was a narrow and long one, and his course lay within it for nearly an hour, during which the passengers had gradually diminished to about that number which is ordinarily seen at noon in Broadway near the Park—so vast a difference is there between a London populace and that of the most frequented American city. A second turn brought us into a square, brilliantly lighted, and overflowing with life. The old manner of the stranger re-appeared. His chin fell upon his breast, while his eyes rolled wildly from under his knit brows, in every direction, upon those who hemmed him in. He urged his way steadily and perseveringly. I was surprised, however, to find, upon his having made the circuit of the square, that he turned and retraced his steps. Still more was I astonished to see him repeat the same walk several times—once nearly detecting me as he came round with a sudden movement.

In this exercise he spent another hour, at the end of which we met with far less interruption from passengers than at first. The rain fell fast; the air grew cool; and the people were retiring to their homes. With a gesture of impatience, the wanderer passed into a bye-street comparatively deserted. Down this, some quarter of a mile long, he rushed with an activity I could not have dreamed of seeing in one so aged, and which put me to much trouble in pursuit. A few minutes brought us to a large and busy bazaar, with the localities of which the stranger appeared well acquainted, and where his original demeanor again became apparent, as he forced his way to and fro, without aim, among the host of buyers and sellers.

During the hour and a half, or thereabouts, which we passed in this place, it required much caution on my part to keep him within reach without attracting his observation. Luckily I wore a pair of caoutchouc[10] over-shoes, and could move about in perfect silence. At no moment did he see that I watched him. He entered shop after shop, priced nothing, spoke no word, and looked at all objects with a wild and vacant stare. I was now utterly amazed at his behaviour, and firmly resolved that we should not part until I had satisfied myself in some measure respecting him.

A loud-toned clock struck eleven, and the company were fast deserting the bazaar. A shop-keeper, in putting up a shutter, jostled the old man, and at the instant I saw a strong shudder come over his frame. He hurried into the street, looked anxiously around him for an instant, and then ran with incredible swiftness through many crooked and people-less lanes, until we emerged once more upon the great thoroughfare whence we had started—the street of the D—— Hotel. It no longer wore, however, the same aspect. It was still brilliant with gas; but the rain fell fiercely, and there were few persons to be seen. The stranger grew pale. He walked moodily some paces up the once populous avenue, then, with a heavy sigh, turned in the direction of the river, and, plunging through a great variety of devious ways, came out, at length, in view of one of the principal theatres. It was about being closed, and the audience were thronging from the doors. I saw the old man gasp as if for breath while he threw himself amid the crowd; but I thought that the intense agony of his countenance had, in some measure, abated. His head again fell upon his breast; he appeared as I had seen him at first. I observed that he now took the course in which had gone the greater number of the audience—but, upon the whole, I was at a loss to comprehend the waywardness of his actions.

As he proceeded, the company grew more scattered, and his old uneasiness and vacillation were resumed. For some time he followed closely a party of some ten or twelve roisterers; but from this number one by one dropped off, until three only remained together, in a narrow and gloomy lane little frequented. The stranger paused, and, for a moment, seemed lost in thought; then, with every mark of agitation, pursued rapidly a route which brought us to the verge of the city, amid regions very different from those we had hitherto traversed. It was the most noisome quarter of London, where every thing wore the worst impress of the most deplorable poverty, and of the most desperate crime. By the dim light of an accidental lamp, tall, antique, worm-eaten, wooden tenements were seen tottering to their fall, in directions so many and capricious that scarce the semblance of a passage was discernible between them. The paving-stones lay at random, displaced from their beds by the rankly-growing grass. Horrible filth festered in the dammed-up gutters.

The whole atmosphere teemed with desolation. Yet, as we proceeded, the sounds of human life revived by sure degrees, and at length large bands of the most abandoned of a London populace were seen reeling to and fro. The spirits of the old man again flickered up, as a lamp which is near its death-hour. Once more he strode onward with elastic tread. Suddenly a corner was turned, a blaze of light burst upon our sight, and we stood before one of the huge suburban temples of Intemperance—one of the palaces of the fiend, Gin.

It was now nearly day-break; but a number of wretched inebriates still pressed in and out of the flaunting entrance. With a half shriek of joy the old man forced a passage within, resumed at once his original bearing, and stalked backward and forward, without apparent object, among the throng. He had not been thus long occupied, however, before a rush to the doors gave token that the host was closing them for the night. It was something even more intense than despair that I then observed upon the countenance of the singular being whom I had watched so pertinaciously. Yet he did not hesitate in his career, but, with a mad energy, retraced his steps at once, to the heart of the mighty London. Long and swiftly he fled, while I followed him in the wildest amazement, resolute not to abandon a scrutiny in which I now felt an interest all-absorbing. The sun arose while we proceeded, and, when we had once again reached that most thronged mart of the populous town, the street of the D—— Hotel, it presented an appearance of human bustle and activity scarcely inferior to what I had seen on the evening before. And here, long, amid the momently increasing confusion, did I persist in my pursuit of the stranger. But, as usual, he walked to and fro, and during the day did not pass from out the turmoil of that street. And, as the shades of the second evening came on, I grew wearied unto death, and, stopping fully in front of the wanderer, gazed at him steadfastly in the face. He noticed me not, but resumed his solemn walk, while I, ceasing to follow, remained absorbed in contemplation. "This old man," I said at length, "is the type and the genius of deep crime. He refuses to be alone. *He is the man of the crowd.* It will be in vain to follow; for I shall learn no more of him, nor of his deeds. The worst heart of the world is a grosser book than the 'Hortulus Animæ,'[11] and perhaps it is but one of the great mercies of God that *'er lasst sich nicht lesen.'*"

The Murders in the Rue Morgue[1]

What song the Syrens sang, or what name Achilles assumed when he hid himself among women, although puzzling questions, are not beyond *all* conjecture.

Sir Thomas Browne[2]

THE mental features discoursed of as the analytical, are, in themselves, but little susceptible of analysis. We appreciate them only in their effects. We know of them, among other things, that they are always to their possessor, when inordinately possessed, a source of the liveliest enjoyment. As the strong man exults in his physical ability, delighting in such exercises as call his muscles into action, so glories the analyst in that moral activity which *disentangles.* He derives pleasure from even the most trivial occupations bringing his talent into play. He is fond of enigmas, of conundrums, of hieroglyphics; exhibiting in his solutions of each a degree of *acumen* which appears to the ordinary apprehension præternatural. His results, brought about by the very soul and essence of method, have, in truth, the whole air of intuition.

The faculty of re-solution is possibly much invigorated by mathematical study, and especially by that highest branch of it which, unjustly, and merely on account of its retrograde operations, has been called, as if *par excellence*, analysis. Yet to calculate is not in itself to analyse. A chess-player, for example, does the one without effort at the other. It follows that the game of chess, in its effects upon mental character, is greatly misunderstood. I am not now writing a treatise, but simply prefacing a somewhat peculiar narrative by observations very much at random; I will, therefore, take occasion to assert that the higher powers of the reflective intellect are more decidedly and more usefully tasked by the unostentatious game of draughts than by all the elaborate frivolity of chess. In this latter, where the pieces have different and *bizarre* motions, with various and variable values, what is only complex is mistaken (a not unusual error) for what is profound. The *attention* is here called powerfully into play. If it flag for an instant, an oversight is committed, resulting in injury or defeat. The possible moves being not only manifold but involute, the chances of such oversights are multiplied; and in nine cases out of ten it is the more concentrative rather than the more acute player who conquers. In draughts, on the contrary, where the moves are *unique* and have but little variation, the probabilities of inadvertence are diminished, and the mere attention being left comparatively unemployed, what advantages are obtained by either party are obtained by superior *acumen*. To be less abstract—Let us suppose a game of draughts where the pieces are reduced to four kings, and where, of course, no oversight is to be expected. It is obvious that here the victory can be decided (the players being at all equal) only by some *recherché*[3] movement, the result of some strong exertion of the intellect. Deprived of ordinary resources, the analyst throws himself into the spirit of his opponent, identifies himself therewith, and not unfrequently sees thus, at a glance, the sole methods (sometimes indeed absurdly simple ones) by which he may seduce into error or hurry into miscalculation.

Whist has long been noted for its influence upon what is termed the calculating power; and men of the highest order of intellect have been known to take an apparently unaccountable delight in it, while eschewing chess as frivolous. Beyond doubt there is nothing of a similar nature so greatly tasking the faculty of analysis. The best chess-player in Christendom *may* be little more than the best player of chess; but proficiency in whist implies capacity for success in all those more important undertakings where mind struggles with mind. When I say proficiency, I mean that perfection in the game which includes a comprehension of *all* the sources whence legitimate advantage may be derived. These are not only manifold but multiform, and lie frequently among recesses of thought altogether inaccessible to the ordinary understanding. To observe attentively is to remember distinctly; and, so far, the concentrative chess-player will do very well at whist; while the rules of Hoyle[4] (themselves based upon the mere mechanism of the game) are sufficiently and generally comprehensible. Thus to have a retentive memory, and to proceed by "the book," are points commonly regarded as the sum total of good playing. But it is in matters beyond the limits of mere rule that the skill of the analyst is evinced. He makes, in silence, a host of observations and inferences. So, perhaps, do his companions; and the difference in the extent of the information obtained, lies not so much in the validity of the inference as in the quality of the observation. The necessary knowledge is that of *what* to observe. Our player confines himself not at all; nor, because the game is the object, does he reject deductions from things external to the game. He examines the countenance of his partner, comparing it carefully with that of each of his opponents. He considers the mode of assorting the cards in each hand; often counting trump by trump, and honor by honor, through the glances bestowed by their holders upon each. He notes every variation of face as the play progresses, gathering a fund of thought from the differences in the expression of certainty, of surprise, of triumph, or of chagrin. From the manner of gathering up a trick he judges whether the person taking it can make another in the suit. He recognises what is played through feint, by the air with which it is thrown upon the table. A casual or inadvertent word; the accidental dropping or turning of a card, with the accompanying anxiety or carelessness in regard to its concealment; the counting of the tricks, with the order of their arrangement; embarrassment, hesitation, eagerness or trepidation—all afford, to his apparently intuitive perception, indications of the true state of affairs. The first two or three rounds having been played, he is in full possession of the contents of each hand, and thenceforward puts down his cards with as absolute a precision of purpose as if the rest of the party had turned outward the faces of their own.

The analytical power should not be confounded with simple ingenuity; for while the analyst is necessarily ingenious, the ingenious man is often remarkably incapable of analysis. The constructive or combining power, by which ingenuity is usually manifested, and to which the phrenologists (I believe erroneously) have assigned a separate organ,[5] supposing it a primitive faculty, has been so frequently seen in those whose intellect bordered otherwise upon idiocy, as to have attracted general observation among writers on morals. Between ingenuity and the analytic ability there exists a difference far greater, indeed, than that between the fancy and the imagination, but of a character very strictly analogous. It will be found, in fact, that the ingenious are always fanciful, and the *truly* imaginative never otherwise than analytic.

The narrative which follows will appear to the reader somewhat in the light of a commentary upon the propositions just advanced.

Residing in Paris during the spring and part of the summer of 18—, I there became acquainted with a Monsieur C. Auguste Dupin. This young gentleman was of an excellent—indeed of an illustrious family, but, by a variety of untoward events, had been reduced to such poverty that the energy of his character succumbed beneath it, and he ceased to bestir himself in the world, or to care for the retrieval of his fortunes. By courtesy of his creditors, there still remained in his possession a small remnant of his patrimony; and, upon the income arising from this, he managed, by means of a rigorous economy, to procure the necessaries of life, without troubling himself about its superfluities. Books, indeed, were his sole luxuries, and in Paris these are easily obtained.

Our first meeting was at an obscure library in the Rue Montmartre, where the accident of our both being in search of the same very rare and very remarkable volume, brought us into closer communion. We saw each other again and again. I was deeply interested in the little family history which he detailed to me with all that candor which a Frenchman indulges whenever mere self is his theme. I was astonished, too, at the vast extent of his reading; and, above all, I felt my soul enkindled within me by the wild fervor, and the vivid freshness of his imagination. Seeking in Paris the objects I then sought, I felt that the society of such a man would be to me a treasure beyond price; and this feeling I frankly confided to him. It was at length arranged that we should live together during my stay in the city; and as my worldly circumstances were somewhat less embarrassed than his own, I was permitted to be at the expense of renting, and furnishing in a style which suited the rather fantastic gloom of our common temper, a time-eaten and grotesque mansion, long deserted through superstitions into which we did not inquire, and tottering to its fall in a retired and desolate portion of the Faubourg St. Germain.

Had the routine of our life at this place been known to the world, we should have been regarded as madmen—although, perhaps, as madmen of a harmless nature. Our seclusion was perfect. We admitted no visitors. Indeed the locality of our retirement had been carefully kept a secret from my own former associates; and it had been many years since Dupin had ceased to know or be known in Paris. We existed within ourselves alone.

It was a freak of fancy in my friend (for what else shall I call it?) to be enamored of the Night for her own sake; and into this *bizarrerie*, as into all his others, I quietly fell; giving myself up to his wild whims with a perfect *abandon*. The sable divinity would not herself dwell with us always; but we could counterfeit her presence. At the first dawn of the morning we closed all the massy shutters of our old building; lighting a couple of tapers which, strongly perfumed, threw out only the ghastliest and feeblest of rays. By the aid of these we then busied our souls in dreams—reading, writing, or conversing, until warned by the clock of the advent of the true Darkness. Then we sallied forth into the streets, arm in arm, continuing the topics of the day, or roaming far and wide until a late hour, seeking, amid the wild lights and shadows of the populous city, that infinity of mental excitement which quiet observation can afford.

At such times I could not help remarking and admiring (although from his rich ideality I had been prepared to expect it) a peculiar analytic ability in Dupin. He seemed, too, to take an eager delight in its exercise—if not exactly in its display— and did not hesitate to confess the pleasure thus derived. He boasted to me, with a low chuckling laugh, that most men, in respect to himself, wore windows in their bosoms, and was wont to follow up such assertions by direct and very startling proofs of his intimate knowledge of my own. His manner at these moments was frigid and abstract; his eyes were vacant in expression; while his voice, usually a rich tenor, rose into a treble which would have sounded petulantly but for the deliberateness and entire distinctness of the enunciation. Observing him in these moods, I often dwelt meditatively upon the old philosophy of the Bi-Part Soul, and amused myself with the fancy of a double Dupin—the creative and the resolvent.

Let it not be supposed, from what I have just said, that I am detailing any mystery, or penning any romance. What I have described in the Frenchman, was merely the result of an excited, or perhaps of a diseased intelligence. But of the character of his remarks at the period in question an example will best convey the idea.

We were strolling one night down a long dirty street, in the vicinity of the Palais Royal. Being both, apparently, occupied with thought, neither of us had spoken a syllable for fifteen minutes at least. All at once Dupin broke forth with these words:

"He is a very little fellow, that's true, and would do better for the *Théâtre des Variétés.*"

"There can be no doubt of that," I replied unwittingly, and not at first observing (so much had I been absorbed in reflection) the extraordinary manner in which the speaker had chimed in with my meditations. In an instant afterward I recollected myself, and my astonishment was profound.

"Dupin," said I, gravely, "this is beyond my comprehension. I do not hesitate to say that I am amazed, and can scarcely credit my senses. How was it possible you should know I was thinking of ——?" Here I paused, to ascertain beyond a doubt whether he really knew of whom I thought.

—— "of Chantilly," said he, "why do you pause? You were remarking to yourself that his diminutive figure unfitted him for tragedy."

This was precisely what had formed the subject of my reflections. Chantilly was a *quondam*[6] cobbler of the Rue St. Denis, who, becoming stage-mad, had attempted the *role* of Xerxes, in Crébillon's tragedy so called, and been notoriously Pasquinaded[7] for his pains.

"Tell me, for Heaven's sake," I exclaimed, "the method—if method there is—by which you have been enabled to fathom my soul in this matter." In fact I was even more startled than I would have been willing to express.

"It was the fruiterer," replied my friend, "who brought you to the conclusion that the mender of soles was not of sufficient height for Xerxes *et id genus omne.*"[8]

"The fruiterer!—you astonish me—I know no fruiterer whomsoever."

"The man who ran up against you as we entered the street—it may have been fifteen minutes ago."

I now remembered that, in fact, a fruiterer, carrying upon his head a large basket of apples, had nearly thrown me down, by accident, as we passed from the Rue C—— into the thoroughfare where we stood; but what this had to do with Chantilly I could not possibly understand.

There was not a particle of *charlatânerie* about Dupin. "I will explain," he said, "and that you may comprehend all clearly, we will first retrace the course of your meditations, from the moment in which I spoke to you until that of the *rencontre* with the fruiterer in question. The larger links of the chain run thus—Chantilly, Orion, Dr. Nichols, Epicurus, Stereotomy, the street stones, the fruiterer."

There are few persons who have not, at some period of their lives, amused themselves in retracing the steps by which particular conclusions of their own minds have been attained. The occupation is often full of interest; and he who attempts it for the first time is astonished by the apparently illimitable distance and incoherence between the starting-point and the goal. What, then, must have been my amazement when I heard the Frenchman speak what he had just spoken, and when I could not help acknowledging that he had spoken the truth. He continued:

"We had been talking of horses, if I remember aright, just before leaving the Rue C——. This was the last subject we discussed. As we crossed into this street, a fruiterer, with a large basket upon his head, brushing quickly past us, thrust you upon a pile of paving-stones collected at a spot where the causeway is undergoing repair. You stepped upon one of the loose fragments, slipped, slightly strained your ankle, appeared vexed or sulky, muttered a few words, turned to look at the pile, and then proceeded in silence. I was not particularly attentive to what you did; but observation has become with me, of late, a species of necessity.

"You kept your eyes upon the ground—glancing, with a petulant expression, at the holes and ruts in the pavement, (so that I saw you were still thinking of the stones,) until we reached the little alley called Lamartine, which has been paved, by way of experiment, with the overlapping and riveted blocks. Here your countenance brightened up, and perceiving your lips move, I could not doubt that you murmured the word 'stereotomy,' a term very affectedly applied to this species of pavement. I knew that you could not say to yourself 'stereotomy' without being brought to think of atomies, and thus of the theories of Epicurus; and since, when we discussed this subject not very long ago, I mentioned to you how singularly, yet with how little notice, the vague guesses of that noble Greek had met with confirmation in the late nebular cosmogony, I felt that you could not avoid casting your eyes upward to the great *nebula* in Orion, and I certainly expected that you would do so. You did look up; and I was now assured that I had correctly followed your steps. But in that bitter *tirade* upon Chantilly, which appeared in yesterday's '*Musée*,' the satirist, making some disgraceful allusions to the cobbler's change of name upon assuming the buskin, quoted a Latin line about which we have often conversed. I mean the line

Perdidit antiquum litera prima sonum[9]

I had told you that this was in reference to Orion, formerly written Urion; and, from certain pungencies connected with this explanation, I was aware that you could not have forgotten it. It was clear, therefore, that you would not fail to combine the two ideas of Orion and Chantilly. That you did combine them I saw by the character of the smile which passed over your lips. You thought of the poor cobbler's immolation. So far, you had been stooping in your gait; but now I saw you draw yourself up to your full height. I was then sure that you reflected upon the diminutive figure of Chantilly. At this point I interrupted your meditations to remark that as, in fact, he *was* a very little fellow—that Chantilly—he would do better at the *Théâtre des Variétés*."

Not long after this, we were looking over an evening edition of the "Gazette des Tribunaux," when the following paragraphs arrested our attention.

"EXTRAORDINARY MURDERS.—This morning, about three o'clock, the inhabitants of the Quartier St. Roch were aroused from sleep by a succession of terrific shrieks, issuing, apparently, from the fourth story of a house in the Rue Morgue, known to be in the sole occupancy of one Madame L'Espanaye, and her daughter, Mademoiselle Camille L'Espanaye. After some delay, occasioned by a fruitless attempt to procure admission in the usual manner, the gateway was broken in with a crowbar, and eight or ten of the neighbors entered, accompanied by two *gendarmes*. By this time the cries had ceased; but, as the party rushed up the first flight of stairs, two or more rough voices, in angry contention, were distinguished, and seemed to proceed from the upper part of the house. As the second landing was reached, these sounds, also, had ceased, and everything remained perfectly quiet.

The party spread themselves, and hurried from room to room. Upon arriving at a large back chamber in the fourth story, (the door of which, being found locked, with the key inside, was forced open,) a spectacle presented itself which struck every one present not less with horror than with astonishment.

"The apartment was in the wildest disorder—the furniture broken and thrown about in all directions. There was only one bedstead; and from this the bed had been removed, and thrown into the middle of the floor. On a chair lay a razor, besmeared with blood. On the hearth were two or three long and thick tresses of grey human hair, also dabbled in blood, and seeming to have been pulled out by the roots. Upon the floor were found four Napoleons, an ear-ring of topaz, three large silver spoons, three smaller of *metal d'Alger*,[10] and two bags, containing nearly four thousand francs in gold. The drawers of a *bureau*, which stood in one corner, were open, and had been, apparently, rifled, although many articles still remained in them. A small iron safe was discovered under the *bed* (not under the bedstead). It was open, with the key still in the door. It had no contents beyond a few old letters, and other papers of little consequence.

"Of Madame L'Espanaye no traces were here seen; but an unusual quantity of soot being observed in the fire-place, a search was made in the chimney, and (horrible to relate!) the corpse of the daughter, head downward, was dragged therefrom; it having been thus forced up the narrow aperture for a considerable distance. The body was quite warm. Upon examining it, many excoriations were perceived, no doubt occasioned by the violence with which it had been thrust up and disengaged. Upon the face were many severe scratches, and, upon the throat, dark bruises, and deep indentations of finger nails, as if the deceased had been throttled to death.

"After a thorough investigation of every portion of the house, without farther discovery, the party made its way into a small paved yard in the rear of the building, where lay the corpse of the old lady, with her throat so entirely cut that, upon an attempt to raise her, the head fell off. The body, as well as the head, was fearfully mutilated—the former so much so as scarcely to retain any semblance of humanity.

"To this horrible mystery there is not as yet, we believe, the slightest clew."

The next day's paper had these additional particulars.

"*The Tragedy in the Rue Morgue.* Many individuals have been examined in relation to this most extraordinary and frightful affair." [The word '*affaire*' has not yet, in France, that levity of import which it conveys with us,] "but nothing whatever has transpired to throw light upon it. We give below all the material testimony elicited.

"*Pauline Dubourg*, laundress, deposes that she has known both the deceased for three years, having washed for them during that period. The old lady and her daughter seemed on good terms—very affectionate towards each other. They were excellent pay. Could not speak in regard to their mode or means of living. Believed that Madame L. told fortunes for a living. Was reputed to have money put by. Never met any persons in the house when she called for the clothes or took them home. Was sure that they had no servant in employ. There appeared to be no furniture in any part of the building except in the fourth story.

"*Pierre Moreau*, tobacconist, deposes that he has been in the habit of selling small quantities of tobacco and snuff to Madame L'Espanaye for nearly four years. Was born in the neighborhood, and has always resided there. The deceased and her daughter had occupied the house in which the corpses were found, for more than six years. It was formerly occupied by a jeweller, who under-let the upper rooms to various persons. The house was the property of Madame L. She became dissatisfied with the abuse of the premises by her tenant, and moved into them herself, refusing to let any portion. The old lady was childish. Witness had seen the daughter some five or six times during the six years. The two lived an exceedingly retired life—were reputed to have money. Had heard it said among the neighbors that Madame L. told fortunes—did not believe it. Had never seen any person enter the door except the old lady and her daughter, a porter once or twice, and a physician some eight or ten times.

"Many other persons, neighbors, gave evidence to the same effect. No one was spoken of as frequenting the house. It was not known whether there were any living connexions of Madame L. and her daughter. The shutters of the front windows were seldom opened. Those in the rear were always closed, with the exception of the large back room, fourth story. The house was a good house—not very old.

"*Isidore Musèt, gendarme*, deposes that he was called to the house about three o'clock in the morning, and found some twenty or thirty persons at the gateway, endeavoring to gain admittance. Forced it open, at length, with a bayonet—not with a crowbar. Had but little difficulty in getting it open, on account of its being a double or folding gate, and bolted neither at bottom nor top. The shrieks were continued until the gate was forced—and then suddenly ceased. They seemed to be screams of some person (or persons) in great agony—were loud and drawn out, not short and quick. Witness led the way up stairs. Upon reaching the first landing, heard two voices in loud and angry contention—the one a gruff voice, the other much shriller—a very strange voice. Could distinguish some words of the former, which was that of a Frenchman. Was positive that it was not a woman's voice. Could distinguish the words '*sacré*' and '*diable.*' The shrill voice was that of a foreigner. Could not be sure whether it was the voice of a man or of a woman. Could not make out what was said, but believed the language to be Spanish. The state of the room and of the bodies was described by this witness as we described them yesterday.

"*Henri Duval*, a neighbor, and by trade a silver-smith, deposes that he was one of the party who first entered the house. Corroborates the testimony of Musèt in general. As soon as they forced an entrance, they reclosed the door, to keep out the crowd, which collected very fast, notwithstanding the lateness of the hour. The shrill voice, this witness thinks, was that of an Italian. Was certain it was not French. Could not be sure that it was a man's voice. It might have been a woman's. Was not acquainted with the Italian language. Could not distinguish the words, but was convinced by the intonation that the speaker was an Italian. Knew Madame L. and her daughter. Had conversed with both frequently. Was sure that the shrill voice was not that of either of the deceased.

"—— *Odenheimer, restaurateur*. This witness volunteered his testimony. Not speaking French, was examined through an interpreter. Is a native of Amsterdam. Was passing the house at the time of the shrieks. They lasted for several minutes—probably ten. They were long and loud—very awful and distressing. Was one of those who entered the building. Corroborated the previous evidence in every respect but one. Was sure that the shrill voice was that of a man—of a Frenchman. Could not distinguish the words uttered. They were loud and quick—unequal—spoken apparently in fear as well as in anger. The voice was harsh—not so much shrill as harsh. Could not call it a shrill voice. The gruff voice said repeatedly '*sacré*,' '*diable*,' and once '*mon Dieu*.'

"*Jules Mignaud*, banker, of the firm of Mignaud et Fils, Rue Deloraine. Is the elder Mignaud. Madame L'Espanaye had some property. Had opened an account with his banking house in the spring of the year —— (eight years previously). Made frequent deposits in small sums. Had checked for nothing until the third day before her death, when she took out in person the sum of 4000 francs. This sum was paid in gold, and a clerk sent home with the money.

"*Adolphe Le Bon*, clerk to Mignaud et Fils, deposes that on the day in question, about noon, he accompanied Madame L'Espanaye to her residence with the 4000 francs, put up in two bags. Upon the door being opened, Mademoiselle L. appeared and took from his hands one of the bags, while the old lady relieved him of the other. He then bowed and departed. Did not see any person in the street at the time. It is a bye-street—very lonely.

"*William Bird*, tailor, deposes that he was one of the party who entered the house. Is an Englishman. Has lived in Paris two years. Was one of the first to ascend the stairs. Heard the voices in contention. The gruff voice was that of a Frenchman. Could make out several words, but cannot now remember all. Heard distinctly '*sacré*' and '*mon Dieu*.' There was a sound at the moment as if of several persons struggling—a scraping and scuffling sound. The shrill voice was very loud—louder than the gruff one. Is sure that it was not the voice of an Englishman. Appeared to be that of a German. Might have been a woman's voice. Does not understand German.

"Four of the above-named witnesses, being recalled, deposed that the door of the chamber in which was found the body of Mademoiselle L. was locked on the inside when the party reached it. Every thing was perfectly silent—no groans or noises of any kind. Upon forcing the door no person was seen. The windows, both of the back and front room, were down and firmly fastened from within. A door between the two rooms was closed, but not locked. The door leading from the front room into the passage was locked, with the key on the inside. A small room in the front of the house, on the fourth story, at the head of the passage, was open, the door being ajar. The room was crowded with old beds, boxes, and so forth. These were carefully removed and searched. There was not an inch of any portion of the house which was not carefully searched. Sweeps were sent up and down the chimneys. The house was a four story one, with garrets (*mansardes*.) A trap-door on the roof was nailed down very securely—did not appear to have been opened for years. The time elapsing between the hearing of the voices in contention and the breaking open of the room door, was variously stated by the witnesses. Some made it as short as three minutes—some as long as five. The door was opened with difficulty.

"*Alfonzo Garcio*, undertaker, deposes that he resides in the Rue Morgue. Is a native of Spain. Was one of the party who entered the house. Did not proceed up stairs. Is nervous, and was apprehensive of the consequences of agitation. Heard the voices in contention. The gruff voice was that of a Frenchman. Could not distinguish what was said. The shrill voice was that of an Englishman—is sure of this. Does not understand the English language, but judges by the intonation.

"*Alberto Montani*, confectioner, deposes that he was among the first to ascend the stairs. Heard the voices in question. The gruff voice was that of a Frenchman. Distinguished several words. The speaker appeared to be expostulating. Could not make out the words of the shrill voice. Spoke quick and unevenly. Thinks it the voice of a Russian. Corroborates the general testimony. Is an Italian. Never conversed with a native of Russia.

"Several witnesses, recalled, here testified that the chimneys of all the rooms on the fourth story were too narrow to admit the passage of a human being. By 'sweeps' were meant cylindrical sweeping-brushes, such as are employed by those who clean chimneys. These brushes were passed up and down every flue in the house. There is no back passage by which any one could have descended while the party proceeded up stairs. The body of Mademoiselle L'Espanaye was so firmly wedged in the chimney that it could not be got down until four or five of the party united their strength.

"*Paul Dumas*, physician, deposes that he was called to view the bodies about day-break. They were both then lying on the sacking of the bedstead in the chamber where Mademoiselle L. was found. The corpse of the young lady was much bruised and excoriated. The fact that it had been thrust up the chimney would sufficiently account for these appearances. The throat was greatly chafed. There were several deep scratches just below the chin, together with a series of livid spots which were evidently the impression of fingers. The face was fearfully discolored, and the eye-balls protruded. The tongue had been partially bitten through. A large bruise was discovered upon the pit of the stomach, produced, apparently, by the pressure of a knee. In the opinion of M. Dumas, Mademoiselle L'Espanaye had been throttled to death by some person or persons unknown. The corpse of the mother was horribly mutilated. All the bones of the right leg and arm were more or less shattered. The left *tibia* much splintered, as well as all the ribs of the left side. Whole body dreadfully bruised and discolored. It was not possible to say how the injuries had been inflicted. A heavy club of wood, or a broad bar of iron—a chair—any large, heavy, and obtuse weapon would have produced such results, if wielded by the hands of a very powerful man. No woman could have inflicted the blows with any weapon. The head of the deceased, when seen by witness, was entirely separated from the body, and was also greatly shattered. The throat had evidently been cut with some very sharp instrument—probably with a razor.

"*Alexandre Etienne*, surgeon, was called with M. Dumas to view the bodies. Corroborated the testimony, and the opinions of M. Dumas.

"Nothing farther of importance was elicited, although several other persons were examined. A murder so mysterious, and so perplexing in all its particulars, was never before committed in Paris—if indeed a murder has been committed at all. The police are entirely at fault—an unusual occurrence in affairs of this nature. There is not, however, the shadow of a clew apparent."

The evening edition of the paper stated that the greatest excitement still continued in the Quartier St. Roch—that the premises in question had been carefully re-searched, and fresh examinations of witnesses instituted, but all to no purpose. A postscript, however, mentioned that Adolphe Le Bon had been arrested and imprisoned—although nothing appeared to criminate him, beyond the facts already detailed.

Dupin seemed singularly interested in the progress of this affair—at least so I judged from his manner, for he made no comments. It was only after the announcement that Le Bon had been imprisoned, that he asked me my opinion respecting the murders.

I could merely agree with all Paris in considering them an insoluble mystery. I saw no means by which it would be possible to trace the murderer.

"We must not judge of the means," said Dupin, "by this shell of an examination. The Parisian police, so much extolled for *acumen*, are cunning, but no more. There is no method in their proceedings, beyond the method of the moment. They make a vast parade of measures; but, not unfrequently, these are so ill adapted to the objects proposed, as to put us in mind of Monsieur Jourdain's calling for his *robe-de-chambre—pour mieux entendre la musique*.[11] The results attained by them are not unfrequently surprising, but, for the most part, are brought about by simple diligence and activity. When these qualities are unavailing, their schemes fail. Vidocq,[12] for example, was a good guesser, and a persevering man. But, without educated thought, he erred continually by the very intensity of his investigations. He impaired his vision by holding the object too close. He might see, perhaps, one or two points with unusual clearness, but in so doing he, necessarily, lost sight of the matter as a whole. Thus there is such a thing as being too profound. Truth is not always in a well. In fact, as regards the more important knowledge, I do believe that she is invariably superficial. The depth lies in the valleys where we seek her, and not upon the mountain-tops where she is found. The modes and sources of this kind of error are well typified in the contemplation of the heavenly bodies. To look at a star by glances—to view it in a side-long way, by turning toward it the exterior portions of the *retina* (more susceptible of feeble impressions of light than the interior), is to behold the star distinctly—is to have the best appreciation of its lustre—a lustre which grows dim just in proportion as we turn our vision *fully* upon it. A greater number of rays actually fall upon the eye in the latter case, but, in the former, there is the more refined capacity for comprehension. By undue profundity we perplex and enfeeble thought; and it is possible to make even Venus herself vanish from the firmament by a scrutiny too sustained, too concentrated, or too direct.

"As for these murders, let us enter into some examinations for ourselves, before we make up an opinion respecting them. An inquiry will afford us amusement," [I thought this an odd term, so applied, but said nothing] "and, besides, Le Bon once rendered me a service for which I am not ungrateful. We will go and see the premises with our own eyes. I know G——, the Prefect of Police, and shall have no difficulty in obtaining the necessary permission."

The permission was obtained, and we proceeded at once to the Rue Morgue. This is one of those miserable thoroughfares which intervene between the Rue Richelieu and the Rue St. Roch. It was late in the afternoon when we reached it; as this quarter is at a great distance from that in which we resided. The house was readily found; for there were still many persons gazing up at the closed shutters, with an objectless curiosity, from the opposite side of the way. It was an ordinary Parisian house, with a gateway, on one side of which was a glazed watch-box, with a sliding panel in the window, indicating a *loge de concierge*. Before going in we walked up the street, turned down an alley, and then, again turning, passed in the rear of the building—Dupin, meanwhile, examining the whole neighborhood, as well as the house, with a minuteness of attention for which I could see no possible object.

Retracing our steps, we came again to the front of the dwelling, rang, and, having shown our credentials, were admitted by the agents in charge. We went up stairs—into the chamber where the body of Mademoiselle L'Espanaye had been found, and where both the deceased still lay. The disorders of the room had, as usual, been suffered to exist. I saw nothing beyond what had been stated in the "Gazette des Tribunaux." Dupin scrutinized every thing—not excepting the bodies of the victims. We then went into the other rooms, and into the yard; a *gendarme* accompanying us throughout. The examination occupied us until dark, when we took our departure. On our way home my companion stepped in for a moment at the office of one of the daily papers.

I have said that the whims of my friend were manifold, and that *Je les ménageais:*—for this phrase there is no English equivalent.¹³ It was his humor, now, to decline all conversation on the subject of the murder, until about noon the next day. He then asked me, suddenly, if I had observed any thing *peculiar* at the scene of the atrocity.

There was something in his manner of emphasizing the word "peculiar," which caused me to shudder, without knowing why.

"No, nothing *peculiar*," I said; "nothing more, at least, than we both saw stated in the paper."

"The 'Gazette,'" he replied, "has not entered, I fear, into the unusual horror of the thing. But dismiss the idle opinions of this print. It appears to me that this mystery is considered insoluble, for the very reason which should cause it to be regarded as easy of solution—I mean for the *outré*¹⁴ character of its features. The police are confounded by the seeming absence of motive—not for the murder itself—but for the atrocity of the murder. They are puzzled, too, by the seeming impossibility of reconciling the voices heard in contention, with the facts that no one was discovered up stairs but the assassinated Mademoiselle L'Espanaye, and that there were no means of egress without the notice of the party ascending. The wild disorder of the room; the corpse thrust, with the head downward, up the chimney; the frightful mutilation of the body of the old lady; these considerations, with those just mentioned, and others which I need not mention, have sufficed to paralyze the powers, by putting completely at fault the boasted *acumen*, of the government agents. They have fallen into the gross but common error of confounding the unusual with the abstruse. But it is by these deviations from the plane of the ordinary, that reason feels its way, if at all, in its search for the true. In investigations such as we are now pursuing, it should not be so much asked 'what has occurred,' as 'what has occurred that has never occurred before.' In fact, the facility with which I shall arrive, or have arrived, at the solution of this mystery, is in the direct ratio of its apparent insolubility in the eyes of the police."

I stared at the speaker in mute astonishment.

"I am now awaiting," continued he, looking toward the door of our apartment—"I am now awaiting a person who, although perhaps not the perpetrator of these butcheries, must have been in some measure implicated in their perpetration. Of the worst portion of the crimes committed, it is probable that he is innocent. I hope that I am right in this supposition; for upon it I build my expectation of reading the entire riddle. I look for the man here—in this room—every moment. It is true that he may not arrive; but the probability is that he will. Should he come, it will be necessary to detain him. Here are pistols; and we both know how to use them when occasion demands their use."

I took the pistols, scarcely knowing what I did, or believing what I heard, while Dupin went on, very much as if in a soliloquy. I have already spoken of his abstract manner at such times. His discourse was addressed to myself; but his voice, although by no means loud, had that intonation which is commonly employed in speaking to some one at a great distance. His eyes, vacant in expression, regarded only the wall.

"That the voices heard in contention," he said, "by the party upon the stairs, were not the voices of the women themselves, was fully proved by the evidence. This relieves us of all doubt upon the question whether the old lady could have first destroyed the daughter, and afterward have committed suicide. I speak of this point chiefly for the sake of method; for the strength of Madame L'Espanaye would have been utterly unequal to the task of thrusting her daughter's corpse up the chimney as it was found; and the nature of the wounds upon her own person entirely preclude the idea of self-destruction. Murder, then, has been committed by some third party; and the voices of this third party were those heard in contention. Let me now advert—not to the whole testimony respecting these voices—but to what was *peculiar* in that testimony. Did you observe any thing peculiar about it?"

I remarked that, while all the witnesses agreed in supposing the gruff voice to be that of a Frenchman, there was much disagreement in regard to the shrill, or, as one individual termed it, the harsh voice.

"That was the evidence itself," said Dupin, "but it was not the peculiarity of the evidence. You have observed nothing distinctive. Yet there *was* something to be observed. The witnesses, as you remark, agreed about the gruff voice; they were here unanimous. But in regard to the shrill voice, the peculiarity is—not that they disagreed—but that, while an Italian, an Englishman, a Spaniard, a Hollander, and a Frenchman attempted to describe it, each one spoke of it as that *of a foreigner*. Each is sure that it was not the voice of one of his own countrymen. Each likens it—not to the voice of an individual of any nation with whose language he is conversant—but the converse. The Frenchman supposes it the voice of a Spaniard, and 'might have distinguished some words *had he been acquainted with the Spanish*.' The Dutchman maintains it to have been that of a Frenchman; but we find it stated that '*not understanding French this witness was examined through an interpreter*.' The Englishman thinks it the voice of a German, and '*does not understand German*.' The Spaniard 'is sure' that it was that of an Englishman, but 'judges by the intonation' altogether, '*as he has no knowledge of the English*.' The Italian believes it the voice of a Russian, but '*has never conversed with a native of Russia*.' A second Frenchman differs, moreover, with the first, and is positive that the voice was that of an Italian; but, *not being cognizant of that tongue*, is, like the Spaniard, 'convinced by the intonation.' Now, how strangely unusual must that voice have really been, about which such testimony as this *could* have been elicited!—in whose *tones*, even, denizens of the five great divisions of Europe could recognise nothing familiar! You will say that it might have been the voice of an Asiatic—of an African. Neither Asiatics nor Africans abound in Paris; but, without denying the inference, I will now merely call your attention to three points. The voice is termed by one witness 'harsh rather than shrill.' It is represented by two others to have been 'quick and *unequal*.' No words—no sounds resembling words—were by any witness mentioned as distinguishable.

"I know not," continued Dupin, "what impression I may have made, so far, upon your own understanding; but I do not hesitate to say that legitimate deductions even from this portion of the testimony—the portion respecting the gruff and shrill voices—are in themselves sufficient to engender a suspicion which should give direction to all farther progress in the investigation of the mystery. I said 'legitimate deductions;' but my meaning is not thus fully expressed. I designed to imply that the deductions are the *sole* proper ones, and that the suspicion arises *inevitably* from them as the single result. What the suspicion is, however, I will not say just yet. I merely wish you to bear in mind that, with myself, it was sufficiently forcible to give a definite form—a certain tendency—to my inquiries in the chamber.

"Let us now transport ourselves, in fancy, to this chamber. What shall we first seek here? The means of egress employed by the murderers. It is not too much to say that neither of us believe in præternatural events. Madame and Mademoiselle L'Espanaye were not destroyed by spirits. The doers of the deed were material, and escaped materially. Then how? Fortunately, there is but one mode of reasoning upon the point, and that mode *must* lead us to a definite decision.—Let us examine, each by each, the possible means of egress. It is clear that the assassins were in the room where Mademoiselle L'Espanaye was found, or at least in the room adjoining, when the party ascended the stairs. It is then only from these two apartments that we have to seek issues. The police have laid bare the floors, the ceilings, and the masonry of the walls, in every direction. No *secret* issues could have escaped their vigilance. But, not trusting to *their* eyes, I examined with my own. There were, then, *no* secret issues. Both doors leading from the rooms into the passage were securely locked, with the keys inside. Let us turn to the chimneys. These, although of ordinary width for some eight or ten feet above the hearths, will not admit, throughout their extent, the body of a large cat. The impossibility of egress, by means already stated, being thus absolute, we are reduced to the windows. Through those of the front room no one could have escaped without notice from the crowd in the street. The murderers *must* have passed, then, through those of the back room. Now, brought to this conclusion in so unequivocal a manner as we are, it is not our part, as reasoners, to reject it on account of apparent impossibilities. It is only left for us to prove that these apparent 'impossibilities' are, in reality, not such.

"There are two windows in the chamber. One of them is unobstructed by furniture, and is wholly visible. The lower portion of the other is hidden from view by the head of the unwieldy bedstead which is thrust close up against it. The former was found securely fastened from within. It resisted the utmost force of those who endeavored to raise it. A large gimlet-hole had been pierced in its frame to the left, and a very stout nail was found fitted therein, nearly to the head. Upon examining the other window, a similar nail was seen similarly fitted in it; and a vigorous attempt to raise this sash, failed also. The police were now entirely satisfied that egress had not been in these directions. And, *therefore*, it was thought a matter of supererogation to withdraw the nails and open the windows.

"My own examination was somewhat more particular, and was so for the reason I have just given—because here it was, I knew, that all apparent impossibilities *must* be proved to be not such in reality.

"I proceeded to think thus—*à posteriori*. The murderers *did* escape from one of these windows. This being so, they could not have re-fastened the sashes from the inside, as they were found fastened;—the consideration which put a stop, through its obviousness, to the scrutiny of the police in this quarter. Yet the sashes *were* fastened. They *must*, then, have the power of fastening themselves. There was no escape from this conclusion. I stepped to the unobstructed casement, withdrew the nail with some difficulty, and attempted to raise the sash. It resisted all my efforts, as I had anticipated. A concealed spring must, I now knew, exist; and this corroboration of my idea convinced me that my premises, at least, were correct, however mysterious still appeared the circumstances attending the nails. A careful search soon brought to light the hidden spring. I pressed it, and, satisfied with the discovery, forbore to upraise the sash.

"I now replaced the nail and regarded it attentively. A person passing out through this window might have reclosed it, and the spring would have caught—but the nail could not have been replaced. The conclusion was plain, and again narrowed in the field of my investigations. The assassins *must* have escaped through the other window. Supposing, then, the springs upon each sash to be the same, as was probable, there *must* be found a difference between the nails, or at least between the modes of their fixture. Getting upon the sacking of the bedstead, I looked over the head-board minutely at the second casement. Passing my hand down behind the board, I readily discovered and pressed the spring, which was, as I had supposed, identical in character with its neighbor. I now looked at the nail. It was as stout as the other, and apparently fitted in the same manner—driven in nearly up to the head.

"You will say that I was puzzled; but if you think so, you must have misunderstood the nature of the inductions. To use a sporting phrase, I had not been once 'at fault.' The scent had never for an instant been lost. There was no flaw in any link of the chain. I had traced the secret to its ultimate result,—and that result was *the nail*. It had, I say, in every respect, the appearance of its fellow in the other window; but this fact was an absolute nullity (conclusive as it might seem to be) when compared with the consideration that here, at this point, terminated the clew. 'There *must* be something wrong,' I said, 'about the nail.' I touched it; and the head, with about a quarter of an inch of the shank, came off in my fingers. The rest of the shank was in the gimlet-hole, where it had been broken off. The fracture was an old one (for its edges were incrusted with rust), and had apparently been accomplished by the blow of a hammer, which had partially imbedded, in the top of the bottom sash, the head portion of the nail. I now carefully replaced this head portion in the indentation whence I had taken it, and the resemblance to a perfect nail was complete—the fissure was invisible. Pressing the spring, I gently raised the sash for a few inches; the head went up with it, remaining firm in its bed. I closed the window, and the semblance of the whole nail was again perfect.

"The riddle, so far, was now unriddled. The assassin had escaped through the window which looked upon the bed. Dropping of its own accord upon his exit (or perhaps purposely closed), it had become fastened by the spring; and it was the retention of this spring which had been mistaken by the police for that of the nail,—farther inquiry being thus considered unnecessary.

"The next question is that of the mode of descent. Upon this point I had been satisfied in my walk with you around the building. About five feet and a half from the casement in question there runs a lightning-rod. From this rod it would have been impossible for any one to reach the window itself, to say nothing of entering it. I observed, however, that the shutters of the fourth story were of the peculiar kind called by Parisian carpenters *ferrades*—a kind rarely employed at the present day, but frequently seen upon very old mansions at Lyons and Bourdeaux. They are in the form of an ordinary door, (a single, not a folding door) except that the lower half is latticed or worked in open trellis—thus affording an excellent hold for the hands. In the present instance these shutters are fully three feet and a half broad. When we saw them from the rear of the house, they were both about half open—that is to say, they stood off at right angles from the wall. It is probable that the police, as well as myself, examined the back of the tenement; but, if so, in looking at these *ferrades* in the line of their breadth (as they must have done), they did not perceive this great breadth itself, or, at all events, failed to take it into due consideration. In fact, having once satisfied themselves that no egress could have been made in this quarter, they would naturally bestow here a very cursory examination. It was clear to me, however, that the shutter belonging to the window at the head of the bed, would, if swung fully back to the wall, reach to within two feet of the lightning-rod. It was also evident that, by exertion of a very unusual degree of activity and courage, an entrance into the window, from the rod, might have been thus effected.—By reaching to the distance of two feet and a half (we now suppose the shutter open to its whole extent) a robber might have taken a firm grasp upon the trellis-work. Letting go, then, his hold upon the rod, placing his feet securely against the wall, and springing boldly from it, he might have swung the shutter so as to close it, and, if we imagine the window open at the time, might even have swung himself into the room.

"I wish you to bear especially in mind that I have spoken of a *very* unusual degree of activity as requisite to success in so hazardous and so difficult a feat. It is my design to show you, first, that the thing might possibly have been accomplished:—but, secondly and *chiefly*, I wish to impress upon your understanding the *very extraordinary*—the almost præternatural character of that agility which could have accomplished it.

"You will say, no doubt, using the language of the law, that 'to make out my case,' I should rather undervalue, than insist upon a full estimation of the activity required in this matter. This may be the practice in law, but it is not the usage of reason. My ultimate object is only the truth. My immediate purpose is to lead you to place in juxta-position, that *very unusual* activity of which I have just spoken, with that *very peculiar* shrill (or harsh) and *unequal* voice, about whose nationality no two persons could be found to agree, and in whose utterance no syllabification could be detected."

At these words a vague and half-formed conception of the meaning of Dupin flitted over my mind. I seemed to be upon the verge of comprehension, without power to comprehend—as men, at times, find themselves upon the brink of remembrance, without being able, in the end, to remember. My friend went on with his discourse.

"You will see," he said, "that I have shifted the question from the mode of egress to that of ingress. It was my design to convey the idea that both were effected in the same manner, at the same point. Let us now revert to the interior of the room. Let us survey the appearances here. The drawers of the bureau, it is said, had been rifled, although many articles of apparel still remained within them. The conclusion here is absurd. It is a mere guess—a very silly one—and no more. How are we to know that the articles found in the drawers were not all these drawers had originally contained? Madame L'Espanaye and her daughter lived an exceedingly retired life—saw no company—seldom went out—had little use for numerous changes of habiliment. Those found were at least of as good quality as any likely to be possessed by these ladies. If a thief had taken any, why did he not take the best—why did he not take all? In a word, why did he abandon four thousand francs in gold to encumber himself with a bundle of linen? The gold *was* abandoned. Nearly the whole sum mentioned by Monsieur Mignaud, the banker, was discovered, in bags, upon the floor. I wish you, therefore, to discard from your thoughts the blundering idea of *motive*, engendered in the brains of the police by that portion of the evidence which speaks of money delivered at the door of the house. Coincidences ten times as remarkable as this (the delivery of the money, and murder committed within three days upon the party receiving it), happen to all of us every hour of our lives, without attracting even momentary notice. Coincidences, in general, are great stumbling-blocks in the way of that class of thinkers who have been educated to know nothing of the theory of probabilities—that theory to which the most glorious objects of human research are indebted for the most glorious of illustration. In the present instance, had the gold been gone, the fact of its delivery three days before would have formed something more than a coincidence. It would have been corroborative of this idea of motive. But, under the real circumstances of the case, if we are to suppose gold the motive of this outrage, we must also imagine the perpetrator so vacillating an idiot as to have abandoned his gold and his motive together.

"Keeping now steadily in mind the points to which I have drawn your attention—that peculiar voice, that unusual agility, and that startling absence of motive in a murder so singularly atrocious as this—let us glance at the butchery itself. Here is a woman strangled to death by manual strength, and thrust up a chimney, head downward. Ordinary assassins employ no such modes of murder as this. Least of all, do they thus dispose of the murdered. In the manner of thrusting the corpse up the chimney, you will admit that there was something *excessively outré*—something altogether irreconcilable with our common notions of human action, even when we suppose the actors the most depraved of men. Think, too, how great must have been that strength which could have thrust the body *up* such an aperture so forcibly that the united vigor of several persons was found barely sufficient to drag it *down!*

"Turn, now, to other indications of the employment of a vigor most marvellous. On the hearth were thick tresses—very thick tresses—of grey human hair. These had been torn out by the roots. You are aware of the great force necessary in tearing thus from the head even twenty or thirty hairs together. You saw the locks in question as well as myself. Their roots (a hideous sight!) were clotted with fragments of the flesh of the scalp—sure token of the prodigious power which had been exerted in uprooting perhaps half a million of hairs at a time. The throat of the old lady was not merely cut, but the head absolutely severed from the body: the instrument was a mere razor. I wish you also to look at the *brutal* ferocity of these deeds. Of the bruises upon the body of Madame L'Espanaye I do not speak. Monsieur Dumas, and his worthy coadjutor Monsieur Etienne, have pronounced that they were inflicted by some obtuse instrument; and so far these gentlemen are very correct. The obtuse instrument was clearly the stone pavement in the yard, upon which the victim had fallen from the window which looked in upon the bed. This idea, however simple it may now seem, escaped the police for the same reason that the breadth of the shutters escaped them—because, by the affair of the nails, their perceptions had been hermetically sealed against the possibility of the windows having ever been opened at all.

"If now, in addition to all these things, you have properly reflected upon the odd disorder of the chamber, we have gone so far as to combine the ideas of an agility astounding, a strength superhuman, a ferocity brutal, a butchery without motive, a *grotesquerie* in horror absolutely alien from humanity, and a voice foreign in tone to the ears of men of many nations, and devoid of all distinct or intelligible syllabification. What result, then, has ensued? What impression have I made upon your fancy?"

I felt a creeping of the flesh as Dupin asked me the question. "A madman," I said, "has done this deed—some raving maniac, escaped from a neighboring *Maison de Santé*."

"In some respects," he replied, "your idea is not irrelevant. But the voices of madmen, even in their wildest paroxysms, are never found to tally with that peculiar voice heard upon the stairs. Madmen are of some nation, and their language, however incoherent in its words, has always the coherence of syllabification. Besides, the hair of a madman is not such as I now hold in my hand. I disentangled this little tuft from the rigidly clutched fingers of Madame L'Espanaye. Tell me what you can make of it."

"Dupin!" I said, completely unnerved; "this hair is most unusual—this is no *human* hair."

"I have not asserted that it is," said he; "but, before we decide this point, I wish you to glance at the little sketch I have here traced upon this paper. It is a *fac-simile* drawing of what has been described in one portion of the testimony as 'dark bruises, and deep indentations of finger nails,' upon the throat of Mademoiselle L'Espanaye, and in another, (by Messrs. Dumas and Etienne,) as a 'series of livid spots, evidently the impression of fingers.'

"You will perceive," continued my friend, spreading out the paper upon the table before us, "that this drawing gives the idea of a firm and fixed hold. There is no *slipping* apparent. Each finger has retained—possibly until the death of the victim— the fearful grasp by which it originally imbedded itself. Attempt, now, to place all your fingers, at the same time, in the respective impressions as you see them."

I made the attempt in vain.

"We are possibly not giving this matter a fair trial," he said. "The paper is spread out upon a plane surface; but the human throat is cylindrical. Here is a billet of wood, the circumference of which is about that of the throat. Wrap the drawing around it, and try the experiment again."

I did so; but the difficulty was even more obvious than before. "This," I said, "is the mark of no human hand."

"Read now," replied Dupin, "this passage from Cuvier."[15]

It was a minute anatomical and generally descriptive account of the large fulvous Ourang-Outang of the East Indian Islands. The gigantic stature, the prodigious strength and activity, the wild ferocity, and the imitative propensities of these mammalia are sufficiently well known to all. I understood the full horrors of the murder at once.

"The description of the digits," said I, as I made an end of reading, "is in exact accordance with this drawing. I see that no animal but an Ourang-Outang, of the species here mentioned, could have impressed the indentations as you have traced them. This tuft of tawny hair, too, is identical in character with that of the beast of Cuvier. But I cannot possibly comprehend the particulars of this frightful mystery. Besides, there were *two* voices heard in contention, and one of them was unquestionably the voice of a Frenchman."

"True; and you will remember an expression attributed almost unanimously, by the evidence, to this voice,—the expression, '*mon Dieu!*' This, under the circumstances, has been justly characterized by one of the witnesses (Montani, the confectioner,) as an expression of remonstrance or expostulation. Upon these two words, therefore, I have mainly built my hopes of a full solution of the riddle. A Frenchman was cognizant of the murder. It is possible—indeed it is far more than probable—that he was innocent of all participation in the bloody transactions which took place. The Ourang-Outang may have escaped from him. He may have traced it to the chamber; but, under the agitating circumstances which ensued, he could never have re-captured it. It is still at large. I will not pursue these guesses—for I have no right to call them more—since the shades of reflection upon which they are based are scarcely of sufficient depth to be appreciable by my own intellect, and since I could not pretend to make them intelligible to the understanding of another. We will call them guesses then, and speak of them as such. If the Frenchman in question is indeed, as I suppose, innocent of this atrocity, this advertisement, which I left last night, upon our return home, at the office of 'Le Monde,' (a paper devoted to the shipping interest, and much sought by sailors,) will bring him to our residence."

He handed me a paper, and I read thus:

CAUGHT—*In the Bois de Boulogne, early in the morning of the —— inst., (the morning of the murder,) a very large, tawny Ourang-Outang of the Bornese species. The owner, (who is ascertained to be a sailor, belonging to a Maltese vessel,) may have the animal again, upon identifying it satisfactorily, and paying a few charges arising from its capture and keeping. Call at No. ——, Rue ——, Fauborg St. Germain—au troisième.*

"How was it possible," I asked, "that you should know the man to be a sailor, and belonging to a Maltese vessel?"

"I do *not* know it," said Dupin. "I am not *sure* of it. Here, however, is a small piece of ribbon, which from its form, and from its greasy appearance, has evidently been used in tying the hair in one of those long *queues* of which sailors are so fond. Moreover, this knot is one which few besides sailors can tie, and is peculiar to the Maltese. I picked the ribbon up at the foot of the lightning-rod. It could not have belonged to either of the deceased. Now if, after all, I am wrong in my induction from this ribbon, that the Frenchman was a sailor belonging to a Maltese vessel, still I can have done no harm in saying what I did in the advertisement. If I am in error, he will merely suppose that I have been misled by some circumstance into which he will not take the trouble to inquire. But if I am right, a great point is gained. Cognizant although innocent of the murder, the Frenchman will naturally hesitate about replying to the advertisement—about demanding the Ourang-Outang. He will reason thus:—'I am innocent; I am poor; my Ourang-Outang is of great value—to one in my circumstances a fortune of itself—why should I lose it through idle apprehensions of danger? Here it is, within my grasp. It was found in the Bois de Boulogne—at a vast distance from the scene of that butchery. How can it ever be suspected that a brute beast should have done the deed? The police are at fault—they have failed to procure the slightest clew. Should they even trace the animal, it would be impossible to prove me cognizant of the murder, or to implicate me in guilt on account of that cognizance. Above all, *I am known*. The advertiser designates me as the possessor of the beast. I am not sure to what limit his knowledge may extend. Should I avoid claiming a property of so great value, which it is known that I possess, I will render the animal at least, liable to suspicion. It is not my policy to attract attention either to myself or to the beast. I will answer the advertisement, get the Ourang-Outang, and keep it close until this matter has blown over.'"

At this moment we heard a step upon the stairs.

"Be ready," said Dupin, "with your pistols, but neither use them nor show them until at a signal from myself."

The front door of the house had been left open, and the visiter had entered, without ringing, and advanced several steps upon the staircase. Now, however, he seemed to hesitate. Presently we heard him descending. Dupin was moving quickly to the door, when we again heard him coming up. He did not turn back a second time, but stepped up with decision, and rapped at the door of our chamber.

"Come in," said Dupin, in a cheerful and hearty tone.

A man entered. He was a sailor, evidently,—a tall, stout, and muscular-looking person, with a certain dare-devil expression of countenance, not altogether unprepossessing. His face, greatly sunburnt, was more than half hidden by whisker and *mustachio*. He had with him a huge oaken cudgel, but appeared to be otherwise unarmed. He bowed awkwardly, and bade us "good evening," in French accents, which, although somewhat Neufchatelish, were still sufficiently indicative of a Parisian origin.

"Sit down, my friend," said Dupin. "I suppose you have called about the Ourang-Outang. Upon my word, I almost envy you the possession of him; a remarkably fine, and no doubt a very valuable animal. How old do you suppose him to be?"

The sailor drew a long breath, with the air of a man relieved of some intolerable burden, and then replied, in an assured tone:

"I have no way of telling—but he can't be more than four or five years old. Have you got him here?"

"Oh, no; we had no conveniences for keeping him here. He is at a livery stable in the Rue Dubourg, just by. You can get him in the morning. Of course you are prepared to identify the property?"

"To be sure I am, sir."

"I shall be sorry to part with him," said Dupin.

"I don't mean that you should be at all this trouble for nothing, sir," said the man. "Couldn't expect it. Am very willing to pay a reward for the finding of the animal— that is to say, any thing in reason."

"Well," replied my friend, "that is all very fair, to be sure. Let me think!—what should I have? Oh! I will tell you. My reward shall be this. You shall give me all the information in your power about these murders in the Rue Morgue."

Dupin said the last words in a very low tone, and very quietly. Just as quietly, too, he walked toward the door, locked it, and put the key in his pocket. He then drew a pistol from his bosom and placed it, without the least flurry, upon the table.

The sailor's face flushed up as if he were struggling with suffocation. He started to his feet and grasped his cudgel; but the next moment he fell back into his seat, trembling violently, and with the countenance of death itself. He spoke not a word. I pitied him from the bottom of my heart.

"My friend," said Dupin, in a kind tone, "you are alarming yourself unnecessarily— you are indeed. We mean you no harm whatever. I pledge you the honor of a gentleman, and of a Frenchman, that we intend you no injury. I perfectly well know that you are innocent of the atrocities in the Rue Morgue. It will not do, however, to deny that you are in some measure implicated in them. From what I have already said, you must know that I have had means of information about this matter—means of which you could never have dreamed. Now the thing stands thus. You have done nothing which you could have avoided—nothing, certainly, which renders you culpable. You were not even guilty of robbery, when you might have robbed with impunity. You have nothing to conceal. You have no reason for concealment. On the other hand, you are bound by every principle of honor to confess all you know. An innocent man is now imprisoned, charged with that crime of which you can point out the perpetrator."

The sailor had recovered his presence of mind, in a great measure, while Dupin uttered these words; but his original boldness of bearing was all gone.

"So help me God," said he, after a brief pause, "I *will* tell you all I know about this affair;—but I do not expect you to believe one half I say—I would be a fool indeed if I did. Still, I *am* innocent, and I will make clean breast if I die for it."

What he stated was, in substance, this. He had lately made a voyage to the Indian Archipelago. A party, of which he formed one, landed at Borneo, and passed into the interior on an excursion of pleasure. Himself and a companion had captured the Ourang-Outang. This companion dying, the animal fell into his own exclusive possession. After great trouble, occasioned by the intractable ferocity of his captive during the home voyage, he at length succeeded in lodging it safely at his own residence in Paris, where, not to attract toward himself the unpleasant curiosity of his neighbors, he kept it carefully secluded, until such time as it should recover from a wound in the foot, received from a splinter on board ship. His ultimate design was to sell it.

Returning home from some sailors' frolic on the night, or rather in the morning of the murder, he found the beast occupying his own bed-room, into which it had broken from a closet adjoining, where it had been, as was thought, securely confined. Razor in hand, and fully lathered, it was sitting before a looking-glass, attempting the operation of shaving, in which it had no doubt previously watched its master through the key-hole of the closet. Terrified at the sight of so dangerous a weapon in the possession of an animal so ferocious, and so well able to use it, the man, for some moments, was at a loss what to do. He had been accustomed, however, to quiet the creature, even in its fiercest moods, by the use of a whip, and to this he now resorted. Upon sight of it, the Ourang-Outang sprang at once through the door of the chamber, down the stairs, and thence, through a window, unfortunately open, into the street.

The Frenchman followed in despair; the ape, razor still in hand, occasionally stopping to look back and gesticulate at its pursuer, until the latter had nearly come up with it. It then again made off. In this manner the chase continued for a long time. The streets were profoundly quiet, as it was nearly three o'clock in the morning. In passing down an alley in the rear of the Rue Morgue, the fugitive's attention was arrested by a light gleaming from the open window of Madame L'Espanaye's chamber, in the fourth story of her house. Rushing to the building, it perceived the lightning-rod, clambered up with inconceivable agility, grasped the shutter, which was thrown fully back against the wall, and, by its means, swung itself directly upon the headboard of the bed. The whole feat did not occupy a minute. The shutter was kicked open again by the Ourang-Outang as it entered the room.

The sailor, in the meantime, was both rejoiced and perplexed. He had strong hopes of now recapturing the brute, as it could scarcely escape from the trap into which it had ventured, except by the rod, where it might be intercepted as it came down. On the other hand, there was much cause for anxiety as to what it might do in the house. This latter reflection urged the man still to follow the fugitive. A lightning-rod is ascended without difficulty, especially by a sailor; but, when he had arrived as high as the window, which lay far to his left, his career was stopped; the most that he could accomplish was to reach over so as to obtain a glimpse of the interior of the room. At this glimpse he nearly fell from his hold through excess of horror. Now it was that those hideous shrieks arose upon the night, which had startled from slumber the inmates of the Rue Morgue. Madame L'Espanaye and her daughter, habited in their night clothes, had apparently been occupied in arranging some papers in the iron chest already mentioned, which had been wheeled into the middle of the room. It was open, and its contents lay beside it on the floor. The victims must have been sitting with their backs toward the window; and, from the time elapsing between the ingress of the beast and the screams, it seems probable that it was not immediately perceived. The flapping-to of the shutter would naturally have been attributed to the wind.

As the sailor looked in, the gigantic animal had seized Madame L'Espanaye by the hair, (which was loose, as she had been combing it,) and was flourishing the razor about her face, in imitation of the motions of a barber. The daughter lay prostrate and motionless; she had swooned. The screams and struggles of the old lady (during which the hair was torn from her head) had the effect of changing the probably pacific purposes of the Ourang-Outang into those of wrath. With one determined sweep of its muscular arm it nearly severed her head from her body. The sight of blood inflamed its anger into phrenzy. Gnashing its teeth, and flashing fire from its eyes, it flew upon the body of the girl, and imbedded its fearful talons in her throat, retaining its grasp until she expired. Its wandering and wild glances fell at this moment upon the head of the bed, over which the face of its master, rigid with horror, was just discernible. The fury of the beast, who no doubt bore still in mind the dreaded whip, was instantly converted into fear. Conscious of having deserved punishment, it seemed desirous of concealing its bloody deeds, and skipped about the chamber in an agony of nervous agitation; throwing down and breaking the furniture as it moved, and dragging the bed from the bedstead. In conclusion, it seized first the corpse of the daughter, and thrust it up the chimney, as it was found; then that of the old lady, which it immediately hurled through the window headlong.

As the ape approached the casement with its mutilated burden, the sailor shrank aghast to the rod, and, rather gliding than clambering down it, hurried at once home—dreading the consequences of the butchery, and gladly abandoning, in his terror, all solicitude about the fate of the Ourang-Outang. The words heard by the party upon the staircase were the Frenchman's exclamations of horror and affright, commingled with the fiendish jabberings of the brute.

I have scarcely anything to add. The Ourang-Outang must have escaped from the chamber, by the rod, just before the breaking of the door. It must have closed the window as it passed through it. It was subsequently caught by the owner himself, who obtained for it a very large sum at the *Jardin des Plantes*.[16] Le Bon was instantly released, upon our narration of the circumstances (with some comments from Dupin) at the *bureau* of the Prefect of Police. This functionary, however well disposed to my friend, could not altogether conceal his chagrin at the turn which affairs had taken, and was fain to indulge in a sarcasm or two, about the propriety of every person minding his own business.

"Let him talk," said Dupin, who had not thought it necessary to reply. "Let him discourse; it will ease his conscience. I am satisfied with having defeated him in his own castle. Nevertheless, that he failed in the solution of this mystery, is by no means matter for wonder which he supposes it; for, in truth, our friend the Prefect is somewhat too cunning to be profound. In his wisdom is no *stamen*. It is all head and no body, like the pictures of the Goddess Laverna,—or, at best, all head and shoulders, like a codfish. But he is a good creature after all. I like him especially for one master stroke of cant, by which he has attained his reputation for ingenuity. I mean the way he has '*de nier ce qui est, et d'expliquer ce qui n'est pas.*'"[17]

A Descent into the Maelström[1]

The ways of God in Nature, as in Providence, are not as *our* ways; nor are the models that we frame any way commensurate to the vastness, profundity, and unsearchableness of His works, *which have a depth in them greater than the well of Democritus.*

Joseph Glanville[2]

WE had now reached the summit of the loftiest crag. For some minutes the old man seemed too much exhausted to speak.

"Not long ago," said he at length, "and I could have guided you on this route as well as the youngest of my sons; but, about three years past, there happened to me an event such as never happened before to mortal man—or at least such as no man ever survived to tell of—and the six hours of deadly terror which I then endured have broken me up body and soul. You suppose me a *very* old man—but I am not. It took less than a single day to change these hairs from a jetty black to white, to weaken my limbs, and to unstring my nerves, so that I tremble at the least exertion, and am frightened at a shadow. Do you know I can scarcely look over this little cliff without getting giddy?"

The "little cliff," upon whose edge he had so carelessly thrown himself down to rest that the weightier portion of his body hung over it, while he was only kept from falling by the tenure of his elbow on its extreme and slippery edge—this "little cliff" arose, a sheer unobstructed precipice of black shining rock, some fifteen or sixteen hundred feet from the world of crags beneath us. Nothing would have tempted me to within half a dozen yards of its brink. In truth so deeply was I excited by the perilous position of my companion, that I fell at full length upon the ground, clung to the shrubs around me, and dared not even glance upward at the sky—while I struggled in vain to divest myself of the idea that the very foundations of the mountain were in danger from the fury of the winds. It was long before I could reason myself into sufficient courage to sit up and look out into the distance.

"You must get over these fancies," said the guide, "for I have brought you here that you might have the best possible view of the scene of that event I mentioned—and to tell you the whole story with the spot just under your eye."

"We are now," he continued, in that particularizing manner which distinguished him—"we are now close upon the Norwegian coast—in the sixty-eighth degree of latitude—in the great province of Nordland—and in the dreary district of Lofoden. The mountain upon whose top we sit is Helseggen, the Cloudy. Now raise yourself up a little higher—hold on to the grass if you feel giddy—so—and look out, beyond the belt of vapor beneath us, into the sea."

I looked dizzily, and beheld a wide expanse of ocean, whose waters wore so inky a hue as to bring at once to my mind the Nubian geographer's account of the *Mare Tenebrarum*.[3] A panorama more deplorably desolate no human imagination can conceive. To the right and left, as far as the eye could reach, there lay outstretched, like ramparts of the world, lines of horridly black and beetling cliff, whose character of gloom was but the more forcibly illustrated by the surf which reared high up against it its white and ghastly crest, howling and shrieking for ever. Just opposite the promontory upon whose apex we were placed, and at a distance of some five or six miles out at sea, there was visible a small, bleak-looking island; or, more properly, its position was discernible through the wilderness of surge in which it was enveloped. About two miles nearer the land, arose another of smaller size, hideously craggy and barren, and encompassed at various intervals by a cluster of dark rocks.

The appearance of the ocean, in the space between the more distant island and the shore, had something very unusual about it. Although, at the time, so strong a gale was blowing landward that a brig in the remote offing lay to under a double-reefed trysail, and constantly plunged her whole hull out of sight, still there was here nothing like a regular swell, but only a short, quick, angry cross dashing of water in every direction—as well in the teeth of the wind as otherwise. Of foam there was little except in the immediate vicinity of the rocks.

"The island in the distance," resumed the old man, "is called by the Norwegians Vurrgh. The one midway is Moskoe. That a mile to the northwest is Ambaaren. Yonder are Islesen, Hotholm, Keildhelm, Suarven, and Buckholm. Farther off— between Moskoe and Vurggh—are Otterholm, Flimen, Sandflesen, and Stockholm. These are the true names of the places—but why it has been thought necessary to name them at all, is more than either you or I can understand. Do you hear any thing? Do you see any change in the water?"

We had now been about ten minutes upon the top of Helseggen, to which we had ascended from the interior of Lofoden, so that we had caught no glimpse of the sea until it had burst upon us from the summit. As the old man spoke, I became aware of a loud and gradually increasing sound, like the moaning of a vast herd of buffaloes upon an American prairie; and at the same moment I perceived that what seamen term the *chopping* character of the ocean beneath us, was rapidly changing into a current which set to the eastward. Even while I gazed, this current acquired a monstrous velocity. Each moment added to its speed—to its headlong impetuosity. In five minutes the whole sea, as far as Vurrgh, was lashed into ungovernable fury; but it was between Moskoe and the coast that the main uproar held its sway. Here the vast bed of the waters, seamed and scarred into a thousand conflicting channels, burst suddenly into phrensied convulsion—heaving, boiling, hissing— gyrating in gigantic and innumerable vortices, and all whirling and plunging on to the eastward with a rapidity which water never elsewhere assumes except in precipitous descents.

In a few minutes more, there came over the scene another radical alteration. The general surface grew somewhat more smooth, and the whirlpools, one by one, disappeared, while prodigious streaks of foam became apparent where none had been seen before. These streaks, at length, spreading out to a great distance, and entering into combination, took unto themselves the gyratory motion of the subsided vortices, and seemed to form the germ of another more vast. Suddenly—very suddenly—this assumed a distinct and definite existence, in a circle of more than a mile in diameter. The edge of the whirl was represented by a broad belt of gleaming spray; but no particle of this slipped into the mouth of the terrific funnel, whose interior, as far as the eye could fathom it, was a smooth, shining, and jet-black wall of water, inclined to the horizon at an angle of some forty-five degrees, speeding dizzily round and round with a swaying and sweltering motion, and sending forth to the winds an appalling voice, half shriek, half roar, such as not even the mighty cataract of Niagara ever lifts up in its agony to Heaven.

The mountain trembled to its very base, and the rock rocked. I threw myself upon my face, and clung to the scant herbage in an excess of nervous agitation.

"This," said I at length, to the old man—"this *can* be nothing else than the great whirlpool of the Maelström."

"So it is sometimes termed," said he. "We Norwegians call it the Moskoe-ström, from the island of Moskoe in the midway."

The ordinary accounts of this vortex had by no means prepared me for what I saw. That of Jonas Ramus,[4] which is perhaps the most circumstantial of any, cannot impart the faintest conception either of the magnificence, or of the horror of the scene—or of the wild bewildering sense of *the novel* which confounds the beholder. I am not sure from what point of view the writer in question surveyed it, nor at what time; but it could neither have been from the summit of Helseggen, nor during a storm. There are some passages of his description, nevertheless, which may be quoted for their details, although their effect is exceedingly feeble in conveying an impression of the spectacle.

"Between Lofoden and Moskoe," he says, "the depth of the water is between thirty-six and forty fathoms; but on the other side, toward Ver (Vurrgh) this depth decreases so as not to afford a convenient passage for a vessel, without the risk of splitting on the rocks, which happens even in the calmest weather. When it is flood, the stream runs up the country between Lofoden and Moskoe with a boisterous rapidity; but the roar of its impetuous ebb to the sea is scarce equalled by the loudest and most dreadful cataracts; the noise being heard several leagues off, and the vortices or pits are of such an extent and depth, that if a ship comes within its attraction, it is inevitably absorbed and carried down to the bottom, and there beat to pieces against the rocks; and when the water relaxes, the fragments thereof are thrown up again. But these intervals of tranquillity are only at the turn of the ebb and flood, and in calm weather, and last but a quarter of an hour, its violence gradually returning. When the stream is most boisterous, and its fury heightened by a storm, it is dangerous to come within a Norway mile of it. Boats, yachts, and ships have been carried away by not guarding against it before they were within its reach. It likewise happens frequently, that whales come too near the stream, and are overpowered by its violence; and then it is impossible to describe their howlings and bellowings in their fruitless struggles to disengage themselves. A bear once, attempting to swim from Lofoden to Moskoe, was caught by the stream and borne down, while he roared terribly, so as to be heard on shore. Large stocks of firs and pine trees, after being absorbed by the current, rise again broken and torn to such a degree as if bristles grew upon them. This plainly shows the bottom to consist of craggy rocks, among which they are whirled to and fro. This stream is regulated by the flux and reflux of the sea—it being constantly high and low water every six hours. In the year 1645, early in the morning of Sexagesima Sunday,[5] it raged with such noise and impetuosity that the very stones of the houses on the coast fell to the ground."

In regard to the depth of the water, I could not see how this could have been ascertained at all in the immediate vicinity of the vortex. The "forty fathoms" must have reference only to portions of the channel close upon the shore either of Moskoe or Lofoden. The depth in the centre of the Moskoe-ström must be immeasurably greater; and no better proof of this fact is necessary than can be obtained from even the sidelong glance into the abyss of the whirl which may be had from the highest crag of Helseggen. Looking down from this pinnacle upon the howling Phlegethon[6] below, I could not help smiling at the simplicity with which the honest Jonas Ramus records, as a matter difficult of belief, the anecdotes of the whales and the bears; for it appeared to me, in fact, a self-evident thing, that the largest ship of the line in existence, coming within the influence of that deadly attraction, could resist it as little as a feather the hurricane, and must disappear bodily and at once.

The attempts to account for the phenomenon—some of which, I remember, seemed to me sufficiently plausible in perusal—now wore a very different and unsatisfactory aspect. The idea generally received is that this, as well as three smaller vortices among the Ferroe islands,[7] "have no other cause than the collision of waves rising and falling, the flux and reflux, against a ridge of rocks and shelves, which confines the water so that it precipitates itself like a cataract; and thus the higher the flood rises, the deeper must the fall be, and the natural result of all is a whirlpool or vortex, the prodigious suction of which is sufficiently known by lesser experiments."— These are the words of the Encyclopædia Britannica. Kircher and others imagine that in the centre of the channel of the Maelström is an abyss penetrating the globe, and issuing in some very remote part—the Gulf of Bothnia[8] being somewhat decidedly named in one instance. This opinion, idle in itself, was the one to which, as I gazed, my imagination most readily assented; and, mentioning it to the guide, I was rather surprised to hear him say that, although it was the view almost universally entertained of the subject by the Norwegians, it nevertheless was not his own. As to the former notion he confessed his inability to comprehend it; and here I agreed with him—for, however conclusive on paper, it becomes altogether unintelligible, and even absurd, amid the thunder of the abyss.

"You have had a good look at the whirl now," said the old man, "and if you will creep round this crag, so as to get in its lee, and deaden the roar of the water, I will tell you a story that will convince you I ought to know something of the Moskoe-ström."

I placed myself as desired, and he proceeded.

"Myself and my two brothers once owned a schooner-rigged smack of about seventy tons burthen, with which we were in the habit of fishing among the islands beyond Moskoe, nearly to Vurrgh. In all violent eddies at sea there is good fishing, at proper opportunities, if one has only the courage to attempt it; but among the whole of the Lofoden coastmen, we three were the only ones who made a regular business of going out to the islands, as I tell you. The usual grounds are a great way lower down to the southward. There fish can be got at all hours, without much risk, and therefore these places are preferred. The choice spots over here among the rocks, however, not only yield the finest variety, but in far greater abundance; so that we often got in a single day, what the more timid of the craft could not scrape together in a week. In fact, we made it a matter of desperate speculation—the risk of life standing instead of labor, and courage answering for capital.

"We kept the smack in a cove about five miles higher up the coast than this; and it was our practice, in fine weather, to take advantage of the fifteen minutes' slack to push across the main channel of the Moskoe-ström, far above the pool, and then drop down upon anchorage somewhere near Otterholm, or Sandflesen, where the eddies are not so violent as elsewhere. Here we used to remain until nearly time for slack-water again, when we weighed and made for home. We never set out upon this expedition without a steady side wind for going and coming—one that we felt sure would not fail us before our return—and we seldom made a mis-calculation upon this point. Twice, during six years, we were forced to stay all night at anchor on account of a dead calm, which is a rare thing indeed just about here; and once we had to remain on the grounds nearly a week, starving to death, owing to a gale which blew up shortly after our arrival, and made the channel too boisterous to be thought of. Upon this occasion we should have been driven out to sea in spite of everything, (for the whirlpools threw us round and round so violently, that, at length, we fouled our anchor and dragged it) if it had not been that we drifted into one of the innumerable cross currents—here to-day and gone to-morrow—which drove us under the lee of Flimen, where, by good luck, we brought up.

"I could not tell you the twentieth part of the difficulties we encountered 'on the grounds'—it is a bad spot to be in, even in good weather—but we made shift always to run the gauntlet of the Moskoe-ström itself without accident; although at times my heart has been in my mouth when we happened to be a minute or so behind the slack. The wind sometimes was not as strong as we thought it at starting, and then we made rather less way than we could wish, while the current rendered the smack unmanageable. My eldest brother had a son eighteen years old, and I had two stout boys of my own. These would have been of great assistance at such times, in using the sweeps, as well as afterward in fishing—but, somehow, although we ran the risk ourselves, we had not the heart to let the young ones get into the danger—for, after all is said and done, it *was* a horrible danger, and that is the truth.

"It is now within a few days of three years since what I am going to tell you occurred. It was on the tenth day of July, 18—, a day which the people of this part of the world will never forget—for it was one in which blew the most terrible hurricane that ever came out of the heavens. And yet all the morning, and indeed until late in the afternoon, there was a gentle and steady breeze from the south-west, while the sun shone brightly, so that the oldest seaman among us could not have foreseen what was to follow.

"The three of us—my two brothers and myself—had crossed over to the islands about two o'clock P. M., and had soon nearly loaded the smack with fine fish, which, we all remarked, were more plenty that day than we had ever known them. It was just seven, *by my watch*, when we weighed and started for home, so as to make the worst of the Ström at slack water, which we knew would be at eight.

"We set out with a fresh wind on our starboard quarter, and for some time spanked along at a great rate, never dreaming of danger, for indeed we saw not the slightest reason to apprehend it. All at once we were taken aback by a breeze from over Helseggen. This was most unusual—something that had never happened to us before—and I began to feel a little uneasy, without exactly knowing why. We put the boat on the wind, but could make no headway at all for the eddies, and I was upon the point of proposing to return to the anchorage, when, looking astern, we saw the whole horizon covered with a singular copper-colored cloud that rose with the most amazing velocity.

"In the meantime the breeze that had headed us off fell away, and we were dead becalmed, drifting about in every direction. This state of things, however, did not last long enough to give us time to think about it. In less than a minute the storm was upon us—in less than two the sky was entirely overcast—and what with this and the driving spray, it became suddenly so dark that we could not see each other in the smack.

"Such a hurricane as then blew it is folly to attempt describing. The oldest seaman in Norway never experienced any thing like it. We had let our sails go by the run before it cleverly took us; but, at the first puff, both our masts went by the board as if they had been sawed off—the mainmast taking with it my youngest brother, who had lashed himself to it for safety.

"Our boat was the lightest feather of a thing that ever sat upon water. It had a complete flush deck, with only a small hatch near the bow, and this hatch it had always been our custom to batten down when about to cross the Ström, by way of precaution against the chopping seas. But for this circumstance we should have foundered at once—for we lay entirely buried for some moments. How my elder brother escaped destruction I cannot say, for I never had an opportunity of ascertaining. For my part, as soon as I had let the foresail run, I threw myself flat on deck, with my feet against the narrow gunwale of the bow, and with my hands grasping a ring-bolt near the foot of the foremast. It was mere instinct that prompted me to do this—which was undoubtedly the very best thing I could have done—for I was too much flurried to think.

"For some moments we were completely deluged, as I say, and all this time I held my breath, and clung to the bolt. When I could stand it no longer I raised myself upon my knees, still keeping hold with my hands, and thus got my head clear. Presently our little boat gave herself a shake, just as a dog does in coming out of the water, and thus rid herself, in some measure, of the seas. I was now trying to get the better of the stupor that had come over me, and to collect my senses so as to see what was to be done, when I felt somebody grasp my arm. It was my elder brother, and my heart leaped for joy, for I had made sure that he was overboard—but the next moment all this joy was turned into horror—for he put his mouth close to my ear, and screamed out the word 'Moskoe-ström!'

"No one ever will know what my feelings were at that moment. I shook from head to foot as if I had had the most violent fit of the ague. I knew what he meant by that one word well enough—I knew what he wished to make me understand. With the wind that now drove us on, we were bound for the whirl of the Ström, and nothing could save us!

"You perceive that in crossing the Ström *channel*, we always went a long way up above the whirl, even in the calmest weather, and then had to wait and watch carefully for the slack—but now we were driving right upon the pool itself, and in such a hurricane as this! 'To be sure,' I thought, 'we shall get there just about the slack—there is some little hope in that'—but in the next moment I cursed myself for being so great a fool as to dream of hope at all. I knew very well that we were doomed, had we been ten times a ninety-gun ship.

"By this time the first fury of the tempest had spent itself, or perhaps we did not feel it so much, as we scudded before it, but at all events the seas, which at first had been kept down by the wind, and lay flat and frothing, now got up into absolute mountains. A singular change, too, had come over the heavens. Around in every direction it was still as black as pitch, but nearly overhead there burst out, all at once, a circular rift of clear sky—as clear as I ever saw—and of a deep bright blue—and through it there blazed forth the full moon with a lustre that I never before knew her to wear. She lit up every thing about us with the greatest distinctness—but, oh God, what a scene it was to light up!

"I now made one or two attempts to speak to my brother—but, in some manner which I could not understand, the din had so increased that I could not make him hear a single word, although I screamed at the top of my voice in his ear. Presently he shook his head, looking as pale as death, and held up one of his fingers, as if to say '*listen!*'

"At first I could not make out what he meant—but soon a hideous thought flashed upon me. I dragged my watch from its fob. It was not going. I glanced at its face by the moonlight, and then burst into tears as I flung it far away into the ocean. *It had run down at seven o'clock! We were behind the time of the slack, and the whirl of the Ström was in full fury!*

"When a boat is well built, properly trimmed, and not deep laden, the waves in a strong gale, when she is going large, seem always to slip from beneath her—which appears very strange to a landsman—and this is what is called *riding*, in sea phrase. Well, so far we had ridden the swells very cleverly; but presently a gigantic sea happened to take us right under the counter, and bore us with it as it rose—up— up—as if into the sky. I would not have believed that any wave could rise so high. And then down we came with a sweep, a slide, and a plunge, that made me feel sick and dizzy, as if I was falling from some lofty mountain-top in a dream. But while we were up I had thrown a quick glance around—and that one glance was all sufficient. I saw our exact position in an instant. The Moskoe-ström whirlpool was about a quarter of a mile dead ahead—but no more like the every-day Moskoe-ström, than the whirl as you now see it is like a mill-race. If I had not known where we were, and what we had to expect, I should not have recognised the place at all. As it was, I involuntarily closed my eyes in horror. The lids clenched themselves together as if in a spasm.

"It could not have been more than two minutes afterward until we suddenly felt the waves subside, and were enveloped in foam. The boat made a sharp half turn to larboard, and then shot off in its new direction like a thunderbolt. At the same moment the roaring noise of the water was completely drowned in a kind of shrill shriek—such a sound as you might imagine given out by the waste-pipes of many thousand steam-vessels, letting off their steam all together. We were now in the belt of surf that always surrounds the whirl; and I thought, of course, that another moment would plunge us into the abyss—down which we could only see indistinctly on account of the amazing velocity with which we were borne along. The boat did not seem to sink into the water at all, but to skim like an air-bubble upon the surface of the surge. Her starboard side was next the whirl, and on the larboard arose the world of ocean we had left. It stood like a huge writhing wall between us and the horizon.

"It may appear strange, but now, when we were in the very jaws of the gulf, I felt more composed than when we were only approaching it. Having made up my mind to hope no more, I got rid of a great deal of that terror which unmanned me at first. I suppose it was despair that strung my nerves.

"It may look like boasting—but what I tell you is truth—I began to reflect how magnificent a thing it was to die in such a manner, and how foolish it was in me to think of so paltry a consideration as my own individual life, in view of so wonderful a manifestation of God's power. I do believe that I blushed with shame when this idea crossed my mind. After a little while I became possessed with the keenest curiosity about the whirl itself. I positively felt a *wish* to explore its depths, even at the sacrifice I was going to make; and my principal grief was that I should never be able to tell my old companions on shore about the mysteries I should see. These, no doubt, were singular fancies to occupy a man's mind in such extremity—and I have often thought since, that the revolutions of the boat around the pool might have rendered me a little light-headed.

"There was another circumstance which tended to restore my self-possession; and this was the cessation of the wind, which could not reach us in our present situation—for, as you saw yourself, the belt of surf is considerably lower than the general bed of the ocean, and this latter now towered above us, a high, black, mountainous ridge. If you have never been at sea in a heavy gale, you can form no idea of the confusion of mind occasioned by the wind and spray together. They blind, deafen, and strangle you, and take away all power of action or reflection. But we were now, in a great measure, rid of these annoyances—just as death-condemned felons in prison are allowed petty indulgences, forbidden them while their doom is yet uncertain.

"How often we made the circuit of the belt it is impossible to say. We careered round and round for perhaps an hour, flying rather than floating, getting gradually more and more into the middle of the surge, and then nearer and nearer to its horrible inner edge. All this time I had never let go of the ring-bolt. My brother was at the stern, holding on to a small empty water-cask which had been securely lashed under the coop of the counter, and was the only thing on deck that had not been swept overboard when the gale first took us. As we approached the brink of the pit he let go his hold upon this, and made for the ring, from which, in the agony of his terror, he endeavored to force my hands, as it was not large enough to afford us both a secure grasp. I never felt deeper grief than when I saw him attempt this act— although I knew he was a madman when he did it—a raving maniac through sheer fright. I did not care, however, to contest the point with him. I knew it could make no difference whether either of us held on at all; so I let him have the bolt, and went astern to the cask. This there was no great difficulty in doing; for the smack flew round steadily enough, and upon an even keel—only swaying to and fro, with the immense sweeps and swelters of the whirl. Scarcely had I secured myself in my new position, when we gave a wild lurch to starboard, and rushed headlong into the abyss. I muttered a hurried prayer to God, and thought all was over.

"As I felt the sickening sweep of the descent, I had instinctively tightened my hold upon the barrel, and closed my eyes. For some seconds I dared not open them— while I expected instant destruction, and wondered that I was not already in my death-struggles with the water. But moment after moment elapsed. I still lived. The sense of falling had ceased; and the motion of the vessel seemed much as it had been before, while in the belt of foam, with the exception that she now lay more along. I took courage, and looked once again upon the scene.

"Never shall I forget the sensations of awe, horror, and admiration with which I gazed about me. The boat appeared to be hanging, as if by magic, midway down, upon the interior surface of a funnel vast in circumference, prodigious in depth, and whose perfectly smooth sides might have been mistaken for ebony, but for the bewildering rapidity with which they spun around, and for the gleaming and ghastly radiance they shot forth, as the rays of the full moon, from that circular rift amid the clouds which I have already described, streamed in a flood of golden glory along the black walls, and far away down into the inmost recesses of the abyss.

"At first I was too much confused to observe anything accurately. The general burst of terrific grandeur was all that I beheld. When I recovered myself a little, however, my gaze fell instinctively downward. In this direction I was able to obtain an unobstructed view, from the manner in which the smack hung on the inclined surface of the pool. She was quite upon an even keel—that is to say, her deck lay in a plane parallel with that of the water—but this latter sloped at an angle of more than forty-five degrees, so that we seemed to be lying upon our beam-ends. I could not help observing, nevertheless, that I had scarcely more difficulty in maintaining my hold and footing in this situation, than if we had been upon a dead level; and this, I suppose, was owing to the speed at which we revolved.

"The rays of the moon seemed to search the very bottom of the profound gulf; but still I could make out nothing distinctly, on account of a thick mist in which everything there was enveloped, and over which there hung a magnificent rainbow, like that narrow and tottering bridge which Mussulmen[9] say is the only pathway between Time and Eternity. This mist, or spray, was no doubt occasioned by the clashing of the great walls of the funnel, as they all met together at the bottom—but the yell that went up to the Heavens from out of that mist, I dare not attempt to describe.

"Our first slide into the abyss itself, from the belt of foam above, had carried us a great distance down the slope; but our farther descent was by no means proportionate. Round and round we swept—not with any uniform movement—but in dizzying swings and jerks, that sent us sometimes only a few hundred yards—sometimes nearly the complete circuit of the whirl. Our progress downward, at each revolution, was slow, but very perceptible.

"Looking about me upon the wide waste of liquid ebony on which we were thus borne, I perceived that our boat was not the only object in the embrace of the whirl. Both above and below us were visible fragments of vessels, large masses of building timber and trunks of trees, with many smaller articles, such as pieces of house furniture, broken boxes, barrels and staves. I have already described the unnatural curiosity which had taken the place of my original terrors. It appeared to grow upon me as I drew nearer and nearer to my dreadful doom. I now began to watch, with a strange interest, the numerous things that floated in our company. I *must* have been delirious—for I even sought *amusement* in speculating upon the relative velocities of their several descents toward the foam below. 'This fir tree,' I found myself at one time saying, 'will certainly be the next thing that takes the awful plunge and disappears,'—and then I was disappointed to find that the wreck of a Dutch merchant ship overtook it and went down before. At length, after making several guesses of this nature, and being deceived in all—this fact—the fact of my invariable miscalculation—set me upon a train of reflection that made my limbs again tremble, and my heart beat heavily once more.

"It was not a new terror that thus affected me, but the dawn of a more exciting *hope*. This hope arose partly from memory, and partly from present observation. I called to mind the great variety of buoyant matter that strewed the coast of Lofoden, having been absorbed and then thrown forth by the Moskoe-ström. By far the greater number of the articles were shattered in the most extraordinary way—so chafed and roughened as to have the appearance of being stuck full of splinters—but then I distinctly recollected that there were *some* of them which were not disfigured at all. Now I could not account for this difference except by supposing that the roughened fragments were the only ones which had been *completely absorbed*—that the others had entered the whirl at so late a period of the tide, or, for some reason, had descended so slowly after entering, that they did not reach the bottom before the turn of the flood came, or of the ebb, as the case might be. I conceived it possible, in either instance, that they might thus be whirled up again to the level of the ocean, without undergoing the fate of those which had been drawn in more early, or absorbed more rapidly. I made, also, three important observations. The first was, that, as a general rule, the larger the bodies were, the more rapid their descent—the second, that, between two masses of equal extent, the one spherical, and the other *of any other shape*, the superiority in speed of descent was with the sphere—the third, that, between two masses of equal size, the one cylindrical, and the other of any other shape, the cylinder was absorbed the more slowly. Since my escape, I have had several conversations on this subject with an old school-master of the district; and it was from him that I learned the use of the words 'cylinder' and 'sphere.' He explained to me—although I have forgotten the explanation—how what I observed was, in fact, the natural consequence of the forms of the floating fragments—and showed me how it happened that a cylinder, swimming in a vortex, offered more resistance to its suction, and was drawn in with greater difficulty than an equally bulky body, of any form whatever.[10]

"There was one startling circumstance which went a great way in enforcing these observations, and rendering me anxious to turn them to account, and this was that, at every revolution, we passed something like a barrel, or else the yard or the mast of a vessel, while many of these things, which had been on our level when I first opened my eyes upon the wonders of the whirlpool, were now high up above us, and seemed to have moved but little from their original station.

"I no longer hesitated what to do. I resolved to lash myself securely to the water cask upon which I now held, to cut it loose from the counter, and to throw myself with it into the water. I attracted my brother's attention by signs, pointed to the floating barrels that came near us, and did everything in my power to make him understand what I was about to do. I thought at length that he comprehended my design—but, whether this was the case or not, he shook his head despairingly, and refused to move from his station by the ring-bolt. It was impossible to reach him; the emergency admitted of no delay; and so, with a bitter struggle, I resigned him to his fate, fastened myself to the cask by means of the lashings which secured it to the counter, and precipitated myself with it into the sea, without another moment's hesitation.

"The result was precisely what I had hoped it might be. As it is myself who now tell you this tale—as you see that I *did* escape—and as you are already in possession of the mode in which this escape was effected, and must therefore anticipate all that I have farther to say—I will bring my story quickly to conclusion. It might have been an hour, or thereabout, after my quitting the smack, when, having descended to a vast distance beneath me, it made three or four wild gyrations in rapid succession, and, bearing my loved brother with it, plunged headlong, at once and forever, into the chaos of foam below. The barrel to which I was attached sunk very little farther than half the distance between the bottom of the gulf and the spot at which I leaped overboard, before a great change took place in the character of the whirlpool. The slope of the sides of the vast funnel became momently less and less steep. The gyrations of the whirl grew, gradually, less and less violent. By degrees, the froth and the rainbow disappeared, and the bottom of the gulf seemed slowly to uprise. The sky was clear, the winds had gone down, and the full moon was setting radiantly in the west, when I found myself on the surface of the ocean, in full view of the shores of Lofoden, and above the spot where the pool of the Moskoe-ström *had been*. It was the hour of the slack—but the sea still heaved in mountainous waves from the effects of the hurricane. I was borne violently into the channel of the Ström, and in a few minutes was hurried down the coast into the 'grounds' of the fishermen. A boat picked me up—exhausted from fatigue—and (now that the danger was removed) speechless from the memory of its horror. Those who drew me on board were my old mates and daily companions—but they knew me no more than they would have known a traveller from the spirit-land. My hair which had been raven-black the day before, was as white as you see it now. They say too that the whole expression of my countenance had changed. I told them my story—they did not believe it. I now tell it to *you*—and I can scarcely expect you to put more faith in it than did the merry fishermen of Lofoden."

Never Bet the Devil Your Head
A Tale With a Moral[1]

"CON *tal que las costumbres de un autor*," says Don Thomas De Las Torres, in the preface to his "Amatory Poems" "*sean puras y castas, importo muy poco que no sean igualmente severas sus obras*"[2]—meaning, in plain English, that, provided the morals of an author are pure, personally, it signifies nothing what are the morals of his books. We presume that Don Thomas is now in Purgatory for the assertion. It would be a clever thing, too, in the way of poetical justice, to keep him there until his "Amatory Poems" get out of print, or are laid definitely upon the shelf through lack of readers. Every fiction *should have* a moral; and, what is more to the purpose, the critics have discovered that every fiction *has*. Philip Melancthon, some time ago, wrote a commentary upon the "Batrachomyomachia"[3] and proved that the poet's object was to excite a distaste for sedition. Pierre La Seine, going a step farther, shows that the intention was to recommend to young men temperance in eating and drinking. Just so, too, Jacobus Hugo has satisfied himself that, by Euenis, Homer meant to insinuate John Calvin; by Antinöus, Martin Luther; by the Lotophagi, Protestants in general; and by the Harpies, the Dutch. Our more modern Scholiasts are equally acute. These fellows demonstrate a hidden meaning in "The Antediluvians," a parable in "Powhatan," new views in "Cock Robin," and transcendentalism in "Hop O' My Thumb."[4] In short, it has been shown that no man can sit down to write without a very profound design. Thus to authors in general much trouble is spared. A novelist, for example, need have no care of his moral. It is there—that is to say it is somewhere—and the moral and the critics can take care of themselves. When the proper time arrives, all that the gentleman intended, and all that he did not intend, will be brought to light, in the "Dial," or the "Down-Easter," together with all that he ought to have intended, and the rest that he clearly meant to intend:—so that it will all come very straight in the end.

There is no just ground, therefore, for the charge brought against me by certain ignoramuses—that I have never written a moral tale, or, in more precise words, a tale with a moral. They are not the critics predestined to bring me out, and *develop* my morals:—that is the secret. By and by the "North American Quarterly Humdrum" will make them ashamed of their stupidity.[5] In the meantime, by way of staying execution—by way of mitigating the accusations against me—I offer the sad history appended;—a history about whose obvious moral there can be no question whatever, since he who runs may read it in the large capitals which form the title of the tale. I should have credit for this arrangement—a far wiser one than that of La Fontaine and others, who reserve the impression to be conveyed until the last moment, and thus sneak it in at the fag end of their fables.

Defuncti injuriâ ne afficiantur was a law of the twelve tables,[6] and *De mortuis nil nisi bonum* is an excellent injunction—even if the dead in question be nothing but dead small beer. It is not my design, therefore, to vituperate my deceased friend Toby Dammit. He was a sad dog, it is true, and a dog's death it was that he died; but he himself was not to blame for his vices. They grew out of a personal defect in his mother. She did her best in the way of flogging him while an infant—for duties to her well-regulated mind were always pleasures, and babies, like tough steaks, or the modern Greek olive trees, are invariably the better for beating—but, poor woman! she had the misfortune to be left-handed, and a child flogged left-handedly had better be left unflogged. The world revolves from right to left. It will not do to whip a baby from left to right. If each blow in the proper direction drives an evil propensity out, it follows that every thump in an opposite one knocks its quota of wickedness in. I was often present at Toby's chastisements, and, even by the way in which he kicked, I could perceive that he was getting worse and worse every day. At last I saw, through the tears in my eyes, that there was no hope of the villain at all, and one day when he had been cuffed until he grew so black in the face that one might have mistaken him for a little African, and no effect had been produced beyond that of making him wriggle himself into a fit, I could stand it no longer, but went down upon my knees forthwith, and, uplifting my voice, made prophecy of his ruin.

The fact is that his precocity in vice was awful. At five months of age he used to get into such passions that he was unable to articulate. At six months, I caught him gnawing a pack of cards. At seven months he was in the constant habit of catching and kissing the female babies. At eight months he peremptorily refused to put his signature to the Temperance pledge. Thus he went on increasing in iniquity, month after month, until, at the close of the first year, he not only insisted upon wearing *moustaches*, but had contracted a propensity for cursing and swearing, and for backing his assertions by bets.

Through this latter most ungentlemanly practice, the ruin which I had predicted to Toby Dammit overtook him at last. The fashion had "grown with his growth and strengthened with his strength," so that, when he came to be a man, he could scarcely utter a sentence without interlarding it with a proposition to gamble. Not that he actually *laid* wagers—no. I will do my friend the justice to say that he would as soon have laid eggs. With him the thing was a mere formula—nothing more. His expressions on this head had no meaning attached to them whatever. They were simple if not altogether innocent expletives—imaginative phrases wherewith to round off a sentence. When he said "I'll bet you so and so," nobody ever thought of taking him up; but still I could not help thinking it my duty to put him down. The habit was an immoral one, and so I told him. It was a vulgar one—this I begged him to believe. It was discountenanced by society—here I said nothing but the truth. It was forbidden by act of Congress—here I had not the slightest intention of telling a lie. I remonstrated—but to no purpose. I demonstrated—in vain. I entreated—he smiled. I implored—he laughed. I preached—he sneered. I threatened—he swore. I kicked him—he called for the police. I pulled his nose—he blew it, and offered to bet the Devil his head that I would not venture to try that experiment again.

Poverty was another vice which the peculiar physical deficiency of Dammit's mother had entailed upon her son. He was detestably poor; and this was the reason, no doubt, that his expletive expressions about betting, seldom took a pecuniary turn. I will not be bound to say that I ever heard him make use of such a figure of speech as "I'll bet you a dollar." It was usually "I'll bet you what you please," or "I'll bet you what you dare," or "I'll bet you a trifle," or else, more significantly still, "*I'll bet the Devil my head.*"

This latter form seemed to please him best:—perhaps because it involved the least risk; for Dammit had become excessively parsimonious. Had any one taken him up, his head was small, and thus his loss would have been small too. But these are my own reflections, and I am by no means sure that I am right in attributing them to him. At all events the phrase in question grew daily in favor, notwithstanding the gross impropriety of a man's betting his brains like banknotes:—but this was a point which my friend's perversity of disposition would not permit him to comprehend. In the end, he abandoned all other forms of wager, and gave himself up to "*I'll bet the Devil my head,*" with a pertinacity and exclusiveness of devotion that displeased not less than it surprised me. I am always displeased by circumstances for which I cannot account. Mysteries force a man to think, and so injure his health. The truth is, there was something in *the air* with which Mr. Dammit was wont to give utterance to his offensive expression—something in his *manner* of enunciation—which at first interested, and afterwards made me very uneasy—something which, for want of a more definite term at present, I must be permitted to call *queer*; but which Mr. Coleridge would have called mystical, Mr. Kant pantheistical, Mr. Carlyle twistical, and Mr. Emerson[7] hyperquizzitistical. I began not to like it at all. Mr. Dammit's soul was in a perilous state. I resolved to bring all my eloquence into play to save it. I vowed to serve him as St. Patrick, in the Irish chronicle, is said to have served the toad, that is to say, "awaken him to a sense of his situation." I addressed myself to the task forthwith. Once more I betook myself to remonstrance. Again I collected my energies for a final attempt at expostulation.

When I had made an end of my lecture, Mr. Dammit indulged himself in some very equivocal behaviour. For some moments he remained silent, merely looking me inquisitively in the face. But presently he threw his head to one side, and elevated his eyebrows to great extent. Then he spread out the palms of his hands and shrugged up his shoulders. Then he winked with the right eye. Then he repeated the operation with the left. Then he shut them both up very tight. Then he opened them both so very wide that I became seriously alarmed for the consequences. Then, applying his thumb to his nose, he thought proper to make an indescribable movement with the rest of his fingers. Finally, setting his arms a-kimbo, he condescended to reply.

I can call to mind only the heads of his discourse. He would be obliged to me if I would hold my tongue. He wished none of my advice. He despised all my insinuations. He was old enough to take care of himself. Did I still think him baby Dammit? Did I mean to say anything against his character? Did I intend to insult him? Was I a fool? Was my maternal parent aware, in a word, of my absence from the domiciliary residence? He would put this latter question to me as to a man of veracity, and he would bind himself to abide by my reply. Once more he would demand explicitly if my mother knew that I was out. My confusion, he said, betrayed me, and he would be willing to bet the Devil his head that she did not.

Mr. Dammit did not pause for my rejoinder. Turning upon his heel, he left my presence with undignified precipitation. It was well for him that he did so. My feelings had been wounded. Even my anger had been aroused. For once I would have taken him up upon his insulting wager. I would have won for the Arch-Enemy Mr. Dammit's little head—for the fact is, my mamma *was* very well aware of my merely temporary absence from home.

But *Khoda shefa midêhed*[8]—Heaven gives relief—as the Musselmen say when you tread upon their toes. It was in pursuance of my duty that I had been insulted, and I bore the insult like a man. It now seemed to me, however, that I had done all that could be required of me, in the case of this miserable individual, and I resolved to trouble him no longer with my counsel, but to leave him to his conscience and himself. But although I forebore to intrude with my advice, I could not bring myself to give up his society altogether. I even went so far as to humor some of his less reprehensible propensities; and there were times when I found myself lauding his wicked jokes, as epicures do mustard, with tears in my eyes:—so profoundly did it grieve me to hear his evil talk.

One fine day, having strolled out together arm in arm, our route led us in the direction of a river. There was a bridge, and we resolved to cross it. It was roofed over, by way of protection from the weather, and the arch-way, having but few windows, was thus very uncomfortably dark. As we entered the passage, the contrast between the external glare, and the interior gloom, struck heavily upon my spirits. Not so upon those of the unhappy Dammit, who offered to bet the Devil his head that I was hipped. He seemed to be in an unusual good humor. He was excessively lively—so much so that I entertained I know not what of uneasy suspicion. It is not impossible that he was affected with the transcendentals. I am not well enough versed, however, in the diagnosis of this disease to speak with decision upon the point; and unhappily there were none of my friends of the "Dial" present. I suggest the idea, nevertheless, because of a certain species of austere Merry-Andrewism which seemed to beset my poor friend, and caused him to make quite a Tom-Fool of himself. Nothing would serve him but wriggling and skipping about under and over everything that came in his way; now shouting out, and now lisping out, all manner of odd little and big words, yet preserving the gravest face in the world all the time. I really could not make up my mind whether to kick or to pity him. At length, having passed nearly across the bridge, we approached the termination of the foot-way, when our progress was impeded by a turnstile of some height. Through this I made my way quietly, pushing it around as usual. But this turn would not serve the turn of Mr. Dammit. He insisted upon leaping the stile, and said he could cut a pigeon-wing[9] over it in the air. Now this, conscientiously speaking, I did not think he could do. The best pigeon-winger over all kinds of style, was my friend Mr. Carlyle, and as I knew *he* could not do it, I would not believe it could be done by Toby Dammit. I therefore told him, in so many words, that he was a braggadocio, and could not do what he said. For this, I had reason to be sorry afterwards;—for he straightway offered to *bet the Devil his head* that he could.

I was about to reply, notwithstanding my previous resolutions, with some remonstrance against his impiety, when I heard, close at my elbow, a slight cough, which sounded very much like the ejaculation *"ahem!"* I started, and looked about me in surprise. My glance at length fell into a nook of the frame-work of the bridge, and upon the figure of a little lame old gentleman of venerable aspect. Nothing could be more reverend than his whole appearance; for, he not only had on a full suit of black, but his shirt was perfectly clean and the collar turned very neatly down over a white cravat, while his hair was parted in front like a girl's. His hands were clasped pensively together over his stomach, and his two eyes were carefully rolled up into the top of his head.

Upon observing him more closely, I perceived that he wore a black silk apron over his small-clothes; and that this was a thing which I thought very odd. Before I had time to make any remark, however, upon so singular a circumstance, he interrupted me with a second *"ahem!"*

To this observation I was not immediately prepared to reply. The fact is, remarks of this laconic nature are nearly unanswerable. I have known a Quarterly Review *non-plused* by the word *"Fudge!"* I am not ashamed to say, therefore, that I turned to Mr. Dammit for assistance.

"Dammit," said I, "what are you about? don't you hear?—the gentleman says *'ahem!'"* I looked sternly at my friend while I thus addressed him; for to say the truth, I felt particularly puzzled, and when a man is particularly puzzled he must knit his brows and look savage, or else he is pretty sure to look like a fool.

"Dammit," observed I—although this sounded very much like an oath, than which nothing was farther from my thoughts—"Dammit," I suggested—"the gentleman says *'ahem!'"*

I do not attempt to defend my remark on the score of profundity; I did not think it profound myself; but I have noticed that the effect of our speeches is not always proportionate with their importance in our own eyes; and if I had shot Mr. D. through and through with a Paixhan bomb, or knocked him in the head with the "Poets and Poetry of America,"[10] he could hardly have been more discomfited than when I addressed him with those simple words—"Dammit, what are you about?—don't you hear?—the gentleman says *'ahem!'"*

"You don't say so?" gasped he at length, after turning more colors than a pirate runs up, one after the other, when chased by a man-of-war. "Are you quite sure he said *that?* Well, at all events I am in for it now, and may as well put a bold face upon the matter. Here goes, then—*ahem!*"

At this the little old gentleman seemed pleased—God only knows why. He left his station at the nook of the bridge, limped forward with a gracious air, took Dammit by the hand and shook it cordially, looking all the while straight up in his face with an air of the most unadulterated benignity which it is possible for the mind of man to imagine.

"I am quite sure you will win it, Dammit," said he with the frankest of all smiles, "but we are obliged to have a trial you know, for the sake of mere form."

"Ahem!" replied my friend, taking off his coat with a deep sigh, tying a pocket-handkerchief around his waist, and producing an unaccountable alteration in his countenance by twisting up his eyes, and bringing down the corners of his mouth— "ahem!" And "ahem," said he again, after a pause; and not another word more than "ahem!" did I ever know him to say after that. "Aha!" thought I, without expressing myself aloud—"this is quite a remarkable silence on the part of Toby Dammit, and is no doubt a consequence of his verbosity upon a previous occasion. One extreme induces another. I wonder if he has forgotten the many unanswerable questions which he propounded to me so fluently on the day when I gave him my last lecture? At all events, he is cured of the transcendentals."

"Ahem!" here replied Toby, just as if he had been reading my thoughts, and looking like a very old sheep in a reverie.

The old gentleman now took him by the arm, and led him more into the shade of the bridge—a few paces back from the turnstile. "My good fellow," said he, "I make it a point of conscience to allow you this much run. Wait here, till I take my place by the stile, so that I may see whether you go over it handsomely, and transcendentally, and don't omit any flourishes of the pigeon-wing. A mere form, you know. I will say 'one, two, three, and away.' Mind you start at the word 'away.'" Here he took his position by the stile, paused a moment as if in profound reflection, then *looked up* and, I thought, smiled very slightly, then tightened the strings of his apron, then took a long look at Dammit, and finally gave the word as agreed upon—

One—two—three—and away!

Punctually, at the word "away," my poor friend set off in a strong gallop. The stile was not very high, like Mr. Lord's[11]—nor yet very low, like that of Mr. Lord's reviewers, but upon the whole I made sure that he would clear it. And then what if he did not?—ah, that was the question—what if he did not? "What right," said I, "had the old gentleman to make any other gentleman jump? The little old dot-and-carry-one! who is *he?* If he asks *me* to jump, I won't do it, that's flat, and I don't care who *the devil he is.*" The bridge, as I say, was arched and covered in, in a very ridiculous manner, and there was a most uncomfortable echo about it at all times— an echo which I never before so particularly observed as when I uttered the four last words of my remark.

But what I said, or what I thought, or what I heard, occupied only an instant. In less than five seconds from his starting, my poor Toby had taken the leap. I saw him run nimbly, and spring grandly from the floor of the bridge, cutting the most awful flourishes with his legs as he went up. I saw him high in the air, pigeon-winging it to admiration just over the top of the stile; and of course I thought it an unusually singular thing that he did not *continue* to go over. But the whole leap was the affair of a moment, and, before I had a chance to make any profound reflections, down came Mr. Dammit on the flat of his back, on the same side of the stile from which he had started. In the same instant I saw the old gentleman limping off at the top of his speed, having caught and wrapped up in his apron something that fell heavily into it from the darkness of the arch just over the turnstile. At all this I was much astonished; but I had no leisure to think, for Mr. Dammit lay particularly still, and I concluded that his feelings had been hurt, and that he stood in need of my assistance. I hurried up to him and found that he had received what might be termed a serious injury. The truth is, he had been deprived of his head, which after a close search I could not find anywhere:—so I determined to take him home, and send for the homœopathists.[12] In the mean time a thought struck me, and I threw open an adjacent window of the bridge; when the sad truth flashed upon me at once. About five feet just above the top of the turnstile, and crossing the arch of the foot-path so as to constitute a brace, there extended a flat iron bar, lying with its breadth horizontally, and forming one of a series that served to strengthen the structure throughout its extent. With the edge of this brace it appeared evident that the neck of my unfortunate friend had come precisely in contact.

He did not long survive his terrible loss. The homœopathists did not give him little enough physic, and what little they did give him he hesitated to take. So in the end he grew worse, and at length died, a lesson to all riotous livers. I bedewed his grave with my tears, worked a *bar* sinister on his family escutcheon,[13] and, for the general expenses of his funeral, sent in my very moderate bill to the transcendentalists. The scoundrels refused to pay it, so I had Mr. Dammit dug up at once, and sold him for dog's meat.

The Masque of the Red Death[1]

THE "Red Death" had long devastated the country. No pestilence had ever been so fatal, or so hideous. Blood was its Avatar[2] and its seal—the redness and the horror of blood. There were sharp pains, and sudden dizziness, and then profuse bleeding at the pores, with dissolution. The scarlet stains upon the body and especially upon the face of the victim, were the pest ban which shut him out from the aid and from the sympathy of his fellow-men. And the whole seizure, progress and termination of the disease, were the incidents of half an hour.

But the Prince Prospero[3] was happy and dauntless and sagacious. When his dominions were half depopulated, he summoned to his presence a thousand hale and light-hearted friends from among the knights and dames of his court, and with these retired to the deep seclusion of one of his castellated abbeys. This was an extensive and magnificent structure, the creation of the prince's own eccentric yet august taste. A strong and lofty wall girdled it in. This wall had gates of iron. The courtiers, having entered, brought furnaces and massy hammers and welded the bolts. They resolved to leave means neither of ingress or egress to the sudden impulses of despair or of frenzy from within. The abbey was amply provisioned.

With such precautions the courtiers might bid defiance to contagion. The external world could take care of itself. In the meantime it was folly to grieve, or to think. The prince had provided all the appliances of pleasure. There were buffoons, there were improvisatori, there were ballet-dancers, there were musicians, there was Beauty, there was wine. All these and security were within. Without was the "Red Death."

It was toward the close of the fifth or sixth month of his seclusion, and while the pestilence raged most furiously abroad, that the Prince Prospero entertained his thousand friends at a masked ball of the most unusual magnificence.

It was a voluptuous scene, that masquerade. But first let me tell of the rooms in which it was held. There were seven—an imperial suite. In many palaces, however, such suites form a long and straight vista, while the folding doors slide back nearly to the walls on either hand, so that the view of the whole extent is scarcely impeded. Here the case was very different; as might have been expected from the duke's love of the *bizarre*. The apartments were so irregularly disposed that the vision embraced but little more than one at a time. There was a sharp turn at every twenty or thirty yards, and at each turn a novel effect. To the right and left, in the middle of each wall, a tall and narrow Gothic window looked out upon a closed corridor which pursued the windings of the suite. These windows were of stained glass whose color varied in accordance with the prevailing hue of the decorations of the chamber into which it opened. That at the eastern extremity was hung, for example, in blue—and vividly blue were its windows. The second chamber was purple in its ornaments and tapestries, and here the panes were purple. The third was green throughout, and so were the casements. The fourth was furnished and lighted with orange—the fifth with white—the sixth with violet. The seventh apartment was closely shrouded in black velvet tapestries that hung all over the ceiling and down the walls, falling in heavy folds upon a carpet of the same material and hue. But in this chamber only, the color of the windows failed to correspond with the decorations. The panes here were scarlet—a deep blood color. Now in no one of the seven apartments was there any lamp or candelabrum, amid the profusion of golden ornaments that lay scattered to and fro or depended from the roof. There was no light of any kind emanating from lamp or candle within the suite of chambers. But in the corridors that followed the suite, there stood, opposite to each window, a heavy tripod, bearing a brazier of fire that projected its rays through the tinted glass and so glaringly illumined the room. And thus were produced a multitude of gaudy and fantastic appearances. But in the western or black chamber the effect of the fire-light that streamed upon the dark hangings through the blood-tinted panes, was ghastly in the extreme, and produced so wild a look upon the countenances of those who entered, that there were few of the company bold enough to set foot within its precincts at all.

It was in this apartment, also, that there stood against the western wall, a gigantic clock of ebony. Its pendulum swung to and fro with a dull, heavy, monotonous clang; and when the minute-hand made the circuit of the face, and the hour was to be stricken, there came from the brazen lungs of the clock a sound which was clear and loud and deep and exceedingly musical, but of so peculiar a note and emphasis that, at each lapse of an hour, the musicians of the orchestra were constrained to pause, momentarily, in their performance, to harken to the sound; and thus the waltzers perforce ceased their evolutions; and there was a brief disconcert of the whole gay company; and, while the chimes of the clock yet rang, it was observed that the giddiest grew pale, and the more aged and sedate passed their hands over their brows as if in confused reverie or meditation. But when the echoes had fully ceased, a light laughter at once pervaded the assembly; the musicians looked at each other and smiled as if at their own nervousness and folly, and made whispering vows, each to the other, that the next chiming of the clock should produce in them no similar emotion; and then, after the lapse of sixty minutes, (which embrace three thousand and six hundred seconds of the Time that flies,) there came yet another chiming of the clock, and then were the same disconcert and tremulousness and meditation as before.

But, in spite of these things, it was a gay and magnificent revel. The tastes of the duke were peculiar. He had a fine eye for colors and effects. He disregarded the *decora* of mere fashion. His plans were bold and fiery, and his conceptions glowed with barbaric lustre. There are some who would have thought him mad. His followers felt that he was not. It was necessary to hear and see and touch him to be *sure* that he was not.

He had directed, in great part, the moveable embellishments of the seven chambers, upon occasion of this great *fête*; and it was his own guiding taste which had given character to the masqueraders. Be sure they were grotesque. There were much glare and glitter and piquancy and phantasm—much of what has been since seen in "Hernani."[4] There were arabesque figures with unsuited limbs and appointments. There were delirious fancies such as the madman fashions. There was much of the beautiful, much of the wanton, much of the *bizarre*, something of the terrible, and not a little of that which might have excited disgust. To and fro in the seven chambers there stalked, in fact, a multitude of dreams. And these—the dreams—writhed in and about, taking hue from the rooms, and causing the wild music of the orchestra to seem as the echo of their steps. And, anon, there strikes the ebony clock which stands in the hall of the velvet. And then, for a moment, all is still, and all is silent save the voice of the clock. The dreams are stiff-frozen as they stand. But the echoes of the chime die away—they have endured but an instant—and a light, half-subdued laughter floats after them as they depart. And now again the music swells, and the dreams live, and writhe to and fro more merrily than ever, taking hue from the many tinted windows through which stream the rays from the tripods. But to the chamber which lies most westwardly of the seven, there are now none of the maskers who venture: for the night is waning away; and there flows a ruddier light through the blood-colored panes; and the blackness of the sable drapery appals; and to him whose foot falls upon the sable carpet, there comes from the near clock of ebony a muffled peal more solemnly emphatic than any which reaches *their* ears who indulge in the more remote gaieties of the other apartments.

But these other apartments were densely crowded, and in them beat feverishly the heart of life. And the revel went whirlingly on, until at length there commenced the sounding of midnight upon the clock. And then the music ceased, as I have told; and the evolutions of the waltzers were quieted; and there was an uneasy cessation of all things as before. But now there were twelve strokes to be sounded by the bell of the clock; and thus it happened, perhaps, that more of thought crept, with more of time, into the meditations of the thoughtful among those who revelled. And thus, too, it happened, perhaps, that before the last echoes of the last chime had utterly sunk into silence, there were many individuals in the crowd who had found leisure to become aware of the presence of a masked figure which had arrested the attention of no single individual before. And the rumor of this new presence having spread itself whisperingly around, there arose at length from the whole company a buzz, or murmur, expressive of disapprobation and surprise—then, finally, of terror, of horror, and of disgust.

In an assembly of phantasms such as I have painted, it may well be supposed that no ordinary appearance could have excited such sensation. In truth the masquerade license of the night was nearly unlimited; but the figure in question had out-Heroded Herod,[5] and gone beyond the bounds of even the prince's indefinite decorum. There are chords in the hearts of the most reckless which cannot be touched without emotion. Even with the utterly lost, to whom life and death are equally jests, there are matters of which no jest can be made. The whole company, indeed, seemed now deeply to feel that in the costume and bearing of the stranger neither wit nor propriety existed. The figure was tall and gaunt, and shrouded from head to foot in the habiliments of the grave. The mask which concealed the visage was made so nearly to resemble the countenance of a stiffened corpse that the closest scrutiny must have had difficulty in detecting the cheat. And yet all this might have been endured, if not approved, by the mad revellers around. But the mummer had gone so far as to assume the type of the Red Death. His vesture was dabbled in *blood*— and his broad brow, with all the features of the face, was besprinkled with the scarlet horror.

When the eyes of Prince Prospero fell upon this spectral image (which with a slow and solemn movement, as if more fully to sustain its *rôle*, stalked to and fro among the waltzers) he was seen to be convulsed, in the first moment with a strong shudder either of terror or distaste; but, in the next, his brow reddened with rage.

"Who dares?" he demanded hoarsely of the courtiers who stood near him—"who dares insult us with this blasphemous mockery? Seize him and unmask him—that we may know whom we have to hang at sunrise, from the battlements!"

It was in the eastern or blue chamber in which stood the Prince Prospero as he uttered these words. They rang throughout the seven rooms loudly and clearly—for the prince was a bold and robust man, and the music had become hushed at the waving of his hand.

It was in the blue room where stood the prince, with a group of pale courtiers by his side. At first, as he spoke, there was a light rushing movement of this group in the direction of the intruder, who at the moment was also near at hand, and now, with deliberate and stately step, made closer approach to the speaker. But from a certain nameless awe with which the mad assumptions of the mummer had inspired the whole party, there were found none who put forth hand to seize him; so that, unimpeded, he passed within a yard of the prince's person; and, while the vast assembly, as if with one impulse, shrank from the centres of the rooms to the walls, he made his way uninterruptedly, but with the same solemn and measured step which had distinguished him from the first, through the blue chamber to the purple— through the purple to the green—through the green to the orange—through this again to the white—and even thence to the violet, ere a decided movement had been made to arrest him. It was then, however, that the Prince Prospero, maddening with rage and the shame of his own momentary cowardice, rushed hurriedly through the six chambers, while none followed him on account of a deadly terror that had seized upon all. He bore aloft a drawn dagger, and had approached, in rapid impetuosity, to within three or four feet of the retreating figure, when the latter, having attained the extremity of the velvet apartment, turned suddenly and confronted his pursuer. There was a sharp cry—and the dagger dropped gleaming upon the sable carpet, upon which, instantly afterwards, fell prostrate in death the Prince Prospero. Then, summoning the wild courage of despair, a throng of the revellers at once threw themselves into the black apartment, and, seizing the mummer, whose tall figure stood erect and motionless within the shadow of the ebony clock, gasped in unutterable horror at finding the grave-cerements and corpse-like mask which they handled with so violent a rudeness, untenanted by any tangible form.

And now was acknowledged the presence of the Red Death. He had come like a thief in the night.[6] And one by one dropped the revellers in the blood-bedewed halls of their revel, and died each in the despairing posture of his fall. And the life of the ebony clock went out with that of the last of the gay. And the flames of the tripods expired. And Darkness and Decay and the Red Death held illimitable dominion over all.

The Pit and the Pendulum[1]

Impia tortorum longas hic turba furores
Sanguinis innocui, non satiata, aluit.
Sospite nunc patrià, fracto nunc funeris antro,
Mors ubi dira fuit vita salusque patent.

[Quatrain composed for the gates of a Market to be erected upon the site of the Jacobin Club House at Paris.][2]

I WAS sick—sick unto death with that long agony; and when they at length unbound me, and I was permitted to sit, I felt that my senses were leaving me. The sentence—the dread sentence of death—was the last of distinct accentuation which reached my ears. After that, the sound of the inquisitorial voices seemed merged in one dreamy indeterminate hum. It conveyed to my soul the idea of *revolution*—perhaps from its association in fancy with the burr of a millwheel. This only for a brief period; for presently I heard no more. Yet, for a while, I saw; but with how terrible an exaggeration! I saw the lips of the black-robed judges.[3] They appeared to me white—whiter than the sheet upon which I trace these words—and thin even to grotesqueness; thin with the intensity of their expression of firmness—of immoveable resolution—of stern contempt of human torture. I saw that the decrees of what to me was Fate, were still issuing from those lips. I saw them writhe with a deadly locution. I saw them fashion the syllables of my name; and I shuddered because no sound succeeded. I saw, too, for a few moments of delirious horror, the soft and nearly imperceptible waving of the sable draperies which enwrapped the walls of the apartment. And then my vision fell upon the seven tall candles upon the table. At first they wore the aspect of charity, and seemed white slender angels who would save me; but then, all at once, there came a most deadly nausea over my spirit, and I felt every fibre in my frame thrill as if I had touched the wire of a galvanic battery, while the angel forms became meaningless spectres, with heads of flame, and I saw that from them there would be no help. And then there stole into my fancy, like a rich musical note, the thought of what sweet rest there must be in the grave. The thought came gently and stealthily, and it seemed long before it attained full appreciation; but just as my spirit came at length properly to feel and entertain it, the figures of the judges vanished, as if magically, from before me; the tall candles sank into nothingness; their flames went out utterly; the blackness of darkness supervened; all sensations appeared swallowed up in a mad rushing descent as of the soul into Hades. Then silence, and stillness, and night were the universe.

I had swooned; but still will not say that all of consciousness was lost. What of it there remained I will not attempt to define, or even to describe; yet all was not lost. In the deepest slumber—no! In delirium—no! In a swoon—no! In death—no! even in the grave all *is not* lost. Else there is no immortality for man. Arousing from the most profound of slumbers, we break the gossamer web of *some* dream. Yet in a second afterward, (so frail may that web have been) we remember not that we have dreamed. In the return to life from the swoon there are two stages; first, that of the sense of mental or spiritual; secondly, that of the sense of physical, existence. It seems probable that if, upon reaching the second stage, we could recall the impressions of the first, we should find these impressions eloquent in memories of the gulf beyond. And that gulf is—what? How at least shall we distinguish its shadows from those of the tomb? But if the impressions of what I have termed the first stage, are not, at will, recalled, yet, after long interval, do they not come unbidden, while we marvel whence they come? He who has swooned, is not he who finds strange palaces and wildly familiar faces in coals that glow; is not he who beholds floating in mid-air the sad visions that the many may not view; is not he who ponders ever the perfume of some novel flower—is not he whose brain grows bewildered with the meaning of some musical cadence which has never before arrested his attention.

Amid frequent and thoughtful endeavors to remember; amid earnest struggles to regather some token of the state of seeming nothingness into which my soul had lapsed, there have been moments when I have dreamed of success; there have been brief, very brief periods when I have conjured up remembrances which the lucid reason of a later epoch assures me could have had reference only to that condition of seeming unconsciousness. These shadows of memory tell, indistinctly, of tall figures that lifted and bore me in silence down—down—still down—till a hideous dizziness oppressed me at the mere idea of the interminableness of the descent. They tell also of a vague horror at my heart, on account of that heart's unnatural stillness. Then comes a sense of sudden motionlessness throughout all things; as if those who bore me (a ghastly train!) had outrun, in their descent, the limits of the limitless, and paused from the wearisomeness of their toil. After this I call to mind flatness and dampness; and then all is *madness*—the madness of a memory which busies itself among forbidden things.

Very suddenly there came back to my soul motion and sound—the tumultuous motion of the heart, and, in my ears, the sound of its beating. Then a pause in which all is blank. Then again sound, and motion, and touch—a tingling sensation pervading my frame. Then the mere consciousness of existence, without thought—a condition which lasted long. Then, very suddenly, *thought*, and shuddering terror, and earnest endeavor to comprehend my true state. Then a strong desire to lapse into insensibility. Then a rushing revival of soul and a successful effort to move. And now a full memory of the trial, of the judges, of the sable draperies, of the sentence, of the sickness, of the swoon. Then entire forgetfulness of all that followed; of all that a later day and much earnestness of endeavor have enabled me vaguely to recall.

So far, I had not opened my eyes. I felt that I lay upon my back, unbound. I reached out my hand, and it fell heavily upon something damp and hard. There I suffered it to remain for many minutes, while I strove to imagine where and *what* I could be. I longed, yet dared not to employ my vision. I dreaded the first glance at objects around me. It was not that I feared to look upon things horrible, but that I grew aghast lest there should be *nothing* to see. At length, with a wild desperation at heart, I quickly unclosed my eyes. My worst thoughts, then, were confirmed. The blackness of eternal night encompassed me. I struggled for breath. The intensity of the darkness seemed to oppress and stifle me. The atmosphere was intolerably close. I still lay quietly, and made effort to exercise my reason. I brought to mind the inquisitorial proceedings, and attempted from that point to deduce my real condition. The sentence had passed; and it appeared to me that a very long interval of time had since elapsed. Yet not for a moment did I suppose myself actually dead. Such a supposition, notwithstanding what we read in fiction, is altogether inconsistent with real existence;—but where and in what state was I? The condemned to death, I knew, perished usually at the *auto-da-fes*,[4] and one of these had been held on the very night of the day of my trial. Had I been remanded to my dungeon, to await the next sacrifice, which would not take place for many months? This I at once saw could not be. Victims had been in immediate demand. Moreover, my dungeon, as well as all the condemned cells at Toledo, had stone floors, and light was not altogether excluded.

A fearful idea now suddenly drove the blood in torrents upon my heart, and for a brief period, I once more relapsed into insensibility. Upon recovering, I at once started to my feet, trembling convulsively in every fibre. I thrust my arms wildly above and around me in all directions. I felt nothing; yet dreaded to move a step, lest I should be impeded by the walls of a *tomb*. Perspiration burst from every pore, and stood in cold big beads upon my forehead. The agony of suspense, grew at length intolerable, and I cautiously moved forward, with my arms extended, and my eyes straining from their sockets, in the hope of catching some faint ray of light. I proceeded for many paces; but still all was blackness and vacancy. I breathed more freely. It seemed evident that mine was not, at least, the most hideous of fates.

And now, as I still continued to step cautiously onward, there came thronging upon my recollection a thousand vague rumors of the horrors of Toledo. Of the dungeons there had been strange things narrated—fables I had always deemed them—but yet strange, and too ghastly to repeat, save in a whisper. Was I left to perish of starvation in this subterranean world of darkness; or what fate, perhaps even more fearful, awaited me? That the result would be death, and a death of more than customary bitterness, I knew too well the character of my judges to doubt. The mode and the hour were all that occupied or distracted me.

My outstretched hands at length encountered some solid obstruction. It was a wall, seemingly of stone masonry—very smooth, slimy, and cold. I followed it up; stepping with all the careful distrust with which certain antique narratives had inspired me. This process, however, afforded me no means of ascertaining the dimensions of my dungeon; as I might make its circuit, and return to the point whence I set out, without being aware of the fact; so perfectly uniform seemed the wall. I therefore sought the knife which had been in my pocket, when led into the inquisitorial chamber; but it was gone; my clothes had been exchanged for a wrapper of coarse serge. I had thought of forcing the blade in some minute crevice of the masonry, so as to identify my point of departure. The difficulty, nevertheless, was but trivial; although, in the disorder of my fancy, it seemed at first insuperable. I tore a part of the hem from the robe and placed the fragment at full length, and at right angles to the wall. In groping my way around the prison, I could not fail to encounter this rag upon completing the circuit. So, at least I thought: but I had not counted upon the extent of the dungeon, or upon my own weakness. The ground was moist and slippery. I staggered onward for some time, when I stumbled and fell. My excessive fatigue induced me to remain prostrate; and sleep soon overtook me as I lay.

Upon awaking, and stretching forth an arm, I found beside me a loaf and a pitcher with water. I was too much exhausted to reflect upon this circumstance, but ate and drank with avidity. Shortly afterward, I resumed my tour around the prison, and with much toil, came at last upon the fragment of the serge. Up to the period when I fell I had counted fifty-two paces, and upon resuming my walk, I had counted forty-eight more;—when I arrived at the rag. There were in all, then, a hundred paces; and, admitting two paces to the yard, I presumed the dungeon to be fifty yards in circuit. I had met, however, with many angles in the wall, and thus I could form no guess at the shape of the vault; for vault I could not help supposing it to be.

I had little object—certainly no hope—in these researches; but a vague curiosity prompted me to continue them. Quitting the wall, I resolved to cross the area of the enclosure. At first I proceeded with extreme caution, for the floor, although seemingly of solid material, was treacherous with slime. At length, however, I took courage, and did not hesitate to step firmly; endeavoring to cross in as direct a line as possible. I had advanced some ten or twelve paces in this manner, when the remnant of the torn hem of my robe became entangled between my legs. I stepped on it, and fell violently on my face.

In the confusion attending my fall, I did not immediately apprehend a somewhat startling circumstance, which yet, in a few seconds afterward, and while I still lay prostrate, arrested my attention. It was this—my chin rested upon the floor of the prison, but my lips and the upper portion of my head, although seemingly at a less elevation than the chin, touched nothing. At the same time my forehead seemed bathed in a clammy vapor, and the peculiar smell of decayed fungus arose to my nostrils. I put forward my arm, and shuddered to find that I had fallen at the very brink of a circular pit, whose extent, of course, I had no means of ascertaining at the moment. Groping about the masonry just below the margin, I succeeded in dislodging a small fragment, and let it fall into the abyss. For many seconds I hearkened to its reverberations as it dashed against the sides of the chasm in its descent; at length there was a sullen plunge into water, succeeded by loud echoes. At the same moment there came a sound resembling the quick opening, and as rapid closing of a door overhead, while a faint gleam of light flashed suddenly through the gloom, and as suddenly faded away.

I saw clearly the doom which had been prepared for me, and congratulated myself upon the timely accident by which I had escaped. Another step before my fall, and the world had seen me no more. And the death just avoided, was of that very character which I had regarded as fabulous and frivolous in the tales respecting the Inquisition. To the victims of its tyranny, there was the choice of death with its direst physical agonies, or death with its most hideous moral horrors. I had been reserved for the latter. By long suffering my nerves had been unstrung, until I trembled at the sound of my own voice, and had become in every respect a fitting subject for the species of torture which awaited me.

Shaking in every limb, I groped my way back to the wall; resolving there to perish rather than risk the terrors of the wells, of which my imagination now pictured many in various positions about the dungeon. In other conditions of mind I might have had courage to end my misery at once by a plunge into one of these abysses; but now I was the veriest of cowards. Neither could I forget what I had read of these pits—that the *sudden* extinction of life formed no part of their most horrible plan.

Agitation of spirit kept me awake for many long hours; but at length I again slumbered. Upon arousing, I found by my side, as before, a loaf and a pitcher of water. A burning thirst consumed me, and I emptied the vessel at a draught. I must have been drugged; for scarcely had I drunk, before I became irresistibly drowsy. A deep sleep fell upon me—a sleep like that of death. How long it lasted, of course, I know not; but when, once again, I unclosed my eyes, the objects around me were visible. By a wild sulphurous lustre, the origin of which I could not at first determine, I was enabled to see the extent and aspect of the prison.

In its size I had been greatly mistaken. The whole circuit of its walls did not exceed twenty-five yards. For some minutes this fact occasioned me a world of vain trouble; vain indeed! for what could be of less importance, under the terrible circumstances which environed me, than the mere dimensions of my dungeon? But my soul took a wild interest in trifles, and I busied myself in endeavors to account for the error I had committed in my measurement. The truth at length flashed upon me. In my first attempt at exploration I had counted fifty-two paces, up to the period when I fell; I must then have been within a pace or two of the fragment of serge; in fact, I had nearly performed the circuit of the vault. I then slept, and upon awaking, I must have returned upon my steps—thus supposing the circuit nearly double what it actually was. My confusion of mind prevented me from observing that I began my tour with the wall to the left, and ended it with the wall to the right.

I had been deceived, too, in respect to the shape of the enclosure. In feeling my way I had found many angles, and thus deduced an idea of great irregularity; so potent is the effect of total darkness upon one arousing from lethargy or sleep! The angles were simply those of a few slight depressions, or niches, at odd intervals. The general shape of the prison was square. What I had taken for masonry seemed now to be iron, or some other metal, in huge plates, whose sutures or joints occasioned the depression. The entire surface of this metallic enclosure was rudely daubed in all the hideous and repulsive devices to which the charnel superstition of the monks has given rise. The figures of fiends in aspects of menace, with skeleton forms, and other more really fearful images, overspread and disfigured the walls. I observed that the outlines of these monstrosities were sufficiently distinct, but that the colors seemed faded and blurred, as if from the effects of a damp atmosphere. I now noticed the floor, too, which was of stone. In the centre yawned the circular pit from whose jaws I had escaped; but it was the only one in the dungeon.

All this I saw indistinctly and by much effort: for my personal condition had been greatly changed during slumber. I now lay upon my back, and at full length, on a species of low framework of wood. To this I was securely bound by a long strap resembling a surcingle.[5] It passed in many convolutions about my limbs and body, leaving at liberty only my head, and my left arm to such extent that I could, by dint of much exertion, supply myself with food from an earthen dish which lay by my side on the floor. I saw, to my horror, that the pitcher had been removed. I say to my horror; for I was consumed with intolerable thirst. This thirst it appeared to be the design of my persecutors to stimulate: for the food in the dish was meat pungently seasoned.

Looking upward, I surveyed the ceiling of my prison. It was some thirty or forty feet overhead, and constructed much as the side walls. In one of its panels a very singular figure riveted my whole attention. It was the painted figure of Time as he is commonly represented, save that, in lieu of a scythe, he held what, at a casual glance, I supposed to be the pictured image of a huge pendulum such as we see on antique clocks. There was something, however, in the appearance of this machine which caused me to regard it more attentively. While I gazed directly upward at it (for its position was immediately over my own) I fancied that I saw it in motion. In an instant afterward the fancy was confirmed. Its sweep was brief, and of course slow. I watched it for some minutes, somewhat in fear, but more in wonder. Wearied at length with observing its dull movement, I turned my eyes upon the other objects in the cell.

A slight noise attracted my notice, and, looking to the floor, I saw several enormous rats traversing it. They had issued from the well, which lay just within view to my right. Even then, while I gazed, they came up in troops, hurriedly, with ravenous eyes, allured by the scent of the meat. From this it required much effort and attention to scare them away.

It might have been half an hour, perhaps even an hour, (for I could take but imperfect note of time) before I again cast my eyes upward. What I then saw confounded and amazed me. The sweep of the pendulum had increased in extent by nearly a yard. As a natural consequence, its velocity was also much greater. But what mainly disturbed me was the idea that it had perceptibly *descended*. I now observed— with what horror it is needless to say—that its nether extremity was formed of a crescent of glittering steel, about a foot in length from horn to horn; the horns upward, and the under edge evidently as keen as that of a razor. Like a razor also, it seemed massy and heavy, tapering from the edge into a solid and broad structure above. It was appended to a weighty rod of brass, and the whole *hissed* as it swung through the air.

I could no longer doubt the doom prepared for me by monkish ingenuity in torture. My cognizance of the pit had become known to the inquisitorial agents—

the pit whose horrors had been destined for so bold a recusant as myself—*the pit*, typical of hell, and regarded by rumor as the Ultima Thule[6] of all their punishments. The plunge into this pit I had avoided by the merest of accidents, and I knew that surprise, or entrapment into torment, formed an important portion of all the grotesquerie of these dungeon deaths. Having failed to fall, it was no part of the demon plan to hurl me into the abyss; and thus (there being no alternative) a different and a milder destruction awaited me. Milder! I half smiled in my agony as I thought of such application of such a term.

What boots it to tell of the long, long hours of horror more than mortal, during which I counted the rushing vibrations of the steel! Inch by inch—line by line—with a descent only appreciable at intervals that seemed ages—down and still down it came! Days passed—it might have been that many days passed—ere it swept so closely over me as to fan me with its acrid breath. The odor of the sharp steel forced itself into my nostrils. I prayed—I wearied heaven with my prayer for its more speedy descent. I grew frantically mad, and struggled to force myself upward against the sweep of the fearful scimitar. And then I fell suddenly calm, and lay smiling at the glittering death, as a child at some rare bauble.

There was another interval of utter insensibility; it was brief; for, upon again lapsing into life there had been no perceptible descent in the pendulum. But it might have been long; for I knew there were demons who took note of my swoon, and who could have arrested the vibration at pleasure. Upon my recovery, too, I felt very—oh, inexpressibly sick and weak, as if through long inanition. Even amid the agonies of that period, the human nature craved food. With painful effort I outstretched my left arm as far as my bonds permitted, and took possession of the small remnant which had been spared me by the rats. As I put a portion of it within my lips, there rushed to my mind a half formed thought of joy—of hope. Yet what business had *I* with hope? It was, as I say, a half formed thought—man has many such which are never completed. I felt that it was of joy—of hope; but I felt also that it had perished in its formation. In vain I struggled to perfect—to retain it. Long suffering had nearly annihilated all my ordinary powers of mind. I was an imbecile—an idiot.

The vibration of the pendulum was at right angles to my length. I saw that the crescent was designed to cross the region of the heart. It would fray the serge of my robe—it would return and repeat its operations—again—and again. Notwithstanding its terrifically wide sweep (some thirty feet or more) and the hissing vigor of its descent, sufficient to sunder these very walls of iron, still the fraying of my robe would be all that, for several minutes, it would accomplish. And at this thought I paused. I dared not go farther than this reflection. I dwelt upon it with a pertinacity of attention—as if, in so dwelling, I could arrest *here* the descent of the steel. I forced myself to ponder upon the sound of the crescent as it should pass across the garment—upon the peculiar thrilling sensation which the friction of cloth produces on the nerves. I pondered upon all this frivolity until my teeth were on edge.

Down—steadily down it crept. I took a frenzied pleasure in contrasting its downward with its lateral velocity. To the right—to the left—far and wide—with the shriek of a damned spirit; to my heart with the stealthy pace of the tiger! I alternately laughed and howled as the one or the other idea grew predominant.

Down—certainly, relentlessly down! It vibrated within three inches of my bosom! I struggled violently, furiously, to free my left arm. This was free only from the elbow to the hand. I could reach the latter, from the platter beside me, to my mouth, with great effort, but no farther. Could I have broken the fastenings above the elbow, I would have seized and attempted to arrest the pendulum. I might as well have attempted to arrest an avalanche!

Down—still unceasingly—still inevitably down! I gasped and struggled at each vibration. I shrunk convulsively at its every sweep. My eyes followed its outward or upward whirls with the eagerness of the most unmeaning despair; they closed themselves spasmodically at the descent, although death would have been a relief, oh! how unspeakable! Still I quivered in every nerve to think how slight a sinking of the machinery would precipitate that keen, glistening axe upon my bosom. It was *hope* that prompted the nerve to quiver—the frame to shrink. It was *hope*—the hope that triumphs on the rack—that whispers to the death-condemned even in the dungeons of the Inquisition.

I saw that some ten or twelve vibrations would bring the steel in actual contact with my robe, and with this observation there suddenly came over my spirit all the keen, collected calmness of despair. For the first time during many hours—or perhaps days—I *thought*. It now occurred to me that the bandage, or surcingle, which enveloped me, was *unique*. I was tied by no separate cord. The first stroke of the razor-like crescent athwart any portion of the band, would so detach it that it might be unwound from my person by means of my left hand. But how fearful, in that case, the proximity of the steel! The result of the slightest struggle how deadly! Was it likely, moreover, that the minions of the torturer had not foreseen and provided for this possibility! Was it probable that the bandage crossed my bosom in the track of the pendulum? Dreading to find my faint, and, as it seemed, my last hope frustrated, I so far elevated my head as to obtain a distinct view of my breast. The surcingle enveloped my limbs and body close in all directions—*save in the path of the destroying crescent.*

Scarcely had I dropped my head back into its original position, when there flashed upon my mind what I cannot better describe than as the unformed half of that idea of deliverance to which I have previously alluded, and of which a moiety only floated indeterminately through my brain when I raised food to my burning lips. The whole thought was now present—feeble, scarcely sane, scarcely definite—but still entire. I proceeded at once, with the nervous energy of despair, to attempt its execution.

For many hours the immediate vicinity of the low framework upon which I lay, had been literally swarming with rats. They were wild, bold, ravenous; their red eyes glaring upon me as if they waited but for motionlessness on my part to make me their prey. "To what food," I thought, "have they been accustomed in the well."

They had devoured, in spite of all my efforts to prevent them, all but a small remnant of the contents of the dish. I had fallen into an habitual see-saw, or wave of the hand about the platter: and, at length, the unconscious uniformity of the movement deprived it of effect. In their voracity the vermin frequently fastened their sharp fangs in my fingers. With the particles of the oily and spicy viand which now remained, I thoroughly rubbed the bandage wherever I could reach it; then, raising my hand from the floor, I lay breathlessly still.

At first the ravenous animals were startled and terrified at the change—at the cessation of movement. They shrank alarmedly back; many sought the well. But this was only for a moment. I had not counted in vain upon their voracity. Observing that I remained without motion, one or two of the boldest leaped upon the frame-work, and smelt at the surcingle. This seemed the signal for a general rush. Forth from the well they hurried in fresh troops. They clung to the wood—they overran it, and leaped in hundreds upon my person. The measured movement of the pendulum disturbed them not at all. Avoiding its strokes they busied themselves with the anointed bandage. They pressed—they swarmed upon me in ever accumulating heaps. They writhed upon my throat; their cold lips sought my own; I was half stifled by their thronging pressure; disgust, for which the world has no name, swelled my bosom, and chilled, with a heavy clamminess, my heart. Yet one minute, and I felt that the struggle would be over. Plainly I perceived the loosening of the bandage. I knew that in more than one place it must be already severed. With a more than human resolution I lay *still*.

Nor had I erred in my calculations—nor had I endured in vain. I at length felt that I was *free*. The surcingle hung in ribands from my body. But the stroke of the pendulum already pressed upon my bosom. It had divided the serge of the robe. It had cut through the linen beneath. Twice again it swung, and a sharp sense of pain shot through every nerve. But the moment of escape had arrived. At a wave of my hand my deliverers hurried tumultuously away. With a steady movement—cautious, sidelong, shrinking, and slow—I slid from the embrace of the bandage and beyond the reach of the scimitar. For the moment, at least, *I was free*.

Free!—and in the grasp of the Inquisition! I had scarcely stepped from my wooden bed of horror upon the stone floor of the prison, when the motion of the hellish machine ceased and I beheld it drawn up, by some invisible force, through the ceiling. This was a lesson which I took desperately to heart. My every motion was undoubtedly watched. Free!—I had but escaped death in one form of agony, to be delivered unto worse than death in some other. With that thought I rolled my eyes nervously around on the barriers of iron that hemmed me in. Something unusual—some change which, at first, I could not appreciate distinctly—it was obvious, had taken place in the apartment. For many minutes of a dreamy and trembling abstraction, I busied myself in vain, unconnected conjecture. During this period, I became aware, for the first time, of the origin of the sulphurous light which illumined the cell. It proceeded from a fissure, about half an inch in width, extending entirely around the prison at the base of the walls, which thus appeared, and were, completely separated from the floor. I endeavored, but of course in vain, to look through the aperture.

As I arose from the attempt, the mystery of the alteration in the chamber broke at once upon my understanding. I have observed that, although the outlines of the figures upon the walls were sufficiently distinct, yet the colours seemed blurred and indefinite. These colors had now assumed, and were momentarily assuming, a startling and most intense brilliancy, that gave to the spectral and fiendish portraitures an aspect that might have thrilled even firmer nerves than my own. Demon eyes, of a wild and ghastly vivacity, glared upon me in a thousand directions, where none had been visible before, and gleamed with the lurid lustre of a fire that I could not force my imagination to regard as unreal.

Unreal!—Even while I breathed there came to my nostrils the breath of the vapour of heated iron! A suffocating odour pervaded the prison! A deeper glow settled each moment in the eyes that glared at my agonies! A richer tint of crimson diffused itself over the pictured horrors of blood. I panted! I gasped for breath! There could be no doubt of the design of my tormentors—oh! most unrelenting! oh! most demoniac of men! I shrank from the glowing metal to the centre of the cell. Amid the thought of the fiery destruction that impended, the idea of the coolness of the well came over my soul like balm. I rushed to its deadly brink. I threw my straining vision below. The glare from the enkindled roof illumined its inmost recesses. Yet, for a wild moment, did my spirit refuse to comprehend the meaning of what I saw. At length it forced—it wrestled its way into my soul—it burned itself in upon my shuddering reason.—Oh! for a voice to speak!—oh! horror!—oh! any horror but this! With a shriek, I rushed from the margin, and buried my face in my hands—weeping bitterly.

The heat rapidly increased, and once again I looked up, shuddering as with a fit of the ague. There had been a second change in the cell—and now the change was obviously in the *form*. As before, it was in vain that I, at first, endeavored to appreciate or understand what was taking place. But not long was I left in doubt. The Inquisitorial vengeance had been hurried by my two-fold escape, and there was to be no more dallying with the King of Terrors. The room had been square. I saw that two of its iron angles were now acute—two, consequently, obtuse. The fearful difference quickly increased with a low rumbling or moaning sound. In an instant the apartment had shifted its form into that of a lozenge. But the alteration stopped not here—I neither hoped nor desired it to stop. I could have clasped the red walls to my bosom as a garment of eternal peace. "Death," I said, "any death but that of the pit!" Fool! might I have not known that *into the pit* it was the object of the burning iron to urge me? Could I resist its glow? or, if even that, could I withstand its pressure? And now, flatter and flatter grew the lozenge, with a rapidity that left me no time for contemplation. Its centre, and of course, its greatest width, came just over the yawning gulf. I shrank back—but the closing walls pressed me resistlessly onward. At length for my seared and writhing body there was no longer an inch of foothold on the firm floor of the prison. I struggled no more, but the agony of my soul found vent in one loud, long, and final scream of despair. I felt that I tottered upon the brink—I averted my eyes—

There was a discordant hum of human voices! There was a loud blast as of many trumpets! There was a harsh grating as of a thousand thunders! The fiery walls rushed back! An outstretched arm caught my own as I fell, fainting, into the abyss. It was that of General Lasalle.[7] The French army had entered Toledo. The Inquisition was in the hands of its enemies.

The Tell-Tale Heart[1]

TRUE!—nervous—very, very dreadfully nervous I had been and am; but why *will* you say that I am mad? The disease had sharpened my senses—not destroyed—not dulled them. Above all was the sense of hearing acute. I heard all things in the heaven and in the earth. I heard many things in hell. How, then, am I mad? Hearken! and observe how healthily—how calmly I can tell you the whole story.

It is impossible to say how first the idea entered my brain; but once conceived, it haunted me day and night. Object there was none. Passion there was none. I loved the old man. He had never wronged me. He had never given me insult. For his gold I had no desire. I think it was his eye! yes, it was this! He had the eye of a vulture—a pale blue eye, with a film over it. Whenever it fell upon me, my blood ran cold; and so by degrees—very gradually—I made up my mind to take the life of the old man, and thus rid myself of the eye forever.

Now this is the point. You fancy me mad. Madmen know nothing. But you should have seen *me*. You should have seen how wisely I proceeded—with what caution—with what foresight—with what dissimulation I went to work! I was never kinder to the old man than during the whole week before I killed him. And every night, about midnight, I turned the latch of his door and opened it—oh so gently! And then, when I had made an opening sufficient for my head, I put in a dark lantern, all closed, closed, so that no light shone out, and then I thrust in my head. Oh, you would have laughed to see how cunningly I thrust it in! I moved it slowly—very, very slowly, so that I might not disturb the old man's sleep. It took me an hour to place my whole head within the opening so far that I could see him as he lay upon his bed. Ha!—would a madman have been so wise as this? And then, when my head was well in the room, I undid the lantern cautiously—oh, so cautiously—cautiously (for the hinges creaked)—I undid it just so much that a single thin ray fell upon the vulture eye. And this I did for seven long nights—every night just at midnight—but I found the eye always closed; and so it was impossible to do the work; for it was not the old man who vexed me, but his Evil Eye. And every morning, when the day broke, I went boldly into the chamber, and spoke courageously to him, calling him by name in a hearty tone, and inquiring how he had passed the night. So you see he would have been a very profound old man, indeed, to suspect that every night, just at twelve, I looked in upon him while he slept.

Upon the eighth night I was more than usually cautious in opening the door. A watch's minute hand moves more quickly than did mine. Never before that night, had I *felt* the extent of my own powers—of my sagacity. I could scarcely contain my feelings of triumph. To think that there I was, opening the door, little by little, and he not even to dream of my secret deeds or thoughts. I fairly chuckled at the idea; and perhaps he heard me; for he moved on the bed suddenly, as if startled. Now you may think that I drew back—but no. His room was as black as pitch with the thick darkness, (for the shutters were close fastened, through fear of robbers,) and so I knew that he could not see the opening of the door, and I kept pushing it on steadily, steadily.

I had my head in, and was about to open the lantern, when my thumb slipped upon the tin fastening, and the old man sprang up in the bed, crying out—"Who's there?"

I kept quite still and said nothing. For a whole hour I did not move a muscle, and in the meantime I did not hear him lie down. He was still sitting up in the bed listening;—just as I have done, night after night, hearkening to the death watches[2] in the wall.

Presently I heard a slight groan, and I knew it was the groan of mortal terror. It was not a groan of pain or of grief—oh, no!—it was the low stifled sound that arises from the bottom of the soul when overcharged with awe. I knew the sound well.

Many a night, just at midnight, when all the world slept, it has welled up from my own bosom, deepening, with its dreadful echo, the terrors that distracted me. I say I knew it well. I knew what the old man felt, and pitied him, although I chuckled at heart. I knew that he had been lying awake ever since the first slight noise, when he had turned in the bed. His fears had been ever since growing upon him. He had been trying to fancy them causeless, but could not. He had been saying to himself—"It is nothing but the wind in the chimney—it is only a mouse crossing the floor," or "it is merely a cricket which has made a single chirp." Yes, he has been trying to comfort himself with these suppositions: but he had found all in vain. *All in vain*; because Death, in approaching him had stalked with his black shadow before him, and enveloped the victim. And it was the mournful influence of the unperceived shadow that caused him to feel—although he neither saw nor heard—to *feel* the presence of my head within the room.

When I had waited a long time, very patiently, without hearing him lie down, I resolved to open a little—a very, very little crevice in the lantern. So I opened it— you cannot imagine how stealthily, stealthily—until, at length a single dim ray, like the thread of the spider, shot from out the crevice and fell full upon the vulture eye.

It was open—wide, wide open—and I grew furious as I gazed upon it. I saw it with perfect distinctness—all a dull blue, with a hideous veil over it that chilled the very marrow in my bones; but I could see nothing else of the old man's face or person: for I had directed the ray as if by instinct, precisely upon the damned spot.

And have I not told you that what you mistake for madness is but over acuteness of the senses?—now, I say, there came to my ears a low, dull, quick sound, such as a watch makes when enveloped in cotton. I knew *that* sound well, too. It was the beating of the old man's heart. It increased my fury, as the beating of a drum stimulates the soldier into courage.

But even yet I refrained and kept still. I scarcely breathed. I held the lantern motionless. I tried how steadily I could maintain the ray upon the eye. Meantime the hellish tattoo of the heart increased. It grew quicker and quicker, and louder and louder every instant. The old man's terror *must* have been extreme! It grew louder, I say, louder every moment!—do you mark me well? I have told you that I am nervous: so I am. And now at the dead hour of the night, amid the dreadful silence of that old house, so strange a noise as this excited me to uncontrollable terror. Yet, for some minutes longer I refrained and stood still. But the beating grew louder, louder! I thought the heart must burst. And now a new anxiety seized me—the sound would be heard by a neighbour! The old man's hour had come! With a loud yell, I threw open the lantern and leaped into the room. He shrieked once—once only. In an instant I dragged him to the floor, and pulled the heavy bed over him. I then smiled gaily, to find the deed so far done. But, for many minutes, the heart beat on with a muffled sound. This, however, did not vex me; it would not be heard through the wall. At length it ceased. The old man was dead. I removed the bed and examined the corpse. Yes, he was stone, stone dead. I placed my hand upon the heart and held it there many minutes. There was no pulsation. He was stone dead. His eye would trouble me no more.

If still you think me mad, you will think so no longer when I describe the wise precautions I took for the concealment of the body. The night waned, and I worked hastily, but in silence. First of all I dismembered the corpse. I cut off the head and the arms and the legs.

I then took up three planks from the flooring of the chamber, and deposited all between the scantlings. I then replaced the boards so cleverly, so cunningly, that no human eye—not even *his*—could have detected any thing wrong. There was nothing to wash out—no stain of any kind—no blood-spot whatever. I had been too wary for that. A tub had caught all—ha! ha!

When I had made an end of these labors, it was four o'clock—still dark as midnight. As the bell sounded the hour, there came a knocking at the street door. I went down to open it with a light heart,—for what had I *now* to fear? There entered three men, who introduced themselves, with perfect suavity, as officers of the police. A shriek had been heard by a neighbour during the night; suspicion of foul play had been aroused; information had been lodged at the police office, and they (the officers) had been deputed to search the premises.

I smiled,—for *what* had I to fear? I bade the gentlemen welcome. The shriek, I said, was my own in a dream. The old man, I mentioned, was absent in the country. I took my visitors all over the house. I bade them search—search *well*. I led them, at length, to *his* chamber. I showed them his treasures, secure, undisturbed. In the enthusiasm of my confidence, I brought chairs into the room, and desired them *here* to rest from their fatigues, while I myself, in the wild audacity of my perfect triumph, placed my own seat upon the very spot beneath which reposed the corpse of the victim.

The officers were satisfied. My *manner* had convinced them. I was singularly at ease. They sat, and while I answered cheerily, they chatted of familiar things. But, ere long, I felt myself getting pale and wished them gone. My head ached, and I fancied a ringing in my ears: but still they sat and still they chatted. The ringing became more distinct:—it continued and became more distinct: I talked more freely to get rid of the feeling: but it continued and gained definitiveness—until, at length, I found that the noise was *not* within my ears.

No doubt I now grew *very* pale;—but I talked more fluently, and with a heightened voice. Yet the sound increased—and what could I do? It was *a low, dull, quick sound—much such a sound as a watch makes when enveloped in cotton*. I gasped for breath—and yet the officers heard it not. I talked more quickly—more vehemently; but the noise steadily increased. I arose and argued about trifles, in a high key and with violent gesticulations; but the noise steadily increased. Why *would* they not be gone? I paced the floor to and fro with heavy strides, as if excited to fury by the observations of the men—but the noise steadily increased. Oh God! what *could* I do? I foamed—I raved—I swore! I swung the chair upon which I had been sitting, and grated it upon the boards, but the noise arose over all and continually increased. It grew louder—louder—*louder!* And still the men chatted pleasantly, and smiled. Was it possible they heard not? Almighty God!—no, no! They heard!—they suspected—they *knew!*—they were making a mockery of my horror!—this I thought, and this I think. But anything was better than this agony! Anything was more tolerable than this derision! I could bear those hypocritical smiles no longer! I felt that I must scream or die!—and now—again!—hark! louder! louder! louder! *louder!—*

"Villains!" I shrieked, "dissemble no more! I admit the deed!—tear up the planks!—here, here!—it is the beating of his hideous heart!"

The Gold-Bug[1]

What ho! what ho! this fellow is dancing mad!
He hath been bitten by the Tarantula.
All in the Wrong[2]

MANY years ago, I contracted an intimacy with a Mr. William Legrand. He was of an ancient Huguenot family, and had once been wealthy; but a series of misfortunes had reduced him to want. To avoid the mortification consequent upon his disasters, he left New Orleans, the city of his forefathers, and took up his residence at Sullivan's Island,[3] near Charleston, South Carolina.

This Island is a very singular one. It consists of little else than the sea sand, and is about three miles long. Its breadth at no point exceeds a quarter of a mile. It is separated from the main land by a scarcely perceptible creek, oozing its way through a wilderness of reeds and slime, a favorite resort of the marsh-hen. The vegetation, as might be supposed, is scant, or at least dwarfish. No trees of any magnitude are to be seen. Near the western extremity, where Fort Moultrie stands, and where are some miserable frame buildings, tenanted, during summer, by the fugitives from Charleston dust and fever, may be found, indeed, the bristly palmetto; but the whole island, with the exception of this western point, and a line of hard, white beach on the seacoast, is covered with a dense undergrowth of the sweet myrtle, so much prized by the horticulturists of England. The shrub here often attains the height of fifteen or twenty feet, and forms an almost impenetrable coppice, burthening the air with its fragrance.

In the inmost recesses of this coppice, not far from the eastern or more remote end of the island, Legrand had built himself a small hut, which he occupied when I first, by mere accident, made his acquaintance. This soon ripened into friendship—for there was much in the recluse to excite interest and esteem. I found him well educated, with unusual powers of mind, but infected with misanthropy, and subject to perverse moods of alternate enthusiasm and melancholy. He had with him many books, but rarely employed them. His chief amusements were gunning and fishing, or sauntering along the beach and through the myrtles, in quest of shells or entomological specimens;—his collection of the latter might have been envied by a Swammerdamm.[4] In these excursions he was usually accompanied by an old negro, called Jupiter, who had been manumitted before the reverses of the family, but who could be induced, neither by threats nor by promises, to abandon what he considered his right of attendance upon the footsteps of his young "Massa Will." It is not improbable that the relatives of Legrand, conceiving him to be somewhat unsettled in intellect, had contrived to instil this obstinacy into Jupiter, with a view to the supervision and guardianship of the wanderer.

The winters in the latitude of Sullivan's Island are seldom very severe, and in the fall of the year it is a rare event indeed when a fire is considered necessary. About the middle of October, 18—, there occurred, however, a day of remarkable chilliness.

Just before sunset I scrambled my way through the evergreens to the hut of my friend, whom I had not visited for several weeks—my residence being, at that time, in Charleston, a distance of nine miles from the Island, while the facilities of passage and re-passage were very far behind those of the present day. Upon reaching the hut I rapped, as was my custom, and getting no reply, sought for the key where I knew it was secreted, unlocked the door and went in. A fine fire was blazing upon the hearth. It was a novelty, and by no means an ungrateful one. I threw off an overcoat, took an arm-chair by the crackling logs, and awaited patiently the arrival of my hosts.

Soon after dark they arrived, and gave me a most cordial welcome. Jupiter, grinning from ear to ear, bustled about to prepare some marsh-hens for supper. Legrand was in one of his fits—how else shall I term them?—of enthusiasm. He had found an unknown bivalve, forming a new genus, and, more than this, he had hunted down and secured, with Jupiter's assistance, a *scarabæus*[5] which he believed to be totally new, but in respect to which he wished to have my opinion on the morrow.

"And why not to-night?" I asked, rubbing my hands over the blaze, and wishing the whole tribe of *scarabæi* at the devil.

"Ah, if I had only known you were here!" said Legrand, "but it's so long since I saw you; and how could I foresee that you would pay me a visit this very night of all others? As I was coming home I met Lieutenant G——, from the fort, and, very foolishly, I lent him the bug; so it will be impossible for you to see it until the morning. Stay here to-night, and I will send Jup down for it at sunrise. It is the loveliest thing in creation!"

"What?—sunrise?"

"Nonsense! no!—the bug. It is of a brilliant gold color—about the size of a large hickory-nut—with two jet black spots near one extremity of the back, and another, somewhat longer, at the other. The *antennæ* are—"

"Dey aint *no* tin in him, Massa Will, I keep a tellin on you," here interrupted Jupiter; "de bug is a goole bug, solid, ebery bit of him, inside and all, sep him wing—neber feel half so hebby a bug in my life."

"Well, suppose it is, Jup," replied Legrand, somewhat more earnestly, it seemed to me, than the case demanded, "is that any reason for your letting the birds burn? The color"—here he turned to me—"is really almost enough to warrant Jupiter's idea. You never saw a more brilliant metallic lustre than the scales emit—but of this you cannot judge till to-morrow. In the mean time I can give you some idea of the shape." Saying this, he seated himself at a small table, on which were a pen and ink, but no paper. He looked for some in a drawer, but found none.

"Never mind," said he at length, "this will answer;" and he drew from his waistcoat pocket a scrap of what I took to be very dirty foolscap, and made upon it a rough drawing with the pen. While he did this, I retained my seat by the fire, for I was still chilly. When the design was complete, he handed it to me without rising. As I received it, a loud growl was heard, succeeded by a scratching at the door. Jupiter opened it, and a large Newfoundland, belonging to Legrand, rushed in, leaped upon my shoulders, and loaded me with caresses; for I had shown him much attention during previous visits. When his gambols were over, I looked at the paper, and, to speak the truth, found myself not a little puzzled at what my friend had depicted.

"Well!" I said, after contemplating it for some minutes, "this *is* a strange *scarabæus*, I must confess: new to me: never saw anything like it before—unless it was a skull, or a death's-head—which it more nearly resembles than anything else that has come under *my* observation."

"A death's head!" echoed Legrand—"Oh—yes—well, it has something of that appearance upon paper, no doubt. The two upper black spots look like eyes, eh? and the longer one at the bottom like a mouth—and then the shape of the whole is oval."

"Perhaps so," said I; "but, Legrand, I fear you are no artist. I must wait until I see the beetle itself, if I am to form any idea of its personal appearance."

"Well, I don't know," said he, a little nettled, "I draw tolerably—*should* do it at least—have had good masters, and flatter myself that I am not quite a blockhead."

"But, my dear fellow, you are joking then," said I, "this is a very passable *skull*— indeed, I may say that it is a very *excellent* skull, according to the vulgar notions about such specimens of physiology—and your *scarabæus* must be the queerest *scarabæus* in the world if it resembles it. Why, we may get up a very thrilling bit of superstition upon this hint. I presume you will call the bug *scarabæus caput hominis*,[6] or something of that kind—there are many similar titles in the Natural Histories. But where are the *antennæ* you spoke of?"

"The *antennæ!*" said Legrand, who seemed to be getting unaccountably warm upon the subject; "I am sure you must see the *antennæ*. I made them as distinct as they are in the original insect, and I presume that is sufficient."

"Well, well," I said, "perhaps you have—still I don't see them;" and I handed him the paper without additional remark, not wishing to ruffle his temper; but I was much surprised at the turn affairs had taken; his ill humor puzzled me—and, as for the drawing of the beetle, there were positively *no antennæ* visible, and the whole *did* bear a very close resemblance to the ordinary cuts of a death's-head.

He received the paper very peevishly, and was about to crumple it, apparently to throw it in the fire, when a casual glance at the design seemed suddenly to rivet his attention. In an instant his face grew violently red—in another as excessively pale. For some minutes he continued to scrutinize the drawing minutely where he sat. At length he arose, took a candle from the table, and proceeded to seat himself upon a sea-chest in the farthest corner of the room. Here again he made an anxious examination of the paper; turning it in all directions. He said nothing, however, and his conduct greatly astonished me; yet I thought it prudent not to exacerbate the growing moodiness of his temper by any comment. Presently he took from his coat pocket a wallet, placed the paper carefully in it, and deposited both in a writing-desk, which he locked. He now grew more composed in his demeanor; but his original air of enthusiasm had quite disappeared. Yet he seemed not so much sulky as abstracted. As the evening wore away he became more and more absorbed in reverie, from which no sallies of mine could arouse him. It had been my intention to pass the night at the hut, as I had frequently done before, but, seeing my host in this mood, I deemed it proper to take leave. He did not press me to remain, but, as I departed, he shook my hand with even more than his usual cordiality.

It was about a month after this (and during the interval I had seen nothing of Legrand) when I received a visit, at Charleston, from his man, Jupiter. I had never seen the good old negro look so dispirited, and I feared that some serious disaster had befallen my friend.

"Well, Jup," said I, "what is the matter now?—how is your master?"

"Why, to speak de troof, massa, him not so berry well as mought be."

"Not well! I am truly sorry to hear it. What does he complain of?"

"Dar! dat's it!—him neber plain of notin—but him berry sick for all dat."

"*Very* sick, Jupiter!—why didn't you say so at once? Is he confined to bed?"

"No, dat he aint!—he aint find nowhar—dat's just whar de shoe pinch—my mind is got to be berry hebby bout poor Massa Will."

"Jupiter, I should like to understand what it is you are talking about. You say your master is sick. Hasn't he told you what ails him?"

"Why, massa, taint worf while for to git mad about de matter—Massa Will say noffin at all aint de matter wid him—but den what make him go about looking dis here way, wid he head down and he soldiers up, and as white as a gose? And den he keeps a syphon all de time—"

"Keeps a what, Jupiter?"

"Keeps a syphon wid de figgurs on de slate—de queerest figgurs I ebber did see. Ise gittin to be skeered, I tell you. Hab for to keep mighty tight eye pon him noovers. Todder day he gib me slip fore de sun up and was gone de whole ob de blessed day. I had a big stick ready cut for to gib him deuced good beating when he did come—but Ise sich a fool dat I hadn't de heart arter all—he look so berry poorly."

"Eh?—what?—ah yes!—upon the whole I think you had better not be too severe with the poor fellow—don't flog him, Jupiter—he can't very well stand it—but can you form no idea of what has occasioned this illness, or rather this change of conduct? Has anything unpleasant happened since I saw you?"

"No, massa, dey aint bin noffin onpleasant *since* den—'twas *fore* den I'm feared—'twas de berry day you was dare."

"How? what do you mean?"

"Why massa, I mean de bug—dare now."

"The what?"

"De bug—I'm berry sartain dat Massa Will bin bit somewhere bout de head by dat goole-bug."

"And what cause have you, Jupiter, for such a supposition?"

"Claws enuff, massa, and mouff too. I nebber did see sich a deuced bug—he kick and he bite ebery ting what cum near him. Massa Will cotch him fuss, but had for to let him go gin mighty quick, I tell you—den was de time he must ha got de bite. I didn't like de look ob de bug mouff, myself, no how, so I wouldn't take hold ob him wid my finger, but I cotch him wid a piece ob paper dat I found. I rap him up in de paper and stuff piece ob it in he mouff—dat was de way."

"And you think, then, that your master was really bitten by the beetle, and that the bite made him sick?"

"I don't tink noffin about it—I nose it. What make him dream bout de goole so much, if taint cause he bit by de goole-bug? Ise heerd bout dem goole-bugs fore dis."

"But how do you know he dreams about gold?"

"How I know? why cause he talk about it in he sleep—dat's how I nose."

"Well, Jup, perhaps you are right; but to what fortunate circumstance am I to attribute the honor of a visit from you to-day?"

"What de matter, massa?"

"Did you bring any message from Mr. Legrand?"

"No, massa, I bring dis here pissel;" and here Jupiter handed me a note which ran thus:

MY DEAR—

Why have I not seen you for so long a time? I hope you have not been so foolish as to take offence at any little *brusquerie* of mine; but no, that is improbable.

Since I saw you I have had great cause for anxiety. I have something to tell you, yet scarcely know how to tell it, or whether I should tell it at all.

I have not been quite well for some days past, and poor old Jup annoys me, almost beyond endurance, by his well-meant attentions. Would you believe it?—he had prepared a huge stick, the other day, with which to chastise me for giving him the slip, and spending the day, *solus*, among the hills on the main land. I verily believe that my ill looks alone saved me a flogging.

I have made no addition to my cabinet since we met.

If you can, in any way, make it convenient, come over with Jupiter. *Do* come. I wish to see you *to-night*, upon business of importance. I assure you that it is of the *highest* importance.

Ever yours,   WILLIAM LEGRAND.

There was something in the tone of this note which gave me great uneasiness. Its whole style differed materially from that of Legrand. What could he be dreaming of? What new crotchet possessed his excitable brain? What "business of the highest importance" could *he* possibly have to transact? Jupiter's account of him boded no good. I dreaded lest the continued pressure of misfortune had, at length, fairly unsettled the reason of my friend. Without a moment's hesitation, therefore, I prepared to accompany the negro.

Upon reaching the wharf, I noticed a scythe and three spades, all apparently new, lying in the bottom of the boat in which we were to embark.

"What is the meaning of all this, Jup?" I inquired.

"Him syfe, massa, and spade."

"Very true; but what are they doing here?"

"Him de syfe and de spade what Massa Will sis pon my buying for him in de town, and de debbils own lot of money I had to gib for em."

"But what, in the name of all that is mysterious, is your 'Massa Will' going to do with scythes and spades?"

"Dat's more dan *I* know, and debbil take me if I don't blieve 'tis more dan he know, too. But it's all cum ob de bug."

Finding that no satisfaction was to be obtained of Jupiter, whose whole intellect seemed to be absorbed by "de bug," I now stepped into the boat and made sail. With a fair and strong breeze we soon ran into the little cove to the northward of Fort Moultrie, and a walk of some two miles brought us to the hut. It was about three in the afternoon when we arrived. Legrand had been awaiting us in eager expectation. He grasped my hand with a nervous *empressement* which alarmed me and strengthened the suspicions already entertained. His countenance was pale even to ghastliness, and his deep-set eyes glared with unnatural lustre. After some inquiries respecting his health, I asked him, not knowing what better to say, if he had yet obtained the *scarabæus* from Lieutenant G——.

"Oh, yes," he replied, coloring violently, "I got it from him the next morning. Nothing should tempt me to part with that *scarabæus*. Do you know that Jupiter is quite right about it?"

"In what way?" I asked, with a sad foreboding at heart.

"In supposing it to be a bug of *real gold*." He said this with an air of profound seriousness, and I felt inexpressibly shocked.

"This bug is to make my fortune," he continued, with a triumphant smile, "to reinstate me in my family possessions. Is it any wonder, then, that I prize it? Since Fortune has thought fit to bestow it upon me, I have only to use it properly and I shall arrive at the gold of which it is the index. Jupiter, bring me that *scarabæus!*"

"What! de bug, massa? I'd rudder not go fer trubble dat bug—you mus git him for your own self." Hereupon Legrand arose, with a grave and stately air, and brought me the beetle from a glass case in which it was enclosed. It was a beautiful *scarabæus*, and, at that time, unknown to naturalists—of course a great prize in a scientific point of view. There were two round, black spots near one extremity of the back, and a long one near the other. The scales were exceedingly hard and glossy, with all the appearance of burnished gold. The weight of the insect was very remarkable, and, taking all things into consideration, I could hardly blame Jupiter for his opinion respecting it; but what to make of Legrand's concordance with that opinion, I could not, for the life of me, tell.

"I sent for you," said he, in a grandiloquent tone, when I had completed my examination of the beetle, "I sent for you, that I might have your counsel and assistance in furthering the views of Fate and of the bug"—

"My dear Legrand," I cried, interrupting him, "you are certainly unwell, and had better use some little precautions. You shall go to bed, and I will remain with you a few days, until you get over this. You are feverish and"—

"Feel my pulse," said he.

I felt it, and, to say the truth, found not the slightest indication of fever.

"But you may be ill and yet have no fever. Allow me this once to prescribe for you. In the first place, go to bed. In the next"—

"You are mistaken," he interposed, "I am as well as I can expect to be under the excitement which I suffer. If you really wish me well, you will relieve this excitement."

"And how is this to be done?"

"Very easily. Jupiter and myself are going upon an expedition into the hills, upon the main land, and, in this expedition, we shall need the aid of some person in whom we can confide. You are the only one we can trust. Whether we succeed or fail, the excitement which you now perceive in me will be equally allayed."

"I am anxious to oblige you in any way," I replied; "but do you mean to say that this infernal beetle has any connection with your expedition into the hills?"

"It has."

"Then, Legrand, I can become a party to no such absurd proceeding."

"I am sorry—very sorry—for we shall have to try it by ourselves."

"Try it by yourselves! The man is surely mad!—but stay!—how long do you propose to be absent?"

"Probably all night. We shall start immediately, and be back, at all events, by sunrise."

"And will you promise me, upon your honor, that when this freak of yours is over, and the bug business (good God!) settled to your satisfaction, you will then return home and follow my advice implicitly, as that of your physician?"

"Yes; I promise; and now let us be off, for we have no time to lose."

With a heavy heart I accompanied my friend. We started about four o'clock—Legrand, Jupiter, the dog, and myself. Jupiter had with him the scythe and spades—the whole of which he insisted upon carrying—more through fear, it seemed to me, of trusting either of the implements within reach of his master, than from any excess of industry or complaisance. His demeanor was dogged in the extreme, and "dat deuced bug" were the sole words which escaped his lips during the journey. For my own part, I had charge of a couple of dark lanterns, while Legrand contented himself with the *scarabæus*, which he carried attached to the end of a bit of whip-cord; twirling it to and fro, with the air of a conjuror, as he went. When I observed this last, plain evidence of my friend's aberration of mind, I could scarcely refrain from tears. I thought it best, however, to humor his fancy, at least for the present, or until I could adopt some more energetic measures with a chance of success. In the mean time I endeavored, but all in vain, to sound him in regard to the object of the expedition. Having succeeded in inducing me to accompany him, he seemed unwilling to hold conversation upon any topic of minor importance, and to all my questions vouchsafed no other reply than "we shall see!"

We crossed the creek at the head of the island by means of a skiff, and, ascending the high grounds on the shore of the main land, proceeded in a northwesterly direction, through a tract of country excessively wild and desolate, where no trace of a human footstep was to be seen. Legrand led the way with decision; pausing only for an instant, here and there, to consult what appeared to be certain landmarks of his own contrivance upon a former occasion.

In this manner we journeyed for about two hours, and the sun was just setting when we entered a region infinitely more dreary than any yet seen. It was a species of table land, near the summit of an almost inaccessible hill, densely wooded from base to pinnacle, and interspersed with huge crags that appeared to lie loosely upon the soil, and in many cases were prevented from precipitating themselves into the valleys below, merely by the support of the trees against which they reclined. Deep ravines, in various directions, gave an air of still sterner solemnity to the scene.

The natural platform to which we had clambered was thickly overgrown with brambles, through which we soon discovered that it would have been impossible to force our way but for the scythe; and Jupiter, by direction of his master, proceeded to clear for us a path to the foot of an enormously tall tulip-tree, which stood, with some eight or ten oaks, upon the level, and far surpassed them all, and all other trees which I had then ever seen, in the beauty of its foliage and form, in the wide spread of its branches, and in the general majesty of its appearance. When we reached this tree, Legrand turned to Jupiter, and asked him if he thought he could climb it. The old man seemed a little staggered by the question, and for some moments made no reply. At length he approached the huge trunk, walked slowly around it, and examined it with minute attention. When he had completed his scrutiny, he merely said,

"Yes, massa, Jup climb any tree he ebber see in he life."

"Then up with you as soon as possible, for it will soon be too dark to see what we are about."

"How far mus go up, massa?" inquired Jupiter.

"Get up the main trunk first, and then I will tell you which way to go—and here—stop! take this beetle with you."

"De bug, Massa Will!—de goole bug!" cried the negro, drawing back in dismay— "what for mus tote de bug way up de tree?—d—n if I do!"

"If you are afraid, Jup, a great big negro like you, to take hold of a harmless little dead beetle, why you can carry it up by this string—but, if you do not take it up with you in some way, I shall be under the necessity of breaking your head with this shovel."

"What de matter now, massa?" said Jup, evidently shamed into compliance; "always want for to raise fuss wid old nigger. Was only funnin any how. *Me* feered de bug! what I keer for de bug?" Here he took cautiously hold of the extreme end of the string, and, maintaining the insect as far from his person as circumstances would permit, prepared to ascend the tree.

In youth, the tulip-tree, or *Liriodendron Tulipiferum*, the most magnificent of American foresters, has a trunk peculiarly smooth, and often rises to a great height without lateral branches; but, in its riper age, the bark becomes gnarled and uneven, while many short limbs make their appearance on the stem. Thus the difficulty of ascension, in the present case, lay more in semblance than in reality. Embracing the huge cylinder, as closely as possible, with his arms and knees, seizing with his hands some projections, and resting his naked toes upon others, Jupiter, after one or two narrow escapes from falling, at length wriggled himself into the first great fork, and seemed to consider the whole business as virtually accomplished. The *risk* of the achievement was, in fact, now over, although the climber was some sixty or seventy feet from the ground.

"Which way mus go now, Massa Will?" he asked.

"Keep up the largest branch—the one on this side," said Legrand. The negro obeyed him promptly, and apparently with but little trouble; ascending higher and higher, until no glimpse of his squat figure could be obtained through the dense foliage which enveloped it. Presently his voice was heard in a sort of halloo.

"How much fudder is got for go?"

"How high up are you?" asked Legrand.

"Ebber so fur," replied the negro; "can see de sky fru de top ob de tree."

"Never mind the sky, but attend to what I say. Look down the trunk and count the limbs below you on this side. How many limbs have you passed?"

"One, two, tree, four, fibe—I done pass fibe big limb, massa, pon dis side."

"Then go one limb higher."

In a few minutes the voice was heard again, announcing that the seventh limb was attained.

"Now Jup," cried Legrand, evidently much excited, "I want you to work your way out upon that limb as far as you can. If you see anything strange, let me know."

By this time what little doubt I might have entertained of my poor friend's insanity, was put finally at rest. I had no alternative but to conclude him stricken with lunacy, and I became seriously anxious about getting him home. While I was pondering upon what was best to be done, Jupiter's voice was again heard.

"Mos feerd for to ventur pon dis limb berry far—tis dead limb putty much all de way."

"Did you say it was a *dead* limb, Jupiter?" cried Legrand in a quavering voice.

"Yes, massa, him dead as de door-nail—done up for sartain—done departed dis here life."

"What in the name of heaven shall I do?" asked Legrand, seemingly in the greatest distress.

"Do!" said I, glad of an opportunity to interpose a word, "why come home and go to bed. Come now!—that's a fine fellow. It's getting late, and, besides, you remember your promise."

"Jupiter," cried he, without heeding me in the least, "do you hear me?"

"Yes, Massa Will, hear you ebber so plain."

"Try the wood well, then, with your knife, and see if you think it *very* rotten."

"Him rotten, massa, sure nuff," replied the negro in a few moments, "but not so berry rotten as mought be. Mought ventur out leetle way pon de limb by myself, dat's true."

"By yourself!—what do you mean?"

"Why I mean de bug. 'Tis *berry* hebby bug. Spose I drop him down fuss, and den de limb won't break wid just de weight ob one nigger."

"You infernal scoundrel!" cried Legrand, apparently much relieved, "what do you mean by telling me such nonsense as that? As sure as you drop that beetle I'll break your neck. Look here, Jupiter, do you hear me?"

"Yes, massa, needn't hollo at poor nigger dat style."

"Well! now listen!—if you will venture out on the limb as far as you think safe, and not let go the beetle, I'll make you a present of a silver dollar as soon as you get down."

"I'm gwine, Massa Will—deed I is," replied the negro very promptly—"mos out to the eend now."

"*Out to the end!*" here fairly screamed Legrand, "do you say you are out to the end of that limb?"

"Soon be to de eend, massa—o-o-o-o-oh! Lor-gol-a-marcy! what *is* dis here pon de tree?"

"Well!" cried Legrand, highly delighted, "what is it?"

"Why taint noffin but a skull—somebody bin lef him head up de tree, and de crows done gobble ebery bit ob de meat off."

"A skull, you say!—very well!—how is it fastened to the limb?—what holds it on?"

"Sure nuff, massa; mus look. Why dis berry curous sarcumstance, pon my word—dare's a great big nail in de skull, what fastens ob it on to de tree."

"Well now, Jupiter, do exactly as I tell you—do you hear?"

"Yes, massa."

"Pay attention, then!—find the left eye of the skull."

"Hum! hoo! dat's good! why dare aint no eye lef at all."

"Curse your stupidity! do you know your right hand from your left?"

"Yes, I nose dat—nose all bout dat—tis my lef hand what I chops de wood wid."

"To be sure! you are left-handed; and your left eye is on the same side as your left hand. Now, I suppose, you can find the left eye of the skull, or the place where the left eye has been. Have you found it?"

Here was a long pause. At length the negro asked,

"Is de lef eye of de skull pon de same side as de lef hand of de skull, too?—cause de skull aint got not a bit ob a hand at all—nebber mind! I got de lef eye now—here de lef eye! what mus do wid it?"

"Let the beetle drop through it, as far as the string will reach—but be careful and not let go your hold of the string."

"All dat done, Massa Will; mighty easy ting for to put de bug fru de hole—look out for him dare below!"

During this colloquy no portion of Jupiter's person could be seen; but the beetle, which he had suffered to descend, was now visible at the end of the string, and glistened, like a globe of burnished gold, in the last rays of the setting sun, some of which still faintly illumined the eminence upon which we stood. The *scarabæus* hung quite clear of any branches, and, if allowed to fall, would have fallen at our feet. Legrand immediately took the scythe, and cleared with it a circular space, three or four yards in diameter, just beneath the insect, and, having accomplished this, ordered Jupiter to let go the string and come down from the tree.

Driving a peg, with great nicety, into the ground, at the precise spot where the beetle fell, my friend now produced from his pocket a tape-measure. Fastening one end of this at that point of the trunk of the tree which was nearest the peg, he unrolled it till it reached the peg, and thence farther unrolled it, in the direction already established by the two points of the tree and the peg, for the distance of fifty feet—Jupiter clearing away the brambles with the scythe. At the spot thus attained a second peg was driven, and about this, as a centre, a rude circle, about four feet in diameter, described. Taking now a spade himself, and giving one to Jupiter and one to me, Legrand begged us to set about digging as quickly as possible.

To speak the truth, I had no especial relish for such amusement at any time, and, at that particular moment, would most willingly have declined it; for the night was coming on, and I felt much fatigued with the exercise already taken; but I saw no mode of escape, and was fearful of disturbing my poor friend's equanimity by a refusal. Could I have depended, indeed, upon Jupiter's aid, I would have had no hesitation in attempting to get the lunatic home by force; but I was too well assured of the old negro's disposition, to hope that he would assist me, under any circumstances, in a personal contest with his master. I made no doubt that the latter had been infected with some of the innumerable Southern superstitions about money buried, and that his phantasy had received confirmation by the finding of the *scarabæus*, or, perhaps, by Jupiter's obstinacy in maintaining it to be "a bug of real gold." A mind disposed to lunacy would readily be led away by such suggestions—especially if chiming in with favorite preconceived ideas—and then I called to mind the poor fellow's speech about the beetle's being "the index of his fortune." Upon the whole, I was sadly vexed and puzzled, but, at length, I concluded to make a virtue of necessity—to dig with a good will, and thus the sooner to convince the visionary, by ocular demonstration, of the fallacy of the opinions he entertained.

The lanterns having been lit, we all fell to work with a zeal worthy a more rational cause; and, as the glare fell upon our persons and implements, I could not help thinking how picturesque a group we composed, and how strange and suspicious our labors must have appeared to any interloper who, by chance, might have stumbled upon our whereabouts.

We dug very steadily for two hours. Little was said; and our chief embarrassment lay in the yelpings of the dog, who took exceeding interest in our proceedings. He, at length, became so obstreperous that we grew fearful of his giving the alarm to some stragglers in the vicinity;—or, rather, this was the apprehension of Legrand;—for myself, I should have rejoiced at any interruption which might have enabled me to get the wanderer home. The noise was, at length, very effectually silenced by Jupiter, who, getting out of the hole with a dogged air of deliberation, tied the brute's mouth up with one of his suspenders, and then returned, with a grave chuckle, to his task.

When the time mentioned had expired, we had reached a depth of five feet, and yet no signs of any treasure became manifest. A general pause ensued, and I began to hope that the farce was at an end. Legrand, however, although evidently much disconcerted, wiped his brow thoughtfully and recommenced. We had excavated the entire circle of four feet diameter, and now we slightly enlarged the limit, and went to the farther depth of two feet. Still nothing appeared. The gold-seeker, whom I sincerely pitied, at length clambered from the pit, with the bitterest disappointment imprinted upon every feature, and proceeded, slowly and reluctantly, to put on his coat, which he had thrown off at the beginning of his labor. In the mean time I made no remark. Jupiter, at a signal from his master, began to gather up his tools. This done, and the dog having been unmuzzled, we turned in profound silence towards home.

We had taken, perhaps, a dozen steps in this direction, when, with a loud oath, Legrand strode up to Jupiter, and seized him by the collar. The astonished negro opened his eyes and mouth to the fullest extent, let fall the spades, and fell upon his knees.

"You scoundrel," said Legrand, hissing out the syllables from between his clenched teeth—"you infernal black villain!—speak, I tell you!—answer me this instant, without prevarication!—which—which is your left eye?"

"Oh, my golly, Massa Will! aint dis here my lef eye for sartain?" roared the terrified Jupiter, placing his hand upon his *right* organ of vision, and holding it there with a desperate pertinacity, as if in immediate dread of his master's attempt at a gouge.

"I thought so!—I knew it! hurrah!" vociferated Legrand, letting the negro go, and executing a series of curvets and caracols,[7] much to the astonishment of his valet, who, arising from his knees, looked, mutely, from his master to myself, and then from myself to his master.

"Come! we must go back," said the latter, "the game's not up yet;" and he again led the way to the tulip-tree.

"Jupiter," said he, when we reached its foot, "come here! was the skull nailed to the limb with the face outwards, or with the face to the limb?"

"De face was out, massa, so dat de crows could get at de eyes good, widout any trouble."

"Well, then, was it this eye or that through which you dropped the beetle?"—here Legrand touched each of Jupiter's eyes.

"Twas dis eye, massa—de lef eye—jis as you tell me," and here it was his right eye that the negro indicated.

"That will do—we must try it again."

Here my friend, about whose madness I now saw, or fancied that I saw, certain indications of method, removed the peg which marked the spot where the beetle fell, to a spot about three inches to the westward of its former position. Taking, now, the tape-measure from the nearest point of the trunk to the peg, as before, and continuing the extension in a straight line to the distance of fifty feet, a spot was indicated, removed, by several yards, from the point at which we had been digging.

Around the new position a circle, somewhat larger than in the former instance, was now described, and we again set to work with the spades. I was dreadfully weary, but, scarcely understanding what had occasioned the change in my thoughts, I felt no longer any great aversion from the labor imposed. I had become most unaccountably interested—nay, even excited. Perhaps there was something, amid all the extravagant demeanor of Legrand—some air of forethought, or of deliberation, which impressed me. I dug eagerly, and now and then caught myself actually looking, with something that very much resembled expectation, for the fancied treasure, the vision of which had demented my unfortunate companion. At a period when such vagaries of thought most fully possessed me, and when we had been at work perhaps an hour and a half, we were again interrupted by the violent howlings of the dog. His uneasiness, in the first instance, had been, evidently, but the result of playfulness or caprice, but he now assumed a bitter and serious tone. Upon Jupiter's again attempting to muzzle him, he made furious resistance, and, leaping into the hole, tore up the mould frantically with his claws. In a few seconds he had uncovered a mass of human bones, forming two complete skeletons, intermingled with several buttons of metal, and what appeared to be the dust of decayed woolen. One or two strokes of a spade upturned the blade of a large Spanish knife, and, as we dug farther, three or four loose pieces of gold and silver coin came to light.

At sight of these the joy of Jupiter could scarcely be restrained, but the countenance of his master wore an air of extreme disappointment. He urged us, however, to continue our exertions, and the words were hardly uttered when I stumbled and fell forward, having caught the toe of my boot in a large ring of iron that lay half buried in the loose earth.

We now worked in earnest, and never did I pass ten minutes of more intense excitement. During this interval we had fairly unearthed an oblong chest of wood, which, from its perfect preservation and wonderful hardness, had plainly been subjected to some mineralizing process—perhaps that of the Bi-chloride of Mercury. This box was three feet and a half long, three feet broad, and two and a half feet deep. It was firmly secured by bands of wrought iron, riveted, and forming a kind of open trellis-work over the whole. On each side of the chest, near the top, were three rings of iron—six in all—by means of which a firm hold could be obtained by six persons. Out utmost united endeavors served only to disturb the coffer very slightly in its bed.

We at once saw the impossibility of removing so great a weight. Luckily, the sole fastenings of the lid consisted of two sliding bolts. These we drew back—trembling and panting with anxiety. In an instant, a treasure of incalculable value lay gleaming before us. As the rays of the lanterns fell within the pit, there flashed upwards a glow and a glare, from a confused heap of gold and of jewels, that absolutely dazzled our eyes.

I shall not pretend to describe the feelings with which I gazed. Amazement was, of course, predominant. Legrand appeared exhausted with excitement, and spoke very few words. Jupiter's countenance wore, for some minutes, as deadly a pallor as it is possible, in the nature of things, for any negro's visage to assume. He seemed stupefied—thunderstricken. Presently he fell upon his knees in the pit, and, burying his naked arms up to the elbows in gold, let them there remain, as if enjoying the luxury of a bath. At length, with a deep sigh, he exclaimed, as if in a soliloquy,

"And dis all cum ob de goole-bug! de putty goole-bug! de poor little goole-bug, what I boosed in dat sabage kind ob style! Aint you shamed ob yourself, nigger?—answer me dat!"

It became necessary, at last, that I should arouse both master and valet to the expediency of removing the treasure. It was growing late, and it behooved us to make exertion, that we might get every thing housed before daylight. It was difficult to say what should be done, and much time was spent in deliberation—so confused were the ideas of all. We, finally, lightened the box by removing two thirds of its contents, when we were enabled, with some trouble, to raise it from the hole. The articles taken out were deposited among the brambles, and the dog left to guard them, with strict orders from Jupiter neither, upon any pretence, to stir from the spot, nor to open his mouth until our return. We then hurriedly made for home with the chest; reaching the hut in safety, but after excessive toil, at one o'clock in the morning. Worn out as we were, it was not in human nature to do more immediately. We rested until two, and had supper; starting for the hills immediately afterwards, armed with three stout sacks, which, by good luck, were upon the premises. A little before four we arrived at the pit, divided the remainder of the booty, as equally as might be, among us, and, leaving the holes unfilled, again set out for the hut, at which, for the second time, we deposited our golden burthens, just as the first faint streaks of the dawn gleamed from over the tree-tops in the East.

We were now thoroughly broken down; but the intense excitement of the time denied us repose. After an unquiet slumber of some three or four hours' duration, we arose, as if by preconcert, to make examination of our treasure.

The chest had been full to the brim, and we spent the whole day, and the greater part of the next night, in a scrutiny of its contents. There had been nothing like order or arrangement. Every thing had been heaped in promiscuously. Having assorted all with care, we found ourselves possessed of even vaster wealth than we had at first supposed. In coin there was rather more than four hundred and fifty thousand dollars—estimating the value of the pieces, as accurately as we could, by the tables of the period. There was not a particle of silver. All was gold of antique date and of great variety—French, Spanish, and German money, with a few English guineas, and some counters, of which we had never seen specimens before. There were several very large and heavy coins, so worn that we could make nothing of their inscriptions. There was no American money. The value of the jewels we found more difficulty in estimating. There were diamonds—some of them exceedingly large and fine—a hundred and ten in all, and not one of them small; eighteen rubies of remarkable brilliancy;—three hundred and ten emeralds, all very beautiful; and twenty-one sapphires, with an opal. These stones had all been broken from their settings and thrown loose in the chest. The settings themselves, which we picked out from among the other gold, appeared to have been beaten up with hammers, as if to prevent identification. Besides all this, there was a vast quantity of solid gold ornaments;—nearly two hundred massive finger and ear rings;—rich chains—thirty of these, if I remember;—eighty-three very large and heavy crucifixes;—five gold censers of great value;—a prodigious golden punch-bowl, ornamented with richly chased vine-leaves and Bacchanalian figures; with two sword-handles exquisitely embossed, and many other smaller articles which I cannot recollect. The weight of these valuables exceeded three hundred and fifty pounds avoirdupois; and in this estimate I have not included one hundred and ninety-seven superb gold watches; three of the number being worth each five hundred dollars, if one. Many of them were very old, and as time keepers valueless; the works having suffered, more or less, from corrosion—but all were richly jewelled and in cases of great worth. We estimated the entire contents of the chest, that night, at a million and a half of dollars; and, upon the subsequent disposal of the trinkets and jewels (a few being retained for our own use), it was found that we had greatly undervalued the treasure.

When, at length, we had concluded our examination, and the intense excitement of the time had, in some measure, subsided, Legrand, who saw that I was dying with impatience for a solution of this most extraordinary riddle, entered into a full detail of all the circumstances connected with it.

"You remember," said he, "the night when I handed you the rough sketch I had made of the *scarabæus*. You recollect also, that I became quite vexed at you for insisting that my drawing resembled a death's-head. When you first made this assertion I thought you were jesting; but afterwards I called to mind the peculiar spots on the back of the insect, and admitted to myself that your remark had some little foundation in fact. Still, the sneer at my graphic powers irritated me—for I am considered a good artist—and, therefore, when you handed me the scrap of parchment, I was about to crumple it up and throw it angrily into the fire."

"The scrap of paper, you mean," said I.

"No; it had much of the appearance of paper, and at first I supposed it to be such, but when I came to draw upon it, I discovered it, at once, to be a piece of very thin parchment. It was quite dirty, you remember. Well, as I was in the very act of crumpling it up, my glance fell upon the sketch at which you had been looking, and you may imagine my astonishment when I perceived, in fact, the figure of a death's-head just where, it seemed to me, I had made the drawing of the beetle. For a moment I was too much amazed to think with accuracy. I knew that my design was very different in detail from this—although there was a certain similarity in general outline. Presently I took a candle, and seating myself at the other end of the room, proceeded to scrutinize the parchment more closely. Upon turning it over, I saw my own sketch upon the reverse, just as I had made it. My first idea, now, was mere surprise at the really remarkable similarity of outline—at the singular coincidence involved in the fact, that unknown to me, there should have been a skull upon the other side of the parchment, immediately beneath my figure of the *scarabæus*, and that this skull, not only in outline, but in size, should so closely resemble my drawing. I say the singularity of this coincidence absolutely stupefied me for a time. This is the usual effect of such coincidences. The mind struggles to establish a connexion—a sequence of cause and effect—and, being unable to do so, suffers a species of temporary paralysis. But, when I recovered from this stupor, there dawned upon me gradually a conviction which startled me even far more than the coincidence. I began distinctly, positively, to remember that there had been *no* drawing upon the parchment when I made my sketch of the *scarabæus*. I became perfectly certain of this; for I recollected turning up first one side and then the other, in search of the cleanest spot. Had the skull been then there, of course I could not have failed to notice it. Here was indeed a mystery which I felt it impossible to explain; but, even at that early moment, there seemed to glimmer, faintly, within the most remote and secret chambers of my intellect, a glow-worm-like conception of that truth which last night's adventure brought to so magnificent a demonstration. I arose at once, and putting the parchment securely away, dismissed all farther reflection until I should be alone.

"When you had gone, and when Jupiter was fast asleep, I betook myself to a more methodical investigation of the affair. In the first place I considered the manner in which the parchment had come into my possession. The spot where we discovered the *scarabæus* was on the coast of the main land, about a mile eastward of the island, and but a short distance above high water mark. Upon my taking hold of it, it gave me a sharp bite, which caused me to let it drop. Jupiter, with his accustomed caution, before seizing the insect, which had flown towards him, looked about him for a leaf, or something of that nature, by which to take hold of it. It was at this moment that his eyes, and mine also, fell upon the scrap of parchment, which I then supposed to be paper. It was lying half buried in the sand, a corner sticking up. Near the spot where we found it, I observed the remnants of the hull of what appeared to have been a ship's long boat. The wreck seemed to have been there for a very great while; for the resemblance to boat timbers could scarcely be traced.

"Well, Jupiter picked up the parchment, wrapped the beetle in it, and gave it to me. Soon afterwards we turned to go home, and on the way met Lieutenant G—. I showed him the insect, and he begged me to let him take it to the fort. Upon my consenting, he thrust it forthwith into his waistcoat pocket, without the parchment in which it had been wrapped, and which I had continued to hold in my hand during his inspection. Perhaps he dreaded my changing my mind, and thought it best to make sure of the prize at once—you know how enthusiastic he is on all subjects connected with Natural History. At the same time, without being conscious of it, I must have deposited the parchment in my own pocket.

"You remember that when I went to the table, for the purpose of making a sketch of the beetle, I found no paper where it was usually kept. I looked in the drawer, and found none there. I searched my pockets, hoping to find an old letter, when my hand fell upon the parchment. I thus detail the precise mode in which it came into my possession; for the circumstances impressed me with peculiar force.

"No doubt you will think me fanciful—but I had already established a kind of *connexion*. I had put together two links of a great chain. There was a boat lying upon a sea-coast, and not far from the boat was a parchment—*not a paper*—with a skull depicted upon it. You will, of course, ask 'where is the connection?' I reply that the skull, or death's-head, is the well-known emblem of the pirate. The flag of the death's-head is hoisted in all engagements.

"I have said that the scrap was parchment, and not paper. Parchment is durable—almost imperishable. Matters of little moment are rarely consigned to parchment; since, for the mere ordinary purposes of drawing or writing, it is not nearly so well adapted as paper. This reflection suggested some meaning—some relevancy—in the death's-head. I did not fail to observe, also, the *form* of the parchment. Although one of its corners had been, by some accident, destroyed, it could be seen that the original form was oblong. It was just such a slip, indeed, as might have been chosen for a memorandum—for a record of something to be long remembered and carefully preserved."

"But," I interposed, "you say that the skull was *not* upon the parchment when you made the drawing of the beetle. How then do you trace any connexion between the boat and the skull—since this latter, according to your own admission, must have been designed (God only knows how or by whom) at some period subsequent to your sketching the *scarabæus?*"

"Ah, hereupon turns the whole mystery; although the secret, at this point, I had comparatively little difficulty in solving. My steps were sure, and could afford but a single result. I reasoned, for example, thus: When I drew the *scarabæus*, there was no skull apparent upon the parchment. When I had completed the drawing I gave it to you, and observed you narrowly until you returned it. *You*, therefore, did not design the skull, and no one else was present to do it. Then it was not done by human agency. And nevertheless it was done.

"At this stage of my reflections I endeavored to remember, and *did* remember, with entire distinctness, every incident which occurred about the period in question. The weather was chilly (oh rare and happy accident!), and a fire was blazing upon the hearth. I was heated with exercise and sat near the table. You, however, had drawn a chair close to the chimney. Just as I placed the parchment in your hand, and as you were in the act of inspecting it, Wolf, the Newfoundland, entered, and leaped upon your shoulders. With your left hand you caressed him and kept him off, while your right, holding the parchment, was permitted to fall listlessly between your knees, and in close proximity to the fire. At one moment I thought the blaze had caught it, and was about to caution you, but, before I could speak, you had withdrawn it, and were engaged in its examination. When I considered all these particulars, I doubted not for a moment that *heat* had been the agent in bringing to light, upon the parchment, the skull which I saw designed upon it. You are well aware that chemical preparations exist, and have existed time out of mind, by means of which it is possible to write upon either paper or vellum, so that the characters shall become visible only when subjected to the action of fire. Zaffre, digested in *aqua regia*,[8] and diluted with four times its weight of water, is sometimes employed; a green tint results. The regulus of cobalt, dissolved in spirit of nitre, gives a red. These colors disappear at longer or shorter intervals after the material written upon cools, but again become apparent upon the re-application of heat.

"I now scrutinized the death's-head with care. Its outer edges—the edges of the drawing nearest the edge of the vellum—were far more *distinct* than the others. It was clear that the action of the caloric had been imperfect or unequal. I immediately kindled a fire, and subjected every portion of the parchment to a glowing heat. At first, the only effect was the strengthening of the faint lines in the skull; but, upon persevering in the experiment, there became visible, at the corner of the slip, diagonally opposite to the spot in which the death's-head was delineated, the figure of what I at first supposed to be a goat. A closer scrutiny, however, satisfied me that it was intended for a kid."

"Ha! ha!" said I, "to be sure I have no right to laugh at you—a million and a half of money is too serious a matter for mirth—but you are not about to establish a third link in your chain—you will not find any especial connexion between your pirates and a goat—pirates, you know, have nothing to do with goats; they appertain to the farming interest."

"But I have just said that the figure was *not* that of a goat."

"Well, a kid then—pretty much the same thing."

"Pretty much, but not altogether," said Legrand. "You may have heard of one *Captain* Kidd.⁹ I at once looked upon the figure of the animal as a kind of punning or hieroglyphical signature. I say signature; because its position upon the vellum suggested this idea. The death's-head at the corner diagonally opposite, had, in the same manner, the air of a stamp, or seal. But I was sorely put out by the absence of all else—of the body to my imagined instrument—of the text for my context."

"I presume you expected to find a letter between the stamp and the signature."

"Something of that kind. The fact is, I felt irresistibly impressed with a presentiment of some vast good fortune impending. I can scarcely say why. Perhaps, after all, it was rather a desire than an actual belief;—but do you know that Jupiter's silly words, about the bug being of solid gold, had a remarkable effect upon my fancy? And then the series of accidents and coincidences—these were so *very* extraordinary. Do you observe how mere an accident it was that these events should have occurred upon the *sole* day of all the year in which it has been, or may be, sufficiently cool for fire, and that without the fire, or without the intervention of the dog at the precise moment in which he appeared, I should never have become aware of the death's-head, and so never the possessor of the treasure?"

"But proceed—I am all impatience."

"Well; you have heard, of course, the many stories current—the thousand vague rumors afloat about money buried, somewhere upon the Atlantic coast, by Kidd and his associates. These rumors must have had some foundation in fact. And that the rumors have existed so long and so continuous, could have resulted, it appeared to me, only from the circumstance of the buried treasure still *remaining* entombed. Had Kidd concealed his plunder for a time, and afterwards reclaimed it, the rumors would scarcely have reached us in their present unvarying form. You will observe that the stories told are all about money-seekers, not about money-finders. Had the pirate recovered his money, there the affair would have dropped. It seemed to me that some accident—say the loss of a memorandum indicating its locality—had deprived him of the means of recovering it, and that this accident had become known to his followers, who otherwise might never have heard that treasure had been concealed at all, and who, busying themselves in vain, because unguided attempts, to regain it, had given first birth, and then universal currency, to the reports which are now so common. Have you ever heard of any important treasure being unearthed along the coast?"

"Never."

"But that Kidd's accumulations were immense, is well known. I took it for granted, therefore, that the earth still held them; and you will scarcely be surprised when I tell you that I felt a hope, nearly amounting to certainty, that the parchment so strangely found, involved a lost record of the place of deposit."

"But how did you proceed?"

"I held the vellum again to the fire, after increasing the heat; but nothing appeared. I now thought it possible that the coating of dirt might have something to do with the failure; so I carefully rinsed the parchment by pouring warm water over it, and, having done this, I placed it in a tin pan, with the skull downwards, and put the pan upon a furnace of lighted charcoal. In a few minutes, the pan having become thoroughly heated, I removed the slip, and, to my inexpressible joy, found it spotted, in several places, with what appeared to be figures arranged in lines. Again I placed it in the pan, and suffered it to remain another minute. Upon taking it off, the whole was just as you see it now."

Here Legrand, having re-heated the parchment, submitted it to my inspection. The following characters were rudely traced, in a red tint, between the death's-head and the goat:

53‡‡†305))6*;4826)4‡.)4‡);806*;48†8¶60))85;1‡(;:‡*8†83(88)
5*†;46(;88*96*?;8)*‡(;485);5*†2:*‡(;4956*2(5*—4)8¶8*;40692
85;)6†8)4‡‡;1(‡9;48081;8:8†1;48†85;4)485†528806*81(‡9;48;
(88;4(‡?34;48)4‡;161;:188; ‡?;

"But," said I, returning him the slip, "I am as much in the dark as ever. Were all the jewels of Golconda[10] awaiting me upon my solution of this enigma, I am quite sure that I should be unable to earn them."

"And yet," said Legrand, "the solution is by no means so difficult as you might be lead to imagine from the first hasty inspection of the characters. These characters, as any one might readily guess, form a cipher—that is to say, they convey a meaning; but then, from what is known of Kidd, I could not suppose him capable of constructing any of the more abstruse cryptographs. I made up my mind, at once, that this was of a simple species—such, however, as would appear, to the crude intellect of the sailor, absolutely insoluble without the key."

"And you really solved it?"

"Readily; I have solved others of an abstruseness ten thousand times greater. Circumstances, and a certain bias of mind, have led me to take interest in such riddles, and it may well be doubted whether human ingenuity can construct an enigma of the kind which human ingenuity may not, by proper application, resolve. In fact, having once established connected and legible characters, I scarcely gave a thought to the mere difficulty of developing their import.

"In the present case—indeed in all cases of secret writing—the first question regards the *language* of the cipher; for the principles of solution, so far, especially, as the more simple ciphers are concerned, depend upon, and are varied by, the genius of the particular idiom. In general, there is no alternative but experiment (directed by probabilities) of every tongue known to him who attempts the solution, until the true one be attained. But, with the cipher now before us, all difficulty was removed by the signature. The pun upon the word 'Kidd' is appreciable in no other language than the English. But for this consideration I should have begun my attempts with the Spanish and French, as the tongues in which a secret of this kind would most naturally have been written by a pirate of the Spanish main. As it was, I assumed the cryptograph to be English.

"You observe there are no divisions between the words. Had there been divisions, the task would have been comparatively easy. In such case I should have commenced with a collation and analysis of the shorter words, and, had a word of a single letter occurred, as is most likely, (*a* or *I*, for example,) I should have considered the solution as assured. But, there being no division, my first step was to ascertain the predominant letters, as well as the least frequent. Counting all, I constructed a table, thus:

Of the character 8 there are 33.
;	"	26.
4	"	19.
‡)	"	16.
*	"	13.
5	"	12.
6	"	11.
† 1	"	8.
0	"	6.
9 2	"	5.
: 3	"	4.
?	"	3.
¶	"	2.
—.	"	1.

"Now, in English, the letter which most frequently occurs is *e*. Afterwards, the succession runs thus: *a o i d h n r s t u y c f g l m w b k p q x z. E* predominates so remarkably that an individual sentence of any length is rarely seen, in which it is not the prevailing character.

"Here, then, we have, in the very beginning, the groundwork for something more than a mere guess. The general use which may be made of the table is obvious   but, in this particular cipher, we shall only very partially require its aid. As our predominant character is 8, we will commence by assuming it as the *e* of the natural alphabet. To verify the supposition, let us observe if the 8 be seen often in couples— for *e* is doubled with great frequency in English—in such words, for example, as 'meet,' 'fleet,' 'speed,' 'seen,' 'been,' 'agree,' &c. In the present instance we see it doubled no less than five times, although the cryptograph is brief.

"Let us assume 8, then, as *e*. Now, of all *words* in the language, 'the' is most usual; let us see, therefore, whether there are not repetitions of any three characters, in the same order of collocation, the last of them being 8. If we discover repetitions of such letters, so arranged, they will most probably represent the word 'the.' Upon inspection, we find no less than seven such arrangements, the characters being ;48.

We may, therefore, assume that ; represents *t*, 4 represents *h*, and 8 represents *e*—the last being now well confirmed. Thus a great step has been taken.

"But, having established a single word, we are enabled to establish a vastly important point; that is to say, several commencements and terminations of other words. Let us refer, for example, to the last instance but one, in which the combination ;48 occurs—not far from the end of the cipher. We know that the ; immediately ensuing is the commencement of a word, and, of the six characters succeeding this 'the,' we are cognizant of no less than five. Let us set these characters down, thus, by the letters we know them to represent, leaving a space for the unknown—

t eeth.

"Here, we are enabled, at once, to discard the '*th*,' as forming no portion of the word commencing with the first *t*; since, by experiment of the entire alphabet for a letter adapted to the vacancy, we perceive that no word can be formed of which this *th* can be a part. We are thus narrowed into

t ee,

and, going through the alphabet, if necessary, as before, we arrive at the word 'tree,' as the sole possible reading. We thus gain another letter, *r*, represented by (, with the words 'the tree' in juxtaposition.

"Looking beyond these words, for a short distance, we again see the combination ;48, and employ it by way of *termination* to what immediately precedes. We have thus this arrangement:

the tree ;4(‡?34 the,

or, substituting the natural letters, where known, it reads thus:

the tree thr‡?3h the.

"Now, if, in place of the unknown characters, we leave blank spaces, or substitute dots, we read thus:

he tree thr. . .h the,

when the word '*through*' makes itself evident at once. But this discovery gives us three new letters, *o*, *u* and *g*, represented by ‡ ? and 3.

"Looking now, narrowly, through the cipher for combinations of known characters, we find, not very far from the beginning, this arrangement,

83(88, or egree,

which, plainly, is the conclusion of the word 'degree,' and gives us another letter, *d*, represented by †.

"Four letters beyond the word 'degree,' we perceive the combination

;48(;88.

"Translating the known characters, and representing the unknown by dots, as before, we read thus:

th rtee.

an arrangement immediately suggestive of the word 'thirteen,' and again furnishing us with two new characters, *i* and *n*, represented by 6 and *.

"Referring, now, to the beginning of the cryptograph, we find the combination,

53‡‡†.

"Translating, as before, we obtain

. good,

which assures us that the first letter is *A*, and that the first two words are 'A good.'

"It is now time that we arrange our key, as far as discovered, in a tabular form, to avoid confusion. It will stand thus:

5	represents	a
†	"	d
8	"	e
3	"	g
4	"	h
6	"	i
*	"	n
‡	"	o
(	"	r
;	"	t

"We have, therefore, no less than ten of the most important letters represented, and it will be unnecessary to proceed with the details of the solution. I have said enough to convince you that ciphers of this nature are readily soluble, and to give you some insight into the *rationale* of their development. But be assured that the specimen before us appertains to the very simplest species of cryptograph. It now only remains to give you the full translation of the characters upon the parchment, as unriddled. Here it is:

'*A good glass in the bishop's hostel in the devil's seat forty-one degrees and thirteen minutes northeast and by north main branch seventh limb east side shoot from the left eye of the death's-head a bee line from the tree through the shot fifty feet out.*'"

"But," said I, "the enigma seems still in as bad a condition as ever. How is it possible to extort a meaning from all this jargon about 'devil's seats,' 'death's-heads,' and 'bishop's hotels?'"

"I confess," replied Legrand, "that the matter still wears a serious aspect, when regarded with a casual glance. My first endeavor was to divide the sentence into the natural division intended by the cryptographist."

"You mean, to punctuate it?"

"Something of that kind."

"But how was it possible to effect this?"

"I reflected that it had been a *point* with the writer to run his words together without division, so as to increase the difficulty of solution. Now, a not over-acute man, in pursuing such an object, would be nearly certain to overdo the matter.

When, in the course of his composition, he arrived at a break in his subject which would naturally require a pause, or a point, he would be exceedingly apt to run his characters, at this place, more than usually close together. If you will observe the MS., in the present instance, you will easily detect five such cases of unusual crowding. Acting upon this hint, I made the division thus:

'A good glass in the Bishop's hostel in the Devil's seat—forty-one degrees and thirteen minutes—northeast and by north—main branch seventh limb east side— shoot from the left eye of the death's-head—a bee-line from the tree through the shot fifty feet out.'"

"Even this division," said I, "leaves me still in the dark."

"It left me also in the dark," replied Legrand, "for a few days; during which I made diligent inquiry, in the neighborhood of Sullivan's Island, for any building which went by the name of the 'Bishop's Hotel;' for, of course, I dropped the obsolete word 'hostel.' Gaining no information on the subject, I was on the point of extending my sphere of search, and proceeding in a more systematic manner, when, one morning, it entered into my head, quite suddenly, that this 'Bishop's Hostel' might have some reference to an old family, of the name of Bessop, which, time out of mind, had held possession of an ancient manor-house, about four miles to the northward of the Island. I accordingly went over to the plantation, and re-instituted my inquiries among the older negroes of the place. At length one of the most aged of the women said that she had heard of such a place as *Bessop's Castle*, and thought that she could guide me to it, but that it was not a castle, nor a tavern, but a high rock.

"I offered to pay her well for her trouble, and, after some demur, she consented to accompany me to the spot. We found it without much difficulty, when, dismissing her, I proceeded to examine the place. The 'castle' consisted of an irregular assemblage of cliffs and rocks—one of the latter being quite remarkable for its height as well as for its insulated and artificial appearance. I clambered to its apex, and then felt much at a loss as to what should be next done.

"While I was busied in reflection, my eyes fell upon a narrow ledge in the eastern face of the rock, perhaps a yard below the summit upon which I stood. This ledge projected about eighteen inches, and was not more than a foot wide, while a niche in the cliff just above it, gave it a rude resemblance to one of the hollow-backed chairs used by our ancestors. I made no doubt that here was the 'devil's-seat' alluded to in the MS., and now I seemed to grasp the full secret of the riddle.

"The 'good glass,' I knew, could have reference to nothing but a telescope; for the word 'glass' is rarely employed in any other sense by seamen. Now here, I at once saw, was a telescope to be used, and a definite point of view, *admitting no variation*, from which to use it. Nor did I hesitate to believe that the phrases, 'forty-one degrees and thirteen minutes,' and 'northeast and by north,' were intended as directions for the levelling of the glass. Greatly excited by these discoveries, I hurried home, procured a telescope, and returned to the rock.

"I let myself down to the ledge, and found that it was impossible to retain a seat upon it except in one particular position. This fact confirmed my preconceived idea. I proceeded to use the glass. Of course, the 'forty-one degrees and thirteen minutes' could allude to nothing but elevation above the visible horizon, since the horizontal direction was clearly indicated by the words, 'northeast and by north.' This latter direction I at once established by means of a pocket-compass; then, pointing the glass as nearly at an angle of forty-one degrees of elevation as I could do it by guess, I moved it cautiously up or down, until my attention was arrested by a circular rift or opening in the foliage of a large tree that overtopped its fellows in the distance. In the centre of this rift I perceived a white spot, but could not, at first, distinguish what it was. Adjusting the focus of the telescope, I again looked, and now made it out to be a human skull.

"Upon this discovery I was so sanguine as to consider the enigma solved; for the phrase 'main branch, seventh limb, east side,' could refer only to the position of the skull upon the tree, while 'shoot from the left eye of the death's-head' admitted, also, of but one interpretation, in regard to a search for buried treasure. I perceived that the design was to drop a bullet from the left eye of the skull, and that a bee-line, or, in other words, a straight line, drawn from the nearest point of the trunk through 'the shot,' (or the spot where the bullet fell,) and thence extended to a distance of fifty feet, would indicate a definite point—and beneath this point I thought it at least *possible* that a deposit of value lay concealed."

"All this," I said, "is exceedingly clear, and, although ingenious, still simple and explicit. When you left the Bishop's Hotel, what then?"

"Why, having carefully taken the bearings of the tree, I turned homewards. The instant that I left 'the devil's seat,' however, the circular rift vanished; nor could I get a glimpse of it afterwards, turn as I would. What seems to me the chief ingenuity in this whole business, is the fact (for repeated experiment has convinced me it *is* a fact) that the circular opening in question is visible from no other attainable point of view than that afforded by the narrow ledge upon the face of the rock.

"In this expedition to the 'Bishop's Hotel' I had been attended by Jupiter, who had, no doubt, observed, for some weeks past, the abstraction of my demeanor, and took especial care not to leave me alone. But, on the next day, getting up very early, I contrived to give him the slip, and went into the hills in search of the tree. After much toil I found it. When I came home at night my valet proposed to give me a flogging. With the rest of the adventure I believe you are as well acquainted as myself."

"I suppose," said I, "you missed the spot, in the first attempt at digging, through Jupiter's stupidity in letting the bug fall through the right instead of through the left eye of the skull."

"Precisely. This mistake made a difference of about two inches and a half in the 'shot'—that is to say, in the position of the peg nearest the tree; and had the treasure been *beneath* the 'shot,' the error would have been of little moment; but 'the shot,' together with the nearest point of the tree, were merely two points for the establishment of a line of direction; of course the error, however trivial in the beginning, increased as we proceeded with the line, and by the time we had gone fifty feet, threw us quite off the scent. But for my deep-seated impressions that treasure was here somewhere actually buried, we might have had all our labor in vain."

"But your grandiloquence, and your conduct in swinging the beetle—how excessively odd! I was sure you were mad. And why did you insist upon letting fall the bug, instead of a bullet, from the skull?"

"Why, to be frank, I felt somewhat annoyed by your evident suspicions touching my sanity, and so resolved to punish you quietly, in my own way, by a little bit of sober mystification. For this reason I swung the beetle, and for this reason I let it fall from the tree. An observation of yours about its great weight suggested the latter idea."

"Yes, I perceive; and now there is only one point which puzzles me. What are we to make of the skeletons found in the hole?"

"That is a question I am no more able to answer than yourself. There seems, however, only one plausible way of accounting for them—and yet it is dreadful to believe in such atrocity as my suggestion would imply. It is clear that Kidd—if Kidd indeed secreted this treasure, which I doubt not—it is clear that he must have had assistance in the labor. But this labor concluded, he may have thought it expedient to remove all participants in his secret. Perhaps a couple of blows with a mattock were sufficient, while his coadjutors were busy in the pit; perhaps it required a dozen—who shall tell?"

The Black Cat[1]

FOR the most wild, yet most homely narrative which I am about to pen, I neither expect nor solicit belief. Mad indeed would I be to expect it, in a case where my very senses reject their own evidence. Yet, mad am I not—and very surely do I not dream. But to-morrow I die, and to-day I would unburthen my soul. My immediate purpose is to place before the world, plainly, succinctly, and without comment, a series of mere household events. In their consequences, these events have terrified—have tortured—have destroyed me. Yet I will not attempt to expound them. To me, they have presented little but Horror—to many they will seem less terrible than *barroques*.[2] Hereafter, perhaps, some intellect may be found which will reduce my phantasm to the common-place—some intellect more calm, more logical, and far less excitable than my own, which will perceive, in the circumstances I detail with awe, nothing more than an ordinary succession of very natural causes and effects.

From my infancy I was noted for the docility and humanity of my disposition. My tenderness of heart was even so conspicuous as to make me the jest of my companions. I was especially fond of animals, and was indulged by my parents with a great variety of pets. With these I spent most of my time, and never was so happy as when feeding and caressing them. This peculiarity of character grew with my growth, and, in my manhood, I derived from it one of my principal sources of pleasure. To those who have cherished an affection for a faithful and sagacious dog, I need hardly be at the trouble of explaining the nature or the intensity of the gratification thus derivable. There is something in the unselfish and self-sacrificing love of a brute, which goes directly to the heart of him who has had frequent occasion to test the paltry friendship and gossamer fidelity of mere *Man*.

I married early, and was happy to find in my wife a disposition not uncongenial with my own. Observing my partiality for domestic pets, she lost no opportunity of procuring those of the most agreeable kind. We had birds, gold-fish, a fine dog, rabbits, a small monkey, and *a cat*.

This latter was a remarkably large and beautiful animal, entirely black, and sagacious to an astonishing degree. In speaking of his intelligence, my wife, who at heart was not a little tinctured with superstition, made frequent allusion to the ancient popular notion, which regarded all black cats as witches in disguise. Not that she was ever *serious* upon this point—and I mention the matter at all for no better reason than that it happens, just now, to be remembered.

Pluto—this was the cat's name—was my favorite pet and playmate. I alone fed him, and he attended me wherever I went about the house. It was even with difficulty that I could prevent him from following me through the streets.

Our friendship lasted, in this manner, for several years, during which my general temperament and character—through the instrumentality of the Fiend Intemperance—had (I blush to confess it) experienced a radical alteration for the worse. I grew, day by day, more moody, more irritable, more regardless of the feelings of others. I suffered myself to use intemperate language to my wife. At length, I even offered her personal violence. My pets, of course, were made to feel the change in my disposition. I not only neglected, but ill-used them. For Pluto, however, I still retained sufficient regard to restrain me from maltreating him, as I made no scruple of maltreating the rabbits, the monkey, or even the dog, when by accident, or through affection, they came in my way. But my disease grew upon me—for what disease is like Alcohol!—and at length even Pluto, who was now becoming old, and consequently somewhat peevish—even Pluto began to experience the effects of my ill temper.

One night, returning home, much intoxicated, from one of my haunts about town, I fancied that the cat avoided my presence. I seized him; when, in his fright at my violence, he inflicted a slight wound upon my hand with his teeth. The fury of a demon instantly possessed me. I knew myself no longer. My original soul seemed, at once, to take its flight from my body; and a more than fiendish malevolence, gin-nurtured, thrilled every fibre of my frame. I took from my waistcoat-pocket a pen-knife, opened it, grasped the poor beast by the throat, and deliberately cut one of its eyes from the socket! I blush, I burn, I shudder, while I pen the damnable atrocity.

When reason returned with the morning—when I had slept off the fumes of the night's debauch—I experienced a sentiment half of horror, half of remorse, for the crime of which I had been guilty; but it was, at best, a feeble and equivocal feeling, and the soul remained untouched. I again plunged into excess, and soon drowned in wine all memory of the deed.

In the meantime the cat slowly recovered. The socket of the lost eye presented, it is true, a frightful appearance, but he no longer appeared to suffer any pain. He went about the house as usual, but, as might be expected, fled in extreme terror at my approach. I had so much of my old heart left, as to be at first grieved by this evident dislike on the part of a creature which had once so loved me. But this feeling soon gave place to irritation. And then came, as if to my final and irrevocable overthrow, the spirit of PERVERSENESS. Of this spirit philosophy takes no account. Yet I am not more sure that my soul lives, than I am that perverseness is one of the primitive impulses of the human heart—one of the indivisible primary faculties, or sentiments, which give direction to the character of Man. Who has not, a hundred times, found himself committing a vile or a silly action, for no other reason than because he knows he should *not*? Have we not a perpetual inclination, in the teeth of our best judgment, to violate that which is *Law*, merely because we understand it to be such? This spirit of perverseness, I say, came to my final overthrow. It was this unfathomable longing of the soul *to vex itself*—to offer violence to its own nature—to do wrong for the wrong's sake only—that urged me to continue and finally to consummate the injury I had inflicted upon the unoffending brute. One morning, in cool blood, I slipped a noose about its neck and hung it to the limb of a tree;—hung it with the tears streaming from my eyes, and with the bitterest remorse at my heart;—hung it *because* I knew that it had loved me, and *because* I felt it had given me no reason of offence;—hung it *because* I knew that in so doing I was committing a sin—a deadly sin that would so jeopardize my immortal soul as to place it—if such a thing were possible—even beyond the reach of the infinite mercy of the Most Merciful and Most Terrible God.

On the night of the day on which this cruel deed was done, I was aroused from sleep by the cry of fire. The curtains of my bed were in flames. The whole house was blazing. It was with great difficulty that my wife, a servant, and myself, made our escape from the conflagration. The destruction was complete. My entire worldly wealth was swallowed up, and I resigned myself thenceforward to despair.

I am above the weakness of seeking to establish a sequence of cause and effect, between the disaster and the atrocity. But I am detailing a chain of facts—and wish not to leave even a possible link imperfect. On the day succeeding the fire, I visited the ruins. The walls, with one exception, had fallen in. This exception was found in a compartment wall, not very thick, which stood about the middle of the house, and against which had rested the head of my bed. The plastering had here, in great measure, resisted the action of the fire—a fact which I attributed to its having been recently spread. About this wall a dense crowd were collected, and many persons seemed to be examining a particular portion of it with very minute and eager attention. The words "strange!" "singular!" and other similar expressions, excited my curiosity. I approached and saw, as if graven in *bas relief*³ upon the white surface, the figure of a gigantic *cat*. The impression was given with an accuracy truly marvellous. There was a rope about the animal's neck.

When I first beheld this apparition—for I could scarcely regard it as less—my wonder and my terror were extreme. But at length reflection came to my aid. The cat, I remembered, had been hung in a garden adjacent to the house. Upon the alarm of fire, this garden had been immediately filled by the crowd—by some one of whom the animal must have been cut from the tree and thrown, through an open window, into my chamber. This had probably been done with the view of arousing me from sleep. The falling of other walls had compressed the victim of my cruelty into the substance of the freshly-spread plaster; the lime of which, with the flames, and the *ammonia* from the carcass, had then accomplished the portraiture as I saw it.

Although I thus readily accounted to my reason, if not altogether to my conscience, for the startling fact just detailed, it did not the less fail to make a deep impression upon my fancy. For months I could not rid myself of the phantasm of the cat; and, during this period, there came back into my spirit a half-sentiment that seemed, but was not, remorse. I went so far as to regret the loss of the animal, and to look about me, among the vile haunts which I now habitually frequented, for another pet of the same species, and of somewhat similar appearance, with which to supply its place.

One night as I sat, half stupefied, in a den of more than infamy, my attention was suddenly drawn to some black object, reposing upon the head of one of the immense hogsheads of Gin, or of Rum, which constituted the chief furniture of the apartment. I had been looking steadily at the top of this hogshead for some minutes, and what now caused me surprise was the fact that I had not sooner perceived the object thereupon. I approached it, and touched it with my hand. It was a black cat—a very large one—fully as large as Pluto, and closely resembling him in every respect but one. Pluto had not a white hair upon any portion of his body; but this cat had a large, although indefinite splotch of white, covering nearly the whole region of the breast.

Upon my touching him, he immediately arose, purred loudly, rubbed against my hand, and appeared delighted with my notice. This, then, was the very creature of which I was in search. I at once offered to purchase it of the landlord; but this person made no claim to it—knew nothing of it—had never seen it before.

I continued my caresses, and, when I prepared to go home, the animal evinced a disposition to accompany me. I permitted it to do so; occasionally stooping and patting it as I proceeded. When it reached the house it domesticated itself at once, and became immediately a great favorite with my wife.

For my own part, I soon found a dislike to it arising within me. This was just the reverse of what I had anticipated; but—I know not how or why it was—its evident fondness for myself rather disgusted and annoyed. By slow degrees, these feelings of disgust and annoyance rose into the bitterness of hatred. I avoided the creature; a certain sense of shame, and the remembrance of my former deed of cruelty, preventing me from physically abusing it. I did not, for some weeks, strike, or otherwise violently ill use it; but gradually—very gradually—I came to look upon it with unutterable loathing, and to flee silently from its odious presence, as from the breath of a pestilence.

What added, no doubt, to my hatred of the beast, was the discovery, on the morning after I brought it home, that, like Pluto, it also had been deprived of one of its eyes. This circumstance, however, only endeared it to my wife, who, as I have already said, possessed, in a high degree, that humanity of feeling which had once been my distinguishing trait, and the source of many of my simplest and purest pleasures.

With my aversion to this cat, however, its partiality for myself seemed to increase. It followed my footsteps with a pertinacity which it would be difficult to make the reader comprehend. Whenever I sat, it would crouch beneath my chair, or spring upon my knees, covering me with its loathsome caresses. If I arose to walk it would get between my feet and thus nearly throw me down, or, fastening its long and sharp claws in my dress, clamber, in this manner, to my breast. At such times, although I longed to destroy it with a blow, I was yet withheld from so doing, partly by a memory of my former crime, but chiefly—let me confess it at once—by absolute *dread* of the beast.

This dread was not exactly a dread of physical evil—and yet I should be at a loss how otherwise to define it. I am almost ashamed to own—yes, even in this felon's cell, I am almost ashamed to own—that the terror and horror with which the animal inspired me, had been heightened by one of the merest chimæras it would be possible to conceive. My wife had called my attention, more than once, to the character of the mark of white hair, of which I have spoken, and which constituted the sole visible difference between the strange beast and the one I had destroyed. The reader will remember that this mark, although large, had been originally very indefinite; but, by slow degrees—degrees nearly imperceptible, and which for a long time my Reason struggled to reject as fanciful—it had, at length, assumed a rigorous distinctness of outline. It was now the representation of an object that I shudder to name—and for this, above all, I loathed, and dreaded, and would have rid myself of the monster *had I dared*—it was now, I say, the image of a hideous—of a ghastly thing—of the GALLOWS!—oh, mournful and terrible engine of Horror and of Crime—of Agony and of Death!

And now was I indeed wretched beyond the wretchedness of mere Humanity. And a *brute beast*—whose fellow I had contemptuously destroyed—*a brute beast* to work out for *me*—for me a man, fashioned in the image of the High God—so much of insufferable wo! Alas! neither by day nor by night knew I the blessing of Rest any more! During the former the creature left me no moment alone; and, in the latter, I started, hourly, from dreams of unutterable fear, to find the hot breath of *the thing* upon my face, and its vast weight—an incarnate Night-Mare[4] that I had no power to shake off—incumbent eternally upon my *heart!*

Beneath the pressure of torments such as these, the feeble remnant of the good within me succumbed. Evil thoughts became my sole intimates—the darkest and most evil of thoughts. The moodiness of my usual temper increased to hatred of all things and of all mankind; while, from the sudden, frequent, and ungovernable outbursts of a fury to which I now blindly abandoned myself, my uncomplaining wife, alas! was the most usual and the most patient of sufferers.

One day she accompanied me, upon some household errand, into the cellar of the old building which our poverty compelled us to inhabit. The cat followed me down the steep stairs, and, nearly throwing me headlong, exasperated me to madness. Uplifting an axe, and forgetting, in my wrath, the childish dread which had hitherto stayed my hand, I aimed a blow at the animal which, of course, would have proved instantly fatal had it descended as I wished. But this blow was arrested by the hand of my wife. Goaded, by the interference, into a rage more than demoniacal, I withdrew my arm from her grasp and buried the axe in her brain. She fell dead upon the spot, without a groan.

This hideous murder accomplished, I set myself forthwith, and with entire deliberation, to the task of concealing the body. I knew that I could not remove it from the house, either by day or by night, without the risk of being observed by the neighbors. Many projects entered my mind. At one period I thought of cutting the corpse into minute fragments, and destroying them by fire. At another, I resolved to dig a grave for it in the floor of the cellar. Again, I deliberated about casting it in the well in the yard—about packing it in a box, as if merchandize, with the usual arrangements, and so getting a porter to take it from the house. Finally I hit upon what I considered a far better expedient than either of these. I determined to wall it up in the cellar—as the monks of the middle ages are recorded to have walled up their victims.

For a purpose such as this the cellar was well adapted. Its walls were loosely constructed, and had lately been plastered throughout with a rough plaster, which the dampness of the atmosphere had prevented from hardening. Moreover, in one of the walls was a projection, caused by a false chimney, or fireplace, that had been filled up, and made to resemble the rest of the cellar. I made no doubt that I could readily displace the bricks at this point, insert the corpse, and wall the whole up as before, so that no eye could detect any thing suspicious.

And in this calculation I was not deceived. By means of a crow-bar I easily dislodged the bricks, and, having carefully deposited the body against the inner wall, I propped it in that position, while, with little trouble, I re-laid the whole structure as it originally stood. Having procured mortar, sand, and hair, with every possible precaution, I prepared a plaster which could not be distinguished from the old, and with this I very carefully went over the new brick-work. When I had finished, I felt satisfied that all was right. The wall did not present the slightest appearance of having been disturbed. The rubbish on the floor was picked up with the minutest care. I looked around triumphantly, and said to myself—"Here at least, then, my labor has not been in vain."

My next step was to look for the beast which had been the cause of so much wretchedness; for I had, at length, firmly resolved to put it to death. Had I been able to meet with it, at the moment, there could have been no doubt of its fate; but it appeared that the crafty animal had been alarmed at the violence of my previous anger, and forebore to present itself in my present mood. It is impossible to describe, or to imagine, the deep, the blissful sense of relief which the absence of the detested creature occasioned in my bosom. It did not make its appearance during the night— and thus for one night at least, since its introduction into the house, I soundly and tranquilly slept; aye, *slept* even with the burden of murder upon my soul!

The second and the third day passed, and still my tormentor came not. Once again I breathed as a freeman. The monster, in terror, had fled the premises forever! I should behold it no more! My happiness was supreme! The guilt of my dark deed disturbed me but little. Some few inquiries had been made, but these had been readily answered. Even a search had been instituted—but of course nothing was to be discovered. I looked upon my future felicity as secured.

Upon the fourth day of the assassination, a party of the police came, very unexpectedly, into the house, and proceeded again to make rigorous investigation of the premises. Secure, however, in the inscrutability of my place of concealment, I felt no embarrassment whatever. The officers bade me accompany them in their search. They left no nook or corner unexplored. At length, for the third or fourth time, they descended into the cellar. I quivered not in a muscle. My heart beat calmly as that of one who slumbers in innocence. I walked the cellar from end to end. I folded my arms upon my bosom, and roamed easily to and fro. The police were thoroughly satisfied and prepared to depart. The glee at my heart was too strong to be restrained. I burned to say if but one word, by way of triumph, and to render doubly sure their assurance of my guiltlessness.

"Gentlemen," I said at last, as the party ascended the steps, "I delight to have allayed your suspicions. I wish you all health, and a little more courtesy. By the bye, gentlemen, this—this is a very well constructed house." [In the rabid desire to say something easily, I scarcely knew what I uttered at all.]—"I may say an *excellently* well constructed house. These walls—are you going, gentlemen?—these walls are solidly put together;" and here, through the mere phrenzy of bravado, I rapped heavily, with a cane which I held in my hand, upon that very portion of the brick-work behind which stood the corpse of the wife of my bosom.

But may God shield and deliver me from the fangs of the Arch-Fiend! No sooner had the reverberation of my blows sunk into silence, than I was answered by a voice from within the tomb!—by a cry, at first muffled and broken, like the sobbing of a child, and then quickly swelling into one long, loud, and continuous scream, utterly anomalous and inhuman—a howl—a wailing shriek, half of horror and half of triumph, such as might have arisen only out of hell, conjointly from the throats of the damned in their agony and of the demons that exult in the damnation.

Of my own thoughts it is folly to speak. Swooning, I staggered to the opposite wall. For one instant the party upon the stairs remained motionless, through extremity of terror and of awe. In the next, a dozen stout arms were toiling at the wall. It fell bodily. The corpse, already greatly decayed and clotted with gore, stood erect before the eyes of the spectators. Upon its head, with red extended mouth and solitary eye of fire, sat the hideous beast whose craft had seduced me into murder, and whose informing voice had consigned me to the hangman. I had walled the monster up within the tomb!

The Premature Burial[1]

There are certain themes of which the interest is all-absorbing, but which are too entirely horrible for the purposes of legitimate fiction. These the mere romanticist must eschew, if he do not wish to offend, or to disgust. They are with propriety handled, only when the severity and majesty of Truth sanctify and sustain them. We thrill, for example, with the most intense of "pleasurable pain," over the accounts of the Passage of the Beresina, of the Earthquake at Lisbon, of the Plague at London, of the Massacre of St. Bartholomew, or of the stifling of the hundred and twenty-three prisoners in the Black Hole at Calcutta.[2] But, in these accounts, it is the fact—it is the reality—it is the history which excites. As inventions, we should regard them with simple abhorrence.

I have mentioned some few of the more prominent and august calamities on record; but, in these, it is the extent, not less than the character of the calamity, which so vividly impresses the fancy. I need not remind the reader that, from the long and weird catalogue of human miseries, I might have selected many individual instances more replete with essential suffering than any of these vast generalities of disaster. The true wretchedness, indeed—the ultimate woe—is particular, not diffuse. That the ghastly extremes of agony are endured by man the unit, and never by man the mass—for this let us thank a merciful God!

To be buried while alive, is beyond question, the most terrific of these extremes which has ever fallen to the lot of mere mortality. That it has frequently, very frequently, so fallen, will scarcely be denied by those who think. The boundaries which divide Life from Death, are at best shadowy and vague. Who shall say where the one ends, and where the other begins? We know that there are diseases in which occur total cessations of all the apparent functions of vitality, and yet in which these cessations are merely suspensions, properly so called. They are only temporary pauses in the incomprehensible mechanism. A certain period elapses, and some unseen mysterious principle again sets in motion the magic pinions and the wizard wheels. The silver cord was not forever loosed, nor the golden bowl irreparably broken. But where, meantime, was the soul?

Apart, however, from the inevitable conclusion, *à priori*, that such causes must produce such effects—that the well known occurrence of such cases of suspended animation must naturally give rise, now and then, to premature interments—apart from this consideration, we have the direct testimony of medical and ordinary experience, to prove that a vast number of such interments have actually taken place. I might refer at once, if necessary, to a hundred well authenticated instances. One of very remarkable character, and of which the circumstances may be fresh in the memory of some of my readers, occurred, not very long ago, in the neighboring city of Baltimore, where it occasioned a painful, intense, and widely extended excitement. The wife of one of the most respectable citizens—a lawyer of eminence and a member of Congress—was seized with a sudden and unaccountable illness, which completely baffled the skill of her physicians. After much suffering she died, or was supposed to die. No one suspected, indeed, or had reason to suspect, that she was not actually dead. She presented all the ordinary appearances of death. The face assumed the usual pinched and sunken outline. The lips were of the usual marble pallor. The eyes were lustreless. There was no warmth. Pulsation had ceased. For three days the body was preserved unburied, during which it had acquired a stony rigidity. The funeral, in short, was hastened, on account of the rapid advance of what was supposed to be decomposition.

The lady was deposited in her family vault, which, for three subsequent years, was undisturbed. At the expiration of this term, it was opened for the reception of a sarcophagus;—but, alas! how fearful a shock awaited the husband, who, personally, threw open the door. As its portals swung outwardly back, some white-apparrelled object fell rattling within his arms. It was the skeleton of his wife in her yet unmouldered shroud.

A careful investigation rendered it evident that she had revived within two days after her entombment—that her struggles within the coffin had caused it to fall from a ledge, or shelf, to the floor, where it was so broken as to permit her escape. A lamp which had been accidentally left, full of oil, within the tomb, was found empty; it might have been exhausted, however, by evaporation. On the uppermost of the steps which led down into the dread chamber, was a large fragment of the coffin, with which it seemed that she had endeavored to arrest attention, by striking the iron door. While thus occupied, she probably swooned, or possibly died, through sheer terror; and, in falling, her shroud became entangled in some iron-work which projected interiorly. Thus she remained, and thus she rotted, erect.

In the year 1810, a case of living inhumation happened in France, attended with circumstances which go far to warrant the assertion that truth is, indeed, stranger than fiction. The heroine of the story was a Mademoiselle Victorine Lafourcade, a young girl of illustrious family, of wealth, and of great personal beauty. Among her numerous suitors was Julien Bossuet, a poor *littérateur*, or journalist, of Paris. His talents and general amiability had recommended him to the notice of the heiress, by whom he seems to have been truly beloved; but her pride of birth decided her, finally, to reject him, and to wed a Monsieur Rénelle, a banker, and a diplomatist of some eminence. After marriage, however, this gentleman neglected, and perhaps, even more positively ill-treated her. Having passed with him some wretched years, she died,—at least her condition so closely resembled death as to deceive every one who saw her. She was buried—not in a vault—but in an ordinary grave in the village of her nativity. Filled with despair, and still inflamed by the memory of a profound attachment, the lover journeys from the capital to the remote province in which the village lies, with the romantic purpose of disinterring the corpse, and possessing himself of its luxuriant tresses. He reaches the grave. At midnight he unearths the coffin, opens it, and is in the act of detaching the hair, when he is arrested by the unclosing of the beloved eyes. In fact, the lady had been buried alive. Vitality had not altogether departed; and she was aroused, by the caresses of her lover, from the lethargy which had been mistaken for death. He bore her frantically to his lodgings in the village. He employed certain powerful restoratives suggested by no little medical learning. In fine, she revived. She recognized her preserver. She remained with him until, by slow degrees, she fully recovered her original health. Her woman's heart was not adamant, and this last lesson of love sufficed to soften it. She bestowed it upon Bossuet. She returned no more to her husband, but concealing from him her resurrection, fled with her lover to America. Twenty years afterwards, the two returned to France, in the persuasion that time had so greatly altered the lady's appearance that her friends would be unable to recognize her. They were mistaken, however; for, at the first meeting, Monsieur Rénelle did actually recognize and make claim to his wife. This claim she resisted; and a judicial tribunal sustained her in her resistance; deciding that the peculiar circumstances, with the long lapse of years, had extinguished, not only equitably but legally, the authority of the husband.

The "Chirurgical Journal" of Leipsic—a periodical, of high authority and merit, which some American bookseller would do well to translate and republish—records, in a late number, a very distressing event of the character in question.

An officer of artillery, a man of gigantic stature and of robust health, being thrown from an unmanageable horse, received a very severe contusion upon the head, which rendered him insensible at once; the skull was slightly fractured; but no immediate danger was apprehended. Trepanning was accomplished successfully. He was bled, and many other of the ordinary means of relief were adopted. Gradually, however, he fell into a more and more hopeless state of stupor; and, finally, it was thought that he died.

The weather was warm; and he was buried, with indecent haste, in one of the public cemeteries. His funeral took place on Thursday. On the Sunday following, the grounds of the cemetery were, as usual, much thronged with visiters; and, about noon, an intense excitement was created by the declaration of a peasant that, while sitting upon the grave of the officer, he had distinctly felt a commotion of the earth, as if occasioned by some one struggling beneath. At first little attention was paid to the man's asseveration; but his evident terror, and the dogged obstinacy with which he persisted in his story, had, at length, their natural effect upon the crowd. Spades were hurriedly procured, and the grave, which was shamefully shallow, was, in a few minutes, so far thrown open that the head of its occupant appeared. He was then, seemingly, dead; but he sat nearly erect within his coffin, the lid of which, in his furious struggles, he had partially uplifted.

He was forthwith conveyed to the nearest Hospital, and there pronounced to be still living, although in an asphytic condition.[3] After some hours he revived, recognized individuals of his acquaintance, and, in broken sentences, spoke of his agonies in the grave.

From what he related, it was clear that he must have been conscious of life for more than an hour, while inhumed, before lapsing into insensibility. The grave was carelessly and loosely filled with an exceedingly porous soil; and thus some air was necessarily admitted. He heard the footsteps of the crowd overhead, and endeavored to make himself heard in turn. It was the tumult within the grounds of the cemetery, he said, which appeared to awaken him from a deep sleep—but no sooner was he awake than he became fully aware of the awful horrors of his position.

This patient, it is recorded, was doing well, and seemed to be in a fair way of ultimate recovery, but fell a victim to the quackeries of medical experiment. The galvanic battery was applied; and he suddenly expired in one of those ecstatic paroxysms which, occasionally, it superinduces.

The mention of the galvanic battery, nevertheless, recalls to my memory a well known and very extraordinary case in point, where its action proved the means of restoring to animation a young attorney of London who had been interred for two days. This occurred in 1831, and created, at the time, a very profound sensation wherever it was made the subject of converse.

The patient, Mr. Edward Stapleton, had died, apparently, of typhus fever, accompanied with some anomalous symptoms which had excited the curiosity of his medical attendants. Upon his seeming decease, his friends were requested to sanction a *post mortem* examination, but declined to permit it. As often happens when such refusals are made, the practitioners resolved to disinter the body and dissect it at leisure, in private. Arrangements were easily effected with some of the numerous corps of body-snatchers with which London abounds; and, upon the third night after the funeral, the supposed corpse was unearthed from a grave eight feet deep, and deposited in the operation chamber of one of the private hospitals.

An incision of some extent had been actually made in the abdomen, when the fresh and undecayed appearance of the subject suggested an application of the battery. One experiment succeeded another, and the customary effects supervened, with nothing to characterize them in any respect, except, upon one or two occasions, a more than ordinary degree of life-likeliness in the convulsive action.

It grew late. The day was about to dawn; and it was thought expedient, at length, to proceed at once to the dissection. A student, however, was especially desirous of testing a theory of his own, and insisted upon applying the battery to one of the pectoral muscles. A rough gash was made, and a wire hastily brought in contact; when the patient, with a hurried but quite unconvulsive movement, arose from the table, stepped into the middle of the floor, gazed about him uneasily for a few seconds, and then—spoke. What he said was unintelligible; but words were uttered; the syllabification was distinct. Having spoken, he fell heavily to the floor.

For some moments all were paralyzed with awe—but the urgency of the case soon restored them their presence of mind. It was seen that Mr. Stapleton was alive, although in a swoon. Upon exhibition of ether he revived and was rapidly restored to health, and to the society of his friends—from whom, however, all knowledge of his resuscitation was withheld, until a relapse was no longer to be apprehended. Their wonder—their rapturous astonishment—may be conceived.

The most thrilling peculiarity of this incident, nevertheless, is involved in what Mr. S. himself asserts. He declares that at no period was he altogether insensible—that, dully and confusedly, he was aware of every thing which happened to him, from the moment in which he was pronounced *dead* by his physicians, to that in which he fell swooning to the floor of the Hospital. "I am alive" were the uncomprehended words which, upon recognizing the locality of the dissecting-room, he had endeavored, in his extremity, to utter.

It were an easy matter to multiply such histories as these—but I forbear—for, indeed, we have no need of such to establish the fact that premature interments occur. When we reflect how very rarely, from the nature of the case, we have it in our power to detect them, we must admit that they may *frequently* occur without our cognizance. Scarcely, in truth, is a graveyard ever encroached upon, for any purpose, to any great extent, that skeletons are not found in postures which suggest the most fearful of suspicions.

Fearful indeed the suspicion—but more fearful the doom! It may be asserted, without hesitation, that *no* event is so terribly well adapted to inspire the supremeness of bodily and of mental distress, as is burial before death. The unendurable oppression of the lungs—the stifling fumes from the damp earth—the clinging of the death garments—the rigid embrace of the narrow house—the blackness of the absolute Night—the silence like a sea that overwhelms—the unseen but palpable presence of the Conqueror Worm—these things, with thoughts of the air and grass above, with memory of dear friends who would fly to save us if but informed of our fate, and with consciousness that of this fate they can *never* be informed—that our hopeless portion is that of the really dead—these considerations, I say, carry into the heart, which still palpitates, a degree of appalling and intolerable horror from which the most daring imagination must recoil. We know of nothing so agonizing upon Earth—we can dream of nothing half so hideous in the realms of the nethermost Hell. And thus all narratives upon this topic have an interest profound; an interest, nevertheless, which, through the sacred awe of the topic itself, very properly and very peculiarly depends upon our conviction of the *truth* of the matter narrated. What I have now to tell, is of my own actual knowledge—of my own positive and personal experience.

For several years I had been subject to attacks of the singular disorder which physicians have agreed to term catalepsy, in default of a more definitive title. Although both the immediate and the predisposing causes, and even the actual diagnosis, of this disease, are still mysteries, its obvious and apparent character is sufficiently well understood. Its variations seem to be chiefly of degree. Sometimes the patient lies, for a day only, or even for a shorter period, in a species of exaggerated lethargy. He is senseless and externally motionless; but the pulsation of the heart is still faintly perceptible; some traces of warmth remain; a slight color lingers within the centre of the cheek; and, upon application of a mirror to the lips, we can detect a torpid, unequal, and vacillating action of the lungs. Then again the duration of the trance is for weeks—even for months; while the closest scrutiny, and the most rigorous medical tests, fail to establish any material distinction between the state of the sufferer and what we conceive of absolute death. Very usually, he is saved from premature interment solely by the knowledge of his friends that he has been previously subject to catalepsy, by the consequent suspicion excited, and, above all, by the non-appearance of decay. The advances of the malady are, luckily, gradual. The first manifestations, although marked, are unequivocal. The fits grow successively more and more distinctive, and endure each for a longer term than the preceding. In this lies the principal security from inhumation. The unfortunate whose *first* attack should be of the extreme character which is occasionally seen, would almost inevitably be consigned alive to the tomb.

My own case differed in no important particular from those mentioned in medical books. Sometimes, without any apparent cause, I sank, little by little, into a condition of hemi-syncope, or half swoon; and, in this condition, without pain, without ability to stir, or, strictly speaking, to think, but with a dull lethargic consciousness of life and of the presence of those who surrounded my bed, I remained, until the crisis of the disease restored me, suddenly, to perfect sensation. At other times I was quickly and impetuously smitten. I grew sick, and numb, and chilly, and dizzy, and so fell prostrate at once. Then, for weeks, all was void, and black, and silent, and Nothing became the universe. Total annihilation could be no more. From these latter attacks I awoke, however, with a gradation slow in proportion to the suddenness of the seizure. Just as the day dawns to the friendless and houseless beggar who roams the streets throughout the long desolate winter night—just so tardily—just so wearily— just so cheerily came back the light of the Soul to me.

Apart from the tendency to trance, however, my general health appeared to be good; nor could I perceive that it was at all affected by the one prevalent malady— unless, indeed, an idiosyncrasy in my ordinary *sleep* may be looked upon as superinduced. Upon awaking from slumber, I could never gain, at once, thorough possession of my senses, and always remained, for many minutes, in much bewilderment and perplexity;—the mental faculties in general, but the memory in especial, being in a condition of absolute abeyance.

In all that I endured there was no physical suffering, but of moral distress an infinitude. My fancy grew charnal. I talked "of worms, of tombs and epitaphs." I was lost in reveries of death, and the idea of premature burial held continual possession of my brain. The ghastly Danger to which I was subjected, haunted me day and night. In the former, the torture of meditation was excessive—in the latter, supreme. When the grim Darkness overspread the Earth, then, with very horror of thought, I shook—shook as the quivering plumes upon the hearse. When Nature could endure wakefulness no longer, it was with a struggle that I consented to sleep—for I shuddered to reflect that, upon awaking, I might find myself the tenant of a grave. And when, finally, I sank into slumber, it was only to rush at once into a world of phantasms, above which, with vast, sable, overshadowing wings, hovered, predominant, the one sepulchral Idea.

From the innumerable images of gloom which thus oppressed me in dreams, I select for record but a solitary vision. Methought I was immersed in a cataleptic trance of more than usual duration and profundity. Suddenly there came an icy hand upon my forehead, and an impatient, gibbering voice whispered the word "Arise!" within my ear.

I sat erect. The darkness was total. I could not see the figure of him who had aroused me. I could call to mind neither the period at which I had fallen into the trance, nor the locality in which I then lay. While I remained motionless, and busied in endeavors to collect my thoughts, the cold hand grasped me fiercely by the wrist, shaking it petulantly, while the gibbering voice said again:

"Arise! did I not bid thee arise?"

"And who," I demanded, "art thou?"

"I have no name in the regions which I inhabit," replied the voice mournfully; "I was mortal, but am fiend. I was merciless, but am pitiful. Thou dost feel that I shudder.—My teeth chatter as I speak, yet it is not with the chilliness of the night— of the night without end. But this hideousness is insufferable. How canst *thou* tranquilly sleep? I cannot rest for the cry of these great agonies. These sights are more than I can bear. Get thee up! Come with me into the outer Night, and let me unfold to thee the graves. Is not this a spectacle of woe?—Behold!"

I looked; and the unseen figure, which still grasped me by the wrist, had caused to be thrown open the graves of all mankind; and from each issued the faint phosphoric radiance of decay; so that I could see into the innermost recesses, and there view the shrouded bodies in their sad and solemn slumbers with the worm. But, alas! the real sleepers were fewer, by many millions, than those who slumbered not at all; and there was a feeble struggling; and there was a general sad unrest; and from out the depths of the countless pits there came a melancholy rustling from the garments of the buried. And, of those who seemed tranquilly to repose, I saw that a vast number had changed, in a greater or less degree, the rigid and uneasy position in which they had originally been entombed. And the voice again said to me, as I gazed:

"Is it not—oh, is it *not* a pitiful sight?"—but, before I could find words to reply, the figure had ceased to grasp my wrist, the phosphoric lights expired, and the graves were closed with a sudden violence, while from out them arose a tumult of despairing cries, saying again—"Is it not—oh, God! is it *not* a very pitiful sight?"

Phantasies such as these, presenting themselves at night, extended their terrific influence far into my waking hours.—My nerves became thoroughly unstrung, and I fell a prey to perpetual horror. I hesitated to ride, or to walk, or to indulge in any exercise that would carry me from home. In fact I no longer dared trust myself out of the immediate presence of those who were aware of my proneness to catalepsy, lest, falling into one of my usual fits, I should be buried before my real condition could be ascertained. I doubted the care, the fidelity of my dearest friends. I dreaded that, in some trance of more than customary duration, they might be prevailed upon to regard me as irrecoverable. I even went so far as to fear that, as I occasioned much trouble, they might be glad to consider any very protracted attack as sufficient excuse for getting rid of me altogether. It was in vain they endeavored to reassure me by the most solemn promises. I exacted the most sacred oaths, that under no circumstances they would bury me until decomposition had so materially advanced as to render farther preservation impossible. And, even then, my mortal terrors would listen to no reason—would accept no consolation. I entered into a series of elaborate precautions. Among other things, I had the family vault so remodelled as to admit of being readily opened from within. The slightest pressure upon a long lever that extended far into the tomb would cause the iron portals to fly back. There were arrangements also for the free admission of air and light, and convenient receptacles for food and water, within immediate reach of the coffin intended for my reception. This coffin was warmly and softly padded, and was provided with a lid, fashioned upon the principle of the vault-door, with the addition of springs so contrived that the feeblest movement of the body would be sufficient to set it at liberty. Besides all this, there was suspended from the roof of the tomb, a large bell, the rope of which, it was designed, should extend through a hole in the coffin, and so be fastened to one of the hands of the corpse. But, alas! what avails the vigilance against the Destiny of man? Not even these well contrived securities sufficed to save from the uttermost agonies of living inhumation, a wretch to these agonies foredoomed!

There arrived an epoch—as often before there had arrived—in which I found myself emerging from total unconsciousness into the first feeble and indefinite sense of existence.—Slowly—with a tortoise gradation—approached the faint gray dawn of the psychal day. A torpid uneasiness. An apathetic endurance of dull pain. No care— no hope—no effort. Then, after long interval, a ringing in the ears; then, after a lapse still longer, a pricking or tingling sensation in the extremities; then a seemingly eternal period of pleasurable quiescence, during which the awakening feelings are struggling into thought; then a brief re-sinking into non-entity; then a sudden recovery. At length the slight quivering of an eyelid, and immediately thereupon, an electric shock of a terror, deadly and indefinite, which sends the blood in torrents from the temples to the heart. And now the first positive effort to think. And now the first endeavor to remember. And now a partial and evanescent success. And now the memory has so far regained its dominion that, in some measure, I am cognizant of my state. I feel that I am not awaking from ordinary sleep. I recollect that I have been subject to catalepsy. And now, at last, as if by the rush of an ocean, my shuddering spirit is overwhelmed by the one grim Danger—by the one spectral and ever-prevalent Idea.

For some minutes after this fancy possessed me, I remained without motion. And why? I could not summon courage to move. I dared not make the effort which was to satisfy me of my fate—and yet there was something at my heart which whispered me *it was sure*. Despair—such as no other species of wretchedness ever calls into being—despair alone urged me, after long irresolution, to uplift the heavy lids of my eyes. I uplifted them. It was dark—all dark. I knew that the fit was over. I knew that the crisis of my disorder had long passed. I knew that I had now fully recovered the use of my visual faculties—and yet it was dark—all dark—the intense and utter raylessness of the Night that endureth for evermore.

I endeavored to shriek; and my lips and my parched tongue moved convulsively together in the attempt—but no voice issued from the cavernous lungs, which, oppressed as if by the weight of some incumbent mountain, gasped and palpitated, with the heart, at every elaborate and struggling inspiration.

The movement of the jaws, in this effort to cry aloud, showed me that they were bound up, as is usual with the dead. I felt, too, that I lay upon some hard substance; and by something similar my sides were, also, closely compressed. So far, I had not ventured to stir any of my limbs—but now I violently threw up my arms, which had been lying at length, with the wrists crossed. They struck a solid wooden substance, which extended above my person at an elevation of not more than six inches from my face. I could no longer doubt that I reposed within a coffin at last.

And now, amid all my infinite miseries, came sweetly the cherub Hope—for I thought of my precautions. I writhed, and made spasmodic exertions to force open the lid: it would not move. I felt my wrists for the bell-rope: it was not to be found. And now the Comforter fled forever, and a still sterner Despair reigned triumphant; for I could not help perceiving the absence of the paddings which I had so carefully prepared—and then, too, there came suddenly to my nostrils the strong peculiar odor of moist earth. The conclusion was irresistible. I was *not* within the vault. I had fallen into a trance while absent from home—while among strangers—when, or how, I could not remember—and it was they who had buried me as a dog—nailed up in some common coffin—and thrust, deep, deep, and forever, into some ordinary and nameless *grave*.

As this awful conviction forced itself, thus, into the innermost chambers of my soul, I once again struggled to cry aloud. And in this second endeavor I succeeded. A long, wild, and continuous shriek, or yell, of agony, resounded through the realms of the subterrene Night.

"Hillo! hillo, there!" said a gruff voice in reply.

"What the devil's the matter now?" said a second.

"Get out o' that!" said a third.

"What do you mean by yowling in that ere kind of style, like a cattymount?"[4] said a fourth; and hereupon I was seized and shaken without ceremony, for several minutes, by a junto of very rough-looking individuals. They did not arouse me from my slumber—for I was wide awake when I screamed—but they restored me to the full possession of my memory.

This adventure occurred near Richmond, in Virginia. Accompanied by a friend, I had proceeded, upon a gunning expedition, some miles down the banks of James River. Night approached, and we were overtaken by a storm. The cabin of a small sloop lying at anchor in the stream, and laden with garden mould, afforded us the only available shelter. We made the best of it, and passed the night on board. I slept in one of the only two berths in the vessel—and the berths of a sloop of sixty or seventy tons, need scarcely be described. That which I occupied had no bedding of any kind. Its extreme width was eighteen inches. The distance of its bottom from the deck overhead, was precisely the same. I found it a matter of exceeding difficulty to squeeze myself in. Nevertheless, I slept soundly; and the whole of my vision—for it was no dream, and no nightmare—arose naturally from the circumstances of my position—from my ordinary bias of thought—and from the difficulty, to which I have alluded, of collecting my senses, and especially of regaining my memory, for a long time after awaking from slumber. The men who shook me were the crew of the sloop, and some laborers engaged to unload it. From the load itself came the earthy smell. The bandage about the jaws was a silk handkerchief in which I had bound up my head, in default of my customary nightcap.

The tortures endured, however, were indubitably quite equal, for the time, to those of actual sepulture. They were fearfully—they were inconceivably hideous; but out of Evil proceeded Good; for their very excess wrought in my spirit an inevitable revulsion. My soul acquired tone—acquired temper. I went abroad. I took vigorous exercise. I breathed the free air of Heaven. I thought upon other subjects than Death. I discarded my medical books. "Buchan"[5] I burned. I read no "Night

Thoughts"—no fustian about churchyards—no bugaboo tales—*such as this*. From that memorable night, I dismissed forever my charnal apprehensions, and with them vanished the cataleptic disorder, of which, perhaps, they had been less the consequence than the cause.

There are moments when, even to the sober eye of Reason, the world of our sad Humanity may assume the semblance of a Hell—but the imagination of man is no Carathis, to explore with impunity its every cavern. Alas! the grim legion of sepulchral terrors cannot be regarded as altogether fanciful—but, like the Demons in whose company Afrasiab[6] made his voyage down the Oxus, they must sleep, or they will devour us—they must be suffered to slumber, or we perish.

The Purloined Letter[1]

Nil sapientiae odiosius acumine nimio.

Seneca[2]

AT Paris, just after dark one gusty evening in the autumn of 18—, I was enjoying the twofold luxury of meditation and a meerschaum,[3] in company with my friend C. Auguste Dupin, in his little back library, or book-closet, *au troisiême, No. 33, Rue Dunôt, Faubourg St. Germain.* For one hour at least we had maintained a profound silence; while each, to any casual observer, might have seemed intently and exclusively occupied with the curling eddies of smoke that oppressed the atmosphere of the chamber. For myself, however, I was mentally discussing certain topics which had formed matter for conversation between us at an earlier period of the evening; I mean the affair of the Rue Morgue, and the mystery attending the murder of Marie Rogêt.[4] I looked upon it, therefore, as something of a coincidence, when the door of our apartment was thrown open and admitted our old acquaintance, Monsieur G—, the Prefect of the Parisian police.

We gave him a hearty welcome; for there was nearly half as much of the entertaining as of the contemptible about the man, and we had not seen him for several years. We had been sitting in the dark, and Dupin now arose for the purpose of lighting a lamp, but sat down again, without doing so, upon G.'s saying that he had called to consult us, or rather to ask the opinion of my friend, about some official business which had occasioned a great deal of trouble.

"If it is any point requiring reflection," observed Dupin, as he forebore to enkindle the wick, "we shall examine it to better purpose in the dark."

"That is another of your odd notions," said the Prefect, who had a fashion of calling every thing "odd" that was beyond his comprehension, and thus lived amid an absolute legion of "oddities."

"Very true," said Dupin, as he supplied his visiter with a pipe, and rolled towards him a comfortable chair.

"And what is the difficulty now?" I asked. "Nothing more in the assassination way, I hope?"

"Oh no; nothing of that nature. The fact is, the business is *very* simple indeed, and I make no doubt that we can manage it sufficiently well ourselves; but then I thought Dupin would like to hear the details of it, because it is so excessively *odd*."

"Simple and odd," said Dupin.

"Why, yes; and not exactly that, either. The fact is, we have all been a good deal puzzled because the affair *is* so simple, and yet baffles us altogether."

"Perhaps it is the very simplicity of the thing which puts you at fault," said my friend.

"What nonsense you *do* talk!" replied the Prefect, laughing heartily.

"Perhaps the mystery is a little *too* plain," said Dupin.

"Oh, good heavens! who ever heard of such an idea?"

"A little *too* self-evident."

"Ha! ha! ha!—ha! ha! ha!—ho! ho! ho!" roared our visiter, profoundly amused, "oh, Dupin, you will be the death of me yet!"

"And what, after all, *is* the matter on hand?" I asked.

"Why, I will tell you," replied the Prefect, as he gave a long, steady, and contemplative puff, and settled himself in his chair. "I will tell you in a few words; but, before I begin, let me caution you that this is an affair demanding the greatest secrecy, and that I should most probably lose the position I now hold, were it known that I confided it to any one."

"Proceed," said I.

"Or not," said Dupin.

"Well then; I have received personal information, from a very high quarter, that a certain document of the last importance, has been purloined from the royal apartments. The individual who purloined it is known; this beyond a doubt; he was seen to take it. It is known, also, that it still remains in his possession."

"How is this known?" asked Dupin.

"It is clearly inferred," replied the Prefect, "from the nature of the document, and from the non-appearance of certain results which would at once arise from its passing *out* of the robber's possession;—that is to say, from his employing it as he must design in the end to employ it."

"Be a little more explicit," I said.

"Well, I may venture so far as to say that the paper gives its holder a certain power in a certain quarter where such power is immensely valuable." The Prefect was fond of the cant of diplomacy.

"Still I do not quite understand," said Dupin.

"No? Well; the disclosure of the document to a third person, who shall be nameless, would bring in question the honor of a personage of most exalted station; and this fact gives the holder of the document an ascendancy over the illustrious personage whose honor and peace are so jeopardized."

"But this ascendancy," I interposed, "would depend upon the robber's knowledge of the loser's knowledge of the robber. Who would dare—"

"The thief," said G., "is the Minister D——, who dares all things, those unbecoming as well as those becoming a man. The method of the theft was not less ingenious than bold. The document in question—a letter, to be frank—had been received by the personage robbed while alone in the royal *boudoir*. During its perusal she was suddenly interrupted by the entrance of the other exalted personage from whom especially it was her wish to conceal it. After a hurried and vain endeavor to thrust it in a drawer, she was forced to place it, open as it was, upon a table. The address, however, was uppermost, and, the contents thus unexposed, the letter escaped notice. At this juncture enters the Minister D——. His lynx eye immediately perceives the paper, recognises the handwriting of the address, observes the confusion of the personage addressed, and fathoms her secret. After some business transactions, hurried through in his ordinary manner, he produces a letter somewhat similar to the one in question, opens it, pretends to read it, and then places it in close juxtaposition to the other. Again he converses, for some fifteen minutes, upon the public affairs. At length, in taking leave, he takes also from the table the letter to which he had no claim. Its rightful owner saw, but, of course, dared not call attention to the act, in the presence of the third personage who stood at her elbow. The minister decamped; leaving his own letter—one of no importance—upon the table."

"Here, then," said Dupin to me, "you have precisely what you demand to make the ascendancy complete—the robber's knowledge of the loser's knowledge of the robber."

"Yes," replied the Prefect; "and the power thus attained has, for some months past, been wielded, for political purposes, to a very dangerous extent. The personage robbed is more thoroughly convinced, every day, of the necessity of reclaiming her letter. But this, of course, cannot be done openly. In fine, driven to despair, she has committed the matter to me."

"Than whom," said Dupin, amid a perfect whirlwind of smoke, "no more sagacious agent could, I suppose, be desired, or even imagined."

"You flatter me," replied the Prefect; "but it is possible that some such opinion may have been entertained."

"It is clear," said I, "as you observe, that the letter is still in possession of the minister; since it is this possession, and not any employment of the letter, which bestows the power. With the employment the power departs."

"True," said G.; "and upon this conviction I proceeded. My first care was to make thorough search of the minister's hotel; and here my chief embarrassment lay in the necessity of searching without his knowledge. Beyond all things, I have been warned of the danger which would result from giving him reason to suspect our design."

"But," said I, "you are quite *au fait* in these investigations. The Parisian police have done this thing often before."

"O yes; and for this reason I did not despair. The habits of the minister gave me, too, a great advantage. He is frequently absent from home all night. His servants are by no means numerous. They sleep at a distance from their master's apartment, and, being chiefly Neapolitans, are readily made drunk. I have keys, as you know, with which I can open any chamber or cabinet in Paris. For three months a night has not passed, during the greater part of which I have not been engaged, personally, in ransacking the D—— Hotel. My honor is interested, and, to mention a great secret, the reward is enormous. So I did not abandon the search until I had become fully satisfied that the thief is a more astute man than myself. I fancy that I have investigated every nook and corner of the premises in which it is possible that the paper can be concealed."

"But is it not possible," I suggested, "that although the letter may be in possession of the minister, as it unquestionably is, he may have concealed it elsewhere than upon his own premises?"

"This is barely possible," said Dupin. "The present peculiar condition of affairs at court, and especially of those intrigues in which D—— is known to be involved, would render the instant availability of the document—its susceptibility of being produced at a moment's notice—a point of nearly equal importance with its possession."

"Its susceptibility of being produced?" said I.

"That is to say, of being *destroyed*," said Dupin.

"True," I observed; "the paper is clearly then upon the premises. As for its being upon the person of the minister, we may consider that as out of the question."

"Entirely," said the Prefect. "He has been twice waylaid, as if by footpads,[5] and his person rigorously searched under my own inspection."

"You might have spared yourself this trouble," said Dupin. "D——, I presume, is not altogether a fool, and, if not, must have anticipated these waylayings, as a matter of course."

"Not *altogether* a fool," said G., "but then he's a poet, which I take to be only one remove from a fool."

"True," said Dupin, after a long and thoughtful whiff from his meerschaum, "although I have been guilty of certain doggrel myself."

"Suppose you detail," said I, "the particulars of your search."

"Why the fact is, we took our time, and we searched *every where*. I have had long experience in these affairs. I took the entire building, room by room; devoting the nights of a whole week to each. We examined, first, the furniture of each apartment. We opened every possible drawer; and I presume you know that, to a properly trained police agent, such a thing as a *secret* drawer is impossible. Any man is a dolt who permits a 'secret' drawer to escape him in a search of this kind. The thing is *so* plain. There is a certain amount of bulk—of space—to be accounted for in every cabinet. Then we have accurate rules. The fiftieth part of a line could not escape us. After the cabinets we took the chairs. The cushions we probed with the fine long needles you have seen me employ. From the tables we removed the tops."

"Why so?"

"Sometimes the top of a table, or other similarly arranged piece of furniture, is removed by the person wishing to conceal an article; then the leg is excavated, the article deposited within the cavity, and the top replaced. The bottoms and tops of bedposts are employed in the same way."

"But could not the cavity be detected by sounding?" I asked.

"By no means, if, when the article is deposited, a sufficient wadding of cotton be placed around it. Besides, in our case, we were obliged to proceed without noise."

"But you could not have removed—you could not have taken to pieces *all* articles of furniture in which it would have been possible to make a deposit in the manner you mention. A letter may be compressed into a thin spiral roll, not differing much in shape or bulk from a large knitting-needle, and in this form it might be inserted into the rung of a chair, for example. You did not take to pieces all the chairs?"

"Certainly not; but we did better—we examined the rungs of every chair in the hotel, and, indeed, the jointings of every description of furniture, by the aid of a most powerful microscope. Had there been any traces of recent disturbance we should not have failed to detect it instantly. A single grain of gimlet-dust, for example, would have been as obvious as an apple. Any disorder in the glueing—any unusual gaping in the joints—would have sufficed to insure detection."

"I presume you looked to the mirrors, between the boards and the plates, and you probed the beds and the bed-clothes, as well as the curtains and carpets."

"That of course; and when we had absolutely completed every particle of the furniture in this way, then we examined the house itself. We divided its entire surface into compartments, which we numbered, so that none might be missed; then we scrutinized each individual square inch throughout the premises, including the two houses immediately adjoining, with the microscope, as before."

"The two houses adjoining!" I exclaimed; "you must have had a great deal of trouble."

"We had; but the reward offered is prodigious."

"You include the *grounds* about the houses?"

"All the grounds are paved with brick. They gave us comparatively little trouble. We examined the moss between the bricks, and found it undisturbed."

"You looked among D——'s papers, of course, and into the books of the library?"

"Certainly; we opened every package and parcel; we not only opened every book, but we turned over every leaf in each volume, not contenting ourselves with a mere shake, according to the fashion of some of our police officers. We also measured the thickness of every book-*cover*, with the most accurate admeasurement, and applied to each the most jealous scrutiny of the microscope. Had any of the bindings been recently meddled with, it would have been utterly impossible that the fact should have escaped observation. Some five or six volumes, just from the hands of the binder, we carefully probed, longitudinally, with the needles."

"You explored the floors beneath the carpets?"

"Beyond doubt. We removed every carpet, and examined the boards with the microscope."

"And the paper on the walls?"

"Yes."

"You looked into the cellars?"

"We did."

"Then," I said, "you have been making a miscalculation, and the letter is *not* upon the premises, as you suppose."

"I fear you are right there," said the Prefect. "And now, Dupin, what would you advise me to do?"

"To make a thorough re-search of the premises."

"That is absolutely needless," replied G——. "I am not more sure that I breathe than I am that the letter is not at the Hotel."

"I have no better advice to give you," said Dupin. "You have, of course, an accurate description of the letter?"

"Oh yes!"—And here the Prefect, producing a memorandum-book, proceeded to read aloud a minute account of the internal, and especially of the external appearance of the missing document. Soon after finishing the perusal of this description, he took his departure, more entirely depressed in spirits than I had ever known the good gentleman before.

In about a month afterwards he paid us another visit, and found us occupied very nearly as before. He took a pipe and a chair and entered into some ordinary conversation. At length I said,—

"Well, but G——, what of the purloined letter? I presume you have at last made up your mind that there is no such thing as overreaching the Minister?"

"Confound him, say I—yes; I made the re-examination, however, as Dupin suggested—but it was all labor lost, as I knew it would be."

"How much was the reward offered, did you say?" asked Dupin.

"Why, a very great deal—a *very* liberal reward—I don't like to say how much, precisely; but one thing I *will* say, that I wouldn't mind giving my individual check for fifty thousand francs to any one who could obtain me that letter. The fact is, it is becoming of more and more importance every day; and the reward has been lately doubled. If it were trebled, however, I could do no more than I have done."

"Why, yes," said Dupin, drawlingly, between the whiffs of his meerschaum, "I really—think, G——, you have not exerted yourself—to the utmost in this matter. You might—do a little more, I think, eh?"

"How?—in what way?"

"Why—puff, puff—you might—puff, puff—employ counsel in the matter, eh?— puff, puff, puff. Do you remember the story they tell of Abernethy?"

"No; hang Abernethy!"

"To be sure! hang him and welcome. But, once upon a time, a certain rich miser conceived the design of spunging upon this Abernethy for a medical opinion. Getting up, for this purpose, an ordinary conversation in a private company, he insinuated his case to the physician, as that of an imaginary individual.

"'We will suppose,' said the miser, 'that his symptoms are such and such; now, doctor, what would *you* have directed him to take?'

"'Take!' said Abernethy, 'why, take *advice*, to be sure.'"

"But," said the Prefect, a little discomposed, "I am *perfectly* willing to take advice, and to pay for it. I would *really* give fifty thousand francs to any one who would aid me in the matter."

"In that case," replied Dupin, opening a drawer, and producing a check-book, "you may as well fill me up a check for the amount mentioned. When you have signed it, I will hand you the letter."

I was astounded. The Prefect appeared absolutely thunder-stricken. For some minutes he remained speechless and motionless, looking incredulously at my friend with open mouth, and eyes that seemed starting from their sockets; then, apparently recovering himself in some measure, he seized a pen, and after several pauses and vacant stares, finally filled up and signed a check for fifty thousand francs, and handed it across the table to Dupin. The latter examined it carefully and deposited it in his pocket-book; then, unlocking an *escritoire*, took thence a letter and gave it to the Prefect. This functionary grasped it in a perfect agony of joy, opened it with a trembling hand, cast a rapid glance at its contents, and then, scrambling and struggling to the door, rushed at length unceremoniously from the room and from the house, without having uttered a syllable since Dupin had requested him to fill up the check.

When he had gone, my friend entered into some explanations.

"The Parisian police," he said, "are exceedingly able in their way. They are persevering, ingenious, cunning, and thoroughly versed in the knowledge which their duties seem chiefly to demand. Thus, when G—— detailed to us his mode of searching the premises at the Hotel D——, I felt entire confidence in his having made a satisfactory investigation—so far as his labors extended."

"So far as his labors extended?" said I.

"Yes," said Dupin. "The measures adopted were not only the best of their kind, but carried out to absolute perfection. Had the letter been deposited within the range of their search, these fellows would, beyond a question, have found it."

I merely laughed—but he seemed quite serious in all that he said.

"The measures, then," he continued, "were good in their kind, and well executed; their defect lay in their being inapplicable to the case, and to the man. A certain set of highly ingenious resources are, with the Prefect, a sort of Procrustean bed,[6] to which he forcibly adapts his designs. But he perpetually errs by being too deep or too shallow, for the matter in hand; and many a schoolboy is a better reasoner than he. I knew one about eight years of age, whose success at guessing in the game of 'even and odd' attracted universal admiration. This game is simple, and is played with marbles. One player holds in his hand a number of these toys, and demands of another whether that number is even or odd. If the guess is right, the guesser wins one; if wrong, he loses one. The boy to whom I allude won all the marbles of the school. Of course he had some principle of guessing; and this lay in mere observation and admeasurement of the astuteness of his opponents. For example, an arrant simpleton is his opponent, and, holding up his closed hand, asks, 'are they even or odd?' Our schoolboy replies, 'odd,' and loses; but upon the second trial he wins, for he then says to himself, 'the simpleton had them even upon the first trial, and his amount of cunning is just sufficient to make him have them odd upon the second; I will therefore guess odd;'—he guesses odd, and wins. Now, with a simpleton a degree above the first, he would have reasoned thus: 'This fellow finds that in the first instance I guessed odd, and, in the second, he will propose to himself, upon the first impulse, a simple variation from even to odd, as did the first simpleton; but then a second thought will suggest that this is too simple a variation, and finally he will decide upon putting it even as before. I will therefore guess even;'—he guesses even, and wins. Now this mode of reasoning in the schoolboy, whom his fellows termed 'lucky,'—what, in its last analysis, is it?"

"It is merely," I said, "an identification of the reasoner's intellect with that of his opponent."

"It is," said Dupin; "and, upon inquiring of the boy by what means he effected the *thorough* identification in which his success consisted, I received answer as follows: 'When I wish to find out how wise, or how stupid, or how good, or how wicked is any one, or what are his thoughts at the moment, I fashion the expression of my face, as accurately as possible, in accordance with the expression of his, and then wait to see what thoughts or sentiments arise in my mind or heart, as if to match or correspond with the expression.' This response of the schoolboy lies at the bottom of all the spurious profundity which has been attributed to Rochefoucault, to La Bougive, to Machiavelli, and to Campanella."[7]

"And the identification," I said, "of the reasoner's intellect with that of his opponent, depends, if I understand you aright, upon the accuracy with which the opponent's intellect is admeasured."

"For its practical value it depends upon this," replied Dupin; "and the Prefect and his cohort fail so frequently, first, by default of this identification, and, secondly, by ill-admeasurement, or rather through non-admeasurement, of the intellect with which they are engaged. They consider only their *own* ideas of ingenuity; and, in searching for anything hidden, advert only to the modes in which *they* would have hidden it. They are right in this much—that their own ingenuity is a faithful representative of that of *the mass*; but when the cunning of the individual felon is diverse in character from their own, the felon foils them, of course. This always happens when it is above their own, and very usually when it is below. They have no variation of principle in their investigations; at best, when urged by some unusual emergency—by some extraordinary reward—they extend or exaggerate their old modes of *practice*, without touching their principles. What, for example, in this case of D——, has been done to vary the principle of action? What is all this boring, and probing, and sounding, and scrutinizing with the microscope, and dividing the surface of the building into registered square inches—what is it all but an exaggeration *of the application* of the one principle or set of principles of search, which are based upon the one set of notions regarding human ingenuity, to which the Prefect, in the long routine of his duty, has been accustomed? Do you not see he has taken it for granted that *all* men proceed to conceal a letter,—not exactly in a gimlet-hole bored in a chair-leg—but, at least, in *some* out-of-the-way hole or corner suggested by the same tenor of thought which would urge a man to secrete a letter in a gimlet-hole bored in a chair-leg? And do you not see also, that such *recherchés*[8] nooks for concealment are adapted only for ordinary occasions, and would be adopted only by ordinary intellects; for, in all cases of concealment, a disposal of the article concealed—a disposal of it in this *recherché* manner,—is, in the very first instance, presumable and presumed; and thus its discovery depends, not at all upon the acumen, but altogether upon the mere care, patience, and determination of the seekers; and where the case is of importance—or, what amounts to the same thing in the policial eyes, when the reward is of magnitude,—the qualities in question have *never* been known to fail. You will now understand what I meant in suggesting that, had the purloined letter been hidden any where within the limits of the Prefect's examination—in other words, had the principle of its concealment been comprehended within the principles of the Prefect—its discovery would have been a matter altogether beyond question. This functionary, however, has been thoroughly mystified; and the remote source of his defeat lies in the supposition that the Minister is a fool, because he has acquired renown as a poet. All fools are poets; this the Prefect *feels*; and he is merely guilty of a *non distributio medii*[9] in thence inferring that all poets are fools."

"But is this really the poet?" I asked. "There are two brothers, I know; and both have attained reputation in letters. The Minister I believe has written learnedly on the Differential Calculus. He is a mathematician, and no poet."

"You are mistaken; I know him well; he is both. As poet *and* mathematician, he would reason well; as mere mathematician, he could not have reasoned at all, and thus would have been at the mercy of the Prefect."

"You surprise me," I said, "by these opinions, which have been contradicted by the voice of the world. You do not mean to set at naught the well-digested idea of centuries. The mathematical reason has long been regarded as *the* reason *par excellence.*"

"'*Il y a à parièr,*'" replied Dupin, quoting from Chamfort, "'*que toute idée publique, toute convention reçue, est une sottise, car elle a convenue au plus grande nombre.*'[10] The mathematicians, I grant you, have done their best to promulgate the popular error to which you allude, and which is none the less an error for its promulgation as truth. With an art worthy a better cause, for example, they have insinuated the term 'analysis' into application to algebra. The French are the originators of this particular deception; but if a term is of any importance—if words derive any value from applicability—then 'analysis' conveys 'algebra' about as much as, in Latin, '*ambitus*' implies 'ambition,' '*religio*' 'religion,' or '*homines honesti,*' a set of *honorable* men."[11]

"You have a quarrel on hand, I see," said I, "with some of the algebraists of Paris; but proceed."

"I dispute the availability, and thus the value, of that reason which is cultivated in any especial form other than the abstractly logical. I dispute, in particular, the reason educed by mathematical study. The mathematics are the science of form and quantity; mathematical reasoning is merely logic applied to observation upon form and quantity. The great error lies in supposing that even the truths of what is called *pure* algebra, are abstract or general truths. And this error is so egregious that I am confounded at the universality with which it has been received. Mathematical axioms are *not* axioms of general truth. What is true of *relation*—of form and quantity—is often grossly false in regard to morals, for example. In this latter science it is very usually *un*true that the aggregated parts are equal to the whole. In chemistry also the axiom fails. In the consideration of motive it fails; for two motives, each of a given value, have not, necessarily, a value when united, equal to the sum of their values apart. There are numerous other mathematical truths which are only truths within the limits of *relation*. But the mathematician argues, from his *finite truths*, through habit, as if they were of an absolutely general applicability—as the world indeed imagines them to be. Bryant,[12] in his very learned 'Mythology,' mentions an analogous source of error, when he says that 'although the Pagan fables are not believed, yet we forget ourselves continually, and make inferences from them as existing realities.' With the algebraists, however, who are Pagans themselves, the 'Pagan fables' *are* believed, and the inferences are made, not so much through lapse of memory, as through an unaccountable addling of the brains. In short, I never yet encountered the mere mathematician who could be trusted out of equal roots, or one who did not clandestinely hold it as a point of his faith that x^2+px was absolutely and unconditionally equal to q. Say to one of these gentlemen, by way of experiment, if you please, that you believe occasions may occur where x^2+px is *not* altogether equal to q, and, having made him understand what you mean, get out of his reach as speedily as convenient, for, beyond doubt, he will endeavor to knock you down.

"I mean to say," continued Dupin, while I merely laughed at his last observations, "that if the Minister had been no more than a mathematician, the Prefect would have been under no necessity of giving me this check. I knew him, however, as both mathematician and poet, and my measures were adapted to his capacity, with reference to the circumstances by which he was surrounded. I knew him as a courtier, too, and as a bold *intriguant*.[13] Such a man, I considered, could not fail to be aware of the ordinary policial modes of action. He could not have failed to anticipate—and events have proved that he did not fail to anticipate—the waylayings to which he was subjected. He must have foreseen, I reflected, the secret investigations of his premises. His frequent absences from home at night, which were hailed by the Prefect as certain aids to his success, I regarded only as *ruses*, to afford opportunity for thorough search to the police, and thus the sooner to impress them with the conviction to which G——, in fact, did finally arrive—the conviction that the letter was not upon the premises. I felt, also, that the whole train of thought, which I was at some pains in detailing to you just now, concerning the invariable principle of policial action in searches for articles concealed—I felt that this whole train of thought would necessarily pass through the mind of the Minister. It would imperatively lead him to despise all the ordinary *nooks* of concealment. *He* could not, I reflected, be so weak as not to see that the most intricate and remote recess of his hotel would be as open as his commonest closets to the eyes, to the probes, to the gimlets, and to the microscopes of the Prefect. I saw, in fine, that he would be driven, as a matter of course, to *simplicity*, if not deliberately induced to it as a matter of choice. You will remember, perhaps, how desperately the Prefect laughed when I suggested, upon our first interview, that it was just possible this mystery troubled him so much on account of its being so *very* self-evident."

"Yes," said I, "I remember his merriment well. I really thought he would have fallen into convulsions."

"The material world," continued Dupin, "abounds with very strict analogies to the immaterial; and thus some color of truth has been given to the rhetorical dogma, that metaphor, or simile, may be made to strengthen an argument, as well as to embellish a description. The principle of the *vis inertiæ*, for example, seems to be identical in physics and metaphysics. It is not more true in the former, that a large body is with more difficulty set in motion than a smaller one, and that its subsequent *momentum* is commensurate with this difficulty, than it is, in the latter, that intellects of the vaster capacity, while more forcible, more constant, and more eventful in their movements than those of inferior grade, are yet the less readily moved, and more embarrassed and full of hesitation in the first few steps of their progress. Again: have you ever noticed which of the street signs, over the shop-doors, are the most attractive of attention?"

"I have never given the matter a thought," I said.

"There is a game of puzzles," he resumed, "which is played upon a map. One party playing requires another to find a given word—the name of town, river, state or empire—any word, in short, upon the motley and perplexed surface of the chart. A novice in the game generally seeks to embarrass his opponents by giving them the most minutely lettered names; but the adept selects such words as stretch, in large characters, from one end of the chart to the other. These, like the over-largely lettered signs and placards of the street, escape observation by dint of being excessively obvious; and here the physical oversight is precisely analogous with the moral inapprehension by which the intellect suffers to pass unnoticed those considerations which are too obtrusively and too palpably self-evident. But this is a point, it appears, somewhat above or beneath the understanding of the Prefect. He never once thought it probable, or possible, that the Minister had deposited the letter immediately beneath the nose of the whole world, by way of best preventing any portion of that world from perceiving it.

"But the more I reflected upon the daring, dashing, and discriminating ingenuity of D——; upon the fact that the document must always have been *at hand*, if he intended to use it to good purpose; and upon the decisive evidence, obtained by the Prefect, that it was not hidden within the limits of that dignitary's ordinary search— the more satisfied I became that, to conceal this letter, the Minister had resorted to the comprehensive and sagacious expedient of not attempting to conceal it at all.

"Full of these ideas, I prepared myself with a pair of green spectacles, and called one fine morning, quite by accident, at the Ministerial hotel. I found D—— at home, yawning, lounging, and dawdling, as usual, and pretending to be in the last extremity of *ennui*. He is, perhaps, the most really energetic human being now alive—but that is only when nobody sees him.

"To be even with him, I complained of my weak eyes, and lamented the necessity of the spectacles, under cover of which I cautiously and thoroughly surveyed the whole apartment, while seemingly intent only upon the conversation of my host.

"I paid especial attention to a large writing-table near which he sat, and upon which lay confusedly, some miscellaneous letters and other papers, with one or two musical instruments and a few books. Here, however, after a long and very deliberate scrutiny, I saw nothing to excite particular suspicion.

"At length my eyes, in going the circuit of the room, fell upon a trumpery fillagree[14] card-rack of pasteboard, that hung dangling by a dirty blue ribbon, from a little brass knob just beneath the middle of the mantel-piece. In this rack, which had three or four compartments, were five or six visiting cards and a solitary letter. This last was much soiled and crumpled. It was torn nearly in two, across the middle—as if a design, in the first instance, to tear it entirely up as worthless, had been altered, or stayed, in the second. It had a large black seal, bearing the D—— cipher *very* conspicuously, and was addressed, in a diminutive female hand, to D——, the minister, himself. It was thrust carelessly, and even, as it seemed, contemptuously, into one of the uppermost divisions of the rack.

"No sooner had I glanced at this letter, than I concluded it to be that of which I was in search. To be sure, it was, to all appearance, radically different from the one of which the Prefect had read us so minute a description. Here the seal was large and black, with the D—— cipher; there it was small and red, with the ducal arms of the S—— family. Here, the address, to the Minister, was diminutive and feminine; there the superscription, to a certain royal personage, was markedly bold and decided; the size alone formed a point of correspondence. But, then, the *radicalness* of these differences, which was excessive; the dirt; the soiled and torn condition of the paper, so inconsistent with the *true* methodical habits of D——, and so suggestive of a design to delude the beholder into an idea of the worthlessness of the document; these things, together with the hyper-obtrusive situation of this document, full in the view of every visiter, and thus exactly in accordance with the conclusions to which I had previously arrived; these things, I say, were strongly corroborative of suspicion, in one who came with the intention to suspect.

"I protracted my visit as long as possible, and, while I maintained a most animated discussion with the Minister, upon a topic which I knew well had never failed to interest and excite him, I kept my attention really riveted upon the letter. In this examination, I committed to memory its external appearance and arrangement in the rack; and also fell, at length, upon a discovery which set at rest whatever trivial doubt I might have entertained. In scrutinizing the edges of the paper, I observed them to be more *chafed* than seemed necessary. They presented the *broken* appearance which is manifested when a stiff paper, having been once folded and pressed with a folder, is refolded in a reversed direction, in the same creases or edges which had formed the original fold. This discovery was sufficient. It was clear to me that the letter had been turned, as a glove, inside out, re-directed, and re-sealed. I bade the Minister good morning, and took my departure at once, leaving a gold snuff-box upon the table.

"The next morning I called for the snuff-box, when we resumed, quite eagerly, the conversation of the preceding day. While thus engaged, however, a loud report, as if of a pistol, was heard immediately beneath the windows of the hotel, and was succeeded by a series of fearful screams, and the shoutings of a terrified mob. D——rushed to a casement, threw it open, and looked out. In the meantime, I stepped to the card-rack, took the letter, put it in my pocket, and replaced it by a *fac-simile*, (so far as regards externals,) which I had carefully prepared at my lodgings—imitating the D—— cipher, very readily, by means of a seal formed of bread.

"The disturbance in the street had been occasioned by the frantic behavior of a man with a musket. He had fired it among a crowd of women and children. It proved, however, to have been without ball, and the fellow was suffered to go his way as a lunatic or a drunkard. When he had gone, D—— came from the window, whither I had followed him immediately upon securing the object in view. Soon afterwards I bade him farewell. The pretended lunatic was a man in my own pay."

"But what purpose had you," I asked, "in replacing the letter by a *fac-simile?* Would it not have been better, at the first visit, to have seized it openly, and departed?"

"D——," replied Dupin, "is a desperate man, and a man of nerve. His hotel, too, is not without attendants devoted to his interests. Had I made the wild attempt you suggest, I might never have left the Ministerial presence alive. The good people of Paris might have heard of me no more. But I had an object apart from these considerations. You know my political prepossessions. In this matter, I act as a partisan of the lady concerned. For eighteen months the Minister has had her in his power. She has now him in hers—since, being unaware that the letter is not in his possession, he will proceed with his exactions as if it was. Thus will he inevitably commit himself, at once, to his political destruction. His downfall, too, will not be more precipitate than awkward. It is all very well to talk about the *facilis descensus Averni*;[15] but in all kinds of climbing, as Catalani said of singing, it is far more easy to get up than to come down. In the present instance I have no sympathy—at least no pity—for him who descends. He is that *monstrum horrendum*, an unprincipled man of genius. I confess, however, that I should like very well to know the precise character of his thoughts, when, being defied by her whom the Prefect terms 'a certain personage,' he is reduced to opening the letter which I left for him in the card-rack."

"How? did you put any thing particular in it?"

"Why—it did not seem altogether right to leave the interior blank—that would have been insulting. D——, at Vienna once, did me an evil turn, which I told him, quite good-humoredly, that I should remember. So, as I knew he would feel some curiosity in regard to the identity of the person who had outwitted him, I thought it a pity not to give him a clue. He is well acquainted with my MS., and I just copied into the middle of the blank sheet the words—

"'——   ——Un dessein si funeste,
S'il n'est digne d'Atrée, est digne de Thyeste.

They are to be found in Crébillon's 'Atrée.'"[16]

The System of Dr. Tarr and Prof. Fether[1]

DURING the autumn of 18—, while on a tour through the extreme Southern provinces of France, my route led me within a few miles of a certain *Maison de Santé*, or private Mad-House, about which I had heard much, in Paris, from my medical friends. As I had never visited a place of the kind, I thought the opportunity too good to be lost; and so proposed to my traveling companion, (a gentleman with whom I had made casual acquaintance, a few days before,) that we should turn aside, for an hour or so, and look through the establishment. To this he objected—pleading haste, in the first place, and, in the second, a very usual horror at the sight of a lunatic. He begged me, however, not to let any mere courtesy toward himself interfere with the gratification of my curiosity, and said that he would ride on leisurely, so that I might overtake him during the day, or, at all events, during the next. As he bade me good-bye, I bethought me that there might be some difficulty in obtaining access to the premises, and mentioned my fears on this point. He replied that, in fact, unless I had personal knowledge of the superintendent, Monsieur Maillard, or some credential in the way of a letter, a difficulty might be found to exist, as the regulations of these private mad-houses were more rigid than the public hospital laws. For himself, he added, he had, some years since, made the acquaintance of Maillard, and would so far assist me as to ride up to the door and introduce me; although his feelings on the subject of lunacy would not permit of his entering the house.

I thanked him, and, turning from the main-road, we entered a grass-grown by-path, which, in half an hour, nearly lost itself in a dense forest, clothing the base of a mountain. Through this dank and gloomy wood we rode some two miles, when the *Maison de Santé* came in view. It was a fantastic *château*, much dilapidated, and indeed scarcely tenantable through age and neglect. Its aspect inspired me with absolute dread, and, checking my horse, I half resolved to turn back. I soon, however, grew ashamed of my weakness, and proceeded.

As we rode up to the gate-way, I perceived it slightly open, and the visage of a man peering through. In an instant afterward, this man came forth, accosted my companion by name, shook him cordially by the hand, and begged him to alight. It was Monsieur Maillard himself. He was a portly, fine-looking gentleman of the old school, with a polished manner, and a certain air of gravity, dignity, and authority which was very impressive.

My friend, having presented me, mentioned my desire to inspect the establishment, and received Monsieur Maillard's assurance that he would show me all attention, now took leave, and I saw him no more.

When he had gone, the superintendent ushered me into a small and exceedingly neat parlor, containing, among other indications of refined taste, many books, drawings, pots of flowers, and musical instruments. A cheerful fire blazed upon the hearth. At a piano, singing an aria from Bellini, sat a young and very beautiful woman, who, at my entrance, paused in her song, and received me with graceful courtesy. Her voice was low, and her whole manner subdued. I thought, too, that I perceived the traces of sorrow in her countenance, which was excessively, although, to my taste, not unpleasingly pale. She was attired in deep mourning, and excited in my bosom a feeling of mingled respect, interest, and admiration.

I had heard, at Paris, that the institution of Monsieur Maillard was managed upon what is vulgarly termed the "system of soothing"—that all punishments were avoided—that even confinement was seldom resorted to—that the patients, while secretly watched, were left much apparent liberty, and that most of them were permitted to roam about the house and grounds, in the ordinary apparel of persons in right mind.

Keeping these impressions in view, I was cautious in what I said before the young lady; for I could not be sure that she was sane; and, in fact, there was a certain restless brilliancy about her eyes which half led me to imagine she was not. I confined my remarks, therefore, to general topics, and to such as I thought would not be displeasing or exciting even to a lunatic. She replied in a perfectly rational manner to all that I said; and even her original observations were marked with the soundest good sense; but a long acquaintance with the metaphysics of *mania*, had taught me to put no faith in such evidence of sanity, and I continued to practice, throughout the interview, the caution with which I commenced it.

Presently a smart footman in livery brought in a tray with fruit, wine, and other refreshments, of which I partook, the lady soon afterwards leaving the room. As she departed I turned my eyes in an inquiring manner toward my host.

"No," he said, "oh, no—a member of my family—my niece, and a most accomplished woman."

"I beg a thousand pardons for the suspicion," I replied, "but of course you will know how to excuse me. The excellent administration of your affairs here is well understood in Paris, and I thought it just possible, you know—"

"Yes, yes—say no more—or rather it is myself who should thank you for the commendable prudence you have displayed. We seldom find so much of forethought in young men; and, more than once, some unhappy *contre-temps* has occurred in consequence of thoughtlessness on the part of our visitors. While my former system was in operation, and my patients were permitted the privilege of roaming to and fro at will, they were often aroused to a dangerous frenzy by injudicious persons who called to inspect the house. Hence I was obliged to enforce a rigid system of exclusion; and none obtained access to the premises upon whose discretion I could not rely."

"While your *former* system was in operation!" I said, repeating his words—"do I understand you, then, to say that the 'soothing system' of which I have heard so much, is no longer in force?"

"It is now," he replied, "several weeks since we have concluded to renounce it forever."

"Indeed! you astonish me!"

"We found it, sir," he said, with a sigh, "absolutely necessary to return to the old usages. The *danger* of the soothing system was, at all times, appalling; and its advantages have been much overrated. I believe, sir, that in this house it has been given a fair trial, if ever in any. We did every thing that rational humanity could suggest. I am sorry that you could not have paid us a visit at an earlier period, that you might have judged for yourself. But I presume you are conversant with the soothing practice—with its details."

"Not altogether. What I have heard has been at third or fourth hand."

"I may state the system, then, in general terms, as one in which the patients were *menagés*, humored. We contradicted *no* fancies which entered the brains of the mad. On the contrary, we not only indulged but encouraged them; and many of our most permanent cures have been thus effected. There is no argument which so touches the feeble reason of the madman as the *argumentum ad absurdum*. We have had men, for example, who fancied themselves chickens. The cure was, to insist upon the thing as a fact—to accuse the patient of stupidity in not sufficiently perceiving it to be a fact—and thus to refuse him any other diet for a week than that which properly appertains to a chicken. In this manner a little corn and gravel were made to perform wonders."

"But was this species of acquiescence all?"

"By no means. We put much faith in amusements of a simple kind, such as music, dancing, gymnastic exercises generally, cards, certain classes of books, and so forth. We affected to treat each individual as if for some ordinary physical disorder; and the word 'lunacy' was never employed. A great point was to set each lunatic to guard the actions of all the others. To repose confidence in the understanding or discretion of a madman, is to gain him body and soul. In this way we were enabled to dispense with an expensive body of keepers."

"And you had no punishments of any kind?"

"None."

"And you never confined your patients?"

"Very rarely. Now and then, the malady of some individual growing to a crisis, or taking a sudden turn of fury, we conveyed him to a secret cell, lest his disorder should infect the rest, and there kept him until we could dismiss him to his friends— for with the raging maniac we have nothing to do. He is usually removed to the public hospitals."

"And you have now changed all this—and you think for the better?"

"Decidedly. The system had its disadvantages, and even its dangers. It is now, happily, exploded throughout all the *Maisons de Santé* of France."

"I am very much surprised," I said, "at what you tell me; for I made sure that, at this moment, no other method of treatment for mania existed in any portion of the country."

"You are young yet, my friend," replied my host, "but the time will arrive when you will learn to judge for yourself of what is going on in the world, without trusting to the gossip of others. Believe nothing you hear, and only one half that you see. Now, about our *Maisons de Santé*, it is clear that some ignoramus has misled you. After dinner, however, when you have sufficiently recovered from the fatigue of your ride, I will be happy to take you over the house, and introduce to you a system which, in my opinion, and in that of every one who has witnessed its operation, is incomparably the most effectual as yet devised."

"Your own?" I inquired—"one of your own invention?"

"I am proud," he replied, "to acknowledge that it is—at least in some measure."

In this manner I conversed with Monsieur Maillard for an hour or two, during which he showed me the gardens and conservatories of the place.

"I cannot let you see my patients," he said, "just at present. To a sensitive mind there is always more or less of the shocking in such exhibitions; and I do not wish to spoil your appetite for dinner. We will dine. I can give you some veal *à la St. Menehoult*, with cauliflowers in *velouté* sauce—after that a glass *Clos de Vougeôt*—then your nerves will be sufficiently steadied."

At six, dinner was announced; and my host conducted me into a large *salle à manger*, where a very numerous company were assembled—twenty-five or thirty in all. They were, apparently, people of rank—certainly of high breeding—although their habiliments, I thought, were extravagantly rich, partaking somewhat too much of the ostentatious finery of the *vielle cour*.[2] I noticed that at least two-thirds of these guests were ladies; and some of the latter were by no means accoutered in what a Parisian would consider good taste at the present day. Many females, for example, whose age could not have been less than seventy, were bedecked with a profusion of jewelry, such as rings, bracelets, and ear-rings, and wore their bosoms and arms shamefully bare. I observed, too, that very few of the dresses were well made—or, at least, that very few of them fitted the wearers. In looking about, I discovered the interesting girl to whom Monsieur Maillard had presented me in the parlor; but my surprise was great to see her wearing a hoop and farthingale, with high-heeled shoes, and a dirty cap of Brussels lace, so much too large for her that it gave her face a ridiculously diminutive expression. When I had first seen her she was attired, most becomingly, in deep mourning. There was an air of oddity, in short, about the dress of the whole party, which, at first, caused me to recur to my original idea of the "soothing system," and to fancy that Monsieur Maillard had been willing to deceive me until after dinner, that I might experience no uncomfortable feelings during the repast, at finding myself dining with lunatics; but I remembered having been informed, in Paris, that the southern provincialists were a peculiarly eccentric people, with a vast number of antiquated notions; and then, too, upon conversing with several members of the company, my apprehensions were immediately and fully dispelled.

The dining-room itself, although perhaps sufficiently comfortable, and of good dimensions, had nothing too much of elegance about it. For example, the floor was uncarpeted; in France, however, a carpet is frequently dispensed with. The windows, too, were without curtains; the shutters, being shut, were securely fastened with iron bars, applied diagonally, after the fashion of our ordinary shop-shutters. The apartment, I observed, formed, in itself, a wing of the *château*, and thus the windows were on three sides of the parallelogram; the door being at the other. There were no less than ten windows in all.

The table was superbly set out. It was loaded with plate, and more than loaded with delicacies. The profusion was absolutely barbaric. There were meats enough to have feasted the Anakim.[3] Never, in all my life, had I witnessed so lavish, so wasteful an expenditure of the good things of life. There seemed very little taste, however, in the arrangements; and my eyes, accustomed to quiet lights, were sadly offended by the prodigious glare of a multitude of wax candles, which, in silver *candelabra*, were deposited upon the table, and all about the room, wherever it was possible to find a place. There were several active servants in attendance; and, upon a large table, at the farther end of the apartment, were seated seven or eight people with fiddles, fifes, trombones, and a drum. These fellows annoyed me very much, at intervals, during the repast, by an infinite variety of noises, which were intended for music, and which appeared to afford much entertainment to all present, with the exception of myself.

Upon the whole, I could not help thinking that there was much of the *bizarre* about every thing I saw—but then the world is made up of all kinds of persons, with all modes of thought, and all sorts of conventional customs. I had traveled so much as to be quite an adept in the *nil admirari*,[4] so I took my seat very coolly at the right hand of my host, and, having an excellent appetite, did justice to the good cheer set before me.

The conversation, in the mean time, was spirited and general. The ladies, as usual, talked a great deal. I soon found that nearly all the company were well educated; and my host was a world of good-humored anecdote in himself. He seemed quite willing to speak of his position as superintendent of a *Maison de Santé*; and, indeed, the topic of lunacy was, much to my surprise, a favorite one with all present. A great many amusing stories were told, having reference to the *whims* of the patients.

"We had a fellow here once," said a fat little gentleman, who sat at my right—"a fellow that fancied himself a tea-pot; and, by the way, is it not especially singular how often this particular crotchet has entered the brain of the lunatic? There is scarcely an insane asylum in France which cannot supply a human tea-pot. *Our* gentleman was a Britannia-ware tea-pot, and was careful to polish himself every morning with buckskin and whiting."

"And then," said a tall man, just opposite, "we had here, not long ago, a person who had taken it into his head that he was a donkey—which, allegorically speaking, you will say, was quite true. He was a troublesome patient; and we had much ado to keep him within bounds. For a long time he would eat nothing but thistles; but of this idea we soon cured him by insisting upon his eating nothing else. Then he was perpetually kicking out his heels—so—so—"

"Mr. De Kock! I will thank you to behave yourself!" here interrupted an old lady, who sat next to the speaker. "Please keep your feet to yourself! You have spoiled my brocade! Is it necessary, pray, to illustrate a remark in so practical a style? Our friend, here, can surely comprehend you without all this. Upon my word, you are nearly as great a donkey as the poor unfortunate imagined himself. Your acting is very natural, as I live!"

"*Mille pardons! ma'mselle!*" replied Monsieur De Kock, thus addressed—"a thousand pardons! I had no intention of offending. Ma'mselle Laplace—Monsieur De Kock will do himself the honor of taking wine with you."

Here Monsieur De Kock bowed low, kissed his hand with much ceremony, and took wine with Ma'mselle Laplace.

"Allow me, *mon ami*," now said Monsieur Maillard, addressing myself, "allow me to send you a morsel of this veal *à la St. Menehoult*—you will find it particularly fine."

At this instant three sturdy waiters had just succeeded in depositing safely upon the table an enormous dish, or trencher, containing what I supposed to be the "*monstrum, horrendum, informe, ingens, cui lumen ademptum.*"[5] A closer scrutiny assured me, however, that it was only a small calf roasted whole, and set upon its knees, with an apple in its mouth, as is the English fashion of dressing a hare.

"Thank you, no," I replied; "to say the truth, I am not particularly partial to veal *à la St.*—what is it?—for I do not find that it altogether agrees with me. I will change my plate, however, and try some of the rabbit."

There were several side-dishes on the table, containing what appeared to be the ordinary French rabbit—a very delicious *morceau*, which I can recommend.

"Pierre," cried the host, "change this gentleman's plate, and give him a side-piece of this rabbit *au-chât*."[6]

"This what?" said I.

"This rabbit *au-chât*."

"Why, thank you—upon second thoughts, no. I will just help myself to some of the ham."

There is no knowing what one eats, thought I to myself, at the tables of these people of the province. I will have none of their rabbit *au-chât*—and, for the matter of that, none of their *cat-au-rabbit* either.

"And then," said a cadaverous looking personage, near the foot of the table, taking up the thread of the conversation where it had been broken off—"and then, among other oddities, we had a patient, once upon a time, who very pertinaciously maintained himself to be a Cordova cheese, and went about, with a knife in his hand, soliciting his friends to try a small slice from the middle of his leg."

"He was a great fool, beyond doubt," interposed some one, "but not to be compared with a certain individual whom we all know, with the exception of this strange gentleman. I mean the man who took himself for a bottle of champagne, and always went off with a pop and a fizz, in this fashion."

Here the speaker, very rudely, as I thought, put his right thumb in his left cheek, withdrew it with a sound resembling the popping of a cork, and then, by a dexterous movement of the tongue upon the teeth, created a sharp hissing and fizzing, which lasted for several minutes, in imitation of the frothing of champagne. This behavior, I saw plainly, was not very pleasing to Monsieur Maillard; but that gentleman said nothing, and the conversation was resumed by a very lean little man in a big wig.

"And then there was an ignoramus," said he, "who mistook himself for a frog; which, by the way, he resembled in no little degree. I wish you could have seen him, sir"—here the speaker addressed myself—"it would have done your heart good to see the natural airs that he put on. Sir, if that man was *not* a frog, I can only observe that it is a pity he was not. His croak thus—o-o-o-o-gh—o-o-o-o-gh! was the finest note in the world—B flat; and when he put his elbows upon the table thus—after taking a glass or two of wine—and distended his mouth, thus, and rolled up his eyes, thus, and winked them, with excessive rapidity, thus, why then, sir, I take it upon myself to say, positively, that you would have been lost in admiration of the genius of the man."

"I have no doubt of it," I said.

"And then," said somebody else, "then there was Petit Gaillard, who thought himself a pinch of snuff, and was truly distressed because he could not take himself between his own finger and thumb."

"And then there was Jules Desoulières, who was a very singular genius, indeed, and went mad with the idea that he was a pumpkin. He persecuted the cook to make him up into pies—a thing which the cook indignantly refused to do. For my part, I am by no means sure that a pumpkin pie *à la Desoulières*, would not have been very capital eating, indeed!"

"You astonish me!" said I; and I looked inquisitively at Monsieur Maillard.

"Ha! ha! ha!" said that gentleman—"he! he! he!—hi! hi! hi!—ho! ho! ho!—hu! hu! hu!—very good indeed! You must not be astonished, *mon ami*; our friend here is a wit—a *drôle*—you must not understand him to the letter."

"And then," said some other one of the party, "then there was Bouffon Le Grand—another extraordinary personage in his way. He grew deranged through love, and fancied himself possessed of two heads. One of these he maintained to be the head of Cicero; the other he imagined a composite one, being Demosthenes' from the top of the forehead to the mouth, and Lord Brougham[7] from the mouth to the chin. It is not impossible that he was wrong; but he would have convinced you of his being in the right; for he was a man of great eloquence. He had an absolute passion for oratory, and could not refrain from display. For example, he used to leap upon the dinner-table, thus, and—and—"

Here a friend, at the side of the speaker, put a hand upon his shoulder, and whispered a few words in his ear; upon which he ceased talking with great suddenness, and sank back within his chair.

"And then," said the friend, who had whispered, "there was Boullard, the tee-totum.[8] I call him the tee-totum, because, in fact, he was seized with the droll, but not altogether irrational crotchet, that he had been converted into a tee-totum. You would have roared with laughter to see him spin. He would turn round upon one heel by the hour, in this manner—so—"

Here the friend whom he had just interrupted by a whisper, performed an exactly similar office for himself.

"But then," cried an old lady, at the top of her voice, "your Monsieur Boullard was a madman, and a very silly madman at best; for who, allow me to ask you, ever heard of a human tee-totum? The thing is absurd. Madame Joyeuse was a more sensible person, as you know. She had a crotchet, but it was instinct with common sense, and gave pleasure to all who had the honor of her acquaintance. She found, upon mature deliberation, that, by some accident, she had been turned into a chicken-cock; but, as such, she behaved with propriety. She flapped her wings with prodigious effect—so—so—so—and, as for her crow, it was delicious! Cock-a-doodle-doo!—cock-a-doodle-doo!—cock-a-doodle-de-doo-doo-dooo-do-o-o-o-o-o!"

"Madame Joyeuse, I will thank you to behave yourself!" here interrupted our host, very angrily. "You can either conduct yourself as a lady should do, or you can quit the table forthwith—take your choice."

The lady, (whom I was much astonished to hear addressed as Madame Joyeuse, after the description of Madame Joyeuse she had just given,) blushed up to the eyebrows, and seemed exceedingly abashed at the reproof. She hung down her head, and said not a syllable in reply. But another and younger lady resumed the theme. It was my beautiful girl of the little parlor!

"Oh, Madame Joyeuse *was* a fool!" she exclaimed; "but there was really much sound sense, after all, in the opinion of Eugénie Salsafette. She was a very beautiful and painfully modest young lady, who thought the ordinary mode of habiliment indecent, and wished to dress herself, always, by getting outside, instead of inside of her clothes. It is a thing very easily done, after all. You have only to do so—and then so—so—so—and then so—so—so—and then—"

"Mon dieu! Mam'selle Salsafette!" here cried a dozen voices at once. "What *are* you about?—forbear!—that is sufficient!—we see, very plainly, how it is done!—hold! hold!!" and several persons were already leaping from their seats to withhold Mam'selle Salsafette from putting herself upon a par with the Medicean Venus,[9] when the point was very effectually and suddenly accomplished by a series of loud screams, or yells, from some portion of the main body of the chateau.

My nerves were very much affected, indeed, by these yells; but the rest of the company I really pitied. I never saw any set of reasonable people so thoroughly frightened in my life. They all grew as pale as so many corpses, and, shrinking within their seats, sat quivering and gibbering with terror, and listening for a repetition of the sound. It came again—louder and seemingly nearer—and then a third time *very* loud, and then a fourth time with a vigor evidently diminished. At this apparent dying away of the noise, the spirits of the company were immediately regained, and all was life and anecdote as before. I now ventured to inquire the cause of the disturbance.

"A mere *bagatelle*,"[10] said Monsieur Maillard. "We are used to these things, and care really very little about them. The lunatics, every now and then, get up a howl in concert; one starting another, as is sometimes the case with a bevy of dogs at night. It occasionally happens, however, that the *concerto* yells are succeeded by a simultaneous effort at breaking loose; when, of course, some little danger is to be apprehended."

"And how many have you in charge?"

"At present, we have not more than ten, altogether."

"Principally females, I presume?"

"Oh, no—every one of them men, and stout fellows, too, I can tell you."

"Indeed! I have always understood that the majority of lunatics were of the gentler sex."

"It is generally so, but not always. Some time ago, there were about twenty-seven patients here; and, of that number, no less than eighteen were women; but lately, matters have changed very much, as you see."

"Yes—have changed very much, as you see," here interrupted the gentleman who had broken the shins of Ma'mselle Laplace.

"Yes—have changed very much, as you see!" chimed in the whole company at once.

"Hold your tongues, every one of you!" said my host, in a great rage. Whereupon the whole company maintained a dead silence for nearly a minute. As for one lady, she obeyed Monsieur Maillard to the letter, and thrusting out her tongue, which was an excessively long one, held it very resignedly, with both hands, until the end of the entertainment.

"And this gentlewoman," said I, to Monsieur Maillard, bending over and addressing him in a whisper—"this good lady who has just spoken, and who gives us the cock-a-doodle-de-doo—she, I presume, is harmless—quite harmless, eh?"

"Harmless!" ejaculated he, in unfeigned surprise, "why—why what *can* you mean?"

"Only slightly touched?" said I, touching my head. "I take it for granted that she is not particularly—not dangerously affected, eh?"

"*Mon Dieu!* what *is* it you imagine? This lady, my particular old friend, Madame Joyeuse, is as absolutely sane as myself. She has her little eccentricities, to be sure—but then, you know, all old women—all *very* old women are more or less eccentric!"

"To be sure," said I—"to be sure—and then the rest of these ladies and gentlemen—"

"Are my friends and keepers," interrupted Monsieur Maillard, drawing himself up with *hauteur*—"my very good friends and assistants."

"What! all of them?" I asked—"the women and all?"

"Assuredly," he said—"we could not do at all without the women; they are the best lunatic-nurses in the world; they have a way of their own, you know; their bright eyes have a marvellous effect;—something like the fascination of the snake, you know."

"To be sure," said I—"to be sure! They behave a little odd, eh?—they are a little *queer*, eh?—don't you think so?"

"Odd!—queer!—why, do you *really* think so? We are not very prudish, to be sure, here in the South—do pretty much as we please—enjoy life, and all that sort of thing, you know—"

"To be sure," said I—"to be sure."

"And then, perhaps, this *Clos de Vougeôt* is a little heady, you know—a little *strong*—you understand, eh?"

"To be sure," said I—"to be sure. By the bye, monsieur, did I understand you to say that the system you have adopted, in place of the celebrated soothing system, was one of very vigorous severity?"

"By no means. Our confinement is necessarily close; but the treatment—the medical treatment, I mean—is rather agreeable to the patients than otherwise."

"And the new system is one of your own invention?"

"Not altogether. Some portions of it are referable to Professor Tarr, of whom you have, necessarily, heard; and, again, there are modifications in my plan which I am happy to acknowledge as belonging of right to the celebrated Fether, with whom, if I mistake not, you have the honor of an intimate acquaintance."

"I am quite ashamed to confess," I replied, "that I have never even heard the name of either gentleman before."

"Good Heavens!" ejaculated my host, drawing back his chair abruptly, and uplifting his hands. "I surely do not hear you aright! You did not intend to say, eh? that you had never *heard* either of the learned Doctor Tarr, or of the celebrated Professor Fether?"

"I am forced to acknowledge my ignorance," I replied; "but the truth should be held inviolate above all things. Nevertheless, I feel humbled to the dust, not to be acquainted with the works of these no doubt extraordinary men. I will seek out their writings forthwith, and peruse them with deliberate care. Monsieur Maillard, you have really—I must confess it—you have *really* made me ashamed of myself!"

And this was the fact.

"Say no more, my good young friend," he said kindly, pressing my hand—"join me now in a glass of Sauterne."

We drank. The company followed our example, without stint. They chatted—they jested—they laughed—they perpetrated a thousand absurdities—the fiddles shrieked—the drum row-de-dowed—the trombones bellowed like so many brazen bulls of Phalaris—and the whole scene, growing gradually worse and worse, as the wines gained the ascendancy, became at length a sort of Pandemonium *in petto*.[11] In the mean time, Monsieur Maillard and myself, with some bottles of Sauterne and Vougeôt between us, continued our conversation at the top of the voice. A word spoken in an ordinary key stood no more chance of being heard than the voice of a fish from the bottom of Niagara Falls.

"And, sir," said I, screaming in his ear, "you mentioned something, before dinner, about the danger incurred in the old system of soothing. How is that?"

"Yes," he replied, "there was, occasionally, very great danger, indeed. There is no accounting for the caprices of madmen; and, in my opinion, as well as in that of Doctor Tarr and Professor Fether, it is *never* safe to permit them to run at large unattended. A lunatic may be 'soothed,' as it is called, for a time, but, in the end, he is very apt to become obstreperous. His cunning, too, is proverbial, and great. If he has a project in view, he conceals his design with a marvelous wisdom; and the dexterity with which he counterfeits sanity, presents, to the metaphysician, one of the most singular problems in the study of mind. When a madman appears *thoroughly* sane, indeed, it is high time to put him in a straight-jacket."

"But the *danger*, my dear sir, of which you were speaking—in your own experience—during your control of this house—have you had practical reason to think liberty hazardous, in the case of a lunatic?"

"Here?—in my own experience?—why, I may say, yes. For example:—no *very* long while ago, a singular circumstance occurred in this very house. The 'soothing system,' you know, was then in operation, and the patients were at large. They behaved remarkably well—especially so—any one of sense might have known that some devilish scheme was brewing from that particular fact, that the fellows behaved so *remarkably* well. And, sure enough, one fine morning the keepers found themselves pinioned hand and foot, and thrown into the cells, where they were attended, as if *they* were the lunatics, by the lunatics themselves, who had usurped the offices of the keepers."

"You don't tell me so! I never heard of any thing so absurd in my life?"

"Fact—it all came to pass by means of a stupid fellow—a lunatic—who, by some means, had taken it into his head that he had invented a better system of government than any ever heard of before—of lunatic government, I mean. He wished to give his invention a trial, I suppose—and so he persuaded the rest of the patients to join him in a conspiracy for the overthrow of the reigning powers."

"And he really succeeded?"

"No doubt of it. The keepers and kept were soon made to exchange places. Not that exactly either—for the madmen had been free, but the keepers were shut up in cells forthwith, and treated, I am sorry to say, in a very cavalier manner."

"But I presume a counter revolution was soon effected. This condition of things could not have long existed. The country people in the neighborhood—visiters coming to see the establishment—would have given the alarm."

"There you are out. The head rebel was too cunning for that. He admitted no visiters at all—with the exception, one day, of a very stupid-looking young gentleman of whom he had no reason to be afraid. He let him in to see the place—just by way of variety—to have a little fun with him. As soon as he had gammoned him sufficiently, he let him out, and sent him about his business."

"And *how* long, then, did the madmen reign?"

"Oh, a very long time, indeed—a month certainly—how much longer I can't precisely say. In the mean time, the lunatics had a jolly season of it—that you may swear. They doffed their own shabby clothes, and made free with the family wardrobe and jewels. The cellars of the *château* were well stocked with wine; and these madmen are just the devils that know how to drink it. They lived well, I can tell you."

"And the treatment—what was the particular species of treatment which the leader of the rebels put into operation?"

"Why, as for that, a madman is not necessarily a fool, as I have already observed, and it is my honest opinion that his treatment was a much better treatment than that which it superseded. It was a very capital system, indeed—simple—neat—no trouble at all—in fact it was delicious—it was—"

Here my host's observations were cut short by another series of yells, of the same character as those which had previously disconcerted us. This time, however, they seemed to proceed from persons rapidly approaching.

"Gracious Heavens!" I ejaculated—"the lunatics have most undoubtedly broken loose."

"I very much fear it is so," replied Monsieur Maillard, now becoming excessively pale. He had scarcely finished the sentence, before loud shouts and imprecations were heard beneath the windows; and, immediately afterward, it became evident that some persons outside were endeavoring to gain entrance into the room. The door was beaten with what appeared to be a sledge-hammer, and the shutters were wrenched and shaken with prodigious violence.

A scene of the most terrible confusion ensued. Monsieur Maillard, to my excessive astonishment, threw himself under the side-board. I had expected more resolution at his hands. The members of the orchestra, who, for the last fifteen minutes, had been seemingly too much intoxicated to do duty, now sprang all at once to their feet and to their instruments, and, scrambling upon their table, broke out, with one accord, into "Yankee Doodle," which they performed, if not exactly in tune, at least with an energy superhuman, during the whole of the uproar.

Meantime, upon the main dining-table, among the bottles and glasses, leaped the gentleman who, with such difficulty, had been restrained from leaping there before. As soon as he fairly settled himself, he commenced an oration, which, no doubt, was a very capital one, if it could only have been heard. At the same moment, the man with the tee-totum predilections, set himself to spinning around the apartment, with immense energy, and with arms outstretched at right angles with his body; so that he had all the air of a tee-totum in fact, and knocked every body down that happened to get in his way. And now, too, hearing an incredible popping and fizzing of champagne, I discovered, at length, that it proceeded from the person who performed the bottle of that delicate drink during dinner. And then, again, the frog-man croaked away as if the salvation of his soul depended upon every note that he uttered. And, in the midst of all this, the continuous braying of a donkey arose over all. As for my old friend, Madame Joyeuse, I really could have wept for the poor lady, she appeared so terribly perplexed. All she did, however, was to stand up in a corner, by the fire-place, and sing out incessantly, at the top of her voice, "Cock-a-doodle-de-dooooooooh!"

And now came the climax—the catastrophe of the drama. As no resistance, beyond whooping and yelling and cock-a-doodle-ing, was offered to the encroachments of the party without, the ten windows were very speedily, and almost simultaneously, broken in. But I shall never forget the emotions of wonder and horror with which I gazed, when, leaping through these windows, and down among us *pêle-mêle*, fighting, stamping, scratching, and howling, there rushed a perfect army of what I took to be Chimpanzees, Ourang-Outangs, or big black baboons of the Cape of Good Hope!

I received a terrible beating—after which I rolled under a sofa, and lay still. After lying there some fifteen minutes, however, during which time I listened with all my ears to what was going on in the room, I came to some satisfactory *dénouement* of this tragedy. Monsieur Maillard, it appeared, in giving me the account of the lunatic who had excited his fellows to rebellion, had been merely relating his own exploits. This gentleman had, indeed, some two or three years before, been the superintendent of the establishment; but grew crazy himself, and so became a patient. This fact was unknown to the traveling companion who introduced me. The keepers, ten in number, having been suddenly overpowered, were first well tarred, then carefully feathered, and then shut up in underground cells. They had been so imprisoned for more than a month, during which period Monsieur Maillard had generously allowed them not only the tar and feathers (which constituted his "system") but some bread, and abundance of water. The latter was pumped on them daily. At length, one escaping through a sewer, gave freedom to all the rest.

The "soothing system," with important modifications, has been resumed at the *château;* yet I cannot help agreeing with Monsieur Maillard, that his own "treatment" was a very capital one of its kind. As he justly observed, it was "simple—neat—and gave no trouble at all—not the least."

I have only to add that, although I have searched every library in Europe for the works of Doctor *Tarr* and Professor *Fether*, I have, up to the present day, utterly failed in my endeavors at procuring an edition.

The Balloon-Hoax[1]

[Astounding News by Express, *via* Norfolk!—The Atlantic crossed in Three Days! Signal Triumph of Mr. Monck Mason's Flying Machine!—Arrival at Sullivan's Island, near Charleston, S.C., of Mr. Mason, Mr. Robert Holland, Mr. Henson, Mr. Harrison Ainsworth, and four others, in the Steering Balloon, "Victoria," after a passage of Seventy-five Hours from Land to Land! Full Particulars of the Voyage![2]

The subjoined *jeu d'esprit*[3] with the preceding heading in magnificent capitals, well interspersed with notes of admiration, was originally published, as matter of fact, in the "New-York Sun," a daily newspaper, and therein fully subserved the purpose of creating indigestible aliment for the *quidnuncs*[4] during the few hours intervening between a couple of the Charleston mails. The rush for the "sole paper which had the news," was something beyond even the prodigious; and, in fact, if (as some assert) the "Victoria" *did* not absolutely accomplish the voyage recorded, it will be difficult to assign a reason why she *should* not have accomplished it.]

THE great problem is at length solved! The air, as well as the earth and the ocean, has been subdued by science, and will become a common and convenient highway for mankind. *The Atlantic has been actually crossed in a Balloon!* and this too without difficulty—without any great apparent danger—with thorough control of the machine—and in the inconceivably brief period of seventy-five hours from shore to shore! By the energy of an agent at Charleston, S.C., we are enabled to be the first to furnish the public with a detailed account of this most extraordinary voyage, which was performed between Saturday, the 6th instant, at 11, A.M., and 2, P.M., on Tuesday, the 9th instant, by Sir Everard Bringhurst; Mr. Osborne, a nephew of Lord Bentinck's; Mr. Monck Mason and Mr. Robert Holland, the well-known æronauts; Mr. Harrison Ainsworth, author of "Jack Sheppard," &c.; and Mr. Henson, the projector of the late unsuccessful flying machine—with two seamen from Woolwich—in all, eight persons. The particulars furnished below may be relied on as authentic and accurate in every respect, as, with a slight exception, they are copied *verbatim* from the joint diaries of Mr. Monck Mason and Mr. Harrison Ainsworth, to whose politeness our agent is also indebted for much verbal information respecting the balloon itself, its construction, and other matters of interest. The only alteration in the MS. received, has been made for the purpose of throwing the hurried account of our agent, Mr. Forsyth, in a connected and intelligible form.

THE BALLOON.

Two very decided failures, of late—those of Mr. Henson and Sir George Cayley—had much weakened the public interest in the subject of aerial navigation. Mr. Henson's scheme (which at first was considered very feasible even by men of science,) was founded upon the principle of an inclined plane, started from an eminence by an extrinsic force, applied and continued by the revolution of impinging vanes, in form and number resembling the vanes of a windmill. But, in all the experiments made with models at the Adelaide Gallery, it was found that the operation of these fans not only did not propel the machine, but actually impeded its flight. The only propelling force it ever exhibited, was the mere *impetus* acquired from the descent of the inclined plane; and this *impetus* carried the machine farther when the vanes were at rest, than when they were in motion—a fact which sufficiently demonstrates their inutility; and in the absence of the propelling, which was also the *sustaining* power, the whole fabric would necessarily descend. This consideration led Sir George Cayley to think only of adapting a propeller to some machine having of itself an independent power of support—in a word, to a balloon; the idea, however, being novel, or original, with Sir George, only so far as regards the mode of its application to practice. He exhibited a model of his invention at the Polytechnic Institution. The propelling principle, or power, was here, also, applied to interrupted surfaces, or vanes, put in revolution. These vanes were four in number, but were found entirely ineffectual in moving the balloon, or in aiding its ascending power. The whole project was thus a complete failure.

It was at this juncture that Mr. Monck Mason (whose voyage from Dover to Weilburg in the balloon, "Nassau," occasioned so much excitement in 1837,) conceived the idea of employing the principle of the Archimedean screw for the purpose of propulsion through the air—rightly attributing the failure of Mr. Henson's scheme, and of Sir George Cayley's, to the interruption of surface in the independent vanes. He made the first public experiment at Willis's Rooms, but afterwards removed his model to the Adelaide Gallery.

Like Sir George Cayley's balloon, his own was an ellipsoid. Its length was thirteen feet six inches—height, six feet eight inches. It contained about three hundred and twenty cubic feet of gas, which, if pure hydrogen, would support twenty-one pounds upon its first inflation, before the gas has time to deteriorate or escape. The weight of the whole machine and apparatus was seventeen pounds—leaving about four pounds to spare. Beneath the centre of the balloon, was a frame of light wood, about nine feet long, and rigged on to the balloon itself with a network in the customary manner. From this framework was suspended a wicker basket or car.

The screw consists of an axis of hollow brass tube, eighteen inches in length, through which, upon a semi-spiral inclined at fifteen degrees, pass a series of a steel wire radii, two feet long, and thus projecting a foot on either side. These radii are connected at the outer extremities by two bands of flattened wire—the whole in this manner forming the framework of the screw, which is completed by a covering of oiled silk cut into gores, and tightened so as to present a tolerably uniform surface. At each end of its axis this screw is supported by pillars of hollow brass tube descending from the hoop. In the lower ends of these tubes are holes in which the pivots of the axis revolve. From the end of the axis which is next the car, proceeds a shaft of steel, connecting the screw with the pinion of a piece of spring machinery fixed in the car. By the operation of this spring, the screw is made to revolve with great rapidity, communicating a progressive motion to the whole. By means of the rudder, the machine was readily turned in any direction. The spring was of great power, compared with its dimensions, being capable of raising forty-five pounds upon a barrel of four inches diameter, after the first turn, and gradually increasing as it was wound up. It weighed, altogether, eight pounds six ounces. The rudder was a light frame of cane covered with silk, shaped somewhat like a battledoor, and was about three feet long, and at the widest, one foot. Its weight was about two ounces. It could be turned *flat*, and directed upwards or downwards, as well as to the right or left; and thus enabled the æronaut to transfer the resistance of the air which in an inclined position it must generate in its passage, to any side upon which he might desire to act; thus determining the balloon in the opposite direction.

This model (which, through want of time, we have necessarily described in an imperfect manner,) was put in action at the Adelaide Gallery, where it accomplished a velocity of five miles per hour; although, strange to say, it excited very little interest in comparison with the previous complex machine of Mr. Henson—so resolute is the world to despise anything which carries with it an air of simplicity. To accomplish the great desideratum of ærial navigation, it was very generally supposed that some exceedingly complicated application must be made of some unusually profound principle in dynamics.

So well satisfied, however, was Mr. Mason of the ultimate success of his invention, that he determined to construct immediately, if possible, a balloon of sufficient capacity to test the question by a voyage of some extent—the original design being to cross the British Channel, as before, in the Nassau balloon. To carry out his views, he solicited and obtained the patronage of Sir Everard Bringhurst and Mr. Osborne, two gentlemen well known for scientific acquirement, and especially for the interest they have exhibited in the progress of ærostation. The project, at the desire of Mr. Osborne, was kept a profound secret from the public—the only persons entrusted with the design being those actually engaged in the construction of the machine, which was built (under the superintendence of Mr. Mason, Mr. Holland, Sir Everard Bringhurst, and Mr. Osborne,) at the seat of the latter gentleman near Penstruthal, in Wales. Mr. Henson, accompanied by his friend Mr. Ainsworth, was admitted to a private view of the balloon, on Saturday last—when the two gentlemen made final arrangements to be included in the adventure. We are not informed for what reason the two seamen were also included in the party—but, in the course of a day or two, we shall put our readers in possession of the minutest particulars respecting this extraordinary voyage.

The balloon is composed of silk, varnished with the liquid gum caoutchouc.[5] It is of vast dimensions, containing more than 40,000 cubic feet of gas; but as coal gas was employed in place of the more expensive and inconvenient hydrogen, the supporting power of the machine, when fully inflated, and immediately after inflation, is not more than about 2500 pounds. The coal gas is not only much less costly, but is easily procured and managed.

For its introduction into common use for purposes of aerostation, we are indebted to Mr. Charles Green. Up to his discovery, the process of inflation was not only exceedingly expensive, but uncertain. Two, and even three days, have frequently been wasted in futile attempts to procure a sufficiency of hydrogen to fill a balloon, from which it had great tendency to escape owing to its extreme subtlety, and its affinity for the surrounding atmosphere. In a balloon sufficiently perfect to retain its contents of coal-gas unaltered, in quality or amount, for six months, an equal quantity of hydrogen could not be maintained in equal purity for six weeks.

The supporting power being estimated at 2500 pounds, and the united weights of the party amounting only to about 1200, there was left a surplus of 1300, of which again 1200 was exhausted by ballast, arranged in bags of different sizes, with their respective weights marked upon them—by cordage, barometers, telescopes, barrels containing provision for a fortnight, water-casks, cloaks, carpet-bags, and various other indispensable matters, including a coffee-warmer, contrived for warming coffee by means of slack-lime, so as to dispense altogether with fire, if it should be judged prudent to do so. All these articles, with the exception of the ballast, and a few trifles, were suspended from the hoop over head. The car is much smaller and lighter, in proportion, than the one appended to the model. It is formed of a light wicker, and is wonderfully strong, for so frail looking a machine. Its rim is about four feet deep. The rudder is also very much larger, in proportion, than that of the model; and the screw is considerably smaller. The balloon is furnished besides, with a grapnel, and a guide-rope; which latter is of the most indispensable importance. A few words, in explanation, will here be necessary for such of our readers as are not conversant with the details of aerostation.

As soon as the balloon quits the earth, it is subjected to the influence of many circumstances tending to create a difference in its weight; augmenting or diminishing its ascending power. For example, there may be a disposition of dew upon the silk, to the extent, even, of several hundred pounds; ballast has then to be thrown out, or the machine may descend. This ballast being discarded, and a clear sunshine evaporating the dew, and at the same time expanding the gas in the silk, the whole will again rapidly ascend. To check this ascent, the only resource is, (or rather *was*, until Mr. Green's invention of the guide-rope,) the permission of the escape of gas from the valve; but, in the loss of gas, is a proportionate general loss of ascending power; so that, in a comparatively brief period, the best constructed balloon must necessarily exhaust all its resources, and come to the earth. This was the great obstacle to voyages of length.

The guide-rope remedies the difficulty in the simplest manner conceivable. It is merely a very long rope which is suffered to trail from the car, and the effect of which is to prevent the balloon from changing its level in any material degree. If, for example, there should be a deposition of moisture upon the silk, and the machine begins to descend in consequence, there will be no necessity for discharging ballast to remedy the increase of weight, for it is remedied, or counteracted, in an exactly just proportion, by the deposit on the ground of just so much of the end of the rope as is necessary. If, on the other hand, any circumstances should cause undue levity, and consequent ascent, this levity is immediately counteracted by the additional weight of rope upraised from the earth. Thus, the balloon can neither ascend or descend, except within very narrow limits, and its resources, either in gas or ballast, remain comparatively unimpaired. When passing over an expanse of water, it becomes necessary to employ small kegs of copper or wood, filled with liquid ballast of a lighter nature than water. These float, and serve all the purposes of a mere rope on land. Another most important office of the guide-rope, is to point out the *direction* of the balloon. The rope *drags*, either on land or sea, while the balloon is free; the latter, consequently, is always in advance, when any progress whatever is made: a comparison, therefore, by means of the compass, of the relative positions of the two objects, will always indicate the *course*. In the same way, the angle formed by the rope with the vertical axis of the machine, indicates the *velocity*. When there is *no* angle—in other words, when the rope hangs perpendicularly, the whole apparatus is stationary; but the larger the angle, that is to say, the farther the balloon precedes the end of the rope, the greater the velocity; and the converse.

As the original design was to cross the British Channel, and alight as near Paris as possible, the voyagers had taken the precaution to prepare themselves with passports directed to all parts of the Continent, specifying the nature of the expedition, as in the case of the Nassau voyage, and entitling the adventurers to exemption from the usual formalities of office: unexpected events, however, rendered these passports superfluous.

The inflation was commenced very quietly at daybreak, on Saturday morning, the 6th instant, in the Court-Yard of Weal-Vor House, Mr. Osborne's seat, about a mile from Penstruthal, in North Wales; and at 7 minutes past 11, every thing being ready for departure, the balloon was set free, rising gently but steadily, in a direction nearly South; no use being made, for the first half hour, of either the screw or the rudder. We proceed now with the journal, as transcribed by Mr. Forsyth from the joint MSS. of Mr. Monck Mason, and Mr. Ainsworth. The body of the journal, as given, is in the hand-writing of Mr. Mason, and a P. S. is appended, each day, by Mr. Ainsworth, who has in preparation, and will shortly give the public a more minute, and no doubt, a thrillingly interesting account of the voyage.

THE JOURNAL.

Saturday, April the 6th.—Every preparation likely to embarrass us, having been made over night, we commenced the inflation this morning at daybreak; but owing to a thick fog, which encumbered the folds of the silk and rendered it unmanageable, we did not get through before nearly eleven o'clock. Cut loose, then, in high spirits, and rose gently but steadily, with a light breeze at North, which bore us in the direction of the British Channel. Found the ascending force greater than we had expected; and as we arose higher and so got clear of the cliffs, and more in the sun's rays, our ascent became very rapid. I did not wish, however, to lose gas at so early a period of the adventure, and so concluded to ascend for the present. We soon ran out our guide-rope; but even when we had raised it clear of the earth, we still went up very rapidly. The balloon was unusually steady, and looked beautifully. In about ten minutes after starting, the barometer indicated an altitude of 15,000 feet. The weather was remarkably fine, and the view of the subjacent country—a most romantic one when seen from any point,—was now especially sublime. The numerous deep gorges presented the appearance of lakes, on account of the dense vapors with which they were filled, and the pinnacles and crags to the South East, piled in inextricable confusion, resembled nothing so much as the giant cities of eastern fable. We were rapidly approaching the mountains in the South; but our elevation was more than sufficient to enable us to pass them in safety. In a few minutes we soared over them in fine style; and Mr. Ainsworth, with the seamen, were surprised at their apparent want of altitude when viewed from the car, the tendency of great elevation in a balloon being to reduce inequalities of the surface below, to nearly a dead level. At half-past eleven still proceeding nearly South, we obtained our first view of the Bristol Channel; and, in fifteen minutes afterwards, the line of breakers on the coast appeared immediately beneath us, and we were fairly out at sea. We now resolved to let off enough gas to bring our guide-rope, with the buoys affixed, into the water. This was immediately done, and we commenced a gradual descent. In about twenty minutes our first buoy dipped, and at the touch of the second soon afterwards, we remained stationary as to elevation. We were all now anxious to test the efficiency of the rudder and screw, and we put them both into requisition forthwith, for the purpose of altering our direction more to the eastward, and in a line for Paris. By means of the rudder we instantly effected the necessary change of direction, and our course was brought nearly at right angles to that of the wind; when we set in motion the spring of the screw, and were rejoiced to find it propel us readily as desired. Upon this we gave nine hearty cheers, and dropped in the sea a bottle, enclosing a slip of parchment with a brief account of the principle of the invention. Hardly, however, had we done with our rejoicings, when an unforeseen accident occurred which discouraged us in no little degree. The steel rod connecting the spring with the propeller was suddenly jerked out of place, at the car end, (by a swaying of the car through some movement of one of the two seamen we had taken up,) and in an instant hung dangling out of reach, from the pivot of the axis of the screw. While we were endeavoring to regain it, our attention being completely absorbed, we became involved in a strong current of wind from the East, which bore us, with rapidly increasing force, towards the Atlantic. We soon found ourselves driving out to sea at the rate of not less, certainly, than fifty or sixty miles an hour, so that we came up with Cape Clear, at some forty miles to our North, before we had secured the rod, and had time to think what we were about. It was now that Mr. Ainsworth made an extraordinary, but to my fancy, a by no means unreasonable or chimerical proposition, in which he was instantly seconded by Mr. Holland—viz.: that we should take advantage of the strong gale which bore us on, and in place of beating back to Paris, make an attempt to reach the coast of North America. After slight reflection I gave a willing assent to this bold proposition, which (strange to say) met with objection from the two seamen only. As the stronger party, however, we overruled their fears, and kept resolutely upon our course. We steered due West; but as the trailing of the buoys materially impeded our progress, and we had the balloon abundantly at command, either for ascent or descent, we first threw out fifty pounds of ballast, and then wound up (by means of a windlass) so much of a rope as brought it quite clear of the sea. We perceived the effect of this manœuvre immediately, in a vastly increased rate of progress; and, as the gale freshened, we flew with a velocity nearly inconceivable; the guide-rope flying out behind the car, like a streamer from a vessel. It is needless to say that a very short time sufficed us to lose sight of the coast. We passed over innumerable vessels of all kinds, a few of which were endeavoring to beat up, but the most of them lying to. We occasioned the greatest excitement on board all—an excitement greatly relished by ourselves, and especially by our two men, who, now under the influence of a dram of Geneva, seemed resolved to give all scruple, or fear, to the wind. Many of the vessels fired signal guns; and in all we were saluted with loud cheers (which we heard with surprising distinctness) and the waving of caps and handkerchiefs. We kept on in this manner throughout the day, with no material incident, and, as the shades of night closed around us, we made a rough estimate of the distance traversed. It could not have been less than five hundred miles, and was probably much more. The propeller was kept in constant operation, and, no doubt, aided our progress materially. As the sun went down, the gale freshened into an absolute hurricane, and the ocean beneath was clearly visible on account of its phosphorescence. The wind was from the East all night, and gave us the brightest omen of success. We suffered no little from cold, and the dampness of the atmosphere was most unpleasant; but the ample space in the car enabled us to lie down, and by means of cloaks and a few blankets, we did sufficiently well.

P. S. (by Mr. Ainsworth). The last nine hours have been unquestionably the most exciting of my life. I can conceive nothing more sublimating than the strange peril and novelty of an adventure such as this. May God grant that we succeed! I ask not success for mere safety to my insignificant person, but for the sake of human knowledge and—for the vastness of the triumph. And yet the feat is only so evidently feasible that the sole wonder is why men have scrupled to attempt it before. One single gale such as now befriends us—let such a tempest whirl forward a balloon for four or five days (these gales often last longer) and the voyager will be easily borne, in that period, from coast to coast. In view of such a gale the broad Atlantic becomes a mere lake. I am more struck, just now, with the supreme silence which reigns in the sea beneath us, notwithstanding its agitation, than with any other phenomenon presenting itself. The waters give up no voice to the heavens. The immense flaming ocean writhes and is tortured uncomplainingly. The mountainous surges suggest the idea of innumerable dumb gigantic fiends struggling in impotent agony. In a night such as is this to me, a man *lives*—lives a whole century of ordinary life—nor would I forego this rapturous delight for that of a whole century of ordinary existence.

Sunday, the seventh. [Mr. Mason's MS.] This morning the gale, by 10, had subsided to an eight or nine knot breeze, (for a vessel at sea,) and bears us, perhaps, thirty miles per hour, or more. It has veered however, very considerably to the north; and now, at sundown, we are holding our course due west, principally by the screw and rudder, which answer their purposes to admiration. I regard the project as thoroughly successful, and the easy navigation of the air in any direction (not exactly in the teeth of a gale) as no longer problematical. We could not have made head against the strong wind of yesterday; but, by ascending, we might have got out of its influence, if requisite. Against a pretty stiff breeze, I feel convinced, we can make our way with the propeller. At noon, to-day, ascended to an elevation of nearly 25,000 feet, by discharging ballast. Did this to search for a more direct current, but found none so favorable as the one we are now in. We have an abundance of gas to take us across this small pond, even should the voyage last three weeks. I have not the slightest fear for the result. The difficulty has been strangely exaggerated and misapprehended. I can choose my current, and should I find *all* currents against me, I can make very tolerable headway with the propeller. We have had no incidents worth recording. The night promises fair.

P. S. [By Mr. Ainsworth.] I have little to record, except the fact (to me quite a surprising one), that, at an elevation equal to that of Cotopaxi,[6] I experienced neither very intense cold, nor headache, nor difficulty of breathing; neither, I find, did Mr. Mason, nor Mr. Holland, nor Sir Everard. Mr. Osborne complained of constriction of the chest—but this soon wore off. We have flown at a great rate during the day, and we must be more than half way across the Atlantic. We have passed over some twenty or thirty vessels of various kinds, and all seem to be delightfully astonished. Crossing the ocean in a balloon is not so difficult a feat after all. *Omne ignotum pro magnifico.*[7] *Mem* : at 25,000 feet elevation the sky appears nearly black, and the stars are distinctly visible; while the sea does not seem convex (as one might suppose) but absolutely and most unequivocally *concave.*[8]

Monday, the 8th. [Mr. Mason's MS.] This morning we had again some little trouble with the rod of the propeller, which must be entirely remodelled, for fear of serious accident—I mean the steel rod—not the vanes. The latter could not be improved. The wind has been blowing steadily and strongly from the northeast all day; and so far fortune seems bent upon favoring us. Just before day, we were all somewhat alarmed at some odd noises and concussions in the balloon, accompanied with the apparent rapid subsidence of the whole machine. These phenomena were occasioned by the expansion of the gas, through increase of heat in the atmosphere, and the consequent disruption of the minute particles of ice with which the network had become encrusted during the night. Threw down several bottles to the vessels below. Saw one of them picked up by a large ship—seemingly one of the New York line packets. Endeavored to make out her name, but could not be sure of it. Mr. Osborne's telescope made it out something like "Atalanta." It is now 12, at night, and we are still going nearly west, at a rapid pace. The sea is peculiarly phosphorescent.

P. S. [By Mr. Ainsworth.] It is now 2, A. M., and nearly calm, as well as I can judge—but it is very difficult to determine this point, since we move *with* the air so completely. I have not slept since quitting Wheal-Vor, but can stand it no longer, and must take a nap. We cannot be far from the American coast.

Tuesday, the 9th. [Mr. Ainsworth's M. S.] *One, P. M. We are in full view of the low coast of South Carolina.* The great problem is accomplished. We have crossed the Atlantic—fairly and *easily* crossed it in a balloon! God be praised! Who shall say that anything is impossible hereafter?

———

The Journal here ceases. Some particulars of the descent were communicated, however, by Mr. Ainsworth to Mr. Forsyth. It was nearly dead calm when the voyagers first came in view of the coast, which was immediately recognised by both the seamen, and by Mr. Osborne. The latter gentleman having acquaintances at Fort Moultrie,[9] it was immediately resolved to descend in its vicinity. The balloon was brought over the beach (the tide being out and the sand hard, smooth, and admirably adapted for a descent,) and the grapnel let go, which took firm hold at once. The inhabitants of the island, and of the fort, thronged out, of course, to see the balloon; but it was with the greatest difficulty that any one could be made to credit the actual voyage—*the crossing of the Atlantic.* The grapnel caught at 2, P. M., precisely; and thus the whole voyage was completed in seventy-five hours; or rather less, counting from shore to shore. No serious accident occurred. No real danger was at any time apprehended. The balloon was exhausted and secured without trouble; and when the MS. from which this narrative is compiled was despatched from Charleston, the party were still at Fort Moultrie. Their farther intentions were not ascertained; but we can safely promise our readers some additional information either on Monday or in the course of the next day, at farthest.

This is unquestionably the most stupendous, the most interesting, and the most important undertaking, ever accomplished or even attempted by man. What magnificent events may ensue, it would be useless now to think of determining.

The Literary Life of Thingum Bob, Esq.

LATE EDITOR OF THE "GOOSETHERUMFOODLE."
BY HIMSELF.[1]

I am now growing in years, and—since I understand that Shakespeare and Mr. Emmons[2] are deceased—it is not impossible that I may even die. It has occurred to me, therefore, that I may as well retire from the field of Letters and repose upon my laurels. But I am ambitious of signalizing my abdication of the literary sceptre by some important bequest to posterity; and, perhaps, I cannot do a better thing than just pen for it an account of my earlier career. My name, indeed, has been so long and so constantly before the public eye, that I am not only willing to admit the naturalness of the interest which it has everywhere excited, but ready to satisfy the extreme curiosity which it has inspired. In fact it is no more than the duty of him who achieves greatness, to leave behind him, in his ascent, such landmarks as may guide others to be great. I propose, therefore, in the present paper, (which I had some idea of calling "Memoranda to serve for the Literary History of America,") to give a detail of those important, yet feeble and tottering first steps, by which, at length, I attained the high road to the pinnacle of human renown.

Of one's *very* remote ancestors it is superfluous to say much. My father, Thomas Bob, Esq., stood for many years at the summit of his profession, which was that of a merchant-barber, in the city of Smug. His warehouse was the resort of all the principal people of the place, and especially of the editorial corps—a body which inspires all about it with profound veneration and awe. For my own part, I regarded them as Gods, and drank in with avidity the rich wit and wisdom which continuously flowed from their august mouths during the process of what is styled "lather." My first moment of positive inspiration must be dated from that ever-memorable epoch, when the brilliant conductor of the "Gad-Fly," in the intervals of the important process just mentioned, recited aloud, before a conclave of our apprentices, an inimitable poem in honor of the "Only Genuine Oil-of-Bob," (so called from its talented inventor, my father,) and for which effusion the editor of the "Fly" was remunerated with a regal liberality, by the firm of Thomas Bob and company, merchant barbers.

The genius of the stanzas to the "Oil-of-Bob" first breathed into me, I say, the divine *afflatus*.[3] I resolved at once to become a great man and to commence by becoming a great poet. That very evening I fell upon my knees at the feet of my father.

"Father," I said, "pardon me!—but I have a soul above lather. It is my firm intention to cut the shop. I would be an editor—I would be a poet—I would pen stanzas to the 'Oil-of-Bob.' Pardon me and aid me to be great!"

"My dear Thingum," replied my father, (I had been christened Thingum after a wealthy relative so surnamed,) "My dear Thingum," he said, raising me from my knees by the ears—"Thingum, my boy, you're a trump, and take after your father in having a soul. You have an immense head, too, and it must hold a great many brains. This I have long seen, and therefore had thoughts of making you a lawyer. The business, however, has grown ungenteel, and that of a politician don't pay. Upon the whole you judge wisely;—the trade of editor is best:—and if you can be a poet at the same time,—as most of the editors are, by the by,—why you will kill two birds with one stone. To encourage you in the beginning of things, I will allow you a garret; pen, ink and paper; a rhyming dictionary; and a copy of the 'Gad-Fly.' I suppose you would scarcely demand any more."

"I would be an ungrateful villain if I did," I replied with enthusiasm. "Your generosity is boundless. I will repay it by making you the father of a genius."

Thus ended my conference with the best of men, and immediately upon its termination, I betook myself with zeal to my poetical labors; as upon these, chiefly, I founded my hopes of ultimate elevation to the editorial chair.

In my first attempts at composition I found the stanzas to "The Oil-of-Bob" rather a draw-back than otherwise. Their splendor more dazzled than enlightened me. The contemplation of their excellence tended, naturally, to discourage me by comparison with my own abortions; so that for a long time I labored in vain. At length there came into my head one of those exquisitely original ideas which now and then *will* permeate the brain of a man of genius. It was this:—or, rather, thus was it carried into execution. From the rubbish of an old book-stall, in a very remote corner of the town, I got together several antique and altogether unknown or forgotten volumes. The bookseller sold them to me for a song. From one of these, which purported to be a translation of one Dante's "Inferno," I copied with remarkable neatness a long passage about a man named Ugolino, who had a parcel of brats. From another which contained a good many old plays by some person whose name I forget, I extracted in the same manner, and with the same care, a great number of lines about "angels" and "ministers saying grace," and "goblins damned," and more besides of that sort. From a third, which was the composition of some blind man or other, either a Greek or a Choctaw—I cannot be at the pains of remembering every trifle exactly—I took about fifty verses beginning with "Achilles' wrath," and "grease," and something else. From a fourth, which I recollect was also the work of a blind man, I selected a page or two all about "hail" and "holy light;"[4] and although a blind man has no business to write about light, still the verses were sufficiently good in their way.

Having made fair copies of these poems I signed every one of them "Oppodeldoc," (a fine sonorous name,) and, doing each up nicely in a separate envelope, I despatched one to each of the four principal Magazines, with a request for speedy insertion and prompt pay. The result of this well conceived plan, however, (the success of which would have saved me much trouble in after life,) served to convince me that some editors are not to be bamboozled, and gave the *coup-de-grace* (as they say in France,) to my nascent hopes, (as they say in the city of the transcendentals.)

The fact is, that each and every one of the Magazines in question, gave Mr. "Oppodeldoc" a complete using-up, in the "Monthly Notices to Correspondents." The "Hum-Drum" gave him a dressing after this fashion:

"'Oppodeldoc,' (whoever he is,) has sent us a long *tirade* concerning a bedlamite whom he styles 'Ugolino,' who had a great many children that should have been all whipped and sent to bed without their suppers. The whole affair is exceedingly tame—not to say *flat*. 'Oppodeldoc,' (whoever he is,) is entirely devoid of imagination—and imagination, in our humble opinion, is not only the soul of POESY, but also its very heart. 'Oppodeldoc,' (whoever he is,) has the audacity to demand of us, for his twattle, a 'speedy insertion and prompt pay.' We neither insert nor purchase any stuff of the sort. There can be no doubt, however, that he would meet with a ready sale for all the balderdash he can scribble, at the office of either the 'Rowdy-Dow,' the 'Lollipop,' or the 'Goosetherumfoodle.'"

All this, it must be acknowledged, was very severe upon "Oppodeldoc"—but the unkindest cut was putting the word POESY in small caps. In those five preeminent letters what a world of bitterness is there not involved!

But "Oppodeldoc" was punished with equal severity in the "Rowdy-dow," which spoke thus:

"We have received a most singular and insolent communication from a person, (whoever he is,) signing himself 'Oppodeldoc'—thus desecrating the greatness of the illustrious Roman Emperor so named. Accompanying the letter of 'Oppdeldoc,' (whoever he is,) we find sundry lines of most disgusting and unmeaning rant about 'angels and ministers of grace'—rant such as no madman short of a Nat Lee,[5] or an 'Oppodeldoc,' could possibly perpetrate. And for this trash of trash, we are modestly requested to 'pay promptly.' No sir—no! We pay for nothing of *that* sort. Apply to the 'Hum-Drum,' the 'Lollipop,' or the 'Goosetherumfoodle.' These *periodicals* will undoubtedly accept any literary offal you may send them—and as undoubtedly *promise* to pay for it."

This was bitter indeed upon poor "Oppodeldoc;" but, in this instance, the weight of the satire falls upon the "Hum-Drum," the "Lollipop," and the "Goosetherumfoodle," who are pungently styled "*periodicals*"—in Italics, too—a thing that must have cut them to the heart.

Scarcely less savage was the "Lollipop," which thus discoursed:

"Some *individual*, who rejoices in the appellation 'Oppodeldoc,' (to what low uses are the names of the illustrious dead too often applied!) has enclosed us some fifty or sixty *verses*, commencing after this fashion:

Achilles' wrath, to Greece the direful spring
Of woes unnumbered, &c., &c., &c., &c.

'Oppodeldoc,' (whoever he is,) is respectfully informed that there is not a printer's devil in our office who is not in the daily habit of composing better *lines*. Those of 'Oppodeldoc' will not *scan*. 'Oppodeldoc' should learn to *count*. But why he should have conceived the idea that *we*, (of all others, *we*!) would disgrace our pages with his ineffable nonsense, is utterly beyond comprehension. Why, the absurd twattle is scarcely good enough for the 'Hum-Drum,' the 'Rowdy-Dow,' the 'Goosetherumfoodle'—things that are in the practice of publishing 'Mother Goose's Melodies' as original lyrics. And 'Oppodeldoc,' (whoever he is,) has even the assurance to demand *pay* for this drivel.

Does 'Oppodeldoc,' (whoever he is,) know—is he aware that we could not be paid to insert it?"

As I perused this I felt myself growing gradually smaller and smaller, and when I came to the point at which the editor sneered at the poem as "*verses*," there was little more than an ounce of me left. As for "Oppodeldoc" I began to experience *compassion* for the poor fellow. But the "Goosetherumfoodle" showed, if possible, less mercy than the "Lollipop." It was the "Goosetherumfoodle" that said:

"A wretched poetaster, who signs himself 'Oppodeldoc,' is silly enough to fancy that *we* will print and *pay for* a medley of incoherent and ungrammatical bombast which he has transmitted to us, and which commences with the following most *intelligible* line:

"Hail, Holy Light! Offspring of Heaven, first born."

"We say, 'most *intelligible*.' 'Oppodeldoc,' (whoever he is,) will be kind enough to tell us, perhaps, how '*hail*' can be '*holy light*.' We always regarded it as *frozen rain*. Will he inform us, also, how frozen rain can be, at one and the same time, both 'holy light,' (whatever that is,) and an 'offspring?'—which latter term, (if we understand any thing about English,) is only employed, with propriety, in reference to small babies of about six weeks old. But it is preposterous to descant upon such absurdity—although 'Oppodeldoc,' (whoever he is,) has the unparalleled effrontery to suppose that we will not only 'insert' his ignorant ravings, but (absolutely) *pay for them!*

"Now this is fine—it is rich!—and we have half a mind to punish this young scribbler for his egotism, by really publishing his effusion, *verbatim et literatim*,[6] as he has written it. We could inflict no punishment so severe, and we *would* inflict it, but for the boredom which we should cause our readers in so doing.

"Let 'Oppodeldoc,' (whoever he is,) send any future *composition* of like character to the 'Hum-Drum,' the 'Lollipop,' or the 'Rowdy-Dow.' *They* will 'insert' it. *They* 'insert' every month just such stuff. Send it to them. WE are not to be insulted with impunity."

This made an end of me; and as for the "Hum-Drum," the "Rowdy-Dow," and the "Lollipop," I never could comprehend how they survived it. The putting *them* in the smallest possible *minion*, (*that* was the rub—thereby insinuating their lowness—their baseness,) while WE stood looking down upon them in gigantic capitals!—oh it was *too* bitter!—it was wormwood—it was gall. Had I been either of these periodicals I would have spared no pains to have the "Goosetherumfoodle" prosecuted. It might have been done under the Act for the "Prevention of Cruelty to Animals." As for "Oppodeldoc," (whoever he was,) I had by this time lost all patience with the fellow, and sympathized with him no longer. He was a fool, beyond doubt, (whoever he was,) and got not a kick more than he deserved.

The result of my experiment with the old books, convinced me, in the first place, that "honesty is the best policy," and, in the second, that if I could not write better than Mr. Dante, and the two blind men, and the rest of the old set, it would, at least, be a difficult matter to write worse. I took heart, therefore, and determined to prosecute the "entirely original," (as they say on the covers of the magazines,) at whatever cost of study and pains. I again placed before my eyes, as a model, the brilliant stanzas on "The Oil-of-Bob," by the editor of the "Gad-Fly," and resolved to construct an Ode on the same sublime theme, in rivalry of what had already been done.

With my first verse I had no material difficulty. It ran thus:

> To pen an Ode upon the "Oil-of-Bob."

Having carefully looked out, however, all the legitimate rhymes to "Bob," I found it impossible to proceed. In this dilemma I had recourse to paternal aid; and, after some hours of mature thought, my father and myself thus constructed the poem:

> To pen an Ode upon the "Oil-of-Bob"
> Is all sorts of a job.
>   (Signed,)   SNOB.

To be sure this composition was of no very great length—but I "have yet to learn" as they say in the Edinburgh Review, that the mere extent of a literary work has any thing to do with its merit. As for the Quarterly cant about "sustained effort," it is impossible to see the sense of it. Upon the whole, therefore, I was satisfied with the success of my maiden attempt, and now the only question regarded the disposal I should make of it. My father suggested that I should send it to the "Gad-Fly"—but there were two reasons which operated to prevent me from so doing. I dreaded the jealousy of the editor—and I had ascertained that he did not pay for original contributions. I therefore, after due deliberation, consigned the article to the more dignified pages of the "Lollipop," and awaited the event in anxiety, but with resignation.

In the very next published number I had the proud satisfaction of seeing my poem printed at length, as the leading article, with the following significant words, prefixed in italics and between brackets:

["We call the attention of our readers to the subjoined admirable stanzas on "The Oil-of-Bob." We need say nothing of their sublimity, or of their pathos:—it is impossible to peruse them without tears. Those who have been nauseated with a sad dose on the same august topic from the goose-quill of the editor of the "Gad-Fly," will do well to compare the two compositions.

P. S. We are consumed with anxiety to probe the mystery which envelops the evident pseudonym "Snob." May we not hope for a personal interview?"]

All this was scarcely more than justice, but it was, I confess, rather more than I had expected:—I acknowledge this, be it observed, to the everlasting disgrace of my country and of mankind. I lost no time, however, in calling upon the editor of the "Lollipop," and had the good fortune to find this gentleman at home. He saluted me with an air of profound respect, slightly blended with a fatherly and patronizing admiration, wrought in him, no doubt, by my appearance of extreme youth and inexperience. Begging me to be seated, he entered at once upon the subject of my poem;—but modesty will ever forbid me to repeat the thousand compliments which he lavished upon me. The eulogies of Mr. Crab, (such was the editor's name,) were, however, by no means fulsomely indiscriminate. He analyzed my composition with much freedom and great ability—not hesitating to point out a few trivial defects—a circumstance which elevated him highly in my esteem. The "Gad-Fly" was, of course, brought upon the *tapis*, and I hope never to be subjected to a criticism so searching, or to rebukes so withering, as were bestowed by Mr. Crab upon that unhappy effusion. I had been accustomed to regard the editor of the "Gad-Fly" as something superhuman; but Mr. Crab soon disabused me of that idea. He set the literary as well as the personal character of the Fly (so Mr. C. satirically designated the rival editor,) in its true light. He, the Fly, was very little better than he should be. He had written infamous things. He was a penny-a-liner, and a buffoon. He was a villain. He had composed a tragedy which set the whole country in a guffaw, and a farce which deluged the universe in tears. Besides all this, he had the impudence to pen what he meant for a lampoon upon himself, (Mr. Crab,) and the temerity to style him "an ass." Should I at any time wish to express my opinion of Mr. Fly, the pages of the "Lollipop," Mr. Crab assured me, were at my unlimited disposal. In the meantime, as it was very certain that I would be attacked in the Fly for my attempt at composing a rival poem on "The Oil-of-Bob," he (Mr. Crab,) would take it upon himself to attend, pointedly, to my private and personal interests. If I were not made a man of at once, it should not be the fault of himself, (Mr. Crab.)

Mr. Crab having now paused in his discourse, (the latter portion of which I found it impossible to comprehend,) I ventured to suggest something about the remuneration which I had been taught to expect for my poem, by an announcement on the cover of the "Lollipop," declaring that it, (the "Lollipop,") "insisted upon being permitted to pay exorbitant prices for all accepted contributions;—frequently expending more money for a single brief poem than the whole annual cost of the 'Hum-Drum,' the 'Rowdy-Dow,' and the 'Goosetherumfoodle' combined."

As I mentioned the word "remuneration," Mr. Crab first opened his eyes, and then his mouth, to quite a remarkable extent; causing his personal appearance to resemble that of a highly-agitated elderly duck in the act of quacking;—and in this condition he remained, (ever and anon pressing his hands tightly to his forehead, as if in a state of desperate bewilderment) until I had nearly made an end of what I had to say.

Upon my conclusion, he sank back into his seat, as if much overcome, letting his arms fall lifelessly by his side, but keeping his mouth still rigorously open, after the fashion of the duck. While I remained in speechless astonishment at behaviour so alarming, he suddenly leaped to his feet and made a rush at the bell-rope; but just as he reached this, he appeared to have altered his intention, whatever it was, for he dived under a table and immediately re-appeared with a cudgel. This he was in the act of uplifting, (for what purpose I am at a loss to imagine,) when, all at once, there came a benign smile over his features, and he sank placidly back in his chair.

"Mr. Bob," he said, (for I had sent up my card before ascending myself,) "Mr. Bob, you are a young man, I presume—*very?*"

I assented; adding that I had not yet concluded my third lustrum.[7]

"Ah!" he replied, "very good! I see how it is—say no more! Touching this matter of compensation, what you observe is very just: in fact it is excessively so. But—ah—ah— the *first* contribution—the *first*, I say—it is never the Magazine custom to pay for—you comprehend, eh? The truth is, we are usually the *recipients* in such case." [Mr. Crab smiled blandly as he emphasized the word "recipients."] "For the most part, we are *paid* for the insertion of a maiden attempt—especially in verse. In the second place, Mr. Bob, the Magazine rule is never to disburse what we term in France the *argent comptant*:⁸—I have no doubt you understand. In a quarter or two after publication of the article—or in a year or two—we make no objection to giving our note at nine months:—provided always that we can so arrange our affairs as to be quite certain of a 'burst up' in six. I really *do* hope, Mr. Bob, that you will look upon this explanation as satisfactory." Here Mr. Crab concluded, and the tears stood in his eyes.

Grieved to my soul at having been, however innocently, the cause of pain to so eminent and so sensitive a man, I hastened to apologize, and to reassure him, by expressing my perfect coincidence with his views, as well as my entire appreciation of the delicacy of his position. Having done all this in a neat speech, I took leave.

One fine morning, very shortly afterwards, "I awoke and found myself famous." The extent of my renown will be best estimated by reference to the editorial opinions of the day. These opinions, it will be seen, were embodied in critical notices of the number of the "Lollipop" containing my poem, and are perfectly satisfactory, conclusive and clear with the exception, perhaps, of the hieroglyphical marks "*Sep.* 15—1 *t.*"⁹ appended to each of the critiques.

The "Owl," a journal of profound sagacity, and well known for the deliberate gravity of its literary decisions—the "Owl," I say, spoke as follows:

"'THE LOLLIPOP!' The October number of this delicious Magazine surpasses its predecessors, and sets competition at defiance. In the beauty of its typography and paper—in the number and excellence of its steel plates—as well as in the literary merit of its contributions—the 'Lollipop' compares with its slow-paced rivals as Hyperion with a Satyr. The 'Hum-Drum,' the 'Rowdy-Dow,' and the 'Goosetherumfoodle,' excel, it is true, in braggadocio, but, in all other points, give us the 'Lollipop!' How this celebrated journal can sustain its evidently tremendous expenses, is more than we can understand. To be sure, it has a circulation of 100,000, and its subscription-list has increased one fourth during the last month; but, on the other hand, the sums it disburses constantly for contributions are inconceivable. It is reported that Mr. Slyass received no less than thirty-seven and a half cents for his inimitable paper on 'Pigs.' With Mr. CRAB, as editor, and with such names upon the list of contributors as SNOB and Slyass, there can be no such word as 'fail' for the 'Lollipop.' Go and subscribe. *Sep.* 15—1 *t.*"

I must say that I was gratified with this high-toned notice from a paper so respectable as the "Owl." The placing my name—that is to say my *nom de guerre*— in priority of station to that of the great Slyass, was a compliment as happy as I felt it to be deserved.

My attention was next arrested by these paragraphs in the "Toad"—a print highly distinguished for its uprightness, and independence—for its entire freedom from sycophancy and subservience to the givers of dinners.

"The 'Lollipop' for October is out in advance of all its contemporaries, and infinitely surpasses them, of course, in the splendor of its embellishments, as well as in the richness of its literary contents. The 'Hum-Drum,' the 'Rowdy-Dow,' and the 'Goosetherumfoodle' excel, we admit, in braggadocio, but, in all other points, give us the 'Lollipop.' How this celebrated Magazine can sustain its evidently tremendous expenses, is more than we can understand. To be sure, it has a circulation of 200,000, and its subscription list has increased one third during the last fortnight, but on the other hand, the sums it disburses, monthly, for contributions, are fearfully great. We learn that Mr. Mumblethumb received no less than fifty cents for his late 'Monody in a Mud-Puddle.'

"Among the original contributors to the present number we notice, (besides the eminent editor, Mr. CRAB,) such men as SNOB, Slyass, and Mumblethumb. Apart from the editorial matter, the most valuable paper, nevertheless, is, we think, a poetical gem by 'Snob,' on the 'Oil-of-Bob'—but our readers must not suppose, from the title of this incomparable *bijou*,[10] that it bears any similitude to some balderdash on the same subject by a certain contemptible individual whose name is unmentionable to ears polite. The *present* poem 'On the Oil-of-Bob,' has excited universal anxiety and curiosity in respect to the owner of the evident pseudonym, 'Snob'—a curiosity which, happily, we have it in our power to satisfy. 'Snob' is the *nom-de-plume* of Mr. Thingum Bob, of this city,—a relative of the great Mr. Thingum, (after whom he is named,) and otherwise connected with the most illustrious families of the State. His father, Thomas Bob, Esq., is an opulent merchant in Smug. *Sep.* 15—1 *t*."

This generous approbation touched me to the heart—the more especially as it emanated from a source so avowedly—so proverbially pure as the "Toad." The word "balderdash," as applied to the "Oil-of-Bob" of the Fly, I considered singularly pungent and appropriate. The words "gem" and "*bijou*," however, used in reference to my composition, struck me as being, in some degree, feeble. They seemed to me to be deficient in force. They were not sufficiently *pronouncés*, (as we have it in France.)

I had hardly finished reading the "Toad," when a friend placed in my hands a copy of the "Mole," a daily, enjoying high reputation for the keenness of its perception about matters in general, and for the open, honest, above-ground style of its editorials. The "Mole" spoke of the "Lollipop" as follows:

"We have just received the 'Lollipop' for October, and *must* say that never before have we perused any single number of any periodical which afforded us a felicity so supreme. We speak advisedly. The 'Hum-Drum,' the 'Rowdy-Dow' and the 'Goosetherumfoodle' must look well to their laurels. These prints, no doubt, surpass every thing in loudness of pretension, but, in all other points, give us the 'Lollipop!' How this celebrated Magazine can sustain its evidently tremendous expenses, is more than we can comprehend. To be sure, it has a circulation of 300,000; and its subscription-list has increased one half within the last week, but then the sum it disburses, monthly, for contributions, is astoundingly enormous. We have it upon good authority, that Mr. Fatquack received no less than sixty-two cents and a half for his late Domestic Nouvelette, the 'Dish-Clout.'

"The contributors to the number before us are Mr. CRAB, (the eminent editor,) SNOB, Mumblethumb, Fatquack and others; but, after the inimitable compositions of the editor himself, we prefer a diamond-like effusion from the pen of a rising poet who writes over the signature 'Snob'—a *nom de guerre* which we predict will one day extinguish the radiance of 'BOZ.' 'SNOB,' we learn, is a Mr. THINGUM BOB, sole heir of a wealthy merchant of this city, Thomas Bob, Esq., and a near relative of the distinguished Mr. Thingum. The title of Mr. B's admirable poem is the 'Oil-of-Bob'—a somewhat unfortunate name, by-the-bye, as some contemptible vagabond connected with the penny press has already disgusted the town with a great deal of drivel upon the same topic. There will be no danger, however, of confounding the compositions. *Sep.* 15—1 *t.*"

The generous approbation of so clear-sighted a journal as the "Mole" penetrated my soul with delight. The only objection which occurred to me was, that the terms "contemptible vagabond" might have been better written "*odious and* contemptible, *wretch, villain* and vagabond." This would have sounded more gracefully, I think. "Diamond-like," also, was scarcely, it will be admitted, of sufficient intensity to express what the "Mole" evidently *thought* of the brilliancy of the "Oil-of-Bob."

On the same afternoon in which I saw these notices in the "Owl," the "Toad," and the "Mole," I happened to meet with a copy of the "Daddy-Long-Legs," a periodical proverbial for the extreme extent of its understanding. And it was the "Daddy-Long-Legs" which spoke thus:

"The 'Lollipop'!! This gorgeous Magazine is already before the public for October. The question of pre-eminence is forever put to rest, and hereafter it will be excessively preposterous in the 'Hum-Drum,' the 'Rowdy-Dow,' or the 'Goosetherumfoodle,' to make any farther spasmodic attempts at competition. These journals may excel the 'Lollipop' in outcry, but, in all other points, give us the 'Lollipop!' How this celebrated Magazine can sustain its evidently tremendous expenses, is past comprehension. To be sure it has a circulation of precisely half a million, and its subscription-list has increased seventy-five per cent. within the last couple of days; but then the sums it disburses, monthly, for contributions, are scarcely credible; we are cognizant of the fact, that Mademoiselle Cribalittle received no less than eighty-seven cents and half for her late valuable Revolutionary Tale, entitled 'The York-Town Katy-Did, and the Bunker-Hill Katy-Didn't.'

"The most able papers in the present number, are, of course, those furnished by the editor, (the eminent Mr. CRAB,) but there are numerous magnificent contributions from such names as SNOB; Mademoiselle Cribalittle; Slyass; Mrs. Fibalittle; Mumblethum; Mrs. Squibalittle; and, last, though not least, Fatquack. The world may well be challenged to produce so rich a galaxy of genius.

"The poem over the signature 'SNOB' is, we find, attracting universal commendation, and, we are constrained to say, deserves, if possible, even more applause than it has received. The 'Oil-of-Bob' is the title of this masterpiece of eloquence and art. One or two of our readers *may* have a *very* faint, although sufficiently disgusting recollection of a poem (?) similarly entitled, the perpetration of a miserable penny-a-liner, mendicant, and cut-throat, connected in the capacity of scullion, we believe, with one of the indecent prints about the purlieus of the city; we beg them, for God's sake, not to confound the compositions. The author of *the* 'Oil-of-Bob,' is, we hear, THINGUM

BOB, Esq., a gentleman of high genius, and a scholar. 'Snob' is merely a *nom-de-guerre.* *Sept.* 15—1 *t.*"

I could scarcely restrain my indignation while I perused the concluding portions of this diatribe. It was clear to me that the yea-nay manner—not to say the gentleness—the positive forbearance with which the "Daddy-Long-Legs" spoke of that pig, the editor of the "Gad-Fly"—it was evident to me, I say, that this gentleness of speech could proceed from nothing else than a partiality for the Fly—whom it was clearly the intention of the "Daddy-Long-Legs" to elevate into reputation at my expense. Any one, indeed, might perceive, with half an eye, that, had the real design of the "Daddy" been what it wished to appear, it, (the "Daddy,") might have expressed itself in terms more direct, more pungent, and altogether more to the purpose. The words "penny-a-liner," "mendicant," "scullion," and "cut-throat," were epithets so intentionally inexpressive and equivocal, as to be worse than nothing when applied to the author of the very worst stanzas ever penned by one of the human race. We all know what is meant by "damning with faint praise," and, on the other hand, who could fail seeing through the covert purpose of the "Daddy"— that of glorifying with feeble abuse?

What the "Daddy" chose to say of the Fly, however, was no business of mine. What it said of myself *was*. After the noble manner in which the "Owl," the "Toad," the "Mole," had expressed themselves in respect to my ability, it was rather too much to be coolly spoken of by a thing like the "Daddy-Long-Legs," as merely "a gentleman of high genius and a scholar." Gentleman indeed! I made up my mind, at once, either to get a written apology from the "Daddy-Long-Legs," or to call it out.

Full of this purpose, I looked about me to find a friend whom I could entrust with a message to his Daddyship, and, as the editor of the "Lollipop" had given me marked tokens of regard, I at length concluded to seek assistance upon the present occasion.

I have never yet been able to account, in a manner satisfactory to my own understanding, for the *very* peculiar countenance and demeanor with which Mr. Crab listened to me, as I unfolded to him my design. He again went though the scene of the bell-rope and cudgel, and did not omit the duck. At one period I thought he really intended to quack. His fit, nevertheless, finally subsided as before, and he began to act and speak in a rational way. He declined bearing the cartel, however, and in fact, dissuaded me from sending it at all; but was candid enough to admit that the "Daddy-Long-Legs" had been disgracefully in the wrong—more especially in what related to the epithets "gentleman and scholar."

Towards the end of this interview with Mr. Crab, who really appeared to take a paternal interest in my welfare, he suggested to me that I might turn an honest penny and, at the same time, advance my reputation, by occasionally playing Thomas Hawk for the "Lollipop."

I begged Mr. Crab to inform me who was Mr. Thomas Hawk, and how it was expected that I should play him.

Here Mr. Crab again "made great eyes," (as we say in Germany,) but at length, recovering himself from a profound attack of astonishment, he assured me that he employed the words "Thomas Hawk" to avoid the colloquialism, Tommy, which was low—but that the true idea was Tommy Hawk—or tomahawk—and that by "playing tomahawk" he referred to scalping, brow-beating and otherwise using-up the herd of poor-devil authors.

I assured my patron that, if this was all, I was perfectly resigned to the task of playing Thomas Hawk. Hereupon Mr. Crab desired me to use-up the editor of the "Gad-Fly" forthwith, in the fiercest style within the scope of my ability, and as a specimen of my powers. This I did, upon the spot, in a review of the original "Oil-of-Bob," occupying thirty-six pages of the "Lollipop." I found playing Thomas Hawk, indeed, a far less onerous occupation than poetizing; for I went upon *system* altogether, and thus it was easy to do the thing thoroughly and well. My practice was this. I bought auction copies (cheap) of "Lord Brougham's Speeches," "Cobbett's Complete Works," the "New Slang-Syllabus," the "Whole Art of Snubbing," "Prentice's Billingsgate," (folio edition,) and "Lewis G. Clarke on Tongue."[11] These works I cut up thoroughly with a curry-comb, and then, throwing the shreds into a sieve, sifted out carefully all that might be thought decent, (a mere trifle); reserving the hard phrases, which I threw into a large tin pepper-castor with longitudinal holes, so that an entire sentence could get through without material injury. The mixture was then ready for use. When called upon to play Thomas Hawk, I anointed a sheet of fools-cap with the white of a gander's egg; then, shredding the thing to be reviewed as I had previously shredded the books,—only with more care, so as to get every word separate—I threw the latter shreds in with the former, screwed on the lid of the castor, gave it a shake, and so dusted out the mixture upon the egg'd foolscap; where it stuck. The effect was beautiful to behold. It was captivating. Indeed the reviews I brought to pass by this simple expedient have never been approached, and were the wonder of the world. At first, through bashfulness—the result of inexperience—I was a little put out by a certain inconsistency—a certain air of the *bizarre*, (as we say in France,) worn by the composition as a whole. All the phrases did not *fit*, (as we say in the Anglo-Saxon.) Many were quite awry. Some, even, were up-side-down; and there were none of them which were not, in some measure, injured, in regard to effect, by this latter species of accident, when it occurred:—with the exception of Mr. Lewis Clarke's paragraphs, which were so vigorous, and altogether stout, that they seemed not particularly disconcerted by any extreme of position, but looked equally happy and satisfactory, whether on their heads, or on their heels.

What became of the editor of the "Gad-Fly," after the publication of my criticism on his "Oil-of-Bob," it is somewhat difficult to determine. The most reasonable conclusion is, that he wept himself to death. At all events he disappeared instantaneously from the face of the earth, and no man has seen even the ghost of him since.

This matter having been properly accomplished, and the Furies appeased, I grew at once into high favor with Mr. Crab. He took me into his confidence, gave me a permanent situation as Thomas Hawk of the "Lollipop," and as, for the present, he could afford me no salary, allowed me to profit, at discretion, by his advice.

"My Dear Thingum," said he to me one day after dinner, "I respect your abilities and love you as a son. You shall be my heir. When I die I will bequeath you the

'Lollipop.' In the meantime I will make a man of you—I *will*—provided always that you follow my counsel. The first thing to do is to get rid of the old bore."

"Boar?" said I inquiringly—"pig, eh?—*aper?* (as we say in Latin)—who?—where?"

"Your father," said he.

"Precisely," I replied,—"pig."

"You have your fortune to make, Thingum," resumed Mr. Crab, "and that governor of yours is a millstone about your neck. We must cut him at once." [Here I took out my knife.] "We must cut him," continued Mr. Crab, "decidedly and forever. He won't do—he *won't.* Upon second thoughts, you had better kick him, or cane him, or something of that kind."

"What do you say," I suggested modestly, "to my kicking him in the first instance, caning him afterwards, and winding up by tweaking his nose?"

Mr. Crab looked at me musingly for some moments, and then answered:

"I think, Mr. Bob, that what you propose would answer sufficiently well—indeed remarkably well—that is to say, as far as it went—but barbers are exceedingly hard to cut, and I think, upon the whole, that, having performed upon Thomas Bob the operations you suggest, it would be advisable to blacken, with your fists, both his eyes, very carefully and thoroughly, to prevent his ever seeing you again in fashionable promenades. After doing this, I really do not perceive that you can do any more. However—it might be just as well to roll him once or twice in the gutter, and then put him in charge of the police. Any time the next morning you can call at the watch-house and swear an assault."

I was much affected by the kindness of feeling towards me personally, which was evinced in this excellent advice of Mr. Crab, and I did not fail to profit by it forthwith. The result was, that I got rid of the old bore, and began to feel a little independent and gentleman-like. The want of money, however, was, for a few weeks, a source of some discomfort; but at length, by carefully putting to use my two eyes, and observing how matters went just in front of my nose, I perceived how the thing was to be brought about. I say "thing"—be it observed—for they tell me the Latin for it is *rem.* By the way, talking of Latin, can any one tell me the meaning of *quocunque*—or what is the meaning of *modo?*[12]

My plan was exceedingly simple. I bought, for a song, a sixteenth of the "Snapping-Turtle:"—that was all. The thing was *done,* and I put money in my purse. There were some trivial arrangements afterwards, to be sure; but these formed no portion of the plan. They were a consequence—a result. For example, I bought pen, ink and paper, and put them into furious activity. Having thus completed a Magazine article, I gave it, for appellation, "FOL-LOL, *by the Author of* 'THE OIL-OF-BOB,'" and enveloped it to the "Goosetherumfoodle." That journal, however, having pronounced it "twattle" in the "Monthly Notices to Correspondents," I reheaded the paper "'Hey-Diddle-Diddle' by THINGUM BOB, Esq., Author of the Ode on 'The Oil-of-Bob,' *and* Editor of the 'Snapping-Turtle.'" With this amendment, I reenclosed it to the "Goosetherumfoodle," and, while I awaited a reply, published daily, in the "Turtle," six columns of what may be termed philosophical and analytical investigation of the literary merits of the "Goosetherumfoodle" as well as of the personal character of the editor of the "Goosetherumfoodle." At the end of a week the "Goosetherumfoodle" discovered that it had, by some odd mistake, "confounded a stupid article, headed 'Hey-Diddle-Diddle' and composed by some unknown ignoramus, with a gem of resplendent lustre similarly entitled, the work of Thingum Bob, Esq., the celebrated author of 'The Oil-of-Bob.'" The "Goosetherumfoodle" deeply "regretted this very natural accident," and promised, moreover, an insertion of the *genuine* 'Hey-Diddle-Diddle' in the very next number of the Magazine.

The fact is I *thought*—I *really* thought—I thought at the time—I thought *then*—and have no reason for thinking otherwise *now*—that the "Goosetherumfoodle" *did* make a mistake. With the best intentions in the world, I never knew any thing that made as many singular mistakes as the "Goosetherumfoodle." From that day I took a liking to the "Goosetherumfoodle," and the result was I soon saw into the very depths of its literary merits, and did not fail to expatiate upon them, in the "Turtle," whenever a fitting opportunity occurred. And it is to be regarded as a very peculiar coincidence—as one of those positively *remarkable* coincidences which set a man to serious thinking—that just such a total revolution of opinion—just such entire *bouleversement*, (as we say in French,)—just such thorough *topsiturviness*, (if I may be permitted to employ a rather forcible term of the Choctaws,) as happened, *pro* and *con*, between myself on the one part, and the "Goosetherumfoodle" on the other, did actually again happen, in a brief period afterwards, and with precisely similar circumstances, in the case of myself and the "Rowdy-Dow," and in the case of myself and the "Hum-Drum."

Thus it was that, by a master-stroke of genius, I at length consummated my triumphs by "putting money in my purse" and thus may be said really and fairly to have commenced that brilliant and eventful career which rendered me illustrious, and which now enables me to say, with Chateaubriand, "I have made history"—"*J'ai fait l'histoire.*"

I have indeed "made history." From the bright epoch which I now record, my actions—my works—are the property of mankind. They are familiar to the world. It is, then, needless for me to detail how, soaring rapidly, I fell heir to the "Lollipop"—how I merged this journal in the "Hum-Drum"—how again I made purchase of the "Rowdy-Dow," thus combining the three periodicals—how, lastly, I effected a bargain for the sole remaining rival, and united all the literature of the country in one magnificent Magazine, known every where as the

"Rowdy-Dow, Lollipop, Hum-Drum,
and
GOOSETHERUMFOODLE."

Yes; I have made history. My fame is universal. It extends to the uttermost ends of the earth. You cannot take up a common newspaper in which you shall not see some allusion to the immortal THINGUM BOB. It is Mr. Thingum Bob said so, and Mr. Thingum Bob wrote this, and Mr. Thingum Bob did that. But I am meek and expire with an humble heart. After all, what is it?—this indescribable something which men will persist in terming "genius?" I agree with Buffon—with Hogarth—it is but *diligence* after all.

Look at *me!*—how I labored—how I toiled—how I wrote! Ye Gods, did I *not* write? I knew not the word "ease." By day I adhered to my desk, and at night, a pale student, I consumed the midnight oil. You should have seen me—you *should*. I leaned to the right. I leaned to the left. I sat forward. I sat backward. I sat upon end. I sat *tête baissée*, (as they have it in the Kickapoo,) bowing my head close to the alabaster page. And, through all, I—*wrote*. Through joy and through sorrow, I—*wrote*. Through hunger and through thirst, I—*wrote*. Through good report and through ill report, I—*wrote*. *What* I wrote it is unnecessary to say. The *style!*—that was the thing. I caught it from Fatquack—whizz!—fizz!—and I am giving you a specimen of it now.

Some Words with a Mummy[1]

THE SYMPOSIUM of the preceding evening had been a little too much for my nerves. I had a wretched headache, and was desperately drowsy. Instead of going out, therefore, to spend the evening as I had proposed, it occurred to me that I could not do a wiser thing than just eat a mouthful of supper and go immediately to bed.

A *light* supper of course. I am exceedingly fond of Welsh rabbit. More than a pound at once, however, may not at all times be advisable. Still, there can be no material objection to two. And really between two and three, there is merely a single unit of difference. I ventured, perhaps, upon four. My wife will have it five;—but, clearly, she has confounded two very distinct affairs. The abstract number, five, I am willing to admit; but, concretely, it has reference to bottles of Brown Stout, without which, in the way of condiment, Welsh rabbit is to be eschewed.

Having thus concluded a frugal meal, and donned my night-cap, with the serene hope of enjoying it till noon the next day, I placed my head upon the pillow, and through the aid of a capital conscience, fell into a profound slumber forthwith.

But when were the hopes of humanity fulfilled? I could not have completed my third snore when there came a furious ringing at the street-door bell, and then an impatient thumping at the knocker, which awakened me at once. In a minute afterward, and while I was still rubbing my eyes, my wife thrust in my face a note from my old friend, Doctor Ponnonner. It ran thus:

Come to me by all means, my dear good friend, as soon as you receive this. Come and help us to rejoice. At last, by long persevering diplomacy, I have gained the assent of the Directors of the City Museum, to my examination of the Mummy—you know the one I mean. I have permission to unswathe it and open it, if desirable. A few friends only will be present—you, of course. The Mummy is now at my house, and we shall begin to unroll it at eleven to-night.[2]

Yours ever,

PONNONNER.

By the time I had reached the "Ponnonner," it struck me that I was as wide awake as a man need be. I leaped out of bed in an ecstasy, overthrowing all in my way; dressed myself with a rapidity truly marvellous; and set off, at the top of my speed, for the Doctor's.

There I found a very eager company assembled. They had been awaiting me with much impatience; the Mummy was extended upon the dining table; and the moment I entered, its examination was commenced.

It was one of a pair brought, several years previously, by Captain Arthur Sabretash, a cousin of Ponnonner's, from a tomb near Eleithias, in the Lybian Mountains, a considerable distance above Thebes on the Nile. The grottoes at this point, although less magnificent than the Theban sepulchres, are of higher interest, on account of affording more numerous illustrations of the private life of the Egyptians. The chamber from which our specimen was taken, was said to be very rich in such illustrations; the walls being completely covered with fresco paintings and bas-reliefs, while statues, vases, and Mosaic work of rich patterns, indicated the vast wealth of the deceased.

The treasure had been deposited in the Museum precisely in the same condition in which Captain Sabretash had found it;—that is to say, the coffin had not been disturbed. For eight years it had thus stood, subject only externally to public inspection. We had now, therefore, the complete Mummy at our disposal; and to those who are aware how very rarely the unransacked antique reaches our shores, it will be evident, at once, that we had great reason to congratulate ourselves upon our good fortune.

Approaching the table, I saw on it a large box, or case, nearly seven feet long, and perhaps three feet wide, by two feet and a half deep. It was oblong—not coffin-shaped. The material was at first supposed to be the wood of the sycamore (*platanus*), but, upon cutting into it, we found it to be pasteboard, or more properly, *papier maché*, composed of papyrus. It was thickly ornamented with paintings, representing funeral scenes, and other mournful subjects, interspersed among which in every variety of position, were certain series of hieroglyphical characters intended, no doubt, for the name of the departed. By good luck, Mr. Gliddon[3] formed one of our party; and he had no difficulty in translating the letters, which were simply phonetic, and represented the word, *Allamistakeo*.

We had some difficulty in getting this case open without injury, but, having at length accomplished the task, we came to a second, coffin-shaped, and very considerably less in size than the exterior one, but resembling it precisely in every other respect. The interval between the two was filled with resin, which had, in some degree, defaced the colors of the interior box.

Upon opening this latter (which we did quite easily,) we arrived at a third case, also coffin-shaped, and varying from the second one in no particular, except in that of its material, which was cedar, and still emitted the peculiar and highly aromatic odor of that wood. Between the second and the third case there was no interval: the one fitting accurately within the other.

Removing the third case, we discovered and took out the body itself. We had expected to find it, as usual, enveloped in frequent rolls, or bandages, of linen, but, in place of these, we found a sort of sheath, made of papyrus, and coated with a layer of plaster, thickly gilt and painted. The paintings represented subjects connected with the various supposed duties of the soul, and its presentation to different divinities, with numerous identical human figures, intended, very probably, as portraits of the persons embalmed. Extending from head to foot, was a columnar, or perpendicular inscription in phonetic hieroglyphics, giving again his name and titles, and the names and titles of his relations.

Around the neck thus ensheathed, was a collar of cylindrical glass beads, diverse in color, and so arranged as to form images of deities, of the scarabæus, etc., with the winged globe. Around the small of the waist was a similar collar, or belt.

Stripping off the papyrus, we found the flesh in excellent preservation, with no perceptible odor. The color was reddish. The skin was hard, smooth and glossy. The teeth and hair were in good condition. The eyes (it seemed) had been removed, and glass ones substituted, which were very beautiful and wonderfully life-like, with the exception of somewhat too determined a stare. The finger and the nails were brilliantly gilded.

Mr. Gliddon was of opinion, from the redness of the epidermis, that the embalment had been effected altogether by asphaltum; but, on scraping the surface with a steel instrument, and throwing into the fire some of the powder thus obtained, the flavor of camphor and other sweet-scented gums became apparent.

We searched the corpse very carefully for the usual openings through which the entrails are extracted, but, to our surprise, we could discover none. No member of the party was at that period aware that entire or unopened mummies are not unfrequently met. The brain it was customary to withdraw through the nose; the intestines through an incision in the side; the body was then shaved, washed, and salted; then laid aside for several weeks, when the operation of embalming, properly so called, began.

As no trace of an opening could be found, Doctor Ponnonner was preparing his instruments for dissection, when I observed that it was then past two o'clock. Hereupon it was agreed to postpone the internal examination until the next evening; and we were about to separate for the present, when some one suggested an experiment or two with the Voltaic pile.[4]

The application of electricity to a Mummy three or four thousand years old at the least, was an idea, if not very sage, still sufficiently original, and we all caught at it at once. About one tenth in earnest and nine tenths in jest, we arranged a battery in the Doctor's study, and conveyed thither the Egyptian.

It was only after much trouble that we succeeded in laying bare some portions of the temporal muscle which appeared of less stony rigidity than other parts of the frame, but which, as we had anticipated, of course, gave no indication of galvanic susceptibility when brought in contact with the wire. This the first trial, indeed, seemed decisive, and, with a hearty laugh at our own absurdity, we were bidding each other good night, when my eyes, happening to fall upon those of the Mummy, were there immediately riveted in amazement. My brief glance, in fact, had sufficed to assure me that the orbs which we had all supposed to be glass, and which were originally noticeable for a certain wild stare, were now so far covered by the lids that only a small portion of the *tunica albuginea* remained visible.

With a shout I called attention to the fact, and it became immediately obvious to all.

I cannot say that I was *alarmed* at the phenomenon, because "alarmed" is, in my case, not exactly the word. It is possible, however, that, but for the Brown Stout, I might have been a little nervous. As for the rest of the company, they really made no attempt at concealing the downright fright which possessed them. Doctor Ponnonner was a man to be pitied. Mr. Gliddon, by some peculiar process, rendered himself invisible. Mr. Silk Buckingham,[5] I fancy, will scarcely be so bold as to deny that he made his way, upon all fours, under the table.

After the first shock of astonishment, however, we resolved, as a matter of course, upon farther experiment forthwith. Our operations were now directed against the great toe of the right foot. We made an incision over the outside of the exterior *os sesamoideum pollicis pedis*, and thus got at the root of the *abductor* muscle. Re-adjusting the battery, we now applied the fluid to the bisected nerves—when, with a movement of exceeding life-likeness, the Mummy first drew up its right knee so as to bring it nearly in contact with the abdomen, and then, straightening the limb with inconceivable force, bestowed a kick upon Doctor Ponnonner which had the effect of discharging that gentleman, like an arrow from a catapult, through a window into the street below.

We rushed out *en masse* to bring in the mangled remains of the victim, but had the happiness to meet him upon the staircase, coming up in an unaccountable hurry, brimfull of the most ardent philosophy, and more than ever impressed with the necessity of prosecuting our experiments with rigor and with zeal.

It was by his advice, accordingly, that we made, upon the spot, a profound incision into the tip of the subject's nose, while the Doctor himself, laying violent hands upon it, pulled it into vehement contact with the wire.

Morally and physically—figuratively and literally—was the effect electric. In the first place, the corpse opened its eyes and winked very rapidly for several minutes, as does Mr. Barnes in the pantomime; in the second place, it sneezed; in the third, it sat upon end; in the fourth, it shook its fist in Doctor Ponnonner's face; in the fifth, turning to Messieurs Gliddon and Buckingham, it addressed them, in very capital Egyptian, thus:

"I must say, gentlemen, that I am as much surprised as I am mortified, at your behaviour. Of Doctor Ponnonner nothing better was to be expected. He is a poor little fat fool who *knows* no better. I pity and forgive him. But you, Mr. Gliddon—and you, Silk—who have travelled and resided in Egypt until one might imagine you to the manor born—you, I say, who have been so much among us that you speak Egyptian fully as well, I think, as you write your mother tongue—you, whom I have always been led to regard as the firm friend of the mummies—I really did anticipate more gentlemanly conduct from *you*. What am I to think of your standing quietly by and seeing me thus unhandsomely used? What am I to suppose by your permitting Tom, Dick and Harry to strip me of my coffins, and my clothes, in this wretchedly cold climate? In what light (to come to the point) am I to regard your aiding and abetting that miserable little villain, Doctor Ponnonner, in pulling me by the nose?"

It will be taken for granted, no doubt, that upon hearing this speech under the circumstances, we all either made for the door, or fell into violent hysterics, or went off in a general swoon. One of these three things was, I say, to be expected. Indeed each and all of these lines of conduct might have been very plausibly pursued. And, upon my word, I am at a loss to know how or why it was that we pursued neither the one or the other. But, perhaps, the true reason is to be sought in the spirit of the age, which proceeds by the rule of contraries altogether, and is now usually admitted as the solution of everything in the way of paradox and impossibility. Or, perhaps, after all, it was only the Mummy's exceedingly natural and matter-of-course air that divested his words of the terrible. However this may be, the facts are clear, and no member of our party betrayed any very particular trepidation, or seemed to consider that any thing had gone very especially wrong.

For my part I was convinced it was all right, and merely stepped aside, out of the range of the Egyptian's fist. Doctor Ponnonner thrust his hands into his breeches' pockets, looked hard at the Mummy, and grew excessively red in the face. Mr. Gliddon stroked his whiskers and drew up the collar of his shirt. Mr. Buckingham hung down his head, and put his right thumb into the left corner of his mouth.

The Egyptian regarded him with a severe countenance for some minutes, and at length, with a sneer, said:

"Why don't you speak, Mr. Buckingham? Did you hear what I asked you, or not? *Do* take your thumb out of your mouth!"

Mr. Buckingham, hereupon, gave a slight start, took his right thumb out of the left corner of his mouth, and, by way of indemnification, inserted his left thumb in the right corner of the aperture above-mentioned.

Not being able to get an answer from Mr. B., the figure turned peevishly to Mr. Gliddon, and, in a peremptory tone, demanded in general terms what we all meant.

Mr. Gliddon replied at great length, in phonetics; and but for the deficiency of American printing-offices in hieroglyphical type, it would afford me much pleasure to record here, in the original, the whole of his very excellent speech.

I may as well take this occasion to remark, that all the subsequent conversation in which the Mummy took a part, was carried on in primitive Egyptian, through the medium (so far as concerned myself and other untravelled members of the company)—through the medium, I say, of Messieurs Gliddon and Buckingham, as interpreters. These gentlemen spoke the mother-tongue of the mummy with inimitable fluency and grace; but I could not help observing that (owing, no doubt, to the introduction of images entirely modern, and, of course, entirely novel to the stranger,) the two travelers were reduced, occasionally, to the employment of sensible forms for the purpose of conveying a particular meaning. Mr. Gliddon, at one period, for example, could not make the Egyptian comprehend the term "politics," until he sketched upon the wall, with a bit of charcoal, a little carbuncle-nosed gentleman, out at elbows, standing upon a stump, with his left leg drawn back, his right arm thrown forward, with the fist shut, the eyes rolled up toward Heaven, and the mouth open at an angle of ninety degrees. Just in the same way Mr. Buckingham failed to convey the absolutely modern idea, "wig," until, (at Doctor Ponnonner's suggestion,) he grew very pale in the face, and consented to take off his own.

It will be readily understood that Mr. Gliddon's discourse turned chiefly upon the vast benefits accruing to science from the unrolling and disembowelling of mummies; apologizing, upon this score, for any disturbance that might have occasioned *him*, in particular, the individual Mummy called Allamistakeo; and concluding with a mere hint, (for it could scarcely be considered more,) that, as these little matters were now explained, it might be as well to proceed with the investigation intended. Here Doctor Ponnonner made ready his instruments.

In regard to the latter suggestions of the orator, it appears that Allamistakeo had certain scruples of conscience, the nature of which I did not distinctly learn; but he expressed himself satisfied with the apologies tendered, and, getting down from the table, shook hands with the company all round.

When this ceremony was at an end, we immediately busied ourselves in repairing the damages which our subject had sustained from the scalpel. We sewed up the wound in his temple, bandaged his foot, and applied a square inch of black plaster to the tip of his nose.

It was now observed that the Count, (this was the title, it seems, of Allamistakeo,) had a slight fit of shivering—no doubt from the cold. The doctor immediately repaired to his wardrobe, and soon returned with a black dress coat, made in Jennings' best manner, a pair of sky-blue plaid pantaloons with straps, a pink gingham *chemise*, a flapped vest of brocade, a white sack overcoat, a walking cane with a hook, a hat with no brim, patent-leather boots, straw-colored kid gloves, an eye-glass, a pair of whiskers, and a waterfall cravat. Owing to the disparity of size between the Count and doctor, (the proportion being as two to one,) there was some little difficulty adjusting these habiliments upon the person of the Egyptian; but when all was arranged, he might have been said to be dressed. Mr. Gliddon, therefore, gave him his arm, and led him to a comfortable chair by the fire, while the doctor rang the bell upon the spot and ordered a supply of cigars and wine.

The conversation soon grew animated. Much curiosity was, of course, expressed in regard to the somewhat remarkable fact of Allamistakeo's still remaining alive.

"I should have thought," observed Mr. Buckingham, "that it is high time you were dead."

"Why," replied the Count, very much astonished, "I am little more than seven hundred years old! My father lived a thousand, and was by no means in his dotage when he died."

Here ensued a brisk series of questions and computations, by means of which it became evident that the antiquity of the Mummy had been grossly misjudged. It had been five thousand and fifty years, and some months, since he had been consigned to the catacombs at Eleithias.

"But my remark," resumed Mr. Buckingham, "had no reference to your age at the period of interment; (I am willing to grant, in fact, that you are still a young man,) and my allusion was to the immensity of time during which, by your own showing, you must have been done up in asphaltum."

"In what?" said the Count.

"In asphaltum," persisted Mr. B.

"Ah, yes; I have some faint notion of what you mean; it might be made to answer, no doubt,—but in my time we employed scarcely anything else than the Bichloride of Mercury."

"But what we are especially at a loss to understand," said Doctor Ponnonner, "is how it happens that, having been dead and buried in Egypt five thousand years ago, you are here to-day all alive, and looking so delightfully well."

"Had I been, as you say, *dead*," replied the Count, "it is more than probable that dead I should still be; for I perceive you are yet in the infancy of Galvanism, and cannot accomplish with it what was a common thing among us in the old days. But the fact is, I fell into catalepsy, and it was considered by my best friends that I was either dead or should be; they accordingly embalmed me at once—I presume you are aware of the chief principle of the embalming process?"

"Why, not altogether."

"Ah, I perceive;—a deplorable condition of ignorance! Well, I cannot enter into details just now: but it is necessary to explain that to embalm, (properly speaking,) in Egypt, was to arrest indefinitely *all* the animal functions subjected to the process. I use the word 'animal' in its widest sense, as including the physical not more than the moral and *vital* being. I repeat that the leading principle of embalment consisted, with us, in the immediately arresting, and holding in perpetual *abeyance, all* the animal functions subjected to the process. To be brief, in whatever condition the individual was, at the period of embalment, in that condition he remained. Now, as it is my good fortune to be of the blood of the Scarabœus, I was embalmed *alive*, as you see me at present."

"The blood of the Scarabœus!" exclaimed Doctor Ponnonner.

"Yes. The Scarabœus was the *insignium*, or the 'arms,' of a very distinguished and a very rare patrician family. To be 'of the blood of the Scarabœus,' is merely to be one of that family of which the Scarabœus is the *insignium*. I speak figuratively."

"But what has this to do with your being alive?"

"Why it is the general custom, in Egypt, to deprive a corpse, before embalment, of its bowels and brains; the race of the Scarabœi alone did not coincide with the custom. Had I not been a Scarabœus, therefore, I should have been without bowels and brains; and without either it is inconvenient to live."

"I perceive that;" said Mr. Buckingham, "and I presume that all the *entire* mummies that come to hand are of the race of Scarabœi."

"Beyond doubt."

"I thought," said Mr. Gliddon very meekly, "that the Scarabœus was one of the Egyptian gods."

"One of the Egyptian *what?*" exclaimed the Mummy, starting to its feet.

"Gods!" repeated the traveler.

"Mr. Gliddon I really am ashamed to hear you talk in this style," said the Count, resuming his chair. "No nation upon the face of the earth has ever acknowledged more than *one god*. The Scarabœus, the Ibis, etc., were with us, (as similar creatures have been with others) the symbols, or *media*, through which we offered worship to a Creator too august to be more directly approached."

There was here a pause. At length the colloquy was renewed by Doctor Ponnonner.

"It is not improbable, then, from what you have explained," said he, "that among the catacombs near the Nile, there may exist other mummies of the Scarabœus tribe, in a condition of vitality."

"There can be no question of it," replied the Count; all the Scarabœi embalmed accidentally while alive, are alive now. Even some of those *purposely* so embalmed, may have been overlooked by their executors, and still remain in the tombs."

"Will you be kind enough to explain," I said, "what you mean by 'purposely so embalmed?'"

"With great pleasure," answered the Mummy, after surveying me leisurely through his eye-glass—for it was the first time I had ventured to address him a direct question.

"With great pleasure," said he. "The usual duration of man's life, in my time, was about eight hundred years. Few men died, unless by most extraordinary accident, before the age of six hundred; few lived longer than a decade of centuries; but eight were considered the natural term. After the discovery of the embalming principle, as I have already described it to you, it occurred to our philosophers that a laudable curiosity might be gratified, and, at the same time, the interests of science much advanced, by living this natural term in instalments. In the case of history, indeed, experience demonstrated that something of this kind was indispensable. An historian, for example, having attained the age of five hundred, would write a book with great labor and then get himself carefully embalmed; leaving instructions to his executors *pro tem.*, that they should cause him to be revivified after the lapse of a certain period—say five or six hundred years. Resuming existence at the expiration of this term, he would invariably find his great work converted into a species of hap-hazard notebook—that is to say, into a kind of literary arena for the conflicting guesses, riddles, and personal squabbles of whole herds of exasperated commentators. These guesses, etc., which passed under the name of annotations or emendations, were found so completely to have enveloped, distorted, and overwhelmed the text, that the author had to go about with a lantern to discover his own book. When discovered, it was never worth the trouble of the search. After re-writing it throughout, it was regarded as the bounden duty of the historian to set himself to work, immediately, in correcting from his own private knowledge and experience, the traditions of the day concerning the epoch at which he had originally lived. Now this process of re-scription and personal rectification, pursued by various individual sages, from time to time, had the effect of preventing our history from degenerating into absolute fable."

"I beg your pardon," said Doctor Ponnonner at this point, laying his hand gently upon the arm of the Egyptian—"I beg your pardon, sir, but may I presume to interrupt you for one moment?"

"By all means, *sir*," replied the Count, drawing up.

"I merely wished to ask you a question," said the Doctor. "You mentioned the historian's personal correction of *traditions* respecting his own epoch. Pray, sir, upon an average, what proportion of these Kabbala were usually found to be right?"[6]

"The Kabbala, as you properly term them, sir, were generally discovered to be precisely on a par with the facts recorded in the un-re-written histories themselves;— that is to say, not one individual iota of either, was ever known, under any circumstances, to be not totally and radically wrong."

"But since it is quite clear," resumed the Doctor, "that at least five thousand years have elapsed since your entombment, I take it for granted that your histories at that period, if not your traditions, were sufficiently explicit on that one topic of universal interest, the Creation, which took place, as I presume you are aware, only about ten centuries before."

"Sir!" said Count Allamistakeo.

The Doctor repeated his remarks, but it was only after much additional explanation, that the foreigner could be made to comprehend them. The latter at length said, hesitatingly:

"The ideas you have suggested are to me, I confess, utterly novel. During my time I never knew any one to entertain so singular a fancy as that the universe (or this world if you will have it so) ever had a beginning at all. I remember, once, and once only, hearing something remotely hinted, by a man of many speculations, concerning the origin *of the human race*; and by this individual the very word *Adam*, (or Red Earth) which you make use of, was employed. He employed it, however, in a generical sense, with reference to the spontaneous germination from rank soil (just as a thousand of the lower *genera* of creatures are germinated)—the spontaneous germination, I say, of five vast hordes of men, simultaneously upspringing in five distinct and nearly equal divisions of the globe."[7]

Here, in general, the company shrugged their shoulders, and one or two of us touched our foreheads with a very significant air. Mr. Silk Buckingham, first glancing slightly at the occiput and then at the siniciput of Allamistakeo, spoke as follows:—

"The long duration of human life in your time, together with the occasional practice of passing it, as you have explained, in instalments, must have had, indeed, a strong tendency to the general development and conglomeration of knowledge. I presume, therefore, that we are to attribute the marked inferiority of the old Egyptians in all particulars of science, when compared with the moderns, and more especially with the Yankees, altogether to the superior solidity of the Egyptian skull."

"I confess again," replied the Count with much suavity, "that I am somewhat at a loss to comprehend you; pray, to what particulars of science do you allude?"

Here our whole party, joining voices, detailed, at great length, the assumptions of phrenology and the marvels of animal magnetism.[8]

Having heard us to an end, the Count proceeded to relate a few anecdotes, which rendered it evident that prototypes of Gall and Spurzheim had flourished and faded in Egypt so long ago as to have been nearly forgotten, and that the manœuvres of Mesmer were really very contemptible tricks when put in collation with the positive miracles of the Theban *savans*, who created lice and a great many other similar things.

I here asked the Count if his people were able to calculate eclipses. He smiled rather contemptuously, and said they were.

This put me a little out, but I began to make other inquiries in regard to his astronomical knowledge, when a member of the company, who had never as yet opened his mouth, whispered in my ear that, for information on this head, I had better consult Ptolemy, (whoever Ptolemy is) as well as one Plutarch *de facie lunœ*.[9]

I then questioned the Mummy about burning-glasses and lenses, and, in general, about the manufacture of glass; but I had not made an end of my queries before the silent member again touched me quietly on the elbow, and begged me for God's sake to take a peep at Diodorus Siculus.[10] As for the Count, he merely asked me, in the way of reply, if we moderns possessed any such microscopes as would enable us to cut cameos in the style of the Egyptians. While I was thinking how I should answer this question, little Doctor Ponnonner committed himself in a very extraordinary way.

"Look at our architecture!" he exclaimed, greatly to the indignation of both the travelers, who pinched him black and blue to no purpose.

"Look," he cried with enthusiasm, "at the Bowling-Green Fountain[11] in New York! or if this be too vast a contemplation, regard for a moment the Capitol at

Washington, D. C.!"—and the good little medical man went on to detail very minutely the proportions of the fabric to which he referred. He explained that the portico alone was adorned with no less than four and twenty columns, five feet in diameter, and ten feet apart.

The Count said that he regretted not being able to remember, just at that moment, the precise dimensions of any one of the principal buildings of the city of Aznac, whose foundations were laid in the night of Time, but the ruins of which were still standing, at the epoch of his entombment, in a vast plain of sand to the westward of Thebes. He recollected, however, (talking of porticoes) that one affixed to an inferior palace in a kind of suburb called Carnac, consisted of a hundred and forty-four columns, thirty-seven feet each in circumference, and twenty-five feet apart. The approach to this portico, from the Nile, was through an avenue two miles long, composed of sphynxes, statues and obelisks, twenty, sixty, and a hundred feet in height. The palace itself (as well as he could remember) was, in one direction, two miles long, and might have been, altogether, about seven in circuit. Its walls were richly painted all over, within and without, with hieroglyphics. He would not pretend to *assert* that even fifty or sixty of the Doctor's Capitols might have been built within these walls, but he was by no means sure that two or three hundred of them might not have been squeezed in with some trouble. That palace at Carnac was an insignificant little building after all. He, (the Count) however, could not conscientiously refuse to admit the ingenuity, magnificence, and superiority of the Fountain at the Bowling-Green, as described by the Doctor. Nothing like it, he was forced to allow, had ever been seen in Egypt or elsewhere.

I here asked the Count what he had to say to our railroads.

"Nothing," he replied, "in particular." They were rather slight, rather ill-conceived, and clumsily put together. They could not be compared, of course, with the vast, level, direct, iron-grooved causeways, upon which the Egyptians conveyed entire temples and solid obelisks of a hundred and fifty feet in altitude.

I spoke of our gigantic mechanical forces.

He agreed that we knew something in that way, but inquired how I should have gone to work in getting up the imposts on the lintels of even the little palace at Carnac.

This question I concluded not to hear, and demanded if he had any idea of Artesian wells; but he simply raised his eye-brows; while Mr. Gliddon, winked at me very hard, and said, in a low tone, that one had been recently discovered by the engineers employed to bore for water in the Great Oasis.

I then mentioned our steel; but the foreigner elevated his nose, and asked me if our steel could have executed the sharp curved work seen on the obelisks, and which was wrought altogether by edge-tools of copper.

This disconcerted us so greatly that we thought it advisable to vary the attack to Metaphysics. We sent for a copy of a book called the "Dial,"[12] and read out of it a chapter or two about something which is not very clear, but which the Bostonians call the Great Movement or Progress.

The Count merely said that Great Movements were awfully common things in his day, and as for Progress it was at one time quite a nuisance, but it never progressed.

We then spoke of the great beauty and importance of Democracy, and were at much trouble in impressing the Count with a due sense of the advantages we enjoyed in living where there was suffrage *ad libitum*, and no king.

He listened with marked interest, and in fact seemed not a little amused. When we had done, he said that, a great while ago, there had occurred something of a very similar sort. Thirteen Egyptian provinces determined all at once to be free, and so set a magnificent example to the rest of mankind. They assembled their wise men, and concocted the most ingenious constitution it is possible to conceive. For a while they managed remarkably well; only their habit of bragging was prodigious. The thing ended, however, in the consolidation of the thirteen states, with some fifteen or twenty others, into the most odious and insupportable despotism that ever was heard of upon the face of the Earth.

I asked what was the name of the usurping tyrant.

As well as the Count could recollect, it was *Mob*.

Not knowing what to say to this, I raised my voice, and deplored the Egyptian ignorance of steam.

The Count looked at me with much astonishment, but made no answer. The silent gentleman, however, gave me a violent nudge in the ribs with his elbows—told me I had sufficiently exposed myself for once—and demanded if I was really such a fool as not to know that the modern steam engine is derived from the invention of Hero, through Solomon de Caus.[13]

We were now in imminent danger of being discomfited; but, as good luck would have it, Doctor Ponnonner, having rallied, returned to our rescue, and inquired if the people of Egypt would seriously pretend to rival the moderns in the all-important particular of dress.

The Count, at this, glanced downward to the straps of his pantaloons, and then, taking hold of the end of one of his coat-tails, held it up close to his eyes for some minutes. Letting it fall, at last, his mouth extended itself very gradually from ear to ear; but I do not remember that he said anything in the way of reply.

Hereupon we recovered our spirits, and the Doctor, approaching the mummy with great dignity, desired it to say candidly, upon its honor as a gentleman, if the Egyptians had comprehended, at *any* period, the manufacture of either Ponnonner's lozenges, or Brandreth's pills.[14]

We looked, with profound anxiety, for an answer;—but in vain. It was not forthcoming. The Egyptian blushed and hung down his head. Never was triumph more consummate; never was defeat borne with so ill a grace. Indeed I could not endure the spectacle of the poor Mummy's mortification. I reached my hat, bowed to him stiffly, and took leave.

Upon getting home I found it past four o'clock, and went immediately to bed. It is now ten, A. M. I have been up since seven, penning these memoranda for the benefit of my family and of mankind. The former I shall behold no more. My wife is a shrew. The truth is, I am heartily sick of this life and of the nineteenth century in general. I am convinced that everything is going wrong. Besides, I am anxious to know who will be President in 2045. As soon, therefore, as I shave and swallow a cup of coffee, I shall just step over to Ponnonner's and get embalmed for a couple of hundred years.

The Imp of the Perverse[1]

In the consideration of the faculties and impulses—of the *prima mobilia*[2] of the human soul, the phrenologists[3] have failed to make room for a propensity which, although obviously existing as a radical, primitive, irreducible sentiment, has been equally overlooked by the moralists who have preceded them. In the pure arrogance of the reason we have all overlooked it. We have suffered its existence to escape our senses solely through want of belief—of faith—whether it be faith in Revelation or faith in the inner teachings of the spirit. Its idea has not occurred to us, simply because of its seeming supererogation. We saw no *need* for the propensity in question. We could not perceive its necessity. We could not understand—that is to say, we could not have understood, had the notion of this *primum mobile* ever obtruded itself—in what manner it might be made to further the objects of humanity, either temporal or eternal. It cannot be denied that all metaphysicianism has been concocted *à priori*.[4] The intellectual or logical man, rather than the understanding or observant man, set himself to imagine designs—to dictate purposes to God. Having thus fathomed to his satisfaction the intentions of Jehovah, out of these intentions he reared his innumerable systems of Mind. In the matter of Phrenology, for example, we first determined, naturally enough, that it was the design of Deity that man should eat. We then assigned to man an organ of Alimentiveness, and this organ is the scourge by which Deity compels man to his food. Again, having settled it to be God's will that man should continue his species, we discovered an organ of Amativeness forthwith. And so with Combativeness, with Ideality, with Causality, with Constructiveness; so, in short, with every organ, whether representing a propensity, a moral sentiment, or a faculty of the pure intellect. And in these arrangements of the *principia* of human action, the Spurzheimites, whether right or wrong, in part, or upon the whole, have but followed, in principle, the footsteps of their predecessors; deducing and establishing every thing from the preconceived destiny of man, and upon the ground of the *objects* of his Creator.

It would have been safer—if classify we must—to classify upon the basis of what man usually or occasionally did, and was always occasionally doing, rather than upon the basis of what we took it for granted the Deity intended him to do. If we cannot comprehend God in his visible works, how then in his inconceivable thoughts that call the works into being? If we cannot understand him in his objective creatures, how then in his substantive moods and phases of creation?

Induction *à posteriori* would have brought Phrenology to admit, as an innate and primitive principle of human action, a paradoxical something which, for want of a better term, we may call *Perverseness*. In the sense I intend, it is, in fact, a *mobile* without motive—a motive not *motivirt*. Through its promptings we act without comprehensible object. Or if this shall be understood as a contradiction in terms, we may so far modify the proposition as to say that through its promptings we act for the reason that we should *not*. In theory, no reason can be more unreasonable, but in reality there is none so strong. With certain minds, under certain circumstances, it becomes absolutely irresistible. I am not more sure that I breathe, than that the conviction of the wrong or impolicy of an action is often the one unconquerable *force* which impels us, and alone impels us, to its prosecution. Nor will this overwhelming tendency to do wrong for the wrong's sake, admit of analysis, or resolution into ulterior elements. It is a radical, a primitive impulse—elementary. It will be said, I am aware, that when we persist in acts because we feel that we should *not* persist in them, our conduct is but a modification of that which ordinarily springs from the Combativeness of Phrenology. But a glance will show the fallacy of this idea. The phrenological Combativeness has for its essence the necessity of self-defence. It is our safeguard against injury. Its principle regards our well-being; and thus the desire to be well must be excited simultaneously with any principle which shall be merely a modification of Combativeness. But in the case of that something which I term Perverseness, the desire to be well is not only *not* aroused, but a strongly antagonistical sentiment prevails.

An appeal to one's own heart is, after all, the best reply to the sophistry just noticed. No one who trustingly consults his own soul will be disposed to deny the entire radicalness of the propensity in question. It is not more incomprehensible than distinct. There lives no man who, at some period, has not been tormented, for example, by an earnest desire to tantalize a listener by circumlocution. The speaker, in such case, is aware that he displeases; he has every intention to please; he is usually curt, precise, and clear; the most laconic and luminous language is struggling for utterance upon his tongue; it is only with difficulty that he restrains himself from giving it flow; he dreads and deprecates the anger of him whom he addresses; yet a shadow seems to flit across the brain, and suddenly the thought strikes that, by certain involutions and parentheses, anger may be engendered. That single thought is enough. The impulse increases to a wish—the wish to a desire—the desire to an uncontrollable longing—and the longing, in defiance of all consequences, is indulged.

Again:—We have a task before us which must be speedily performed. We know that it will be ruinous to make delay. The most important crisis of our life calls, trumpet-tongued, for immediate energy and action. We glow—we are consumed with eagerness to commence the work, and our whole souls are on fire with anticipation of the glorious result. It must—it shall be undertaken to-day—and yet we put it off until to-morrow. And why? There is no answer except that we feel *perverse*—employing the word with no comprehension of the principle. To-morrow arrives, and with it a more impatient anxiety to do our duty; but with this very increase of anxiety arrives, also, a nameless—a positively fearful, because unfathomable, craving for delay. This craving gathers strength as the moments fly. The last hour for action is at hand. We tremble with the violence of the conflict within us—of the definite with the indefinite—of the Substance with the Shadow; but, if the contest have proceeded thus far, it is the Shadow which prevails. We struggle in vain. The clock strikes and is the knell of our welfare, but at the same time is the chanticleer-note to the Thing that has so long overawed us. It flies. It disappears. We are free. The old energy returns. We will labor *now*—alas, it is *too late!*

And yet again:—We stand upon the brink of a precipice. We peer into the abyss. We grow sick and dizzy. Our first impulse is to shrink from the danger, and yet, unaccountably, we remain. By slow degrees our sickness, and dizziness, and horror, become merged in a cloud of unnameable feeling. By gradations still more imperceptible this cloud assumes shape, as did the vapor from the bottle out of which arose the Genius in the Arabian Nights. But out of this *our* cloud on the precipice's edge, there grows into palpability a shape far more terrible than any Genius or any Demon of a tale. And yet it is but a *Thought*, although one which chills the very marrow of our bones with the fierceness of the delight of its horror. It is merely the idea of what would be our sensations during the sweeping precipitancy of a fall from such a height. And this fall—this rushing annihilation—for the very reason that it involves that one most ghastly and loathsome of all the most ghastly and loathsome images of death and suffering which have ever presented themselves to our imagination—*for this very cause* do we now the most impetuously desire it. And because our reason most strenuously deters us from the brink, *therefore* do we the more unhesitatingly approach it. There is no passion in Nature of so demoniac an impatience as the passion of him who, shuddering upon the edge of a precipice, thus meditates a plunge. To indulge, even for a moment, in any attempt at *thought*, is to be inevitably lost; for reflection but urges us to forbear, and *therefore* it is, I say, that we *cannot*. If there be no friendly arm to check us, or if we fail in a sudden effort to throw ourselves backward from the danger, and so out of its sight, we plunge and are destroyed.

Examine these and similar actions as we will, we shall find them resulting solely from the spirit of the *Perverse*. We perpetrate them merely because we feel that we should *not*. Beyond or behind this there is no principle that men, in their fleshly nature, can understand; and were it not occasionally known to operate in furtherance of good, we might deem the anomalous feeling a direct instigation of the Arch-fiend.

I have premised thus much that I may be able, in some degree, to give an intelligible answer to your queries—that I may explain to you why I am here—that I may assign something like a reason for my wearing these fetters and tenanting the cell of the condemned. Had I not been thus prolix, you might either have misunderstood me altogether, or, with the rabble, you might have fancied me mad.

It is impossible that any deed could have been wrought with more thorough deliberation. For weeks—for months—I pondered upon the means of the murder. I rejected a thousand schemes because their accomplishment involved a *chance* of detection. At length, in reading some French memoirs, I found an account of a nearly fatal illness that occurred to Madame Pilau, through the agency of a candle accidentally poisoned. The idea struck my fancy at once. I knew my victim's habit of reading in bed. I knew, too, that his apartment was narrow and ill-ventilated. But I need not vex you with impertinent details. I need not describe the easy artifices by which I substituted, in his candle-stand, a wax-light of my own making for the one which I there found. The next morning he was dead in his bed, and the verdict was "Death by the visitation of God."

Having inherited his estate, all went merrily with me for years. The idea of detection never obtruded itself. Of the remains of the fatal taper I had myself carefully disposed, nor had I left the shadow of a clue by which it would be possible to convict or even to suspect me of the crime.

It is inconceivable how rich a sentiment of satisfaction arose in my bosom as I reflected upon my *absolute* security. For a very long period of time I reveled in this sentiment. It afforded me, I believe, more real delight than all the mere worldly advantages accruing from my sin.

There arrived at length an epoch, after which this pleasurable feeling took to itself a new tone, and grew, by scarcely perceptible gradations, into a haunting and harassing thought—a thought that harassed because it haunted.

I could scarcely get rid of it for an instant. It is quite a common thing to be thus annoyed by the ringing in our ears, or memories, of the burden of an ordinary song, or some unimpressive snatches from an opera. Nor will we be the less tormented though the song in itself be good, or the opera-air meritorious. In this manner, at last, I would perpetually find myself pondering upon my impunity and security, and very frequently would catch myself repeating, in a low, under-tone, the phrases "I am safe—I am safe."

One day, while sauntering listlessly about the streets, I arrested myself in the act of murmuring, half aloud, these customary syllables. In a fit of petulance at my indiscretion I remodeled them thus:—"I am safe—I am safe—yes, *if I do not prove fool enough to make open confession.*"

No sooner had I uttered these words, than I felt an icy chill creep to my heart. I had had (long ago, during childhood) some experience in those fits of Perversity whose nature I have been at so much trouble in explaining, and I remembered that in no instance had I successfully resisted their attacks. And now my own casual self-suggestion—that I might possibly prove fool enough to make open confession—confronted me, as if the very ghost of him I had murdered, and beckoned me on to death.

At first I made strong effort to shake off this nightmare of the soul. I whistled—I laughed aloud—I walked vigorously—faster and still faster. At length I saw—or fancied that I saw—a vast and formless shadow that seemed to dog my footsteps, approaching me from behind, with a cat-like and stealthy pace. It was then that I *ran*. I felt a wild desire to shriek aloud. Every succeeding wave of thought overwhelmed me with new terror—for alas! I understood too well that *to think*, in my condition, was to be undone. I still quickened my steps. I bounded like a madman through the crowded thoroughfares. But now the populace took alarm and pursued. Then—then I felt the consummation of my Fate. Could I have torn out my tongue I would have done it. But a rough voice from some member of the crowd now resounded in my ears, and a rougher grasp seized me by the arm. I turned—I gasped for breath. For a moment I experienced all the pangs of suffocation—I became blind, and deaf, and giddy—and at this instant it was no mortal hand, I knew, that struck me violently with a broad and massive palm upon the back. At that blow the long imprisoned secret burst forth from my soul.

They say that I spoke with distinct enunciation, but with emphasis and passionate hurry, as if in dread of interruption before concluding the brief but pregnant sentences that consigned me to the hangman and to Hell.

The Facts in the Case of M. Valdemar[1]

An article of ours, thus entitled, was published in the last number of Mr. Colton's "American Review," and has given rise to some discussion—especially in regard to the truth or falsity of the statements made. It does not become *us*, of course, to offer one word on the point at issue. We have been requested to reprint the article, and do so with pleasure. We leave it to speak for itself. We may observe, however, that there are a certain class of people who pride themselves upon Doubt, as a profession.—*Ed. B. J.*[2]

Of course I shall not pretend to consider it any matter for wonder, that the extraordinary case of M. Valdemar has excited discussion. It would have been a miracle had it not—especially under the circumstances. Through the desire of all parties concerned, to keep the affair from the public, at least for the present, or until we had farther opportunities for investigation—through our endeavors to effect this—a garbled or exaggerated account made its way into society, and became the source of many unpleasant misrepresentations, and, very naturally, of a great deal of disbelief.

It is now rendered necessary that I give the *facts*—as far as I comprehend them myself. They are, succinctly, these:

My attention, for the last three years, had been repeatedly drawn to the subject of Mesmerism;[3] and, about nine months ago, it occurred to me, quite suddenly, that in the series of experiments made hitherto, there had been a very remarkable and most unaccountable omission:—no person had as yet been mesmerized *in articulo mortis.*[4] It remained to be seen, first, whether, in such condition, there existed in the patient any susceptibility to the magnetic influence; secondly, whether, if any existed, it was impaired or increased by the condition; thirdly, to what extent, or for how long a period, the encroachments of Death might be arrested by the process. There were other points to be ascertained, but these most excited my curiosity—the last in especial, from the immensely important character of its consequences.

In looking around me for some subject by whose means I might test these particulars, I was brought to think of my friend, M. Ernest Valdemar, the well-known compiler of the "Bibliotheca Forensica," and author (under the *nom de plume* of Issachar Marx) of the Polish versions of "Wallenstein" and "Gargantua."[5] M. Valdemar, who has resided principally at Harlaem, N. Y., since the year 1839, is (or was) particularly noticeable for the extreme spareness of his person—his lower limbs much resembling those of John Randolph;[6] and, also, for the whiteness of his whiskers, in violent contrast to the blackness of his hair—the latter, in consequence, being very generally mistaken for a wig. His temperament was markedly nervous, and rendered him a good subject for mesmeric experiment. On two or three occasions I had put him to sleep with little difficulty, but was disappointed in other results which his peculiar constitution had naturally led me to anticipate. His will was at no period positively, or thoroughly, under my control, and in regard to *clairvoyance*, I could accomplish with him nothing to be relied upon. I always attributed my failure at these points to the disordered state of his health. For some months previous to my becoming acquainted with him, his physicians had declared him in a confirmed phthisis.[7] It was his custom, indeed, to speak calmly of his approaching dissolution, as of a matter neither to be avoided nor regretted.

When the ideas to which I have alluded first occurred to me, it was of course very natural that I should think of M. Valdemar. I knew the steady philosophy of the man too well to apprehend any scruples from *him;* and he had no relatives in America who would be likely to interfere. I spoke to him frankly upon the subject; and, to my surprise, his interest seemed vividly excited. I say to my surprise; for, although he had always yielded his person freely to my experiments, he had never before given me any tokens of sympathy with what I did. His disease was of that character which would admit of exact calculation in respect to the epoch of its termination in death; and it was finally arranged between us that he would send for me about twenty-four hours before the period announced by his physicians as that of his decease.

It is now rather more than seven months since I received, from M. Valdemar himself, the subjoined note:

MY DEAR P——,

You may as well come *now*. D—— and F—— are agreed that I cannot hold out beyond to-morrow midnight; and I think they have hit the time very nearly.

VALDEMAR.

I received this note within half an hour after it was written, and in fifteen minutes more I was in the dying man's chamber. I had not seen him for ten days, and was appalled by the fearful alteration which the brief interval had wrought in him. His face wore a leaden hue; the eyes were utterly lustreless; and the emaciation was so extreme that the skin had been broken through by the cheek-bones. His expectoration was excessive. The pulse was barely perceptible. He retained, nevertheless, in a very remarkable manner, both his mental power and a certain degree of physical strength. He spoke with distinctness—took some palliative medicines without aid—and, when I entered the room, was occupied in penciling memoranda in a pocket-book. He was propped up in the bed by pillows. Doctors D—— and F—— were in attendance.

After pressing Valdemar's hand, I took these gentlemen aside, and obtained from them a minute account of the patient's condition. The left lung had been for eighteen months in a semi-osseous or cartilaginous state, and was, of course, entirely useless for all purposes of vitality. The right, in its upper portion, was also partially, if not thoroughly, ossified, while the lower region was merely a mass of purulent tubercles, running one into another. Several extensive perforations existed; and, at one point, permanent adhesion to the ribs had taken place. These appearances in the right lobe were of comparatively recent date. The ossification had proceeded with very unusual rapidity; no sign of it had been discovered a month before, and the adhesion had only been observed during the three previous days. Independently of the phthisis, the patient was suspected of aneurism of the aorta; but on this point the osseous symptoms rendered an exact diagnosis impossible. It was the opinion of both physicians that M. Valdemar would die about midnight on the morrow (Sunday). It was then seven o'clock on Saturday evening.

On quitting the invalid's bed-side to hold conversation with myself, Doctors D—— and F—— had bidden him a final farewell. It had not been their intention to return; but, at my request, they agreed to look in upon the patient about ten the next night.

When they had gone, I spoke freely with M. Valdemar on the subject of his approaching dissolution, as well as, more particularly, of the experiment proposed. He still professed himself quite willing and even anxious to have it made, and urged me to commence it at once. A male and a female nurse were in attendance; but I did not feel myself altogether at liberty to engage in a task of this character with no more reliable witnesses than these people, in case of sudden accident, might prove. I therefore postponed operations until about eight the next night, when the arrival of a medical student with whom I had some acquaintance, (Mr. Theodore L——l,) relieved me from farther embarrassment. It had been my design, originally, to wait for the physicians; but I was induced to proceed, first, by the urgent entreaties of M. Valdemar, and secondly, by my conviction that I had not a moment to lose, as he was evidently sinking fast.

Mr. L——l was so kind as to accede to my desire that he would take notes of all that occurred; and it is from his memoranda that what I now have to relate is, for the most part, either condensed or copied *verbatim.*

It wanted about five minutes of eight when, taking the patient's hand, I begged him to state, as distinctly as he could, to Mr. L——l, whether he (M. Valdemar) was entirely willing that I should make the experiment of mesmerizing him in his then condition.

He replied feebly, yet quite audibly, "Yes, I wish to be mesmerized"—adding immediately afterwards, "I fear you have deferred it too long."

While he spoke thus, I commenced the passes which I had already found most effectual in subduing him. He was evidently influenced with the first lateral stroke of my hand across his forehead; but although I exerted all my powers, no farther perceptible effect was induced until some minutes after ten o'clock, when Doctors D—— and F—— called, according to appointment. I explained to them, in a few words, what I designed, and as they opposed no objection, saying that the patient was already in the death agony, I proceeded without hesitation—exchanging, however, the lateral passes for downward ones, and directing my gaze entirely into the right eye of the sufferer.

By this time his pulse was imperceptible and his breathing was stertorous, and at intervals of half a minute.

This condition was nearly unaltered for a quarter of an hour. At the expiration of this period, however, a natural although a very deep sigh escaped the bosom of the dying man, and the stertorous breathing ceased—that is to say, its stertorousness was no longer apparent; the intervals were undiminished. The patient's extremities were of an icy coldness.

At five minutes before eleven I perceived unequivocal signs of the mesmeric influence. The glassy roll of the eye was changed for that expression of uneasy *inward* examination which is never seen except in cases of sleep-waking, and which it is quite impossible to mistake. With a few rapid lateral passes I made the lids quiver, as in incipient sleep, and with a few more I closed them altogether. I was not satisfied, however, with this, but continued the manipulations vigorously, and with the fullest exertion of the will, until I had completely stiffened the limbs of the slumberer, after placing them in a seemingly easy position. The legs were at full length; the arms were nearly so, and reposed on the bed at a moderate distance from the loins. The head was very slightly elevated.

When I had accomplished this, it was fully midnight, and I requested the gentlemen present to examine M. Valdemar's condition. After a few experiments, they admitted him to be in an unusually perfect state of mesmeric trance. The curiosity of both the physicians was greatly excited. Dr. D—— resolved at once to remain with the patient all night, while Dr. F—— took leave with a promise to return at day-break. Mr. L——l and the nurses remained.

We left M. Valdemar entirely undisturbed until about three o'clock in the morning, when I approached him and found him in precisely the same condition as when Dr. F—— went away—that is to say, he lay in the same position; the pulse was imperceptible; the breathing was gentle (scarcely noticeable, unless through the application of a mirror to the lips); the eyes were closed naturally; and the limbs were as rigid and as cold as marble. Still, the general appearance was certainly not that of death.

As I approached M. Valdemar I made a kind of half effort to influence his right arm into pursuit of my own, as I passed the latter gently to and fro above his person. In such experiments with this patient I had never perfectly succeeded before, and assuredly I had little thought of succeeding now; but to my astonishment, his arm very readily, although feebly, followed every direction I assigned it with mine. I determined to hazard a few words of conversation.

"M. Valdemar," I said, "are you asleep?" He made no answer, but I perceived a tremor about the lips, and was thus induced to repeat the question, again and again. At its third repetition, his whole frame was agitated by a very slight shivering; the eye-lids unclosed themselves so far as to display a white line of the ball; the lips moved sluggishly, and from between them, in a barely audible whisper, issued the words:

"Yes;—asleep now. Do not wake me!—let me die so!"

I here felt the limbs and found them as rigid as ever. The right arm, as before, obeyed the direction of my hand. I questioned the sleep-waker again:

"Do you still feel pain in the breast, M. Valdemar?"

The answer now was immediate, but even less audible than before:

"No pain—I am dying."

I did not think it advisable to disturb him farther just then, and nothing more was said or done until the arrival of Dr. F——, who came a little before sunrise, and expressed unbounded astonishment at finding the patient still alive. After feeling the pulse and applying a mirror to the lips, he requested me to speak to the sleep-waker again. I did so, saying:

"M. Valdemar, do you still sleep?"

As before, some minutes elapsed ere a reply was made; and during the interval the dying man seemed to be collecting his energies to speak. At my fourth repetition of the question, he said very faintly, almost inaudibly:

"Yes; still asleep—dying."

It was now the opinion, or rather the wish, of the physicians, that M. Valdemar should be suffered to remain undisturbed in his present apparently tranquil condition, until death should supervene—and this, it was generally agreed, must now take place within a few minutes. I concluded, however, to speak to him once more, and merely repeated my previous question.

While I spoke, there came a marked change over the countenance of the sleep-waker. The eyes rolled themselves slowly open, the pupils disappearing upwardly; the skin generally assumed a cadaverous hue, resembling not so much parchment as white paper; and the circular hectic spots which, hitherto, had been strongly defined in the centre of each cheek, *went out* at once. I use this expression, because the suddenness of their departure put me in mind of nothing so much as the extinguishment of a candle by a puff of the breath. The upper lip, at the same time, writhed itself away from the teeth, which it had previously covered completely; while the lower jaw fell with an audible jerk, leaving the mouth widely extended, and disclosing in full view the swollen and blackened tongue. I presume that no member of the party then present had been unaccustomed to death-bed horrors; but so hideous beyond conception was the appearance of M. Valdemar at this moment, that there was a general shrinking back from the region of the bed.

I now feel that I have reached a point of this narrative at which every reader will be startled into positive disbelief. It is my business, however, simply to proceed.

There was no longer the faintest sign of vitality in M. Valdemar; and concluding him to be dead, we were consigning him to the charge of the nurses, when a strong vibratory motion was observable in the tongue. This continued for perhaps a minute. At the expiration of this period, there issued from the distended and motionless jaws a voice—such as it would be madness in me to attempt describing. There are, indeed, two or three epithets which might be considered as applicable to it in part; I might say, for example, that the sound was harsh, and broken and hollow; but the hideous whole is indescribable, for the simple reason that no similar sounds have ever jarred upon the ear of humanity. There were two particulars, nevertheless, which I thought then, and still think, might fairly be stated as characteristic of the intonation—as well adapted to convey some idea of its unearthly peculiarity. In the first place, the voice seemed to reach our ears—at least mine—from a vast distance, or from some deep cavern within the earth. In the second place, it impressed me (I fear, indeed, that it will be impossible to make myself comprehended) as gelatinous or glutinous matters impress the sense of touch.

I have spoken both of "sound" and of "voice." I mean to say that the sound was one of distinct—of even wonderfully, thrillingly distinct—syllabification. M. Valdemar *spoke*—obviously in reply to the question I had propounded to him a few minutes before. I had asked him, it will be remembered, if he still slept. He now said:

"Yes;   no;—I *have been* sleeping—and now—now—*I am dead.*"

No person present even affected to deny, or attempted to repress, the unutterable, shuddering horror which these few words, thus uttered, were so well calculated to convey. Mr. L——l (the student) swooned. The nurses immediately left the chamber, and could not be induced to return. My own impressions I would not pretend to render intelligible to the reader. For nearly an hour, we busied ourselves, silently—without the utterance of a word—in endeavors to revive Mr. L——l. When he came to himself, we addressed ourselves again to an investigation of M. Valdemar's condition.

It remained in all respects as I have last described it, with the exception that the mirror no longer afforded evidence of respiration. An attempt to draw blood from the arm failed. I should mention, too, that this limb was no farther subject to my will. I endeavored in vain to make it follow the direction of my hand. The only real indication, indeed, of the mesmeric influence, was now found in the vibratory movement of the tongue, whenever I addressed M. Valdemar a question. He seemed to be making an effort at reply, but had no longer sufficient volition. To queries put to him by any other person than myself he seemed utterly insensible—although I endeavored to place each member of the company in mesmeric *rapport* with him. I believe that I have now related all that is necessary to an understanding of the sleep-waker's state at this epoch. Other nurses were procured; and at ten o'clock I left the house in company with the two physicians and Mr. L——l.

In the afternoon we all called again to see the patient. His condition remained precisely the same. We had now some discussion as to the propriety and feasibility of awakening him; but we had little difficulty in agreeing that no good purpose would be served by so doing. It was evident that, so far, death (or what is usually termed death) had been arrested by the mesmeric process. It seemed clear to us all that to awaken M. Valdemar would be merely to insure his instant, or at least his speedy dissolution.

From this period until the close of last week—*an interval of nearly seven months*—we continued to make daily calls at M. Valdemar's house, accompanied, now and then, by medical and other friends. All this time the sleep-waker remained *exactly* as I have last described him. The nurses' attentions were continual.

It was on Friday last that we finally resolved to make the experiment of awakening, or attempting to awaken him; and it is the (perhaps) unfortunate result of this latter experiment which has given rise to so much discussion in private circles—to so much of what I cannot help thinking unwarranted popular feeling.

For the purpose of relieving M. Valdemar from the mesmeric trance, I made use of the customary passes. These, for a time, were unsuccessful. The first indication of revival was afforded by a partial descent of the iris. It was observed, as especially remarkable, that this lowering of the pupil was accompanied by the profuse out-flowing of a yellowish ichor[8] (from beneath the lids) of a pungent and highly offensive odor.

It now was suggested that I should attempt to influence the patient's arm, as heretofore. I made the attempt and failed. Dr. F—— then intimated a desire to have me put a question. I did so as follows:

"M. Valdemar, can you explain to us what are your feelings or wishes now?"

There was an instant return of the hectic circles on the cheeks; the tongue quivered, or rather rolled violently in the mouth (although the jaws and lips remained as rigid as before;) and at length the same hideous voice which I have already described, broke forth:

"For God's sake!—quick!—quick!—put me to sleep—or, quick!—waken me!—quick!—*I say to you that I am dead!*"

I was thoroughly unnerved, and for an instant remained undecided what to do. At first I made an endeavor to re-compose the patient; but, failing in this through total abeyance of the will, I retraced my steps and as earnestly struggled to awaken him. In this attempt I soon saw that I should be successful—or at least I soon fancied that my success would be complete—and I am sure that all in the room were prepared to see the patient awaken.

For what really occurred, however, it is quite impossible that any human being could have been prepared.

As I rapidly made the mesmeric passes, amid ejaculations of "dead! dead!" absolutely *bursting* from the tongue and not from the lips of the sufferer, his whole frame at once—within the space of a single minute, or even less, shrunk—crumbled—absolutely *rotted* away beneath my hands. Upon the bed, before that whole company, there lay a nearly liquid mass of loathsome—of detestable putrescence.

The Cask of Amontillado[1]

THE thousand injuries of Fortunato I had borne as I best could; but when he ventured upon insult, I vowed revenge. You, who so well know the nature of my soul, will not suppose, however, that I gave utterance to a threat. *At length* I would be avenged; this was a point definitively settled—but the very definitiveness with which it was resolved, precluded the idea of risk. I must not only punish, but punish with impunity. A wrong is unredressed when retribution overtakes its redresser. It is equally unredressed when the avenger fails to make himself felt as such to him who has done the wrong.

It must be understood, that neither by word nor deed had I given Fortunato cause to doubt my good will. I continued, as was my wont, to smile in his face, and he did not perceive that my smile *now* was at the thought of his immolation.

He had a weak point—this Fortunato—although in other regards he was a man to be respected and even feared. He prided himself on his connoisseurship in wine. Few Italians have the true virtuoso spirit. For the most part their enthusiasm is adopted to suit the time and opportunity—to practise imposture upon the British and Austrian *millionaires*. In painting and gemmary[2] Fortunato, like his countrymen, was a quack—but in the matter of old wines he was sincere. In this respect I did not differ from him materially: I was skilful in the Italian vintages myself, and bought largely whenever I could.

It was about dusk, one evening during the supreme madness of the carnival season,[3] that I encountered my friend. He accosted me with excessive warmth, for he had been drinking much. The man wore motley. He had on a tight-fitting parti-striped dress, and his head was surmounted by the conical cap and bells. I was so pleased to see him, that I thought I should never have done wringing his hand.

I said to him—"My dear Fortunato, you are luckily met. How remarkably well you are looking to-day! But I have received a pipe of what passes for Amontillado,[4] and I have my doubts."

"How?" said he. "Amontillado? A pipe? Impossible! And in the middle of the carnival!"

"I have my doubts," I replied; "and I was silly enough to pay the full Amontillado price without consulting you in the matter. You were not to be found, and I was fearful of losing a bargain."

"Amontillado!"

"I have my doubts."

"Amontillado!"

"And I must satisfy them."

"Amontillado!"

"As you are engaged, I am on my way to Luchesi. If any one has a critical turn, it is he. He will tell me——"

"Luchesi cannot tell Amontillado from Sherry."

"And yet some fools will have it that his taste is a match for your own."

"Come, let us go."

"Whither?"

"To your vaults."

"My friend, no; I will not impose upon your good nature. I perceive you have an engagement. Luchesi——"

"I have no engagement;—come."

"My friend, no. It is not the engagement, but the severe cold with which I perceive you are afflicted. The vaults are insufferably damp. They are encrusted with nitre."[5]

"Let us go, nevertheless. The cold is merely nothing. Amontillado! You have been imposed upon. And as for Luchesi, he cannot distinguish Sherry from Amontillado."

Thus speaking, Fortunato possessed himself of my arm. Putting on a mask of black silk, and drawing a *roquelaire*[6] closely about my person, I suffered him to hurry me to my palazzo.

There were no attendants at home; they had absconded to make merry in honor of the time. I had told them that I should not return until the morning, and had given them explicit orders not to stir from the house. These orders were sufficient, I well knew, to insure their immediate disappearance, one and all, as soon as my back was turned.

I took from their sconces two flambeaux,[7] and giving one to Fortunato, bowed him through several suites of rooms to the archway that led into the vaults. I passed down a long and winding staircase, requesting him to be cautious as he followed. We came at length to the foot of the descent, and stood together on the damp ground of the catacombs of the Montresors.

The gait of my friend was unsteady, and the bells upon his cap jingled as he strode.

"The pipe," said he.

"It is farther on," said I; "but observe the white web-work which gleams from these cavern walls."

He turned towards me, and looked into my eyes with two filmy orbs that distilled the rheum of intoxication.

"Nitre?" he asked, at length.

"Nitre," I replied. "How long have you had that cough?"

"Ugh! ugh! ugh!—ugh! ugh! ugh!—ugh! ugh! ugh!—ugh! ugh! ugh!—ugh! ugh! ugh!"

My poor friend found it impossible to reply for many minutes.

"It is nothing," he said, at last.

"Come," I said, with decision, "we will go back; your health is precious. You are rich, respected, admired, beloved; you are happy, as once I was. You are a man to be missed. For me it is no matter. We will go back; you will be ill, and I cannot be responsible. Besides, there is Luchesi——"

"Enough," he said; "the cough is a mere nothing; it will not kill me. I shall not die of a cough."

"True—true," I replied; "and, indeed, I had no intention of alarming you unnecessarily—but you should use all proper caution. A draught of this Medoc will defend us from the damps."

Here I knocked off the neck of a bottle which I drew from a long row of its fellows that lay upon the mould.

"Drink," I said, presenting him the wine.

He raised it to his lips with a leer. He paused and nodded to me familiarly, while his bells jingled.

"I drink," he said, "to the buried that repose around us."

"And I to your long life."

He again took my arm, and we proceeded.

"These vaults," he said, "are extensive."

"The Montresors," I replied, "were a great and numerous family."

"I forget your arms."[8]

"A huge human foot d'or, in a field azure; the foot crushes a serpent rampant whose fangs are imbedded in the heel."

"And the motto?"

"*Nemo me impune lacessit.*"[9]

"Good!" he said.

The wine sparkled in his eyes and the bells jingled. My own fancy grew warm with the Medoc. We had passed through walls of piled bones, with casks and puncheons intermingling, into the inmost recesses of the catacombs. I paused again, and this time I made bold to seize Fortunato by an arm above the elbow.

"The nitre!" I said; "see, it increases. It hangs like moss upon the vaults. We are below the river's bed. The drops of moisture trickle among the bones. Come, we will go back ere it is too late. Your cough——"

"It is nothing," he said; "let us go on. But first, another draught of the Medoc."

I broke and reached him a flaçon of De Grâve. He emptied it at a breath. His eyes flashed with a fierce light. He laughed and threw the bottle upwards with a gesticulation I did not understand.

I looked at him in surprise. He repeated the movement—a grotesque one.

"You do not comprehend?" he said.

"Not I," I replied.

"Then you are not of the brotherhood."

"How?"

"You are not of the masons."[10]

"Yes, yes," I said, "yes, yes."

"You? Impossible! A mason?"

"A mason," I replied.

"A sign," he said.

"It is this," I answered, producing a trowel from beneath the folds of my *roquelaire*.

"You jest," he exclaimed, recoiling a few paces. "But let us proceed to the Amontillado."

"Be it so," I said, replacing the tool beneath the cloak, and again offering him my arm. He leaned upon it heavily. We continued our route in search of the Amontillado. We passed through a range of low arches, descended, passed on, and descending again, arrived at a deep crypt, in which the foulness of the air caused our flambeaux rather to glow than flame.

At the most remote end of the crypt there appeared another less spacious. Its walls had been lined with human remains, piled to the vault overhead, in the fashion of the great catacombs of Paris. Three sides of this interior crypt were still ornamented in this manner. From the fourth the bones had been thrown down, and lay promiscuously upon the earth, forming at one point a mound of some size. Within the wall thus exposed by the displacing of the bones, we perceived a still interior recess, in depth about four feet, in width three, in height six or seven. It seemed to have been constructed for no especial use within itself, but formed merely the interval between two of the colossal supports of the roof of the catacombs, and was backed by one of their circumscribing walls of solid granite.

It was in vain that Fortunato, uplifting his dull torch, endeavored to pry into the depth of the recess. Its termination the feeble light did not enable us to see.

"Proceed," I said; "herein is the Amontillado. As for Luchesi——"

"He is an ignoramus," interrupted my friend, as he stepped unsteadily forward, while I followed immediately at his heels. In an instant he had reached the extremity of the niche, and finding his progress arrested by the rock, stood stupidly bewildered. A moment more and I had fettered him to the granite. In its surface were two iron staples, distant from each other about two feet, horizontally. From one of these depended a short chain, from the other a padlock. Throwing the links about his waist, it was but the work of a few seconds to secure it. He was too much astounded to resist. Withdrawing the key I stepped back from the recess.

"Pass your hand," I said, "over the wall; you cannot help feeling the nitre. Indeed it is *very* damp. Once more let me *implore* you to return. No? Then I must positively leave you. But I must first render you all the little attentions in my power."

"The Amontillado!" ejaculated my friend, not yet recovered from his astonishment.

"True," I replied; "the Amontillado."

As I said these words I busied myself among the pile of bones of which I have before spoken. Throwing them aside, I soon uncovered a quantity of building stone and mortar. With these materials and with the aid of my trowel, I began vigorously to wall up the entrance of the niche.

I had scarcely laid the first tier of the masonry when I discovered that the intoxication of Fortunato had in a great measure worn off. The earliest indication I had of this was a low moaning cry from the depth of the recess. It was *not* the cry of a drunken man. There was then a long and obstinate silence. I laid the second tier, and the third, and the fourth; and then I heard the furious vibrations of the chain. The noise lasted for several minutes, during which, that I might hearken to it with the more satisfaction, I ceased my labors and sat down upon the bones. When at last the clanking subsided, I resumed the trowel, and finished without interruption the fifth, the sixth, and the seventh tier. The wall was now nearly upon a level with my breast. I again paused, and holding the flambeaux over the mason-work, threw a few feeble rays upon the figure within.

A succession of loud and shrill screams, bursting suddenly from the throat of the chained form, seemed to thrust me violently back. For a brief moment I hesitated—I trembled. Unsheathing my rapier, I began to grope with it about the recess: but the thought of an instant reassured me. I placed my hand upon the solid fabric of the catacombs, and felt satisfied. I reapproached the wall. I replied to the yells of him who clamored. I re-echoed—I aided—I surpassed them in volume and in strength. I did this, and the clamorer grew still.

It was now midnight, and my task was drawing to a close. I had completed the eighth, the ninth, and the tenth tier. I had finished a portion of the last and the eleventh; there remained but a single stone to be fitted and plastered in. I struggled with its weight; I placed it partially in its destined position. But now there came from out the niche a low laugh that erected the hairs upon my head. It was succeeded by a sad voice, which I had difficulty in recognising as that of the noble Fortunato. The voice said—

"Ha! ha! ha!—he! he!—a very good joke indeed—an excellent jest. We will have many a rich laugh about it at the palazzo—he! he! he!—over our wine—he! he! he!"

"The Amontillado!" I said.

"He! he! he!—he! he! he!—yes, the Amontillado. But is it not getting late? Will not they be awaiting us at the palazzo, the Lady Fortunato and the rest? Let us be gone."

'Yes," I said, "let us be gone."

"*For the love of God, Montresor!*"

"Yes," I said, "for the love of God!"

But to these words I hearkened in vain for a reply. I grew impatient. I called aloud—

"Fortunato!"

No answer. I called again—

"Fortunato!"

No answer still. I thrust a torch through the remaining aperture and let it fall within. There came forth in return only a jingling of the bells. My heart grew sick—on account of the dampness of the catacombs. I hastened to make an end of my labor. I forced the last stone into its position; I plastered it up. Against the new masonry I re-erected the old rampart of bones. For the half of a century no mortal has disturbed them. *In pace requiescat!*[11]

Hop-Frog[1]

I NEVER knew any one so keenly alive to a joke as the king was. He seemed to live only for joking. To tell a good story of the joke kind, and to tell it well, was the surest road to his favor. Thus it happened that his seven ministers were all noted for their accomplishments as jokers. They all took after the king, too, in being large, corpulent, oily men, as well as inimitable jokers. Whether people grow fat by joking, or whether there is something in fat itself which predisposes to a joke, I have never been quite able to determine; but certain it is that a lean joker is a *rara avis in terris*.[2]

About the refinements, or, as he called them, the "ghosts" of wit, the king troubled himself very little. He had an especial admiration for *breadth* in a jest, and would often put up with *length*, for the sake of it. Over-niceties wearied him. He would have preferred Rabelais's "Gargantua," to the "Zadig" of Voltaire:[3] and, upon the whole, practical jokes suited his taste far better than verbal ones.

At the date of my narrative, professing jesters had not altogether gone out of fashion at court. Several of the great continental "powers" still retained their "fools," who wore motley, with caps and bells, and who were expected to be always ready with sharp witticisms, at a moment's notice, in consideration of the crumbs that fell from the royal table.

Our king, as a matter of course, retained his "fool." The fact is, he *required* something in the way of folly—if only to counterbalance the heavy wisdom of the seven wise men who were his ministers—not to mention himself.

His fool, or professional jester, was not *only* a fool, however. His value was trebled in the eyes of the king, by the fact of his being also a dwarf and a cripple. Dwarfs were as common at court, in those days, as fools; and many monarchs would have found it difficult to get through their days (days are rather longer at court than elsewhere) without both a jester to laugh *with*, and a dwarf to laugh *at*. But, as I have already observed, your jesters, in ninety-nine cases out of a hundred, are fat, round and unwieldy—so that it was no small source of self-gratulation with our king that, in Hop-Frog (this was the fool's name,) he possessed a triplicate treasure in one person.

I believe the name "Hop-Frog" was *not* that given to the dwarf by his sponsors at baptism, but it was conferred upon him, by general consent of the seven ministers, on account of his inability to walk as other men do. In fact, Hop-Frog could only get along by a sort of interjectional gait—something between a leap and a wriggle—a movement that afforded illimitable amusement, and of course consolation, to the king, for (notwithstanding the protuberance of his stomach and a constitutional swelling of the head) the king, by his whole court, was accounted a capital figure.

But although Hop-Frog, through the distortion of his legs, could move only with great pain and difficulty along a road or floor, the prodigious muscular power which nature seemed to have bestowed upon his arms, by way of compensation for deficiency in the lower limbs, enabled him to perform many feats of wonderful dexterity, where trees or ropes were in question, or anything else to climb. At such exercises he certainly much more resembled a squirrel, or a small monkey, than a frog.

I am not able to say, with precision, from what country Hop-Frog originally came. It was from some barbarous region, however, that no person ever heard of—a vast distance from the court of our king. Hop-Frog, and a young girl very little less dwarfish than himself (although of exquisite proportions, and a marvellous dancer,) had been forcibly carried off from their respective homes in adjoining provinces, and sent as presents to the king, by one of his ever-victorious generals.

Under these circumstances, it is not to be wondered at that a close intimacy arose between the two little captives. Indeed, they soon became sworn friends. Hop-Frog, who, although he made a great deal of sport, was by no means popular, had it not in his power to render Trippetta many services; but *she*, on account of her grace and exquisite beauty (although a dwarf,) was universally admired and petted: so she possessed much influence; and never failed to use it, whenever she could, for the benefit of Hop-Frog.

On some grand state occasion—I forget what—the king determined to have a masquerade; and whenever a masquerade, or anything of that kind, occurred at our court, then the talents both of Hop-Frog and Trippetta were sure to be called in play. Hop-Frog, in especial, was so inventive in the way of getting up pageants, suggesting novel characters, and arranging costume, for masked balls, that nothing could be done, it seems, without his assistance.

The night appointed for the *fête* had arrived. A gorgeous hall had been fitted up, under Trippetta's eye, with every kind of device which could possibly give *éclat* to a masquerade. The whole court was in a fever of expectation. As for costumes and characters, it might well be supposed that everybody had come to a decision on such points. Many had made up their minds (as to what *rôles* they should assume) a week, or even a month, in advance; and, in fact, there was not a particle of indecision anywhere—except in the case of the king and his seven ministers. Why *they* hesitated I never could tell, unless they did it by way of a joke. More probably, they found it difficult, on account of being so fat, to make up their minds. At all events, time flew; and, as a last resource, they sent for Trippetta and Hop-Frog.

When the two little friends obeyed the summons of the king, they found him sitting at his wine with the seven members of his cabinet council; but the monarch appeared to be in a very ill humor. He knew that Hop-Frog was not fond of wine; for it excited the poor cripple almost to madness; and madness is no comfortable feeling. But the king loved his practical jokes, and took pleasure in forcing Hop-Frog to drink and (as the king called it) "to be merry."

"Come here, Hop-Frog," said he, as the jester and his friend entered the room: "swallow this bumper to the health of your absent friends [here Hop-Frog sighed,] and then let us have the benefit of your invention. We want characters—*characters*, man—something novel—out of the way. We are wearied with this everlasting sameness. Come, drink! the wine will brighten your wits."

Hop-Frog endeavored, as usual, to get up a jest in reply to these advances from the king; but the effort was too much. It happened to be the poor dwarf's birthday, and the command to drink to his "absent friends" forced the tears to his eyes. Many large, bitter drops fell into the goblet as he took it, humbly, from the hand of the tyrant.

"Ah! ha! ha! ha!" roared the latter, as the dwarf reluctantly drained the beaker. "See what a glass of good wine can do! Why, your eyes are shining already!"

Poor fellow! his large eyes *gleamed*, rather than shone; for the effect of wine on his excitable brain was not more powerful than instantaneous. He placed the goblet nervously on the table, and looked round upon the company with a half-insane stare. They all seemed highly amused at the success of the king's "*joke*."

"And now to business," said the prime minister, a *very* fat man.

"Yes," said the king; "come, Hop-Frog, lend us your assistance. Characters, my fine fellow; we stand in need of characters—all of us—ha! ha! ha!" and as this was seriously meant for a joke, his laugh was chorused by the seven.

Hop-Frog also laughed, although feebly and somewhat vacantly.

"Come, come," said the king, impatiently, "have you nothing to suggest?"

"I am endeavoring to think of something *novel*," replied the dwarf, abstractedly, for he was quite bewildered by the wine.

"Endeavoring!" cried the tyrant, fiercely; "what do you mean by *that*? Ah, I perceive. You are sulky, and want more wine. Here, drink this!" and he poured out another goblet full and offered it to the cripple, who merely gazed at it, gasping for breath.

"Drink, I say!" shouted the monster, "or by the fiends—"

The dwarf hesitated. The king grew purple with rage. The courtiers smirked. Trippetta, pale as a corpse, advanced to the monarch's seat, and, falling on her knees before him, implored him to spare her friend.

The tyrant regarded her, for some moments, in evident wonder at her audacity. He seemed quite at a loss what to do or say—how most becomingly to express his indignation. At last, without uttering a syllable, he pushed her violently from him, and threw the contents of the brimming goblet in her face.

The poor girl got up as best she could, and, not daring even to sigh, resumed her position at the foot of the table.

There was a dead silence for about a half a minute, during which the falling of a leaf, or of a feather, might have been heard. It was interrupted by a low, but harsh and protracted *grating* sound which seemed to come at once from every corner of the room.

"What—what—*what* are you making that noise for?" demanded the king, turning furiously to the dwarf.

The latter seemed to have recovered, in great measure, from his intoxication, and looking fixedly but quietly into the tyrant's face, merely ejaculated:

"I—I? How could it have been me?"

"The sound appeared to come from without," observed one of the courtiers. "I fancy it was the parrot at the window, whetting his bill upon his cage-wires."

"True," replied the monarch, as if much relieved by the suggestion; "but, on the honor of a knight, I could have sworn that it was the gritting of this vagabond's teeth."

Hereupon the dwarf laughed (the king was too confirmed a joker to object to any one's laughing), and displayed a set of large, powerful, and very repulsive teeth. Moreover, he avowed his perfect willingness to swallow as much wine as desired. The monarch was pacified; and having drained another bumper with no very perceptible ill effect, Hop-Frog entered at once, and with spirit, into the plans for the masquerade.

"I cannot tell what was the association of idea," observed he, very tranquilly, and as if he had never tasted wine in his life, "but *just after* your majesty had struck the girl and thrown the wine in her face—*just after* your majesty had done this, and while the parrot was making that odd noise outside the window, there came into my mind a capital diversion—one of my own country frolics—often enacted among us, at our masquerades: but here it will be new altogether. Unfortunately, however, it requires a company of eight persons, and—"

"Here we *are*!" cried the king, laughing at his acute discovery of the coincidence; "eight to a fraction—I and my seven ministers. Come! what is the diversion?"

"We call it," replied the cripple, "the Eight Chained Ourang-Outangs, and it really is excellent sport if well enacted."

"*We* will enact it," remarked the king, drawing himself up, and lowering his eyelids.

"The beauty of the game," continued Hop-Frog, "lies in the fright it occasions among the women."

"Capital!" roared in chorus the monarch and his ministry.

"*I* will equip you as ourang-outangs," proceeded the dwarf; "leave all that to me. The resemblance shall be so striking, that the company of masqueraders will take you for real beasts—and of course, they will be as much terrified as astonished."

"O, this is exquisite!" exclaimed the king. "Hop-Frog! I will make a man of you."

"The chains are for the purpose of increasing the confusion by their jangling. You are supposed to have escaped, *en masse*, from your keepers. Your majesty cannot conceive the *effect* produced, at a masquerade, by eight chained ourang-outangs, imagined to be real ones by most of the company; and rushing in with savage cries, among the crowd of delicately and gorgeously habited men and women. The *contrast* is inimitable."

"It *must* be," said the king: and the council arose hurriedly (as it was growing late), to put in execution the scheme of Hop-Frog.

His mode of equipping the party as ourang-outangs was very simple, but effective enough for his purposes. The animals in question had, at the epoch of my story, very rarely been seen in any part of the civilized world; and as the imitations made by the dwarf were sufficiently beast-like and more than sufficiently hideous, their truthfulness to nature was thus thought to be secured.

The king and his ministers were first encased in tight-fitting stockinet shirts and drawers. They were then saturated with tar. At this stage of the process, some one of the party suggested feathers; but the suggestion was at once overruled by the dwarf, who soon convinced the eight, by ocular demonstration, that the hair of such a brute as the ourang outang was much more efficiently represented by *flax*. A thick coating of the latter was accordingly plastered upon the coating of tar. A long chain was now procured. First, it was passed about the waist of the king, *and tied*; then about another of the party, and also tied; then about all successively, in the same manner. When this chaining arrangement was complete, and the party stood as far apart from each other as possible, they formed a circle; and to make all things appear natural, Hop-Frog passed the residue of the chain, in two diameters, at right angles, across the circle, after the fashion adopted, at the present day, by those who capture Chimpanzees, or other large apes, in Borneo.

The grand saloon in which the masquerade was to take place, was a circular room, very lofty, and receiving the light of the sun only through a single window at top. At night (the season for which the apartment was especially designed,) it was illuminated principally by a large chandelier, depending by a chain from the centre of the sky-light, and lowered, or elevated, by means of a counter-balance as usual; but (in order not to look unsightly) this latter passed outside the cupola and over the roof.

The arrangements of the room had been left to Trippetta's superintendance; but, in some particulars, it seems, she had been guided by the calmer judgment of her friend the dwarf. At his suggestion it was that, on this occasion, the chandelier was removed. Its waxen drippings (which, in weather so warm, it was quite impossible to prevent,) would have been seriously detrimental to the rich dresses of the guests, who, on account of the crowded state of the saloon, could not *all* be expected to keep from out its centre—that is to say, from under the chandelier. Additional sconces were set in various parts of the hall, out of the way; and a flambeau, emitting sweet odor, was placed in the right hand of each of the Caryatides[4] that stood against the wall—some fifty or sixty altogether.

The eight ourang-outangs, taking Hop-Frog's advice, waited patiently until midnight (when the room was thoroughly filled with masqueraders) before making their appearance. No sooner had the clock ceased striking, however, than they rushed, or rather rolled in, all together—for the impediment of their chains caused most of the party to fall, and all to stumble as they entered.

The excitement among the masqueraders was prodigious, and filled the heart of the king with glee. As had been anticipated, there were not a few of the guests who supposed the ferocious-looking creatures to be beasts of *some* kind in reality, if not precisely ourang-outangs. Many of the women swooned with affright; and had not the king taken the precaution to exclude all weapons from the saloon, his party might soon have expiated their frolic in their blood. As it was, a general rush was made for the doors; but the king had ordered them to be locked immediately upon his entrance; and, at the dwarf's suggestion, the keys had been deposited with *him*.

While the tumult was at its height, and each masquerader attentive only to his own safety—(for, in fact, there was much *real* danger from the pressure of the excited crowd,)—the chain by which the chandelier ordinarily hung, and which had been drawn up on its removal, might have been seen very gradually to descend, until its hooked extremity came within three feet of the floor.

Soon after this, the king and his seven friends, having reeled about the hall in all directions, found themselves, at length, in its centre, and, of course, in immediate contact with the chain. While they were thus situated, the dwarf, who had followed closely at their heels, inciting them to keep up the commotion, took hold of their own chain at the intersection of the two portions which crossed the circle diametrically and at right angles. Here, with the rapidity of thought, he inserted the hook from which the chandelier had been wont to depend; and, in an instant, by some unseen agency, the chandelier-chain was drawn so far upward as to take the hook out of reach, and, as an inevitable consequence, to drag the ourang-outangs together in close connection, and face to face.

The masqueraders, by this time, had recovered, in some measure, from their alarm; and, beginning to regard the whole matter as a well-contrived pleasantry, set up a loud shout of laughter at the predicament of the apes.

"Leave them to *me!*" now screamed Hop-Frog, his shrill voice making itself easily heard through all the din. "Leave them to *me*. I fancy *I* know them. If I can only get a good look at them, *I* can soon tell who they are."

Here, scrambling over the heads of the crowd, he managed to get to the wall; when, seizing a flambeau from one of the Caryatides, he returned, as he went, to the centre of the room—leaped, with the agility of a monkey, upon the king's head—and thence clambered a few feet up the chain—holding down the torch to examine the group of ourang-outangs, and still screaming, "*I* shall soon find out who they are!"

And now, while the whole assembly (the apes included) were convulsed with laughter, the jester suddenly uttered a shrill whistle; when the chain flew violently up for about thirty feet—dragging with it the dismayed and struggling ourang-outangs, and leaving them suspended in mid-air between the sky-light and the floor. Hop-Frog, clinging to the chain as it rose, still maintained his relative position in respect to the eight maskers, and still (as if nothing were the matter) continued to thrust his torch down towards them, as though endeavoring to discover who they were.

So thoroughly astonished were the whole company at this ascent, that a dead silence, of about a minute's duration, ensued. It was broken by just such a low, harsh, *grating* sound, as had before attracted the attention of the king and his councillors, when the former threw the wine in the face of Trippetta. But, on the present occasion, there could be no question as to *whence* the sound issued. It came from the fang-like teeth of the dwarf, who ground them and gnashed them as he foamed at the mouth, and glared, with an expression of maniacal rage, into the upturned countenances of the king and his seven companions.

"Ah, ha!" said at length the infuriated jester. "Ah, ha! I begin to see who these people *are*, now!" Here, pretending to scrutinize the king more closely, he held the flambeau to the flaxen coat which enveloped him, and which instantly burst into a sheet of vivid flame. In less than half a minute the whole eight ourang-outangs were blazing fiercely, amid the shrieks of the multitude who gazed at them from below, horror-stricken, and without the power to render them the slightest assistance.

At length the flames, suddenly increasing in virulence, forced the jester to climb higher up the chain, to be out of their reach; and, as he made this movement, the crowd again sank, for a brief instant, into silence. The dwarf seized his opportunity, and once more spoke:

"I now see *distinctly*," he said, "what manner of people these maskers are. They are a great king and his seven privy-councillors—a king who does not scruple to strike a defenceless girl, and his seven councillors who abet him in the outrage. As for myself, I am simply Hop-Frog, the jester—and *this is my last jest.*"

Owing to the high combustibility of both the flax and the tar to which it adhered, the dwarf had scarcely made an end of his brief speech before the work of vengeance was complete. The eight corpses swung in their chains, a fetid, blackened, hideous, and indistinguishable mass. The cripple hurled his torch at them, clambered leisurely to the ceiling, and disappeared through the sky-light.

It is supposed that Trippetta, stationed on the roof of the saloon, had been the accomplice of her friend in his fiery revenge, and that, together, they effected their escape to their own country: for neither was seen again.

NOTES

1. For a discussion of Poe's experience with prize contests, see Leon Jackson, *The Business of Letters: Authorial Economies in Antebellum America* (Stanford, CA: Stanford University Press, 2008).

2. Hawthorne to Poe, Salem, MA, June 17, 1846, eapoe.org, https://www.eapoe.org/misc/letters/t4606170.htm.

3. The best analysis of Poe's style on the sentence level is Brent Zimmerman, *Edgar Allan Poe: Rhetoric and Style* (Montreal: McGill-Queen's University Press, 2005).

4. G. R. Thompson, *Poe's Fiction: Romantic Irony in the Gothic Tales* (Madison: University of Wisconsin Press, 1973).

5. Scott Peeples, "Poe's 'constructiveness' and 'The Fall of the House of Usher,'" *The Cambridge Companion to Edgar Allan Poe*, ed. Kevin J. Hayes (Cambridge: Cambridge University Press, 2002), 178–90.

6. Poe claimed that the hoax "made a far more intense sensation than anything of that character since the 'Moon-Story' of Locke" and that the New York *Sun* offices were "literally besieged, blocked up" due to demand for the paper. "Doings of Gotham," *Columbia Spy*, May 25, 1844.

7. Stefan Andriopoulos, "Arrested in the Moment of Dying: Science, Fiction, and the Reality Effect of Reprinting," *American Literature* 90, no. 3 (2018): 523–51.

8. Poe to Arch Ramsay, New York, December 30, 1846, in *The Collected Letters of Edgar Allan Poe*, eds. John Ward Ostrom, Burton R. Pollin, and Jeffrey A. Savoye (New York: Gordian Press, 2008), 1:610.

9. Carl Ostrowski, "'This Hideous Drama of Revivification': Poe's Fiction and Reprint Culture," *Modern Language Studies* 40, no. 1 (2010): 10–37.

10. Nina Baym, *Novels, Readers, and Reviewers: Responses to Fiction in Antebellum America* (New York: Cornell University Press, 1984).

11. Carl Ostrowski, *Literature and Criminal Justice in Antebellum America* (Amherst: University of Massachusetts Press, 2016).

12. Significant debate surrounds the "Paulding-Drayton review," which appeared in the *Southern Literary Messenger* during Poe's association with the magazine, but I find Joseph V. Ridgely's conclusion that Poe did not write the review convincing. See Ridgely, "The Authorship of the Paulding-Drayton Review," *PSA Newsletter* 20, no. 2 (1992): 1–3, 6. A recent article lends support to this conclusion by way of computer-aided linguistic analysis: Stephen Schöberlein, "Poe or not Poe? A Stylometric Analysis of Edgar Allan Poe's Disputed Writings," *Digital Scholarship in the Humanities* 32, no. 3 (2017): 43–59.

13. Thomas Jefferson, *Notes on the State of Virginia* (London: John Stockdale, 1787), 230.

14. The influential essay that reread slavery back into Poe's Gothic fiction is Joan Dayan, "Amorous Bondage: Poe, Ladies, and Slaves," *American Literature* 66, no. 2 (1994): 239–73.

15. For an overview of the historical literature on separate spheres ideology, as well as a nuanced challenge to simplistic dichotomies of gendered literary spheres in the nineteenth century, see Monika M. Elbert, ed., *Separate Spheres No More: Gender Convergence in American Literature 1830–1930* (Tuscaloosa: University of Alabama Press, 2000).

16. Edgar Allan Poe, "The Literati of New York City—No. IV," *Godey's Magazine and Lady's Book*, August 1846, 72–5.

17. For analysis of the temperance movement's impact on American literature, see David S. Reynolds and Debra J. Rosenthal, eds., *The Serpent in the Cup: Temperance in American Literature* (Amherst: University of Massachusetts Press, 1997).

18. David J. Rothman, *The Discovery of the Asylum: Social Order and Disorder in the New Republic* (rev. ed. Boston: Little, Brown and Company, 1991).

19. John Cleman, "Irresistible Impulses: Edgar Allan Poe and the Insanity Defense," *American Literature* 63, no. 4 (1991): 623–40.

20. Paul Gilmore, "Poe and the Sciences of the Brain," in *The Oxford Handbook of Edgar Allan Poe*, eds. J. Gerald Kennedy and Scott Peeples (New York: Oxford University Press, 2019), 752–72.

21. Jonathan A. Cook, "Poe and the Apocalyptic Sublime: 'The Masque of the Red Death,'" *Religion and the Arts* 23 (2019): 492

22. Rachel Aviv, "What Does It Mean to Die?" *New Yorker*, February 5, 2018.

Ms Found in a Bottle

1. This story first appeared in the Baltimore *Sunday Visiter* of October 19, 1833, a winning entry in the newspaper's literary contest. The source of the present text is Poe's republication of the tale in the *Broadway Journal*, October 11, 1845.

2. **Qui n'a plus . . .** He who has but a moment to live has nothing more to hide. From the play *Atys*, by French dramatist Philippe Quinault (1635–88).

3. **Pyrrhonism** Skepticism.

4. **ignes fatui** I.e., ignis fatuus: a phosphorescent light that hovers over swampy ground at night; anything deceptive or misleading.

5. **jaggeree** I.e., jaggery: a type of cane sugar originating from South Asia (later to be a source of sustenance for the narrator). **Coir** is a fiber derived from coconuts and **ghee** is a kind of butter made in India.

6. **Simoom** A desert wind (Used here loosely to mean a gale).

7. **Sybils** Prophetesses.

Berenice

1. "Berenice" first appeared in the *Southern Literary Messenger* in March 1835. The present text is from Poe's republication of the tale in the *Broadway Journal*, April 4, 1845. Four paragraphs included in the original text but deleted from the *Broadway Journal* publication are included in note #6 below. Poe told Thomas W. White, his editor at the *Southern Literary Messenger*, that the tale originated in a bet that he could not produce an effective tale on a subject "so singular" (see the letter in Part V of this volume). Scholars believe that the subject in question (which Poe does not otherwise specify) is the robbing of graves as a source of teeth for dentists.

2. **Dicebant mihi sodales . . .** My companions told me I might find some little alleviation of my misery, in visiting the grave of my beloved. Poe scholars identify the reference as Ben Zaïat, ancient poet of Baghdad, who died in the second century CE.

3. **Cœlius Secundus Curio . . .** The sixteenth-century Italian Caelius Secundus Curio (1503–69) argued that more souls go to heaven than to hell. Tertullian (*c.* 155–*c.* 240 CE) was an ancient theologian. His quote may be translated, "That the Son of God died is entirely believable simply because it is absurd; that He rose from the dead is certain because it is impossible." St. Austin is St. Augustine (Augustine of Hippo, 354–430 CE).

4. **Halcyon** For as Jove, during the winter season, gives twice seven days of warmth, men have called this clement and temperate time the nurse of the beautiful Halcyon.— *Simonides.* (Poe's note.) Simonides (*c.* 566–468 BCE) was a Greek lyric poet.

5. **idées** Marie Sallé (1707–56) was a ballerina of whom it was said, "her every step was a sentiment." Egæus alters the quotation to "all her teeth were ideas."

6. **completed** The following four paragraphs were included at this point in the first printing of the story, in the *Southern Literary Messenger* in March 1835.

> With a heart full of grief, yet reluctantly, and oppressed with awe, I made my way to the bed-chamber of the departed. The room was large, and very dark, and at every step within its gloomy precincts I encountered the paraphernalia of the grave. The coffin, so a menial told me, lay surrounded by the curtains of yonder bed, and in that coffin, he whisperingly assured me, was all that remained of Berenice. Who was it asked me would I not look upon the corpse? I had seen the lips of no one move, yet the question had been demanded, and the echo of the syllables still lingered in the room. It was impossible to refuse; and with a sense of suffocation I dragged myself to the side of the bed. Gently I uplifted the sable draperies of the curtains.
>
> As I let them fall they descended upon my shoulders, and shutting me thus out from the living, enclosed me in the strictest communion with the deceased.
>
> The very atmosphere was redolent of death. The peculiar smell of the coffin sickened me; and I fancied a deleterious odor was already exhaling from the body. I would have given worlds to escape—to fly from the pernicious influence of mortality—to breathe once again the pure air of the eternal heavens. But I had no longer the power to move—my knees tottered beneath me—and I remained rooted to the spot, and gazing upon the frightful length of the rigid body as it lay outstretched in the dark coffin without a lid.
>
> God of heaven!—is it possible? Is it my brain that reels—or was it indeed the finger of the enshrouded dead that stirred in the white cerement that bound it? Frozen with unutterable awe I slowly raised my eyes to the countenance of the corpse. There had been a band around the jaws, but, I know not how, it was broken asunder. The livid lips were wreathed into a species of smile, and, through the enveloping gloom, once again there glared upon me in too palpable reality, the white and glistening, and ghastly teeth of Berenice. I sprang convulsively from the bed, and, uttering no word, rushed forth a maniac from that apartment of triple horror, and mystery, and death.

Morella

1. "Morella" first appeared in the *Southern Literary Messenger* of April 1835. Poe republished the story in the *Broadway Journal* on June 21, 1845, the source of the present text.

2. *Sympos* Plato's *Symposium.*

3. **Ge-Henna** Gehenna means "hell." In the Bible, the Valley of Hinnon (or Hinnom) acquired this name due to the sacrifice of the children of the valley to the idol Moloch by apostate Israelites.

4. **Morella** The Greek word means "reincarnation." Poe refers to German philosophers Johann Gottlieb Ficthe (1762–1814) and Friedrich Wilhelm Joseph von Schelling (1775–1854).

5. **Pæstum** The rose gardens of the ancient city of Paestum reputedly bloomed twice a year. The Teian is Greek poet Anacreon of Teos (*c. 582–c.* 485 BCE).

6. **lustra** A lustrum equals five years.

Ligeia

1. "Ligeia" first appeared in the Baltimore *American Museum* of September 1838. Poe republished the tale in the *Broadway Journal*, the source of the present text, on September 27, 1845. In the intervening years, Poe had interpolated the poem "The Conqueror Worm." The classic study identifying two divergent ways of interpreting the story is Roy P. Basler, "The Interpretation of 'Ligeia,'" *College English* 5 (1944): 363–72.

2. **Glanvill** Joseph Glanvill (1636–80) was an English philosopher. Poe scholars have not located this epigraph among Glanvill's writings.

3. **Ashtophet** Phoenician fertility goddess.

4. **Nourjahad** Poe refers to a fictional "tribe" in an eighteenth-century novel, *The History of Nourjahad* by Frances Sheridan (1724–66), in which female slaves possess exquisitely beautiful eyes.

5. **Turk** In Islamic mythology, **houri** are maidens waiting on men in Heaven.

6. **Democritus** The Greek philosopher Democritus (*c.* 460–*c.* 370 BCE) reputedly asserted that truth lies in the depths, or at the bottom of a well.

7. **Azrael** Angel of death.

8. **Saracenic** By using the adjective "Saracenic," referring to Islamic armies during the Crusades, Poe suggests that the censer is decorated with geometric patterns as found in Islamic art.

How to Write a Blackwood Article

1. This story first appeared in the Baltimore *American Museum* of November 1838 under the title "The Psyche Zenobia." The present text is from Poe's republication of the story in the *Broadway Journal*, July 12, 1845, by which point Poe had divided it into two separate parts, "How to Write a Blackwood Article" and "The Predicament."

2. *auriculas* Flowers; **agraffas** are "ornamental clasps" (according to Poe editor G. R. Thompson); and a **mantelet** is a shawl or cloak.

3. **society** British aristocrat Lord Brougham founded the Society for the Diffusion of Useful Knowledge in 1828.

4. **sensations** Titles in this paragraph were published in various issues of *Blackwood's Magazine*.

5. **Brandreth's pills** A laxative.

6. *Naturwissenschaft* The titles are *Critique of Pure Reason* and *Metaphysical Foundations of Natural Science* by German philosopher Immanuel Kant (1724–1804). The numerous allusions in the rest of the story constitute Poe's satire of faux erudition in the period's magazines and will not be individually noted.

7. **Channing's** In this paragraph, Poe satirizes the American Transcendentalists. Channing is the poet William Ellery Channing (1780–1842); *The Dial* was a Transcendentalist monthly magazine.

The Predicament

1. "The Predicament" was not a separate story when Poe initially published "The Psyche Zenobia" in the Baltimore *American Museum* of November 1838.

2. **COMUS** John Milton, *Comus* (1634).

The Man That Was Used Up

1. This story first appeared in *Burton's Gentleman's Magazine* in August 1839. Poe republished the story in the *Broadway Journal*, August 9, 1845, the source of the present text. A number of figures who established political reputations during the Indian Wars of the early nineteenth century have been suggested as models for General John A. B. C. Smith, including Richard M. Johnson and Andrew Jackson.

2. **CORNEILLE** Cry, cry, my eyes, and dissolve yourselves with tears! / The one half of my life has sent the other half to the grave. From French playwright Pierre Corneille's *Le Cid* (1637).

3. **Indians** The Kickapoo tribe occupied an area near the Great Lakes before removing to the West in the first half of the nineteenth century. A **bugaboo** is an imaginary object of fear and alarm.

4. *fuit* "In which he bore a large part" (Latin), from the *Aeneid*, by ancient Roman poet Virgil (70–19 BCE). **Horresco referens** (next paragraph): "I shudder at the memory," from the same source.

5. **yesterday** *Othello*, 3.3.330–3.

6. *used up* To be "used up" in the slang of the period meant to be to be thoroughly discredited in print, as in a negative review of a book or performance.

The Fall of the House of Usher

1. Poe first published "The Fall of the House of Usher" in *Burton's Gentleman's Magazine*, September 1839. "The Haunted Palace" was published on its own in April of the same year and then inserted into later printings of the story. The present text is from Poe's *Tales* (New York: Wiley and Putnam, 1845).

2. **De Béranger** "His heart is a lute suspended; as soon as it is touched, it responds." Adapted from "La Refus" by French poet Pierre-Jean de Béranger (1780–1857).

3. **Fuseli** Poe references German composer Carl Maria, Baron von Weber (1786–1826) and Swiss painter Henry Fuseli (1741–1825).

4. **Porphyrogene** Purple, a color befitting royalty.

5. **men** Watson, Dr. Percival, Spallanzani, and especially the Bishop of Landaff —see "Chemical Essays," vol v (Poe's note). Watson is Richard Watson (1737–1816), Bishop of Llandaff in Wales and author of *Essay on the Subjects of Chemistry*, and Spallanzani is Italian naturalist Abbé Lazzaro Spallanzani (1729–99). Poe scholars differ on the identity of Dr. Percival.

6. *Maguntinae* Usher's reading list suggests interest in spiritual and occult matters as well as fantastic journeys. All of the titles are real, though Poe scholars believe he knew of many of the books only second-hand, through encyclopedia and magazine articles.

7. **Canning** Unlike other authors/titles referenced in the story, this clichéd romance (along with the quoted passages) comes wholly from Poe's imagination.

William Wilson

1. This story's initial publication was in *The Gift*, a Christmas annual, in 1839. The present text is from Poe's republication of the story in the *Broadway Journal*, August 30, 1845. Scholars have identified a clear source in a Washington Irving sketch entitled "An Unwritten Drama of Lord Byron." Poe acknowledged the debt in a letter to Irving.

2. **PHARRONIDA** As Poe scholars have noted, lines similar to these can be attributed to English poet William Chamberlayne (1619–89), but they appear in his *Love's Victory*, not *Pharonnida*.

3. **Elah-Gabalus** Heliogabalus (or Elagabulus *c.* 203–22), a Roman emperor noted for depravity.

4. **Bransby** Poe's headmaster at the Stoke Newington School in England was named John Bransby.

5. *peine forte et dure* Strong and long-enduring pain—being pressed to death (French).

6. **lustrum** Five years.

7. *exergues* The exergue on a medal is the inscription beneath the main figure.

8. *que ce siecle de fer* "Oh, the good old days, the Iron Age." From French satirist Voltaire (1694–1778).

9. **nativity** Poe's own birthday was January 19, 1809.

10. **Herod** Cf. *Hamlet*, 3.2.16.

11. **Herodes Atticus** Greek rhetorician (101–77 CE) famed for patronage of public works.

The Man of the Crowd

1. This story first appeared in the magazine *The Casket* for December 1840. The present text is from *Tales* (1845). Scholars have identified a sketch by Charles Dickens, "The Drunkard's Death," as a source.

2. *La Bruyère* "The great misfortune, to be unable to be left alone." From *Les Caractères* by French philosopher Jean de la Bruyère (1645–96).

3. **Gorgias** Poe refers to German philosopher (and mathematician) Gottfried Wilhelm von Leibniz (1646–1716) and ancient Greek philosopher and rhetorician Gorgias (*c.* 485–*c.* 380 BCE). The Greek is from the *Illiad*, "the mist that previously was upon them."

4. **Eupatrids** The ancient nobility of the Greek region of Attica.

5. *bon ton* High style (French).

6. **Lucian** Greek rhetorician and satirist (*c.* 150–*c.* 220 BCE).

7. **Tertullian** Early Christian author; see note 3 to "Berenice," above.

8. **Retzch** German painter and engraver Friedrich August Moritz Retzsch (1779–1857).

9. *roquelaire* A cloak (French).

10. **caoutchouc** A form of rubber.

11. **Hortulus Animæ** According to Barbara Cantalupo (*Poe and the Visual Arts*, University Park, PA: Penn State University Press, 2014, 60–1), "The *Hortulus Animae* (*Little Garden of the Soul*) was a common and very popular prayer book in both its Latin and German forms in the early years of the sixteenth century."

The Murders in the Rue Morgue

1. Poe's first detective story featuring C. Auguste Dupin appeared in *Graham's Lady's and Gentleman's Magazine* in April 1841. The present text is from *Tales* (1845). Among various sources proposed, scholars agree on Voltaire's *Zadig* (1748) as an important one known to Poe.

2. **Sir Thomas Browne** English polymath (1605–82). The quotation is from his work *Hydriotaphia*.

3. *recherché* Poe here seems to mean "rare" or "highly unusual," whereas modern French-English dictionaries define it as "sought-after."

4. **Hoyle** Edmond Hoyle (1672–1769), English author of a treatise on whist.

5. **a separate organ** Phrenology was a popular nineteenth-century pseudo-science in which character traits were inferred from bumps on the skull.

6. *quondam* former (Latin).

7. **Pasquinaded** Publicly satirized or lampooned.

8. *et id genus omne* "and everything of this kind" (Latin). Prosper Jolyot de Crébillon (1674–1762), French author of the tragedy *Xerxes*.

9. **sonum** Poe scholar Thomas Olive Mabbott translates this Latin phrase as "the first letter has lost its original sound" and traces it to Roman poet Ovid (43 BCE–17 or 18 CE).

10. *metal d'Alger* Metal of Algier (French), an alloy of lead, tin, and antimony. Napoleons are gold coins.

11. **musique** "Putting on his dressing gown, the better to listen to music" (French), a quote derived from a play by Jean-Baptiste Poquelin (pen name Molière, 1622–73).

12. **Vidocq** Eugène François Vidocq (1775–1857), the father of French criminology.

13. *ménagais* "I humored him" or "I managed his whims tactfully" (French).

14. *outré* Poe uses this French word to mean "strange" or "bizarre," although modern French to English dictionaries define it as "excessive" or "extravagant."

15. **Cuvier** George Cuvier (1769–1832), French naturalist.

16. *Jardin des Plantes* This Parisian botanical garden houses a zoo.

17. *ce qui n'est pas* Rousseau—Nouvelle Heloise (Poe's note). Poe alludes to a novel by French philosopher Jean-Jacques Rousseau (1712–78). The quotation means, "to deny what is, and to explain what is not."

A Descent into the Maelström

1. This story initially appeared in *Graham's Lady's and Gentleman's Magazine* for May 1841. *Tales* (1845) is the source of the present text.

2. *Glanville* Joseph Glanvill (1636–80), English philosopher. On Democritus, see above note 6 to "Ligeia."

3. *Mare Tenebrarum* Sea of Darkness (Latin). The Nubian geographer is Al-Idrisi (1100–65).

4. **Ramus** Jonas Danilssønn Ramus (1649–1718), Norwegian priest and historian.

5. **Sexagesima Sunday** The second Sunday before the start of Lent.

6. **Phlegethon** A river of the underworld in Greek mythology.

7. **Ferroe islands** I.e., the Faroe Islands, an archipelago in the North Atlantic Ocean.

8. **Gulf of Bothnia** The northernmost arm of the Baltic Sea. Athanasius Kircher (1602–80), German Jesuit scholar.

9. **Mussulmen** A common nineteenth-century designation for Muslims.

10. **whatever** See Archimedes, "*De Incidentibus in Fluido*."—lib. 2 (Poe's note). Archimedes (*c.* 287–*c.* 212 BCE) was an ancient Greek mathematician. Kevin J. Hayes identifies the correct title of this ancient work as *De insidentibus aquae* (*The Annotated Poe*, Cambridge, MA: Belknap Press of Harvard University Press, 2015, 226).

Never Bet the Devil Your Head

1. When this story first appeared in *Graham's Lady's and Gentleman's Magazine* for September 1841, it was entitled "Never Bet Your Head." The present text is from republication in the *Broadway Journal*, August 16, 1845.

2. *obras* Poe provides the translation for this quote from an obscure Spanish author whom scholars identify as Tomás Hermenegildo de Las Torres.

3. **Batrachomyomachia** An ancient Greek comic poem. Philip **Melanchthon** (1497–1560) was a German theologian associated with the Protestant Reformation. It is not necessary to unfold all of the subsequent allusions to see Poe's commentary on the excesses of those who venture to interpret works of literature.

4. **Hop O' My Thumb** Poe mixes allusions to works by his contemporaries with nursery rhymes.

5. **stupidity** In this paragraph and the last, Poe makes fun of magazines edited by the northeastern literati with whom he had a career-long quarrel. The most notable periodicals are *The Dial*, mouthpiece of the Transcendentalist movement, and the staid *North American Review*.

6. **twelve tables** The earliest Roman code of law. The Latin precepts quoted express an injunction not to speak ill of the dead.

7. **Mr. Emerson** American Transcendentalist Ralph Waldo Emerson (1803–82). His intellectual influences included the German philosopher Immanuel Kant (1724–1804) and the British writers Thomas Carlyle (1795–1881) and Samuel Taylor Coleridge (1772–1834).

8. *Khoda shefa midêhed* A Persian saying (translated in the text) attributed to believers in Islam.

9. **pigeon-wing** To cut a pigeon wing is to jump in the air and strike one's legs together.

10. *Poets and Poetry of America* An influential (and presumably hefty) anthology edited by Rufus Griswold, notorious among Poe scholars for besmirching Poe's reputation shortly after his death. A **Paixhan** is a type of artillery shell or cannon.

11. **Mr. Lord's** American poet and clergyman William Wilberforce Lord (1819–1907).

12. **homœopathists** Homeopathy is a form of alternative medicine that involves the ingestion of very low doses of chemical compounds. It was popular in Poe's day.

13. **escutcheon** A field on which a coat of arms is displayed. The bar sinister is the heraldic mark of illegitimate birth.

The Masque of the Red Death

1. When this story first appeared in *Graham's Lady's and Gentleman's Magazine* for May 1842, the title was spelled "The Mask of the Red Death." The present text is from Poe's republication of the story in the *Broadway Journal*, July 19, 1845. An agreed-upon source, or at least inspiration, is Giovanni Boccaccio's *Decameron* (1351–53), a collection of tales whose narrators are gathered in a castle outside Florence to avoid the plague.

2. **Avator** I.e., Avatar: a Sanskrit word denoting the appearance or incarnation of a deity on earth.

3. **Prince Prospero** The name calls to mind the character of Prospero in Shakespeare's *The Tempest* (1611), who also presides over revels.

4. **Hernani** A play by French author Victor Hugo (1802–85).

5. **Herod** Cf. *Hamlet* 3.2.16.

6. **thief in the night** Cf. 1 Thessalonians 5:1-2.

The Pit and the Pendulum

1. Initial appearance was in *The Gift* (1842). The present text is from Poe's republication in the *Broadway Journal*, May 17 and 19, 1845.

2. *Paris* The Latin reads, "Here the furious mob, unappeased, long cherished hatred of innocent blood. Now that the fatherland is saved, and the cave of death destroyed, life and health appear where grim death has been." The Jacobins were radical partisans of the French Revolution.

3. **judges** The persona is tried by the Spanish Inquisition, the body entrusted with maintaining Catholic orthodoxy in Spain and its colonies and legendary for the brutality of its persecutions.

4. *autos-da-fes* Rituals of the Spanish Inquisition where heretics were found guilty and tortured.

5. **surcingle** A girdle or belt.

6. **Ultima Thule** The highest or uttermost point or degree attainable (Greek and Latin).

7. **General Lasalle** Antoine-Charles-Louis, Comte de Lasalle (1775–1809), French cavalry general under Napoleon, here entering the Spanish city of Toledo.

The Tell-Tale Heart

1. This story was first published in James Russell Lowell's short-lived magazine *The Pioneer* for January 1843. The present text is from the *Broadway Journal*, August 23, 1845. A source which Poe is known to have read, because he reviewed the volume in which it appeared, is "Confession Found in a Prison in the Time of Charles the Second," by Charles Dickens.

2. **death watches** Deathwatch beetles are wood-boring insects that make noises in old buildings.

The Gold-Bug

1. "The Gold-Bug" first appeared in Philadelphia's *Dollar Newspaper* on June 21 and 28, 1843. The present text is from *Tales* (1845).

2. *All in the Wrong* According to Hayes (*The Annotated Poe*, 266), the lines actually come from a different play by the Irish writer Arthur Murphy (1727–1805).

3. **Sullivan's Island** Poe had been stationed at Fort Moultrie on Sullivan's Island while in the army. Protestant Huguenots were driven from France in the seventeenth and eighteenth centuries.

4. **Swammerdamm** Jan Swammerdam (1637–80), Dutch naturalist.

5. *scarabœus* A genus consisting of several species of beetle.

6. *scarabœus caput hominis* Man's head beetle (Latin).

7. **executing a series of curvets and caracols** Leaping and prancing about, as would a horseman.

8. **Zaffre . . . *aqua regia*** Zaffre and aqua regia are chemical compounds.

9. **Kidd** Captain William Kidd (1645–1701), legendary Scottish sailor and reputed pirate.

10. **Golconda** I.e., Golkonda, a fort and citadel in southern India, capital of a medieval sultanate, occupying a region whose mines are famous for spectacular gems.

The Black Cat

1. This story initially appeared in the *United States Saturday Post*, August 19, 1843. The source of the present text is *Tales* (1845).

2. *barroques* Weird or bizarre incidents, or, according to Hayes (*The Annotated Poe*, 306), "baroque pearls," which had become "unfashionable in Poe's day."

3. *bas relief* Type of sculpture in which the figures project slightly from the background.

4. **Night-Mare** In folklore, a monster or evil spirit that rides on a person's chest during sleep.

The Premature Burial

1. This story initially appeared in Philadelphia's *Dollar Newspaper*, July 31, 1844. The present text is from Poe's republication of the tale in the *Broadway Journal*, June 14, 1845.

2. **Calcutta** Napoleon's army suffered catastrophic losses when crossing the **Berezina** River during his retreat from Russia in 1812; the Portuguese city of **Lisbon** suffered a devastating earthquake in 1755; London's Great **Plague** took place in 1665–6; the **St. Bartholomew Day's Massacre** was a wave of religious violence against Huguenots that killed tens of thousands in France in 1572; and the Black Hole of Calcutta was a legendarily cramped cell for British captives in 1756.

3. **asphytic condition** Lacking oxygen; suffocating.

4. **cattymount** I.e. catamount, a wild animal of the cat family, such as a cougar or lynx.

5. **Buchan** Poe scholars identify this figure as William Buchan (1729–1805), author of *Domestic Medicine; or The Family Physician*. **Night Thoughts** was a popular book of poems on mortality by Edward Young (1683–1765), an author of the so-called graveyard school.

6. **Afrasiab** Poe scholars trace the two rather obscure underworld-related allusions here (**Carathis** and Afrasiab) to the novel *Stanley* by Horace Binney Wallace (1817–52).

The Purloined Letter

1. Initial publication was in *The Gift* (1844). The present text is from *Tales* (1845).

2. **Seneca** "Nothing is more hateful to wisdom than too much cleverness." Seneca the Younger (*c.* 4 BCE–65 CE), Roman Stoic philosopher.

3. **meerschaum** A pipe for smoking.

4. **Rogêt** Poe alludes to his two previous stories featuring the detective Dupin, "The Murders in the Rue Morgue" (included in this volume) and "The Mystery of Marie Rogêt."

5. **footpads** Highwaymen or robbers who travel on foot.

6. **Procrustean bed** Procrustes was a Greek mythological figure who disfigured his victims by stretching them or cutting off their legs to fit them into an iron bed.

7. **Campanella** Italian philosopher Tommaso Campanella (1569–1639). Also mentioned are French author François de La **Rochefoucauld** (1613–80) and Niccolò **Machiavelli** (1469–1527), Italian political philosopher. Poe editor Mabbott identifies "**La Bougive**" as a printer's error for Jean de la Bruyère (1645–96), French philosopher.

8. *recherchés* Unusual; unexpected; out of the way.

9. *non distributio medii* The logical fallacy known as an undistributed middle (Latin; Dupin explains the nature of the fallacy in his dialogue).

10. *nombre* "It is safe to wager that all received wisdom is nonsense, for it has suited itself to the majority." Sébastien-Roch Nicolas (1741–94), French author.

11. *ambitus . . . religio . . . homenes honesti* In all three cases, the actual meaning of the Latin words differs significantly from what an English speaker would assume based on their sound.

12. **Bryant** Jacob Bryant (1715–1804), British mythographer.

13. *intriguant* A person who engages in political intrigue.

14. **fillagree** I.e. filigree, anything very delicate or fanciful.

15. *Averni* Facilis descensus Avenro, "the descent to Hades is easy" (Latin), from Virgil's *Aeneid*.

16. **Atrée** "Such a baleful scheme, while not worthy of Atreus, is worthy of Thyestes," from *Atrée et Thyeste* by French tragedian Prosper Jolyot de Crébillon (1674–1762).

The System of Dr. Tarr and Prof. Fether

1. This story was first published in *Graham's Magazine of Literature, Art, and Fashion* for November 1845, the source of the present text. A probable source is "The Madhouse of Palermo" by Poe's friend Nathaniel P. Willis.

2. *vielle cour* Old court (French). *Salle à manger* is dining room.

3. **Anakim** A race of giants alluded to in *Genesis* 14.5–6.

4. *nil admirari* "To be surprised by nothing" (Latin).

5. *ademptum* "A monster hideous, vast, and deprived of sight." From Virgil's *Aeneid*.

6. **rabbit** *au-chât* The dish presumably consists of rabbit cooked with cat.

7. **Lord Brougham** Henry Peter Brougham, the Lord Brougham and Vaux (1778–1868). According to Mabbott, Brougham had translated works by the ancient Greek orator Demosthenes.

8. **tee-totum** A four-sided die spun with the fingers in games of chance.

9. **Medicean Venus** A statue of a nude woman.

10. *bagatelle* A mere trifle; a trivial matter (French).

11. *in petto* In secret, in private (Italian). The **brazen bull of Phalaris** was a torture and execution device used in ancient Greece (the condemned person was locked inside and a fire lit underneath).

The Balloon-Hoax

1. Of course, this story was not identified in the title as a hoax when it first appeared in an *Extra* edition of the New York *Sun* on April 13, 1844. The present text is from *The Works of the Late Edgar Allan Poe* (New York: J. S. Redfield, 1850), the posthumous edition prepared by Rufus Griswold.

2. **Voyage** Poe added to the verisimilitude of this attempted hoax by including real-life personnel among its purported participants: William Harrison **Ainsworth** (1805–82), British novelist; Thomas Monck **Mason** (1803–89), British record-setting balloonist; Robert **Hollond** (1808–77), British balloonist; William Samuel Henson (1812–88), British (and later American) inventor and aviation engineer. Sir George **Cayley** (1773–1857), mentioned later in the story, was a pioneering British aeronautical engineer; Charles **Green** (1785–1870) was the most famous British balloonist of his generation; and the **Adelaide Gallery** (actually the National Gallery of Practical Science) was a site for the display of new inventions. Scholars have identified borrowings in the story from previously published accounts of ballooning.

3. *jeu d'esprit* Lighthearted display of wit and cleverness (French).

4. *quidnuncs* Those who seek to know all the latest news or gossip.

5. **caoutchouc** A form of rubber.

6. **Cotopaxi** An active volcano in the Andes, elevation around 19,000 feet.

7. *Omne ignotum pro magnifico* Everything unknown is taken as grand (Latin).

8. *concave Note.*—Mr. Ainsworth has not attempted to account for this phenomena, which, however, is quite susceptible of explanation. A line dropped from an elevation of 25,000 feet, perpendicularly to the surface of the earth (or sea), would form the perpendicular of a right-angled triangle, of which the base would extend from the right angle to the horizon, and the hypotenuse from the horizon to the balloon. But the 25,000 feet of altitude is little or nothing, in comparison with the extent of the prospect. In other words, the base and hypotenuse of the supposed triangle would be so long when compared with the perpendicular, that the two former may be regarded as nearly parallel. In this manner the horizon of the æronaut would appear to be *on a level* with the car. But, as the point immediately beneath him seems, and is, at a great distance below him, it seems, of course, also, at a great distance below the horizon. Hence the impression of *concavity;* and this impression must remain, until the elevation shall bear so great a proportion to the extent of prospect, that the apparent parallelism of the base and hypotenuse disappears—when the earth's real convexity must become apparent. (Poe's note.)

9. **Fort Moultrie** The fort where Poe was stationed during his time in the U.S. Army, 1827–8.

The Literary Life of Thingum Bob, Esq.

1. This satirical tale first appeared in the *Southern Literary Messenger* for December 1844. The source of the present text is the *Broadway Journal*, July 26, 1845.

2. **Mr. Emmons** Richard "Pop" Emmons (1788–1834), author of a notoriously bad epic poem called *The Fredoniad.*

3. *afflatus* Inspiration (Latin).

4. **"holy light"** Thingum Bob cribs poetry from Dante's *Inferno*, Shakespeare's *Hamlet*, Homer's *Iliad*, and John Milton's *Paradise Lost.*

5. **Nat Lee** According to Mabbott, Poe refers to English dramatist Nathaniel Lee (1653–92), who spent time in a mental institution.

6. *verbatim et literatim* Word for word and letter for letter (Latin).

7. **lustrum** A period of five years.

8. *comptant* Ready money (French).

9. *Sep.* **15—1** *t* Mabbott points out that the notation indicates the text is a paid advertisement, to be inserted one time on September 15.

10. *bijou* Jewel (French).

11. **Tongue** Henry Peter **Brougham** (1778–1868), British statesman; William **Cobbett** (1763–1835), British journalist; George Dennison **Prentice** (1802–70), Kentucky newspaper editor; and Lewis Gaylord **Clark** (1808–73), influential editor of *The Knickerbocker* magazine. **Billingsgate** is coarse or abusive language.

12. *quocunque . . . modo* Poe alludes to a quotation from the *Epistles* by ancient Roman poet Horace (65–8 BCE), meaning to make money by any means necessary.

Some Words with a Mummy

1. This story initially appeared in the *American Review* for April 1845. The source of the present text is Poe's republication in the *Broadway Journal*, November 1, 1845. The various sources or inspirations cited by scholars all have to do with Americans' interest in all things related to Egypt, evident in periodical and encyclopedia articles that Poe would have known.

2. **to-night** While it is an urban legend that mummy unwrapping parties were a fad during the Victorian era, dissection of mummies in an academic setting did occur.

3. **Mr. Gliddon** George Gliddon (1809–57), American Egyptologist. Perhaps not incidentally, Gliddon also popularized a variety of nineteenth-century race science, by which human "races" were classified according to their presumed intellectual abilities.

4. **Voltaic pile** An electrical battery.

5. **Mr. Silk Buckingham** James Silk Buckingham (1786–1855), British journalist and travel writer (who had written on his travels in the Middle East).

6. **Kabbala** I.e. cabbala: secret or esoteric knowledge.

7. **globe** Nineteenth-century race scientists debated whether mankind came from a single origin (monogenism) or that different races originated independently in different areas of the world (polygenism).

8. **phrenology . . . animal magnetism** Two influential pseudo-sciences of Poe's time. In the following paragraph, Franz Joseph **Gall** (1758–1828) and Johann **Spurzheim** (1776–1832) were proponents of phrenology; Franz **Mesmer** (1734–1815) was the discoverer of animal magnetism.

9. *de facie lunæ* **Ptolemy** was a Greco-Egyptian astronomer/scientist (*c.* 100–70). Roman historian **Plutarch** (*c.* 46–120 CE) did not write a treatise on the phases of the moon, as implied.

10. **Diodorus Siculus** Ancient Greek historian (first century BCE, precise dates unknown).

11. **Bowling-Green Fountain** Public fountain mocked for the poor taste it supposedly represented.

12. **Dial** *The Dial*, a periodical associated with the New England Transcendentalists.

13. **Solomon de Caus** French engineer Salomon de Caus (1576–1626), credited with inventing a steam-powered machine. **Hero** of Alexandria (*c.* 10–*c.* 70 CE), ancient Greek engineer also so credited.

14. **Brandreth's pills** A patent-medicine laxative.

The Imp of the Perverse

1. This piece first appeared in *Graham's Magazine of Literature, Art, and Fashion* for July 1845, the source of the present text.

2. *prima mobilia* Prime movers (Latin).

3. **phrenologists** Practitioners of the pseudo-science of phrenology divided the human character into various traits (including **amativeness** and **combativeness**, mentioned below) assigned to regions of the brain and purported to ascertain an individual's personality from charting the bumps on his/her skull corresponding with these regions. Johann **Spurzheim** (1776–1832) was an earlier proponent of phrenology.

4. *à priori* I.e. *a priori*, existing in the mind prior to and independent of experience. Contrast *a posteriori*, based upon actual evidence or observation.

The Facts in the Case of M. Valdemar

1. This story first appeared in the *American Review* for December 1845. The source of the present text is the *Broadway Journal*, December 20, 1845. The sources that have been identified reflect widespread interest in the pseudoscience of mesmerism in the 1840s.

2. *B. J.* Poe himself was editing the *Broadway Journal* when this story was reprinted and is the author of this introductory note.

3. **Mesmerism** A medical/psychological practice akin to modern hypnosis. Some practitioners claimed their subjects achieved clairvoyance in the trance state.

4. *in articulo mortis* At the point of death (Latin).

5. **"Wallenstein" and "Gargantua"** *Wallenstein* (a tragedy by German author Johann Christoph Friedrich von Schiller (1759–1805)) and *Gargantua* (a volume of *Gargantua and Pantagruel* by French author François Rabelais (c.1483–1553)) are real literary works, but Valdemar and his pseudonymous Polish translations are, or course, fictional.

6. **John Randolph** Virginia statesman John Randolph (1773–1833) was known for various eccentricities, including an unusual physique evidently the result of his having contracted tuberculosis as a youth and consequently never having gone through puberty.

7. **phthisis** Tuberculosis.

8. **ichor** Watery discharge.

The Cask of Amontillado

1. This story first appeared in *Godey's Magazine and Lady's Book* for November 1846. The present text is from Griswold's 1850 edition of *The Works of the Late Edgar Allan Poe*. An agreed-upon source is Joel Tyler Headley's "A Man Built in a Wall," published in the *Columbian Magazine* in 1844.

2. **gemmary** Expertise with respect to fine gems.

3. **carnival season** A period of festivities in Europe preceding the Catholic observance of Lent.

4. **Amontillado** A particular variety of sherry, a type of wine.

5. **nitre** A naturally occurring chemical compound, potassium nitrate, also called saltpeter.

6. *roquelaire* A man's knee-length cloak.

7. **flambeaux** Plural of "flambeau," a lighted torch.

8. **arms** Coat of arms, the heraldic symbol of a noble family. In Montresor's description of the coat of arms, **d'or** means "gold." The **rampant** serpent rises to strike.

9. **Nemo me impune lacessit** No one insults me with impunity (Latin), the national motto of Scotland.

10. **masons** The international fraternal Order of Freemasons, a semi-secret organization with roots in medieval craftwork. Producing a trowel, Montresor ironically implies that he is a literal mason, a builder in stone or brick.

11. *In pace requiescat* May he rest in peace (Latin).

Hop-Frog

1. This story first appeared in *The Flag of Our Union*, March 17, 1849. The present text is from Griswold's 1850 edition of *The Works of the Late Edgar Allan Poe*.

2. *rara avis in terris* Rare bird on earth (Latin).

3. **Voltaire** The satire of French Renaissance author François **Rabelais's** (*c.* 1483–1553) *Gargantua and Pantagruel* is considerably broader and grosser than the more urbane wit of *Zadig*, written by French Enlightenment author François-Maire Arouet (pen name Voltaire, 1694–1778).

4. **Caryatides** Sculpted female figures serving as architectural supports.

PART III

Poems

POE'S CAREER AS A POET

Poe's earliest ambition—superseded, if at all, later in his career only by the goal of founding a national, high quality literary magazine—was to achieve recognition as a poet. In his preface to *The Raven and Other Poems* (see Part V), Poe identified poetry as "not a purpose, but a passion," one that would have been his "field of choice" had circumstances, presumably financial in nature, permitted. But despite the ubiquity of poetic expression in the nineteenth century (poems could be found in newspapers, magazines, gift books, personal albums, commonplace books, and published volumes that were available in a range of prices and formats) and the international celebrity of poets such as Walter Scott and Lord Byron, the market afforded very few authors the luxury of making a living from their poetry. Writing poems when opportunity offered over the course of his literary career, Poe produced a small but influential body of work that includes some of the most famous English-language poems of the nineteenth century.

Poe's first three published books were all volumes of poetry. Recently estranged from foster father John Allan and living in Boston, Poe published *Tamerlane and Other Poems* there in 1827. The title page attributed authorship only to "a Bostonian"—Boston being the city of Poe's birth. In the 406-line title poem, the fourteenth-century founder of the Timurid Empire speaks in Byronic tones about the conflict between ambition and contentment. Poe brought out a second volume of poetry, *Al Aaraaf, Tamerlane and Minor Poems*, in Baltimore in 1829. "Al Aaraaf" was Poe's formulation for a concept he knew from the Qur'an, describing a place where, as he put it, "men suffer no punishment, yet do not attain that tranquil & even happiness which they suppose to be the characteristic of heavenly enjoyment."[1] (Legends, tales, and characters drawn from Middle Eastern history and culture were fashionable subjects of Anglo-American poetry in the early nineteenth century.) Foreshadowing the interest in astronomy later to be found in *Eureka*, Poe imaginatively combined this locale where the souls of angels and mortals mingle with a supernova discovered by astronomer Tycho Brahe in 1572. Notable to modern readers for including the poem later entitled "Sonnet—To Science," this 72-page volume attracted brief but complimentary public notice from novelist John Neal and magazine editor Sarah Josepha Hale.[2]

The milestone *Poems: Second Edition* (1831) included early versions of a number of Poe's most famous lyrics. The book was published in New York on the strength of a subscription list that included many of Poe's fellow cadets at West Point, to whom the volume was dedicated. Scholars have speculated that Poe's fellow cadets were disappointed by the volume, which did not include the amusing verse satires for which Poe was known among his West Point peers.[3] (By calling the volume a second edition, Poe evidently meant to suppress or ignore his 1827 *Tamerlane and Other Poems*, which had been published anonymously, as noted above.) *Poems: Second Edition* included the first published versions of "To Helen," "Israfel," "The Doomed City" (which would eventually be revised and retitled "The City in the Sea"), and "Irenë," which Poe revised and republished later as "The Sleeper." The volume also included a prefatory letter (excerpted in Part V as "Letter to B—"), a statement of the critical principles Poe would continue to elaborate for the remainder of his career. The volume received a mixed appraisal in the *New-York Mirror*—a forerunner of the similarly named periodical Poe would become associated with in the 1840s—whose reviewer admitted that the poetry "occasionally sparkles with a true poetic expression," but also reported that, at times, "a conflict of beauty and nonsense takes place, in which the latter seems to have the best of it."[4] Despite containing work of remarkable accomplishment, *Poems: Second Edition* did not materially advance Poe's literary ambitions.

Poe continued to write and publish poetry during his years editing major literary magazines. Among the poems included here, "The Haunted Palace" first appeared in the Baltimore *American Museum of Science, Literature, and the Arts* in April 1839. Poe inserted the poem into his short story "The Fall of the House of Usher" when it was published the same year in *Burton's Gentleman's Magazine*. *Graham's Magazine* saw the first publication of "The Conqueror Worm" in January 1843; the poem was added to the short story "Ligeia" two years later, upon the story's republication in *The New World*. In contrast to the indefinite suggestiveness that Poe valued in poetry, both of these poems are essentially allegories, all of whose details line up neatly and coherently once the figurative level of meaning is clear. Poe's decision to embed these poems within stories raises productive interpretive questions. For example, does the insertion of two of Poe's most comprehensible poems within two of his most evasive stories clarify—or does it complicate—the meaning of the stories in which they appear? Poe's mercenary repurposing of previously published work may simply have been an effort to widen exposure to his poetry, the art form he held in the highest esteem.

"The Raven" first appeared in New York's *Evening Mirror* in January 1845, in advance of its scheduled publication in the *American Review* magazine. A prefatory note to the *American Review* publication—which attributed the poem pseudonymously to "Quarles"—called attention to the poem's remarkable versification. Scholars have identified a similar meter in a previously published poem, Elizabeth Barrett Browning's "Lady Geraldine's Courtship" (Poe knew Barrett Browning's poetry well from having reviewed it), but Poe improved upon his model, uniting a compelling narrative with his hypnotic meter and insistent internal rhymes. The poem became an immediate sensation and was reprinted in periodicals across the nation; it was also extensively parodied.[5] These reprintings served to raise Poe's public profile substantially, but under the permissive copyright provisions of the time, they did not provide him directly with any additional income. Thanks in part to the fame generated by "The Raven," however, Poe finally landed a book of poems with a major publisher: Wiley and Putnam of New York brought out *The Raven and Other Poems* in 1845, giving Poe the opportunity to revise and consolidate his body of work while making it accessible to a wider audience than it had ever seen before.

Three of the poems included here come from the last years of Poe's career. "Ulalume" appeared in December 1847 in the *American Review*, the same magazine that had accepted "The Raven." Poe had arranged for the publication of "Annabel Lee" in *Sartain's Union Magazine*, but he died before the poem saw print. Rufus Griswold published the poem in the infamously scurrilous obituary notice he prepared for the *New-York Tribune* issue of October 9, 1849. "The Bells" appeared soon after, in November, its funereal fourth section a fitting dirge for its author's passing. "Alone" was published decades after Poe's death, after having been discovered penned into the album of a youthful acquaintance of Poe's; it is included below in accordance with its probable date of composition, as established by Poe editor Thomas Ollive Mabbott.

APPRECIATING POE'S POETRY

While many commentators have enriched our understanding of Poe's poems in the intervening years, an early, perceptive appraisal by South Carolina novelist and man of letters William Gilmore Simms offers the modern a reader a more than creditable introduction to key elements of Poe's poetry. Simms, a friend (and sometime rival) of Poe, noted in his 1846 review of *The Raven and Other Poems*, "The wild, fanciful and utterly abstract character of these poems, will prove incomprehensible to him who requires that poetry shall embody an axiom in morals, or a maxim in philosophy or society." Warning such readers away from a book sure to offend their tastes, Simms in his positive review labeled Poe "a fantastic and a mystic—a man of dreamy mood and wandering fancies" whose "scheme of a poem requires that his reader shall surrender himself to influences of pure imagination."[6]

Those who, through the years, have dismissed or downplayed the quality of Poe's poetry—including Ralph Waldo Emerson, who judged Poe to be merely a "lyrist," not a true poet—have generally done so because their theories of what a poem should be and do differ from Poe's.[7] Emerson was exactly the type of unsympathetic reader Simms worried about, whose preconceptions about poetry would make Poe's work incomprehensible. But Poe went to some length to explain his aesthetic principles in essays such as "The Philosophy of Composition" and "The Poetic Principle" (see Part V), and his practice bears out his theories. For Poe, the sound (or, as he put it, the music) of a poem was a preeminent consideration. His poems sometimes appeared in periodicals with paragraphs drawing attention to their versification, and in at least one case (the paragraph that accompanied initial publication of "The Raven") the comment was probably authored by Poe himself. Poe foregrounded not what a work of art, particularly a poem, *said*, but the *effect* it had over a reader, requiring readers of his poetry, as Simms realized, to "surrender" themselves to the poem's musical, incantatory charms. Applying the same strict standard of criticism to Poe's poetry that Poe had often applied to others in his critical writings, T. S. Eliot thought that Poe lavished inordinate attention on the sound of the poem, observing an "irresponsibility towards the meaning of words" in some of the work. Eliot believed that certain words in "The Raven," for example, "seem to be inserted either merely to fill out the line to the required measure, or for the sake of the rhyme."[8]

Whatever its drawbacks, this emphasis on sound has been one reason for Poe's enduring and widespread popularity, since non-academic readers of poetry have always recognized and valued Poe's unique sonic effects. Achieving the psychological control over the reading experience that Poe aimed for in poetry meant manipulating the reader not only through sound, but also through emotion. Poe famously (and perhaps, now, notoriously) asserted in "The Philosophy of Composition" that the death of a beautiful woman was "the most poetical" of all subjects because it combined the beautiful with the melancholy. A glance at Poe's output suggests that this after-the-fact explanation of his choice of subject matter for "The Raven" can be taken more or less at face value, since some of his best-known poems ("The Sleeper," "The Raven," "Ulalume," and "Annabel Lee") offer variations on the theme.

For some readers, Poe's emphasis on the music and mood of a poem comes with a corresponding sacrifice of attention to considerations of theme. Simms anticipated such readers when he said that those looking for an "axiom" or a moral in poetry should look elsewhere. Poe consistently spoke out against poetry that he considered overly didactic in nature, arguing that whatever message a poem had to communicate should present merely an "under current" of the work. Poe's value of suggestiveness over clarity when it comes to poetry must be borne in mind. Although annotations of various literary allusions are provided for the poems that follow, expecting an allusion to Homer (in "To Helen"), Greek myth ("Sonnet—To Science"), the Bible ("The City in the Sea"), or any other source to provide the key that unlocks a poem's true interpretation is generally to read against the spirit of Poe's work, which trades in evocative and suggestive moods (or, as Simms put it, the "mystic" and "fantastic") over definite and explicable themes. Certain details of Poe's poems defy interpretation, even if the general drift and subject matter of the poems remain clear enough.

Teachers of Poe's fiction usually, and rightly, devote a certain amount of instruction to challenging the biographical fallacy: no, Poe cannot be equated with the murderers and madmen whose first-person narration drives his fiction, and no, Poe's interest in (and command of) the Gothic does not necessarily find its origins in a uniquely disturbed psyche. If anything, the tendency to conflate Poe's speakers with the author himself is even more pronounced when it comes to the poetry, not least because there is some truth in the conceit. "Ulalume" was composed in the year following the premature death of Poe's beloved wife Virginia, and it does not seem especially naive to believe that the poem on some level constitutes Poe's working through his grief, even if the poem's origin story might also have included a commission on the part of an elocution teacher for Poe to compose a poem eligible for recitation.[9] While readers have always wanted to believe that "Annabel Lee" must be a tribute to the love between Poe and his teenage bride Virginia ("*She* was a child and *I* was a child"), such readers may be somewhat disillusioned to learn that after the poem's publication, more than one woman with whom Poe was romantically linked stepped forward to say that Poe told her the poem was written with her in mind.[10] The early poem "Alone" also speaks to the equivocal biographical element in Poe's poetry. The persona of a poem composed by a writer barely out of his teens claims to have lived through "a most stormy life," suggesting that the pose of the alienated, tortured persona present in much of Poe's work always entailed a certain amount of literary posturing; and yet, even by age twenty, Poe had perhaps suffered enough losses and travails (the early death of his mother; his troubled relationship with foster father John Allan; his truncated engagement to Elmira Royster; his premature departure from the University of Virginia) to give the persona's torment an authenticity grounded in the poet's own suffering.

American poets have struggled to assess Poe's poetic legacy (French poets have embraced Poe's influence with much less ambivalence).[11] Poe's near-contemporary Walt Whitman (Poe was ten years older; the two once met in the offices of the *Broadway Journal*, to which Whitman had contributed an essay)[12] thought that Poe's verses "probably belong among the electric lights of imaginative literature, brilliant and dazzling, but with no heat."[13] Whitman meant that while Poe's versification demonstrated spectacular technical proficiency, the poems failed to depict the warmth of a recognizable human character that Whitman had tried to capture in his own work. Yet Whitman also paid subtle tribute to Poe by echoing the refrain of "The Raven" in certain lines of his poem "Out of the Cradle Endlessly Rocking," which also happens to feature the speech of a bird. In his essay on Poe in the collection *In the American Grain*, William Carlos Williams credited Poe with possessing vigor and originality that were indispensable in establishing a national literary tradition distinct from that of Europe. Yet Williams dismissively claimed that there were only five—"possibly three"—worthwhile poems in Poe's entire body of work.[14] The influential Southern Agrarian poet and critic Allen Tate wrote two essays reassessing Poe's legacy, yet in both of them he focused almost exclusively on the prose. Tate denigrated Poe's sonic techniques in the poetry, saying that "his verse rhythms are for the metronome, not the human ear," and hesitated about whether to define Poe as a poet, preferring instead the designation "a man of letters."[15] Eliot found himself unable to pin down the question of Poe's influence: "I can name positively certain poets whose work has influenced me, I can name others whose work, I am sure, has not . . . but about Poe I shall never be sure."[16] Eliot's conception of his precursor poet as a ghostly presence, whose influence over the scene of composition can be neither asserted nor dismissed with certainty, seems fitting tribute to the designedly evasive, unworldly spirit of the poems included here.

Tate and Eliot were influential critics as well as poets, and the tone of certain of their comments reflects long-standing skepticism in the academy about the seriousness and artistic value of Poe's poetry. But academic opinion of Poe's poetry is trending upward, thanks to Jerome McGann's complex reassessment in *The Poet Edgar Allan Poe: Alien Angel* (2014). McGann reads Poe's poems as radical experimentations with language, consistent with the ideas put forth in Poe's critical writings: "All of Poe's significant poetry is a performative demonstration of his theoretical ideas."[17] McGann's bracing conception of a proto-modernist Poe, whose poetry rejects the consolations of his culture and of the Western poetic tradition, has recently been taken up and extended by John Michael, in *Secular Lyric: The Modernization of the Poem in Poe, Whitman, and Dickinson* (2018).[18] The poems by Poe on which these academic reassessments hinge, as well as those most cherished by non-academic lovers of poetry, are included among the selections below.

SONNET—TO SCIENCE[1]

SCIENCE! true daughter of Old Time thou art!
 Who alterest all things with thy peering eyes.
Why preyest thou thus upon the poet's heart,
 Vulture, whose wings are dull realities?
How should he love thee? or how deem thee wise,
 Who wouldst not leave him in his wandering
To seek for treasure in the jewelled skies,
 Albeit he soared with an undaunted wing?
Hast thou not dragged Diana[2] from her car?
 And driven the Hamadryad[3] from the wood
To seek a shelter in some happier star?
 Hast thou not torn the Naiad[4] from her flood,
The Elfin[5] from the green grass, and from me
The summer dream beneath the tamarind tree?

ALONE[1]

From childhood's hour I have not been
As others were— I have not seen
As others saw— I could not bring
My passions from a common spring—
From the same source I have not taken
My sorrow— I could not awaken
My heart to joy at the same tone—
And all I loved— *I* lov'd alone—
Then—in my childhood—in the dawn
Of a most stormy life— was drawn
From ev'ry depth of good and ill
The mystery which binds me still—
From the torrent, or the fountain—
From the red cliff of the mountain—
From the sun that 'round me roll'd
In its autumn tint of gold—
From the lightning in the sky
As it pass'd me flying by—
From the thunder of the storm—
And the cloud that took the form
(When the rest of Heaven was blue)
Of a demon in my view—

TO HELEN[1]

HELEN, thy beauty is to me
 Like those Nicéan[2] barks of yore,
That gently, o'er a perfumed sea,

The weary, way-worn wanderer bore
To his own native shore.

On desperate seas long wont to roam,
Thy hyacinth[3] hair, thy classic face,
Thy Naiad[4] airs have brought me home
To the glory that was Greece,
And the grandeur that was Rome.

Lo! in yon brilliant window-niche
How statue-like I see thee stand,
The agate[5] lamp within thy hand!
Ah, Psyche,[6] from the regions which
Are Holy-Land!

ISRAFEL[1]

IN Heaven a spirit doth dwell
"Whose heart-strings are a lute;"
None sing so wildly well
As the angel Israfel,
And the giddy stars (so legends tell)
Ceasing their hymns, attend the spell
Of his voice, all mute.

Tottering above
In her highest noon,
The enamoured moon
Blushes with love,
While, to listen, the red levin[2]
(With the rapid Pleiads,[3] even,
Which were seven,)
Pauses in Heaven.

And they say (the starry choir
And the other listening things)
That Israfeli's fire
Is owing to that lyre
By which he sits and sings—
The trembling living wire
Of those unusual strings.

But the skies that angel trod,
Where deep thoughts are a duty—
Where Love's a grown-up God—
Where the Houri[4] glances are
Imbued with all the beauty
Which we worship in a star.

Therefore, thou art not wrong,
  Israfeli, who despisest
An unimpassioned song;
To thee the laurels[5] belong,
  Best bard, because the wisest!
Merrily live, and long!

The ecstasies above
  With thy burning measures suit—
Thy grief, thy joy, thy hate, thy love,
  With the fervour of thy lute—
  Well may the stars be mute!

Yes, Heaven is thine; but this
  Is a world of sweets and sours;
  Our flowers are merely—flowers,
And the shadow of thy perfect bliss
  Is the sunshine of ours.

If I could dwell
Where Israfel
  Hath dwelt, and he where I,
He might not sing so wildly well
  A mortal melody,
While a bolder note than this might swell
  From my lyre within the sky.

THE SLEEPER[1]

AT midnight, in the month of June,
I stand beneath the mystic moon.
An opiate vapour, dewy, dim,
Exhales from out her golden rim,
And, softly dripping, drop by drop,
Upon the quiet mountain top,
Steals drowsily and musically
Into the universal valley.
The rosemary[2] nods upon the grave;
The lily lolls upon the wave;
Wrapping the fog about its breast,
The ruin moulders into rest;
Looking like Lethe,[3] see! the lake
A conscious slumber seems to take,
And would not, for the world, awake.
All Beauty sleeps!—and lo! where lies
Irene, with her Destinies!

Oh, lady bright! can it be right—
This window open to the night?
The wanton airs, from the tree-top,
Laughingly through the lattice drop—
The bodiless airs, a wizard rout,
Flit through thy chamber in and out,
And wave the curtain canopy
So fitfully—so fearfully—
Above the closed and fringéd lid
'Neath which thy slumb'ring soul lies hid,
That, o'er the floor and down the wall,
Like ghosts the shadows rise and fall!
Oh, lady dear, hast thou no fear?
Why and what art thou dreaming here?
Sure thou art come o'er far-off seas,
A wonder to these garden trees!
Strange is thy pallor! strange thy dress!
Strange, above all, thy length of tress,
And this all solemn silentness!

The lady sleeps! Oh, may her sleep,
Which is enduring, so be deep!
Heaven have her in its sacred keep!
This chamber changed for one more holy,
This bed for one more melancholy,
I pray to God that she may lie
Forever with unopened eye,
While the pale sheeted ghosts go by!
My love, she sleeps! Oh, may her sleep,
As it is lasting, so be deep!
Soft may the worms about her creep!
Far in the forest, dim and old,
For her may some tall vault unfold—
Some vault that oft hath flung its black
And wingéd pannels fluttering back,
Triumphant, o'er the crested palls,
Of her grand family funerals—
Some sepulchre, remote, alone,
Against whose portal she hath thrown,
In childhood, many an idle stone—
Some tomb from out whose sounding door
She ne'er shall force an echo more,
Thrilling to think, poor child of sin!
It was the dead who groaned within.

THE CITY IN THE SEA[1]

Lo! Death has reared himself a throne
In a strange city lying alone
Far down within the dim West,
Where the good and the bad and the worst and the best
Have gone to their eternal rest.
There shrines and palaces and towers
(Time-eaten towers that tremble not!)
Resemble nothing that is ours.
Around, by lifting winds forgot,
Resignedly beneath the sky
The melancholy waters lie.

No rays from the holy heaven come down
On the long night-time of that town;
But light from out the lurid sea
Streams up the turrets silently—
Gleams up the pinnacles far and free—
Up domes—up spires—up kingly halls—
Up fanes—up Babylon-like[2] walls—
Up shadowy long-forgotten bowers
Of sculptured ivy and stone flowers—
Up many and many a marvellous shrine
Whose wreathéd friezes intertwine
The viol, the violet, and the vine.

Resignedly beneath the sky
The melancholy waters lie.
So blend the turrets and shadows there
That all seem pendulous in air,
While from a proud tower in the town
Death looks gigantically down.

There open fanes[3] and gaping graves
Yawn level with the luminous waves;
But not the riches there that lie
In each idol's diamond eye—
Not the gaily-jewelled dead
Tempt the waters from their bed;
For no ripples curl, alas!
Along that wilderness of glass—
No swellings tell that winds may be
Upon some far-off happier sea—
No heavings hint that winds have been
On seas less hideously serene.

But lo, a stir is in the air!
The wave—there is a movement there!

As if the towers had thrust aside,
In slightly sinking, the dull tide—
As if their tops had feebly given
A void within the filmy Heaven.
The waves have now a redder glow—
The hours are breathing faint and low—
And when, amid no earthly moans,
Down, down that town shall settle hence,
Hell, rising from a thousand thrones,
Shall do it reverence.

THE HAUNTED PALACE[1]

In the greenest of our valleys
  By good angels tenanted,
Once a fair and stately palace—
  Radiant palace—reared its head.
In the monarch Thought's dominion—
  It stood there!
Never seraph spread a pinion
  Over fabric half so fair!

Banners yellow, glorious, golden,
  On its roof did float and flow,
(This—all this—was in the olden
  Time long ago,)
And every gentle air that dallied,
  In that sweet day,
Along the ramparts plumed and pallid,
  A wingéd odor went away.

Wanderers in that happy valley,
  Through two luminous windows, saw
Spirits moving musically,
  To a lute's well-tuned law,
Round about a throne where, sitting,
  Porphyrogene,[2]
In state his glory well befitting,
  The ruler of the realm was seen.
And all with pearl and ruby glowing
  Was the fair palace door,
Through which came flowing, flowing, flowing,
  And sparkling evermore,
A troop of Echoes, whose sweet duty
  Was but to sing,
In voices of surpassing beauty,
  The wit and wisdom of their king.

But evil things, in robes of sorrow,
　　Assailed the monarch's high estate.
(Ah, let us mourn!—for never morrow
　　Shall dawn upon him desolate!)
And round about his home the glory
　　That blushed and bloomed,
Is but a dim-remembered story
　　Of the old time entombed.

And travellers, now, within that valley,
　　Through the red-litten windows see
Vast forms, that move fantastically
　　To a discordant melody,
While, like a ghastly rapid river,
　　Through the pale door
A hideous throng rush out forever
　　And laugh—but smile no more.

THE CONQUEROR WORM[1]

Lo! 'tis a gala night
　　Within the lonesome latter years!
An angel throng, bewinged, bedight[2]
　　In veils, and drowned in tears,
Sit in a theatre, to see
　　A play of hopes and fears,
While the orchestra breathes fitfully
　　The music of the spheres.[3]

Mimes, in the form of God on high,
　　Mutter and mumble low,
And hither and thither fly—.
　　Mere puppets they, who come and go
At bidding of vast formless things
　　That shift the scenery to and fro,
Flapping from out their Condor wings
　　Invisible Wo!

That motley drama—oh, be sure
　　It shall not be forgot!
With its Phantom chased for evermore,
　　By a crowd that seize it not,
Through a circle that ever returneth in
　　To the self-same spot,
And much of Madness, and more of Sin,
　　And Horror the soul of the plot.

But see, amid the mimic rout
　　A crawling shape intrude!

A blood-red thing that writhes from out
   The scenic solitude!
It writhes!—it writhes!—with mortal pangs
   The mimes become its food,
And seraphs sob at vermin fangs
   In human gore imbued.

Out—out are the lights—out all!
   And, over each quivering form,
The curtain, a funeral pall,
   Comes down with the rush of a storm,
While the angels, all pallid and wan,
   Uprising, unveiling, affirm
That the play is the tragedy, "Man,"
   And its hero the Conqueror Worm.

DREAM-LAND[1]

BY a route obscure and lonely,
Haunted by ill angels only,
Where an Eidolon,[2] named NIGHT,
On a black throne reigns upright,
I have reached these lands but newly
From an ultimate dim Thule—[3]
From a wild weird clime that lieth, sublime,
      Out of SPACE—out of TIME.

Bottomless vales and boundless floods,
And chasms, and caves, and Titan[4] woods,
With forms that no man can discover
For the tears that drip all over;
Mountains toppling evermore
Into seas without a shore;
Seas that restlessly aspire,
Surging, unto skies of fire;
Lakes that endlessly outspread
Their lone waters—lone and dead,—
Their still waters—still and chilly
With the snows of the lolling lily.

By the lakes that thus outspread
Their lone waters, lone and dead,—
Their sad waters, sad and chilly
With the snows of the lolling lily,—
By the mountains—near the river
Murmuring lowly, murmuring ever,—
By the grey woods,—by the swamp
Where the toad and the newt encamp,—

By the dismal tarns and pools
　　Where dwell the Ghouls,—
By each spot the most unholy—
In each nook most melancholy,—
There the traveller meets, aghast,
Sheeted Memories of the Past—
Shrouded forms that start and sigh
As they pass the wanderer by—
White-robed[5] forms of friends long given,
In agony, to the Earth—and Heaven.

For the heart whose woes are legion
'Tis a peaceful, soothing region—
For the spirit that walks in shadow
'Tis—oh 'tis an Eldorado![6]
But the traveller, travelling through it,
May not—dare not openly view it;
Never its mysteries are exposed
To the weak human eye unclosed;
So wills its King, who hath forbid
The uplifting of the fringéd lid;
And thus the sad Soul that here passes
Beholds it but through darkened glasses.[7]

By a route obscure and lonely,
Haunted by ill angels only,
Where an Eidolon, named NIGHT,
On a black throne reigns upright,
I have wandered home but newly
From this ultimate dim Thule.

THE RAVEN[1]

ONCE upon a midnight dreary, while I pondered, weak and weary,
Over many a quaint and curious volume of forgotten lore—
While I nodded, nearly napping, suddenly there came a tapping,
As of some one gently rapping, rapping at my chamber door.
"'Tis some visiter," I muttered, "tapping at my chamber door—
　　　　　　　Only this and nothing more."

Ah, distinctly I remember it was in the bleak December;
And each separate dying ember wrought its ghost upon the floor.
Eagerly I wished the morrow;—vainly I had sought to borrow
From my books surcease of sorrow—sorrow for the lost Lenore—
For the rare and radiant maiden whom the angels name Lenore—
　　　　　　　Nameless *here* for evermore.

And the silken, sad, uncertain rustling of each purple curtain
Thrilled me—filled me with fantastic terrors never felt before;
So that now, to still the beating of my heart, I stood repeating
"'Tis some visiter entreating entrance at my chamber door—
Some late visiter entreating entrance at my chamber door;—
     This it is and nothing more."

Presently my soul grew stronger; hesitating then no longer,
"Sir," said I, "or Madam, truly your forgiveness I implore;
But the fact is I was napping, and so gently you came rapping,
And so faintly you came tapping, tapping at my chamber door,
That I scarce was sure I heard you"—here I opened wide the door;——
     Darkness there and nothing more.

Deep into that darkness peering, long I stood there wondering, fearing,
Doubting, dreaming dreams no mortal ever dared to dream before;
But the silence was unbroken, and the stillness gave no token,
And the only word there spoken was the whispered word, "Lenore?"
This I whispered, and an echo murmured back the word, "Lenore!"
     Merely this and nothing more.

Back into the chamber turning, all my soul within me burning,
Soon again I heard a tapping somewhat louder than before.
"Surely," said I, "surely that is something at my window lattice;
Let me see, then, what thereat is, and this mystery explore—
Let my heart be still a moment and this mystery explore;—
     'Tis the wind and nothing more!"

Open here I flung the shutter, when, with many a flirt and flutter,
In there stepped a stately Raven of the saintly days of yore;
Not the least obeisance made he; not a minute stopped or stayed he;
But, with mien of lord or lady, perched above my chamber door—
Perched upon a bust of Pallas[2] just above my chamber door—
     Perched, and sat, and nothing more.

Then this ebony bird beguiling my sad fancy into smiling,
By the grave and stern decorum of the countenance it wore,
"Though thy crest be shorn and shaven, thou," I said, "art sure no craven,[3]
Ghastly grim and ancient Raven wandering from the Nightly shore—
Tell me what thy lordly name is on the Night's Plutonian[4] shore!"
     Quoth the Raven "Nevermore."

Much I marvelled this ungainly fowl to hear discourse so plainly,
Though its answer little meaning—little relevancy bore;
For we cannot help agreeing that no living human being

Ever yet was blessed with seeing bird above his chamber door—
Bird or beast upon the sculptured bust above his chamber door,
                    With such name as "Nevermore."

But the Raven, sitting lonely on the placid bust, spoke only
That one word, as if his soul in that one word he did outpour.
Nothing farther then he uttered—not a feather then he fluttered—
Till I scarcely more than muttered "Other friends have flown before—
On the morrow *he* will leave me, as my Hopes have flown before."
                    Then the bird said "Nevermore."

Startled at the stillness broken by reply so aptly spoken,
"Doubtless," said I, "what it utters is its only stock and store
Caught from some unhappy master whom unmerciful Disaster
Followed fast and followed faster till his songs one burden bore—
Till the dirges of his Hope that melancholy burden bore
                    Of 'Never—nevermore.'"

But the Raven still beguiling all my fancy into smiling,[5]
Straight I wheeled a cushioned seat in front of bird, and bust and door;
Then, upon the velvet sinking, I betook myself to linking
Fancy unto fancy, thinking what this ominous bird of yore—
What this grim, ungainly, ghastly, gaunt, and ominous bird of yore
                    Meant in croaking "Nevermore."

This I sat engaged in guessing, but no syllable expressing
To the fowl whose fiery eyes now burned into my bosom's core;
This and more I sat divining, with my head at ease reclining
On the cushion's velvet lining that the lamp-light gloated o'er,
But whose velvet-violet lining with the lamp-light gloating o'er,
                    She shall press, ah, nevermore!

Then, methought, the air grew denser, perfumed from an unseen censer[6]
Swung by seraphim whose foot-falls tinkled on the tufted floor.
"Wretch," I cried, "thy God hath lent thee—by these angels he hath sent thee
Respite—respite and nepenthe[7] from thy memories of Lenore;
Quaff, oh quaff this kind nepenthe and forget this lost Lenore!"
                    Quoth the Raven "Nevermore."

"Prophet!" said I, "thing of evil!—prophet still, if bird or devil!—
Whether Tempter sent, or whether tempest tossed thee here ashore,
Desolate yet all undaunted, on this desert land enchanted—
On this home by Horror haunted—tell me truly, I implore—
Is there—*is* there balm in Gilead?[8]—tell me—tell me, I implore!"
                    Quoth the Raven "Nevermore."

"Prophet!" said I, "thing of evil!—prophet still, if bird or devil!
By that Heaven that bends above us—by that God we both adore—
Tell this soul with sorrow laden if, within the distant Aidenn,[9]
It shall clasp a sainted maiden whom the angels name Lenore—
Clasp a rare and radiant maiden whom the angels name Lenore."
            Quoth the Raven "Nevermore."

"Be that word our sign of parting, bird or fiend!" I shrieked, upstarting—
"Get thee back into the tempest and the Night's Plutonian shore!
Leave no black plume as a token of that lie thy soul hath spoken!
Leave my loneliness unbroken!—quit the bust above my door!
Take thy beak from out my heart, and take thy form from off my door!"
            Quoth the Raven "Nevermore."

And the Raven, never flitting, still is sitting, *still* is sitting
On the pallid bust of Pallas just above my chamber door;
And his eyes have all the seeming of a demon's that is dreaming,
And the lamp-light o'er him streaming throws his shadow on the floor;
And my soul from out that shadow that lies floating on the floor
            Shall be lifted—nevermore!

TO – – –
ULALUME: A BALLAD[1]

THE skies they were ashen and sober;
     The leaves they were crispèd and sere—
     The leaves they were withering and sere;
It was night in the lonesome October
     Of my most immemorial year;
It was hard by the dim lake of Auber,
     In the misty mid region of Weir—
It was down by the dank tarn of Auber,
     In the ghoul-haunted woodland of Weir.[2]

Here once, through an alley Titanic,
     Of cypress,[3] I roamed with my Soul—
     Of cypress, with Psyche, my Soul.[4]
These were the days when my heart was volcanic
     As the scoriac[5] rivers that roll—
     As the lavas that restlessly roll
Their sulphurous currents down Yaanek
     In the ultimate climes of the pole—
That groan as they roll down Mount Yaanek
     In the realms of the boreal[6] pole.

Our talk had been serious and sober,
     But our thoughts they were palsied and sere—

Our memories were treacherous and sere—
For we knew not the month was October,
   And we marked not the night of the year—
   (Ah, night of all nights in the year!)
We noted not the dim lake of Auber—
   (Though once we had journeyed down here)—
We remembered not the dank tarn of Auber,
   Nor the ghoul-haunted woodland of Weir.

And now, as the night was senescent[7]
   And star-dials pointed to morn—
   As the star-dials hinted of morn—
At the end of our path a liquescent
   And nebulous lustre was born,
Out of which a miraculous crescent
   Arose with a duplicate horn—
Astarte's[8] bediamonded crescent
   Distinct with its duplicate horn.

And I said—"She is warmer than Dian:[9]
   She rolls through an ether of sighs—
   She revels in a region of sighs:
She has seen that the tears are not dry on
   These cheeks, where the worm never dies,
And has come past the stars of the Lion[10]
   To point us the path to the skies—
   To the Lethean[11] peace of the skies—
Come up, in despite of the Lion,
   To shine on us with her bright eyes—
Come up through the lair of the Lion
   With Love in her luminous eyes."

But Psyche, uplifting her finger,
   Said—"Sadly this star I mistrust—
   Her pallor I strangely mistrust:—
Oh, hasten!—oh, let us not linger!
   Oh, fly!—let us fly!—for we must."
In terror she spoke, letting sink her
   Wings till they trailed in the dust—
In agony sobbed, letting sink her
   Plumes till they trailed in the dust—
   Till they sorrowfully trailed in the dust.

I replied—"This is nothing but dreaming:
   Let us on by this tremulous light!
   Let us bathe in this crystalline light!

Its Sybillic[12] splendor is beaming
   With Hope and in Beauty to-night:—
   See!—it flickers up the sky through the night!
Ah, we safely may trust to its gleaming,
   And be sure it will lead us aright—
We safely may trust to a gleaming
   That cannot but guide us aright,
   Since it flickers up to Heaven through the night."

Thus I pacified Psyche and kissed her,
   And tempted her out of her gloom—
   And conquered her scruples and gloom:
And we passed to the end of the vista,
   And were stopped by the door of a tomb—
   By the door of a legended tomb;
And I said—"What is written, sweet sister,
   On the door of this legended tomb?"
She replied—"Ulalume—Ulalume—
'Tis the vault of thy lost Ulalume!"[13]

Then my heart it grew ashen and sober
   As the leaves that were crispèd and sere—
   As the leaves that were withering and sere,
And I cried—"It was surely October
   On *this* very night of last year
   That I journeyed—I journeyed down here—
   That I brought a dread burden down here—
   On this night of all nights in the year,
   Oh, what demon has tempted me here?
Well I know, now, this dim lake of Auber—
   This misty mid region of Weir—
Well I know, now, this dank tarn of Auber,
   In the ghoul-haunted woodland of Weir."

Said *we*, then—the two, then—"Ah, can it
   Have been that the woodlandish ghouls—
   The pitiful, the merciful ghouls—
To bar up our way and to ban it
   From the secret that lies in these wolds—[14]
   From the thing that lies hidden in these wolds—
Have drawn up the spectre of a planet
   From the limbo of lunary souls—
This sinfully scintillant[15] planet
   From the Hell of the planetary souls?"

THE BELLS[1]

I.

Hear the sledges[2] with the bells—
Silver bells!
What a world of merriment their melody foretells!
How they tinkle, tinkle, tinkle,
In the icy air of night!
While the stars that oversprinkle
All the heavens seem to twinkle
With a crystalline delight;
Keeping time, time, time,
In a sort of Runic[3] rhyme,
To the tintinnabulation[4] that so musically wells
From the bells, bells, bells, bells,
Bells, bells, bells—
From the jingling and the tinkling of the bells.

II.

Hear the mellow wedding bells,
Golden bells!
What a world of happiness their harmony foretells!
Through the balmy air of night
How they ring out their delight!
From the molten-golden notes,
And all in tune,
What a liquid ditty floats
To the turtle-dove that listens, while she gloats
On the moon!
Oh, from out the sounding cells,
What a gush of euphony voluminously wells!
How it swells!
How it dwells
On the future! how it tells
Of the rapture that impels
To the swinging and the ringing
Of the bells, bells, bells,
Of the bells, bells, bells, bells,
Bells, bells, bells—
To the rhyming and the chiming of the bells!

III.

Hear the loud alarum bells—
Brazen bells!
What a tale of terror, now their turbulency tells!
In the startled ear of night

How they scream out their affright!
Too much horrified to speak,
They can only shriek, shriek,
Out of tune.
In a clamorous appealing to the mercy of the fire,
In a mad expostulation with the deaf and frantic fire
Leaping higher, higher, higher,
With a desperate desire,
And a resolute endeavor
Now—now to sit, or never,
By the side of the pale-faced moon.
Oh, the bells, bells, bells!
What a tale their terror tells
Of Despair!
How they clang, and clash, and roar!
What a horror they outpour
On the bosom of the palpitating air!
Yet the ear, it fully knows,
By the twanging
And the clanging,
How the danger ebbs and flows;
Yet the ear distinctly tells,
In the jangling
And the rangling,
How the danger sinks and swells,
By the sinking or the swelling in the anger of the bells—
Of the bells—
Of the bells, bells, bells, bells,
Bells, bells, bells—
In the clamor and the clangor of the bells!

IV.
Hear the tolling of the bells—
Iron bells!
What a world of solemn thought their monody[5] compels
In the silence of the night,
How we shiver with affright
At the melancholy menace of their tone!
For every sound that floats
From the rust within their throats
Is a groan.
And the people—ah, the people—
They that dwell up in the steeple,
All alone,
And who, tolling, tolling, tolling,
In that muffled monotone,

Feel a glory in so rolling
On the human heart a stone—
They are neither man nor woman—
They are neither brute nor human—
They are Ghouls:[6]
And their king it is who tolls;
And he rolls, rolls, rolls,
Rolls
A pæan[7] from the bells!
And his merry bosom swells
With the pæan of the bells!
And he dances, and he yells;
Keeping time, time, time,
In a sort of Runic rhyme,
To the pæan of the bells—
Of the bells:
Keeping time, time, time,
In a sort of Runic rhyme,
To the throbbing of the bells—
Of the bells, bells, bells—
To the sobbing of the bells;
Keeping time, time, time,
As he knells, knells, knells,
In a happy Runic rhyme,
To the rolling of the bells—
Of the bells, bells, bells;
To the tolling of the bells—
Of the bells, bells, bells, bells,
Bells, bells, bells—
To the moaning and the groaning of the bells.

ANNABEL LEE[1]

It was many and many a year ago,
In a kingdom by the sea,
That a maiden there lived whom you may know
By the name of Annabel Lee;—
And this maiden she lived with no other thought
Than to love and be loved by me.

She was a child and *I* was a child,
In this kingdom by the sea,
But we loved with a love that was more than love—
I and my Annabel Lee—
With a love that the wingéd seraphs of Heaven
Coveted her and me.

And this was the reason that, long ago,
   In this kingdom by the sea,
A wind blew out of a cloud by night
   Chilling my Annabel Lee;
So that her high-born kinsmen came
   And bore her away from me,
To shut her up in a sepulchre
   In this kingdom by the sea.

The angels, not half so happy in Heaven,
   Went envying her and me;
Yes! that was the reason (as all men know,
   In this kingdom by the sea)
That the wind came out of the cloud, chilling
   And killing my Annabel Lee.

But our love it was stronger by far than the love
   Of those who were older than we—
   Of many far wiser than we—
And neither the angels in Heaven above
   Nor the demons down under the sea
Can ever dissever my soul from the soul
   Of the beautiful Annabel Lee:—

For the moon never beams without bringing me dreams
   Of the beautiful Annabel Lee;
And the stars never rise but I see the bright eyes
   Of the beautiful Annabel Lee;
And so, all the night-tide, I lie down by the side
Of my darling, my darling, my life and my bride
   In her sepulchre there by the sea—
   In her tomb by the side of the sea.

NOTES

1. Poe to Isaac Lea, Philadelphia, PA, before May 27, 1829, in *The Collected Letters of Edgar Allan Poe*, eds. John Ward Ostrom, Burton R. Pollin, and Jeffrey A. Savoye (New York: Gordian Press, 2008), 1:26

2. Arthur Hobson Quinn, *Edgar Allan Poe: A Critical Biography* (Baltimore, MD: Johns Hopkins University Press, 1998), 165.

3. Kevin J. Hayes, *Poe and the Printed Word* (Cambridge: Cambridge University Press, 2003).

4. "Literary Notices," *New-York Mirror*, May 7, 1831.

5. Eliza Richards surveys these parodies and discusses how they exemplify the reproducibility characteristic of antebellum print culture. Eliza Richards, "Poe's Lyrical Media: The Raven's Returns," in *Poe and the Remapping of Antebellum Print*

Culture, eds. Jerome McGann and J. Gerald Kennedy (Baton Rouge: Louisiana State University Press, 2012), 200–26.

6. This review is quoted in Dwight Thomas and David K. Jackson, *The Poe Log: A Documentary Life of Edgar Allan Poe 1809–1849* (Boston: G. K. Hall & Co., 1987), 628.

7. Without identifying him by name, Emerson (even before publication of "The Raven") astutely tagged Poe in 1844 as "a man of subtle mind, whose head appeared to be a music-box of delicate tunes and rhythms." Ralph Waldo Emerson, "The Poet," *Emerson's Poetry and Prose*, eds. Joel Porte and Saundra Norris (New York: W. W. Norton & Company, Inc., 2001), 185.

8. T. S. Eliot, "From Poe to Valéry," *Hudson Review* 2, no. 3 (1949): 333.

9. Thomas Ollive Mabbott tells of the poem's origin as an elocution exercise in his *Edgar Allan Poe: Complete Poems* (Urbana and Chicago: University of Illinois Press, 2000), 409.

10. Biographer Kenneth Silverman lists the claimants in *Edgar A. Poe: Mournful and Never-Ending Remembrance* (New York: HarperPerennial, 1992), 401.

11. The classic study of Poe's influence in France is Patrick F. Quinn, *The French Face of Edgar Allan Poe* (Carbondale: Southern Illinois Press, 1957).

12. Jerome Loving, *Walt Whitman: The Song of Himself* (Berkeley: University of California Press, 1999), 97.

13. Walt Whitman, *Complete Prose Works* (Philadelphia: David McKay, 1892), 157.

14. William Carlos Williams, *In the American Grain* (New York: New Directions, 1956), 232.

15. Allen Tate, "Our Cousin, Mr. Poe," *Partisan Review*, December 1949, 1217, and "The Angelic Imagination: Poe and the Power of Words," *Kenyon Review* 14, no. 3 (1952): 455.

16. Eliot, "From Poe to Valéry," 327.

17. Jerome McGann, *The Poet Edgar Allan Poe: Alien Angel* (Cambridge, MA: Harvard University Press, 2014), 6.

18. John Michael, *Secular Lyric: The Modernization of the Poem in Poe, Whitman, and Dickinson* (New York: Fordham University Press, 2018).

SONNET—TO SCIENCE

1. The source of the present text is *The Raven and Other Poems* (New York: Wiley and Putnam, 1845). The poem was first published in *Al Aaraaf, Tamerlane, and Minor Poems* (1829).

2. **Diana** Roman goddess of the hunt and the moon, sometimes depicted riding in a chariot across the heavens.

3. **Hamadryad** A mythological Greek creature who lives in a tree.

4. **Naiad** In Greek mythology, a water nymph who presides over fresh water bodies such as fountains, wells, and springs.

5. **Elfin** Elves are supernatural beings from Germanic mythology and folklore.

ALONE

1. The text comes from the poem's initial, posthumous publication in *Scribner's Monthly Magazine*, September 1875.

TO HELEN

1. The text is from *The Raven and Other Poems*. The poem was initially published in *Poems* (1831). **HELEN** Helen is meant to evoke, without necessarily directly or exclusively referring to, Helen of Troy, the beautiful wife of Menelaus whose kidnapping launched the Trojan War, as described in Homer's *Iliad*. A biographical figure, Jane Stith Stanard (the mother of a childhood friend), has also been identified as an inspiration.

2. **Nicéan** Poe apparently alludes to Nike, the ancient Greek goddess of victory, or to one of the ancient cities named for her.

3. **hyacinth** Dark and luxuriantly curling, as the leaves of the hyacinth plant.

4. **Naiad** A water nymph from ancient Greek mythology.

5. **agate** A type of stone characterized by banded colors.

6. **Psyche** The Greek word for soul.

ISRAFEL

1. The text is from *The Raven and Other Poems* (1845). I follow Poe's personal emendation in inserting a hyphen in the phrase "grown-up God" (line 25), as indicated by the Lorimer Graham copy of *The Raven and Other Poems*, which included Poe's corrections. Thomas Ollive Mabbott, ed., *The Raven and Other Poems Reproduced in Facsimile from the Lorimer Graham Copy of the Edition of 1845 with Author's Corrections* (New York: Columbia University Press, 1942). Initial publication was in *Poems* (1831). **ISRAFEL** And the angel Israfel, whose heart-strings are a lute, and who has the sweetest voice of all God's creatures.—KORAN (Poe's note). The angel Israfel had been celebrated in Thomas Moore's poem *Lalla Rookh* (1817), which Poe knew.

2. **levin** Lightning.

3. **Pleiads** The constellation of the Pleiades (also known as the Seven Sisters).

4. **Houri** According to Islamic tradition, beautiful women who attend the faithful in Heaven.

5. **laurels** Laurels were awarded to the best poets in ancient Greek competitions.

THE SLEEPER

1. The text follows *The Raven and Other Poems* with Poe's personal emendations as indicated in Mabbott's facsimile edition of the Lorimer Graham copy, cited above in note 1 to "Israfel." The poem was initially published under the title "Irenë" in *Poems* (1831).

2. **rosemary** This herb and the **lily** (in the next line) were popularly associated with remembrance and death in Poe's time.

3. **Lethe** The river of forgetfulness leading to the underworld in ancient Greek mythology. Spirits drank from it and forgot their earthly lives.

THE CITY IN THE SEA

1. The text is from *The Raven and Other Poems*, with one emendation from the Lorimer Graham facsimile edition, cited above in note 1 to "Israfel": Poe wanted a comma instead of a period at the end of line 51. The poem was initially published as "The Doomed City" in *Poems* (1831). **THE CITY IN THE SEA** Poe's city probably alludes suggestively to the biblical cities of Sodom and Gomorrah (punished by God for their wickedness) and legends of ancient cities lost beneath the sea.

2. **Babylon-like** Babylon was a city of ancient Mesopotamia, associated with wickedness in various passages of the Bible.

3. **fanes** Temples.

THE HAUNTED PALACE

1. The text is from *The Raven and Other Poems*, incorporating Poe's various emendations from the Lorimer Graham copy, cited above in note 1 to "Israfel." The poem was initially published in the Baltimore *American Museum of Science, Literature and Arts*, April 1839.

2. **Porphyrogene** Clothed in purple, the color of royalty.

THE CONQUEROR WORM

1. The text is from *The Raven and Other Poems*, with two changes incorporated from the Lorimer Graham copy, cited above in note 1 to "Israfel." Poe changed "the angels" to "seraphs" in line 31 and changed "And" to "While" in line 37. The poem was initially published in *Graham's Magazine*, January 1843.

2. **bedight** Decked out, arrayed.

3. **music of the spheres** An ancient philosophical concept held that the planetary bodies move in harmony, producing a kind of music.

DREAM-LAND

1. The text is from *The Raven and Other Poems*, with a few minor emendations following Poe's marks in the Lorimer Graham copy, cited above in note 1 to "Israfel." Initial publication was in *Graham's Lady's and Gentlemen's Magazine*, June 1844.

2. **Eidolon** Phantom.

3. **Thule** Thulé was the Greek and Latin name for the most northward region conceivable. Poe uses it figuratively to mean some ultimate point or destination.

4. **Titan** In Greek mythology, Titans were giant deities.

5. **White-robed** White robes are given to the saints in Revelation 6.11.

6. **Eldorado** A fabled city of gold.

7. **darkened glasses** Evidently an allusion to 1 Corinthians 13.12: "For now we see through a glass, darkly; but then face to face."

THE RAVEN

1. The text follows *The Raven and Other Poems* but with Poe's many corrections as indicated in the Lorimer Graham copy, cited in note 1 to "Israfel." Most of Poe's corrections are minor, but two notable changes he indicated were to capitalize "Raven" throughout the poem and to remove the commas following each "Quoth the Raven" phrase in the refrain. The poem was first published in the New York *Evening Mirror*, January 29, 1845. **THE RAVEN** Ravens have long been associated with death (because of their diet of carrion). Poe also knew of traditions crediting ravens with supernatural knowledge. Charles Dickens's *Barnaby Rudge* (1841), which features a talking raven (and which Poe had reviewed), is a probable source.

2. **Pallas** An epithet for Athena, Greek goddess of wisdom (among other virtues).

3. **craven** A cowardly knight's head was sometimes shaved, according to Mabbott.

4. **Plutonian** Pluto was the god of the underworld in ancient Greek mythology.

5. **smiling** "But the Raven still beguiling my sad fancy into smiling" is the variant Mabbott chooses for this line.

6. **censer** A container for burning incense.

7. **nepenthe** In ancient Greek mythology, a drug that induces forgetfulness or assuages pain.

8. **Gilead** From Jeremiah 8.22: "Is there no balm in Gilead?"

9. **Aidenn** An alternate spelling for Eden (used here to signify Heaven).

To ————Ulalume: A Ballad

1. The text is from initial publication of the poem in the *American Whig Review*, December 1847.

2. **Weir** Auber and Weir are imaginary locales, invented for the sonic effects the names contribute to the poem. The same is true of **Mount Yaanek** (line 16 and following).

3. **cypress** An alley of gigantic cypress trees, associated with graveyards and mourning.

4. **Psyche, my Soul** Psyche is the Greek word for "the soul," a reference Poe also uses in "To Helen" above.

5. **scoriac** Scoria is a type of lava.

6. **boreal** Of or relating to the north.

7. **senescent** Growing old.

8. **Astarte's** Astarte is the Greek name for a Middle Eastern goddess of antiquity associated with sexuality and fertility.

9. **Dian** Roman goddess associated here with the moon.

10. **Lion** The constellation of Leo.

11. **Lethean** Associated with Lethe, the ancient river of the underworld (in Greek mythology), whose waters induced forgetfulness of pain.

12. **Sybillic** Sibyls were women to whom powers of prophecy were attributed by ancient Greeks.

13. **Ulalume** Mabbott's assertion that the name combines elements of Latin words meaning "to wail" (*ululare*) and "light" (*lumen*) seems convincing.

14. **wolds** A wold is an elevated tract of open country, but perhaps "wolds" here is synonymous with "woods."

15. **scintillant** Sparkling.

THE BELLS

1. The text is from the New York *Home Journal*, October 27, 1849. Initial, posthumous publication was in *Sartain's Union Magazine*, November 1849 (the magazine was published ahead of its November date).

2. **sledges** Sleighs.

3. **Runic** Consisting of or set down in runes, meaning scripts or alphabets with mystical import.

4. **tintinnabulation** The ringing or sound of bells.

5. **monody** A poem in which the poet/speaker laments another's death.

6. **Ghouls** Evil demons that feed on human corpses.

7. **pæan** A song of praise, joy, or triumph.

Annabel Lee

1. The text is from the *Southern Literary Messenger*, November 1849. Initial publication was in the *New-York Tribune*, October 9, 1849.

PART IV

Eureka: A Prose Poem

A treatise on cosmology is not the departure it may at first seem from a writer previously known for poetry, short fiction, and literary criticism. Long before publishing *Eureka* in 1848, Poe had frequently capitalized on popular cultural trends in his writings. After observing how subjects as varied as South Sea exploration, ballooning, and mesmerism captured the public imagination in magazine and newspaper articles, Poe opportunistically fashioned original literary responses. *Eureka* can be seen in a similar light, as the work of an author with a long-standing interest in scientific subjects who naturally took professional notice of the public appetite for scientific popularizations. In fact, *Eureka* initially took shape as a popular lecture at the New York Society Library, as Poe attempted to raise funds for his cherished project of launching a high-quality literary magazine, *The Stylus*.[1] In other words, the market-savvy Poe identified cosmology as, potentially, a crowd-pleasing, attention-generating subject.

Poe dedicated *Eureka* to the Prussian naturalist Alexander von Humboldt. The first volume of Humboldt's late-career, multi-volume *Kosmos* was an immediate popular sensation when it appeared in the United States in translation in 1845, "establishing him as a household name across the North American continent."[2] The first book included sections on celestial phenomena, geography, and organic life, as Humboldt attempted to unite disparate scientific fields in one holistic survey. Poe's dedication to Humboldt may have been, in part, a marketing strategy designed to draw in Humboldt's popular audience for *Eureka*. At roughly the same time, the anonymously authored *Vestiges of the Natural History of Creation* gained a wide readership upon its publication in London in 1844 (Wiley and Putnam brought out an American edition in 1845, the same year in which they published two volumes by Poe). The author, later revealed to be Scottish publisher Robert Chambers, speculated controversially on the origins and evolution of the universe. Another author Poe had in mind when writing *Eureka* was Scottish astronomer John Pringle Nichol, who published *Views of the Architecture of the Heavens* to acclaim in 1837; an American edition appeared in 1840. Nichol was delivering a series of well-attended lectures on astronomy in New York at the very same time as Poe's lecture took place, in February 1848. Even if *Eureka* was not the publishing success Poe had hoped, then, his calculation as to its potential popularity amid a range of similar books in the mid- to late 1840s was sound.[3]

Whether the astronomy itself outlined in *Eureka* is equally sound is a question on which readers differ. Poe was conversant with the major astronomical findings of the day. He alludes in *Eureka* to the findings of William Herschel, a German-born British astronomer known for building telescopes with which he cataloged stars as well as for the discovery of Uranus. Poe also cites the work of William's son John Herschel, another astronomer of note. Poe repeatedly engages with the work of French astronomer Pierre-Simon Laplace, who is credited with developing the nebular hypothesis of the development of the solar system. Poe's most enthusiastic admirers have claimed not only that he accurately tracked developments in nineteenth-century astronomy, but that he also anticipated a number of twentieth-century insights, including space-time interdependence and the Big Bang.[4] Other readers, however, refer to the "astrophysics about which Poe understood so little" or dismiss the subject of his anticipation of later discoveries as not a "fruitful argument."[5] Poe expressed satisfaction with his own contribution in characteristically hyperbolic terms, avowing to a friend, "What I have propounded will (in good time) revolutionize the world of Physical & Metaphysical Science. I say this calmly—but I say it."[6] This statement seems so outrageous, however, as to invite speculation as to whether the entire performance should be classified as one of Poe's hoaxes.[7] All a non-specialist can say with confidence on the question of *Eureka*'s significance to the history of astronomy is that the jury is still out and will probably remain so until the Big Crunch that the text predicts renders the question moot.

The original title page of *Eureka* identifies the work as a "Prose-Poem," and Poe claimed in his preface, included below, that he wanted the work to be judged as a poem after his death. This classification raises obvious questions in light of well-known pronouncements in Poe's literary criticism. Poe held that a poem by definition had to be short enough to be read in a single sitting and that meter and rhythm were indispensable poetic effects (see "The Philosophy of Composition" and "The Poetic Principle" in Part V of this volume). The book-length *Eureka* obviously satisfies neither criterion. One way to explain the inconsistency is that Poe insisted on the generic classification of a poem as a way of hedging his bets against readers who would discover verifiable faults in *Eureka*'s scientific truth-claims. Laura Saltz points to the contest for cultural authority between science and literature in Poe's day, when science was increasingly the province of professionals working in institutional settings, as opposed to gifted amateurs such as Poe; against this backdrop, the classification of a cosmological treatise as a poem is an attempt "to subordinate the authority of scientific knowledge to the poetic imagination."[8]

At times, Poe seems to use cosmology as the pretense for veering into other subjects. For example, the passage on how the construction of the universe betrays an intricate interdependence in which cause and effect are indistinguishable from each other echoes his pronouncement on literary plots in the review of Edward Bulwer's novel *Night and Morning*, excerpted in Part V. Taking such arguments from analogy even further, some readers have proposed that *Eureka*'s investigation into the relationship between the universe's current state of heterogeneity and its original state of unity masks a political statement.[9] Since its founding, the United States has struggled with the paradox of dividing authority between the many (the states, individual citizens) and the one (the central government). Such arguments have the significant virtue of explaining why certain passages within *Eureka* may not pass scientific muster; any lack of precision or accuracy can be attributed to Poe's using astronomy as a cover for a wholly different set of concerns. What such readings cannot explain is why Poe would go to the trouble of dressing up political opinions in an elaborate cosmological allegory, a literary mode he described in the aforementioned Bulwer review as "at all times an abomination." The simpler explanation seems to be that *Eureka* is what it purports to be, a treatise on cosmology written for a popular audience, incorporating the latest science but also venturing original insights.

The selections included below give the reader a reasonably complete view of Poe's chief concerns in *Eureka*. The book starts off with a pun-filled satirical letter, presumably from the year 2848, aiming to expose the epistemological shortcomings of scientific inquiry in Poe's day. This section of *Eureka* was adapted from a separate Poe story, "Mellonta Tauta," a phrase from Sophocles' *Antigone* that means "these things are in the future." Although the letter's jocular tone is jarringly out of keeping with the serious passages that follow, Poe was clearly invested in the idea, put forward by the letter's reputed author, that the most important scientific breakthroughs derive from a process that could be classified as neither induction nor deduction. Poe contends that paradigm-shifting knowledge is arrived at only through the inspired guesses of figures like Johannes Kepler, German discoverer of the laws of planetary motion, and Archimedes, the ancient Greek philosopher whose famous (if apocryphal) exclamation upon suddenly intuiting a method for determining the volume of an irregular shape gives *Eureka* its title.

Following the spurious letter from the future, remaining excerpts allow readers to trace Poe's main argument defending his view of a universe that began as a single particle, expanded outward, and is currently in a state of contraction. Poe imagines this contraction culminating in the rushing of all matter in the universe back to its original unity, only to radiate outward again from unity to multiplicity, a process of expansion and contraction that he figures as a divine heartbeat. Poe's vision of humanity losing individual identity in a merging with God at the moment of ultimate contraction into unity bears resemblance to the Transcendentalist thought Poe often ridiculed, although critics have noted important differences between Poe's and Emerson's glosses on unity with the divine.[10] Along the way, readers can trace the text's most important digressions and corollary conclusions. These include Poe's speculations about the evolution of superior races on Earth corresponding with the creation of new planets in the solar system; about why the universe cannot be of infinite size, his resolution to the problem astronomers label Olbers' paradox; about the existence or non-existence of a medium known as ether pervading the universe; and about the possibility of alternate universes not governed by the same laws of physics as our own.[11]

from Eureka: A Prose Poem[1]

PREFACE.

———

To the few who love me and whom I love—to those who feel rather than to those who think—to the dreamers and those who put faith in dreams as in the only realities—I offer this Book of Truths, not in its character of Truth-Teller, but for the Beauty that abounds in its Truth; constituting it true. To these I present the composition as an Art-Product alone:—let us say as a Romance; or, if I be not urging too lofty a claim, as a Poem.

What I here propound is true:—therefore it cannot die:—or if by any means it be now trodden down so that it die, it will "rise again to the Life Everlasting."

Nevertheless it is as a Poem only that I wish this work to be judged after I am dead.

E. A. P.

EUREKA:

AN ESSAY ON THE MATERIAL AND SPIRITUAL UNIVERSE

It is with humility really unassumed—it is with a sentiment even of awe—that I pen the opening sentence of this work: for of all conceivable subjects I approach the reader with the most solemn—the most comprehensive—the most difficult—the most august.

What terms shall I find sufficiently simple in their sublimity—sufficiently sublime in their simplicity—for the mere enunciation of my theme?

I design to speak of the *Physical, Metaphysical and Mathematical—of the Material and Spiritual Universe:—of its Essence, its Origin, its Creation, its Present Condition and its Destiny*. I shall be so rash, moreover, as to challenge the conclusions, and thus, in effect, to question the sagacity, of many of the greatest and most justly reverenced of men.

In the beginning, let me as distinctly as possible announce—not the theorem which I hope to demonstrate—for, whatever the mathematicians may assert, there is, in this world at least, *no such thing* as demonstration—but the ruling idea which, throughout this volume, I shall be continually endeavoring to suggest.

My general proposition, then, is this:—*In the Original Unity of the First Thing lies the Secondary Cause of All Things, with the Germ of their Inevitable Annihilation.*

In illustration of this idea, I propose to take such a survey of the Universe that the mind may be able really to receive and to perceive an individual impression.

He who from the top of Ætna[2] casts his eyes leisurely around, is affected chiefly by the *extent* and *diversity* of the scene. Only by a rapid whirling on his heel could he hope to comprehend the panorama in the sublimity of its *oneness*. But as, on the summit of Ætna, *no* man has thought of whirling on his heel, so no man has ever taken into his brain the full uniqueness of the prospect; and so, again, whatever considerations lie involved in this uniqueness, have as yet no practical existence for mankind.

I do not know a treatise in which a survey of the *Universe*—using the word in its most comprehensive and only legitimate acceptation—is taken at all:—and it may be as well here to mention that by the term "Universe," wherever employed without qualification in this essay, I mean to designate *the utmost conceivable expanse of space, with all things, spiritual and material, that can be imagined to exist within the compass of that expanse*. In speaking of what is *ordinarily* implied by the expression, "Universe," I shall take a phrase of limitation—"the Universe of stars." Why this distinction is considered necessary, will be seen in the sequel.

But even of treatises on the really limited, although always assumed as the *un*limited, Universe of *stars*, I know none in which a survey, even of this limited Universe, is so taken as to warrant deductions from its *individuality*. The nearest approach to such a work is made in the "Cosmos" of Alexander Von Humboldt.[3] He presents the subject, however, *not* in its individuality but in its generality. His theme, in its last result, is the law of *each* portion of the merely physical Universe, as this law is related to the laws of *every other* portion of this merely physical Universe. His design is simply syncœretical. In a word, he discusses the universality of material relation, and discloses to the eye of Philosophy whatever inferences have hitherto lain hidden *behind* this universality. But however admirable be the succinctness with which he has treated each particular point of his topic, the mere multiplicity of these points occasions, necessarily, an amount of detail, and thus an involution of idea, which preclude all *individuality* of impression.

It seems to me that, in aiming at this latter effect, and, through it, at the consequences—the conclusions—the suggestions—the speculations—or, if nothing better offer itself, the mere guesses which may result from it—we require something like a mental gyration on the heel. We need so rapid a revolution of all things about the central point of sight that, while the minutiæ vanish altogether, even the more conspicuous objects become blended into one. Among the vanishing minutiæ, in a survey of this kind, would be all exclusively terrestrial matters. The Earth would be considered in its planetary relations alone. A man, in this view, becomes mankind; mankind a member of the cosmical family of Intelligences.

And now, before proceeding to our subject proper, let me beg the reader's attention to an extract or two from a somewhat remarkable letter, which appears to have been found corked in a bottle and floating on the *Mare Tenebrarum*[4]—an ocean well described by the Nubian geographer, Ptolemy Hephestion, but little frequented in modern days unless by the Transcendentalists and some other divers for crotchets. The date of this letter, I confess, surprises me even more particularly than its contents; for it seems to have been written in the year *two* thousand eight hundred and forty-eight. As for the passages I am about to transcribe, they, I fancy, will speak for themselves.

"Do you know, my dear friend," says the writer, addressing, no doubt, a contemporary—"Do you know that it is scarcely more than eight or nine hundred years ago since the metaphysicians first consented to relieve the people of the singular fancy that there exist *but two practicable roads to Truth?* Believe it if you can! It appears, however, that long, long ago, in the night of Time, there lived a Turkish philosopher called Aries and surnamed Tottle." [Here, possibly, the letter-writer means Aristotle; the best names are wretchedly corrupted in two or three thousand years.] "The fame of this great man depended mainly upon his demonstration that sneezing is a natural provision, by means of which over-profound thinkers are enabled to expel superfluous ideas through the nose; but he obtained a scarcely less valuable celebrity as the founder, or at all events as the principal propagator, of what was termed the deductive or *à priori* philosophy. He started with what he maintained to be axioms, or self-evident truths:—and the now well understood fact that *no* truths are *self*-evident, really does not make in the slightest degree against his speculations:—it was sufficient for his purpose that the truths in question were evident at all. From axioms he proceeded, logically, to results. His most illustrious disciples were one Tuclid, a geometrician," [meaning Euclid] "and one Kant,[5] a Dutchman, the originator of that species of Transcendentalism which, with the change merely of a C for a K, now bears his peculiar name.

"Well, Aries Tottle flourished supreme, until the advent of one Hog, surnamed 'the Ettrick shepherd,'[6] who preached an entirely different system, which he called the *à posteriori* or *in*ductive. His plan referred altogether to sensation. He proceeded by observing, analyzing, and classifying facts—*instantiæ Naturæ*, as they were somewhat affectedly called—and arranging them into general laws. In a word, while the mode of Aries rested on *noumena*, that of Hog depended on *phenomena*; and so great was the admiration excited by this latter system that, at its first introduction, Aries fell into general disrepute. Finally, however, he recovered ground, and was permitted to divide the empire of Philosophy with his more modern rival:—the savans contenting themselves with proscribing all *other* competitors, past, present, and to come; putting an end to all controversy on the topic by the promulgation of a Median law, to the effect that the Aristotelian and Baconian roads are, and of right ought to be, the sole possible avenues to knowledge:—'Baconian,' you must know, my dear friend," adds the letter-writer at this point, "was an adjective invented as equivalent to Hog-ian, and at the same time more dignified and euphonious.

"Now I do assure you most positively"—proceeds the epistle—"that I represent these matters fairly; and you can easily understand how restrictions so absurd on their very face must have operated, in those days, to retard the progress of true Science, which makes its most important advances—as all History will show—by seemingly intuitive *leaps*. These ancient ideas confined investigation to crawling; and I need not suggest to you that crawling, among varieties of locomotion, is a very capital thing of its kind;—but because the tortoise is sure of foot, for this reason must we clip the wings of the eagles? For many centuries, so great was the infatuation, about Hog especially, that a virtual stop was put to all thinking, properly so called. No man dared utter a truth for which he felt himself indebted to his soul alone. It mattered not whether the truth was even demonstrably such; for the dogmatizing philosophers of that epoch regarded only *the road* by which it professed to have been attained. The end, with them, was a point of no moment, whatever:—'the means!' they vociferated—'let us look at the means!'—and if, on scrutiny of the means, it was found to come neither under the category Hog, nor under the category Aries (which means ram), why then the savans went no farther, but, calling the thinker a fool and branding him a 'theorist,' would never, thenceforward, have any thing to do either with *him* or with his truths.

"Now, my dear friend," continues the letter-writer, "it cannot be maintained that by the crawling system, exclusively adopted, men would arrive at the maximum amount of truth, even in any long series of ages; for the repression of imagination was an evil not to be counterbalanced even by *absolute* certainty in the snail processes. But their certainty was very far from absolute. The error of our progenitors was quite analogous with that of the wiseacre who fancies he must necessarily see an object the more distinctly, the more closely he holds it to his eyes. They blinded themselves, too, with the impalpable, titillating Scotch snuff of *detail*; and thus the boasted facts of the Hog-ites were by no means always facts—a point of little importance but for the assumption that they always *were*. The vital taint, however, in Baconianism—its most lamentable fount of error—lay in its tendency to throw power and consideration into the hands of merely perceptive men—of those inter-Tritonic minnows, the microscopical savans—the diggers and pedlers of minute *facts*, for the most part in physical science—facts all of which they retailed at the same price upon the highway; their value depending, it was supposed, simply upon the *fact of their fact*, without reference to their applicability or inapplicability in the development of those ultimate and only legitimate facts, called Law.

"Than the persons"—the letter goes on to say—"Than the persons thus suddenly elevated by the Hog-ian philosophy into a station for which they were unfitted—thus transferred from sculleries into the parlors of Science—from its pantries into its pulpits—than these individuals a more intolerant—a more intolerable set of bigots and tyrants never existed on the face of the earth. Their creed, their text and their sermon were, alike, the one word '*fact*'—but, for the most part, even of this one word, they knew not even the meaning. On those who ventured to *disturb* their facts with the view of putting them in order and to use, the disciples of Hog had no mercy whatever. All attempts at generalization were met at once by the words 'theoretical,' 'theory,' 'theorist'—all *thought*, to be brief, was very properly resented as a personal affront to themselves. Cultivating the natural sciences to the exclusion of Metaphysics, the Mathematics, and Logic, many of these Bacon-engendered philosophers—one-idead, one-sided and lame of a leg—were more wretchedly helpless—more miserably ignorant, in view of all the comprehensible objects of knowledge, than the veriest unlettered hind who proves that he knows something at least, in admitting that he knows absolutely nothing.

"Nor had our forefathers any better right to talk about *certainty*, when pursuing, in blind confidence, the *à priori* path of axioms, or of the Ram.[7] At innumerable points this path was scarcely as straight as a ram's-horn. The simple truth is, that the Aristotelians erected their castles upon a basis far less reliable than air; *for no such things as axioms ever existed or can possibly exist at all*. This they must have been very blind, indeed, not to see, or at least to suspect; for, even in their own day, many of their long-admitted 'axioms' had been abandoned:—'*ex nihilo nihil fit*,'[8] for example, and a 'thing cannot act where it is not,' and 'there cannot be antipodes,' and 'darkness cannot proceed from light.' These and numerous similar propositions formerly accepted, without hesitation, as axioms, or undeniable truths, were, even at the period of which I speak, seen to be altogether untenable:—how absurd in these people, then, to persist in relying upon a basis, as immutable, whose mutability had become so repeatedly manifest!

"But, even through evidence afforded by themselves against themselves, it is easy to convict these *à priori* reasoners of the grossest unreason—it is easy to show the futility—the impalpability of their axioms in general. I have now lying before me"—it will be observed that we still proceed with the letter—"I have now lying before me a book printed about a thousand years ago. Pundit assures me that it is decidedly the cleverest ancient work on the topic, which is 'Logic.' The author, who was much esteemed in his day, was one Miller, or Mill;[9] and we find it recorded of him, as a point of some importance, that he rode a mill-horse whom he called Jeremy Bentham:—but let us glance at the volume itself!

"Ah!—'Ability or inability to conceive,' says Mr. Mill very properly, 'is *in no case* to be received as a criterion of axiomatic truth.' Now, that this is a palpable truism no one in his senses will deny. *Not* to admit the proposition, is to insinuate a charge of variability in Truth itself, whose very title is a synonym of the Steadfast. If ability to conceive be taken as a criterion of Truth, then a truth to *David* Hume[10] would very seldom be a truth to *Joe*; and ninety-nine hundredths of what is undeniable in Heaven would be demonstrable falsity upon Earth. The proposition of Mr. Mill, then, is sustained. I will not grant it to be an *axiom*; and this merely because I am showing that *no* axioms exist; but, with a distinction which could not have been cavilled at even by Mr. Mill himself, I am ready to grant that, *if* an axiom *there be*, then the proposition of which we speak has the fullest right to be considered an axiom—that no *more* absolute axiom *is*—and, consequently, that any subsequent proposition which shall conflict with this one primarily advanced, must be either a falsity in itself—that is to say no axiom—or, if admitted axiomatic, must at once neutralize both itself and its predecessor.

"And now, by the logic of their own propounder, let us proceed to test any one of the axioms propounded. Let us give Mr. Mill the fairest of play. We will bring the point to no ordinary issue. We will select for investigation no common-place axiom—no axiom of what, not the less preposterously because only impliedly, he terms his secondary class—as if a positive truth by definition could be either more or less positively a truth:—we will select, I say, no axiom of an unquestionability so questionable as is to be found in Euclid. We will not talk, for example, about such propositions as that two straight lines cannot enclose a space, or that the whole is greater than any one of its parts. We will afford the logician *every* advantage. We will come at once to a proposition which he regards as the acme of the unquestionable— as the quintessence of axiomatic undeniability. Here it is:—'Contradictions cannot *both* be true—that is, cannot cöexist in nature.' Here Mr. Mill means, for instance,— and I give the most forcible instance conceivable—that a tree must be either a tree or *not* a tree—that it cannot be at the same time a tree *and* not a tree:—all which is quite reasonable of itself and will answer remarkably well as an axiom, until we bring it into collation with an axiom insisted upon a few pages before—in other words—words which I have previously employed—until we test it by the logic of its own propounder. 'A tree,' Mr. Mill asserts, 'must be either a tree or *not* a tree.' Very well:—and now let me ask him, *why*. To this little query there is but one response:—I defy any man living to invent a second. The sole answer is this:—'Because we find it *impossible to conceive* that a tree can be any thing else than a tree or not a tree.' This, I repeat, is Mr. Mill's sole answer:—he will not *pretend* to suggest another:— and yet, by his own showing, his answer is clearly no answer at all; for has he not already required us to admit, *as an axiom*, that ability or inability to conceive is *in no case* to be taken as a criterion of axiomatic truth? Thus all—absolutely *all* his argumentation is at sea without a rudder. Let it not be urged that an exception from the general rule is to be made, in cases where the 'impossibility to conceive' is so peculiarly great as when we are called upon to conceive a tree *both* a tree and *not* a tree. Let no attempt, I say, be made at urging this sotticism; for, in the first place, there are no *degrees* of 'impossibility,' and thus no one impossible conception can be *more* peculiarly impossible than another impossible conception:—in the second place, Mr. Mill himself, no doubt after thorough deliberation, has most distinctly, and most rationally, excluded all opportunity for exception, by the emphasis of his proposition, that, *in no case*, is ability or inability to conceive, to be taken as a criterion of axiomatic truth:—in the third place, even were exceptions admissible at all, it remains to be shown how any exception is admissible *here*. That a tree can be both a tree and not a tree, is an idea which the angels, or the devils, *may* entertain, and which no doubt many an earthly Bedlamite,[11] or Transcendentalist, *does*.

"Now I do not quarrel with these ancients," continues the letter-writer, "*so much* on account of the transparent frivolity of their logic—which, to be plain, was baseless, worthless and fantastic altogether—as on account of their pompous and infatuate proscription of all *other* roads to Truth than the two narrow and crooked paths—the one of creeping and the other of crawling—to which, in their ignorant perversity, they have dared to confine the Soul—the Soul which loves nothing so well as to soar in those regions of illimitable intuition which are utterly incognizant of '*path*.'

"By the bye, my dear friend, is it not an evidence of the mental slavery entailed upon those bigoted people by their Hogs and Rams, that in spite of the eternal prating of their savans about *roads* to Truth, none of them fell, even by accident, into what we now so distinctly perceive to be the broadest, the straightest and most available of all mere roads—the great thoroughfare—the majestic highway of the *Consistent*? Is it not wonderful that they should have failed to deduce from the works of God the vitally momentous consideration that *a perfect consistency can be nothing but an absolute truth*? How plain—how rapid our progress since the late announcement of this proposition! By its means, investigation has been taken out of the hands of the ground-moles, and given as a duty, rather than as a task, to the true—to the *only* true thinkers—to the generally-educated men of ardent imagination. These latter—our Keplers—our Laplaces[12]—'speculate'—'theorize'—these are the terms—can you not fancy the shout of scorn with which they would be received by our progenitors, were it possible for them to be looking over my shoulders as I write? The Keplers, I repeat, speculate—theorize—and their theories are merely corrected—reduced—sifted—cleared, little by little, of their chaff of inconsistency—until at length there stands apparent an unencumbered *Consistency*—a consistency which the most stolid admit—because it *is* a consistency—to be an absolute and an unquestionable *Truth*.

"I have often thought, my friend, that it must have puzzled these dogmaticians of a thousand years ago, to determine, even, by which of their two boasted roads it is that the cryptographist attains the solution of the more complicated cyphers—or by which of them Champollion[13] guided mankind to those important and innumerable truths which, for so many centuries, have lain entombed amid the phonetical hieroglyphics of Egypt. In especial, would it not have given these bigots some trouble to determine by which of their two roads was reached the most momentous and sublime of *all* their truths—the truth—the fact of *gravitation*? Newton[14] deduced it from the laws of Kepler. Kepler admitted that these laws he *guessed*—these laws whose investigation disclosed to the greatest of British astronomers that principle, the basis of all (existing) physical principle, in going behind which we enter at once the nebulous kingdom of Metaphysics. Yes!—these vital laws Kepler *guessed*—that is to say, he *imagined* them. Had he been asked to point out either the *deductive* or *inductive* route by which he attained them, his reply might have been—'I know nothing about *routes*—but I *do* know the machinery of the Universe. Here it is. I grasped it with *my soul*—I reached it through mere dint of *intuition*.' Alas, poor ignorant old man! Could not any metaphysician have told him that what he called 'intuition' was but the conviction resulting from *deductions* or *inductions* of which the processes were so shadowy as to have escaped his consciousness, eluded his reason, or bidden defiance to his capacity of expression? How great a pity it is that some 'moral philosopher' had not enlightened him about all this! How it would have comforted him on his death-bed to know that, instead of having gone intuitively and thus unbecomingly, he had, in fact, proceeded decorously and legitimately—that is to say Hog-ishly, or at least Ram-ishly—into the vast halls where lay gleaming, untended, and hitherto untouched by mortal hand—unseen by mortal eye—the imperishable and priceless secrets of the Universe!

"Yes, Kepler was essentially a *theorist*; but this title, *now* of so much sanctity, was, in those ancient days, a designation of supreme contempt. It is only *now* that men begin to appreciate that divine old man—to sympathize with the prophetical and poetical rhapsody of his ever-memorable words. For *my* part," continues the unknown correspondent, "I glow with a sacred fire when I even think of them, and feel that I shall never grow weary of their repetition:—in concluding this letter, let me have the real pleasure of transcribing them once again:—'*I care not whether my work be read now or by posterity. I can afford to wait a century for readers when God himself has waited six thousand years for an observer. I triumph. I have stolen the golden secret of the Egyptians. I will indulge my sacred fury.*'"

Here end my quotations from this very unaccountable and, perhaps, somewhat impertinent epistle; and perhaps it would be folly to comment, in any respect, upon the chimerical, not to say revolutionary, fancies of the writer—whoever he is—fancies so radically at war with the well-considered and well-settled opinions of this age. Let us proceed, then, to our legitimate thesis, *The Universe*.

. . .

As our starting-point, then, let us adopt the *Godhead*. Of this Godhead, *in itself*, he alone is not imbecile—he alone is not impious who propounds—nothing. "*Nous ne connaissons rien,*" says the Baron de Bielfeld[15]—"*Nous ne connaissons rien de la nature ou de l'essence de Dieu:—pour savoir ce qu'il est, il faut être Dieu même.*"— "We know absolutely *nothing* of the nature or essence of God:—in order to comprehend what he is, we should have to be God ourselves."

"*We should have to be God ourselves!*"—With a phrase so startling as this yet ringing in my ears, I nevertheless venture to demand if this our present ignorance of the Deity is an ignorance to which the soul is *everlastingly* condemned.

By *Him*, however—*now*, at least, the Incomprehensible—by Him—assuming him as *Spirit*—that is to say, as *not Matter*—a distinction which, for all intelligible purposes, will stand well instead of a definition—by Him, then, existing as Spirit, let us content ourselves, to-night, with supposing to have been *created*, or made out of Nothing, by dint of his Volition—at some point of Space which we will take as a centre—at some period into which we do not pretend to inquire, but at all events immensely remote—by Him, then again, let us suppose to have been created—*what?* This is a vitally momentous epoch in our considerations. *What* is it that we are justified—that alone we are justified in supposing to have been, primarily and solely, *created?*

We have attained a point where only *Intuition* can aid us:—but now let me recur to the idea which I have already suggested as that alone which we can properly entertain of intuition. It is but *the conviction arising from those inductions or deductions of which the processes are so shadowy as to escape our consciousness, elude our reason, or defy our capacity of expression.* With this understanding, I now assert—that an intuition altogether irresistible, although inexpressible, forces me to the conclusion that what God originally created—that that Matter which, by dint of his Volition, he first made from his Spirit, or from Nihility, *could* have been nothing but Matter in its utmost conceivable state of——what?—of *Simplicity?*

This will be found the sole absolute *assumption* of my Discourse. I use the word "assumption" in its ordinary sense; yet I maintain that even this my primary proposition, is very, very far indeed, from being really a mere assumption. Nothing was ever more certainly—no human conclusion was ever, in fact, more regularly—more rigorously *deduced:*—but, alas! the processes lie out of the human analysis—at all events are beyond the utterance of the human tongue.

Let us now endeavor to conceive what Matter must be, when, or if, in its absolute extreme of *Simplicity.* Here the Reason flies at once to Imparticularity—to a particle—to *one* particle—a particle of *one* kind—of *one* character—of *one* nature—of *one* size—of one form—a particle, therefore, *"without* form and void"[16]—a particle positively a particle at all points—a particle absolutely unique, individual, undivided, and not indivisible only because He who *created* it, by dint of his Will, can by an infinitely less energetic exercise of the same Will, as a matter of course, divide it.

Oneness, then, is all that I predicate of the originally created Matter; but I propose to show that this *Oneness is a principle abundantly sufficient to account for the constitution, the existing phænomena and the plainly inevitable annihilation of at least the material Universe.*

The willing into being the primordial particle, has completed the act, or more properly the *conception,* of Creation. We now proceed to the ultimate purpose for which we are to suppose the Particle created—that is to say, the ultimate purpose so far as our considerations *yet* enable us to see it—the constitution of the Universe from it, the Particle.

This constitution has been effected by *forcing* the originally and therefore normally *One* into the abnormal condition of *Many.* An action of this character implies reäction. A diffusion from Unity, under the conditions, involves a tendency to return into Unity—a tendency ineradicable until satisfied. But on these points I will speak more fully hereafter.

. . .

Discarding now the two equivocal terms, "gravitation" and "electricity," let us adopt the more definite expressions, *"attraction"* and *"repulsion."* The former is the body; the latter the soul: the one is the material; the other the spiritual, principle of the Universe. *No other principles exist. All* phænomena are referable to one, or to the other, or to both combined. So rigorously is this the case—so thoroughly demonstrable is it that attraction and repulsion are the *sole* properties through which we perceive the Universe—in other words, by which Matter is manifested to Mind—that, for all merely argumentative purposes, we are fully justified in assuming that matter *exists* only as attraction and repulsion—that attraction and repulsion *are* matter:—there being no conceivable case in which we may not employ the term "matter" and the terms "attraction" and "repulsion," taken together, as equivalent, and therefore convertible, expressions in Logic.

. . .

Let me now repeat the definition of gravity:—*Every atom, of every body, attracts every other atom, both of its own and of every other body*, with a force which varies inversely as the squares of the distances of the attracting and attracted atom.

Here let the reader pause with me, for a moment, in contemplation of the miraculous—of the ineffable—of the altogether unimaginable complexity of relation involved in the fact that *each atom attracts every other atom*—involved merely in this fact of the attraction, without reference to the law or mode in which the attraction is manifested—involved *merely* in the fact that each atom attracts every other atom *at all*, in a wilderness of atoms so numerous that those which go to the composition of a cannon-ball, exceed, probably, in mere point of number, all the stars which go to the constitution of the Universe.

Had we discovered, simply, that each atom tended to some one favorite point—to some especially attractive atom—we should still have fallen upon a discovery which, in itself, would have sufficed to overwhelm the mind:—but what is it that we are actually called upon to comprehend? That each atom attracts—sympathizes with the most delicate movements of every other atom, and with each and with all at the same time, and forever, and according to a determinate law of which the complexity, even considered by itself solely, is utterly beyond the grasp of the imagination of man. If I propose to ascertain the influence of one mote in a sunbeam upon its neighboring mote, I cannot accomplish my purpose without first counting and weighing all the atoms in the Universe and defining the precise positions of all at one particular moment. If I venture to displace, by even the billionth part of an inch, the microscopical speck of dust which lies now upon the point of my finger, what is the character of that act upon which I have adventured? I have done a deed which shakes the Moon in her path, which causes the Sun to be no longer the Sun, and which alters forever the destiny of the multitudinous myriads of stars that roll and glow in the majestic presence of their Creator.

These ideas—conceptions such as *these*—unthoughtlike thoughts—soul-reveries rather than conclusions or even considerations of the intellect:—ideas, I repeat, such as these, are such as we can alone hope profitably to entertain in any effort at grasping the great principle, *Attraction*.

But now,—*with* such ideas—with such a *vision* of the marvellous complexity of Attraction fairly in his mind—let any person competent of thought on such topics as these, set himself to the task of imagining a *principle* for the phænomena observed—a condition from which they sprang.

Does not so evident a brotherhood among the atoms point to a common parentage? Does not a sympathy so omniprevalent, so ineradicable, and so thoroughly irrespective, suggest a common paternity as its source? Does not one extreme impel the reason to the other? Does not the infinitude of division refer to the utterness of individuality? Does not the entireness of the complex hint at the perfection of the simple? It is *not* that the atoms, as we see them, are divided or that they are complex in their relations—but that they are inconceivably divided and unutterably complex:—it is the extremeness of the conditions to which I now allude, rather than to the conditions themselves. In a word, is it not because the atoms were, at some remote epoch of time, even *more than together*—is it not because originally, and therefore normally, they were *One*—that now, in all circumstances—at all points—in all directions—by all modes of approach—in all relations and through all conditions—they struggle *back* to this absolutely, this irrelatively, this unconditionally *one?*

. . .

I have already given my reasons for presuming Matter to have been diffused by a determinate rather than by a continuous or infinitely continued force. Supposing a continuous force, we should be unable, in the first place, to comprehend a rëaction at all; and we should be required, in the second place, to entertain the impossible conception of an infinite extension of Matter. Not to dwell upon the impossibility of the conception, the infinite extension of Matter is an idea which, if not positively disproved, is at least not in any respect warranted by telescopic observation of the stars—a point to be explained more fully hereafter; and this empirical reason for believing in the original finity of Matter is unempirically confirmed. For example:—Admitting, for the moment, the possibility of understanding Space *filled* with the irradiated atoms—that is to say, admitting, as well as we can, for argument's sake, that the succession of the irradiated atoms had absolutely *no end*—then it is abundantly clear that, even when the Volition of God had been withdrawn from them, and thus the tendency to return into Unity permitted (abstractly) to be satisfied, this permission would have been nugatory and invalid—practically valueless and of no effect whatever. No Rëaction could have taken place; no movement toward Unity could have been made; no Law of Gravity could have obtained.

To explain:—Grant the *abstract* tendency of any one atom to any one other as the inevitable result of diffusion from the normal Unity:—or, what is the same thing, admit any given atom as *proposing* to move in any given direction—it is clear that, since there is an *infinity* of atoms on all sides of the atom proposing to move, it can never actually move toward the satisfaction of its tendency in the direction given, on account of a precisely equal and counterbalancing tendency in the direction diametrically opposite. In other words, exactly as many tendencies to Unity are behind the hesitating atom as before it; for it is a mere sotticism to say that one infinite line is longer or shorter than another infinite line, or that one infinite number is greater or less than another number that is infinite. Thus the atom in question must remain stationary forever. Under the impossible circumstances which we have been merely endeavoring to conceive for argument's sake, there could have been no aggregation of Matter—no stars—no worlds—nothing but a perpetually atomic and inconsequential Universe. In fact, view it as we will, the whole idea of unlimited Matter is not only untenable, but impossible and preposterous.

With the understanding of a *sphere* of atoms, however, we perceive, at once, a *satisfiable* tendency to union. The general result of the tendency each to each, being a tendency of all to the centre, the *general* process of condensation, or approximation, commences immediately, by a common and simultaneous movement, on withdrawal of the Divine Volition; the *individual* approximations, or coalescences—*not* cöalitions—of atom with atom, being subject to almost infinite variations of time, degree, and condition, on account of the excessive multiplicity of relation, arising from the differences of form assumed as characterizing the atoms at the moment of their quitting the Particle Proper; as well as from the subsequent particular inequidistance, each from each.

What I wish to impress upon the reader is the certainty of there arising, at once, (on withdrawal of the diffusive force, or Divine Volition,) out of the condition of the atoms as described, at innumerable points throughout the Universal sphere, innumerable agglomerations, characterized by innumerable specific differences of form, size, essential nature, and distance each from each. The development of Repulsion (Electricity) must have commenced, of course, with the very earliest particular efforts at Unity, and must have proceeded constantly in the ratio of Coalescence—that is to say, *in that of Condensation*, or, again, of Heterogeneity.

Thus the two Principles Proper, *Attraction and Repulsion*—the Material and the Spiritual—accompany each other, in the strictest fellowship, forever. Thus *The Body and The Soul walk hand in hand*.

. . .

After referring, however, the centripetal force to the omniprevalent law of Gravity, it has been the fashion with astronomical treatises, to seek beyond the limits of mere Nature—that is to say, of *Secondary* Cause—a solution of the phænomenon of tangential velocity. This latter they attribute directly to a *First* Cause—to God. The force which carries a stellar body around its primary they assert to have originated in an impulse given immediately by the finger—this is the childish phraseology employed—by the finger of Deity itself. In this view, the planets, fully formed, are conceived to have been hurled from the Divine hand, to a position in the vicinity of the suns, with an impetus mathematically adapted to the masses, or attractive capacities, of the suns themselves. An idea so grossly unphilosophical, although so supinely adopted, could have arisen only from the difficulty of otherwise accounting for the absolutely accurate adaptation, each to each, of two forces so seemingly independent, one of the other, as are the gravitating and tangential. But it should be remembered that, for a long time, the coincidence between the moon's rotation and her sidereal revolution—two matters seemingly far more independent than those now considered—was looked upon as positively miraculous; and there was a strong disposition, even among astronomers, to attribute the marvel to the direct and continual agency of God—who, in this case, it was said, had found it necessary to interpose, specially, among his general laws, a set of subsidiary regulations, for the purpose of forever concealing from mortal eyes the glories, or perhaps the horrors, of the other side of the Moon—of that mysterious hemisphere which has always avoided, and must perpetually avoid, the telescopic scrutiny of mankind. The advance of Science, however, soon demonstrated—what to the philosophical instinct needed *no* demonstration—that the one movement is but a portion—something more, even, than a consequence—of the other.

For my part, I have no patience with fantasies at once so timorous, so idle, and so awkward. They belong to the veriest *cowardice* of thought. That Nature and the God of Nature are distinct, no thinking being can long doubt. By the former we imply merely the laws of the latter. But with the very idea of God, omnipotent, omniscient, we entertain, also, the idea of *the infallibility* of his laws. With Him there being neither Past nor Future—with Him all being *Now*—do we not insult him in supposing his laws so contrived as not to provide for every possible contingency?— or, rather, what idea *can* we have of *any* possible contingency, except that it is at once a result and a manifestation of his laws? He who, divesting himself of prejudice, shall have the rare courage to think absolutely for himself, cannot fail to arrive, in the end, at the condensation of *laws* into *Law*—cannot fail of reaching the conclusion that *each law of Nature is dependent at all points upon all other laws*, and that all are but consequences of one primary exercise of the Divine Volition. Such is the principle of the Cosmogony which, with all necessary deference, I here venture to suggest and to maintain.

In this view, it will be seen that, dismissing as frivolous, and even impious, the fancy of the tangential force having been imparted to the planets immediately by "the finger of God," I consider this force as originating in the rotation of the stars:— this rotation as brought about by the in-rushing of the primary atoms, towards their respective centres of aggregation:—this in-rushing as the consequence of the law of Gravity:—this law as but the mode in which is necessarily manifested the tendency of the atoms to return into imparticularity:—this tendency to return as but the inevitable rëaction of the first and most sublime of Acts—that act by which a God, self-existing and alone existing, became all things at once, through dint of his volition, while all things were thus constituted a portion of God.

. . .

Now this is in precise accordance with what we know of the succession of animals on the Earth. As it has proceeded in its condensation, superior and still superior races have appeared. Is it impossible that the successive geological revolutions which have attended, at least, if not immediately caused, these successive elevations of vitalic character—is it improbable that these revolutions have themselves been produced by the successive planetary discharges from the Sun—in other words, by the successive variations in the solar influence on the Earth? Were this idea tenable, we should not be unwarranted in the fancy that the discharge of yet a new planet, interior to Mercury, may give rise to yet a new modification of the terrestrial surface—a modification from which may spring a race both materially and spiritually superior to Man. These thoughts impress me with all the force of truth—but I throw them out, of course, merely in their obvious character of suggestion.

. . .

No astronomical fallacy is more untenable, and none has been more pertinaciously adhered to, than that of the absolute *illimitation* of the Universe of Stars. The reasons for limitation, as I have already assigned them, *à priori*, seem to me unanswerable; but, not to speak of these, *observation* assures us that there is, in numerous directions around us, certainly, if not in all, a positive limit—or, at the very least, affords us no basis whatever for thinking otherwise. Were the succession of stars endless, then the background of the sky would present us an uniform luminosity, like that displayed by the Galaxy—*since there could be absolutely no point, in all that background, at which would not exist a star*. The only mode, therefore, in which, under such a state of affairs, we could comprehend the *voids* which our telescopes find in innumerable directions, would be by supposing the distance of the invisible background so immense that no ray from it has yet been able to reach us at all. That this *may* be so, who shall venture to deny? I maintain, simply, that we have not even the shadow of a reason for believing that it *is* so.

When speaking of the vulgar propensity to regard all bodies on the Earth as tending merely to the Earth's centre, I observed that, "with certain exceptions to be specified hereafter, every body on the Earth tended not only to the Earth's centre, but in every conceivable direction besides." The "exceptions" refer to those frequent gaps in the Heavens, where our utmost scrutiny can detect not only no stellar bodies, but no indications of their existence:—where yawning chasms, blacker than Erebus, seem to afford us glimpses, through the boundary walls of the Universe of Stars, into the illimitable Universe of Vacancy, beyond. Now as any body, existing on the Earth, chances to pass, either through its own movement or the Earth's, into a line with any one of these voids, or cosmical abysses, it clearly is no longer attracted *in the direction of that void*, and for the moment, consequently, is "heavier" than at any period, either after or before. Independently of the consideration of these voids, however, and looking only at the generally unequable distribution of the stars, we see that the absolute tendency of bodies on the Earth to the Earth's centre, is in a state of perpetual variation.

We comprehend, then, the insulation of our Universe. We perceive the isolation of *that*—of *all* that which we grasp with the senses. We know that there exists one *cluster of clusters*—a collection around which, on all sides, extend the immeasurable wildernesses of a Space *to all human perception* untenanted. But *because* upon the confines of this Universe of Stars we are compelled to pause, through want of farther evidence from the senses, is it right to conclude that, in fact, there *is* no material point beyond that which we have thus been permitted to attain? Have we, or have we not, an analogical right to the inference that this perceptible Universe—that this cluster of clusters—is but one of *a series* of clusters of clusters, the rest of which are invisible through distance—through the diffusion of their light being so excessive, ere it reaches us, as not to produce upon our retinas a light-impression—or from there being no such emanation as light at all, in these unspeakably distant worlds—or, lastly, from the mere interval being so vast, that the electric tidings of their presence in Space, have not yet—through the lapsing myriads of years—been enabled to traverse that interval?

Have we any right to inferences—have we any ground whatever for visions such as these? If we have a right to them in *any* degree, we have a right to their infinite extension.

The human brain has obviously a leaning to the *"Infinite,"* and fondles the phantom of the idea. It seems to long with a passionate fervor for this impossible conception, with the hope of intellectually believing it when conceived. What is general among the whole race of Man, of course no individual of that race can be warranted in considering abnormal; nevertheless, there *may* be a class of superior intelligences, to whom the human bias alluded to may wear all the character of monomania.

My question, however, remains unanswered:—Have we any right to infer—let us say, rather, to imagine—an interminable succession of the "clusters of clusters," or of "Universes" more or less similar?

I reply that the "right," in a case such as this, depends absolutely upon the hardihood of that imagination which ventures to claim the right. Let me declare, only, that, as an individual, I myself feel impelled to the *fancy*—without daring to call it more—that there *does* exist a *limitless* succession of Universes, more or less similar to that of which we have cognizance—to that of which *alone* we shall ever have cognizance—at the very least until the return of our own particular Universe into Unity. *If* such clusters of clusters exist, however—*and they do*—it is abundantly clear that, having had no part in our origin, they have no portion in our laws. They neither attract us, nor we them. Their material—their spirit is not ours—is not that which obtains in any part of our Universe. They could not impress our senses or our souls. Among them and us—considering all, for the moment, collectively—there are no influences in common. Each exists, apart and independently, *in the bosom of its proper and particular God.*

. . .

Our fancies thus occupied with the cosmical distances, let us take the opportunity of referring to the difficulty which we have so often experienced, while pursuing *the beaten path* of astronomical reflection, *in accounting* for the immeasurable voids alluded to—in comprehending why chasms so totally unoccupied and therefore apparently so needless, have been made to intervene between star and star—between cluster and cluster—in understanding, to be brief, a sufficient reason for the Titanic scale, in respect of mere *Space*, on which the Universe is seen to be constructed. A rational cause for this phænomenon, I maintain that Astronomy has palpably failed to assign:—but the considerations through which, in this Essay, we have proceeded step by step, enable us clearly and immediately to perceive that *Space and Duration are one.* That the Universe might *endure* throughout an æra at all commensurate with the grandeur of its component material portions and with the high majesty of its spiritual purposes, it was necessary that the original atomic diffusion be made to so inconceivable an extent as to be only not infinite. It was required, in a word, that the stars should be gathered into visibility from invisible nebulosity—proceed from nebulosity to consolidation—and so grow grey in giving birth and death to unspeakably numerous and complex variations of vitalic development:—it was required that the stars should do all this—should have time thoroughly to accomplish all these Divine purposes—*during the period* in which all things were effecting their return into Unity with a velocity accumulating in the inverse proportion of the squares of the distances at which lay the inevitable End.

Throughout all this we have no difficulty in understanding the absolute accuracy of the Divine *adaptation*. The density of the stars, respectively, proceeds, of course, as their condensation diminishes; condensation and heterogeneity keep pace with each other; through the latter, which is the index of the former, we estimate the vitalic and spiritual development. Thus, in the density of the globes, we have the measure in which their purposes are fulfilled. *As* density proceeds—*as* the divine intentions *are* accomplished—*as* less and still less remains *to be* accomplished—so—in the same ratio—should we expect to find an acceleration of *the End:*—and thus the philosophical mind will easily comprehend that the Divine designs in constituting the stars, advance *mathematically* to their fulfillment:—and more; it will readily give the advance a mathematical expression; it will decide that this advance is inversely proportional with the squares of the distances of all created things from the starting-point and goal of their creation.

Not only is this Divine adaptation, however, mathematically accurate, but there is that about it which stamps it *as divine*, in distinction from that which is merely the work of human constructiveness. I allude to the complete *mutuality* of adaptation. For example; in human constructions a particular cause has a particular effect; a particular intention brings to pass a particular object; but this is all; we see no reciprocity. The effect does not re-act upon the cause; the intention does not change relations with the object. In Divine constructions the object is either design or object as we choose to regard it—and we may take at any time a cause for an effect, or the converse—so that we can never absolutely decide which is which.

To give an instance:—In polar climates the human frame, to maintain its animal heat, requires, for combustion in the capillary system, an abundant supply of highly azotized food, such as train-oil. But again:—in polar climates nearly the sole food afforded man is the oil of abundant seals and whales. Now, whether is oil at hand because imperatively demanded, or the only thing demanded because the only thing to be obtained? It is impossible to decide. There is an absolute *reciprocity of adaptation*.

The pleasure which we derive from any display of human ingenuity is in the ratio of *the approach* to this species of reciprocity. In the construction of *plot*, for example, in fictitious literature, we should aim at so arranging the incidents that we shall not be able to determine, of any one of them, whether it depends from any one other or upholds it. In this sense, of course, *perfection* of *plot* is really, or practically, unattainable—but only because it is a finite intelligence that constructs. The plots of God are perfect. The Universe is a plot of God.

. . .

It is, perhaps, in no little degree, however, our propensity for the continuous—for the analogical—in the present case more particularly for the symmetrical—which has been leading us astray. And, in fact, the sense of the symmetrical is an instinct which may be depended upon with an almost blindfold reliance. It is the poetical essence of the Universe—*of the Universe* which, in the supremeness of its symmetry, is but the most sublime of poems. Now symmetry and consistency are convertible terms:—thus Poetry and Truth are one. A thing is consistent in the ratio of its truth—true in the ratio of its consistency. *A perfect consistency, I repeat, can be nothing but an absolute truth*. We may take it for granted, then, that Man cannot long or widely err, if he suffer himself to be guided by his poetical, which I have maintained to be his truthful, in being his symmetrical, instinct. He must have a care, however, lest, in pursuing too heedlessly the superficial symmetry of forms and motions, he leave out of sight the really essential symmetry of the principles which determine and control them.

That the stellar bodies would finally be merged in one—that, at last, all would be drawn into the substance of *one stupendous central orb already existing*—is an idea which, for some time past, seems, vaguely and indeterminately, to have held possession of the fancy of mankind. It is an idea, in fact, which belongs to the class of the *excessively obvious*. It springs, instantly, from a superficial observation of the cyclic and seemingly *gyrating*, or *vorticial* movements of those individual portions of the Universe which come most immediately and most closely under our observation. There is not, perhaps, a human being, of ordinary education and of average reflective capacity, to whom, at some period, the fancy in question has not occurred, as if spontaneously, or intuitively, and wearing all the character of a very profound and very original conception. This conception, however, so commonly entertained, has never, within my knowledge, arisen out of any abstract considerations. Being, on the contrary, always suggested, as I say, by the vorticial movements about centres, a reason for it, also,—a *cause* for the ingathering of all the orbs into one, *imagined to be already existing*, was naturally sought in the same direction—among these cyclic movements themselves.

Thus it happened that, on announcement of the gradual and perfectly regular decrease observed in the orbit of Enck's comet,[17] at every successive revolution about our Sun, astronomers were nearly unanimous in the opinion that the cause in question was found—that a principle was discovered sufficient to account, physically, for that final, universal agglomeration which, I repeat, the analogical, symmetrical or poetical instinct of Man had predetermined to understand as something more than a simple hypothesis.

This cause—this sufficient reason for the final ingathering—was declared to exist in an exceedingly rare but still material medium pervading space; which medium, by retarding, in some degree, the progress of the comet, perpetually weakened its tangential force; thus giving a predominance to the centripetal; which, of course, drew the comet nearer and nearer at each revolution, and would eventually precipitate it upon the Sun.

All this was strictly logical—admitting the medium or ether; but this ether was assumed, most illogically, on the ground that no *other* mode than the one spoken of could be discovered, of accounting for the observed decrease in the orbit of the comet:—as if from the fact that we could *discover* no other mode of accounting for it, it followed, in any respect, that no other mode of accounting for it existed. It is clear that innumerable causes might operate, in combination, to diminish the orbit, without even a possibility of our ever becoming acquainted with one of them. In the meantime, it has never been fairly shown, perhaps, why the retardation occasioned by the skirts of the Sun's atmosphere, through which the comet passes at perihelion, is not enough to account for the phænomenon. That Enck's comet will be absorbed into the Sun, is probable; that all the comets of the system will be absorbed, is more than merely possible; but, in such case, the principle of absorption must be referred to eccentricity of orbit—to the close approximation to the Sun, of the comets at their perihelia; and is a principle not affecting, in any degree, the ponderous *spheres*, which are to be regarded as the true material constituents of the Universe.—Touching comets, in general, let me here suggest, in passing, that we cannot be far wrong in looking upon them as the *lightning-flashes of the cosmical Heaven.*

The idea of a retarding ether and, through it, of a final agglomeration of all things, seemed at one time, however, to be confirmed by the observation of a positive decrease in the orbit of the solid moon. By reference to eclipses recorded 2500 years ago, it was found that the velocity of the satellite's revolution *then* was considerably less than it is *now*; that on the hypothesis that its motions in its orbit is uniformly in accordance with Kepler's law, and was accurately determined *then*—2500 years ago—it is now in advance of the position it *should* occupy, by nearly 9000 miles. The increase of velocity proved, of course, a diminution of orbit; and astronomers were fast yielding to a belief in an ether, as the sole mode of accounting for the phænomenon, when Lagrange[18] came to the rescue. He showed that, owing to the configurations of the spheroids, the shorter axes of their ellipses are subject to variation in length; the longer axes being permanent; and that this variation is continuous and vibratory—so that every orbit is in a state of transition, either from circle to ellipse, or from ellipse to circle. In the case of the moon, where the shorter axis is *de*creasing, the orbit is passing from circle to ellipse and, consequently, is *de*creasing too; but, after a long series of ages, the ultimate eccentricity will be attained; then the shorter axis will proceed to *in*crease, until the orbit becomes a circle; when the process of shortening will again take place;—and so on forever. In the case of the Earth, the orbit is passing from ellipse to circle. The facts thus demonstrated do away, of course, with all necessity for supposing an ether, and with all apprehension of the system's instability—on the ether's account.

It will be remembered that I have myself assumed what we may term *an ether*. I have spoken of a subtle *influence* which we know to be ever in attendance upon matter, although becoming manifest only through matter's heterogeneity. To this *influence*—without daring to touch it at all in any effort at explaining its awful *nature*—I have referred the various phænomena of electricity, heat, light, magnetism; and more—of vitality, consciousness, and thought—in a word, of spirituality. It will be seen, at once, then, that the ether thus conceived is radically distinct from the ether of the astronomers; inasmuch as theirs is *matter* and mine *not*.

With the idea of a material ether, seems, thus, to have departed altogether the thought of that universal agglomeration so long predetermined by the poetical fancy of mankind:—an agglomeration in which a sound Philosophy might have been warranted in putting faith, at least to a certain extent, if for no other reason than that by this poetical fancy it *had* been so predetermined. But so far as Astronomy— so far as mere Physics have yet spoken, the cycles of the Universe are perpetual—the Universe has no conceivable end. Had an end been demonstrated, however, from so purely collateral a cause as an ether, Man's instinct of the Divine *capacity to adapt*, would have rebelled against the demonstration. We should have been forced to regard the Universe with some such sense of dissatisfaction as we experience in contemplating an unnecessarily complex work of human art. Creation would have affected us as an imperfect *plot* in a romance, where the *dénoûment* is awkwardly brought about by interposed incidents external and foreign to the main subject; instead of springing out of the bosom of the thesis—out of the heart of the ruling idea—instead of arising as a result of the primary proposition—as inseparable and inevitable part and parcel of the fundamental conception of the book.

What I mean by the symmetry of mere surface will now be more clearly understood. It is simply by the blandishment of this symmetry that we have been beguiled into the general idea of which Mädler's hypothesis[19] is but a part—the idea of the vorticial indrawing of the orbs. Dismissing this nakedly physical conception, the symmetry of principle sees the end of all things metaphysically involved in the thought of a beginning; seeks and finds in this origin of all things the *rudiment* of this end; and perceives the impiety of supposing this end likely to be brought about less simply—less directly—less obviously—less artistically—than through *the reäction of the originating Act.*

Recurring, then, to a previous suggestion, let us understand the systems—let us understand each star, with its attendant planets—as but a Titanic atom existing in space with precisely the same inclination for Unity which characterized, in the beginning, the actual atoms after their irradiation throughout the Universal sphere. As these original atoms rushed towards each other in generally straight lines, so let us conceive as at least generally rectilinear, the paths of the system-atoms towards their respective centres of aggregation:—and in this direct drawing together of the systems into clusters, with a similar and simultaneous drawing together of the clusters themselves while undergoing consolidation, we have at length attained the great *Now*—the awful Present—the Existing Condition of the Universe.

Of the still more awful Future a not irrational analogy may guide us in framing an hypothesis. The equilibrium between the centripetal and centrifugal forces of each system, being necessarily destroyed upon attainment of a certain proximity to the nucleus of the cluster to which it belongs, there must occur, at once, a chaotic or seemingly chaotic precipitation, of the moons upon the planets, of the planets upon the suns, and of the suns upon the nuclei; and the general result of this precipitation must be the gathering of the myriad now-existing stars of the firmament into an almost infinitely less number of almost infinitely superior spheres. In being immeasurably fewer, the worlds of that day will be immeasurably greater than our own. Then, indeed, amid unfathomable abysses, will be glaring unimaginable suns. But all this will be merely a climactic magnificence foreboding the great End. Of this End the new genesis described, can be but a very partial postponement. While undergoing consolidation, the clusters themselves, with a speed prodigiously accumulative, have been rushing towards their own general centre—and now, with a thousand-fold electric velocity, commensurate only with their material grandeur and with the spiritual passion of their appetite for oneness, the majestic remnants of the tribe of Stars flash, at length, into a common embrace. The inevitable catastrophe is at hand.

But this catastrophe—what is it? We have seen accomplished the ingathering of the orbs. Henceforward, are we not to understand *one material globe of globes* as constituting and comprehending the Universe? Such a fancy would be altogether at war with every assumption and consideration of this Discourse.

I have already alluded to that absolute *reciprocity of adaptation* which is the idiosyncrasy of the divine Art—stamping it divine. Up to this point of our reflections, we have been regarding the electrical influence as a something by dint of whose repulsion alone Matter is enabled to exist in that state of diffusion demanded for the fulfilment of its purposes:—so far, in a word, we have been considering the influence in question as ordained for Matter's sake—to subserve the objects of matter. With a perfectly legitimate reciprocity, we are now permitted to look at Matter, as created *solely for the sake of this influence*—solely to serve the objects of this spiritual Ether. Through the aid—by the means—through the agency of Matter, and by dint of its heterogeneity—is this Ether manifested—is *Spirit individualized*. It is merely in the development of this Ether, through heterogeneity, that particular masses of Matter become animate—sensitive—and in the ratio of their heterogeneity;—some reaching a degree of sensitiveness involving what we call *Thought* and thus attaining Conscious Intelligence.

In this view, we are enabled to perceive Matter as a Means—not as an End. Its purposes are thus seen to have been comprehended in its diffusion; and with the return into Unity these purposes cease. The absolutely consolidated globe of globes would be *objectless*:—therefore not for a moment could it continue to exist. Matter, created for an end, would unquestionably, on fulfilment of that end, be Matter no longer. Let us endeavor to understand that it would disappear, and that God would remain all in all.

That every work of Divine conception must cöexist and cöexpire with its particular design, seems to me especially obvious; and I make no doubt that, on perceiving the final globe of globes to be *objectless*, the majority of my readers will be satisfied with my "*therefore* it cannot continue to exist." Nevertheless, as the startling thought of its instantaneous disappearance is one which the most powerful intellect cannot be expected readily to entertain on grounds so decidedly abstract, let us endeavor to look at the idea from some other and more ordinary point of view:—let us see how thoroughly and beautifully it is corroborated in an *à posteriori* consideration of Matter as we actually find it.

I have before said that "Attraction and Repulsion being undeniably the sole properties by which Matter is manifested to Mind, we are justified in assuming that Matter *exists* only as Attraction and Repulsion—in other words that Attraction and Repulsion *are* Matter; there being no conceivable case in which we may not employ the term Matter and the terms 'Attraction' and 'Repulsion' taken together, as equivalent, and therefore convertible, expressions in Logic."

Now the very definition of Attraction implies particularity—the existence of parts, particles, or atoms; for we define it as the tendency of "each atom &c. to every other atom" &c. according to a certain law. Of course where there are *no* parts—where there is absolute Unity—where the tendency to oneness is satisfied—there can be no Attraction:—this has been fully shown, and all Philosophy admits it. When, on fulfilment of its purposes, then, Matter shall have returned into its original condition of *One*—a condition which presupposes the expulsion of the separative ether, whose province and whose capacity are limited to keeping the atoms apart until that great day when, this ether being no longer needed, the overwhelming pressure of the finally collective Attraction shall at length just sufficiently predominate[20] and expel it:—when, I say, Matter, finally, expelling the Ether, shall have returned into absolute Unity,—it will then (to speak paradoxically for the moment) be Matter without Attraction and without Repulsion—in other words, Matter without Matter—in other words, again, *Matter no more*. In sinking into Unity, it will sink at once into that Nothingness which, to all Finite Perception, Unity must be—into that Material Nihility from which alone we can conceive it to have been evoked—to have been *created* by the Volition of God.

I repeat then—Let us endeavor to comprehend that the final globe of globes will instantaneously disappear, and that God will remain all in all.

But are we here to pause? Not so. On the Universal agglomeration and dissolution, we can readily conceive that a new and perhaps totally different series of conditions may ensue—another creation and irradiation, returning into itself—another action and reäction of the Divine Will. Guiding our imaginations by that omniprevalent law of laws, the law of periodicity, are we not, indeed, more than justified in entertaining a belief—let us say, rather, in indulging a hope—that the processes we have here ventured to contemplate will be renewed forever, and forever, and forever; a novel Universe swelling into existence, and then subsiding into nothingness, at every throb of the Heart Divine?

And now—this Heart Divine—what is it? *It is our own.*

Let not the merely seeming irreverence of this idea frighten our souls from that cool exercise of consciousness—from that deep tranquillity of self-inspection—through which alone we can hope to attain the presence of this, the most sublime of truths, and look it leisurely in the face.

. . .

No thinking being lives who, at some luminous point of his life of thought, has not felt himself lost amid the surges of futile efforts at understanding, or believing, that anything exists *greater than his own soul*. The utter impossibility of any one's soul feeling itself inferior to another; the intense, overwhelming dissatisfaction and rebellion at the thought;—these, with the omniprevalent aspirations at perfection, are but the spiritual, coincident with the material, struggles towards the original Unity—are, to my mind at least, a species of proof far surpassing what Man terms demonstration, that no one soul *is* inferior to another—that nothing is, or can be, superior to any one soul—that each soul is, in part, its own God—its own Creator:—in a word, that God—the material *and* spiritual God—*now* exists solely in the diffused Matter and Spirit of the Universe; and that the regathering of this diffused Matter and Spirit will be but the re-constitution of the *purely* Spiritual and Individual God.

. . .

NOTES

1. Kenneth Silverman, *Edgar A. Poe: Mournful and Never-Ending Remembrance* (New York: Harper Perennial, 1991), 338.

2. Andrea Wulf, *The Invention of Nature: Alexander von Humboldt's New World* (New York: Alfred A. Knopf, 2016), 248.

3. According to Silverman, *Eureka* "sold poorly." Silverman, *Edgar A. Poe*, 338.

4. David N. Stamos, *Edgar Allan Poe, Eureka, and Scientific Imagination* (Albany: SUNY Press, 2017).

5. John Carlos Rowe, "Space, the Final Frontier: Poe's *Eureka* as Imperial Fantasy," *Poe Studies* 39–40, no. 1–2 (2006): 21; Stuart and Susan F. Levine, "Introduction," in *Edgar Allan Poe: Eureka* (Urbana and Chicago: University of Illinois Press, 2004), xx.

6. Poe to George W. Eveleth, New York, February 29, 1848, in *The Collected Letters of Edgar Allan Poe*, eds. John Ward Ostrom, Burton R. Pollin, and Jeffrey A. Savoye (New York: Gordian Press, 2008), 2:650.

7. G. R. Thompson, while acknowledging the text's importance to understanding the vein of Romantic skepticism that runs through Poe's entire body of work, also calls *Eureka* "Poe's most colossal *hoax*." G. R. Thompson, "Unity, Death, and Nothingness: Poe's Romantic Skepticism," *PMLA* 85, no. 2 (1970): 300 (emphasis in original).

8. Laura Saltz, "Making Sense of *Eureka*," in *The Oxford Handbook of Edgar Allan Poe*, eds. J. Gerald Kennedy and Scott Peeples (New York: Oxford University Press, 2019), 436.

9. Jennifer Rae Greeson, "Poe's 1848: *Eureka*, the Southern Margin, and the Expanding U[niverse] of S[tars]," in *Poe and the Remapping of Antebellum Print Culture*, eds. Jerome McGann and J. Gerald Kennedy (Baton Rouge: Louisiana University Press, 2012), 123–40; W. C. Harris, "Edgar Allan Poe's *Eureka* and the Poetics of Constitution," *American Literary History* 12, no. 1–2 (2000): 1–40.

10. In contrast to transcendentalism, in which the connection between an individual and a transcendental deity is empowering, Poe suggests that the process of merging with an immanent (not transcendent) force is a complete annihilation of individual identity. Matthew Taylor, *Universes Without Us: Posthuman Cosmologies in American Literature* (Minneapolis: University of Minnesota Press, 2013), 30.

11. Briefly, Olbers' paradox holds that the then-current vision of an infinite and static universe could not be reconciled with the observed darkness of the night sky. In an infinite universe, every conceivable line of sight from earth would eventually meet with a star, and the night sky would therefore be filled with light coming from all possible directions. Poe holds instead that the universe is finite and dynamic.

Eureka: A Prose Poem

1. The text is from the first edition. Edgar Allan Poe, *Eureka: A Prose Poem* (New York: Geo. P. Putnam, 1848).

2. **Ætna** Mount Etna, an active volcano on the east coast of Sicily.

3. **Alexander von Humboldt** Friedrich Wilhelm Heinrich Alexander von Humboldt (1769–1859) was a renowned Prussian naturalist. English-language translations of the first volume of his multi-volume *Kosmos* had been published to great acclaim in the years before Poe published *Eureka*.

4. **Mare Tenebrarum** Muslim geographer al-Idrisi (1100–65) used this term for the Atlantic Ocean. Poe misattributes the usage to the ancient Greek author Ptolemy Hephaestion.

5. **Euclid . . . Kant** The ancient Greek mathematician Euclid wrote an influential treatise still used to teach geometry in Poe's day. Poe often invoked (and criticized) German philosopher Immanuel Kant (1724–1804), whose works influenced many British and American authors in the Romantic and Transcendentalist traditions.

6. **Ettrick shepherd** Poe relies on pork-related puns here for his humor. English philosopher and naturalist Francis Bacon (1561–1626) is credited with ushering in the scientific revolution with his emphasis on observing the facts of the natural world. Scottish author James Hogg, who wrote under the pseudonym the "Ettrick shepherd" for one of Poe's favorite magazines, *Blackwood's Magazine*, was not a scientist. Poe has fun with the idea of the corruption of texts over time in his story "Some Words with a Mummy."

7. **Ram** Poe is probably punning on Aries/Ram/Ramus, invoking Petrus Ramus (1515–72), a French humanist associated with the reaction against Aristotelian thought.

8. **ex nihilo nihil fit** Latin, from nothing comes nothing.

9. **Mill** John Stuart Mill (1806–73), British philosopher who promoted the philosophy of utilitarianism originally developed by his predecessor and mentor, English philosopher Jeremy **Bentham** (1748–1832).

10. **Hume** David Hume (1711–76), Scottish Enlightenment historian and philosopher whose skepticism aligns him with empiricists such as Bacon.

11. **Bedlamite** An inhabitant of a mental institution, such as the notorious Bethlem Royal Hospital in London.

12. **Laplaces** Pierre-Simon, marquis de Laplace (1749–1827) was a French polymath, invoked here for his pioneering multi-volume work of astronomy, *Celestial Mechanics* (1799–1825). Johannes **Kepler** (1571–1630) was a German astronomer who developed laws of planetary motion.

13. **Champollion** Jean-François Champollion (1790–1832) is the French scholar known for deciphering Egyptian hieroglyphics.

14. **Newton** Sir Isaac Newton (1642–1727), English physicist and astronomer who formulated the theory of universal gravitation, explaining the laws of planetary motion.

15. **Bielfeld** Jakob Friedrich von Bielfeld (1717–70), German statesman.

16. **void** Genesis 1.2: "And the earth was without form, and void; and darkness *was* upon the face of the deep. And the Spirit of God moved upon the face of the waters."

17. **Enck's comet** The orbit of this previously discovered comet was first computed by German astronomer Johann Franz Encke (1791–1865) in 1819.

18. **Lagrange** Joseph Louis-Lagrange (1736–1813), Italian-French astronomer.

19. **Mädler's hypothesis** Johann Heinrich von Mädler (1794–1874) was a German astronomer who hypothesized that the Sun revolves around a central point in the galaxy.

20. **predominate** "Gravity, therefore, must be the strongest of forces." Poe's note, citing his own statement from earlier in the book.

PART V

Letters, Prefaces, and Critical Writings

Literary criticism was Edgar Allan Poe's initial route to professional recognition. Writing for the *Southern Literary Messenger*, Poe earned notoriety for the severity of his reviews. Michael Allen reads Poe's review style as a conscious attempt to model his writing after what was found in certain popular British magazines Poe admired, such as *Blackwood's* and *Fraser's*, whose reviewers often indulged in harsh personal attacks known as "personalities."[1] Entertainingly caustic reviews were also a way of raising one's personal profile, a means to get ahead in a highly competitive, crowded literary field.[2] Poe's bruising review style is exemplified below in his humorous 1841 takedown of the novel *Guy Fawkes* by British author William Harrison Ainsworth (who, oddly, would later turn up as a thrilled and articulate passenger in Poe's hoaxing account of a transatlantic balloon flight). Poe charges Ainsworth with including "second-hand bits of classical and miscellaneous information" in the novel, a literary failing Poe may have been uniquely qualified to spot, given his own tendency to raid encyclopedias in much the same way. Beyond its entertaining dismissal of *Guy Fawkes* as "*less* than nothing," the review also includes Poe's identification of a golden mean when it comes to narrative commentary, somewhere between purely action-based fiction, which Poe dismisses as tedious, and a "superabundance" of such commentary that leads to didacticism.

Poe's reviews led malicious literary executor Rufus Griswold to dismiss him in his infamous obituary as a "carping grammarian."[3] As an example, note Poe's merciless parsing of British novelist Edward Bulwer's faulty sentences in his review of *Night and Morning*. But this review of Bulwer also expresses influential critical principles Poe consistently championed: his bias in favor of shorter over longer works, his rejection of didacticism in literature (here glossed as "philosophical discussions"), and his emphasis on the supreme artistic value of unity of effect. The definition of plot ("that in which no part can be displaced without ruin to the whole") points to the self-serving quality of some of Poe's criticism: a definition too exacting to be carried out in a novel-length work is perfectly suited to exquisitely plotted short fictions such as the Dupin mysteries or "The Gold-Bug." The grounds on which Poe bases his appreciation of the novel's character Fanny may shed light on the principles at work in his own writings, and antebellum imaginative literature in general, with respect to the characterization of women.

Poe astutely identified Nathaniel Hawthorne as the only active short-story writer whose mastery of the form challenged his own, praising Hawthorne's genius and originality in unusually fulsome language in two reviews published in *Graham's Magazine* in 1842. These reviews promoted an influential theory of the short-story form. In Poe's time, as today, the novel accrued to its author a level of prestige that practitioners of the short story did not enjoy. In the appealingly contrarian spirit that often animates his criticism, Poe disputes the idea that the mere length of a work implies artistic superiority and identifies the short story as the fictional genre (that is, excluding poetry) providing the best opportunity for the display of genius. This position depended upon the emphasis Poe placed on a reader's response to an artistic work. In Poe's view, the success of a work of art was to be judged not on the amount of effort that went into creating it, but on the intensity of its effect on a reader. Longer works sacrificed the unity of effect achievable in a story or poem that a reader could consume in a single sitting. Concentrating on reader response allowed Poe to mount a defense of exactly the kind of fiction he excelled at writing: tales of effect, as Poe styled them, suddenly enjoyed elevated critical status. Terence Whalen speculates persuasively that an aesthetics of effect may have represented Poe's fantasy of being able to predict with more certainty the way a work would land in a mass audience whose tastes could be "dangerously mysterious."[4] The effort Poe expended in distinguishing between tale proper and essay in this set of reviews also served his own ends by privileging self-contained stories (his preferred genre) as opposed to genial meditations foregrounding the authorial voice (as pioneered by Washington Irving in his *Sketchbook of Geoffrey Crayon* (1819–20) and followed, in some works, by Hawthorne).[5]

In the *Graham's* reviews, Poe expresses relief that Hawthorne's work deserves whatever plaudits have been accorded it rather than having been promoted through one of the "impudent *cliques*" that shaped literary opinion. Poe carried out a career-long crusade against the literary cliques and culture of puffing that were ubiquitous in the magazine world of the era. As Sidney P. Moss explains, in an age when publishing was a volatile industry, publishers sought to guarantee sales by leaguing with magazine editors in promoting the reputations of their authors. The leading cliques were located in New York (headed by Lewis Gaylord Clark's magazine *The Knickerbocker*) and Boston (represented by the staid quarterly, the *North American Review*).[6] Poe repeatedly mocked both of these self-appointed coteries of judgment. This stance earned him a reputation as an independent critical voice, on which grounds he was drafted, for a time, into the literary movement known as "Young America," which promoted an international copyright agreement to protect the interests of American authors.[7]

Poe's "Letter to B——," his review of Henry Wadsworth Longfellow's *Ballads and Other Poems*, and his essays "The Philosophy of Composition" and "The Poetic Principle" collectively express his influential theories of poetry. Scholars have identified the major influences on Poe's critical theory as the Scottish Common Sense philosophers Hugh Blair and Lord Kames and the British Romantic poet/essayist Samuel Taylor Coleridge. Robert D. Jacobs traces Poe's interest in literary effect as a kind of stimulus-response dynamic to the Scottish philosophers' interest in Lockean psychology.[8] Meanwhile, Poe's announcement in the "Letter to B——" that poetry has as its immediate object pleasure instead of truth comes almost verbatim from Coleridge's *Biographia Literaria*.[9] In a period when readers expected literature to be both entertaining and enlightening, a poem that embedded a moral sentiment was not considered off-putting. For Poe, however, a poem's embodiment of beauty was spoiled by any overt didacticism. While announcing his sincere admiration for Longfellow's talent, Poe faults the poet for privileging truth over beauty in individual works (a poem in Poe's view may only depict virtue, not preach of it). Poe goes further in the Longfellow review, defining the poet's mission as something beyond singing the beauty of the natural world; the true poet is charged with attempting to capture "supernal" beauty: to satisfy the soul's longing for a beauty presumed to exist in an afterlife. Such a pronouncement could not be in sharper contrast to Ralph Waldo Emerson's call in "The Poet" in 1844 for American poets to sing of such prosaic and earthly matters as political campaigns and fisheries.[10] Poe insists that rhyme and meter are essential to poetry because of the unique capacity of sound (or music) to approach transcendence. In Poe's admirably concise formulation, poetry is "the Rhythmical creation of Beauty."

"The Philosophy of Composition" strikes many readers as combining the features of a critical essay and a hoax. The technique in this famous essay is not unlike his practice in "The Balloon-Hoax": start with plausible propositions and then slowly bring the reader along to assertions that are implausible, if not outlandish. Readers need only consider the fifth paragraph of the essay to see that Poe was fully aware that the process of artistic creation is never as calculated or methodical an affair as the rest of the essay proposes. But the critical principles expressed in Poe's winking account of how he composed "The Raven" are sincere, judging by their agreement with Poe's statements elsewhere and with his own poetic practice: the idea that the correct province of a poem is beauty; the suggestion that the death of a beautiful woman is the most poetical of topics; the insistence on rhyme and meter as necessary elements of a poem; the emphasis on effect (and its corollary, brevity); and the importance of circumscription of space (so effective a technique in many of Poe's tales). Similar ideas are put forward in the posthumously published essay, "The Poetic Principle," notable for its often-quoted proscription against the "heresy of The Didactic" and its championing of art for art's sake.

Publishing "The Philosophy of Composition" in 1846 was in part an attempt to wring additional profit out of a poem for which remuneration was not nearly commensurate with the international sensation it occasioned. Poe's concern with the position of the artist in a print culture that sanctioned unlimited circulation of an author's works without due compensation can be glimpsed in his defense of an international copyright law—and his argument for prompt payment of authors by magazine editors—in "Some Secrets of the Magazine Prison-House." American writers complained throughout the nineteenth century that unauthorized reprinting of popular British works suppressed the cause of American authorship by making publishers unwilling to gamble on comparatively lesser-known domestic writers (their concerns would not be answered with an international copyright agreement until the 1890s). In his short piece on anastatic printing, Poe envisioned this new technological process (a method of printing from plates that would supposedly have made reproduction almost as simple and inexpensive as modern photocopying) potentially enabling a revolution in the relationship between authors and the public. The idea that bypassing the expense of type-setting would allow "poor devil" authors a level playing field against wealthy gentlemen of leisure (who could afford to indemnify publishers against financial loss) appealed to a writer who felt himself at a disadvantage when compared with patrician authors such as Longfellow, but the techno-utopianism of this piece (which anticipates claims later made about the potential of the internet to democratize authorship) proved illusory.

The letters included below fall into two categories: those that reveal something about Poe's emotional life, and those in which he comments directly on some of his best-known works. On the biographical side, the first letter reflects the troubled relationship between Poe and his foster father, John Allan, conveying the overwrought emotional tone of the men's correspondence. By the time of this 1828 letter, the relationship between them had been strained for years. Poe held Allan responsible for neglecting to sufficiently finance his education at the University of Virginia (having accrued debts, Poe left the university after one year), while Allan considered his ward irresponsible and ungrateful. Allan probably dismissed with scorn the nineteen-year-old Poe's pronouncement that Richmond, Virginia—and indeed the entire United States—furnished too narrow a sphere for his literary ambitions. Although Poe and Allan reconciled for a time after this letter, eventually new sources of conflict arose and the relationship permanently ruptured.

Similar volatility emerges from Poe's August 1835 letter to Maria Clemm, mother of the author's soon-to-be bride, thirteen-year-old Virginia Clemm. At his most manipulative, the twenty-six-year-old Poe was capable of threatening suicide should Virginia accept her cousin Neilson Poe's offer to take her in and provide for her education. Shortly after receiving this letter, Maria and Virginia rejected Neilson's offer, Poe married Virginia, and the three of them took up residence in Richmond. The letter foreshadows how much Poe would come to rely upon Muddy (his nickname for mother-in-law Maria) and Virginia to provide a stable, emotionally supportive home life as the family unit moved among various Eastern seaboard cities between 1835 and 1847. Poe's devastation following Virginia's initial illness in 1842 and ensuing death in 1847 is registered in his candid letter of January 1848 to George W. Eveleth. Notwithstanding the Gothic-sounding language to which Poe reverts in recounting the series of recoveries and relapses Virginia suffered, he sounds sincere and self-reflective in discussing his constitutional nervousness and his turn to alcohol during a period of severe emotional stress.

While Poe's April 1835 letter to Thomas W. White, publisher of the *Southern Literary Messenger*, incidentally reveals the author's habit of exaggerating his accomplishments (in the account of his supposed swimming prowess), its true importance lies in Poe's coolly rational defense of the Gothic fiction that would become his trademark. From the very outset of his career, Poe wrote such stories in a calculated bid for popularity, not out of depraved impulses, much less as a byproduct of mental illness or substance abuse, as many readers continue, erroneously, to assume. The February 1836 letter to novelist John Pendleton Kennedy provocatively (yet coyly) opens up the possibility that Poe's Gothic tales contain an element of irony, bringing them to the verge of self-parody.

The brutal economics of authorship in Poe's era are evident in Poe's May 1845 lament to Frederick W. Thomas that at the height of his popularity, after publication of "The Raven" in January, he remained as poor as he had ever been (the ironic reference to enslavement is notable given the institution's presence as a subtext in some of his writings). Poe's claim that he wrote the poem intending to cause a sensation seems best regarded as a retroactive boast, not unlike his tongue-in-cheek description of the poem's genesis in "The Philosophy of Composition." A species of authorial vanity probably accounts for the way Poe encouraged lengthy correspondence regarding details of expression within his works, even to the extent of commenting on supposed errors with Eveleth, an admirer with no particular standing in the world of letters. In his letter to Eveleth of December 1846, Poe admits that the verb "tinkled" may not work as well as intended to describe the sound of angels' footfalls on a carpeted floor in "The Raven," but defends the notion that a light source—streaming from above the raven, itself perched atop a bust over a doorway—could cast the bird's shadow downward onto the floor. If the criticisms have merit, such missteps are attributable to Poe's privileging sound and mood over logic in accordance with his theory of the "indefinite" prevailing in poetry. They also represent precisely the kinds of lapses that Poe pitilessly exposed in his reviews of inferior authors.

In the letter to Philip P. Cooke regarding his three stories featuring French detective C. Auguste Dupin, Poe downplays the performances as merely ingenious. By dismissing the subgenre as unworthy of further exploration, he may have underestimated its enduring appeal among readers, which would be exploited by later writers, starting with Arthur Conan Doyle. The pride Poe takes in diversity of tone and subject matter is consistent with the value he places on variety in his May 1842 review of Hawthorne; that Poe is known today among most readers almost exclusively for Gothic subject matter would perhaps have disappointed him. In singling out "Ligeia" as his best tale, Poe apparently believes it had been significantly improved by the inclusion within the story of his poem, "The Conqueror Worm," since that is the primary revision he had made since agreeing with Cooke, in a letter of September 1839, that the tale deserved a different, and better, ending.

Sadly, Poe never achieved the "great purpose of [his] literary life" briefly described in the August 9, 1846 letter to Cooke: the sole proprietorship of a literary magazine. In the prospectuses he prepared for would-be investors, Poe referred to this project as the *Penn Magazine* or, later, *The Stylus*. Poe envisioned a magazine occupying the top tier of periodicals in the United States, costing five dollars per year and appealing to an exclusive readership (in contrast, *Graham's* cost three dollars per year by subscription).[11] Poe needed substantial capital to begin such a project, since he envisioned sparing no expense in the magazine's physical production and intended to attract the best writers in the country as contributors. Had such a magazine been successful in the way Poe fantasized, it would have lifted him out of poverty and, just as importantly, established him as the pre-eminent critical voice in American letters, with the power to promote or reject writers according to his estimate of their merits. Poignantly, three years before his death at age forty, Poe tells Cooke that only a premature death will deter him from accomplishing this aim.

From "Letter to B——"[1]

A poem, in my opinion, is opposed to a work of science by having, for its *immediate* object, pleasure, not truth; to romance, by having for its object an *indefinite* instead of a *definite* pleasure, being a poem only so far as this object is attained; romance presenting perceptible images with definite, poetry with *in*definite sensations, to which end music is an *essential,* since the comprehension of sweet sound is our most indefinite conception. Music, when combined with a pleasurable idea, is poetry; music without the idea is simply music; the idea without the music is prose from its very definitiveness.

. . .

From Night and Morning.[1] A Novel. *By the author of Pelham, Rienzi, Eugene Aram, &c. 2 vols. Re-published by Harper & Brothers, New York.*

[Poe opens the review with a very long paragraph summarizing key plot elements of Edward Bulwer's novel *Night and Morning,* the subject of the review, before making the observations on plot that follow.]

We do not give this as the plot of "Night and Morning," but as the ground-work of the plot; which latter, woven from the incidents above mentioned, is in itself exceedingly complex. The ground work, as will be seen, is of no very original character—it is even absurdly common-place. We are not asserting too much when we say that every second novel since the flood has turned upon some series of hopeless efforts, either to establish legitimacy, or to prove a will, or to get possession of a great sum of money most unjustly withheld, or to find out a ragamuffin of a father, who had been much better left unfound. But, saying nothing of the basis upon which this story has been erected, the story itself is, in many respects, worthy its contriver.

The word "plot," as commonly accepted, conveys but an indefinite meaning. Most persons think of it as of simple *complexity*; and into this error even so fine a critic as Augustus William Schlegel[2] has obviously fallen, when he confounds its idea with that of the mere *intrigue* in which the Spanish dramas of Cervantes and Calderon[3] abound. But the greatest involution of incident will not result in plot; which, properly defined, is *that in which no part can be displaced without ruin to the whole.* It may be described as a building so dependently constructed, that to change the position of a single brick is to overthrow the entire fabric. In this definition and description, we of course refer only to that infinite perfection which the true artist bears ever in mind—that unattainable goal to which his eyes are always directed, but of the possibility of attaining which he still endeavors, if wise, to cheat himself into the belief. The reading world, however, is satisfied with a less rigid construction of the term. It is content to think that plot a good one, in which none of the *leading* incidents can be *removed* without *detriment* to the mass. Here indeed is a material difference; and in this view of the case the plot of "Night and Morning" is decidedly excellent. Speaking comparatively, and in regard to stories similarly composed, it is one of the best. This the author has evidently designed to make it. For this purpose he has taxed his powers to the utmost. Every page bears marks of excessive elaboration, all tending to one point—a perfect adaptation of the very numerous atoms of a very unusually involute story. The better to attain his object he has resorted to the expedient of writing his book backwards. This is a simple thing in itself, but may not be generally understood. An example will best convey the idea. Drawing near the *dénouement* of his tale, our novelist had proceeded so far as to render it necessary that means should be devised for the discovery of the missing marriage record. This record is in the old bureau—this bureau is at Fernside, originally the seat of Philip's father, but now in possession of one Lord Lilburne, a member of Robert Beaufort's family. Two things now strike the writer—first, that the retrieval of the hero's fortune should be brought about by no less a personage than the heroine—by some lady who should in the end be his bride—and, secondly, that this lady must procure access to Fernside. Up to this period in the narrative, it had been the design to make Camilla Beaufort, Philip's cousin, the heroine; but in such case, the cousin and Lord Lilburne being friends, the document must have been obtained by fair means; whereas foul means are the most dramatic. There would have been no *difficulties* to overcome in introducing Camilla into the house in question. She would have merely rung the bell and walked in. Moreover, in getting the paper, she would have had no chance of getting up a scene. This lady is therefore dropped as the heroine; Mr. Bulwer retraces his steps, creates Fanny, brings Philip to love her, and employs Lilburne, (a courtly villain, invented for all the *high* dirty work, as De Burgh Smith for all the *low* dirty work of the story,) employs Lilburne to abduct her to Fernside, where the capture of the document is at length (more dramatically than naturally) contrived. In short, these latter incidents were emendations, and their really episodical character is easily traced by the critic. What appears first in the published book, was last in the original MS.[4] Many of the most striking portions of the novel were *interleaved* in the same manner—thus giving to afterthought that air of premeditation which is so pleasing. Effect seems to follow cause in the most natural and in the most provident manner, but, in the true construction, the cause (and here we commit no bull) is absolutely brought about by the effect. The many brief, and seemingly insulated chapters met with in the course of the narrative, are the interposed afterthoughts in question.

So careful has been our author in this working-up of his story—in this nice dovetailing of its constituent parts—that it is difficult to detect a blemish in any portion. What he has intended to do he has done well; and his main intention, as we have before hinted, was *perfection of plot*.

. . .

We have defined the word "plot," in a definition of our own to be sure, but in one which we do not the less consider substantially correct; and we have said that it has been a main point with Mr. Bulwer in this his last novel, "Night and Morning," to work up his plot as near perfection as possible. We have asserted, too, that his design is well accomplished; but we do not the less assert that it has been conceived and executed in error.

The interest of plot, referring, as it does, to cultivated thought in the reader, and appealing to considerations analogous with those which are the essence of sculptural taste, is by no means a popular interest; although it has the peculiarity of being appreciated in its atoms by all, while in its totality of beauty it is comprehended but by the few. The pleasure which the many derive from it is disjointed, ineffective, and evanescent; and even in the case of the critical reader it is a pleasure which may be purchased too dearly. A good tale may be written without it. Some of the finest fictions in the world have neglected it altogether. We see nothing of it in Gil Blas, in the Pilgrim's Progress, or in Robinson Crusoe.[5] Thus it is not an essential in story-telling at all; although, well-managed, within proper limits, it is a thing to be desired. At best it is but a secondary and rigidly artistical merit, for which no merit of a higher class—no merit founded in nature—should be sacrificed. But in the book before us *much* is sacrificed for its sake, and every thing is rendered subservient to its purposes. So excessive is, here, the involution of circumstances, that it has been found impossible to dwell for more than a brief period on any particular one. The writer seems in a perpetual flurry to accomplish what, in auctorial parlance, is called "bringing up one's time." He flounders in the vain attempt to keep all his multitudinous incidents at one and the same moment before the eye. His ability has been sadly taxed in the effort—but more sadly the time and temper of the reader. No sooner do we begin to take some slight degree of interest in some cursorily-sketched event, than we are hurried off to some other, for which a new feeling is to be built up, only to be tumbled down, forthwith, as before. And thus, since there is no sufficiently continuous scene in the whole novel, it results that there is not a strongly effective one. Time not being given us in which to become absorbed, we are only permitted to admire, while we are not the less chilled, tantalised, wearied, and displeased. Nature, with natural interest, has been given up a bond-maiden to an elaborate, but still to a misconceived, perverted, and most unsatisfactory Art.

Very little reflection might have sufficed to convince Mr. Bulwer that narratives, even one fourth so long as the one now lying upon our table, are *essentially* inadapted to that nice and complex adjustment of incident at which he has made this desperate attempt. In the wire-drawn romances which have been so long fashionable, (God only knows how or why) the pleasure we derive (if any) is a composite one, and made up of the respective sums of the various pleasurable sentiments experienced in perusal. Without excessive and fatiguing exertion, inconsistent with legitimate interest, the mind cannot comprehend at one time, and in one survey, the numerous individual items which go to establish the whole. Thus the high ideal sense of the *unique* is sure to be wanting:—for, however absolute in itself be the unity of the novel, it must inevitably fail of appreciation. We speak now of that species of unity which is alone worth the attention of the critic—the unity or totality *of effect*.

But we could never bring ourselves to attach any idea of merit to mere *length* in the abstract. A long story does not appear to us necessarily twice as good as one only half so long. The ordinary talk about "continuous and sustained effort" is pure twaddle and nothing more. Perseverance is one thing and genius is another— whatever Buffon or Hogart[6] may assert to the contrary—and notwithstanding that, in many passages of the dogmatical literature of old Rome, such phrases as "*diligentia maxima,*" "*diligentia mirabilis,*" can be construed only as "great talent" or "wonderful ability." Now if the author of "Ernest Maltravers," implicitly following authority like *les moutons de Panurge,*[7] *will* persist in writing long romances because long romances have been written before—if, in short, he cannot be satisfied with the brief tale (a species of composition which admits of the highest development of artistical power in alliance with the wildest vigor of imagination)—he must then content himself, perforce, with a more simply and more rigidly narrative form.

. . .

Giving up his attention to the one point upon which we have commented, our novelist has failed to do himself justice in others. The overstrained effort at perfection of plot has seduced him into absurd sacrifices of verisimilitude, as regards the connexion of his *dramatis personæ* each with each, and each with the main events. However incidental be the appearance of any personage upon the stage, this personage is sure to be linked in, will I nill I, with the matters in hand. Philip, on the stage-coach, for example, converses with but one individual, William Gawtrey; yet this man's fate (not subsequently but previously) is interwoven into that of Philip himself, through the latter's relationship to Lilburne. The hero goes to his mother's grave, and there comes in contact with this Gawtrey's father. He meets Fanny, and Fanny happens to be also involved in his *destiny* (a pet word, conveying a pet idea of the author's) through *her* relationship to Lilburne. The witness in the case of his mother's marriage is missing, and this individual turns up at last in the brother of that very Charles De Burgh Smith with whom so perfectly accidental an intimacy has already been established. The wronged heir proceeds at random to look for a lawyer, and stumbles at once upon the precise one who had figured before in the story, and who knows all about previous investigations. Setting out in search of Liancourt, the first person he sees is that gentleman himself. Entering a horse-bazaar in a remote portion of the country, the steed up for sale at the exact moment of his entrance is recognised as the pet of his better days. Now our quarrel with these coincidences is not that they sometimes, but that they everlastingly occur, and that nothing occurs besides. We find no fault with Philip for chancing, at the identically proper moment, upon the identical men, women, and horses necessary for his own ends and the ends of the story—but we do think it excessively hard that he should *never happen upon anything else.*

In delineation of character, our artist has done little worth notice. His highest merit in this respect is, with a solitary exception, the negative one of not having subjected himself to dispraise. Catharine and Camilla are—pretty well in their way. Philip is very much like all other heroes—perhaps a little more stiff, a little more obstinate, and a little more desperately unlucky than the generality of his class. Sydney is drawn with truth. Plaskwith, Plimmins, and the Mortons, just sufficiently caricatured, are very good outline copies from the shaded originals of Dickens. Of Gawtrey—father and son,—of De Burgh Smith, of Robert Beaufort and of Lilburne, what is it possible to say, except that they belong to that extensive firm of Gawtrey, Smith, Beaufort, Lilburne and company, which has figured in every novel since the days of Charles Grandison, and which is doomed to the same eternal configuration till romance-writing shall be no more?

For Fanny the author distinctly avows a partiality; and he does not err in his preference. We have observed, in some previous review, that *original* characters, so called, can only be critically praised as such, either when presenting qualities known in real life, but never before depicted (a combination nearly impossible) or when presenting qualities which, although unknown, or even known to be hypothetical, are so skilfully adapted to the circumstances around them, that our sense of fitness is not offended, and we find ourselves seeking a reason why those things *might not have been* which we are still satisfied *are not*. Fanny appertains to this latter class of originality—which in itself belongs to the loftier regions of *the Ideal*. Her first movements in the story, before her conception (which we have already characterized as an after-thought) had assumed distinct shape in the brain of the author, are altogether ineffective and frivolous. They consist of the unmeaning affectation and rhodomontade[8] with which it is customary to invest the lunatic in common-place fiction. But the subsequent effects of love upon her mental development are finely imagined and richly painted; and, although reason teaches us their impossibility, yet it is sufficient for the purposes of the artist that fancy delights in believing them possible.

. . .

His [Bulwer's] mere English is grossly defective—turgid, involved, and ungrammatical. There is scarcely a page of "Night and Morning" upon which a schoolboy could not detect at least half a dozen instances of faulty construction. Sentences such as this are continually occurring—"And at last silenced, if not convinced, his eyes closed, and the tears yet wet upon their lashes, fell asleep." Here, strictly speaking, it is the eyes which "fell asleep," and which were "silent if not convinced." The pronoun, "he," is wanting for the verb "fell." The whole would read better thus—"And at last, silent, if not convinced, he closed his eyes, and fell asleep with the tears yet on the lashes." It will be seen that, besides other modifications, we have changed "upon" into "on," and omitted "wet" as superfluous when applied to tear; who ever heard of a dry one? The sentence in question, which occurs at page 83, vol. 1, was the first which arrested our attention on opening the book at random; but its errors are sufficiently illustrative of the *character* of those faults of phraseology in which the work abounds, and which have arisen, not so much through carelessness, as from a peculiar bias in the mind of the writer, leading him, per force, into *involution*, whether here in style, or elsewhere in plot. The beauty of simplicity is not that which can be appreciated by Mr. Bulwer; and whatever may be the true merits of his intelligence, the merit of luminous and precise thought is evidently not one of the number.

. . .

Whenever a startling incident is recorded, our novelist seems to make it a point of conscience that somebody should "fall insensible." Thus at page 172, vol. 1,—"'My brother, my brother, they have taken thee from me,' cried Philip, and he fell insensible,"—and at page 38, vol. 2, "'I was unkind to him at the last,' and with these words she fell upon the corpse insensible," &c. &c. There is a great deal too much of this. An occasional swoon is a thing of no consequence, but "even Stamboul must have an end," and Mr. Bulwer should make an end of his syncopes.[9]

Again. That gentlemen and ladies, when called upon to give alms, or to defray some trifling incidental expense, are in the invariable habit of giving the whole contents of their purses without examination, and, moreover, of "throwing" the purse into the bargain, is an idea most erroneously entertained. At page 55, vol. 1, we are told that Philip, "as he spoke, *slid* his purse into the woman's hand." At page 110, "a hint for money restored Beaufort to his recollection, and he *flung* his purse into the nearest hand outstretched to receive it." At page 87, "Lilburne *tossed* his purse into the hands of his valet, whose face seems to lose its anxious embarrassment at the touch of the gold." It is true that the "anxious embarrassment" of any valet out of a novel, would have been rather increased than diminished by having a purse of gold tossed at his head—but what we wish our readers to observe, is that magnificent contempt of filthy lucre with which the characters of Sir Edward Lytton Bulwer "fling," "slide," "toss," and tumble whole purses of money about!

But the predominant and most important failing of the author of "Devereux," in point of style, is an absolute mania for metaphor—metaphor always running into allegory. Pure allegory is at all times an abomination—a remnant of antique barbarism—appealing only to our faculties of comparison, without even a remote interest for our reason, or for our fancy. Metaphor, its softened image, has indisputable force when sparingly and skilfully employed. Vigorous writers use it rarely indeed. Mr. Bulwer is all metaphor or all allegory—mixed metaphor and unsustained allegory—and nothing if neither. He cannot express a dozen consecutive sentences in an honest and manly manner. He is the king-coxcomb of figures-of-speech. His rage for personification is really ludicrous. The simplest noun becomes animate in his hands. Never, by any accident, does he write even so ordinary a word as time, or temper, or talent, without the capital T. Seldom, indeed, is he content with the dignity and mysticism thus imposed;—for the most part it is TIME, TEMPER AND TALENT. Nor does the common-place character of anything which he wishes to personify exclude it from the prosopopeia.[10] At page 256, volume 1, we have some profound rigmarole, seriously urged, about piemen crying "all hot! all hot!" "in the ear of Infant and Ragged Hunger," thus written; and, at page 207, there is something positively transcendental all about LAW—a very little thing in itself, in some cases—but which Mr. Bulwer, in his book, has thought proper to make quite as big as we have printed it above. Who cannot fancy him, in the former instance, saying to himself, as he gnaws the top of his quill, "that is a fine thought!" and exclaiming in the latter, as he puts his finger to the side of his nose, "ah, how *very* fine an idea that is!"

This absurdity, indeed, is chiefly observable in those philosophical discussions with which he is in the wicked habit of interspersing his fictions, and springs only from a rabid anxiety to look wise—to appear profound—even when wisdom is quite out of place, and profundity the quintessence of folly. A "still small voice"[11] has whispered in his ear that, as to the real matter of fact, *he is shallow*—a whisper which he does not intend to believe, and which, by dint of loud talking in parables, he hopes to prevent from reaching the ears of the public. Now, in truth, the public, great-gander as it is, is content to swallow his romance without much examination, but cannot help turning up its nose at his logic.

. . .

Guy Fawkes; or The Gunpowder Treason. An Historical Romance. *By WILLIAM HARRISON AINSWORTH, Author of "The Tower of London," "Jack Sheppard," &c. Philadelphia. Lea and Blanchard.*[1]

What Mr. William Harrison Ainsworth had been doing before he wrote "Rookwood" is uncertain; but it seems to us that he made his literary *début* with that work. It was generally commended; but we found no opportunity of perusing it. "Crichton" followed, and this we read; for our curiosity was much excited in regard to it by certain discrepancies of critical opinion. In one or two instances it was unequivocally condemned as "flat, stale and unprofitable," although, to be sure, the critics, in these one or two instances, were men of little note. The more prevalent idea appeared to be that the book was a miracle of wit and wisdom, and that Ainsworth who wrote "Crichton," was in fact Crichton *redivivus.*[2] We have now before us a number of a Philadelphia Magazine for the month of April, 1840, in which the learned editor thus speaks of the work in question—"Mr. Ainsworth is a powerful writer; his 'Crichton' *stands at the head of the long list of English novels—unapproachable and alone* . . . This great glory is fairly Mr. Ainsworth's due, and in our humble opinion, *the fact is incontrovertible.*" Upon a perusal of the novel so belauded, we found it a somewhat ingenious admixture of pedantry, bombast, and rigmarole. No man ever read "Crichton" through twice. From beginning to end it is one continued abortive effort at effect. The writer keeps us in a perpetual state of preparation for something magnificent; but the something magnificent never arrives. He is always saying to the reader, directly or indirectly, "*now,* in a *very* brief time, you shall see what you shall see!" The reader turns over the page in expectation, and meets with nothing beyond the same everlasting assurance:—another page and the same result—another and still the same—and so on to the end of the performance. One cannot help fancying the novelist in some perplexing dream—one of those frequently recurring visions, half night-mare half asphyxia, in which the sufferer, although making the most strenuous efforts to *run,* finds a walk or a crawl the *ne plus ultra*[3] of his success in locomotion.

The plot is monstrously improbable, and yet not so much improbable as inconsequential. A German critic would say that the whole is excessively *ill-motivert.*[4] No one action follows necessarily upon any one other. There is, at all times, the greatest parade of *measures,* but measures that have no comprehensible result. The author works busily for a chapter or two with a view of bringing matters in train for a certain end; and then suffers this end to be either omitted—unaccomplished—or brought to pass by accidental and irrelevant circumstances. The reader of taste very soon perceives this defect in the conduct of the story, and, ceasing to feel any interest in marches and countermarches that promise no furtherance of any object, abandons himself to the investigation of the page only which is immediately before him. Despairing of all amusement from the *construction* of the book, he falls back upon its immediate descriptions. But, alas, what is there here to excite any emotion in the bosom of a well-read man, beyond that of contempt? If an occasional interest is aroused, he feels it due, not to the novelist, but to the historical reminiscences which even that novelist's inanity cannot render altogether insipid. The turgid pretension of the style annoys, and the elaborately-interwoven pedantry irritates, insults, and disgusts. He must be blind, indeed, who cannot understand the great pains taken by Mr. Ainsworth to interlard the book in question with second-hand bits of classical and miscellaneous erudition; and he must be equally blind who cannot perceive that *this* is the chicanery which has so impressed the judgment, and dazzled the imagination of such critics as he of the aforesaid Magazine. We know nothing at all of Mr. Ainsworth's scholarship. There are some very equivocal blunders in "Crichton," to be sure; but *Ainsworth* is a classical name, and we must make *very* great allowances for the usual errors of press. We say, however, that, from all that appears in the novel in question, he may be as really ignorant as a bear. True erudition—by which term we here mean only to imply much diversified reading—is certainly discoverable—is positively indicated only in its ultimate and total *results*. We have observed elsewhere, that the mere grouping together of fine things from the greatest multiplicity of the rarest works, or even the apparently natural inweaving into any composition of the sentiments and manner of these works, is an attainment within the reach of every moderately-informed, ingenious, and not indolent man, having access to any ordinary collection of good books. Of all vanities the vanity of the unlettered pedant is the most sickening, and the most transparent.

Mr. Ainsworth having thus earned for himself the kind of renown which "Crichton" could establish with the rabble, made his next appearance before that rabble with "Jack Sheppard." Seeing what we have just seen, we should by no means think it wonderful that this romance threw into the greatest astonishment the little critics who so belauded the one preceding. They could not understand it at all. They would not believe that the same author had written both. Thus they condemned it in loud terms. The Magazine before alluded to, styles it, in round terms, "the most corrupt, flat, and vulgar fabrication in the English language . . . a disgrace to the literature of the day." Corrupt and vulgar it undoubtedly is, but it is by no means so *flat* (if we understand the critic's idea of the term) as the "Crichton" to which it is considered so terribly inferior. By "*flat*" we presume "uninteresting" is intended. To us, at least, no novel was less *interesting* than "Crichton," and the only interest which it *could* have had for any reader must have arisen from admiration excited by the apparently miraculous *learning* of the plagiarist, and from the air of owlish profundity which he contrives to throw over the work. The interest, if any, must have had regard to the author and not to his book. Viewed as a work of art, and without reference to any supposed moral or immoral tendencies, (things with which the critic has nothing to do) "Jack Sheppard" is by no means the *very* wretched composition which some gentlemen would have us believe. Its condemnation has been brought about by the revulsion consequent upon the exaggerated estimate of "Crichton." It is altogether a much better book than "Crichton." Although its incidents are improbable—(the frequent miraculous escapes of the hero, for instance, without competent means) still they are not, as in "Crichton," at the same time inconsequential. Admitting the facts, these facts hang together sufficiently well. Nor is there any bombast of style; this negative merit, to be sure, being no merit of the author's, but an enforced one resulting from the subject. The chief defect of the work is a radical one, the nature and effect of which we were at some pains to point out in a late notice of Captain Marryat's "Poacher."[5] The story being, no doubt, written to order, for Magazine purposes, and in a violent hurry, has been scrambled through by means of *incident* solely. It is totally wanting in the *authorial comment*. The writer never pauses to speak, in his own person, of what is going on. It is possible to have too much of this comment; but it is far easier to have too little. The most tedious books, *ceteris paribus*,[6] are those which have none at all. "Sir Charles Grandison," "Clarissa Harlowe," and the "Ernest Maltravers"[7] of Bulwer embody instances of its superabundance. The genius of the author of "Pelham" is in nothing more evident than in the interest which he has infused into some of his late works *in spite* of their ultra-didacticism. The "Poacher" just mentioned, and "The Arabian Nights"[8] are examples of deficiency in the commenting principle, and are both intolerably tedious *in spite* of their rich variety of incident. The *juste milieu*[9] was never more admirably attained than in De Foe's "Robinson Crusoe" and in the "Caleb Williams" of Godwin.[10] This latter work, from the character of its incidents, affords a fine opportunity of contrast with "Jack Sheppard." In both novels the hero escapes repeatedly from prison. In the work of Ainsworth the escapes are merely narrated. In that of Godwin they are *discussed*. With the latter we become at once absorbed in those details which so manifestly absorb his own soul. We read with the most breathless attention. We close the book with a real regret. The former puts us out of all patience. His marvels have a nakedness which repels. Nothing he relates seems either probable or possible, or of the slightest interest, whether the one or the other. His hero impresses us as a mere chimæra with whom we have no earthly concern, and when he makes his final escape and comes to the gallows, we would feel a very sensible relief, but for the impracticability of hanging up Mr. Ainsworth in his stead. But if "Jack Sheppard" is a miserably inartistical book, still it is by no means so utterly contemptible and silly as the tawdry stuff which has been pronounced *"the best of English novels, standing at the head of the long list unapproachable and alone!"*

Of "The Tower of London" we have read only some detached passages—enough to assure us, however, that the *"work,"* like Yankee razors, has been manufactured merely "to sell." "Guy Fawkes," the book now lying before us, and the last completed production of its author, is positively beneath criticism and beneath contempt. The design of Mr. Ainsworth has been to fill, for a certain sum of money, a stipulated number of pages. There existed a necessity of *engaging* the readers whom especially he now addresses—that is to say the lowest order of the lettered mob—a necessity of enticing them into the commencement of a perusal. For this end the title "Guy Fawkes or The Gunpowder Plot" was all sufficient, at least within the regions of Cockaigne.[11] As for fulfilling any reasonable expectations, derived either from the *ad captandum* title,[12] or from his own notoriety (we dare not say reputation) as a novelist—as for exerting himself for the permanent or continuous amusement of the poor flies whom he had inveigled into his trap—all this, with him, has been a consideration of no moment. He had a *task* to perform, and not a duty. What were his readers to Mr. Ainsworth?—"What Hecuba to him, or he to Hecuba?"[13] The result of such a state of affairs is self-evident. With his *best* exertions, in his earliest efforts, with all the goadings of a sickening vanity which stood him well instead of nobler ambition—with all this, he *could* do—he *has* done—but little; and without them he has now accomplished exactly nothing at all. If ever, indeed, a novel were *less* than nothing, then that novel is "Guy Fawkes." To say a word about it in the way of serious criticism, would be to prove ourselves as great a blockhead as its author. *Macte virtute*, my dear sir—proceed and flourish. In the meantime we bid you a final farewell. Your next volume, which will have some such appellation as "The Ghost of Cock-Lane,"[14] we shall take the liberty of throwing unopened out of the window. Our pigs are not all of the description called learned, but they will have more leisure for its examination than we.

From Ballads and Other Poems. *By Henry Wadsworth Longfellow.*[1] *Author of "Voices of the Night," "Hyperion," &c. Second Edition. John Owen: Cambridge.*

In our last number we had some hasty observations on these "Ballads"—observations which we now propose, in some measure, to amplify and explain.

It may be remembered that, among other points, we demurred to Mr. Longfellow's *themes*, or rather to their general character. We found fault with the too obtrusive nature of their *didacticism*. Some years ago we urged a similar objection to one or two of the longer pieces of Bryant; and neither time nor reflection has sufficed to modify, in the slightest particular, our convictions upon this topic.

We have said that Mr. Longfellow's conception of the *aims* of poesy is erroneous; and that thus, laboring at a disadvantage, he does violent wrong to his own high powers; and now the question is, what *are* his ideas of the aims of the Muse, as we gather these ideas from the *general* tendency of his poems? It will be at once evident that, imbued with the peculiar spirit of German song (a pure conventionality) he regards the inculcation of a *moral* as essential. Here we find it necessary to repeat that we have reference only to the *general* tendency of his compositions; for there are some magnificent exceptions, where, as if by accident, he has permitted his genius to get the better of his conventional prejudice. But didacticism is the prevalent *tone* of his song. His invention, his imagery, his all, is made subservient to the elucidation of some one or more points (but rarely of more than one) which he looks upon as *truth*. And that this mode of procedure will find stern defenders should never excite surprise, so long as the world is full to overflowing with cant and conventicles. There are men who will scramble on all fours through the muddiest sloughs of vice to pick up a single apple of virtue. There are things called men who, so long as the sun rolls, will greet with snuffling huzzas every figure that takes upon itself the semblance of truth, even although the figure, in itself only a "stuffed Paddy," be as much out of place as a toga on the statue of Washington, or out of season as rabbits in the days of the dog-star.

Now with as deep a reverence for "the true" as ever inspired the bosom of mortal man, we would limit, in many respects, its modes of inculcation. We would limit to enforce them. We would not render them impotent by dissipation. The demands of truth are severe. She has no sympathy with the myrtles. All that is indispensible in song is all with which she has nothing to do. To deck her in gay robes is to render her a harlot. It is but making her a flaunting paradox to wreathe her in gems and flowers. Even in stating this our present proposition, we verify our own words—we feel the necessity, in enforcing this *truth*, of descending from metaphor. Let us then be simple and distinct. To convey "the true" we are required to dismiss from the attention all inessentials. We must be perspicuous, precise, terse. We need concentration rather than expansion of mind. We must be calm, unimpassioned, unexcited—in a word, we must be in that peculiar mood which, as nearly as possible, is the exact converse of the poetical. He must be blind indeed who cannot perceive the radical and chasmal difference between the truthful and the poetical modes of inculcation. He must be grossly wedded to conventionalisms who, in spite of this difference, shall still attempt to reconcile the obstinate oils and waters of Poetry and Truth.

Dividing the world of mind into its most obvious and immediately recognisable distinctions, we have the pure intellect, taste, and the moral sense. We place *taste* between the intellect and the moral sense, because it is just this intermediate space which, in the mind, it occupies. It is the connecting link in the triple chain. It serves to sustain a mutual intelligence between the extremes. It appertains, in strict appreciation, to the former, but is distinguished from the latter by so faint a difference, that Aristotle has not hesitated to class some of its operations among the Virtues themselves. But the *offices* of the trio are broadly marked. Just as conscience, or the moral sense, recognises duty; just as the intellect deals with *truth*; so is it the part of taste alone to inform us of BEAUTY. And Poesy is the handmaiden but of Taste. Yet we would not be misunderstood. This handmaiden is not forbidden to moralise—in her own fashion. She is not forbidden to depict—but to reason and preach, of virtue. As, of this latter, conscience recognises the obligation, so intellect teaches the expediency, while taste contents herself with displaying the beauty: waging war with vice merely on the ground of its inconsistency with fitness, harmony, proportion—in a word with το καλον.[2]

An important condition of man's immortal nature is thus, plainly, the sense of the Beautiful. This it is which ministers to his delight in the manifold forms and colors and sounds and sentiments amid which he exists. And, just as the eyes of Amaryllis[3] are repeated in the mirror, or the living lily in the lake, so is the mere *record* of these forms and colors and sounds and sentiments—so is their mere oral or written repetition a duplicate source of delight. But this repetition is not Poesy. He who shall merely sing with whatever rapture, in however harmonious strains, or with however vivid a truth of imitation, of the sights and sounds which greet him in common with all mankind—he, we say, has yet failed to prove his divine title. There is still a longing unsatisfied, which he has been impotent to fulfil. There is still a thirst unquenchable, which to allay he has shown us no crystal springs. This burning thirst belongs to the *immortal* essence of man's nature. It is equally a consequence and an indication of his perennial life. It is the desire of the moth for the star. It is not the mere appreciation of the beauty before us. It is a wild effort to reach the beauty above. It is a forethought of the loveliness to come. It is a passion to be satiated by no sublunary sights, or sounds, or sentiments, and the soul thus athirst strives to allay its fever in futile efforts at *creation*. Inspired with a prescient ecstasy of the beauty beyond the grave, it struggles by multiform novelty of combination among the things and thoughts of Time, to anticipate some portion of that loveliness whose very elements, perhaps, appertain solely to Eternity. And the result of such effort, on the part of souls fittingly constituted, is alone what mankind have agreed to denominate Poetry.

We say this with little fear of contradiction. Yet the spirit of our assertion must be more heeded than the letter. Mankind have *seemed* to define Poesy in a thousand, and in a thousand conflicting definitions. But the war is one only of words. Induction is as well applicable to this subject as to the most palpable and utilitarian; and by its sober processes we find that, in respect to compositions which have been really received as poems, the *imaginative*, or, more popularly, the creative portions *alone* have ensured them to be so received. Yet these works, on account of these portions, having once been so received and so named, it has happened, naturally and inevitably, that other portions totally unpoetic have not only come to be regarded by the popular voice as poetic, but have been made to serve as false standards of perfection, in the adjustment of other poetical claims. Whatever has been found in whatever has been received as a poem, has been blindly regarded as *ex statû*[4] poetic. And this is a species of gross error which scarcely could have made its way into any less intangible topic. In fact that license which appertains to the Muse herself, it has been thought decorous, if not sagacious to indulge, in all examination of her character.

Poesy is thus seen to be a response—unsatisfactory it is true—but still in some measure a response, to a natural and irrepressible demand. Man being what he is, the time could never have been in which Poesy was not. Its first element is the thirst for supernal BEAUTY—a beauty which is not afforded the soul by any existing collocation of earth's forms—a beauty which, perhaps, *no possible* combination of these forms would fully produce. Its second element is the attempt to satisfy this thirst by *novel* combinations among those forms of beauty which already exist—or by novel combinations *of those combinations which our predecessors, toiling in chase of the same phantom, have already set in order.* We thus clearly deduce the *novelty,* the *originality,* the *invention,* the *imagination,* or lastly the *creation* of BEAUTY, (for the terms as here employed are synonimous) as the essence of all Poesy. Nor is this idea so much at variance with ordinary opinion as, at first sight, it may appear. A multitude of antique dogmas on this topic will be found, when divested of extrinsic speculation, to be easily resoluble into the definition now proposed. We do nothing more than present tangibly the vague clouds of the world's idea. We recognize the idea itself floating, unsettled, indefinite, in every attempt which has yet been made to circumscribe the conception of "Poesy" in words. A striking instance of this is observable in the fact that no definition exists, in which either "the beautiful," or some one of those qualities which we have above designated synonimously with "creation," has not been pointed out as the *chief* attribute of the Muse. "Invention," however, or "imagination," is by far more commonly insisted upon. The word ποιησις itself (creation) speaks volumes upon this point. Neither will it be amiss here to mention Count Bielfeld's definition of poetry as *"L'art d'exprimer les pensées par la fiction."*[5] With this definition (of which the philosophy is profound to a certain extent) the German terms *Dichthunst,* the art of fiction, and *Dichten,* to feign, which are used for *"poetry"* and *"to make verses,"* are in full and remarkable accordance. It is, nevertheless, in the *combination* of the two omni-prevalent ideas that the novelty and, we believe, the force of our own proposition is to be found.

So far, we have spoken of Poesy as of an abstraction alone. As such, it is obvious that it may be applicable in various moods. The sentiment may develop itself in Sculpture, in Painting, in Music, or otherwise. But our present business is with its development in words—that development to which, in practical acceptation, the world has agreed to limit the term. And at this point there is one consideration which induces us to pause. We cannot make up our minds to admit (as some have admitted) the inessentiality of rhythm. On the contrary, the universality of its use in the earliest poetical efforts of all mankind would be sufficient to assure us, not merely of its congeniality with the Muse, or of its adaptation to her purposes, but of its elementary and indispensible importance. But here we must, perforce, content ourselves with mere suggestion; for this topic is of a character which would lead us too far. We have already spoken of Music as one of the moods of poetical development. It is in Music, perhaps, that the soul most nearly attains that end upon which we have commented—the creation of supernal beauty. It may be, indeed, that this august aim is here even partially or imperfectly attained, *in fact*. The *elements* of that beauty which is felt in sound, *may be* the mutual or common heritage of Earth and Heaven. In the soul's struggles at combination it is thus not impossible that a harp may strike notes not unfamiliar to the angels. And in this view the wonder may well be less that all attempts at defining the character or sentiment of the deeper musical impressions, has been found absolutely futile. Contenting ourselves, therefore, with the firm conviction, that music (in its modifications of rhythm and rhyme) is of so vast a moment in Poesy, as *never* to be neglected by him who is truly poetical—is of so mighty a force in furthering the great aim intended that he is mad who rejects its assistance—content with this idea we shall not pause to maintain its absolute essentiality, for the mere sake of rounding a definition. We will but add, at this point, that the highest possible development of the Poetical Sentiment is to be found in the union of song with music, in its popular sense. The old Bards and Minnesingers[6] possessed, in the fullest perfection, the finest and truest elements of Poesy; and Thomas Moore,[7] singing his own ballads, is but putting the final touch to their completion as poems.

To recapitulate, then, we would define in brief the Poetry of words as the *Rhythmical Creation of Beauty*. Beyond the limits of Beauty its province does not extend. Its sole arbiter is Taste. With the Intellect or with the Conscience it has only collateral relations. It has no dependence, unless incidentally, upon either Duty or *Truth*. That our definition will necessarily exclude much of what, through a supine toleration, has been hitherto ranked as poetical, is a matter which affords us not even momentary concern. We address but the thoughtful, and heed only their approval—with our own. If our suggestions are truthful, then "after many days"[8] shall they be understood as truth, even though found in contradiction of *all* that has been hitherto so understood. If false shall we not be the first to bid them die?

We would reject, of course, all such matters as "Armstrong on Health," a revolting production; Pope's "Essay on Man," which may well be content with the title of an "Essay in Rhyme;" "Hudibras"[9] and other merely humorous pieces. We do not gainsay the peculiar merits of either of these latter compositions—but deny them the position held. In a notice, month before last, of Brainard's Poems,[10] we took occasion to show that the common use of a certain instrument, (rhythm) had tended, more than aught else, to confound humorous verse with poetry. The observation is now recalled to corroborate what we have just said in respect to the vast effect or force of melody in itself—an effect which could elevate into even momentary confusion with the highest efforts of mind, compositions such as are the greater number of satires or burlesques.

Of the poets who have appeared most fully instinct with the principles now developed, we may mention *Keats*[11] as the most remarkable. He is the sole British poet who has never erred in his themes. Beauty is always his aim.

We have thus shown our ground of objection to the general *themes* of Professor Longfellow. In common with all who claim the sacred title of poet, he should limit his endeavors to the creation of novel moods of beauty, in form, in color, in sound, in sentiment; for over all this wide range has the poetry of words dominion. To what the world terms *prose* may be safely and properly left all else. The artist who doubts of his thesis, may always resolve his doubt by the single question—"might not this matter be as well or better handled in *prose?*" If it *may*, then is it no subject for the Muse. In the general acceptation of the term *Beauty* we are content to rest; being careful only to suggest that, in our peculiar views, it must be understood as inclusive of *the sublime*.

Of the pieces which constitute the present volume, there are not more than one or two thoroughly fulfilling the idea above proposed; although the volume as a whole is by no means so chargeable with didacticism as Mr. Longfellow's previous book. We would mention as poems *nearly true*, "The Village Blacksmith;" "The Wreck of the Hesperus" and especially "The Skeleton in Armor." In the first-mentioned we have the *beauty* of simple-mindedness as a genuine thesis; and this thesis is inimitably handled until the concluding stanza, where the spirit of legitimate poesy is aggrieved in the pointed antithetical deduction of a *moral* from what has gone before. In "The Wreck of the Hesperus" we have the *beauty* of child-like confidence and innocence, with that of the father's stern courage and affection. But, with slight exception, those particulars of the storm here detailed are not poetic subjects. Their thrilling *horror* belongs to prose, in which it could be far more effectively discussed, as Professor Longfellow may assure himself at any moment by experiment. There *are* points of a tempest which afford the loftiest and truest poetical themes—points in which pure beauty is found, or, better still, beauty heightened into the sublime, by terror. But when we read, among other similar things, that

> The salt sea was frozen on her breast,
> The salt tears in her eyes,

we feel, if not positive disgust, at least a chilling sense of the inappropriate. In the "Skeleton in Armor" we find a pure and perfect thesis artistically treated. We find the beauty of bold courage and self-confidence, of love and maiden devotion, of reckless adventure, and finally of life-contemning grief. Combined with all this we have numerous *points* of beauty apparently insulated, but all aiding the main effect or impression. The heart is stirred, and the mind does not lament its mal-instruction. The metre is simple, sonorous, well-balanced and fully adapted to the subject. Upon the whole, there are fewer truer poems than this. It has but one defect—an important one. The prose remarks prefacing the narrative are really *necessary*. But every work of art should contain within itself all that is requisite for its own comprehension. And this remark is especially true of the ballad. In poems of magnitude the mind of the reader is not, at all times, enabled to include, in one comprehensive survey, the proportions and proper adjustment of the whole. He is pleased, if at all, with particular passages; and the sum of his pleasure is compounded of the sums of the pleasurable sentiments inspired by these individual passages in the progress of perusal. But, in pieces of less extent, the pleasure is *unique*, in the proper acceptation of this term—the understanding is employed, without difficulty, in the contemplation of the picture *as a whole*; and thus its effect will depend, in great measure, upon the perfection of its finish, upon the nice adaptation of its constituent parts, and especially, upon what is rightly termed by

Schlegel[12] *the unity or totality of interest*. But the practice of prefixing explanatory passages is utterly at variance with such unity. By the prefix, we are either put in possession of the subject of the poem; or some hint, historic fact, or suggestion, is thereby afforded, not included in the body of the piece, which, without the hint, is incomprehensible. In the latter case, while perusing the poem, the reader must revert, in mind at least, to the prefix, for the necessary explanation. In the former, the poem being a mere paraphrase of the prefix, the interest is divided between the prefix and the paraphrase. In either instance the totality of effect is destroyed.

. . .

Twice-Told Tales. *By Nathaniel Hawthorne. James Monroe & Co.: Boston.*[1]

We have always regarded the *Tale* (using this word in its popular acceptation) as affording the best prose opportunity for display of the highest talent. It has peculiar advantages which the novel does not admit. It is, of course, a far finer field than the essay. It has even points of superiority over the poem. An accident has deprived us, this month, of our customary space for review; and thus nipped in the bud a design long cherished of treating this subject in detail; taking Mr. Hawthorne's volumes as a text. In May we shall endeavor to carry out our intention. At present we are forced to be brief.

With rare exception—in the case of Mr. Irving's "Tales of a Traveller"[2] and a few other works of a like cast—we have had no American tales of high merit. We have had no skilful compositions—nothing which could bear examination as works of art. Of twattle called tale-writing we have had, perhaps, more than enough. We have had a superabundance of the Rosa-Matilda effusions—gilt-edged paper all *couleur de rose:*[3] a full allowance of cut-and-thrust blue-blazing melodramaticisms; a nauseating surfeit of low miniature copying of low life, much in the manner, and with about half the merit, of the Dutch herrings and decayed cheeses of Van Tuyssel— of all this, *eheu jam satis!*[4]

Mr. Hawthorne's volumes appear to us misnamed in two respects. In the first place they should not have been called "Twice-Told Tales"—for this is a title which will not bear *repetition*. If in the first collected edition they were twice-told, of course now they are thrice-told.—May we live to hear them told a hundred times! In the second place, these compositions are by no means all "Tales." The most of them are essays properly so called. It would have been wise in their author to have modified his title, so as to have had reference to all included. This point could have been easily arranged.

But under whatever titular blunders we receive this book, it is most cordially welcome. We have seen no prose composition by any American which can compare with *some* of these articles in the higher merits, or indeed in the lower; while there is not a single piece which would do dishonor to the best of the British essayists.

"The Rill from the Town Pump" which, through the *ad captandum*[5] nature of its title, has attracted more of public notice than any one other of Mr. Hawthorne's compositions, is, perhaps, the *least* meritorious. Among his best, we may briefly mention "The Hollow of the Three Hills;" "The Minister's Black Veil;" "Wakefield;" "Mr. Higginbotham's Catastrophe;" "Fancy's Show-Box;" "Dr. Heidegger's Experiment;" "David Swan;" "The Wedding Knell;" and "The White Old Maid." It is remarkable that all these, with one exception, are from the first volume.

The style of Mr. Hawthorne is purity itself. His *tone* is singularly effective—wild, plaintive, thoughtful, and in full accordance with his themes. We have only to object that there is insufficient diversity in these themes themselves, or rather in their character. His *originality* both of incident and of reflection is very remarkable; and this trait alone would ensure him at least *our* warmest regard and commendation. We speak here chiefly of the tales; the essays are not so markedly novel. Upon the whole we look upon him as one of the few men of indisputable genius to whom our country has as yet given birth. As such, it will be our delight to do him honor; and lest, in these undigested and cursory remarks, without proof and without explanation, we should appear to do him *more* honor than is his due, we postpone all farther comment until a more favorable opportunity.

Twice-Told Tales. By *Nathaniel Hawthorne. Two Volumes. Boston: James Munroe and Co.*[1]

We said a few hurried words about Mr. Hawthorne in our last number, with the design of speaking more fully in the present. We are still, however, pressed for room, and must necessarily discuss his volumes more briefly and more at random than their high merits deserve.

The book professes to be a collection of *tales*, yet is, in two respects, misnamed. These pieces are now in their third republication, and, of course, are thrice-told. Moreover, they are by no means *all* tales, either in the ordinary or in the legitimate understanding of the term. Many of them are pure essays; for example, "Sights from a Steeple," "Sunday at Home," "Little Annie's Ramble," "A Rill from the Town-Pump," "The Toll-Gatherer's Day," "The Haunted Mind," "The Sister Years," "Snow-Flakes," "Night Sketches," and "Foot-Prints on the Sea-Shore." We mention these matters chiefly on account of their discrepancy with that marked precision and finish by which the body of the work is distinguished.

Of the Essays just named, we must be content to speak in brief. They are each and all beautiful, without being characterised by the polish and adaptation so visible in the tales proper. A painter would at once note their leading or predominant feature, and style it *repose*. There is no attempt at effect. All is quiet, thoughtful, subdued. Yet this repose may exist simultaneously with high originality of thought; and Mr. Hawthorne has demonstrated the fact. At every turn we meet with novel combinations; yet these combinations never surpass the limits of the quiet. We are soothed as we read; and withal is a calm astonishment that ideas so apparently obvious have never occurred or been presented to us before. Herein our author differs materially from Lamb or Hunt or Hazlitt[2]—who, with vivid originality of manner and expression, have less of the true novelty of thought than is generally supposed, and whose originality, at best, has an uneasy and meretricious quaintness, replete with startling effects unfounded in nature, and inducing trains of reflection which lead to no satisfactory result. The Essays of Hawthorne have much of the character of Irving, with more of originality, and less of finish; while, compared with the Spectator, they have a vast superiority at all points. The Spectator, Mr. Irving, and Mr. Hawthorne have in common that tranquil and subdued manner which we have chosen to denominate *repose*; but, in the case of the two former, this repose is attained rather by the absence of novel combination, or of originality, than otherwise, and consists chiefly in the calm, quiet, unostentatious expression of commonplace thoughts, in an unambitious unadulterated Saxon. In them, by strong effort, we are made to conceive the absence of all. In the essays before us the absence of effort is too obvious to be mistaken, and a strong under-current of *suggestion* runs continuously beneath the upper stream of the tranquil thesis. In short, these effusions of Mr. Hawthorne are the product of a truly imaginative intellect, restrained, and in some measure repressed, by fastidiousness of taste, by constitutional melancholy and by indolence.

But it is of his tales that we desire principally to speak. The tale proper, in our opinion, affords unquestionably the fairest field for the exercise of the loftiest talent, which can be afforded by the wide domains of mere prose. Were we bidden to say how the highest genius could be most advantageously employed for the best display of its own powers, we should answer, without hesitation—in the composition of a rhymed poem, not to exceed in length what might be perused in an hour. Within this limit alone can the highest order of true poetry exist. We need only here say, upon this topic, that, in almost all classes of composition, the unity of effect or impression is a point of the greatest importance. It is clear, moreover, that this unity cannot be thoroughly preserved in productions whose perusal cannot be completed at one sitting. We may continue the reading of a prose composition, from the very nature of prose itself, much longer than we can persevere, to any good purpose, in the perusal of a poem. This latter, if truly fulfilling the demands of the poetic sentiment, induces an exaltation of the soul which cannot be long sustained. All high excitements are necessarily transient. Thus a long poem is a paradox. And, without unity of impression, the deepest effects cannot be brought about. Epics were the offspring of an imperfect sense of Art, and their reign is no more. A poem *too* brief may produce a vivid, but never an intense or enduring impression. Without a certain continuity of effort—without a certain duration or repetition of purpose—the soul is never deeply moved. There must be the dropping of the water upon the rock. De Béranger[3] has wrought brilliant things—pungent and spirit-stirring—but, like all immassive bodies, they lack *momentum*, and thus fail to satisfy the Poetic Sentiment. They sparkle and excite, but, from want of continuity, fail deeply to impress. Extreme brevity will degenerate into epigrammatism; but the sin of extreme length is even more unpardonable. *In medio tutissimus ibis*.[4]

Were we called upon however to designate that class of composition which, next to such a poem as we have suggested, should best fulfil the demands of high genius—should offer it the most advantageous field of exertion—we should unhesitatingly speak of the prose tale, as Mr. Hawthorne has here exemplified it. We allude to the short prose narrative, requiring from a half-hour to one or two hours in its perusal. The ordinary novel is objectionable, from its length, for reasons already stated in substance. As it cannot be read at one sitting, it deprives itself, of course, of the immense force derivable from *totality*. Worldly interests intervening during the pauses of perusal, modify, annul, or counteract, in a greater or less degree, the impressions of the book. But simple cessation in reading would, of itself, be sufficient to destroy the true unity. In the brief tale, however, the author is enabled to carry out the fulness of his intention, be it what it may. During the hour of perusal the soul of the reader is at the writer's control. There are no external or extrinsic influences—resulting from weariness or interruption.

A skilful literary artist has constructed a tale. If wise, he has not fashioned his thoughts to accommodate his incidents; but having conceived, with deliberate care, a certain unique or single *effect* to be wrought out, he then invents such incidents—he then combines such events as may best aid him in establishing this preconceived effect. If his very initial sentence tend not to the outbringing of this effect, then he has failed in his first step. In the whole composition there should be no word written, of which the tendency, direct or indirect, is not to the one pre-established design. And by such means, with such care and skill, a picture is at length painted which leaves in the mind of him who contemplates it with a kindred art, a sense of the fullest satisfaction. The idea of the tale has been presented unblemished, because undisturbed; and this is an end unattainable by the novel. Undue brevity is just as exceptionable here as in the poem; but undue length is yet more to be avoided.

We have said that the tale has a point of superiority even over the poem. In fact, while the *rhythm* of this latter is an essential aid in the development of the poem's highest idea—the idea of the Beautiful—the artificialities of this rhythm are an inseparable bar to the development of all points of thought or expression which have their basis in *Truth*. But Truth is often, and in very great degree, the aim of the tale. Some of the finest tales are tales of ratiocination. Thus the field of this species of composition, if not in so elevated a region on the mountain of Mind, is a table-land of far vaster extent than the domain of the mere poem. Its products are never so rich, but infinitely more numerous, and more appreciable by the mass of mankind. The writer of the prose tale, in short, may bring to his theme a vast variety of modes or inflections of thought and expression—(the ratiocinative, for example, the sarcastic or the humorous) which are not only antagonistical to the nature of the poem, but absolutely forbidden by one of its most peculiar and indispensable adjuncts; we allude, of course, to rhythm. It may be added, here, *par parenthèse*, that the author who aims at the purely beautiful in a prose tale is laboring at a great disadvantage. For Beauty can be better treated in the poem. Not so with terror, or passion, or horror, or a multitude of such other points. And here it will be seen how full of prejudice are the usual animadversions against those *tales of effect* many fine examples of which were found in the earlier numbers of Blackwood. The impressions produced were wrought in a legitimate sphere of action, and constituted a legitimate although sometimes an exaggerated interest. They were relished by every man of genius: although there were found many men of genius who condemned them without just ground. The true critic will but demand that the design intended be accomplished, to the fullest extent, by the means most advantageously applicable.

We have very few American tales of real merit—we may say, indeed, none, with the exception of "The Tales of a Traveller" of Washington Irving, and these "Twice-Told Tales" of Mr. Hawthorne. Some of the pieces of Mr. John Neal[5] abound in vigor and originality; but in general, his compositions of this class are excessively diffuse, extravagant, and indicative of an imperfect sentiment of Art. Articles at random are, now and then, met with in our periodicals which might be advantageously compared with the best effusions of the British Magazines; but, upon the whole, we are far behind our progenitors in this department of literature.

Of Mr. Hawthorne's Tales we would say, emphatically, that they belong to the highest region of Art—an Art subservient to genius of a very lofty order. We had supposed, with good reason for so supposing, that he had been thrust into his present position by one of the impudent *cliques* which beset our literature, and whose pretensions it is our full purpose to expose at the earliest opportunity; but we have been most agreeably mistaken. We know of few compositions which the critic can more honestly commend than these "Twice-Told Tales." As Americans, we feel proud of the book.

Mr. Hawthorne's distinctive trait is invention, creation, imagination, originality—a trait which, in the literature of fiction, is positively worth all the rest. But the nature of originality, so far as regards its manifestation in letters, is but imperfectly understood. The inventive or original mind as frequently displays itself in novelty of *tone* as in novelty of matter. Mr. Hawthorne is original at *all* points.

It would be a matter of some difficulty to designate the best of these tales; we repeat that, without exception, they are beautiful. "Wakefield" is remarkable for the skill with which an old idea—a well-known incident—is worked up or discussed. A man of whims conceives the purpose of quitting his wife and residing *incognito*, for twenty years, in her immediate neighborhood. Something of this kind actually happened in London. The force of Mr. Hawthorne's tale lies in the analysis of the motives which must or might have impelled the husband to such folly, in the first instance, with the possible causes of his perseverance. Upon this thesis a sketch of singular power has been constructed.

"The Wedding Knell" is full of the boldest imagination—an imagination fully controlled by taste. The most captious critic could find no flaw in this production.

"The Minister's Black Veil" is a masterly composition of which the sole defect is that to the rabble its exquisite skill will be *caviare*. The *obvious* meaning of this article will be found to smother its insinuated one. The *moral* put into the mouth of the dying minister will be supposed to convey the *true* import of the narrative; and that a crime of dark dye, (having reference to the "young lady") has been committed, is a point which only minds congenial with that of the author will perceive.

"Mr. Higginbotham's Catastrophe" is vividly original and managed most dexterously.

"Dr. Heidegger's Experiment" is exceedingly well imagined, and executed with surpassing ability. The artist breathes in every line of it.

"The White Old Maid" is objectionable, even more than the "Minister's Black Veil," on the score of its mysticism. Even with the thoughtful and analytic, there will be much trouble in penetrating its entire import.

"The Hollow of the Three Hills" we would quote in full, had we space;—not as evincing higher talent than any of the other pieces, but as affording an excellent example of the author's peculiar ability. The subject is commonplace. A witch subjects the Distant and the Past to the view of a mourner. It has been the fashion to describe, in such cases, a mirror in which the images of the absent appear; or a cloud of smoke is made to arise, and thence the figures are gradually unfolded. Mr. Hawthorne has wonderfully heightened his effect by making the ear, in place of the eye, the medium by which the fantasy is conveyed. The head of the mourner is enveloped in the cloak of the witch, and within its magic folds there arise sounds which have an all-sufficient intelligence. Throughout this article also, the artist is conspicuous—not more in positive than in negative merits. Not only is all done that should be done, but (what perhaps is an end with more difficulty attained) there is nothing done which should not be. Every word *tells*, and there is not a word which does *not* tell.

In "Howe's Masquerade" we observe something which resembles a plagiarism— but which *may be* a very flattering coincidence of thought. We quote the passage in question.

"*With a dark flush of wrath* upon his brow they saw the general *draw his sword* and *advance to meet* the figure *in the cloak* before the latter had stepped one pace upon the floor.

'*Villain, unmuffle yourself,*' cried he, 'you pass no farther!'

"The figure, without blenching a hair's breadth from the sword which was pointed at his breast, made a solemn pause, and *lowered the cape of the cloak* from his face, yet not sufficiently for the spectators to catch a glimpse of it. But Sir William Howe had evidently seen enough. The sternness of his countenance gave place to a look of wild amazement, if not horror, while he recoiled several steps from the figure, *and let fall his sword* upon the floor."—See vol. 2, page 20.

The idea here is, that the figure in the cloak is the phantom or reduplication of Sir William Howe; but in an article called "William Wilson," one of the "Tales of the Grotesque and Arabesque," we have not only the same idea, but the same idea similarly presented in several respects. We quote two paragraphs, which our readers may compare with what has been already given. We have italicized, above, the immediate particulars of resemblance.

"The brief moment in which I averted my eyes had been sufficient to produce, apparently, a material change in the arrangement at the upper or farther end of the room. A large mirror, it appeared to me, now stood where none had been perceptible before: and as I stepped up to it in extremity of terror, mine own image, but with features all pale and dabbled in blood, *advanced* with a feeble and tottering gait to meet me.

"Thus it appeared I say, but was not. It was Wilson, who then stood before me in the agonies of dissolution. Not a line in all the marked and singular lineaments of that face which was not even identically mine own. *His mask and cloak lay where he had thrown them, upon the floor.*"—Vol. 2. p. 57.

Here it will be observed that, not only are the two general conceptions identical, but there are various *points* of similarity. In each case the figure seen is the wraith or duplication of the beholder. In each case the scene is a masquerade. In each case the figure is cloaked. In each, there is a quarrel—that is to say, angry words pass between the parties. In each the beholder is enraged. In each the cloak and sword fall upon the floor. The "villain, unmuffle yourself," of Mr. H. is precisely paralleled by a passage at page 56 of "William Wilson."[6]

In the way of objection we have scarcely a word to say of these tales. There is, perhaps, a somewhat too general or prevalent *tone*—a tone of melancholy and mysticism. The subjects are insufficiently varied. There is not so much of *versatility* evinced as we might well be warranted in expecting from the high powers of Mr. Hawthorne. But beyond these trivial exceptions we have really none to make. The style is purity itself. Force abounds. High imagination gleams from every page. Mr. Hawthorne is a man of the truest genius. We only regret that the limits of our Magazine will not permit us to pay him that full tribute of commendation, which, under other circumstances, we should be so eager to pay.

Some Secrets of the Magazine Prison-House[1]

The want of an International Copy-Right Law,[2] by rendering it nearly impossible to obtain anything from the booksellers in the way of remuneration for literary labor, has had the effect of forcing many of our very best writers into the service of the Magazines and Reviews, which with a pertinacity that does them credit, keep up in a certain or uncertain degree the good old saying, that even in the thankless field of Letters the laborer is worthy of his hire. How—by dint of what dogged instinct of the honest and proper, these journals have contrived to persist in their paying practices, in the very teeth of the opposition got up by the Fosters and Leonard Scotts,[3] who furnish for eight dollars any four of the British periodicals for a year, is a point we have had much difficulty in settling to our satisfaction, and we have been forced to settle it, at last, upon no more reasonable ground than that of a still lingering *esprit de patrie*.[4] That Magazines can live, and not only live but thrive, and not only thrive but afford to disburse money for original contributions, are facts which can only be solved, under the circumstances, by the really fanciful but still agreeable supposition, that there is somewhere still existing an ember not altogether quenched among the fires of good feeling for letters and literary men, that once animated the American bosom.

It would *not do* (perhaps this is the idea) to let our poor devil authors absolutely starve, while we grow fat, in a literary sense, on the good things of which we unblushingly pick the pocket of all Europe: it would not be exactly the thing *comme il faut*,[5] to permit a positive atrocity of this kind: and hence we have Magazines, and hence we have a portion of the public who subscribe to these Magazines (through sheer pity), and hence we have Magazine publishers (who sometimes take upon themselves the duplicate title of "editor *and* proprietor,")—publishers, we say, who, under certain conditions of good conduct, occasional puffs, and decent subserviency at all times, make it a point of conscience to encourage the poor devil author with a dollar or two, more or less as he behaves himself properly and abstains from the indecent habit of turning up his nose.

We hope, however, that we are not so prejudiced or so vindictive as to insinuate that what certainly does look like illiberality on the part of them (the Magazine publishers) is really an illiberality chargeable to *them*. In fact, it will be seen at once, that what we have said has a tendency directly the reverse of any such accusation. These publishers pay *something*—other publishers nothing at all. Here certainly is a difference—although a mathematician might contend that the difference might be infinitesimally small. Still, these Magazine editors and proprietors *pay* (that is the word), and with your true poor-devil author the smallest favors are sure to be thankfully received. No: the illiberality lies at the door of the demagogue-ridden public, who suffer their anointed delegates (or perhaps arointed[6]—which is it?) to insult the common sense of them (the public) by making orations in our national halls on the beauty and conveniency of robbing the Literary Europe on the highway, and on the gross absurdity in especial of admitting so unprincipled a principle, that a man has any right and title either to his own brains or the flimsy material that he chooses to spin out of them, like a confounded caterpillar as he is. If anything of this gossamer character stands in need of protection, why we have our hands full at once with the silk-worms and the *morus multicaulis*.[7]

But if we cannot, under the circumstances, complain of the absolute illiberality of the Magazine publishers (since pay they do), there is at least one particular in which we have against them good grounds of accusation. Why (since pay they must) do they not pay with a good grace, and *promptly*. Were we in an ill humor at this moment, we could a tale unfold which would erect the hair on the head of Shylock.[8] A young author, struggling with Despair itself in the shape of a ghastly poverty, which has no alleviation—no sympathy from an every-day world, that cannot understand his necessities, and that would pretend not to understand them if it comprehended them ever so well—this young author is politely requested to compose an article, for which he will "be handsomely paid." Enraptured, he neglects perhaps for a month the sole employment which affords him the chance of a livelihood, and having starved through the month (he and his family) completes at length the month of starvation and the article, and despatches the latter (with a broad hint about the former) to the pursy "editor" and bottle-nosed "proprietor" who has condescended to honor him (the poor devil) with his patronage. A month (starving still), and no reply. Another month—still none. Two months more—still none. A second letter, modestly hinting that the article may not have reached its destination—still no reply. At the expiration of six additional months, personal application is made at the "editor and proprietor"'s office. Call again. The poor devil goes out, and does not fail to call again. Still call again;—and call again is the word for three or four months more. His patience exhausted, the article is demanded. No—he can't have it—(the truth is, it was too good to be given up so easily)—"it is in print," and "contributions of this character are never paid for (it is a *rule* we have) under six months after publication. Call in six months after the issue of your affair, and your money is ready for you—for we are business men, ourselves—prompt." With this the poor devil is satisfied, and makes up his mind that the "editor and proprietor" is a gentleman, and that of course he (the poor devil) will wait as requested. And it is supposable that he would have waited if he could—but Death in the meantime would not. He dies, and by the good luck of his decease (which came by starvation) the fat "editor and proprietor" is fatter henceforward and for ever to the amount of five and twenty dollars, very cleverly saved, to be spent generously in canvas-backs and champagne.

There are two things which we hope the reader will not do, as he runs over this article: first, we hope that he will not believe that we write from any personal experience of our own, for we have only the reports of actual sufferers to depend upon, and second, that he will not make any personal application of our remarks to any Magazine publisher now living, it being well known that they are all as remarkable for their generosity and urbanity, as for their intelligence, and appreciation of Genius.

From "Anastatic Printing"[1]

It is admitted by every one that of late there has been a rather singular invention, called Anastatic Printing, and that this invention may possibly lead, in the course of time, to some rather remarkable results—among which the one chiefly insisted upon, is the abolition of the ordinary stereotyping process:—but this seems to be the amount, in America at least, of distinct understanding on this subject.

. . .

We are so habituated to new inventions, that we no longer get from newness the vivid interest which should appertain to the new—and no example could be adduced more distinctly showing that the *mere* importance of a novelty will not suffice to gain for it universal attention, than we find in the invention of *Anastatic Printing*. It excites not one fiftieth part of the comment which was excited by the comparatively frivolous invention of Sennefelder;[2]—but he lived in the good old days when a novelty was a novel. Nevertheless, while Lithography opened the way for a very agreeable pastime, it is the province of Anastatic Printing to revolutionize the world.

By means of this discovery any thing written, drawn, or printed, can be made to stereotype itself, with absolute accuracy, in five minutes.

Let us take, for example, a page of this Journal; supposing only one side of the leaf to have printing on it. We dampen the leaf with a certain acid diluted, and then place it between two leaves of blotting-paper to absorb superfluous moisture. We then place the printed side in contact with a zinc plate that lies on the table. The acid in the interspaces between the letters, immediately corrodes the zinc, but the acid on the letters themselves, has no such effect, having been neutralized by the ink. Removing the leaf at the end of five minutes, we find a reversed copy, in slight relief, of the printing on the page—in other words, we have a stereotype plate,[3] from which we can print a vast number of absolute fac-similes of the original printed page—which latter has not been at all injured in the process—that is to say, we can still produce from it (or from any impression of the stereotype plate) new stereotype plates *ad libitum*. Any engraving, or any pen and ink drawing, or any MS. can be stereotyped in precisely the same manner.

The *facts* of this invention are established. The process is in successful operation both in London and Paris. We have seen several specimens of printing done from the plates described, and have now lying before us a leaf (from the London Art-Union) covered with drawing, MS., letter-press, and impressions from wood-cuts—the whole printed from the Anastatic stereotypes, and warranted by the Art-Union to be absolute *fac-similes* of the originals.

The process can scarcely be regarded as a *new* invention—and appears to be rather the modification and successful application of two or three previously ascertained principles—those of etching, electography, lithography, etc. It follows from this that there will be much difficulty in establishing or maintaining a right of patent, and the probability is that the benefits of the process will soon be thrown open to the world. As to the secret—it can only be a secret in name.

That the discovery (if we may so call it) has been made, can excite no surprise in any thinking person—the only matter for surprise is, that it has not been made many years ago. The obviousness of the process, however, in no degree lessens its importance. Indeed its inevitable results enkindle the imagination, and embarrass the understanding.

Every one will perceive, at once, that the ordinary process of stereotyping will be abolished. Through this ordinary process, a publisher, to be sure, is enabled to keep on hand the means of producing edition after edition of any work the certainty of whose sale will justify the cost of stereotyping—which is trifling *in comparison* with that of re-setting the matter. But still, *positively*, this cost (of stereotyping) is great. Moreover, there cannot always be certainty about sales. Publishers frequently are forced to re-set works which they have neglected to stereotype, thinking them unworthy the expense; and many excellent works are not published at all, because small editions do not pay, and the anticipated sales will not warrant the cost of stereotype. *Some* of these difficulties will be at once remedied by the Anastatic Printing, and *all* will be remedied in a brief time. A publisher has only to print as many copies as are immediately demanded. He need print no more than a dozen, indeed, unless he feels perfectly confident of success. Preserving *one* copy, he can from this, at no other cost than that of the zinc, produce with any desirable rapidity, as many impressions as he may think proper. Some idea of the advantages thus accruing may be gleaned from the fact that in several of the London publishing warehouses there is deposited in stereotype plates alone, property to the amount of a million sterling.

The next view of the case, in point of obviousness, is, that if necessary, a hundred thousand impressions per hour, or even infinitely more, can be taken of any newspaper, or similar publication. As many presses can be put in operation as the occasion may require:—indeed there can be no limit to the number of copies producible, provided we have no limit to the number of presses.

The tendency of all this to cheapen information, to diffuse knowledge and amusement, and to bring before the public the very class of works which are most valuable, but least in circulation on account of unsaleability—is what need scarcely be suggested to any one. But benefits such as these are merely the immediate and most obvious—by no means the most important.

For some years, perhaps, the strong spirit of conventionality—of conservatism—will induce authors in general to have recourse, as usual, to the setting of type. A printed book, *now*, is more sightly, and more legible than any MS. and for some years the idea will not be overthrown that this state of things is one of necessity. But by degrees it will be remembered that, while MS. was a *necessity*, men wrote after such fashion that no books printed in modern times have surpassed their MSS. either in accuracy or in beauty. This consideration will lead to the cultivation of a neat and distinct style of handwriting—for authors will perceive the immense advantage of giving their own MSS. directly to the public without the expensive interference of the type-setter, and the often ruinous intervention of the publisher. All that a man of letters need do, will be to pay some attention to legibility of

MS., arrange his pages to suit himself, and stereotype them instantaneously, as arranged. He may intersperse them with his own drawings, or with anything to please his own fancy, in the certainty of being fairly brought before his readers, with all the freshness of his original conception about him.

And at this point we are arrested by a consideration of infinite moment, although of a seemingly shadowy character. The cultivation of accuracy in MS., thus enforced, will tend with an irresistible impetus to every species of improvement in *style*—more especially in the points of concision and distinctness—and this again, in a degree even more noticeable, to precision of thought, and luminous arrangement of matter. There is a very peculiar and easily intelligible reciprocal influence between the thing written and the manner of writing—but the latter has the predominant influence of the two. The more remote effect on philosophy at large, which will inevitably result from improvement of style and thought in the points of concision, distinctness, and accuracy, need only be suggested to be conceived.

As a consequence of attention being directed to neatness and beauty of MS. the antique profession of the scribe will be revived, affording abundant employment to women—their delicacy of organization fitting them peculiarly for such tasks. The female amanuensis, indeed, will occupy very nearly the position of the present male type-setter, whose industry will be diverted perforce into other channels.

These considerations are of vital importance—but there is yet one beyond them all. The value of every book is a compound of its literary value and its physical or mechanical value as the product of physical labor applied to the physical material. But at present the latter value immensely predominates, even in the works of the most esteemed authors. It will be seen, however, that the new condition of things will at once give the ascendancy to the literary value, and thus *by* their literary values will books come to be estimated among men. The wealthy gentleman of elegant leisure will lose the vantage ground now afforded him, and will be forced to tilt on terms of equality with the poor devil author. At present the literary world is a species of anomalous Congress, in which the majority of the members are constrained to listen in silence while all the eloquence proceeds from a privileged few. In the new *régime*, the humblest will speak as often and as freely as the most exalted, and will be sure of receiving just that amount of attention which the intrinsic merit of their speeches may deserve.

From what we have said it will be evident that the discovery of Anastatic Printing will not only not obviate the necessity of copy-right laws, and of an International Law in especial, but will render this necessity more imperative and more apparent. It has been shown that in depressing the value of the *physique* of a book, the invention will proportionally elevate the value of its *morale*, and since it is the latter value alone which the copy-right laws are needed to protect, the necessity of the protection will be only the more urgent and more obvious than ever.

Preface to The Raven and Other Poems[1]

These trifles are collected and republished chiefly with a view to their redemption from the many improvements to which they have been subjected while going "the rounds of the press." I am naturally anxious that if what I have written is to circulate at all, it should circulate as I wrote it. In defence of my own taste, nevertheless, it is incumbent on me to say that I think nothing in this volume of much value to the public, or very creditable to myself. Events not to be controlled have prevented me from making, at any time, any serious effort in what, under happier circumstances, would have been the field of my choice. With me poetry has been not a purpose, but a passion; and the passions should be held in reverence; they must not—they cannot at will be excited, with an eye to the paltry compensations, or the more paltry commendations, of mankind.

The Philosophy of Composition[1]

Charles Dickens, in a note now lying before me, alluding to an examination I once made of the mechanism of "Barnaby Rudge,"[2] says—"By the way, are you aware that Godwin[3] wrote his 'Caleb Williams' backwards? He first involved his hero in a web of difficulties, forming the second volume, and then, for the first, cast about him for some mode of accounting for what had been done."

I cannot think this the *precise* mode of procedure on the part of Godwin—and indeed what he himself acknowledges, is not altogether in accordance with Mr. Dickens' idea—but the author of "Caleb Williams" was too good an artist not to perceive the advantage derivable from at least a somewhat similar process. Nothing is more clear than that every plot, worth the name, must be elaborated to its *dénouement*[4] before any thing be attempted with the pen. It is only with the *dénouement* constantly in view that we can give a plot its indispensable air of consequence, or causation, by making the incidents, and especially the tone at all points, tend to the development of the intention.

There is a radical error, I think, in the usual mode of constructing a story. Either history affords a thesis—or one is suggested by an incident of the day—or, at best, the author sets himself to work in the combination of striking events to form merely the basis of his narrative—designing, generally, to fill in with description, dialogue, or authorial comment, whatever crevices of fact, or action, may, from page to page, render themselves apparent.

I prefer commencing with the consideration of an *effect*. Keeping originality *always* in view—for he is false to himself who ventures to dispose with so obvious and so easily attainable a source of interest—I say to myself, in the first place, "Of the innumerable effects, or impressions, of which the heart, the intellect, or (more generally) the soul is susceptible, what one shall I, on the present occasion, select?" Having chosen a novel, first, and secondly a vivid effect, I consider whether it can best be wrought by incident or tone—whether by ordinary incidents and peculiar tone, or the converse, or by peculiarity both of incident and tone—afterward looking about me (or rather within) for such combinations of event, or tone, as shall best aid me in the construction of the effect.

I have often thought how interesting a magazine paper might be written by any author who would—that is to say, who could—detail, step by step, the processes by which any one of his compositions attained its ultimate point of completion. Why such a paper has never been given to the world, I am much at a loss to say—but, perhaps, the authorial vanity has had more to do with the omission than any one other cause. Most writers—poets in especial—prefer having it understood that they compose by a species of fine frenzy—an ecstatic intuition—and would positively shudder at letting the public take a peep behind the scenes, at the elaborate and vacillating crudities of thought—at the true purposes seized only at the last moment—at the innumerable glimpses of idea that arrived not at the maturity of full view—at the fully matured fancies discarded in despair as unmanageable—at the cautious selections and rejections—at the painful erasures and interpolations—in a word, at the wheels and pinions—the tackle for scene-shifting—the step-ladders and demon-traps—the cock's feathers, the red paint and the black patches, which, in ninety-nine cases out of the hundred, constitute the properties of the literary *histrio*.[5]

I am aware, on the other hand, that the case is by no means common, in which an author is at all in condition to retrace the steps by which his conclusions have been attained. In general, suggestions, having arisen pell-mell, are pursued and forgotten in a similar manner.

For my own part, I have neither sympathy with the repugnance alluded to, nor, at any time, the least difficulty in recalling to mind the progressive steps of any of my compositions; and, since the interest of an analysis, or reconstruction, such as I have considered a *desideratum*,[6] is quite independent of any real or fancied interest in the thing analyzed, it will not be regarded as a breach of decorum on my part to show the *modus operandi*[7] by which some one of my own works was put together. I select "The Raven," as the most generally known. It is my design to render it manifest that no one point in its composition is referrible either to accident or intuition—that the work proceeded, step by step, to its completion with the precision and rigid consequence of a mathematical problem.

Let us dismiss, as irrelevant to the poem *per se*, the circumstance—or say the necessity—which, in the first place, gave rise to the intention of composing *a* poem that should suit at once the popular and the critical taste.

We commence, then, with this intention.

The initial consideration was that of extent. If any literary work is too long to be read at one sitting, we must be content to dispense with the immensely important effect derivable from unity of impression—for, if two sittings be required, the affairs of the world interfere, and every thing like totality is at once destroyed. But since, *ceteris paribus*,[8] no poet can afford to dispense with *any thing* that may advance his design, it but remains to be seen whether there is, in extent, any advantage to counterbalance the loss of unity which attends it. Here I say no, at once. What we term a long poem is, in fact, merely a succession of brief ones—that is to say, of brief poetical effects. It is needless to demonstrate that a poem is such, only inasmuch as it intensely excites, by elevating, the soul; and all intense excitements are, through a psychal[9] necessity, brief. For this reason, at least one half of the "Paradise Lost"[10] is essentially prose—a succession of poetical excitements interspersed, *inevitably*, with corresponding depressions—the whole being deprived, through the extremeness of its length, of the vastly important artistic element, totality, or unity, of effect.

It appears evident, then, that there is a distinct limit, as regards length, to all works of literary art—the limit of a single sitting—and that, although in certain classes of prose composition, such as "Robinson Crusoe,"[11] (demanding no unity,) this limit may be advantageously overpassed, it can never properly be overpassed in a poem. Within this limit, the extent of a poem may be made to bear mathematical relation to its merit—in other words, to the excitement or elevation—again in other words, to the degree of the true poetical effect which it is capable of inducing; for it is clear that the brevity must be in direct ratio of the intensity of the intended effect:—this, with one proviso—that a certain degree of duration is absolutely requisite for the production of any effect at all.

Holding in view these considerations, as well as that degree of excitement which I deemed not above the popular, while not below the critical, taste, I reached at once what I conceived the proper *length* for my intended poem—a length of about one hundred lines. It is, in fact, a hundred and eight.

My next thought concerned the choice of an impression, or effect, to be conveyed: and here I may as well observe that, throughout the construction, I kept steadily in view the design of rendering the work *universally* appreciable. I should be carried too far out of my immediate topic were I to demonstrate a point upon which I have repeatedly insisted, and which, with the poetical, stands not in the slightest need of demonstration—the point, I mean, that Beauty is the sole legitimate province of the poem. A few words, however, in elucidation of my real meaning, which some of my friends have evinced a disposition to misrepresent. That pleasure which is at once the most intense, the most elevating, and the most pure, is, I believe, found in the contemplation of the beautiful. When, indeed, men speak of Beauty, they mean, precisely, not a quality, as is supposed, but an effect—they refer, in short, just to that intense and pure elevation of *soul*—*not* of intellect, or of heart—upon which I have commented, and which is experienced in consequence of contemplating "the beautiful." Now I designate Beauty as the province of the poem, merely because it is an obvious rule of Art that effects should be made to spring from direct causes—that objects should be attained through means best adapted for their attainment—no one as yet having been weak enough to deny that the peculiar elevation alluded to, is *most readily* attained in the poem. Now the object, Truth, or the satisfaction of the intellect, and the object Passion, or the excitement of the heart, are, although attainable, to a certain extent, in poetry, far more readily attainable in prose. Truth, in fact, demands a precision, and Passion, a *homeliness* (the truly passionate will comprehend me) which are absolutely antagonistic to that Beauty which, I maintain, is the excitement, or pleasurable elevation, of the soul. It by no means follows from any thing here said, that passion, or even truth, may not be introduced, and even profitably introduced, into a poem—for they may serve in elucidation, or aid the general effect, as do discords in music, by contrast—but the true artist will always contrive, first, to tone them into proper subservience to the predominant aim, and, secondly, to enveil them, as far as possible, in that Beauty which is the atmosphere and the essence of the poem.

Regarding, then, Beauty as my province, my next question referred to the *tone* of its highest manifestation—and all experience has shown that this tone is one of *sadness*. Beauty of whatever kind, in its supreme development, invariably excites the sensitive soul to tears. Melancholy is thus the most legitimate of all the poetical tones.

The length, the province, and the tone, being thus determined, I betook myself to ordinary induction, with the view of obtaining some artistic piquancy which might serve me as a key-note in the construction of the poem—some pivot upon which the whole structure might turn. In carefully thinking over all the usual artistic effects—or more properly *points*, in the theatrical sense—I did not fail to perceive immediately that no one had been so universally employed as that of the *refrain*. The universality of its employment sufficed to assure me of its intrinsic value, and spared me the necessity of submitting it to analysis. I considered it, however, with regard to its susceptibility of improvement, and soon saw it to be in a primitive condition. As commonly used, the *refrain*, or burden, not only is limited to lyric verse, but depends for its impression upon the force of monotone—both in sound and thought. The pleasure is deduced solely from the sense of identity—of repetition. I resolved to diversify, and so vastly heighten, the effect, by adhering, in general, to the monotone of sound, while I continually varied that of thought: that is to say, I determined to produce continuously novel effects, by the variation *of the application* of the *refrain*—the *refrain* itself remaining, for the most part, unvaried.

These points being settled, I next bethought me of the *nature* of my *refrain*. Since its application was to be repeatedly varied, it was clear that the *refrain* itself must be brief, for there would have been an insurmountable difficulty in frequent variations of application in any sentence of length. In proportion to the brevity of the sentence, would, of course, be the facility of the variation. This led me at once to a single word as the best *refrain*.

The question now arose as to the *character* of the word. Having made up my mind to a *refrain*, the division of the poem into stanzas was, of course, a corollary: the *refrain* forming the close to each stanza. That such a close, to have force, must be sonorous and susceptible of protracted emphasis, admitted no doubt: and these considerations inevitably led me to the long *o* as the most sonorous vowel, in connection with *r* as the most producible consonant.

The sound of the *refrain* being thus determined, it became necessary to select a word embodying this sound, and at the same time in the fullest possible keeping with that melancholy which I had predetermined as the tone of the poem. In such a search it would have been absolutely impossible to overlook the word "Nevermore." In fact, it was the very first which presented itself.

The next *desideratum* was a pretext for the continuous use of the one word "nevermore." In observing the difficulty which I at once found in inventing a sufficiently plausible reason for its continuous repetition, I did not fail to perceive that this difficulty arose solely from the pre-assumption that the word was to be so continuously or monotonously spoken by *a human* being—I did not fail to perceive, in short, that the difficulty lay in the reconciliation of this monotony with the exercise of reason on the part of the creature repeating the word. Here, then, immediately arose the idea of a *non*-reasoning creature capable of speech; and, very naturally, a parrot, in the first instance, suggested itself, but was superseded forthwith by a Raven, as equally capable of speech, and infinitely more in keeping with the intended *tone*.

I had now gone so far as the conception of a Raven—the bird of ill omen—monotonously repeating the one word, "Nevermore," at the conclusion of each stanza, in a poem of melancholy tone, and in length about one hundred lines. Now, never losing sight of the object *supremeness*, or perfection, at all points, I asked myself—"Of all melancholy topics, what, according to the *universal* understanding of mankind, is the *most* melancholy?" Death—was the obvious reply. "And when," I said, "is this most melancholy of topics most poetical?" From what I have already explained at some length, the answer, here also, is obvious—"When it most closely allies itself to *Beauty*: the death, then, of a beautiful woman is, unquestionably, the most poetical topic in the world—and equally is it beyond doubt that the lips best suited for such topic are those of a bereaved lover."

I had now to combine the two ideas, of a lover lamenting his deceased mistress and a Raven continuously repeating the word "Nevermore"—I had to combine these, bearing in mind my design of varying, at every turn, the *application* of the word repeated; but the only intelligible mode of such combination is that of imagining the Raven employing the word in answer to the queries of the lover. And here it was that I saw at once the opportunity afforded for the effect on which I had been depending—that is to say, the effect of the *variation of application*. I saw that I could make the first query propounded by the lover—the first query to which the Raven should reply "Nevermore"—that I could make this first query a commonplace one—the second less so—the third still less, and so on—until at length the lover, startled from his original *nonchalance* by the melancholy character of the word itself—by its frequent repetition—and by a consideration of the ominous reputation of the fowl that uttered it—is at length excited to superstition, and wildly propounds queries of a far different character—queries whose solution he has passionately at heart—propounds them half in superstition and half in that species of despair which delights in self-torture—propounds them not altogether because he believes in the prophetic or demoniac character of the bird (which, reason assures him, is merely repeating a lesson learned by rote) but because he experiences a phrenzied pleasure in so modeling his questions as to receive from the *expected* "Nevermore" the most delicious because the most intolerable of sorrow. Perceiving the opportunity thus afforded me—or, more strictly, thus forced upon me in the progress of the construction—I first established in mind the climax, or concluding query—that to which "Nevermore" should be in the last place an answer—that in reply to which this word "Nevermore" should involve the utmost conceivable amount of sorrow and despair.

Here then the poem may be said to have its beginning—at the end, where all works of art should begin—for it was here, at this point of my preconsiderations, that I first put pen to paper in the composition of the stanza:

"Prophet," said I, "thing of evil! prophet still if bird or devil!
By that heaven that bends above us—by that God we both adore,
Tell this soul with sorrow laden, if within the distant Aidenn,[12]
It shall clasp a sainted maiden whom the angels name Lenore—
Clasp a rare and radiant maiden whom the angels name Lenore."
　　　　　Quoth the raven "Nevermore."

I composed this stanza, at this point, first that, by establishing the climax, I might the better vary and graduate, as regards seriousness and importance, the preceding queries of the lover—and, secondly, that I might definitely settle the rhythm, the metre, and the length and general arrangement of the stanza—as well as graduate the stanzas which were to precede, so that none of them might surpass this in rhythmical effect. Had I been able, in the subsequent composition, to construct more vigorous stanzas, I should, without scruple, have purposely enfeebled them, so as not to interfere with the climacteric effect.

And here I may as well say a few words of the versification. My first object (as usual) was originality. The extent to which this has been neglected, in versification, is one of the most unaccountable things in the world. Admitting that there is little possibility of variety in mere *rhythm*, it is still clear that the possible varieties of metre and stanza are absolutely infinite—and yet, *for centuries, no man, in verse, has ever done, or ever seemed to think of doing, an original thing*. The fact is, originality (unless in minds of very unusual force) is by no means a matter, as some suppose, of impulse or intuition. In general, to be found, it must be elaborately sought, and although a positive merit of the highest class, demands in its attainment less of invention then negation.

Of course, I pretend to no originality in either the rhythm or metre of the "Raven." The former is trochaic—the latter is octameter acatalectic, alternating with heptameter catalectic repeated in the *refrain* of the fifth verse, and terminating with tetrameter catalectic. Less pedantically—the feet employed throughout (trochees) consist of a long syllable followed by a short: the first line of the stanza consists of eight of these feet—the second of seven and a half (in effect two-thirds)—the third of eight—the fourth of seven and a half—the fifth the same—the sixth three and a half. Now, each of these lines, taken individually, has been employed before, and what originality the "Raven" has, is in their *combination into stanza*; nothing even remotely approaching this combination has ever been attempted. The effect of this originality of combination is aided by other unusual, and some altogether novel effects, arising from an extension of the application of the principles of rhyme and alliteration.

The next point to be considered was the mode of bringing together the lover and the Raven—and the first branch of this consideration was the *locale*. For this the most natural suggestion might seem to be a forest, or the fields—but it has always appeared to me that a close *circumscription of space* is absolutely necessary to the effect of insulated incident:—it has the force of a frame to a picture. It has an indisputable moral power in keeping concentrated the attention, and, of course, must not be confounded with mere unity of place.

I determined, then, to place the lover in his chamber—in a chamber rendered sacred to him by memories of her who had frequented it. The room is represented as richly furnished—this in mere pursuance of the ideas I have already explained on the subject of Beauty, as the sole true poetical thesis.

The *locale* being thus determined, I had now to introduce the bird—and the thought of introducing him through the window, was inevitable. The idea of making the lover suppose, in the first instance, that the flapping of the wings of the bird against the shutter, is a "tapping" at the door, originated in a wish to increase, by prolonging, the reader's curiosity, and in a desire to admit the incidental effect arising from the lover's throwing open the door, finding all dark, and thence adopting the half-fancy that it was the spirit of his mistress that knocked.

I made the night tempestuous, first, to account for the Raven's seeking admission, and secondly, for the effect of contrast with the (physical) serenity within the chamber.

I made the bird alight on the bust of Pallas,[13] also for the effect of contrast between the marble and the plumage—it being understood that the bust was absolutely *suggested* by the bird—the bust of *Pallas* being chosen, first, as most in keeping with the scholarship of the lover, and, secondly, for the sonorousness of the word, Pallas, itself.

About the middle of the poem, also, I have availed myself of the force of contrast, with a view of deepening the ultimate impression. For example, an air of the fantastic—approaching as nearly to the ludicrous as was admissible—is given to the Raven's entrance. He comes in "with many a flirt and flutter."

Not the *least obeisance made he*—not a moment stopped or stayed he,
But *with mien of lord or lady*, perched above my chamber door.

In the two stanzas which follow, the design is more obviously carried out:—

Then this ebony bird beguiling my sad fancy into smiling
By the *grave and stern decorum of the countenance it wore*.
"Though thy *crest be shorn and shaven* thou," I said, "art sure no craven,
Ghastly grim and ancient Raven wandering from the nightly shore—
Tell me what thy lordly name is on the Night's Plutonian shore!"
            Quoth the Raven "Nevermore."

———

Much I marvelled *this ungainly fowl* to hear discourse so plainly,
Though its answer little meaning—little relevancy bore;
For we cannot help agreeing that no living human being
Ever yet was blessed with seeing bird above his chamber door—
Bird or beast upon the sculptured bust above his chamber door,
            With such name as "Nevermore."

———

The effect of the *dénouement* being thus provided for, I immediately drop the fantastic for a tone of the most profound seriousness:—this tone commencing in the stanza directly following the one last quoted, with the line,

But the Raven, sitting lonely on that placid bust, spoke only, etc.

From this epoch the lover no longer jests—no longer sees any thing even of the fantastic in the Raven's demeanor. He speaks of him as a "grim, ungainly, ghastly, gaunt, and ominous bird of yore," and feels the "fiery eyes" burning into his "bosom's core." This revolution of thought, or fancy, on the lover's part, is intended to induce a similar one on the part of the reader—to bring the mind into a proper frame for the *dénouement*—which is now brought about as rapidly and as *directly* as possible.

With the *dénouement* proper—with the Raven's reply, "Nevermore," to the lover's final demand if he shall meet his mistress in another world—the poem, in its obvious phase, that of a simple narrative, may be said to have its completion. So far, every thing is within the limits of the accountable—of the real. A raven, having learned by rote the single word "Nevermore," and having escaped from the custody of its owner, is driven, at midnight, through the violence of a storm, to seek admission at a window from which a light still gleams—the chamber-window of a student, occupied half in poring over a volume, half in dreaming of a beloved mistress deceased. The casement being thrown open at the fluttering of the bird's wings, the bird itself perches on the most convenient seat out of the immediate reach of the student, who, amused by the incident and the oddity of the visiter's demeanor, demands of it, in jest and without looking for a reply, its name. The raven addressed, answers with its customary word, "Nevermore"—a word which finds immediate echo in the melancholy heart of the student, who, giving utterance aloud to certain thoughts suggested by the occasion, is again startled by the fowl's repetition of "Nevermore." The student now guesses the state of the case, but is impelled, as I have before explained, by the human thirst for self-torture, and in part by superstition, to propound such queries to the bird as will bring him, the lover, the most of the luxury of sorrow, through the anticipated answer "Nevermore." With the indulgence, to the utmost extreme, of this self-torture, the narration, in what I have termed its first or obvious phase, has a natural termination, and so far there has been no overstepping of the limits of the real.

But in subjects so handled, however skilfully, or with however vivid an array of incident, there is always a certain hardness or nakedness, which repels the artistical eye. Two things are invariably required—first, some amount of complexity, or more properly, adaptation; and, secondly, some amount of suggestiveness—some under current, however indefinite of meaning. It is this latter, in especial, which imparts to a work of art so much of that *richness* (to borrow from colloquy a forcible term) which we are too fond of confounding with *the ideal*. It is the *excess* of the suggested meaning—it is the rendering this the upper instead of the under current of the theme—which turns into prose (and that of the very flattest kind) the so called poetry of the so called transcendentalists.[14]

Holding these opinions, I added the two concluding stanzas of the poem—their suggestiveness being thus made to pervade all the narrative which has preceded them. The under-current of meaning is rendered first apparent in the lines—

"Take thy beak from out *my heart*, and take thy form from off my door!"
        Quoth the Raven "Nevermore."

It will be observed that the words, "from out my heart," involve the first metaphorical expression in the poem. They, with the answer, "Nevermore," dispose the mind to seek a moral in all that has been previously narrated. The reader begins now to regard the Raven as emblematical—but it is not until the very last line of the very last stanza, that the intention of making him emblematical of *Mournful and Never-ending Remembrance* is permitted distinctly to be seen:

> And the Raven, never flitting, still is sitting, still is sitting,
> On the pallid bust of Pallas just above my chamber door;
> And his eyes have all the seeming of a demon's that is dreaming,
> And the lamplight o'er him streaming throws his shadow on the floor
> And my soul *from out that shadow* that lies floating on the floor
>   Shall be lifted—nevermore.

From "The Poetic Principle"[1]

In speaking of the Poetic Principle, I have no design to be either thorough or profound. While discussing, very much at random, the essentiality of what we call Poetry, my principal purpose will be to cite for consideration, some few of those minor English or American poems which best suit my own taste, or which, upon my own fancy, have left the most definite impression. By "minor poems" I mean, of course, poems of little length. And here, in the beginning, permit me to say a few words in regard to a somewhat peculiar principle, which, whether rightfully or wrongfully, has always had its influence in my own critical estimate of the poem. I hold that a long poem does not exist. I maintain that the phrase, "a long poem," is simply a flat contradiction in terms.

I need scarcely observe that a poem deserves its title only inasmuch as it excites, by elevating the soul. The value of the poem is in the ratio of this elevating excitement. But all excitements are, through a psychal necessity, transient. That degree of excitement which would entitle a poem to be so called at all, cannot be sustained throughout a composition of any great length. After the lapse of half an hour, at the very utmost, it flags—fails—a revulsion ensues—and then the poem is, in effect, and in fact, no longer such.

There are, no doubt, many who have found difficulty in reconciling the critical dictum that the "Paradise Lost" is to be devoutly admired throughout, with the absolute impossibility of maintaining for it, during perusal, the amount of enthusiasm which that critical dictum would demand. This great work, in fact, is to be regarded as poetical, only when, losing sight of that vital requisite in all works of Art, Unity, we view it merely as a series of minor poems. If, to preserve its Unity—its totality of effect or impression—we read it (as would be necessary) at a single sitting, the result is but a constant alternation of excitement and depression. After a passage of what we feel to be true poetry, there follows, inevitably, a passage of platitude which no critical pre-judgment can force us to admire; but if, upon completing the work, we read it again, omitting the first book—that is to say, commencing with the second— we shall be surprised at now finding that admirable which we before condemned— that damnable which we had previously so much admired. It follows from all this that the ultimate, aggregate, or absolute effect of even the best epic under the sun, is a nullity:—and this is precisely the fact.

In regard to the Iliad, we have, if not positive proof, at least very good reason for believing it intended as a series of lyrics; but, granting the epic intention, I can say only that the work is based in an imperfect sense of art. The modern epic is, of the supposititious ancient model, but an inconsiderate and blindfold imitation. But the day of these artistic anomalies is over. If, at any time, any very long poem *were* popular in reality, which I doubt, it is at least clear that no very long poem will ever be popular again.

. . .

While the epic mania—while the idea that, to merit in poetry, prolixity is indispensable—has, for some years past, been gradually dying out of the public mind, by mere dint of its own absurdity—we find it succeeded by a heresy too palpably false to be long tolerated, but one which, in the brief period it has already endured, may be said to have accomplished more in the corruption of our Poetical Literature than all its other enemies combined. I allude to the heresy of *The Didactic*. It has been assumed, tacitly and avowedly, directly and indirectly, that the ultimate object of all Poetry is Truth. Every poem, it is said, should inculcate a moral; and by this moral is the poetical merit of the work to be adjudged. We Americans, especially, have patronised this happy idea; and we Bostonians, very especially, have developed it in full. We have taken it into our heads that to write a poem simply for the poem's sake, and to acknowledge such to have been our design, would be to confess ourselves radically wanting in the true Poetic dignity and force:—but the simple fact is, that, would we but permit ourselves to look into our own souls, we should immediately there discover that under the sun there neither exists nor *can* exist any work more thoroughly dignified—more supremely noble than this very poem—this poem *per se*—this poem which is a poem and nothing more—this poem written solely for the poem's sake.

From Poe (Fortress Monroe, VA) to John Allan (Richmond, VA), December 22, 1828[1]

Dear Sir;

I wrote you shortly before leaving Fort Moultrie & am much hurt at receiving no answer. Perhaps my letter has not reached you & under that supposition I will recapitulate its contents. It was chiefly to sollicit [*sic*] your interest in freeing me from the Army of the U. S. in which, (as M[r] Lay's letter from Lieut Howard informed you) — I am at present a soldier. I begged that you would suspend any judgement you might be inclined to form, upon many untoward circumstances, until you heard *of* me again — & begged you to give my dearest love to Ma[2] & solicit her not to let my wayward disposition wear away the affection she used to have for me. I mentioned that all that was necessary to obtain my discharge from the army was your consent in a letter to Lieut J. Howard, who has heard of you by report, & the high character given you by M[r] Lay; this being all that I asked at your hands, I was hurt at your declining to answer my letter . . . It must have been a matter of regret to me, that when those who were strangers took such deep interest in my welfare, <that> you who called me your son should refuse me even the common civility of answering a letter. If it is your wish to forget that I have been your son I am too proud to remind you of it again — I only beg you to remember that you yourself cherished the cause of my leaving your family — Ambition. If it has not taken the channel you wished it, it is not the less certain of its object. Richmond & the U. States were too narrow a sphere & the world shall be my theatre —

As I observed in the letter which you have not received — (you would have answered it if you had) you believe me degraded — but <th> do not believe it — There is that within my heart which has no connection with degradation — I can walk among infection & be uncontaminated. There never was any period of my life when my bosom swelled with a deeper satisfaction, of myself & (except in the injury which I may have done to your feelings) — of my conduct — My father do not throw me aside as *degraded*[.] I will be an honor to your name.

Give my best love to my Ma & to all friends —

If you determine to abandon me — here take [I my] farewell — Neglected — I will be doubly [ambi]tious, & the world shall hear of the son whom you have thought unworthy of your notice. But if you let the love you bear me, outweigh the offence which I have given — then write me my father, quickly. My desire is for the present to be freed from the Army — Since I have been in it my character is one that will bear scrutiny & has merited the esteem of my officers — but I have accomplished my own ends — & I wish to be gone — Write to Lieut Howard — & to Col: House, desiring my discharge — & above all to myself . . .

My dearest love to Ma & all my friends

I am Your affectionate son

Edgar A Poe

From Poe (Baltimore, MD) to Thomas W. White³ (Richmond, VA), April 30, 1835

I noticed the allusion in the Doom. The writer seems to compare my swim with that of Lord Byron,⁴ whereas there can be no comparison between them. Any swimmer "in the falls" in my days, would have swum the Hellespont, and thought nothing of the matter. I swam from Ludlum's wharf to Warwick, (six miles,) in a hot June sun, against one of the strongest tides ever known in the river. It would have been a feat comparatively easy to swim twenty miles in still water. I would not think much of attempting to swim the British Channel from Dover to Calais . . .

A word or two in relation to Berenice. Your opinion of it is very just. The subject is by far too horrible, and I confess that I hesitated in sending it you especially as a specimen of my capabilities. The Tale originated in a bet that I could produce nothing effective on a subject so singular, provided I treated it seriously. But what I wish to say relates to the character of your Magazine more than to any articles I may offer, and I beg you to believe that I have no intention of giving you *advice*, being fully confident that, upon consideration, you will agree with me. The history of all Magazines shows plainly that those which have attained celebrity were indebted for it to articles *similar in nature — to Berenice* — although, I grant you, far superior in style and execution. I say similar in *nature*. You ask me in what does this nature consist? In the ludicrous heightened into the grotesque: the fearful coloured into the horrible: the witty exaggerated into the burlesque: the singular wrought out into the strange and mystical. You may say all this is bad taste. I have my doubts about it.

Nobody is more aware than I am that simplicity is the cant of the day — but take my word for it no one cares any thing about simplicity in their hearts. Believe me also, in spite of what people say to the contrary, that there is nothing easier in the world than to be extremely simple. But whether the articles of which I speak are, or are not in bad taste is little to the purpose. To be appreciated you must be *read*, and these things are invariably sought after with avidity. They are, if you will take notice, the articles which find their way into other periodicals, and into the papers, and in this manner, taking hold upon the public mind they augment the reputation of the source where they originated. Such articles are the "M.S. found in a Mad-house" and the "Monos and Daimonos" of the London New Monthly — the "Confessions of an Opium-Eater" and the "Man in the Bell" of Blackwood.⁵ The two first were written by no less a man than Bulwer — the *Confessions* [being] universally attributed to Coleridge — although unjustly. Thus the first men in [England] have not thought writings of this nature unworthy of their talents, and I have go[od] reason to believe that some very high names valued themselves *principally* upon this species of literature. To be sure originality is an essential in these things — great attention must be paid to style, and much labour spent in their composition, or they will degenerate into the tugid [*sic*] or the absurd. If I am not mistaken you will find Mr Kennedy,⁶ whose writings you admire, and whose Swallow-Barn is unrivalled for purity of style and thought of my opinion in this matter. It is unnecessary for you to pay much attention to the many who will no doubt favour you with their critiques. In respect to Berenice individually I allow that it approaches the very verge of bad taste — but I will not sin quite so egregiously again. I propose to furnish you every month with a Tale of the nature which I have alluded to. The effect — if any — will be estimated better by the circulation of the Magazine than by any comments upon its contents. This much, however, it is necessary to premise, that no two of these Tales will have the slightest resemblance one to the other either in matter or manner — still however preserving the character which I speak of . . .

Yours sincerely

Edgar A Poe

From Poe (Richmond, VA) to Mrs. Maria Clemm⁷ (and Miss Virginia E. Clemm) (Baltimore, MD), August 29, 1835

My dearest Aunty,

I am blinded with tears while writing thi[s] letter — I have no wish to live another hour. Amid sorrow, [*MS torn*] and the deepest anxiety your letter reached — and you well know how little I am able to bear up under the pressure of grief. My bitterest enemy would pity me could he now read my heart — My last my last my only hold on life is cruelly torn away — I have no desire to live and *will not*. But let my duty be done. I love, *you know* I love Virginia passionately devotedly. I cannot express in words the fervent devotion I feel towards my dear little cousin — my own darling. But what can [I] say; Oh think for me for I am incapable of thinking. Al[l my] thoughts are occupied with the supposition that both you & she will prefer to go with N. Poe;⁸ I do sincerely believe that your *comforts* will for the present be secured — I cannot speak as regards your peace — your happiness. You have both tender hearts — and you will always have the reflection that my agony is more than I can bear — that you have driven me to the grave — for love like mine can never be gotten over. It is useless to disguise the truth that when Virginia goes with N. P. that I shall never behold her again — that is absolutely sure. Pity me, my dear Aunty, pity me. I have no one now to fly to — I am among strangers, and my wretchedness is more than I can bear. It is useless to expect advice forom [sic] me — what can I say? — Can I, in honour & in truth say — Virginia! do not go! — do not go where you can be comfortable & perhaps happy — and on the other hand can I calmly resign my — life itself. If she had truly loved me would she not have rejected th offer with scorn? Oh God have mercy on me! If she goes with N. P. what are you to do, my own Aunty,? [sic]

I had procured a sweet little house in a retired situation on [ch]urch hill — newly done up and with a large garden and [eve]ry convenience — at only $5 per month. I have been dreaming [MS torn] every day & night since of the rapture I should feel in [havi]ng my only friends — all I love on Earth with me there, [and] the pride I would take in making you both comfor[table] & in calling her my wife — But the dream is over[.] [Oh G]od have mercy on me. What have I *to live for*? Among strangers with *not one soul to love me* . . .

The tone of your letter wounds me to the soul — Oh Aunty, Aunty you loved me once — how can you be so cruel now? You speak of Virginia acquiring accomplishments, and entering into society — you speak <also of> in so *worldly* a tone. Are you sure she would be more happy. Do you think any one could love her more dearly than I? She will have far — very far better opportunites [sic] of entering into society here than with N. P. Every one here receives me with open arms.

Adieu my dear Aunty. I *cannot advise you.* Ask Virginia. Leave it to her. Let me have, under her own hand, a letter, bidding me *good bye* — forever — and I [m]ay die — my heart will break — but I will say no more.

EAP.

Kiss her for me — a million times [.]
For Virginia,
My love, my own sweetest Sissy, my darling little wifey, thi[nk w]ell before you break the heart of your cousin. Eddy.

From Poe (Richmond, VA) to John P. Kennedy (Baltimore, MD), February 11, 1836

Dᵣ Sir,
. . . You are nearly, but not altogether right in relation to the satire of some of my Tales. Most of them were *intended* for half banter, half satire — although I might not have fully acknowledged this to be their aim even to myself.

. . .

Most sincerely yours

Edgar A Poe

From Poe (Philadelphia, PA) to Philip P. Cooke[9] (Charlestown, VA), September 21, 1839

My Dear Sir,

. . . Touching Ligeia, you are right — all right — throughout. The *gradual* perception of the fact that Ligeia lives again in the person of Rowena, is a far loftier and more thrilling idea than the one I have embodied. It offers, in my opinion, the widest possible scope to the imagination — it might be rendered even sublime. And this idea was mine — had I never written before I should have adopted it — but then there is Morella. Do you remember, there, the *gradual* conviction on the part of the parent that the spirit of the first Morella tenants the person of the second? It was necessary, since Morella was written, to modify Ligeia. I was forced to be content with a sudden half-consciousness, on the part of the narrator, that Ligeia stood before him. One point I have not fully carried out — I should have intimated that the *will* did not perfect its intention — there sh^d have been a relapse — a final one — and Ligeia (who had only succeeded in so much as to convey an idea of the truth to the narrator) should be at length entombed as Rowena — the bodily alterations having gradually faded away.

But since Morella is upon record, I will suffer Ligeia to remain as it is. Your word that it is "intelligible" suffices — and your commentary sustains your word. As for the mob — let them talk on. I should be grieved if I thought they comprehended me here . . .

Sincerely Yours

Edgar A Poe

From Poe (New York, NY) to Frederick W. Thomas[10] (Washington, DC), May 4, 1845

My Dear Thomas,

In the hope that you have not yet *quite* given me up, as gone to Texas, or elsewhere, I sit down to write you a few words . . . For the last three or four months I have been working 14 or 15 hours a day — hard at it all the time — and so, whenever I took pen in hand to write, I found that I was neglecting something that *would be* attended to. I never knew what it was to be a slave before.

And yet, Thomas, I have made no money. I am as poor now as ever I was in my life — except in hope, which is by no means bankable. I have taken a 3d pecuniary interest in the "Broadway Journal",[11] and for every thing I have written for it have been, of course, so much out of pocket. In the end, however, it will pay me well — at least the prospects are good . . .

I send you an early number of the "B. Journal" containing my "Raven". It was copied by Briggs,[12] my associate, before I joined the paper. "The Raven" has had a great "run", Thomas — but I wrote it for the express purpose of running — just as I did the "Gold-Bug", you know. The bird beat the bug, though, all hollow.

Do not forget to write immediately, & believe me

Most sincerely your friend,

Poe

From Poe (New York, NY) to Philip P. Cooke (Millwood, VA), August 9, 1846

My Dear Sir,

. . . You are right about the hair-splitting of my French friend:[13] — that is all done for effect. These tales of ratiocination owe most of their popularity to being something in a new key. I do not mean to say that they are not ingenious — but people think them more ingenious than they are — on account of their method and *air* of method. In the "Murders in the Rue Morgue", for instance, where is the ingenuity of unravelling a web which you yourself (the author) have woven for the express purpose of unravelling? The reader is made to confound the ingenuity of the supposititious Dupin with that of the writer of the story . . .

In this view, one of my chief aims has been the widest diversity of subject, thought, & especially *tone* & manner of handling. Were all my tales now before me in a large volume and as the composition of another — the merit which would principally arrest my attention would be the wide *diversity and* variety . . . There is a vast variety of kinds and, in degree of value, these kinds vary — but each tale is equally good *of its kind*. The loftiest kind is that of the highest imagination — and, for this reason only, "Ligeia" may be called my *best* tale. I have much improved this last since you saw it and I mail you a copy, as well as a copy of my best specimen of analysis — "The Philosophy of Composition." . . .

Touching "The Stylus":[14] — this is the one great purpose of my literary life. Undoubtedly (unless I die) I will accomplish it — but I can afford to lose nothing by precipitancy . . . I wish to establish a journal in which the men of genius may fight their battles; upon some terms of equality, with those dunces the men of talent. But, apart from this, I have *magnificent* objects in view — may I but live to accomplish them!

Most cordially Your friend

Edgar A. Poe

From Poe (New York, NY) to George W. Eveleth[15] (Phillips, ME), December 15, 1846

My Dear Sir,

. . . What you say about the blundering criticism of "the Hartford Review man" is just. For the purposes of poetry it is quite sufficient that a thing is possible — or at least that the improbability be not offensively glaring. It is true that in several ways, as you say, the lamp might have thrown the bird's shadow on the floor. *My* conception was that of the bracket candelabrum affixed against the wall, high up above the door and bust — as is often seen in the English palaces, and even in some of the better houses in New-York.

Your objection to the *tinkling* of the footfalls is far more pointed, and in the course of composition occurred so forcibly to myself that I hesitated to use the term. I finally used it because I saw that it had, in its first conception, been suggested to my mind by the sense of the *supernatural* with which it was, at the moment, filled. No human or physical foot could tinkle on a soft carpet — therefore the tinkling of feet would vividly convey the supernatural impression. This was the idea, and it is good within itself: — but if it fails (as I fear it does) to make itself immediately and generally *felt* according to my intention — then in so much is it badly con[v]eyed, or expressed. Your appreciation of "The Sleeper" delights me. In the higher qualities of poetry, it is better than "The Raven" — but there is not one man in a million who could be brought to agree with me in this opinion. The Raven, of course, is far the better as a work of art — but in the true basis of all art The Sleeper is the superior. I wrote the latter when quite a boy . . . .

Truly Your Friend

Edgar A Poe

From Poe (New York, NY) to George W. Eveleth (Phillips, ME), January 4, 1848

My Dear Sir

. . . — You say — "Can you *hint* to me what was the terrible evil which caused the irregularities so profoundly lamented?" Yes; I can do more than hint. This "evil" was the greatest which can befall a man. Six years ago, a wife, whom I loved as no man ever loved before, ruptured a blood-vessel in singing. Her life was despaired of. I took leave of her forever & underwent all the agonies of her death. She recovered partially and I again hoped. At the end of a year the vessel broke again — I went through precisely the same scene. Again in about a year afterward. Then again — again — again & even once again at varying intervals. Each time I felt all the agonies of her death — and at each accession of the disorder I loved her more dearly & clung to her life with more desperate pertinacity. But I am constitutionally sensitive — nervous in a very unusual degree. I became insane, with long intervals of horrible sanity. During these fits of absolute unconsciousness I drank, God only knows how often or how much. As a matter of course, my enemies referred the insanity to the drink rather than the drink to the insanity. I had indeed, nearly abandoned all hope of a permanent cure when I found one in the *death* of my wife. This I can & do endure as becomes a man — it was the horrible never-ending oscillation between hope & despair which I could *not* longer have endured without the total loss of reason. In the death of what was my life, then, I receive a new but — oh God! how melancholy an existence . . . .

Truly Yours — E A Poe

NOTES

1. Michael Allen, *Poe and the British Magazine Tradition* (New York: Oxford University Press, 1969).

2. Sandra Tomc, *Industry and the Creative Mind: The Eccentric Writer in American Literature and Entertainment, 1790–1860* (Ann Arbor: University of Michigan Press, 2012).

3. "Death of Edgar A. Poe," *New-York Daily Tribune*, October 9, 1849.

4. Terence Whalen, *Edgar Allan Poe and the Masses: The Political Economy of Literature in Antebellum America* (Princeton, NJ: Princeton University Press, 1999), 85.

5. G. R. Thompson, "Literary Politics and the 'Legitimate Sphere': Poe, Hawthorne, and the 'Tale Proper,'" *Nineteenth-Century Literature* 49, no. 2 (1994): 167–95.

6. Sidney P. Moss, *Poe's Literary Battles: The Critic in the Context of His Literary Milieu* (Durham, NC: Duke University Press, 1963).

7. Literary historian Perry Miller had analyzed Poe's brief alignment with Young America as opportunism on Poe's part; one of the movement's leaders, editor Evert Duyckinck, arranged for Poe to publish two volumes in Wiley and Putnam's Library of American Books series. Perry Miller, *The Raven and the Whale: The War of Words and Wits in the Era of Poe and Melville* (New York: Harcourt, Brace and Company, 1956). But more recently, Meredith McGill finds that Young America drafted Poe into its ranks because his stature as an independent critical voice was key to its political and literary aims. Meredith McGill, *American Literature and the Culture of Reprinting, 1834–1853* (Philadelphia: University of Pennsylvania Press, 2003).

8. Robert D. Jacobs, *Poe: Journalist & Critic* (Baton Rouge: Louisiana University Press, 1969).

9. Kenneth Silverman, *Edgar A. Poe: Mournful and Never-Ending Remembrance* (New York: HarperPerennial, 1991), 70. The definitive study of Coleridge's influence on Poe is Edward H. Davidson, *Poe: A Critical Study* (Cambridge, MA: Harvard University Press, 1964).

10. Emerson famously listed some of the subjects of life in the United States awaiting treatment in verse: "Our logrolling, our stumps and their politics, our fisheries, our Negroes, and Indians, our boasts, and our repudiations, the wrath of rogues, and the pusillanimity of honest men, the northern trade, the southern planting, the western clearing, Oregon, and Texas, are yet unsung." Ralph Waldo Emerson, "The Poet," *Emerson's Prose and Poetry*, eds. Joel Porte and Saundra Morris (New York: W. W. Norton & Company, Inc., 2001), 196.

11. Kevin J. Hayes, *Poe and the Printed Word* (Cambridge: Cambridge University Press, 2003).

From "Letter to B——"

1. Poe originally published this letter as a preface to *Poems* (1831). The present text comes from publication in the *Southern Literary Messenger*, July 1836.

From "Night and Morning." A Novel. By the author of Pelham, Rienzi, Eugene Aram, &c. 2 vols. Re-published by Harper & Brothers, New York.

1. *Night and Morning* A novel by Edward Bulwer (1803–73; also known as Edward Bulwer-Lytton), one of Great Britain's leading novelists in the 1840s. The text of the review comes from its appearance in *Graham's Lady's and Gentleman's Magazine*, April 1841.

2. **Schlegel** August Wilhelm von Schlegel (1767–1845), German critic and Romanticist.

3. **Cervantes and Calderon** Miguel de Cervantes (*c.* 1547–1616), Spanish author of *Don Quixote*, considered by many the first modern novel; Pedro Calderón de la Barca (1600–81), Spanish dramatist and poet.

4. **MS** Abbreviation for "manuscript."

5. **Gil Blas . . . Pilgrim's Progress . . . Robinson Crusoe** Three classics of narrative fiction: picaresque novel *Gil Blas* by French author Alain-René Lesage (1668–1747); *Pilgrim's Progress*, an extended allegory by English Puritan John Bunyan (1628–88); and *Robinson Crusoe*, an adventure novel by English author Daniel Defoe (*c.* 1660–1731).

6. **Buffon or Hogart** Poe mentions French naturalist Georges-Louis Leclerc, Comte de Buffon (1707–88) and English artist William Hogarth (1697–1764). A commonplace equating genius with patience can apparently be credited to Buffon.

7. **les moutons de Panurge** The allusion to blindly following authority comes from *Gargantua and Pantagruel* by the French Renaissance author François Rabelais (*c.* 1494–1553).

8. **rhodomontade** Usually spelled rodomontade: pretentious, blustering language.

9. **syncopes** Loss(es) of consciousness. The source of "even Stamboul (Istanbul) must have an end" is unclear, though Poe uses this allusion elsewhere in his writings.

10. **prosopopeia** I.e. prosopopoeia: personification.

11. **"still small voice"** See 1 Kings 19.12.

Guy Fawkes; or The Gunpowder Treason. An Historical Romance. By WILLIAM HARRISON AINSWORTH, Author of "The Tower of London," "Jack Sheppard," & c. Philadelphia. Lea and Blanchard.

1. The text is from *Graham's Lady's and Gentleman's Magazine*, November 1841.

2. *redivivus* Living again (Latin). James Crichton (1560–82), the subject of Ainsworth's novel, was a legendary Scottish polymath.

3. *ne plus ultra* The highest point (Latin).

4. *ill-motivert* Poe means poorly or insufficiently motivated, but his German is in error, according to Burton R. Pollin, *Poe, Creator of Words* (Baltimore, MD: The Edgar Allan Poe Society of Baltimore, 1974).

5. **"Poacher"** A book by British sea adventure novelist Captain Frederick Marryat (1792–1848).

6. *ceteris paribus* Other things being equal (Latin).

7. **"Sir Charles Grandison" . . . "Clarissa Harlowe" . . . "Ernest Maltravers"** Three popular or classic novels: *The History of Sir Charles Grandison* and *Clarissa* by Samuel Richardson (1689–1761), one of the first modern British novelists; and *Ernest Maltravers* by Bulwer. Bulwer was also the author of the novel *Pelham*, mentioned in the next sentence.

8. **"The Arabian Nights"** The English title given to *One Thousand and One Nights*, a collection of stories and folk tales compiled in Arabic during the Islamic Golden Age.

9. *juste milieu* The golden mean (French).

10. **Godwin** British journalist and political radical William Godwin (1756–1836) wrote *Things as They Are; or, The Adventures of Caleb Williams*, a favorite of Poe's. On Defoe, see note 5 to Poe's review of Bulwer's *Night and Morning*, above.

11. **Cockaigne** A mythical land of ease and licentiousness.

12. *ad captandum* **title** A title calculated to "capture the masses" (Latin).

13. **Hecuba** Cf. *Hamlet* 2.2.559.

14. **The Ghost of Cock-Lane** A famous ghost that attracted widespread attention in London in 1762.

From Ballads and Other Poems. By Henry Wadsworth Longfellow. Author of "Voices of the Night," "Hyperion," & c. Second Edition. John Owen: Cambridge.

1. The text is from *Graham's Lady's and Gentleman's Magazine*, April 1842. **Henry Wadsworth Longfellow** Longfellow (1807–82) was the most successful and beloved American poet of his era. Poe simultaneously admired Longfellow's gifts and resented his exalted social position as a member of elite New England society. Later Poe would (wrongly) accuse Longfellow of plagiarism.

2. **το καλον** Beauty (Greek).

3. **Amaryllis** A character from the *Eclogues* by the ancient Roman poet Virgil (70–19 BCE).

4. *ex statû* By definition (Latin).

5. *fiction* According to Poe scholar G. R. Thompson, the definition of poetry as "the art of expressing thoughts by fiction" was found in an eighteenth-century reference work by Baron Jacob von Bielfeld (1717–70). G. R. Thompson, ed., *The Selected Writings of Edgar Allan Poe* (New York. W. W. Norton & Company, 2004), 640, n. 4.

6. **Minnesingers** Performers of love ballads from the Minnesang tradition of medieval Germany. **Bards** performed stories and verses in medieval Britain.

7. **Thomas Moore** Irish poet and singer (1779–1852).

8. **"after many days"** Cf. Ecclesiastes 11.1.

9. **"Armstrong on Health"** . . . **"Essay on Man"** . . . **"Hudibras"** John Armstrong published *The Art of Preserving Health: A Poem* in 1744. The philosophical content and neo-classical style of Alexander Pope (1688–1727) in his *Essay on Man* did not appeal to Poe for obvious reasons, given the definition of poetry advanced in this review. *Hudibras* is a mock epic poem by English satirist Samuel Butler (1613–80).

10. **Brainard's Poems** John Gardiner Calkins Brainard (1795–1828), American lawyer and poet, whose work Poe had discussed in the February 1842 edition of *Graham's Lady's and Gentleman's Magazine*.

11. *Keats* John Keats (1795–1821), one of the great poets of the British Romantic movement.

12. **Schlegel** August Wilhelm von Schlegel (1767–1845), German critic and Romanticist.

Twice-Told Tales. By Nathaniel Hawthorne. James Monroe & Co.: Boston.

1. The text is from *Graham's Lady's and Gentleman's Magazine*, April 1842.

2. **"Tales of a Traveller"** A work by Washington Irving (1783–1859), one of America's most popular and successful authors during Poe's lifetime.

3. *couleur de rose* G. R. Thompson identifies the allusion here to Charlotte Dacre (*c.* 1771–1825), author of sensational novels ("effusions") under the pseudonym Rosa Matilda. Thompson, *Selected Writings of Edgar Allan Poe*, 644, n. 2.

4. **Van Tuyssel . . . *eheu jam satis!*** Enough! (Latin). The name Van Tuyssel sounds like a gesture toward the Renaissance Dutch School of painting, but G. R. Thompson identifies it as a generalized reference to the Dutch subjects of Washington Irving's New York fiction. Perhaps Poe intends to conflate the two. Thompson, *Selected Writings of Edgar Allan Poe*, 644, n. 3.

5. *ad captandum* Latin for "captivating," implying a gullible public.

Twice-Told Tales. By Nathaniel Hawthorne. Two Volumes. Boston: James Munroe and Co.

1. The text is from *Graham's Lady's and Gentleman's Magazine*, May 1842.

2. **Lamb or Hunt or Hazlitt** Charles Lamb (1775–1834), Leigh Hunt (1784–1859), and William Hazlitt (1778–1830) were all renowned British essayists.

3. **De Béranger** Pierre-Jean de Béranger (1780–1857), French poet and songwriter.

4. *In medio tutissimus ibis* You will go most safely by the middle course (Latin).

5. **Mr. John Neal** John Neal (1783–1859) of Maine was a novelist and magazine publisher.

6. Poe's accusation of plagiarism turned out to be completely groundless, since Hawthorne's "Howe's Masquerade" had in fact been first published (as Poe was not aware) before "William Wilson," but the accusation reveals Poe's hypersensitivity on this issue.

Some Secrets of the Magazine Prison-House

1. The text is from the *Broadway Journal*, February 15, 1845.

2. **Copy-Right Law** In the absence of an international copyright law, American publishers could freely reprint works by popular British authors (such as Charles Dickens). This state of affairs presumably made American publishers less willing to risk capital on American authors and depressed writers' wages. Poe was one of many authors who spoke out on the issue.

3. **Fosters and Leonard Scotts** Theodore Foster and Leonard Scott were American publishers who reprinted British magazines.

4. *esprit de patrie* Patriotism.

5. *comme il faut* The right or proper thing to do (French).

6. **arointed** An obsolete verb, found in Shakespeare, meaning "to be gone."

7. *morus multicaulis* A mulberry tree used in silkworm culture.

8. **Shylock** The vengeful villain in Shakespeare's *The Merchant of Venice*.

From "Anastatic Printing"

1. The text is from the *Broadway Journal*, April 12, 1845.

2. **Sennefelder** Johann Alois Senefelder (1771–1834) invented the process of lithography.

3. **stereotype plates** Stereotype plates were made from plaster and captured impressions from a form of type. As Poe explains, they made it possible to reprint works cheaply, but they were expensive to store and publishers did not always know when a work would be popular enough to justify the labor and expense of stereotyping.

Preface to The Raven and Other Poems

1. The text is from *The Raven and Other Poems* (New York: Wiley and Putnam, 1845), but incorporating Poe's minor emendations from the Lorimer Graham copy of the book. Thomas Ollive Mabbott, ed. *The Raven and Other Poems Reproduced in Facsimile from the Lorimer Graham Copy of the Edition of 1845* (New York: Columbia University Press, 1942).

The Philosophy of Composition

1. The text is from *Graham's Magazine of Literature, Art, and Fashion*, April 1846.

2. **"Barnaby Rudge"** In this sly reference, Poe reminds readers that he correctly predicted the ending to Charles Dickens's serialized novel *Barnaby Rudge* (which, incidentally, featured a talking raven) months before the final installment was published.

3. **Godwin** British journalist and political radical William Godwin (1756–1836) wrote *Things as They Are; or, The Adventures of Caleb Williams*, a favorite of Poe's.

4. *dénouement* The final resolution of a plot.

5. *histrio* Actor (Latin). Poe may mean "performance" here.

6. *desideratum* Something wanted or needed.

7. *modus operandi* Mode of operation (Latin).

8. *ceteris paribus* Other things being equal (Latin).

9. **psychal** Psychological (Poe's coinage).

10. **"Paradise Lost"** The famous epic poem by John Milton (1608–74).

11. **"Robinson Crusoe"** An adventure novel by English author Daniel Defoe (*c.* 1660–1731).

12. **Aidenn** Eden, or heaven.

13. **Pallas** Pallas Athena, Greek goddess of wisdom.

14. **transcendentalists** The New England coterie of writers and intellectuals with whom Poe maintained a long-standing artistic grudge.

From "The Poetic Principle"

1. The text is from *Sartain's Union Magazine*, October 1850.

Letters

1. The texts of all letters (which are in the public domain) are taken from *The Collected Letters of Edgar Allan Poe, Third Edition, Two Vols,* eds. John Ward Ostrom, Burton R. Pollin, and Jeffrey A. Savoye (New York: Gordian Press, 2008). The letters were originally edited by John Ward Ostrom; the Gordian Press edition is revised, corrected, and expanded by Burton R. Pollin and Jeffrey A. Savoye. All notes are my own.

2. **Ma** Frances Valentine Allan (1785–1829), Poe's foster mother (the wife of John Allan).

3. **Thomas W. White** White (1788–1843), who would soon engage Poe as his editor, was the proprietor of the *Southern Literary Messenger*, a magazine out of Richmond, Virginia. Poe's story "Berenice" had appeared in the March 1835 edition of the magazine.

4. **Lord Byron** On May 3, 1810, George Gordon, Lord Byron (1788–1824) famously swam the Hellespont strait in Turkey.

5. **Blackwood** *Blackwood's* was a London magazine famous for its publication of Gothic stories. In the following sentence, Edward **Bulwer** (1803–73) was a much-admired novelist. *Confessions of an English Opium-Eater* by Thomas De Quincey (1785–1859) described the author's experiences with that drug. The poet and critic Samuel Taylor **Coleridge** (1772–1834) was one of the leading figures of British Romanticism and a major influence on Poe.

6. **Mr Kennedy** John Pendleton Kennedy (1795–1870), author of the novel *Swallow Barn*, was an early supporter of Poe's writings.

7. **Mrs. Maria Clemm** Clemm (1790–1871) was the mother of Poe's cousin (and soon-to-be wife), Virginia Clemm (1822–47).

8. **N. Poe** Neilson Poe (1809–84), Poe's cousin, was married to Virginia Clemm's half-sister, Josephine. He had offered to take in Virginia to provide for her care and education.

9. **Philip P. Cooke** Philip P. Cooke (1816–50) of Virginia was an author and Poe's friend. Despite reservations about the ending of "Ligeia" expressed in this letter, in a later letter (see below, letter dated August 9, 1846) Poe identified the tale as his best.

10. **Frederick W. Thomas** Thomas (1806–66) was an American writer and editor.

11. **"Broadway Journal"** Poe would take over as proprietor and editor of the *Broadway Journal* in July, 1845, but its prospects were not as good as he predicted, and it ceased publication in January 1846.

12. **Briggs** Charles F. Briggs (1804–77), American journalist and author, had founded the *Broadway Journal* in 1844.

13. **my French friend** The French hero of Poe's detective stories, C. Auguste Dupin.

14. **"The Stylus"** The name of the high-quality literary magazine that Poe hoped to establish.

15. **George W. Eveleth** Eveleth (1819–1908) was a medical student from Maine with whom Poe exchanged a number of revealing letters from 1845 until his death. Here Poe discusses supposed flaws that reviewers discovered in "The Raven."

www.ingramcontent.com/pod-product-compliance
Lightning Source LLC
Chambersburg PA
CBHW071141100726
47908CB00002B/209